The Complete Guide to OSHA Compliance

Robert D. Peterson, J.D.
Robert D. Peterson Law Corporation
Rocklin, California

Joel M. Cohen, CIH
The Cohen Group
San Mateo, California

CRC Press
Taylor & Francis Group
Boca Raton London New York

CRC Press is an imprint of the
Taylor & Francis Group, an **informa** business

CRC Press
Taylor & Francis Group
6000 Broken Sound Parkway NW, Suite 300
Boca Raton, FL 33487-2742

First issued in paperback 2019

© 1996 by Taylor & Francis Group, LLC
CRC Press is an imprint of Taylor & Francis Group, an Informa business

No claim to original U.S. Government works

ISBN-13: 978-0-87371-681-9 (hbk)
ISBN-13: 978-0-367-40146-7 (pbk)

This book contains information obtained from authentic and highly regarded sources. Reasonable efforts have been made to publish reliable data and information, but the author and publisher cannot assume responsibility for the validity of all materials or the consequences of their use. The authors and publishers have attempted to trace the copyright holders of all material reproduced in this publication and apologize to copyright holders if permission to publish in this form has not been obtained. If any copyright material has not been acknowledged please write and let us know so we may rectify in any future reprint.

Except as permitted under U.S. Copyright Law, no part of this book may be reprinted, reproduced, transmitted, or utilized in any form by any electronic, mechanical, or other means, now known or hereafter invented, including photocopying, microfilming, and recording, or in any information storage or retrieval system, without written permission from the publishers.

For permission to photocopy or use material electronically from this work, please access www.copyright.com (http://www.copyright.com/) or contact the Copyright Clearance Center, Inc. (CCC), 222 Rosewood Drive, Danvers, MA 01923, 978-750-8400. CCC is a not-for-profit organization that provides licenses and registration for a variety of users. For organizations that have been granted a photocopy license by the CCC, a separate system of payment has been arranged.

Trademark Notice: Product or corporate names may be trademarks or registered trademarks, and are used only for identification and explanation without intent to infringe.

Library of Congress Card Number 95-42176

Library of Congress Cataloging-in-Publication Data

Cohen, Joel M.
    The complete guide to OSHA compliance / Joel Cohen and Robert Peterson.
        p. cm.
    Includes index.
    ISBN 0-87371-681-7 (alk. paper)
    1. Industrial safety—United States—Handbooks, manuals, etc. 2. Industrial safety—Law and legislation—United States—Handbooks, manuals, etc. I. Peterson, Robert D. II. Title.
    T55.C578 1995
    658.4′08—dc20   95-42176
                                                                                                            CIP

Visit the Taylor & Francis Web site at
http://www.taylorandfrancis.com

and the CRC Press Web site at
http://www.crcpress.com

About the Authors

Robert D. Peterson founded the Robert D. Peterson Law Corporation in 1978 and specializes in the area of OSHA defense litigation. He represents clients in defense of occupational safety and health appeals throughout the country, including both "Fed/OSHA" states and states with their own safety and health programs.

Mr. Peterson is a graduate of Portland State University and the University of Santa Clara School of Law. Prior to establishing the Robert D. Peterson Law Corporation, he served as a Deputy Attorney General for the state of California and as the first Chief Counsel to the California Occupational Safety and Health Appeals Board.

Joel M. Cohen is the founder and President of The Cohen Group, a company which has provided a complete range of environmental and occupational health services to industry and government since 1980.

Mr. Cohen received his Masters of Public Health from the University of Michigan in 1974 and is a Certified Industrial Hygienist. He is also registered in California as an Environmental Assessor and is a certified asbestos consultant. He has published numerous articles and technical journals.

Mr. Peterson and Mr. Cohen are both recognized experts in their fields, have been active in many health and safety-related seminar presentations for various associations, and have co-authored two books on Cal/OSHA compliance.

INTRODUCTION

The federal Occupational Safety and Health Act was enacted in 1970. The Act was intended to assure "so far as possible" a safe and healthy workplace for every working person in the country.

While the Act sets forth a variety of means and methods to accomplish its goal, its enforcement activities constitute its most recognized source of authority. This enforcement authority is implemented by the use of an inspection/citation scheme.

The Act imposes a two-fold responsibility upon an employer. Every employer is to furnish its employees "employment and a place of employment which are free from recognized hazards" and is also to "comply with occupational safety and health standards." The occupational safety and health standards are set forth in Title 29 of the Code of Federal Regulations ("CFR").

To enforce these responsibilities, the Act authorizes the Secretary of Labor to conduct inspections and to issue citations if it is believed that the employer has violated an occupational safety and health regulation. A penalty may also be proposed for alleged violations. In addition, a citation is to establish a reasonable time to abate (correct) the violation.

The employer may file an appeal with the Occupational Safety and Health Review Commission within 15 working days of the receipt of the citation, and a hearing will be scheduled to review the matter. The appeal may contest the violation, any abatement requirements, and the civil penalty.

The Act also allows individual states to assume responsibility for the conduct of their own safety and health programs. Approximately one-half of the states do exercise state jurisdiction over safety and health matters. Of these states, some enforce the federal rules and regulations while some have adopted and enforce their own safety and health standards. Even if the states have assumed jurisdiction of the program, generally only the Secretary of Labor may enforce safety and health on federal properties within the individual states.

To comply with OSHA rules and regulations, an employer must be familiar with what regulations apply to its place(s) of employment. The standards are divided into general areas such as construction, general industry, etc. An employer must review those areas of the OSHA rules to determine which rules and regulations apply to its operation. Additionally, if an employer does business in more than one state, it must become familiar with the occupational safety and health regulations which apply in each state.

This manual, written in lay person's language, provides a general overview of OSHA. It is intended to familiarize the reader with the means of identifying what occupational safety and health regulations might apply to his/her place of employment and to provide direction on how to comply with those rules and regulations. It additionally provides guidance on what to expect from OSHA in the event of an inspection, how to participate in the inspection, and what actions are available in the event one or more citations and penalties are issued as a result of the inspection.

This manual was written for those individuals who have the responsibility for attempting to ensure a safe and healthy place of employment. The manual is not all-inclusive.

It is our sincere hope that this manual will provide you with the "nuts and bolts" information you will need for establishing and maintaining an effective and practical safety program.

TABLE OF CONTENTS

Chapter 1 Understanding OSHA — An Overview 1

Chapter 2 OSHA Recordkeeping 5

    I.   Recordkeeping Requirements for Injuries and Illnesses 5
          A. No Employees 6
          B. Small Employers 6
              1.   Advice 7
          C. Employers in Low Hazard Industries 7
              1.   Recommendation 7
              2.   Advice 8

   II. How to Keep OSHA Records 8
          A. Log and Summary of Occupational Injuries and Illnesses 8
              1.   Advice 12
              2.   Recordable Events 12
              3.   Recommendation 13
              4.   Completion of the Log 13
                  a.   General Information Columns 15
                  b.   Injury Portion of the Log 15
                  c.   Illness Portion of the Log 16
              5.   The Summary of Occupational Injuries and Illnesses 16
          B. The Supplementary Record of Occupational Injuries and Illnesses 17
              1.   Recommendation 18
          C. Reporting a Death or Serious Injury 18
              1.   Recommendation 19

Chapter 3 Regulations that Apply to All Employers 21

    I.   Access to Employee Exposure and Medical Records
        (29 CFR 1910.20 in Appendix 3A) 22
   II. Emergency Action Plan and Fire Protection Plan
        (29 CFR 1910.38 in Appendix 3B) 23
          A. Emergency Action Plan (29 CFR 1910.38[a]) 24
          B. Fire Protection Plan (29 CFR 1910.38[b]) 26
  III. Medical Services and First Aid (29 CFR 1910.151 and
        29 CFR 1926.50 in Appendix 3C) 27

	IV.	Housekeeping (29 CFR 1910.22, 1910.176, and 1926.25 in Appendix 3D)	27
	V.	Hazard Communication Program (29 CFR 1910.1200 in Appendix 3E)	29
		A. What is a Hazardous Substance?	29
		B. Exclusions and Exemptions	30
		C. Required Action	31

Chapter 4 Regulations that Apply to Some Employers 35

I.	Personal Protective Equipment (29 CFR 1910.132 in Appendix 4A)	35
II.	Respiratory Protection (29 CFR 1910.134 in Appendix 4A)	36
III.	Occupational Noise Exposure (29 CFR 1910.95 in Appendix 4C)	39
IV.	Toxic and Hazardous Substances (29 CFR 1910.1000 through 1910.1001 in Appendix 4D)	40
V.	Occupational Exposure to Bloodborne Pathogens (29 CFR 1910.1030 in Appendix 4E)	43
VI.	Occupational Exposures to Hazardous Chemicals in Laboratories (29 CFR 1910.1450 in Appendix 4F)	46
	A. OSHA Laboratory Standard	46
	B. Requirements of Laboratory Standard	46
	1. Employee Exposure Determination	47
	2. Chemical Hygiene Plan	47
	3. Employee Information and Training	48
	4. Medical Consultation	48
	5. Special Precautions	49

Chapter 5 Accident Prevention Plan 51

I.	Responsibility	51
II.	Training	52
III.	Communication	52
IV.	Compliance	52
V.	Inspections	53
VI.	Corrective Measures	53
VII.	Recordkeeping	53
	A. Employee Training	54
	B. Inspections and Corrective Measures	54

Chapter 6 Worker Information and Training 55

I.	General	55
II.	Presenting the Topics	58
III.	Recordkeeping	59
IV.	Supervisor Training	60
V.	Training Under HAZWOPER	60

Chapter 7 OSHA Inspections 63

  I.   Regulatory Authority of the Department of Labor 63
  II.   Scheduling an OSHA Inspection—How and Why 63
  III. Unprogrammed Inspections 64
  IV.   Imminent Danger Inspections 64
  V.   Fatality or Catastrophe Investigations 65
  VI.   Emergency Situations 66
  VII. Complaint and Referral Inspections 66
  VIII. Programmed Inspections 67
  IX.   Comprehensive and Partial Inspections 67
  X.   No Advance Warning 68

Chapter 8 OSHA Citations and Proposed Penalties 69

  I.   Types of Citations 69
  II.   Advice 70

Chapter 9 General Duty Clause 73

  I.   Existing Hazard 73
  II.   Recognizable Hazard 74
  III. Death or Serious Physical Harm 74
  IV.   Feasible, Available Abatement Measures Exist 75

Chapter 10 Avoiding OSHA Inspections and Conduct of Such Inspections 77

  I.   Avoiding an OSHA Inspection 77
  II.   Conduct of Inspection and Dealing with an Inspector 78
        A. Opening Conference 78
        B. Construction 79
        C. Inspection Warrant 79
        D. Advice 80
  III. Inspection Procedure Recommendations 80
        A. Advice 81
  IV.   Walk-Around Inspection 81
  V.   Closing Conference 82

Chapter 11 Appeal or Not? and Appealing a Citation or Penalty 85

  I.   Posting of Citation 85
  II.   Reasons to Appeal 86
        A. Existence of the Violation 86
        B. Amount of Civil Fine 87
        C. Consequences Outside of OSHA 87
        D. Violation Improperly Characterized 88
        E. Possibility of a Repeated Violation 88

	F. Costs and Likelihood of Success	89
	G. Alienate OSHA: Yes or No?	90
III.	Appealing a Citation or Penalty	90
	A. Advice	91
IV.	Informal Conference	92
	A. Advice	93

APPENDICES

1A.	U.S. Department of Labor, Occupational Safety and Health Administration, Regional and Area Offices	97
2A.	Regional Offices of the Bureau of Labor Statistics	105
2B.	A Brief Guide to Recordkeeping Requirements for Occupational Injuries and Illnesses	107
2C.	SIC Code Exemptions	129
2D.	Supplementary Record of Occupational Injuries and Illnesses	131
3A.	29 CFR 1910.20 Access to Employee Exposure and Medical Records	133
3B.	29 CFR 1910.38 Employee Emergency Plans and Fire Prevention Plans	143
3C.	29 CFR 1910.151 Medical Services and First Aid; 29 CFR 1926.50 Medical Services and First Aid	145
3D.	29 CFR 1910.22 General Requirements; 29 CFR 1910.176 Handling Materials—General; 29 CFR 1926.25 Housekeeping	147
3E.	29 CFR 1910.1200 Hazard Communication	149
4A.	29 CFR 1910.132 General Requirements; 29 CFR 1910.133 Eye and Face Protection; 29 CFR 1910.134 Respiratory Protection	175
4B.	29 CFR 1910.146 Permit Required Confined Spaces	183
4C.	29 CFR 1910.95 Occupational Noise Exposure	203
4D.	29 CFR 1910.1000–1910.1001 Air Contaminants	219
4E.	29 CFR 1910.1030 Bloodborne Pathogens	275
4F.	29 CFR 1910.1450 Occupational Exposure to Hazardous Chemicals in Laboratories	289
5A.	Workplace Injury & Illness Prevention Sample Programs	305
6A.	29 CFR 1926.21 Safety Training and Education	339
6B.	29 CFR 1910.120 Hazardous Waste Operations and Emergency Response	341
10A.	Example: Company Inspection Procedure	377
Index		385

The Complete Guide to **OSHA** Compliance

Chapter 1

Understanding OSHA—An Overview

The concern for workers' well-being has extended over many years. The English Parliament enacted landmark labor legislation in 1833 called the Factory Act, which focused on the hours children were permitted to work and provided for inspections of workplaces. Additional legislation was passed in other countries in Europe.

In the U.S., legislation surrounding worker protection began to be enacted in the late 1800s by several states, including New York, Michigan, Massachusetts, and New Jersey. The legislative activity grew considerably after the turn of the century. The Bureau of Mines was created in 1910 and the federal Department of Labor was created in 1913.

State regulations moved faster than the federal programs. State and local government programs and safety standards continued to proliferate until the 1960s. Establishing a national program seemed to be an impossible task. However, the passage of three major pieces of legislation had a significant impact on establishing a national occupational health and safety program. These major pieces of legislation are:

- Metal and Nonmetallic Mine Safety Act of 1966
- Federal Coal Mine Health and Safety Act of 1969, and
- Occupational Safety and Health Act of 1970.

The Occupational Safety and Health Act has had the greatest impact on worker safety and health regulations as we know them today. It was passed at a time when the federal government believed that worker and environmental protection were of utmost importance. About the same time the

Occupational Safety and Health Act was passed, the Federal Hazardous Substances Act of 1966, the National Environmental Policy Act of 1969, the Coal Mine Health and Safety Act of 1969, the Clean Air Act of 1970, the Clean Water Act of 1972, The Environmental Pollution Control Act of 1972, the Safe Drinking Water Act of 1974, and the Toxic Substances Control Act of 1976 were also enacted.

Obviously, the attitude to establish a national piece of legislation to protect workers was strong. At the time the Occupational Safety and Health Act was being discussed, Congress was given the following facts:

- 14,000 deaths were due to job-related accidents
- Nearly 2-1/2 million workers were disabled
- Ten times as many person-days were lost from job-related disabilities as were from strikes
- It was estimated that there would be 300,000 new cases of occupational disease.

The principal tenet of the Occupational Safety and Health Act is to "assure so far as possible every working man and woman in the Nation safe and healthful working conditions and to preserve our human resources." The goals of the Act were to:

- Encourage employers and employees to reduce workplace hazards and to implement new or improve existing safety and health programs.
- Provide for research in occupational safety and health to develop innovative ways of dealing with occupational safety and health problems.
- Establish separate but dependent responsibilities and rights for employers and employees for the achievement of better safety and health conditions.
- Maintain a reporting and recordkeeping system to monitor job-related injuries and illnesses.
- Establish training programs to increase the number and competence of occupational safety and health personnel.
- Develop mandatory job safety and health standards and enforce them effectively.
- Provide for the development, analysis, evaluation and approval of state occupational safety and health programs.

The Occupational Safety and Health Act created several distinct government entities. Most of the power of the Occupational Safety and Health Act resides with the Occupational Safety and Health Administration (OSHA) which is located in the executive branch of the government under the Department of Labor. The specific actions that can be taken by OSHA will be discussed later.

The Occupational Safety and Health Act also established the National Institute for Occupational Safety and Health (NIOSH). NIOSH is the research

UNDERSTANDING OSHA—AN OVERVIEW

arm of OSHA and is responsible for workplace investigations, training and educational programs, recommendations for new health standards, and other related activities. NIOSH is under the Department of Health and Human Services, which was previously called the Department of Health, Education and Welfare.

Other government entities created by the Occupational Safety and Health Act include the Occupational Safety and Health Review Commission, the National Advisory Committee on Occupational Safety and Health, and the National Commission on State Workers' Compensation Laws.

Not all employers are affected by the Occupational Safety and Health Act. The Act covers employers "engaged in business affecting commerce who have employees." This specifically exempts federal workers. Federal agencies are responsible for establishing their own programs that are to be consistent with those established by OSHA. Where rules do not exist, OSHA standards apply. OSHA provisions also do not apply to state and local government employees. Last, federal workers who are under the jurisdiction of another federal agency's rules for health and safety are exempt from the OSHA rules. For example, OSHA's standards and regulations do not apply to those workers who are employed in nuclear power facilities and as longshoremen. These two industries are under the jurisdiction of the Department of Energy (DOE) and the Longshoremen's and Harbor Workers' Compensation Act, respectively. Other groups like railroad workers and miners are also exempt. The Occupational Safety and Health Act also does not cover self-employed persons and farms at which only immediate members of the farm employer's family are employed.

Although federal agencies are exempt from OSHA standards, the Agency conducts workplace inspections in response to worker complaints and for federal workplaces with high hazard jobs. Federal agencies are also required to maintain injury and illness statistics, conduct self-inspections, etc.

The Occupational Safety and Health Act gave power to the states, District of Columbia, and U.S. territories to establish and manage their own occupational safety and health program as long as their rules were "at least as effective" as those enacted by the federal government. States must also cover state and local government workers in their program. States wishing to administer their own program must submit their plans to the Department of Labor for approval. The plan must demonstrate that the state has the ability to provide for:

- Standard-setting
- Enforcement
- Appeals
- Public employee protection
- Sufficient personnel for enforcement
- Training, education and technical assistance programs

There are currently 25 states with approved plans. Although all of these states have established their own enforcement arm, not all states have opted to write their own regulations. Some states have decided to enforce the federal standards as they are written. Other states have decided to establish their own safety and health standards. This is acceptable to the Department of Labor as long as the state's rules are identical to, or at least as stringent as, the federal government's regulations. As the federal government promulgates its regulations, states that establish their own regulations must do so within 6 months following the passage of a federal OSHA regulation. States that have approved plans are shown in Figure 1.1. The plans in Connecticut and New York cover public employees only. In these two states, private sector employees are covered under federal jurisdiction. Contacts for the state plans are shown in Appendix 1A.

Alaska	New York *
Arizona	North Carolina
California	Oregon
Connecticut *	Puerto Rico
Hawaii	South Carolina
Indiana	Tennessee
Iowa	Utah
Kentucky	Vermont
Maryland	Virginia
Michigan	Virgin Islands
Minnesota	Washington
Nevada	Wyoming
New Mexico	

Note * These states cover public employees only. Federal OSHA is responsible for private sector employees.

FIGURE 1.1
States with approved plans.

Chapter 2

OSHA RECORDKEEPING

This chapter covers OSHA recordkeeping requirements for occupational injuries and illnesses. This chapter is *not* all-inclusive, and you are well-advised to review the applicable federal regulations as they are extremely detailed. The applicable federal regulations are set forth in 29 CFR § 1904, et. seq. You should also review the U.S. Department of Labor, Bureau of Labor Statistics, booklet entitled *Recordkeeping Guidelines for Occupational Injuries and Illnesses*. You may obtain a copy of the booklet from one of the regional offices of the Bureau of Labor Statistics. The addresses of the regional offices are set forth in Appendix 2A. An abbreviated guide is also available for your use from the Department of Labor, Bureau of Labor Statistics and is entitled *A Brief Guide to Recordkeeping Requirements for Occupational Injuries and Illnesses*. A copy of the abbreviated guide is set forth in Appendix 2B.

With few limited exceptions, you must complete and maintain the forms discussed in this chapter. This chapter also discusses reporting requirements of a death or a serious injury or illness of a company employee. This chapter is divided into three parts:

- First, recordkeeping requirements for injuries and illnesses
- Second, how to keep OSHA records, including: The Log and Summary of Occupational Injury and Illnesses and The Supplementary Record of Occupational Injuries and Illnesses
- Third, reporting a death or serious injury.

I. RECORDKEEPING REQUIREMENTS FOR INJURIES AND ILLNESSES

If an employee suffers an occupational injury or illness, most employers must complete the documents discussed below. The coverage of the OSHA Act is extensive and covers nearly all employers in the private sector. There are certain limited exceptions to these recordkeeping requirements, which are discussed directly below.

A. No Employees

The following are examples of circumstances where OSHA recordkeeping requirements would *not* apply as there are *no employees* covered by the Fed/OSHA Act.

- Two or more partners operating a small company with no employees would not be covered by the Fed/OSHA Act. Partners are not considered employees.
- Activities of self-employed individuals are not covered by the Fed/OSHA Act. Self-employed individuals are not considered employees under the Act.
- Employers of domestic help in the employer's private residence for the usual purposes of housekeeping and/or child care are not required to keep records for the domestic help.

There are also exemptions from the recordkeeping requirements of OSHA for the following *types* of employers:

- Small employers
- Employers in low hazard industries

B. Small Employers

Although subject to the overall coverage of the Fed/OSHA Act, employers who had *no more than* 10 employees (10 or less) at any point in time during the calendar year immediately preceding a current calendar year need not comply with the recordkeeping requirements of the Act for the current year. For example, if your company employed no more than 10 employees at any point in time in 1994, you need not maintain the OSHA Log in 1995.

In determining your possible classification as a small employer, *the total number* of employees your company may have employed during the calendar year is *not* the determining factor. Rather, it is whether the company employed more than 10 employees *at any one time* during the previous calendar year.

For example, if two partners operate an automotive repair shop throughout the year with nine employees, the small employers exemption may apply to that company, for the partners are not employees. Therefore, as long as the repair shop did not have more than ten employees at any given point in time during the calendar year, it qualifies for the small employer exemption for the following calendar year.

If you have more than one business location ("establishment") under Fed/OSHA jurisdiction, the total number of employees in the entire company is included in this calculation. Therefore, if you have two separate business locations, each of which had six employees during the previous calendar year, you would need to maintain the OSHA injury and illness records during the current year for *both* establishments because the total employment of the company was greater than ten. If, on the other hand, there were never more than ten employees working at the two locations at any point in time during the calendar year, the company would not need to maintain the records in question during the following calendar year.

1. Advice

A few states do require even small employers to maintain OSHA records. If you are in a state plan state, you should check the requirements of your state regarding this requirement.

C. Employers in Low Hazard Industries

The Fed/OSHA Act creates a second exemption from its recordkeeping requirements, which applies to employers in low hazard industries. 29 CFR § 1904.16. This exemption depends upon the company's Standard Industry Classification (SIC) Code. Employers whose establishments are classified in SIC Codes 52–89, (*excluding* 52–54, 70, 75, 76, 79 and 80) need *not* comply with the recordkeeping requirements of the Fed/OSHA Act. See Appendix 2C for a list of the SIC Code exemptions.

1. Recommendation

First, you should determine the SIC Code of your company, for perhaps your company's business may fall under one of the low hazard industry exemptions. If you are uncertain of your SIC code classification, your company's income tax return may include a "principal business activity code" which should reflect a numerical designation which is generally consistent with an SIC code classification. You may also refer to the 1972 edition of the Standard Industrial Classification (SIC) Manual prepared by the Executive Office of the President, Office of Management and Budget, to determine the company's SIC code. This publication might be available in corporate offices and should be available in libraries, or it may be purchased from a government printing office. You may also contact your state officials or the U.S. Department of Labor, Bureau of Labor Statistics Regional Offices (See Appendix 2A), for assistance in determining the company's SIC code.

If you are in a state with an approved state plan, you should determine and comply with the recordkeeping requirements of your state. Some states do *not* exempt employers in low hazard industries from the recordkeeping requirements of the state. Appendix 1A includes state agency addresses and telephone numbers. Also remember to check individual state plans if some of the company's facilities are located in such states.

Large employers with multiple establishments may find that some of their establishments qualify for an exemption while others do not. For example, a manufacturer may have assembly plants and retail sales offices. The manufacturing facilities would not be exempt from OSHA recordkeeping; however, the sales offices might fall under an SIC code exemption as a low hazard type of operation.

If your company happens to be selected to participate in the "Annual Survey of Occupational Injuries and Illnesses" by the Bureau of Labor Statistics, your company would need to complete and maintain the required records for 1 year as a result of the participation in that survey, regardless of an SIC code exemption.

2. Advice

Remember that although OSHA recordkeeping requirements may be unnecessary for small employers and employers in low hazard industries, those employers must still comply with all other safety and health rules and regulations, display the OSHA poster, and orally report any work-related accidents which result in a fatality or the hospitalization of three or more employees to OSHA within 8 hours of learning of the incident.

II. HOW TO KEEP OSHA RECORDS

Only two recordkeeping forms regarding injuries and illnesses are generally used by Fed/OSHA: the Log and Summary of Occupational Injuries and Illnesses, OSHA No. 200 ("the log"), and the Supplemental Record of Occupational Injuries and Illnesses, OSHA No. 101.

A. Log and Summary of Occupational Injuries and Illnesses

The Log and Summary of Occupational Injuries and Illnesses (OSHA No. 200) is a document used for recording and classifying recordable occupational injuries and illnesses, including the extent and outcome of each case. A copy of the log is set forth in Figure 2.1.

The log shows when the occupational injury or illness occurred, to whom, what the injured or ill person's regular job was at the time of the injury and

OSHA RECORDKEEPING

illness exposure, the department in which the person was employed at the time of injury or onset of illness, the kind of injury or illness, the extent and outcome of the injury, any lost time, and the type, extent, and outcome of the illness.

A private equivalent to the log may be used if it contains the same detail as the log itself as long as it is as "readable and comprehensible" to a person not familiar with the equivalent format.

Each recordable injury and illness is to be recorded as early as practicable, but no later than 6 working days after the company has received information that a recordable injury or illness has occurred.

You are required to maintain a log *for each establishment*. An "establishment" is defined as a single physical location where business is conducted or where services or industrial operations are performed, such as a factory, warehouse, or central administrative office. The log must reflect separately the injury and illness experience *of each establishment*.

You may perform the actual preparation and maintenance of the log at a location other than at the establishment to which it pertains. Two requirements exist if the company is to maintain and keep the log at a location other than at the establishment covered by the log. First, sufficient information must be available at the recordkeeping location to allow the log to be accurately completed within 6 workdays; and second, a copy of the log (current to within 45 calendar days) must be present at all times for each establishment in question.

That is, if you complete and retain the log for the factory at your office, send a copy of the log to the factory (the "establishment") every 45 days.

For employees working at a fixed establishment, a copy of the log is to be kept at that establishment. If you have employees who do not report to a fixed location but work elsewhere, the records should be kept at the fixed location to which the employees report each day. For example, employees engaged in activities such as agriculture and construction could fall under this category, although there may be some discretion as to the location of these records. The location of such records depends upon the nature of the operation. If the employees report to a given place each workday but work elsewhere, the records should be kept at the location to which they first report. If, on the other hand, the employees report directly to transient jobsites each day, a construction company has discretion regarding the location of the records. They may be kept at a field office or mobile base of operation, or they may be maintained at an established central location.

Some employees are subject to common supervision, yet do not report or work at a fixed establishment on a regular basis. The records for these employees may be kept at the field office or mobile office of their operations or at an established central location.

Bureau of Labor Statistics
Log and Summary of Occupational
Injuries and Illnesses

NOTE: **This form is required by Public Law 91-596 and must be kept in the establishment for *5 years*. Failure to maintain and post can result in the issuance of citations and assessment of penalties.** ***(See posting requirements on the other side of form.)***

RECORDABLE CASES: You are required to record information about every occupational **death**; every nonfatal occupational **illness**; and those nonfatal occupational in**juries** which involve one or more of the following: loss of consciousness, restriction of work or motion, transfer to another job, or medical treatment (other than first aid) ***(See definitions on the other side of form.)***

Case or File Number	Date of Injury or Onset of Illness	Employee's Name	Occupation	Department	Description of Injury or Illness
Enter a nondupli-cating number which will facilitate com-parisons with supple-mentary records.	Enter Mo./day.	Enter first name or initial, middle initial, last name.	Enter regular job title, not activity employee was per-forming when injured or at onset of illness. In the absence of a formal title, enter a brief description of the employee's duties.	Enter department in which the employee is regularly employed or a description of normal workplace to which employee is assigned, even though temporarily working in another depart-ment at the time of injury or illness.	Enter a brief description of the injury or illness and indicate the part or parts of body affected. Typical entries for this column might be Amputation of 1st joint right forefinger, Strain of lower back, Contact dermatitis on both hands, Electrocution--body
(A)	(B)	(C)	(D)	(E)	(F)
					PREVIOUS PAGE TOTALS →
					TOTALS (Instructions on other side of form.) →

OSHA No. 200 ★U.S.GPO:1990-262-256/15419

FIGURE 2.1
Log and Summary of Occupational Injuries and Illnesses

OSHA RECORDKEEPING 11

U.S. Department of Labor

For Calendar Year 19 _____ Page ____ of ____

Company Name

Establishment Name

Establishment Address

Form Approved
O.M.B. No. 1220-0029
See OMB Disclosure
Statement on reverse.

Extent of and Outcome of INJURY						Type, Extent of, and Outcome of ILLNESS											
Fatalities	Nonfatal Injuries					Type of Illness							Fatalities	Nonfatal Illnesses			
Injury Related	Injuries With Lost Workdays				Injuries Without Lost Workdays	CHECK Only One Column for Each Illness (See other side of form for terminations or permanent transfers.)							Illness Related	Illnesses With Lost Workdays			Illnesses Without Lost Workdays
Enter DATE of death.	Enter a CHECK if injury involves days away from work, or days of restricted work activity, or both.	Enter a CHECK if injury involves days away from work.	Enter number of DAYS away from work.	Enter number of DAYS of restricted work activity.	Enter a CHECK if no entry was made in columns 1 or 2 but the injury is recordable as defined above.	Occupational skin diseases or disorders	Dust diseases of the lungs	Respiratory conditions due to toxic agents	Poisoning (systemic effects of toxic materials)	Disorders due to physical agents	Disorders associated with repeated trauma	All other occupational illnesses	Enter DATE of death.	Enter a CHECK if illness involves days away from work, or days of restricted work activity, or both.	Enter a CHECK if illness involves days away from work.	Enter number of DAYS away from work.	Enter number of DAYS of restricted work activity.	Enter a CHECK if no entry was made in columns 8 or 9.
Mo./day/yr.													Mo./day/yr.				
(1)	(2)	(3)	(4)	(5)	(6)	(a)	(b)	(c)	(d)	(e)	(f)	(g)	(8)	(9)	(10)	(11)	(12)	(13)
										(7)								

Certification of Annual Summary Totals By _____ Title _____ Date _____

OSHA No. 200   POST ONLY THIS PORTION OF THE LAST PAGE NO LATER THAN FEBRUARY 1.

FIGURE 2.1
Log and Summary of Occupational Injuries and Illnesses (Continued)

The records for unsupervised employees such as traveling salespeople, consultants, or engineers who do not report or work at a single establishment, should be maintained at the location from which they are paid or at the location of their company's personnel operations. In any of these cases, such employees should be knowledgeable about the location of the log.

The log must be maintained on a calendar year basis and retained for 5 years following the end of the calendar year in question.

You are not required to maintain a copy of the log for any year during which there were no recordable cases; however, the *summary portion* of the log should be completed with zero entries and retained for the 5-year period.

1. Advice

Since the summary portion of the log is an integral portion of the log, you may want to maintain a copy of the entire log for 5 years, just for the sake of simplicity.

2. Recordable Events

Events which are recordable on the log include:

- Work-related deaths
- Lost work days
- Injuries and illnesses involving medical treatment
- Loss of consciousness
- Restriction of work or motion
- Transfer to another job

First aid treatment is not a recordable event!

The difference between first aid and medical treatment is often significant, not only for OSHA recordkeeping, but also for workers' compensation purposes. The difference between the two treatments is one of degree of treatment, not whether a physician is involved.

First aid is defined as "Any one-time treatment, and any follow-up visit for the purpose of observation, of minor scratches, cuts, burns, splinters, and so forth, which do not ordinarily require medical care. Such one-time treatment, and follow-up visit for the purpose of observation, is considered first aid even though provided by a physician or registered professional personnel."

Medical treatment is defined as "Treatment administered by a physician or by registered professional personnel under the standing orders of a physician. Medical treatment does not include first aid treatment even though provided by a physicians or registered professional personnel." See Figure 2.2 for a list generally acceptable as distinguishing first aid treatment and medical treatment.

A hospital visit (or stay) is not necessarily a controlling factor regarding the issue of the recordability of an event. The focus is also not on the length of a hospital stay, but on whether medical treatment was provided.

Each new recordable injury and illness requires a new entry. Injuries are generally the result of some new incident—such as a trip or slip—and require a new recording. Recurrences, however, do *not* require new entries, merely a revision of an earlier entry.

The distinction between a new incident and the recurrence of a further complication of a previous injury of illness can be complicated. You are referred to Chapter V of the *Recordkeeping Guidelines for Occupational Injuries and Illnesses* (Appendix 2B) to assist you in your decision.

Deciding whether the emergence of illness symptoms constitutes a new event or the recurrence of a previous illness is also often complex, and, as noted above, you should review the recordkeeping booklet for guidance.

The employee need not be presently employed to require a recordable event. As long as the underlying event occurred within the 5-year record retention period, the event is recordable in the year of the injury or illness. This may require changes to a previous year's log.

Entries for previously unrecorded injuries or illnesses which are subsequently discovered or found to be recordable after the end of the year in which the case occurred should be made upon discovery. Log totals should also be modified to reflect any such changes. If an entry previously made is found at a later time to be nonrecordable, that entry may be lined out.

3. Recommendation

Strictly from an OSHA standpoint, if you question whether an injury or illness has occurred, it may be advisable to record the case within 6 workdays of learning of the condition. You may line out the entry at a later date if it is determined not to be recordable. It may be advisable to check with your workers' compensation carrier, however, to determine the ramifications of "overreporting" injuries and illnesses.

4. Completion of the Log

The log consists of three parts including a descriptive portion which identifies the employee and briefly describes an injury or illness, a section covering the extent of the *injuries,* and a similar section on the type and extent of any *illnesses.*

MEDICAL TREATMENT

Treatment of **INFECTION**
Application of **ANTISEPTICS during second or subsequent visit** to medical personnel
Treatment of **SECOND OR THIRD DEGREE BURN(S)**
Application of **SUTURES** (stitches)
Application of **BUTTERFLY ADHESIVE DRESSING(S) STRIP(S)** in lieu of sutures
Removal of **FOREIGN BODIES EMBEDDED IN EYE**
Removal of **FOREIGN BODIES FROM WOUND;** if procedure is **COMPLICATED** because of depth of embedment, size, or location
Use of **PRESCRIPTION MEDICATIONS** (except a single dose administered on first visit for minor injury or discomfort)
Use of hot or cold **SOAKING THERAPY during second or subsequent visit** to medical personnel
Application of hot or cold **COMPRESS(ES) during second or subsequent visit** to medical personnel
CUTTING AWAY DEAD SKIN (surgical debridement)
Application of **HEAT THERAPY during second or subsequent visit** to medical personnel
Use of **WHIRLPOOL BATH THERAPY during second or subsequent visit** to medical personnel
POSITIVE X-RAY DIAGNOSIS fractures, broken bones, etc.)
ADMISSION TO A HOSPITAL or equivalent medical facility **FOR TREATMENT**

FIRST AID TREATMENT

Application of **ANTISEPTICS during first visit** to medical personnel
Treatment of **FIRST DEGREE BURN(S)**
Application of **BANDAGE(S) during any visit** to medical personnel
Use of **ELASTIC BANDAGE(S) during first visit** to medical personnel
Removal of **FOREIGN BODIES NOT EMBEDDED IN EYE** if only irrigation is required
Removal of **FOREIGN BODIES FROM WOUND,** if procedure is **UNCOMPLICATED** and is, for example, by tweezers or other simple technique
Use of **NONPRESCRIPTION MEDICATIONS AND** administration of **single dose of PRESCRIPTION MEDICATION** on first visit for minor injury or discomfort
SOAKING THERAPY on initial visit to medical personnel or removal of bandages by **SOAKING**
Application of hot or cold **COMPRESS(ES) during first visit** to medical personnel
Application of **OINTMENTS** to abrasions to prevent drying or cracking
Application of **HEAT THERAPY during first visit** to medical personnel
Use of **WHIRLPOOL BATH THERAPY during first visit** to medical personnel
NEGATIVE X-RAY DIAGNOSIS
OBSERVATION of injury during visit to medical personnel

FIGURE 2.2
Medical and First Aid Treatment

OSHA RECORDKEEPING

To distinguish an injury from an illness, keep the following distinction in mind. The basic definition of an occupational *injury* includes those incidents which result from a workplace accident or an exposure involving a *single instantaneous incident* in the work environment.

For example, contact with a hot surface which produces a burn as a result of the single instantaneous moment of contact is an injury. On the other hand, sunburn or welding flash burns resulting from *prolonged* exposure are considered illnesses. This distinction is generally referred to as the "single-incident" concept. *Recordkeeping Guidelines for Occupational Injuries and Illnesses* has some excellent examples distinguishing injuries from illnesses.

The columns on the OSHA log are self-explanatory. The directions for the completion of the log are set forth on the reverse side of the form and are comprehensive and easily understood. The following comments are offered for additional assistance in completing the OSHA log.

a. General Information Columns

Column D: You must record the injured or ill employee's *regular* job title even if the employee was working outside his or her regularly assigned job at the time of the injury or illness.

Column E: You must state the department in which the injured or ill person is *regularly* employed. If, for example, an employee is regularly assigned to the maintenance department, but was injured while working in the shipping department, the correct entry would be maintenance.

Column F: While Column F on the log requests a "brief description" of the injury or illness, the entry in this column should be sufficiently detailed. For example, a proper entry regarding a finger amputation would be "amputation-first joint, ring finger, right hand." This details the degree of the injury to the finger on the hand in question.

b. Injury Portion of the Log

Although *all* work-related *deaths* and *illnesses* must be recorded, the recording of work-related *injuries* is limited to certain specific types of cases. Only work injuries involving lost work days, medical treatment, loss of consciousness, restriction of work or motion, or transfer to another job are recordable. Work injuries requiring first aid treatment are *not* recordable. "First aid treatment" is defined above. As noted, the fact that care is provided by a physician does not affect this characterization; that is, if the treatment is properly characterized as first aid treatment, it will remain in that category even if a physician renders the treatment.

Column 1: Column 1 of the injury portion of the log requires the date of death when an occupational injury results in a fatality. Even though the death may not have occurred within 6 working days of the incident, if it occurs within 5 *years* following the end of the calendar year in which the injury occurred and the injury was work-related, the entry in the log must be changed to reflect a fatality. In such a case, any other entries on Columns 2 to 6 would be lined out and the date of death entered in Column 1.

Column 2: If a case involves lost work days or restricted duty due to an injury, check Column 2. Lost work days include days away from work *and* days of restricted work activity. The number of lost work days should *not* include the *day of the injury* or any days which the employee would not regularly have worked (e.g., weekends, paid holidays, vacations).

Column 3 through 6: All of these columns are self-explanatory.

c. *Illness Portion of the Log*

Column 7: You must make only a single entry in one of the Columns 7(a) through 7(g), depending upon which column is applicable.

Column 8: An entry must be made in this column if a fatality does occur within 5 years following the year the illness was initially entered on the log.

Columns 9 through 13: The information required in these columns is similar to that for injuries.

For illnesses only, when a termination or a permanent transfer is involved, you must place an asterisk (*) to the right of the entry in Columns 7(a) through 7(g).

5. *The Summary of Occupational Injuries and Illnesses*

The portion of the log to the right of the dotted vertical line on the form is intended to record injuries and illnesses as discussed directly above and is also to be used to summarize injuries and illnesses in an establishment for the just-completed calendar year. Before preparing the summary you should review the log to ensure that each entry is accurate and correct.

Following the end of the calendar year for which the log was maintained, the summary is prepared by merely totaling the entries in Columns 1 through 13 at the bottom of the columns where indicated. Any asterisks noted on the log need not be totaled. The person certifying the accuracy of the information must complete the certification portion of the log where indicated.

If an injury or illness is continuing at the end of the year, you must *estimate* the number of future work days the employee is likely to lose in the following year as a result of the injury or illness. The estimated number of future lost work days should be added to the number of work days already lost and the combined totals entered on the log as a single entry and included in the summary. In such a situation, the log will need to be revised at a later date to reflect the number of work days that were actually lost.

For example, if an employee is injured in December and has not returned to work as of December 31, the original entry would be in the year of injury. You would calculate the total work days lost up to December 31 and then *estimate* the number of work days the employee is expected to lose the following year. Therefore, if, on December 31, the employee had lost 10 work days and you expect the employee to lose an additional 10 work days the following year, you would put the estimated total of 20 work days in either Column 4 or 5, or 11 or 12 of the log for the year of the injury or illness. When the employee does return to work and is able to perform his or her regular job, you would verify the actual number of lost work days and correct the entries on the log of the year of injury or illness as necessary. No entries would be made on the log of the year the employee returns to work.

You must **post** the summary portion of the log (post *only* that portion of the log to the right of the dotted vertical line) for each establishment for a 1-month period the following year. The summary portion of the log covering the previous calendar year shall be posted no later than February 1 of the following year and shall remain in place until March 1. The summary portion of the log is to be posted during the month of February of the following year even though there were no recordable cases during the previous year. In such a case, zeros would be entered in all the categories on the "totals" line of the summary.

The summary portion of the log must be posted in each establishment to which it pertains in a conspicuous place or in a place(s) where notices to employees are customarily posted.

If some of your employees do not work at a fixed worksite during the period February 1 through March 1, you are required to present or mail a copy of the annual summary to those employees.

If the establishment in question has closed by the time the summary is prepared or a seasonal operation is conducted at the establishment and the site is shut down during the posting period, you need not post the summary. You must, however, provide a copy of the annual summary to those permanent employees who may be employed in the seasonal operation.

As with the log itself, the use of an equivalent form (other than the summary) will be satisfactory as long as it is readable and comprehensible. You must retain the summary for five (5) years following the end of the year to which it relates.

B. The Supplementary Record of Occupational Injuries and Illnesses

For every injury or illness entered on the log, it is necessary to record additional information on the Supplementary Record of Occupational Injuries and Illnesses ("supplementary record"), the OSHA No. 101. (See: Appendix

2D.) This form is intended to provide additional information regarding the injury or illness, including a description of how the injury or illness exposure occurred, any objects or substances involved, an identification of the nature of the injury or illness, as well as the part(s) of the body affected.

If you are required to maintain the log, you are also required to complete the supplementary record in the event of a recordable event.

The supplementary record must be prepared within 6 working days after receipt of information that a recordable case has occurred.

You may use a document other than the OSHA No. 101 as long as the form or forms you use contain the same information as the OSHA form. For example, in many states a workers' compensation report of injury is required to be prepared, and such a form often contains all of the OSHA No. 101 information. In the event that you choose to use such a different form, you should ensure that the form does include all of the information that is required on the OSHA No. 101.

While completion of the OSHA No. 101 is self-explanatory, the following items are highlighted:

The "case or file number" must be the same number used to identify the case or file number in Column A of the log.

Item 8 refers to the employee's regular job title. This will be the same title as set forth in Column D of the log.

Item 9 refers to the department or the division in which the employee is regularly employed. This is the same department as indicated in Column E of the log.

1. Recommendation

Documents such as the supplementary record are often used in litigation occurring as a result of an employee's injury or illness. It is not in the company's best interest to have hurriedly completed the form or speculated as to the *cause* of the accident (paragraph 13 of the OSHA No. 101). The same advice applies to paragraphs 12 and 15 of this supplementary record.

While the supplementary record requests specificity, it may be that you do not know within 6 working days what caused the injuries to the employee or what the employee was doing at the time of his or her injury. You should *not speculate* as to the cause of the injury or illness or as to what the employee may have been doing at the time of the injury. If you do not know or if you are uncertain about these issues, you should indicate your lack of knowledge on the form. A second report prepared at a later date detailing more specific information would seemingly be acceptable to the agency. It may be, however, that the company is never able to determine the cause of the accident, a fact which should be recorded on the OSHA No. 101.

OSHA RECORDKEEPING

C. Reporting a Death or Serious Injury

Federal OSHA regulations require that an employer must *orally* report any work-related incident that resulted in the death of an employee or the hospitalization of three or more employees to OSHA within 8 hours. The 8-hour reporting time begins when the employer or any agent of the employer becomes aware of such an incident. This reporting requirement applies whenever an employee dies or three or more employees are hospitalized within 30 days of the incident as a result of the incident.

The rule requires an employer to make an *oral* report by telephone or in person to the OSHA Area Office nearest the incident site where a fatality or multiple hospitalizations occur. The employer can also choose to use OSHA's toll-free telephone number (800) 321-OSHA. The establishment name, the location and time of the incident, the number of fatalities or hospitalized employees, the company's contact person and his/her telephone number at work, and a brief description of the incident must be included in the report.

It is advisable that you follow up the telephone call in *writing*.

The report must include:

1. The establishment name
2. Location and time of the incident
3. A brief description of the incident
4. The number of fatalities (if any), and the extent of hospitalized employees, any injuries result from the employment accident
5. Identification of a contact person

The Area Director may require additional reports (in writing or otherwise) as he or she deems necessary. Failure to file the reports may result in the issuance of citations and the assessment of penalties. There is no small employer exemption from this reporting requirement.

1. Recommendation

Your company should ensure the existence of a procedure whereby all reportable job-related fatalities, hospitalizations, or injuries to employees are timely reported to the OSHA Area Director. It is also advisable to keep a record of when the company was made aware of the fatality, injury, or the hospitalization, and when the Area Director was contacted. If your company has a place of business within a state which operates its own OSHA program, you must become familiar with the requirements of that state plan.

Chapter 3

REGULATIONS THAT APPLY TO ALL EMPLOYERS

There are several hundred federal OSHA safety and health regulations. Some of the regulations are written for specific industries, e.g., construction, while others are for specific operations, e.g., power press, scaffolding. Still other regulations are written for protection from specific hazards, e.g., asbestos, electrical lockout. Given the fact that certain industries are subject to only a few of the OSHA standards, and others, while potentially subject to virtually all of the standards, are practically affected only by a portion of them, it is important that employers identify the regulations that apply to each of their work activities. This chapter is designed to assist employers who must comply with general workplace safety and health regulations that apply to virtually all employers.

As a general rule, *all employers are subject to the General Industry Standards.* To learn what regulations impact your business, you should:

1. Obtain a copy of the OSHA regulations. They can be found in Title 29 of the Code of Federal Regulations and are available for purchase from the Government Printing Office in Washington, D.C. Review the index for regulations that are likely to impact your business. Section 1910 applies to general industry. Read those regulations.
2. Combine compliance tasks where applicable. Your business may be subject to OSHA, EPA, state, and local government requirements that are similar. In these cases, consider dovetailing your efforts. For example, several agencies have requirements for developing and maintaining hazardous substance inventories. Combine your efforts and develop a single hazardous substance inventory that meets the OSHA Hazard Communication Standard along with the hazardous materials reporting requirements under the Environmental Protection Agency Resource Conservation and Recovery Act (RCRA).
3. Prepare plans or procedures for compliance. Make your plans as clear and straightforward as possible, responding to every point raised in a regulation. Obtain management approval if your plans go beyond what is required for a given regulation.

4. Conduct training programs to inform management about the plans being implemented. Develop an educational program for employees so they will know what is expected of them. Ensure that both groups understand how the company intends to meet the OSHA requirements.
5. Document your program. To the compliance officer, your program is only as good as your records can demonstrate during an inspection. Prepare written compliance programs. Keep written records of any changes made to the program. Maintain written records of all training programs. The records should not only include the names of those who attended, but include as well the date the training was conducted, the name of the instructor, and the class outline and/or agenda.

The following is a summary of regulations that impact nearly every employer.

I. ACCESS TO EMPLOYEE EXPOSURE AND MEDICAL RECORDS (29 CFR 1910.20 in Appendix 3A)

This regulation requires employers to provide employees and their designated representatives (e.g., collective bargaining agent, physician) with access to their exposure and medical records. Employees have a right to examine their personal records.

For the purposes of this regulation, a *medical record* consists of physician and employment questionnaires or histories, laboratory results, medical opinions, diagnoses, treatments, employee medical complaints, etc. Health insurance forms, physical specimens, and records kept for employee assistance programs (e.g., drug rehabilitation, counseling, etc.) are **not** considered medical records for the purposes of OSHA compliance.

An *exposure record* is a record of air monitoring of hazardous airborne substances, biologic monitoring required for employment (e.g., blood lead, urinary arsenic), and Material Safety Data Sheets collected for compliance with the Hazard Communication Standard.

According to this standard, you must:

a. Maintain **medical records** for 30 years beyond the duration of employment. For example, if you have a 15-year employee, you must maintain that person's records for 45 years. Do not comingle medical records with your personnel or insurance claims records.
b. Maintain all **exposure records** for 30 years. These are records directly associated with the assessment of an individual's exposure. If you collected area air samples or other forms of background environmental monitoring that were not directly related to an assessment of personal exposure, these records need only be retained for 1 year.
c. Maintain a Material Safety Data Sheet for 30 years. If you destroyed a Material Safety Data Sheet, you must keep a record of the chemicals that were used, where they were used, and when they were used.

REGULATIONS THAT APPLY TO ALL EMPLOYERS 23

d. Notify employees of their rights to these records. Permit employees (or their representatives) access to **their** records within a reasonable time and manner. You must provide, within 15 days of an employee's request:

- A copy of the record,
- A means of making a copy of the record at no cost to the employee, or loaning the record to the employee,

Develop a written release form for an employee's use in authorizing release of the employee's medical records to a designated representative. The release should include:

- Name and signature of the employee,
- Date of the request,
- Name of the individual or organization that is authorized to release the information,
- Name of the designated representative to receive the information,
- General description of the information to be released,
- General description of the purpose for the release, and
- Date or condition under which the authorization will expire.

A sample request letter is shown in Figure 3.1.

Should you sell your business, all of the above-mentioned records are to be transferred to the new owner and the new owner is responsible to maintain the records.

If your business ceases to exist, and there is no new owner, you must notify your employees of their rights to these records 3 months prior to the business ceasing to exist.

If the business ceases to exist, and there is no new owner, or the owner intends to dispose of records (following the 30-year requirement), the employer may:

- Send the records to the Director of the National Institute for Occupational Safety and Health (NIOSH) if required by another OSHA safety standard; or
- Notify the Director of NIOSH in writing of the impending disposal of the records 3 months prior to their disposal; or
- Large employers who regularly dispose of records required to be preserved for at least 30 years may notify the Director of NIOSH with an annual notification, 3 months prior to the records being disposed.

II. EMERGENCY ACTION PLAN AND FIRE PROTECTION PLAN (29 CFR 1910.38 in Appendix 3B)

While this regulation does not make it clear whether both of these two programs are required for every employer, it is our interpretation and

I, _____, hereby authorize _____
to release to _____ the following medical information from my
personal medical records:

I give my permission for this medical information to be used for the following purpose:
_____, but I do not give permission for any other
use or re-disclosure of this information.

Expiration date:

Employee's name or legal representative:

Signature of employee or legal representative:

Date of signature: _____

FIGURE 3.1
Release of employee medical record information

recommendation that all employers develop and implement these programs and have them available at every place of employment.

The regulation states that small employers (i.e., employers with 10 or fewer employees for **any** time during the year) may communicate their Emergency Action Plan and their Fire Protection Plan orally to the employees. However, some documentation is required to demonstrate to OSHA that the programs are in existence.

A. Emergency Action Plan (29 CFR 1910.38[a])

Employers should develop a written Emergency Action Plan for all foreseeable emergencies, e.g., fire, chemical spill, chemical leak, tornado, hurricane, earthquake, power outage, bomb threat, etc. The plan should be in writing and contain, at a minimum, the following elements:

1. Emergency escape procedures and escape routes (e.g. evacuation routes including the locations where all employees should congregate). Consider various levels of evacuation dependent on the type of emergency, i.e., full building evacuation may not always be appropriate.

REGULATIONS THAT APPLY TO ALL EMPLOYERS

2. Procedures to be followed by employees who remain to operate critical operations that cannot be shut off, or that take time to bring to a low ebb.
3. Procedures to account for all employees following an evacuation. Generally, assigning supervisors the responsibility to perform a head count of their subordinates will suffice.
4. Procedures to be followed by those employees performing rescue and medical duties. Consider including procedures for employees who are part of an emergency response team or fire brigade if you have such groups.
5. Preferred means of reporting emergencies, e.g., call 911, call the receptionist, use the closest fire pull, etc.
6. Names or job titles of persons whom employees can contact for additional information or explanation of duties under the Emergency Action Plan.
7. Establish an alarm system in accordance with 29 CFR 1910.165. Generally, the alarm system should include the following elements:

   a. It should provide for warning for necessary emergency action as provided for in the Emergency Action Plan.
   b. It should be capable of being heard or seen above ambient noise or light levels by all employees. (Consider using flashing lights as well to accommodate the hearing impaired or in areas of high noise levels.)
   c. It should provide a distinctive and recognizable signal to evacuate or to perform actions described in the Emergency Action Plan.
   d. There should be procedures to sound the alarm.
   e. The system must be installed in compliance with the OSHA requirements and local fire and building codes.
   f. The system must be able to be promptly restored following a test or alarm.
   g. The alarm system should be tested at least every 2 months.
   h. A power supply is to be maintained or replaced as often as necessary to operate properly, and a back-up alarm system (e.g., employee runners or telephones) is to be provided should the alarm system be out of operation for any time.
   i. If a manual alarm system is used (e.g., air horn, bull horn) the systems must be located in conspicuous locations and readily accessible.
   j. If the alarm system is used to alert a fire brigade, or other similar purpose, it should be distinctive and not confused with an alarm to evacuate.

All employees should be aware of the means and methods of reporting emergencies, and emergency telephone numbers should be posted near telephones or employee bulletin boards.

You must train your employees on the Emergency Action Plan:

- When the plan is first developed
- Whenever the plan is modified
- If the employee actions change

You should also train a group of employees to help implement this program.

B. Fire Protection Plan (29 CFR 1910.38[b])

Employers should develop a Fire Protection Plan. The plan should be in writing (although OSHA allows for a small employer exemption from writing this plan as well). OSHA's interest in the Fire Protection Plan seems to have intensified since a fire occurred in a chicken processing plant in North Carolina where more than 60 people died.

The requirements of a Fire Protection Plan are similar to those of the Emergency Action Plan, and therefore, you may consider incorporating the requirements of one plan with the requirements of the other plan. Elements of the Fire Protection Plan, at a minimum, include the following:

1. A list of the major workplace fire hazards and their proper handling and storage procedures.
2. A list of potential ignition sources (e.g. welding, smoking, etc.) and their control procedures.
3. Type of fire protection equipment or systems in place to control fires, e.g. fire extinguishers, sprinkler systems, Halon® systems, etc.
4. Names or job titles of employees responsible for maintenance of equipment and fire suppression equipment. Concerning maintenance, OSHA states that the employer "shall regularly and properly maintain, according to established procedures, equipment and systems installed on heat producing equipment to prevent accidental ignition of combustible materials." Maintenance procedures should be included in the written plan.
5. Names or job titles of employees responsible for control of fuel source hazards.
6. Housekeeping procedures regarding the control of the accumulation of flammable and combustible waste materials and residues.

You must inform your employees of the fire hazards, if any, to which they are exposed and train them on this plan as well. Consider dovetailing the training on the Fire Protection Plan with your training on the Emergency Action Plan.

REGULATIONS THAT APPLY TO ALL EMPLOYERS

III. MEDICAL SERVICES AND FIRST AID (29 CFR 1910.151 and 29 CFR 1926.50 in Appendix 3C)

All employers are required to have readily available medical services. The services can be provided in-house, such as through a plant infirmary or nurse's office. Alternatively, the service can be provided by a nearby clinic or hospital. OSHA does not define "near proximity" in this standard, so it is not clear how close the outside services must be to be acceptable. It has been suggested that medical services available within 4 minutes may meet the requirements of this standard.

In the absence of in-house medical services (e.g., a physician or nurse working under a physician's orders) or medical services in close proximity, employers must have on site at least one person trained in first aid (through a reputable course such as that of the American Red Cross) who could render first aid under a physician's orders.

First aid supplies approved by the consulting physician must also be available. The kit is to be maintained in a weatherproof container with individual sealed packages. The employer is to check the contents of the first aid kit regularly. For construction, the contents of the first aid kit are to be verified before being sent out on each job. Expended items are to be replaced (Construction safety orders indicate items are to be replaced at least weekly on each job).

Table 3.1 shows a recommended list of first aid supplies to be made available in the workplace. This list previously appeared in the OSHA regulations, but has since been deleted. The consulting physician should make the final determination of supplies.

Drugs, antiseptics, eye irrigation solutions, inhalants, medicines, should not be included in the first aid kit unless approved by a licensed physician.

If employees may be exposed to "injurious corrosive materials," drench showers and eye washes are to be provided within the work area.

Last, it is advisable to have the emergency telephone numbers (e.g., doctors, hospitals, or ambulance service) posted in a conspicuous location. The standard specifically requires a communication system for contacting an ambulance service or proper equipment to be provided for promptly transporting an injured person to a physician or hospital.

IV. HOUSEKEEPING (29 CFR 1910.22, 1910.176, and 1926.25 in Appendix 3D)

Housekeeping is another important requirement for all places of employment and is addressed in several OSHA regulations. For fixed workplaces (Note: 29 CFR 1910.22 applies to all permanent places of employment

TABLE 3.1
Recommended List of First Aid Supplies

Supplies for First Aid	Type of Supplies Based on Number of Employees			
	1-5	6-15	16-200	Over 200
Dressings in adequate quantities:	x	x	x	x
Adhesive dressings	x	x	x	x
Adhesive tape rolls, 1" wide	x	x	x	x
Eye dressing packet	x	x	x	x
1" gauze bandage roll or compress		x	x	x
2" gauze bandage roll or compress	x	x	x	x
4" gauze bandage roll or compress		x	x	x
Sterile gauze pads, 2" sq.	x	x	x	x
Sterile gauze pads, 4" sq.	x	x	x	x
Sterile surgical pads suitable for pressure dressings		x	x	
Triangular bandages	x	x	x	x
Safety pins	x	x	x	x
Tweezers and scissors	x	x	x	x
Cotton-tipped applicators		x	x	
Forceps			x	x
Emesis basin			x	x
Flashlight	x	x	x	x
Magnifying glass			x	x
Portable oxygen and its breathing equipment				x
Tongue depressors				x
Up-to-date first aid book	x	x	x	x

except where only domestic, mining, or agriculture work is performed), the requirements are as follows:

1. All employment locations must be kept "clean and orderly and in a sanitary condition."
2. Spills must be promptly cleaned up. Mats should be provided around wet work areas.
3. Any protruding objects, such as nails, splinters, loose boards must be removed.

Housekeeping requirements for the construction industry can be found in 29 CFR 1926.25 and require contractors to:

1. Keep all scrap lumber, debris and forms with nails clear from work areas, passageways, stairs, and in buildings and in or around structures.
2. Remove, at regular intervals, combustible scrap and debris.
3. Have waste containers at the job site. The containers must have a top if it is to be used for storage of flammable wastes. Garbage must be removed from the site at regular intervals.

V. HAZARD COMMUNICATION PROGRAM
(29 CFR 1910.1200 in Appendix 3E)

With few exceptions, every employer must comply with the Hazard Communication Standard. This is the safety standard most frequently cited by OSHA and, therefore, we strongly urge all employers, including office environments, to develop and maintain a program for compliance.

The purpose of this regulation is to ensure that employees who are or may be exposed to a hazardous substance understand the physical and health hazards associated with these substances so that they can take appropriate steps to protect themselves. This regulation also requires employers to have on hand information concerning hazardous substances and make it available to their employees.

This standard can be divided into five elements. You must comply with all of the elements in order to avoid citations. The elements are:

1. Develop a *written program* that documents the steps for compliance.
2. Prepare a *list of hazardous substances.* Keep this list current.
3. Compile *Material Safety Data Sheets* on the hazardous substances used in the workplace and make them available to all employees.
4. Ensure that all hazardous substance containers are *properly labeled.*
5. Conduct *training classes* for all affected employees.

A. What Is a Hazardous Substance?

Many employers have difficulties in understanding the difference between a hazardous substance and hazardous waste or hazardous material. Each of these terms holds a unique definition. For the purpose of this regulation, a hazardous substance is a chemical that is reported in one of the following publications:

1. OSHA — 29 CFR 1910, Subpart Z, Toxic and Hazardous Substances.
2. American Conference of Governmental Industrial Hygienists (ACGIH) — Threshold Limit Values for Chemical Substances and Physical Agents in the Work Environment.
3. National Toxicology Program (NTP) — Annual Report on Carcinogens.
4. International Agency for Research on Cancer (IARC) — Monographs.

A hazardous substance may also be defined as any other substance which presents a physical or health hazard as determined by scientific evidence.

Unlike other chemical regulations, there is *no minimum quantity exemption* for this regulation. Even a small bottle of a "hazardous substance" on an employee's desk is sufficient to require an employer to develop a hazard communication standard program.

Many employers handle mixtures, e.g. cleaners, adhesives, etc., rather than individual chemicals. According to this OSHA standard, if the mixture contains 1% or more of a listed "hazardous substance," then the mixture is considered a hazardous substance. Further, if the hazardous ingredient in the mixture is a cancer-causing agent and it is present at the 0.1% or more level, the mixture would again be considered a hazardous substance.

If you are not sure whether the product is a hazardous substance, it is suggested that you assume it is hazardous unless you are notified otherwise by the manufacturer or supplier.

B. Exclusions and Exemptions

There are a few exclusions and industry exemptions from some elements of this standard. These are listed below:

1. Additional labeling is not required on:

    a. Pesticides
    b. Food, drugs, cosmetics, food additives, color additives, or medical or veterinary devices or products
    c. Alcoholic beverages
    d. Consumer products
    e. Agricultural or vegetable seed treated with pesticides

2. The following are completely exempt from this regulation:

    a. Hazardous waste regulated by the EPA
    b. Tobacco products
    c. Wood or wood products (exclusive of other materials)
    d. Articles (manufactured objects, e.g., table, chair, etc.)
    e. Food, drugs, and cosmetics for personal consumption by the employees
    f. Food, drugs, cosmetics, or alcoholic beverages which are packaged for sale in retail trade establishments.
    g. Consumer products sold at retail, unless employee exposure to the substance is greater than the exposure of the consumer to the substance
    h. Drugs administered directly to patients
    i. CERCLA hazardous substances

3. For compliance with Hazard Communication, laboratories must only ensure that:

    a. Incoming containers of chemicals are properly labeled (labels are not to be removed or defaced).
    b. Material Safety Data Sheets on incoming shipments are maintained.

REGULATIONS THAT APPLY TO ALL EMPLOYERS

   c. Material Safety Data Sheets are available to laboratory employees.
   d. Employees are apprised of the hazards.

4. Warehousing, marine cargo handling, and employers who handle other forms of sealed chemical containers must:
   a. Not remove or deface labels of incoming containers.
   b. Maintain copies of Material Safety Data Sheets on incoming shipments.
   c. Obtain Material Safety Data Sheets for sealed containers of hazardous chemicals received without a Material Safety Data Sheet, *if an employee requests such a sheet.*
   d. Ensure that Material Safety Data Sheets are readily accessible to employees.
   e. Provide training to all affected employees.

C. Required Action

You should perform the following actions to comply with this standard.

1. Write a Hazard Communication Compliance Program. The written program should be concise, accurate, and contain the following information:
   a. A list of the hazardous substances in the workplace.
   b. An explanation of how you will meet the requirements of labeling, collecting the Material Safety Data Sheets, and providing employee training and information.
   c. A plan to make employees aware of hazards encountered while performing nonroutine tasks, e.g., cleaning, maintenance.
   d. A plan to make employees aware of chemicals in unlabeled pipes.
   e. A plan to inform outside contractors of any hazardous substances to which their employees may be exposed during the course of their work.

   It is recommended to name an individual who is to be responsible for the implementation and maintenance of this program. That person should be named in the program, and all of your employees should know how to contact this person for additional information. For multiple sites, consider naming a responsible individual for each site, but all reporting to one person who will monitor the program for consistency.

2. Conduct an inventory of the hazardous substances on your work site. The list should include the product name, manufacturer name and address, and location in your facility where the product is being used. Due to some new hazardous materials regulations (e.g., EPA's Community Right-to-Know), some local municipalities may want a copy of

the list with quantities included. Consider local or other regulatory requirements when preparing your list so that you will not have to duplicate effort.

3. Request Material Safety Data Sheets. Based on the results from step 2 above (hazardous substance inventory), request a Material Safety Data Sheet on all listed products from each manufacturer, importer, or distributor. Keep a copy of your request letter. We encourage requesting a Material Safety Data Sheet on consumer products used in your workplace. The individual who receives your request letter will either reply with a letter stating the product does not contain any hazardous substances pursuant to this regulation **or** will send a copy of a Material Safety Data Sheet. On rare occasions, you may not receive a response. Should that occur, write a second letter 30 days following the first request. If no response is received, we suggest finding a more responsive manufacturer.

4. Ensure that all products are properly labeled. Generally, the manufacturer or supplier will have this responsibility. However, it is your responsibility to ensure completeness. Every label must contain the following three items:

    a. Identity of the hazardous substance(s)
    b. Appropriate physical and health hazard warnings
    c. Name and address of the chemical manufacturer, importer, or other responsible party

    If you purchase products in bulk and transfer the products into smaller containers, it is your responsibility to label these smaller "secondary" containers. The labels should include:

    a. Identity of the hazardous substance(s)
    b. Appropriate physical and health hazard warnings

    In lieu of a label, use signs, placards, process sheets, batch tickets, operating procedures or other such written material posted in the work area as long as the alternative labeling method conveys the required information. A Material Safety Data Sheet cannot serve as a label.

    A label is not required on a container if a product is to be in the possession of one employee for one shift and, at the end of that shift, the product will be fully consumed.

5. Conduct employee training. This subsection is the most important element of this regulation. You must provide information and training on hazardous substances to all affected employees. Training is to be provided at the time of initial assignment and whenever a new hazardous substance in introduced into the work area. Employees are to be informed of:

REGULATIONS THAT APPLY TO ALL EMPLOYERS

  a. The elements of the regulation,
  b. The location of any hazardous substances in their work areas, and
  c. The location of the written Hazard Communication Program, including the required list of hazardous substances and the required Material Safety Data Sheets.

Employers also have the obligation to conduct training sessions with their employees where they can be taught how to read a Material Safety Data Sheet and label, how to request Material Safety Data Sheets, and steps to take for additional information. Employees must also be trained on the following topics:

  a. How to detect and observe the presence or release of a hazardous substance in the work area,
  b. Physical and health hazards of the hazardous substances in the work area, and,
  c. How employees can protect themselves from hazards in the work area (including appropriate work practices, personal protective equipment, and emergency procedures).

Training should always be well documented. At a minimum have a sign-in sheet and an outline of topics covered. Always provide employees an opportunity to ask questions during the training. When an answer to a question cannot be immediately provided, advise the group that the answer will be provided to all of them when it has been determined.

Chapter 4

REGULATIONS THAT APPLY TO SOME EMPLOYERS

In addition to the regulations discussed in Chapter 3, OSHA has established regulations which apply to a variety of workplaces. The regulations are specific to work operations or job tasks, including such varied situations as exposure to noise, handling of asbestos, use of a punch press, erection and use of scaffolding, or work in a laboratory. These regulations comprise the largest group of OSHA regulations. Employers are likely to be subject one or more of these specific regulations.

This chapter is devoted to those operation-specific regulations most frequently cited by OSHA and those which have broad-reaching implications for employers. Understand that there are hundreds of these operation-specific regulations. A few of the more common regulations and their general requirements and content are discussed below.

I. PERSONAL PROTECTIVE EQUIPMENT (29 CFR 1910.132 in Appendix 4A)

Personal protective equipment includes items employees may need to use while performing their job tasks such as respirators, safety glasses, face shields, hard hats, etc. If required, you are to ensure that the equipment not only is available for use, but is, in fact, used. You must also ensure that the personal protective equipment is maintained in a reliable and sanitary condition.

OSHA made recent changes to this regulation which went into effect on July 5, 1994. Two provisions, hazard assessment and training requirements, were under administrative stay at the time of this writing.

As currently written, the standard requires each employer to conduct a "hazard assessment" to determine whether hazards are present in the workplace that would require employees to use personal protective equipment (PPE).

An appendix to the regulation offers guidance to employers for conducting the assessment. The appendix indicates that the employer is to conduct a walk-through survey of the work areas and evaluate hazards that would necessitate the use of PPE such as eye, face, head, foot, or hand protection. Such hazards would include employees' exposure to falling objects, sharp objects, electrical hazards, chemical hazards, moving parts, etc. Upon completion of the hazard assessment, if it appears that there would be employee exposures to a hazardous condition, the employer is to select the appropriate PPE, based on the type of hazard and its potential for injury.

The employer must *certify in writing* that the hazard assessment was *conducted*, although it is not clear whether the assessment itself must also be documented. Following the assessment and selection of appropriate PPE, the employer must ensure that the PPE is:

- Properly fitted to the employee.
- In good working order, with all damaged or defective parts replaced.
- Designed to meet the latest editions of the pertinent American National Standards Institute (ANSI) Standards.
- Used by employees trained, and complying with the requirements of the regulation.

The final step for compliance is training. OSHA states that "each employee" must be trained in the use of the PPE and must demonstrate an "understanding" of the training. The employer also must *certify in writing* that the training was provided and was understood. Retraining of an employee is to be provided whenever:

- The employer observes inadequacies in an employee's knowledge or use of PPE.
- Changes in the workplace cause previous training to be obsolete.
- Changes in the type of PPE cause previous training to be obsolete.

Be sure to retain a copy of the documentation which details the conduct of the hazard assessment and the training and any retraining of company employees.

There are specific regulations dealing with particular types of PPE. For example, Section 1910.133 in Appendix 4A sets forth requirements for eye and face protection. Due to the nature and extent that respirators are used in the workplace, the Respiratory Protection Standard is summarized below.

II. RESPIRATORY PROTECTION (29 CFR 1910.134 in Appendix 4A)

Although the use of respiratory protection is mentioned in several OSHA regulations (e.g., asbestos, lead, arsenic), this safety standard is concerned

REGULATIONS THAT APPLY TO SOME EMPLOYERS

with the general aspects of respiratory protection and the need to establish a respiratory protection plan. At the time of publication, OSHA was finalizing an amended Respiratory Protection Standard.

The scope of this standard is unique, in that it states that if employees are being exposed to hazardous dusts, fumes, mists, and the like, it is the employer's responsibility to minimize, if not completely eliminate the exposure by first using *engineering controls* to stop the release of the hazardous substance at its source. Examples of engineering controls include exhaust ventilation, enclosures, and the substitution of less toxic materials.

The standard also states that "when effective engineering controls are not feasible..." then, and only then, should respirators be used. In other words, OSHA demands that respirators be used as the last resort to control personal exposures, not the primary means of control.

According to the standard, if respirators are used, the employer must establish an effective Respiratory Protection Program. Even a paper "dust mask" used to protect against air contaminants could be considered a respirator. The Program must be in writing and include the following elements:

1. **Procedures for the selection and use of respirators.** This section involves how respirators will be selected by the employer and made available to employees. We suggest naming someone responsible for the program.
2. **Respirator selection.** Specify the type of respirators that will be used, where they will be used, and when they will be used.
3. **Employee training.** One of the most critical aspects of an effective program is employee training. Users must be trained on the proper care and use of respirators. Of special note is a fit test. A respirator is only as effective as its fit. The standard refers to a "gas-tight fit." Of particular concern are employees with facial hair which may interfere with a fit. You should consider the adoption of a company policy regarding employees with facial hair and the need for the use of respiratory protection.
4. **Cleaning and sanitizing.** Specify how respirators will be kept clean and frequency for cleaning. Some employers find it cost-effective to use disposable respirators which do not require cleaning, sanitizing or storage since they are designed for a single use.
5. **Storage.** Indicate where and how respirators will be stored. Often, a "zip-lock" bag is used to store the individual respirators. Once so stored, the respirator can then be placed in the worker's locker or in a specially designed respirator cabinet which is located out of the work area.
6. **Inspections.** Generally, there will be several levels of inspections. The user should conduct the first level inspection of his or her respirator before each use. Periodic inspections may also be established to inspect for broken or worn parts. There may also be inspections of emergency respirators which are not assigned to any one individual.

7. **Work area surveillance.** This section refers to air monitoring. Respirators are to be selected on the basis of the hazards present in the workplace. One cannot adequately select a respirator until it has been determined what exposures may be present in the workplace.
8. **Program evaluations.** As with any program, periodic evaluations should be included to measure the program effectiveness. Consider an annual evaluation.
9. **Medical surveillance.** This is likely to be one of the most discussed element of the program requirements. OSHA states that employers "should" ensure that employees assigned to use respirators are medically able to do so. OSHA continues by stating that a physician "shall" determine what health and physical conditions are pertinent. The company should consider adopting a policy regarding the assignment of employees to duties requiring the use of a respirator *and* whether the employees should be assigned a respirator unless a licensed physician has determined that the individual may wear the respirator. Such documentation should be maintained in the employee's medical records.
10. **"Approved" respirators.** Only respirators that carry the Mine Safety and Health Administration (MSHA) and National Institute for Occupational Safety and Health (NIOSH) approvals should be used.

Other issues that effect the use of respirators include the following:

Air Sources/Air Quality: If air is going to be supplied to the respirator by cylinder or air compressor, the air must be of high quality. OSHA specifies "Grade D breathing air as described in Compressed Gas Association Commodity Specification G-7.1-1966." The requirements are as follows:

Carbon monoxide	Less than 20 ppm
Carbon dioxide	Less than 1000 ppm
Condensed hydrocarbons	Less than 5 mg/m^3

Oxygen should never be used in air-line systems.

Air compressors must be carefully placed so that contaminants do not enter the system and get into the breathing air. If oil-lubricated compressors are used to supply air to the respirators, the compressor must be equipped with alarms to indicate system failure or elevated levels of carbon monoxide or temperature. If only high temperature alarms are used, a test for carbon monoxide should be taken for each use or at least weekly. The alarms should be tested periodically and the records of the tests should be maintained.

Confined Spaces/Oxygen-Deficient Atmospheres: Work which takes place in confined spaces where the atmosphere is contaminated at levels that are hazardous or in oxygen-deficient atmospheres which are immediately hazardous to life or health, require specialized procedures and the use of respiratory equipment. OSHA has established stringent regulations for work in confined spaces that can be found in 20 CFR 1910.146 in Appendix 4B. (Note: there are also requirements for agriculture, construction and shipyard employment which can be found in Parts 1928, 1926, and 1915, respectively.) The confined space requirements are not discussed in this publication.

III. OCCUPATIONAL NOISE EXPOSURE
(29 CFR 1910.95 in Appendix 4C)

When employees in a fixed workplace (i.e., excluding construction) are exposed to levels of noise above OSHA's acceptable limit, it is the employer's obligation to develop a Hearing Conservation Program. The acceptable noise exposure varies with duration of exposure as shown below:

Hours	Noise Level (dBA)
8	90
6	92
4	95
3	97
2	100
1.5	102
1	105
0.5	110
<0.25	115

Employee's exposure may not exceed an 8-hour, time-weighted average of 90 dBA. At one half that level, or 85 dBA, the employer must establish and implement an effective Hearing Conservation Program. Employers engaged in oil and gas well drilling and servicing operations are specifically exempted from this standard. The program is to be in writing and is to include the following elements:

1. **Monitoring.** The noise to which employees are exposed must be monitored if there is reason to believe that the employees' exposure may exceed OSHA limits.
2. **Employee notification.** Notify all affected employees who have been found to be exposed to noise in excess of the OSHA limit.
3. **Observation of monitoring.** Provide an opportunity for the employee or an employee representative (for employees represented by a union) to observe the testing. You are not required to have an employee representative present during testing, just afford the opportunity to a representative of the employee group to observe the testing.
4. **Periodic audiometric testing and follow-up.** This is one of the most critical elements of the program. A hearing test is required if one or more employees are exposed to noise in excess of 50% of the OSHA permissible exposure limit (or 85 dBA). A licensed or certified audiologist or other hearing specialist must conduct the audiometric examination of the employees. The test is to include a baseline audiogram to be obtained within 6 months of an employee's first exposure, and annually thereafter. Additional testing may be required if employees are found to have a degree of hearing loss.

5. **Controls.** Engineering controls are the preferred method of reducing or eliminating exposure to noise; examples of engineering controls include the construction of sound-proof enclosures around the noise-emitting source or changing the material flow so that excessive noise is not produced. Another control that is acceptable to OSHA is the use of administrative controls such as job rotation, so that an individual's exposure to noise is limited by time. OSHA believes that the least effective means of controlling noise is the use of personal protective equipment such as ear plugs or muffs. Controls you plan to use should be described in this section of your program.
6. **Hearing protectors.** Hearing protectors (i.e., ear plug or muffs) can be used if it is necessary to keep employees' average exposure (referred to as a time-weighted average) to noise within 85 dBA over an 8-hour work day. It is the employer's responsibility to provide and enforce the use of hearing protectors. Hearing protectors should also be used prior to an employee having a baseline audiogram.
7. **Hearing protector selection.** Hearing protectors vary in their ability to attenuate noise. Factors to consider in the use of hearing protectors include the level of protection they afford the user and their effectiveness in the noise environment in which they will be used. The type of hearing protectors that will be available for employee use and their location for use should be mentioned in this section of the program.
8. **Training.** A training program must be given to all affected employees who work in an environment of 85 dbA or greater level of noise for the workday. The training is to be repeated annually. Employees have access to the training materials.
9. **Recordkeeping.** You are obligated to retain records on the various aspects of this standard as follows:

- Noise exposure measurements: two year retention period
- Audiometric tests: retain for duration of employee's employment

The employee has access to his/her records. All other requirements with records are consistent with "Access to Employee Medical and Exposure Records" which was briefly described in an earlier chapter.

IV. TOXIC AND HAZARDOUS SUBSTANCES (29 CFR 1910.1000 through 1910.1001 in Appendix 4D)

These sections refer to the handling of different hazardous substances, some of which are considered occupational carcinogens. If you believe that your employees may be exposed to one or more airborne contaminants, it is your responsibility to determine if their exposure is within the established limits set by OSHA. These limits of exposure are referred to as Permissible

REGULATIONS THAT APPLY TO SOME EMPLOYERS

Exposure Limits or PELs and are based on a time-weighted average concentration. There are also limits for shorter periods of time, called Short Term Exposure Limits or STELs and Ceiling Limits. A STEL refers to an exposure of 15 minutes during a workday. The Ceiling Limit is the maximum exposure, not to be exceeded for any time during the day. Affected materials are shown in Table 4.1 along with the relevant section number.

Some air contaminants have a PEL, STEL, and Ceiling Limit, while others may only have one limit.

A listing of the exposure limits for contaminants can be found in the regulations. This listing is commonly referred to as the "Z" tables, since the Tables are numbered Z-1-A, Z-2, and Z-3. About 500 of the most common industrial materials are listed in the Z tables. A change to these tables occurred in 1989, where the accepted limits were revised.

At the time of publication of this document, a federal Appeals Court ruled that the procedure OSHA used to establish the 1989 Permissible Exposure Limits (PELS) was scientifically flawed. The court order was temporarily stayed and federal OSHA was deciding if it should appeal the decision.

Since this list is extensive and it covers many industries, your company should consider the implementation of a policy including the following steps:

1. **Evaluate your operations**. Determine what substances are used in your workplace and if employees may become exposed to elevated levels of these materials.
2. **Conduct air monitoring**. Areas or operations that have been identified where workers may be exposed to elevated levels of air contaminants should be measured to determine the extent of exposure. Collecting air samples is not an easy task and should be performed by a qualified individual. Contact your workers' compensation carrier or an industrial hygiene consultant for assistance.

    The sampling survey should be designed to adequately reflect exposure. It may be necessary to sample at various times throughout the day and to monitor several workers performing their tasks. In other words, attempt to collect a "representative" exposure. This may require performing the sampling survey over several days.
3. **Compare air monitoring results**. Once you have received your air monitoring results, compare the measured levels with those PELs listed in the Z tables.
4. **Control elevated exposures**. If your measured levels exceed the PELs, you must control the exposure. There are several ways to reduce exposure such as the use of exhaust ventilation, substituting less hazardous materials for more hazardous ones, wetting down dusty operations, process changes, isolating the employee from the emitting source, etc. Again, your workers' compensation carrier or industrial hygiene consultant can assist in identifying the alternatives for you.

TABLE 4.1
Toxic and Hazardous Substances

Section	Contaminant
1910.1000	Air contaminants
1910.1001	Asbestos
1910.1002	Coal tar pitch volatiles
1910.1003	4-Nitrobiphenyl
1910.1004	alpha-Naphthylamine
1910.1006	Methyl chloromethyl ether
1910.1007	3,3'-Dichlorobenzidine (and its salts)
1910.1008	Bis-Chloromethyl ether
1910.1009	beta-Naphthylamine
1910.1010	Benzidine
1910.1011	4-Aminodiphenyl
1910.1012	Ethyleneimine
1910.1013	beta-Propiolactone
1910.1014	2-Acetylaminofluorene
1910.1015	4-Dimethylaminoazobenzene
1910.1016	N-Nitrosodimethylamine
1910.1017	Vinyl chloride
1910.1018	Inorganic arsenic
1910.1025	Lead
1910.1027	Cadmium
1910.1028	Benzene
1910.1029	Coke oven emissions
1910.1030	Bloodborne pathogens
1910.1043	Cotton dust
1910.1044	1,2-Dibromo-3-chloropropane
1910.1045	Acrylonitrile
1910.1047	Ethylene oxide
1910.1048	Formaldehyde
1910.1050	Methylenedianiline

5. **Notify employees of results**. Share your findings with employees. Explain the sampling and the findings. If corrective action is necessary, tell them what will be done to minimize exposure. If reasonable controls cannot be identified, explain the use of respirators and your respiratory protection program.

Many of the above-listed materials have detailed requirements which go well beyond the Z tables. For example, the requirements for asbestos, lead, arsenic, and formaldehyde require the employer who uses these substances to not only perform exposure monitoring as described, but may also require employee medical surveillance, personal hygiene facilities, use of protective equipment, and required employee training. If you handle any of these materials, be sure to read the regulation.

V. OCCUPATIONAL EXPOSURE TO BLOODBORNE PATHOGENS (29 CFR 1910.1030 in Appendix 4E)

This regulation, which became effective December 1991, applies to all workplaces where there is a potential for occupational exposure to blood and other potentially infectious materials. Many employers believe this regulation to be applicable only to the healthcare industry, but the standard goes well beyond hospitals, physicians' offices, dental offices, residential care facilities, and other healthcare-related employers. This regulation applies to any employer who has employees performing tasks where there could be reasonably anticipated contact with blood or other forms of infectious materials. Non-healthcare industry examples include designated emergency response personnel or teachers who are designated to render first-aid to an injured student.

Blood means human blood, human blood components, and products made from human blood.

Bloodborne Pathogens includes pathogenic microorganisms that are present in human blood. Human immunodeficiency virus (HIV) and hepatitis B are the specifically mentioned concerns.

Other Potentially Infectious Materials includes:

- Semen, vaginal secretions
- Cerebrospinal, synovial fluid
- Pleural, pericardial, peritoneal fluid
- Amniotic fluid
- Fluid visibly contaminated with blood
- All body fluids in situations where it is difficult or impossible to differentiate between fluids.
- Any unfixed tissue or organ (other than intact skin) from a human (living or dead)
- HIV-containing cell, tissue, organ cultures
- HIV- or HBV-containing culture medium, blood, organs, tissues from experimental animals infected with HIV or HBV

To comply, employers who have employees with an "occupational exposure" to bloodborne pathogens must prepare a written Exposure Control Plan that identifies tasks or jobs where exposures to blood or infectious materials may occur, without regard to protective equipment. The Exposure Control Plan must include, at a minimum, the following three sections:

1. **Exposure determination,** which includes all of the following:

   a. Job classifications in which all employees in those job classifications have occupational exposure

b. Job classifications in which some employees have occupational exposure
c. Tasks and procedures or groups of closely related tasks in which occupational exposure may occur and that are performed by employees in the job classifications listed in "b" above

The assessment is made without regard of personal protective equipment

2. **Schedule and method of implementation** (described below)
3. **Procedure for evaluating exposure incidents**

Several methods of compliance or means of minimizing exposure are offered within the standard. These approaches are to be used by the employer. The approach is presented in the employer's "Schedule and Method of Implementation" portion of the Exposure Control Plan. They include:

1. **Universal precautions.** The observance of universal precautions is a widely accepted means of infection control. According to the concept of "Universal Precautions," **all human blood and other potentially contaminated materials and devices are treated as if they are known to be infectious, whether contaminated or not.**
2. **Engineering controls.** The goal of engineering controls is to eliminate or control the source of the potential problem, such as automating a process so that human contact with the contaminated material is not necessary. An example of an engineering control is adding exhaust ventilation to an area that emits an aerosol so that the worker will not breathe the contaminant. With regard to bloodborne pathogens, the use of biosafety cabinets is an important engineering control. Handwashing is also specifically mentioned in the standard. This may be difficult for emergency response personnel where water may not be always available. The use of antiseptic hand cleansers, followed by hand washing when feasible is an acceptable engineering control.

    The standard also discusses the handling of contaminated needles and other sharps. The standard states that these materials are not to be bent, recapped, or removed unless a procedure is used to prevent possible contamination by the handler.
3. **Work practice controls.** This control refers to general work practices such as not eating, drinking, smoking, applying cosmetics, or handling contact lenses in work areas where an occupational exposure to blood or other potentially infectious material may be present. Prohibiting the storing of food and drink with contaminated or infectious materials is another work practice control.
4. **Personal protective equipment.** When there is an occupational exposure to blood or other infectious materials, the employer is to provide, at no cost to the employee, appropriate personal protective equipment. The type of equipment chosen is to be based on the type of exposure, quantity, etc. of material anticipated to be encountered. **Gloves**

REGULATIONS THAT APPLY TO SOME EMPLOYERS

are to be worn when there is a potential for hand contact with the infectious materials. **Masks, eye protection** and **face shields** are to be worn if there is a possibility of splashes, sprays, etc. of infectious materials. **Gowns, aprons,** and **other body clothing** must be worn if there is the possibility of skin contact or contact with street clothing. Selection must be based on the infectious materials and duration of exposure.

5. **Housekeeping.** The employer is to establish an appropriate written schedule for cleaning and methods of decontamination, based on the location, type of surface, type of soil present, and procedures being performed in the area.
6. **Medical wastes (regulated wastes).** What is considered regulated biohazardous waste differs from state to state and from county to county. In general, regulated wastes include the following categories:

   a. Liquid or semi-liquid blood or other potentially infectious material (OPIM).
   b. Items contaminated with blood or OPIM and which would release these substances in a liquid or semi-liquid state if compressed.
   c. Items that are caked with dried blood or OPIM and are capable of releasing these materials during handling.
   d. Contaminated sharps.
   e. Pathological and microbiological wastes containing blood or OPIM.

   The standard also identifies appropriate means of color-coding and labeling the wastes.
7. **Laundry.** Laundry is to be handled as little as possible with a minimum of agitation. It also cannot be sorted or rinsed in the location of use.
8. **Hepatitis B vaccinations.** All employees who have an occupational exposure to blood or infectious materials must be offered the hepatitis B vaccine. The vaccine is to be **made available** at **no cost** to the employee. An employee may decline the vaccination but can receive the vaccination at a later date if he/she changes his/her mind.
9. **Communication.** An employer's ability to comply with a standard is only as good as is the ability to communicate the need for compliance to the employees. OSHA mandates that all exposed individuals receive training and education on the standard. This is accomplished in two ways, as follows:

   1. **Signs and warnings**
   2. **Training.** Training must be provided:

      a. At the time of initial assignment.
      b. Within 90 days after the effective date of the standard.
      c. Annually thereafter.

HIV and HBV Research Laboratories and Production Facilities must follow stringent procedures to ensure employees are not contaminated. These procedures must be delineated in the Exposure Control Plan.

The last element of the standard is **recordkeeping**. Employers must establish acceptable recordkeeping practices for all occupationally exposed individuals. Items to be documented include employee training (annual training is required), incident reporting, and inspections.

Maintaining the confidentiality of these records that may show an employee to be HIV or hepatitis positive is critical. Arrangements should be made in advance for handling these records, should an incident occur.

VI. OCCUPATIONAL EXPOSURES TO HAZARDOUS CHEMICALS IN LABORATORIES (29 CFR 1910.1450 in Appendix 4F)

A. OSHA Laboratory Standard

After more than 10 years in the planning stages, OSHA released the "Lab Standard." As with the Bloodborne Pathogens regulation described above, the Laboratory Standard is broad reaching.

First, the standard applies to all laboratories which are defined as:

> "a facility where the laboratory use of hazardous chemicals occurs. It is a workplace where relatively small quantities of hazardous chemicals are used on a non-production basis."

The standard applies to "laboratory use" of hazardous chemicals. OSHA defines laboratory use of chemicals as:

- Laboratory scale manipulations.
- Multiple chemical procedures or chemicals are used.
- Procedures which are not part of a production process, and do not in any way simulate a production process.
- Protective laboratory practices and equipment are available and in common use to minimize the potential for employee exposure to hazardous chemicals.

If the laboratory is an integral part of a production or manufacturing process, it is exempt from this standard. However, medical research laboratories, analytical testing laboratories, and "R&D" laboratories are included and therefore must comply with the Lab Standard.

B. Requirements of Laboratory Standard

The requirements of this standard can easily be divided into five categories. Each category is summarized below.

REGULATIONS THAT APPLY TO SOME EMPLOYERS

1. Employee Exposure Determination

The assessment phase of the standard requires employers to conduct "initial air monitoring" to characterize and determine the extent of personal exposure to a known airborne contaminant. Sampling will be performed when "there is reason to believe" an exposure exists and it is approaching the OSHA Permissible Exposure Limits. If, however, the employer believes that no exposure exists, or that the exposure is well within acceptable limits, no initial monitoring is required. You are encouraged, however, to conduct air monitoring.

Where elevated levels are found, additional "periodic monitoring" is required. OSHA specifies a frequency for re-sampling for some contaminants, such as some of the highly toxics (e.g., lead, asbestos, arsenic). When levels are within a specified acceptable limit, monitoring may be "terminated."

Employees must be notified within 15 working days in writing of the results of any monitoring. Notification can be individually, or by posting the results.

2. Chemical Hygiene Plan

As a means of protecting employees and to minimize exposure to hazardous chemicals, a written plan must be prepared. The plan must be accessible to all affected employees and include, at a minimum, the following elements:

1. Standard operating procedures relevant to safety and health considerations
2. Criteria for implementing control measures, e.g., engineering controls, personal protective devices
3. Ventilation hood performance evaluations
4. Employee information and training
5. Prior approval for new operations/processes/activities
6. Medical consultation/examinations
7. Designation of a Chemical Hygiene Officer
8. Handling of "select carcinogens" to include:

    a. establishing designated areas
    b. determining containment devices
    c. establishing methods of disposal
    d. instituting methods of decontamination

Naming the Chemical Hygiene Officer ("CHO") requires naming someone of authority who can institute change when needed. OSHA requires the

CHO to be someone who is "qualified by training or experience" to provide technical guidance for the implementation of the Chemical Hygiene Plan.

3. Employee Information and Training

Employee training is another critical element for compliance. The employees need to be apprised of the chemical hazards to which they are exposed in their work areas. The Lab Standard requires employers to provide such training upon initial assignment and prior to be assigned a new job when the hazards are different. At a minimum, the training is to include a discussion of:

1. The existence and content of the OSHA lab standard
2. The location and availability of the Chemical Hygiene Plan
3. Occupational exposure standards, such as OSHA Permissible Exposure Limits
4. Signs and symptoms associated with overexposure to chemicals
5. The location of reference materials such as Material Safety Data Sheets
6. The methods and observations that employees may use to detect the presence or release of hazardous chemicals
7. Work practices, emergency response procedures, and protective equipment to be used

Refresher training is also mandated.

4. Medical Consultation

Whenever a spill, leak, explosion, or other chemical accident occurs that may result in an exposure to a hazardous chemical, the affected laboratory worker is to be provided an opportunity for medical consultation to determine the need for a medical examination. All medical consultations and examinations are to be performed by, or under the direct supervision of, a licensed physician and provided at no cost to the employee. The medical consultation is also to be provided at a reasonable time and place for the employee, without loss of pay.

You should obtain a written opinion from the attending physician for all medical consultations provided under the Lab Standard. The opinion should include recommendations for further medical follow-up, the results of the medical examinations, and any medical conditions that may place your employee at increased risk as a result of the exposure to a hazardous chemical present in the laboratory. Only that information pertinent to the employee's performance in the job should be discussed, so that employee confidential information will not be released.

5. Special Precautions

You are also to provide additional employee protection for work with chemicals that have a high degree of acute toxicity and those chemicals of unknown toxicity, such as reproductive toxins, "select" carcinogens and acutely toxic chemicals. "Select carcinogens" are those substances that are regulated by OSHA as carcinogens, listed as known carcinogens by the National Toxicology Program, or listed as known carcinogens by the International Agency for Research on Cancer. If these types of chemicals are present in the laboratory, the employer is to establish and post a designated area where these materials must be used.

Chapter 5

ACCIDENT PREVENTION PLAN

What about an accident prevention plan? Does your company have such a plan? Should it have such a plan? What should be in an accident prevention plan?

It is not the intent of this manual to advise your company whether it should prepare and enforce an accident prevention plan. It would seem, however, that the existence of such a plan is a necessary tool in the accomplishment of a safe and healthy workplace.

If you are considering the adoption of an accident prevention plan, you should probably give thought to the following issues:

- Responsibility
- Training
- Communication
- Compliance
- Inspections
- Corrective measures
- Recordkeeping

I. RESPONSIBILITY

To have an effective accident prevention plan, some person (or persons) must be responsible for its implementation. Generally, such a person would be a representative of management. This person should have both the responsibility and the authority to ensure compliance with the program. The identity of this person should be known to all company employees to enable the effective flow of communication of safety and health topics between management and employees.

II. TRAINING

The training of company employees about safety and health issues is perhaps the most significant element of the program. Not only is it essential that employees be informed about such matters, but many OSHA regulations require specific training, for example, the Hazard Communication standard. All employees should receive training regarding those aspects of their employment which is necessary to enable the employees to safely perform their job-required tasks. Training regarding that job should be an on-going activity. If an employee moves to a new job, training regarding that job should be accomplished.

III. COMMUNICATION

The methods by which safety and health matters are to be communicated between management and employees should be specified in the company's accident prevention plan. Safety meetings, training programs, company newsletters, postings, anonymous suggestion boxes are typical methods of communicating such topics. The accident prevention plan must provide a two-way street for communication; that is, management and employees must both have access to and be encouraged to use the communication system. Employees must be assured they will suffer no adverse consequences by speaking their mind on matters of safety and health.

IV. COMPLIANCE

All employees, from the top of the organization to the bottom, must understand that the company is serious in its intent to ensure compliance with its accident prevention plan. There are any number of ways that such an understanding may be created. Positive incentives are often a useful tool; if you do comply with the company's safety and health rules, you may expect some reward. Often, just a pat on the back and simple recognition of a job well done is enough to accomplish company goals.

It may be desirable to incorporate disciplinary provisions into the compliance portion of the accident prevention plan. If an employee does not comply with his/her training, the person may expect to be disciplined. Such

ACCIDENT PREVENTION PLAN

a policy should be progressive; that is, the more violations by an employee, the more severe the punishment.

When considering whether to include such a policy in the accident prevention plan, consider the "message" given to an employee if management is aware that the employee has violated a company (or OSHA) rule and it looks the other way. The message is that it is okay to violate the rule. When that employee is eventually injured due to a failure to perform his/her job safely and in accordance with his/her training, what could the employee's response be? *"The company knew I was not following the rules, yet it did not care enough about me to make sure I performed my job safely. In fact, the company tacitly encouraged my unsafe activity."*

V. INSPECTIONS

The company's accident prevention plan should include provisions regarding safety and health inspections. Who should conduct them? When should they be conducted? What should be inspected? All of these questions should be addressed in this portion of your program. You may want to prepare a written checklist that can be used by the person who conducts the inspection. The checklist could include those aspects of your company's operations most likely to expose employees to unsafe or unhealthy working conditions. For example, are guards in place on machinery, or are all employees who should be wearing hearing protection, in fact, wearing such protection?

VI. CORRECTIVE MEASURES

The accident prevention plan should incorporate some method whereby any existing hazardous conditions are corrected. For example, if company maintenance personnel are to correct hazardous conditions, the program should indicate how the maintenance person is to be informed of the condition; what procedural steps are necessary to effect the correction; and how to record the corrective measures. An inspection checklist may document not only safety inspections but those corrective measures taken.

VII. RECORDKEEPING

The only sure-fire method to prove that the company's accident prevention plan has been effectively implemented is to record the activities. At a bare minimum, it is advisable to document the training of the company employees and the conduct of the safety and health inspections and any necessary corrective measures.

A. Employee Training

- Who was present?
- What was discussed?
- When was the training?
- Where was the training?

B. Inspections and Corrective Measures

- Who conducted the inspection?
- What was inspected?
- When was the inspection?
- Where was the inspection?
- What was the result of the inspection?
- What corrective measures were taken?

OSHA has no specific requirements regarding the implementation and requirements of an accident prevention plan. In 1991, California adopted a requirement that all California employers adopt a written Injury and Illness Prevention Program. As such, you may want to refer to the California plan for further guidance. The safety regulation which sets forth the requirements of such a program in California (Title 8, California Code of Regulations § 3203) and a sample Cal/OSHA Injury and Illness Prevention Program is set forth in Appendix 5A.

Chapter 6

WORKER INFORMATION AND TRAINING

I. GENERAL

Many OSHA regulations, including those discussed in the previous chapters, require the employer to provide training to the employees. Regardless of the type of business operated, OSHA requires some amount of employee training. Some of the training that is required is of a **general** nature such as Emergency Action Plan procedures, Fire Protection Plan procedures, proper selection and use of protective equipment, etc. Other regulations have requirements for **specific** topics to be covered in the training. Hazard Communication, Lab Standard, and Bloodborne Pathogens are three examples of OSHA regulations that require very specific training and topics discussed.

For the construction industry, OSHA's regulation titled "Safety Training and Education" (Title 29 CFR 1926.21 in Appendix 6A) states that construction employers must provide their workers with training on the following topics:

1. The recognition and avoidance of unsafe conditions and the regulations applicable to the work environment.
2. Proper handling practices for the use of poisons, caustics, and other harmful substances, and awareness training on personal hygiene and personal protective equipment.
3. Where harmful plants or animals are present on the job site, what are the potential hazards, how to avoid injury, and acceptable first aid procedures to be used in the event of injury.
4. Proper handling practices for flammable liquids, gases, or toxic materials.
5. If they are required to enter into confined or enclosed spaces, the nature of the hazards involved, and appropriate equipment to be used.

Other than the regulatory requirements to train employees, there are many good business reasons to train employees. Studies have shown that the benefits of providing employees with safety and health training include:

- Fewer work-related injuries and illnesses
- Increased productivity
- Lower insurance and workers compensation costs
- A more loyal and dependable workforce

Consider training employees:

- When the training programs are first established.
- When newly hired or when given a new assignment.
- Whenever new substances, processes, procedures, or equipment are introduced into the work environment representing a new hazard.
- Whenever a new or previously unrecognized hazard is brought to your attention.

OSHA's training requirements differ from regulation to regulation. Determine which regulations are applicable to your workplace. Carefully follow the type and format of training as called out in the regulation. OSHA's training requirements fall into one of four categories, as follows:

1. **Performance-oriented requirements**. This type of regulation requires the employer to provide training when the employees' exposure to an airborne contaminant is above an acceptable level, commonly called the Action Level. The Action Level is generally one half of the Permissible Exposure Limit. Training is required only when the employees' exposure to the airborne contaminant exceeds the Action Level. Training is not required if the airborne exposure remains below the Action Level. Examples of OSHA regulations that require training when exposure limits are exceeded include arsenic and noise.
2. **On-site requirements.** This type of regulation requires the employer to provide the employees with training, regardless of exposure. The presence of the materials on site is sufficient justification to require training. Examples of regulations that require this type of training include ionizing radiation and Hazardous Waste Operations and Emergency Response ("Hazwoper").
3. **Periodic training requirements**. Some regulations require the employer to conduct periodic refresher training. Examples of OSHA regulations that require ongoing periodic training include those for asbestos and bloodborne pathogens.
4. **One-time training requirements**. Not every OSHA training program is subject to periodic refresher requirements. Many regulations only require the employer to provide the training once, when the program is first established. Updated or refresher training would only be required

WORKER INFORMATION AND TRAINING

if there has been a change in the workplace, with the employer's method of compliance, or a change in the hazard. For example, Hazard Communication requires employers to train employees on the hazards to which they may be exposed in the handling of hazardous substances. Refresher training is only required if a new substance enters the environment or a change occurred with the existing substances which was brought to the attention of the employer through an updated Material Safety Data Sheet. Although the regulation states that training is required only once, it is advisable to provide employees with refresher training.

To prepare for employee training:

1. Read each regulation that affects your business to determine what are your training requirements. Familiarize yourself with the work that the employees are performing. Not every element of a regulation may be required for your operation. Determine the provisions of the regulation that impact your business. For construction, become aware of the work being performed by other trades on the job site. Their work may affect your employees, such as exposing your employees to the hazardous substances they are using.
2. Determine how the training topic should be presented. OSHA's training requirements seem to follow a similar scheme, i.e., the employer discusses the hazards; safeguards the employees' need to know to avoid exposure; company procedures for handling and monitoring the hazard; and, sources of addition information for the employees to review if desired.

    Some employers conduct the required training during company-wide meetings. The advantage of company-wide training is that all employees will be trained in the same manner, covering the material in the same way. In lieu of this approach, consider smaller group sessions. The small group training is less inhibiting for employees to ask questions and therefore can be a more beneficial experience.

    Consider offering different levels of training. Rather than training employees in large groups, train each operating unit, highlighting how they will be affected by your procedures to meet the OSHA requirement. Offer separate training for supervisors who are directly responsible for employees. In many companies, the supervisors are the trainers. If this is the case with your company, provide your "trainer" with sufficient information so that he/she can answer questions that are likely to be raised during the training.

    Supervisor training should be comprehensive so that the supervisors will have a good grasp of the topic and can more easily pass along the salient points to the subordinates. Realize, however, that not all supervisors are good instructors. Some may feel uncomfortable speaking in front of groups. If this is the case, you may want to script the presentation for the supervisor. This approach has the added benefit of assuring that all employees will hear the same information on a given topic in the same way.

Some employers find the use of outside trainers or consultants to be beneficial. Employees sometimes perceive the topic as more important if an "outside" professional is making the presentation. The use of outside training services, however, may be more costly than providing it in-house. Remember, however, that even if the training is to be completely controlled in-house, there is time and expense in preparing the program. Consider using the outside trainer to conduct the initial training and have subsequent training conducted by supervisors or in-house trainers.

Whoever performs the training, be sure that the person:

- Can give the most effective presentation
- Has the knowledge and experience on the subject
- Can achieve the respect of employees being trained
- Has credibility

3. Training activities should be scheduled to minimize disruption of work activities. Training sessions do not need to be long. A topic can be covered over several meetings.
4. Training location is also important. Pick a relatively quiet, location where distractions and interruptions can be kept to a minimum. The training area should be well lit, and equipped with all of the equipment to be used for the training, e.g., white board, transparency projector, VCR, etc.

II. PRESENTING THE TOPICS

To make a successful educational program, consider the following:

1. Present the information in a credible form. Do not overstate the topic or its severity.
2. Make the training interesting by keeping the subject moving. Consider using training aids such as:

   - Pamphlets or other written handout materials
   - Videotapes, films to strengthen a point or to introduce the topic
   - Hands-on or simulation experience

There are many video tapes, slides, movies available on safety-related topics that can be purchased or rented. These commercially available materials should be used to supplement or strengthen the presenter's material. It is not recommended to use the audio/visual presentation as the sole source of information. The information is available from several sources, including your workers' compensation carrier, trade association, companies in your industry, and local National Safety Council office. Preview the information beforehand. Make sure it is relevant to your operations.

WORKER INFORMATION AND TRAINING

3. Relate the topic to the workplace. Use examples of real life situations. Avoid discussing topics unrelated to the workplace.
4. Give concrete examples of how the topic is relevant to the work area.
5. At the end of the presentation, summarize the important points or have some of the workers restate them for you.

Following training, be sure to have the trainer ask if there are any questions. The trainer should answer the questions if the answer is known. If the correct answer is not known, the trainer should never guess. He/she should find out the right answer and inform the attendees of the correct response.

III. RECORDKEEPING

Keeping good records of training is as important as the training itself. There are several approaches to document the training. Listed below are some of the more commonly used approaches:

1. **Sign in/sign out logs.** Have employees sign for themselves. Under adversarial situations, some employees may refuse to sign a log. If that is the case, assign the task to an employee, to write down names of attendees who refuse to sign. Some employers will videotape the attendees.
2. **Test or quiz.** Some employers use a test or quiz at the conclusion of the training as a means of documenting employees' understanding of the subject matter. This is a very good approach; however, administering the test may be difficult for some employee groups. You may discover that some employees have difficulty in understanding written material or cannot read at all. You need to avoid embarrassing employees, yet everyone should be sufficiently familiar with the material to leave with a passing grade. Be prepared to sit down with some employees to go over questions incorrectly answered.
3. **Certificates or letters of successful completion.** Consider distributing a letter or certificate at the conclusion of the class. Keep a copy of the certificate/letter as a record of attendance.

Keep good records of the class material. At a minimum, the records on the class should include:

1. Training materials, hand-outs, scripts.
2. Information of video, slides, etc.
3. Agenda, topics discussed, with timetable (duration) for the presentation.
4. Date the class was conducted and location.
5. Names of training providers. If an outside training source was used, ask for a letter at the conclusion of the course that will document the instructor's involvement, including date, agenda, duration, and a copy of the class material.

IV. SUPERVISOR TRAINING

As stated above, supervisors generally play a key role in the overall training of employees. Not only are supervisors directly responsible for the day-to-day implementation of the program, but they are to serve as role models for the employees they supervise. A supervisor concerned with safety can have a dramatic influence on employees' safety performance. To perform their role effectively, supervisors should be afforded additional training on safety and health topics. For example, train your supervisors on hazard recognition, accident investigation and safety inspections.

V. TRAINING UNDER HAZWOPER

In March 1989, OSHA promulgated the Hazardous Waste and Emergency Response standard (29 CFR 1910.120 in Appendix 6B) that defined the level of training required for personnel involved in hazardous waste operations and emergency response actions. The standard is now commonly called the HAZWOPER regulation.

The standard covers workers involved in:

- Investigation and clean-up at hazardous waste sites
- Hazardous waste treatment, storage, or disposal (TSD) at facilities licensed under the Environmental Protection Agency's Resource Conservation and Recovery Act (RCRA)
- Any industry that responds to emergencies where hazardous substances may be released.

Not only does the standard require affected employers to develop a written safety and health plan that identifies, evaluates, and controls hazards and sets up emergency response procedures, but *specific training for workers is required*. Contractors who are involved, even incidentally, on one of the above-mentioned sites, must also train their employees **before** coming on site, where they may become exposed to the hazards.

All workers and supervisors covered under this standard must receive training on:

- Names of personnel responsible for site safety and health
- Hazard recognition and prevention
- Safe work practices to minimize risks
- Proper use of engineering controls
- Use and proper fit of personal protective equipment
- Confined space entry procedures
- Spill containment program
- Proper decontamination procedures

WORKER INFORMATION AND TRAINING

- Emergency Response Plan
- Medical Surveillance Requirements

The amount of instruction differs with the nature of the work operations. Workers involved in hazardous waste clean-up who are likely to be exposed to airborne levels of hazardous substances in excess of OSHA's Permissible Exposure Limits (PELs) or who are required to wear respiratory protection must receive the following level of training:

1. 40 hours of general training
2. 3 days of on-site field training
3. 8 hours of annual refresher training
4. Special training for members of emergency response teams (time unspecified)

Workers who may occasionally work at the hazardous waste clean-up site or those involved in site characterization, e.g., groundwater monitoring, surveying, etc., who are **not** exposed to airborne levels of hazardous substances in excess of the PELs and will not be wearing respiratory protection, must receive the following level of training:

1. 24 hours of general training
2. 1 day of on-site field training
3. 8 hours of annual refresher training

Supervisors and/or managers of the above workers must also receive training equivalent in time and content to the training received by those they supervise as well as receive 8 hours of additional specialized hazardous waste management training.

Those who work on Treatment, Storage and Disposal (TSD) sites must receive the following level of training:

1. 24 hours of general training
2. 8 hours of annual refresher training
3. Special training for members of emergency response teams (time unspecified)
4. General emergency awareness training for all facility employees

There are five levels of training for emergency response personnel. These are described below:

1. **First responder training at the "awareness level".** Workers who are likely to witness or discover a release of a hazardous substance and initiate the emergency response must receive sufficient training to demonstrate competency in:

a. Recognition of the presence of hazardous materials in an emergency
   b. The risks involved
   c. Their role in securing the area and calling in the specialists

2. **First responder training at the "operations level".** Workers involved in responding to the release as part of the initial response for the purpose of protecting nearby persons and property, without actually trying to stop the release must have 8 or more hours of training plus "awareness level" competency and be able to demonstrate competency in their specific area.
3. **Hazardous materials ("Hazmat") technicians.** Workers who are responding for the purpose of stopping the release or who must enter the contaminated zone to rescue others or to survey the situation must receive 24 hours of training equivalent to the "operations level" and also be able to demonstrate competency in their specific areas.
4. **Hazardous materials ("Hazmat") specialists.** Workers who are responding to provide support and direct technicians' efforts must receive 24 hours of training equivalent to the Hazmat Technician training and show competency in their areas of specialty.
5. **On-scene incident commander.** Workers who assume control of the incident beyond the first responder awareness level must receive 24 hours of initial training plus special training according to the areas under their control.

All levels must be given annual refresher training which is to be 8 hours in duration or of sufficient content and duration for their level of compentency.

All training should be conducted at a level appropriate to the needs and abilities of the people in the course. Hands-on training and simulations should be included in the course.

A certificate is to be issued to all workers who successfully complete the course. At the time of writing this document, OSHA's certification standard was still in draft stage. Employers should therefore make a careful review of the training program to ensure its completeness. It is also advisable to review the credentials of those who are conducting the training to verify that they are qualified to conduct such a class.

Chapter 7

OSHA INSPECTIONS

This chapter provides information to your company regarding what events may result in an OSHA inspection and the scope of such an inspection. An OSHA inspection often proves to be uneventful, resulting in no citations or fines. Occasionally, however, citations and fines may be issued. Your company should understand its rights and duties during an OSHA inspection and have a sufficient understanding of the process to protect its interests. This chapter explains:

- Events that may trigger an OSHA inspection
- Unprogrammed and programmed inspections
- Comprehensive and partial inspections

I. REGULATORY AUTHORITY OF THE DEPARTMENT OF LABOR

29 CFR 1903 sets forth the regulatory enforcement authority of Fed/OSHA. 29 CFR 1903.1 authorizes the Department of Labor to conduct inspections and to issue citations and proposed penalties for alleged violations of federal health and safety rules and regulations.

29 CFR 1903.3 authorizes Compliance Safety and Health Officers of the Department of Labor ("inspectors") to enter and conduct an inspection without delay and at reasonable times of any factory, plant, establishment, construction site, or any other area, workplace, or environment where work is performed by an employee of an employer.

II. SCHEDULING AN OSHA INSPECTION—HOW AND WHY

There are any number of reasons why OSHA may conduct an inspection of your company. An employee complaint, the occurrence of an accident or a catastrophe, the presence of an imminent hazard, a notification by another agency of the existence of an allegedly unsafe condition, may all result in an OSHA inspection, and even this list is not all-inclusive.

OSHA has a priority system for scheduling inspections. The system is designed to equally distribute available OSHA resources to ensure maximum, feasible protection for all working men and women. The Area Director is responsible for creating inspection priorities. Inspections may be either programmed or unprogrammed. Unprogrammed inspections generally have a higher priority status.

III. UNPROGRAMMED INSPECTIONS

Unprogrammed inspections are generally conducted as the result of the existence of an alleged imminent danger, the occurrence of a fatality or catastrophe, or the receipt of a complaint or referral. The Area Director must prioritize unprogrammed inspections. If, for example, the Area Director has been informed of a job-related fatality at one place of employment and is also in receipt of a complaint received from an employee of a company alleging an unsafe workplace, the Area Director would need to establish the priority of the inspections.

The first priority for an unprogrammed inspection generally involves conditions posing an imminent danger.

IV. IMMINENT DANGER INSPECTIONS

29 U.S.C.A. § 662 defines imminent danger as "...any conditions or practices in any place of employment which are such that a danger exists which could reasonably be expected to cause death or serious physical harm immediately or before the imminence of such danger can be eliminated through the enforcement procedures otherwise provided by this Act."

Any alleged condition or practice which poses an imminent danger is to be inspected immediately. The source of the information regarding the alleged condition or practice is generally not important.

If, upon inspection, the inspector concludes that such a condition or practice exists, he/she is to immediately notify the employer. If the employer voluntarily and permanently eliminates the imminent danger as soon as it is pointed out, a Notice of Alleged Imminent Danger is not to be completed. Voluntary elimination of the danger shall be considered to be accomplished if an employer has removed employees from the danger area and has given satisfactory assurance that the dangerous condition will be eliminated before permitting employees back into the work area in question.

If, after being informed of the imminent danger, the employer does not take steps to reduce employee exposure to the condition, eliminate the im-

imminent danger, or give satisfactory assurance that the danger will be voluntarily eliminated, the inspector is to immediately contact the Area Director for approval to complete and post the OSHA-8 Form, "Notice of Alleged Imminent Danger." The inspector may not stop or shut down the operation or direct employees to take any action, such as leaving the area or discontinuing the practice. Once contacted by an inspector, the Area Director decides whether to order the posting of the Notice of Alleged Imminent Danger and whether to contact legal staff to obtain a temporary restraining order.

A Notice of Alleged Imminent Danger is a notice that an imminent danger is believed to exist and that OSHA may be seeking a temporary restraining order to restrain the employer from permitting employees to work in the area of the danger until it is eliminated; it does not require any particular conduct by an employer, nor does it constitute a citation. It is only with a temporary restraining order that the employer is ordered to abide by the direction of Fed/OSHA.

If it is determined that the Notice of Alleged Imminent Danger is to be posted, the original OSHA-8 Form shall be signed and posted at or near the area in which the exposed employees are working. Where there is no suitable place for posting the OSHA-8 Form, the employer shall be requested to provide a means of posting. Before the inspector leaves the workplace, he/she will advise all affected employees of the hazard and direct their attention to the OSHA-8 Form.

If an OSHA-8 Form has been posted at the worksite, the inspector shall remove the notice as soon as the imminent danger condition or practice has been eliminated or when it has been determined that a temporary restraining order will not be sought.

After an imminent danger has been found, appropriate citations and penalties may be issued. Any additional inspection activity is to take place only after resolution of the imminent danger situation. Any other violations discovered during the remainder of the inspection shall be cited and penalties proposed, whether or not they relate to the imminent danger situation.

The second priority for unprogrammed OSHA inspections involves the investigation of a fatality or catastrophe.

V. FATALITY OR CATASTROPHE INVESTIGATIONS

All job-related fatalities and catastrophes, however reported, are to be investigated by OSHA as thoroughly and expeditiously as resources and other priorities permit. For purposes of this category of inspections, a fatality is defined as an employee death resulting from an employment accident or illness — generally, from an accident or illness caused by or related to a workplace hazard.

A catastrophe is defined as the hospitalization of five or more employees resulting from an employment accident or illness—in general, from an accident caused by a workplace hazard.

Depending on the circumstances surrounding the accident, it may be necessary for the inspector to conduct a complete inspection of the workplace, including other areas or operations within the establishment which may have hazards similar to those that may have caused or contributed to the accident.

Remember to be aware of the requirement to orally report a job-related fatality or an event that resulted in the hospitalization of three or more employees to the nearest Area Director within eight (8) hours.

VI. EMERGENCY SITUATIONS

Emergencies created by fatalities or catastrophes often necessitate immediate rescue work, fire fighting, etc. When equipment which could be used in the rescue operations is available for use, OSHA is to permit its use without citing the employer, even if the equipment does not comply with all existing OSHA rules. OSHA is not to cause a delay in rescue attempts while waiting for equipment which may meet OSHA standards. The use of equipment by private employers which does not comply with OSHA requirements is limited to the actual emergency situation. Citations could be issued for the use of such equipment in a nonrescue operation such as clean-up or reconstruction work.

The third priority of unprogrammed inspections authorizes investigations of complaints and referrals.

VII. COMPLAINT AND REFERRAL INSPECTIONS

An employee complaint may result in an inspection. The complaint may be directed to an inspector or to the Area Director. The complaint must:

- Be in writing
- Be signed
- Set forth with reasonable particularity the grounds of the complaint

To initiate an inspection based upon a complaint or referral, the Area Director must ensure that the complaint satisfies the requirements discussed directly above and determine that there are reasonable grounds to believe an alleged violation exists.

If the Area Director determines that an inspection is warranted, an inspection is to be made as soon as practicable.

If the Area Director determines that an inspection is not warranted, notice of that conclusion must be given to the complainant. The complaining party may then take the complaint to the Assistant Regional Director who will make the final determination of the request. At that stage, the employer may oppose such a review.

If the complainant requests confidentiality, it will be maintained, and the identity of the individual will not be revealed to the employer. If the complaining employee does not request confidentiality, a copy of the complaint must be provided to the employer no later than the time of the inspection.

29 U.S.C.A. § 660 protects employees from discrimination for filing such a complaint.

The inspection does *not* need to be limited to only those matters referred to in the complaint.

VIII. PROGRAMMED INSPECTIONS

Unlike unprogrammed inspections, programmed inspections are inspections of workplaces which have been *scheduled,* based upon objective or neutral selection criteria. The workplaces to be inspected are selected according to national scheduling plans or special emphasis programs.

In scheduling programmed inspections, certain considerations are fundamental to the implementation of OSHA's targeting system. It is OSHA policy that programmed inspections are primarily in the "high-hazard" sectors of employment.

A programmed inspection will generally consist of a comprehensive inspection of the entire worksite. The scope of the inspection may, nevertheless, be limited, in view of resource availability of the Area Director and other enforcement priorities. For example, low-hazard areas at the place of employment (such as office space) may be excluded from such an inspection without affecting the comprehensiveness of that inspection.

IX. COMPREHENSIVE AND PARTIAL INSPECTIONS

Inspections may be comprehensive or partial.

A comprehensive investigation consists of a substantially complete inspection of all potentially high-hazard areas of an establishment.

A partial inspection, on the other hand, consists of an inspection which may be limited to certain potentially hazardous areas, operations, conditions, or practices which may exist at the establishment.

Every inspection, whether programmed or unprogrammed, comprehensive or partial, shall include, in addition to its principal focus:

- A review of the employer's injury and illness records
- An assessment of the employer's hazard communication program
- An assessment of the employer's lockout/tagout program
- An evaluation of the employer's safety and health management program
- A brief walk-around to survey, as deemed appropriate, those areas, conditions, operations, and practices that, based on the exercise of discretion and professional judgment of the inspector, are believed to have the greatest hazard potential

In summary, for example, in the event of a fatality investigation, the inspection would be unprogrammed and would be assigned a higher inspection priority than a complaint investigation. If, in the opinion of the Area Director, a comprehensive inspection of the reporting employer's jobsite is necessary, the Area Director may direct the scope of the fatality investigation to be comprehensive rather than partial.

X. NO ADVANCE WARNING

Generally, no advance warning of an inspection is allowed. Occasionally, an advance notice may be given, for example, in a case of an apparent imminent hazard. If advance notice is given, the employer must promptly notify the authorized representative (if any) of the employees. Failure to so notify may result in a citation or penalty.

Chapter 8

OSHA Citations and Proposed Penalties

This chapter discusses citations and fines that OSHA may issue as a result of violations observed or discovered during an inspection.

Upon completion of an inspection, the inspector prepares a written report which is reviewed by the Area Director. If the documentation substantiates that an employer has violated a safety regulation or any substantive rule, a citation shall be issued to the employer.

The citation must describe the nature of the alleged violation and include a reference to the provisions of the Act, safety regulation, or order alleged to have been violated. Any citation must include a reasonable time for abatement of the alleged violation.

Generally, no citation may be issued more than 6 months after the occurrence of the alleged violation.

The employer shall also be notified of any proposed fine; which amount is determined by the Area Director, who takes into consideration such factors as the size of the employer's business, the gravity of the violation, the good faith of the employer, and the history of previous violations by the employer.

Generally, the amount of any proposed penalty is set forth on the face of the citation.

I. TYPES OF CITATIONS

OSHA citations are classified as **other-than-serious, serious, repeated,** or **willful**.

An **other-than-serious** citation is a violation that is not serious. An other-than-serious violation would generally be issued when a violation of an occupational safety and health regulation does exist, but the most likely result of the condition would probably not result in death or serious physical harm.

A proposed penalty of up to $7000 for each such violation is discretionary. A penalty for an other-than-serious violation may be adjusted downward by as much as 95%, depending on the employer's good faith (demonstrated efforts to comply with the Act), its history of previous violations (hopefully the lack thereof), the gravity of the condition, and the size of the business. When the adjusted penalty amounts to less than $50, no penalty is proposed.

A **serious** violation is defined as existing in a place of employment "...if there is a substantial probability that death or serious physical harm could result from a condition which exists, or from one or more practices, means, methods, operations, or processes which have been adopted or are in use, in such place of employment unless the employer did not, and could not with the exercise of reasonable diligence, know of the presence of the violation." (29 U.S.C.A. § 666(k).)

A mandatory penalty of up to $7000 for each serious violation may be assessed. A penalty for a serious violation may be adjusted based on the employer's good faith, history of previous violations, the gravity of the alleged violation, and the size of the employer's business.

II. ADVICE

As you can see, there is a two-fold test for proving a serious violation. The burden of proving each element of the test rests with OSHA. The inspector will make the first determination of whether each element exists during the initial inspection. OSHA must first prove that there is a substantial probability that death or serious physical harm could occur as a result of an existing condition. Second, the agency must prove that your company either had actual knowledge of the existence of the violation or, with the exercise of reasonable diligence, could have known of the presence of the violation. These are two completely different, unrelated issues. If OSHA is unable to carry its burden of proving both elements of a serious violation, the classification of the citation as serious is improper. The violation could still be upheld, but would usually be modified to allege an other-than-serious violation.

If you do not feel that the agency can prove both elements of a serious violation, after taking into consideration the amount of the civil penalty which may be imposed, you may want to consider filing an appeal from the citation, if for no other reason than to try and have the citation reduced from a serious violation to an other-than-serious violation. If the citation is modified at a hearing, the amount of the civil penalty would be significantly reduced.

A current violation will be classified as **repeated** if your company has been previously cited for a substantially similar condition and the earlier citation (the "underlying citation") has become a final order of the Review Commission. A citation becomes final one of two ways: if no timely appeal from the citation is filed with the Review Commission, or if a decision has denied the appeal of the citation.

While there is no statutory time limit as to how long the underlying citation may support a repeated citation, generally a citation will only be classified as a repeated violation if the present citation is issued within three (3) years of the final order of the underlying citation, or within 3 years of the final abatement date of the underlying citation, whichever is *later*.

If the current citation exists at a different place of employment than the underlying citation, it may or may not be properly classified as a repeated violation.

If the "gravity" of the citation is high (an injury resulting from the violation could be severe), the Area Director will determine if the employer has received any citations at any location *in the nation* over which Fed/OSHA has jurisdiction. If so, the citation may be classified as repeated.

Violations of a *lesser gravity* will generally be classified as repeated under either of two conditions; a violation at a *fixed* place of employment will generally only support a repeated violation if the alleged violation occurs at the same location. At *non-fixed* establishments (such as construction or oil and gas drilling sites) a repeated violation may exist at any site location within the jurisdiction of the same OSHA Area Office.

In summary, if your company has been previously cited within the past 3 years by OSHA for a substantially similar condition, the present citation may be classified as a repeated violation if essentially the same condition exists at the same place of employment at which the previous violation existed. For activities occurring at different locations (such as various construction projects), OSHA will look at the company's citation history throughout the same OSHA Area Office in which the present citation occurred. If a violation of a substantially similar condition occurred within the same OSHA Area Office in question within the previous 3 years, the present citation may be properly classified as repeated.

The penalties assessed for repeated violations increase significantly as the violations continue to occur. Repeated violations can bring a fine of up to $70,000 for each such violation. Repeated violations can become willful.

It may be advisable to consider appealing those citations which could be the basis for possible repeated citations. See Chapter 11.

A **willful** violation is not defined in the enabling legislation. OSHA Instruction CPL 2.45B CH-3 describes a willful violation as existing when the evidence shows either an *intentional* violation or *plain indifference* to the Act or its requirements.

Generally, it has been held that an *intentional* and *knowing* violation has occurred if an employer representative was aware of the requirements of the

Act or of the existence of an applicable standard or regulation and was also aware of a condition or practice which was in violation of those requirements.

It may be that willful conduct has occurred even though an employer representative was not aware of any legal requirements but was aware that an existing condition or practice was hazardous, and the representative made little or no effort to determine the extent of the problem or take corrective action.

Plain indifference exists when it can be established that higher management officials were aware of an OSHA requirement which was applicable to the company's business but made little or no effort to communicate the requirement to lower-level supervisors and employees.

Penalties of up to $70,000 may be proposed for each willful violation with a minimum penalty of $25,000 for each violation. A proposed penalty for a willful violation may be adjusted depending on the size of the business and its history of previous violations. Usually, no credit is given for good faith.

While not a citation per se, a Notification of Failure to Abate an Alleged Violation (OSHA-2B) is to be issued in cases where violations have not been corrected as required. Significant civil penalties can be assessed on a *daily* basis for failure to abate the violation. The Area Director has considerable discretion in calculating the amount of the daily penalty amount.

Chapter 9

GENERAL DUTY CLAUSE

Fed/OSHA requires employers to furnish employment which is free of recognized hazards. As discussed, one method that Fed/OSHA follows to ensure a safe and healthy workplace is by enforcing existing safety and health regulations. It may also enforce the "general duty" clause.

The general duty clause poses requirements which may be separate from and in addition to those included in existing safety rules and regulations. The general duty clause requires an employer to keep employees from being exposed to a recognized hazard which is likely to cause death or serious physical harm.

As the employer, you must recognize the potential for hazardous conditions. If such a condition exists, you must take those steps necessary to eliminate the hazard. If you do not eliminate an existing hazardous condition, you are subject to being cited for a violation of the general duty clause. A violation of the general duty clause consists of four elements:

- An existing hazard to which employees were exposed
- The hazard must be recognized
- The hazard was causing or was likely to cause death or serious physical harm
- Availability of a feasible existing method of abatement

These elements are discussed further below.

I. EXISTING HAZARD

A violation of the general duty clause is the result of the *existence of a hazard* in the workplace. Employee exposure is a requirement; that is, an employer may be in violation of the general duty clause *only* if its *own* employees are exposed to the hazard.

Creation of, or responsibility for, the hazard is not the key. An employer may have created the hazardous condition but, if its employees were not exposed to the condition, it may not be cited for a violation of the general duty clause.

The occurrence of an accident is also not a factor. It may be that an accident is evidence of a hazard, but the accident may also be unrelated to any existing hazard. It is the exposure of an employee to the existence of a hazard that controls.

If any of your employees are exposed to a hazardous condition, your company is subject to being cited for a violation of the general duty clause.

The hazard must be **reasonably foreseeable**. If, for example, combustible gases exist in a location but no source of ignition exists, there could be no violation of the general duty clause since it was not reasonably foreseeable that an explosion could occur.

II. RECOGNIZABLE HAZARD

The hazardous condition must be recognized as a hazard. Recognition of a hazard exists if the employer had actual knowledge of the hazard or if it is a hazard which would be recognized as such within the employer's industry.

The exercise of common sense may also establish knowledge of the existing hazard. If it looks like a duck and quacks like a duck, it is probably a duck, and you should treat it as such. So it is with a recognized hazard. Treat it as such.

III. DEATH OR SERIOUS PHYSICAL HARM

In order to constitute a general duty clause violation, the hazard must be of a magnitude likely to result in death or serious physical harm to the exposed employee(s).

If a hazardous condition exists to which one or more of your company's employees are exposed, but that condition is not likely to result in death or serious physical harm, OSHA may not issue a citation based upon the general duty clause.

Remember, however, that while an existing condition may not be subject to the general duty clause, it may, nevertheless, constitute a violation of an existing occupational safety and health standard. Therefore, when reviewing your company's operations, practices, and procedures, make sure they comply not only with your company's rules and with existing OSHA rules and regulations, but with common sense. Think about the duck.

IV. FEASIBLE, AVAILABLE ABATEMENT MEASURES EXIST

Abatement measures must be available and must be feasible before an employer may be cited for a general duty clause violation; that is, recognized hazards must be preventable.

In summary, your company may be subject to the general duty clause if a recognized hazardous condition exists (or is likely to exist) at your place of employment, which is (or should be) recognizable as a hazard to which your employees are (or are likely to be) exposed, and which may result in death or serious physical harm and an available, feasible method of controlling the condition exists.

Chapter 10

AVOIDING OSHA INSPECTIONS AND CONDUCT OF SUCH INSPECTIONS

This chapter discusses methods of avoiding OSHA inspections. In the event of an inspection, this chapter also discusses what you might expect during such an inspection.

- Avoiding an OSHA inspection
- Conduct of inspection and dealing with an inspector
  - Opening conference
    - Inspection warrant
    - Inspection procedure
  - Walk-around inspection
  - Closing conference

I. AVOIDING AN OSHA INSPECTION

There is no "sure-fire" way to avoid an OSHA inspection. Without question, however, the best way to avoid an OSHA inspection is to maintain a safe workplace in compliance with existing OSHA regulations and your company's own safety and health practices and procedures.

Not only will a safe and healthful workplace tend to reduce the occurrence of injuries and illnesses, but it will reflect a positive commitment by the employer to the health and safety of its employees. Employees are less likely to file a complaint with OSHA if they believe their employer is genuinely concerned with their well-being. The absence of imminent hazards, job-related accidents, and employee complaints will reduce the employer's chances for an unprogrammed OSHA inspection.

If your company has developed and implemented an effective safety and health program and has established a good reputation with OSHA, the agency is more likely to discount unfounded complaints, and it may limit the scope of any inspection which it does conduct.

There are also steps which you may take during an inspection which may yield a positive result.

II. CONDUCT OF INSPECTION AND DEALING WITH AN INSPECTOR

The OSHA Field Operations Manual provides that at the beginning of the inspection, the inspector is to attempt to locate the owner, operator, or agent in charge of the workplace. Once located, the inspector is to present his/her credentials to the employer representative.

If the person in charge is not present, the inspector is to identify the top management official who is available. If neither the person in charge nor a top management official is present, the inspector is to request the presence of such a person.

The inspector will generally wait for a reasonable period of time (perhaps up to one hour) for the arrival of the representative of the employer.

The inspection may commence with the top management official present even if the person in charge never becomes available.

A. Opening Conference

After introductions and the presentation of credentials, the inspector is to conduct an *opening conference* which includes an explanation of the nature and purpose of the inspection, including a description of the general scope of the inspection.

As a part of the opening conference, the inspector will typically request to review certain written documents of the company prior to the commencement of the walk-around inspection (the physical inspection of the jobsite). The inspector will generally ask to review the OSHA Log 200 (OSHA No. 200) and any written programs your company should have implemented, for example, a written safety program and/or the company's written hazard communication program.

It is essential that the company's OSHA Log 200 be accurately maintained and available for review; that all necessary written programs be current and available; and that complete and properly documented safety and health training records exist. Additionally, ensure that all required posters are current and properly posted.

The inspector is to notify the employer of its right to have a representative accompany the inspector during the inspection. A representative of the employees is also given the same opportunity. The inspector is authorized to resolve any disputes as to who is the representative authorized by the employees. If there is no authorized representative of the employees, the inspector is to consult with a reasonable number of employees during the inspection concerning matters of safety and health in the workplace.

Different representatives of the employer and the employees may accompany the inspector during different phases of the inspection as long as the changes will not interfere with the conduct of the inspection.

B. Construction

On multi-employer construction worksites, the inspector is to ask for the superintendent, project manager, or other representative of the general or prime contractor. Once this contact is made, the representative of the general or prime contractor is to identify and assemble representatives of the subcontractors and any employee representatives of the subcontractor companies.

C. Inspection Warrant

An employer does have the right to request that the inspector obtain an *inspection warrant* before commencing the actual inspection of the workplace. 29 CFR 1903.4(a).

If an employer refuses the right of entry or otherwise prohibits the inspector from conducting the inspection, the inspector shall endeavor to determine the reason for such refusal or limitation and shall immediately report the refusal and the reason therefore to the Area Director. The Area Director will consult with the Regional Director, who is authorized to initiate action to obtain an inspection warrant.

The right of entry may not be negotiated with the OSHA inspector. That is, the employer may not require that the inspector agree not to issue a citation or penalty in exchange for allowing the inspector entry to the workplace without the need for an inspection warrant.

D. Advice

There is a difference of opinion regarding the advisability of requiring OSHA to obtain an inspection warrant. Remember that inspectors are human beings and may take such a request personally, which could influence the inspector's state of mind if and when he/she returns with an inspection warrant. OSHA could believe that the company had something to hide by demanding a warrant. Such a belief, proper or not, could result in a more comprehensive and time-consuming inspection than might otherwise have occurred. Since it is not unrealistic to suggest that the more time an OSHA inspector spends at your worksite, the more likely it is a violation may be observed, you may have done more harm than good by making such a request.

On the other hand, it may be that the company has instituted a policy to deny warrantless searches. Perhaps it strongly believes "probable cause" for an inspection does not exist or that there is some other existing condition which makes the inspection unreasonable. Under certain circumstances, the employer may be unwilling to permit an inspection, the result of which may be to require OSHA to seek an inspection warrant.

If it is company policy to require an inspection warrant, it is advisable to explain to the inspector why he/she is not being allowed to conduct an inspection without an inspection warrant. A reasonable explanation of why company policy requires a warrant may go a long way toward smoothing the way for any subsequent inspection in the event that OSHA does obtain an inspection warrant.

Assuming that your company policy is to permit an inspection without a warrant, or if a warrant has been obtained, the inspection will commence.

III. INSPECTION PROCEDURE RECOMMENDATIONS

It is highly advisable that you consider the appointment and training of a "key person." This person should have a basic understanding of the nature and scope of an OSHA inspection and the rights and duties of your company during an OSHA inspection.

Remember that in choosing the key person, he/she will be representing the interests of your company throughout the OSHA inspection. OSHA will consider statements made by the key person to have been made on behalf of the company; that is, he or she will be considered to be speaking for the company. The key person should:

- Verify the inspector's credentials.
- Determine the reason(s) for the inspection.
- Attempt to limit the scope of the inspection.

- Accompany the inspector throughout the inspection.
- Note apparent items of interest to the inspector.
- Note the identity of employees to whom the inspector talks.
- In the event the inspector takes photographs, the key person should take photographs of the same locations or of those items of interest to the inspector. The company's photographs may be taken either during the inspection or shortly thereafter (as long as conditions do not change).
- Taking written notes during the inspection may or may not be a good idea. It must be remembered that there is a possibility that in the event of an appeal of a citation, OSHA may attempt to obtain copies of the key person's notes. To possibly avoid this consequence, it may be advisable to prepare a written report at the request of the company attorney after the inspection is completed.

It is advisable that the key person *not speculate or offer opinions* during an OSHA inspection. The key person should respond to the inspector's questions, but only to the questions, and then as briefly as possible, and only to the extent that the answer is factual. See Appendix 10A for a proposed Company Inspection Procedure.

A. Advice

It only makes sense that company documents regarding safety and health are kept readily available at the workplace. If your key person is familiar with the documents and makes them immediately available to the inspector at the commencement of the inspection, the tenor of the walk-around inspection may be entirely different than if your company's representative appears to be unfamiliar with the basic requirements of OSHA's safety and health rules and regulations. **This is important!** First impressions are often lasting impressions. It is critical that your key person understand this basic fact and that the inspection get started on a positive footing. One other word of advice: **Treat the inspector as you would want to be treated!**

IV. WALK-AROUND INSPECTION

Generally, the scope of the inspection is left to the discretion of OSHA. It may be that in the event of an inspection warrant, the scope of the inspection is described; however, absent some type of limiting condition, there appears to be no restriction upon the authority of OSHA regarding the scope of the inspection.

When an inspector has arrived on your doorstep, your key person should attempt to learn the intent of the inspector. The key person should attempt to limit the scope of the inspection to only that operation, process, equipment, or location which may pose a potentially high-hazard exposure.

The inspection is to be conducted so as to preclude any unreasonable disruption of the operations of the company. Inspectors are to comply with all employer safety and health rules and practices at the establishment being inspected, and they are to wear and use appropriate protective clothing and equipment.

The inspector *does* have the right to talk with company employees in private. This right of confidentiality belongs to the employee. If the employee waives his/her right, you have a right to be present during discussions between the employee and the inspector. Notwithstanding this fact, if the inspector feels strongly about the privacy of the conversation, it may be advisable to allow the conversation to proceed without the presence of the key person, thereby preventing an unneeded confrontation. You may always speak with the employee after the inspection to discuss the conversation between the employee and the inspector.

The inspector has a right to take photographs, conduct sampling, and engage in those types of activities which may be necessary to determine the existence of any unsafe conditions, practices, or methods.

V. CLOSING CONFERENCE

At the conclusion of the inspection, the inspector will generally conduct a *closing conference*. During this meeting, the inspector will confer with your company's key person or other designated representatives and advise such person(s) of any apparent safety or health violations discovered during the inspection. If employee representatives were involved in the inspection, the parties may request separate closing conferences. Where it is otherwise not practicable to hold a joint closing conference, separate closing conferences shall be held.

During the closing conference, the inspector shall describe any alleged violations found during the inspection and indicate the applicable sections of the safety or health standards which may have been violated. Copies of the safety standards are to be given to both the employer and the employee representative. The representatives of both the employer and the employees are to be advised of their right to participate in any subsequent conferences, meetings, or discussions.

During the closing conference, the inspector is also to give the employer a copy of the publication, "Employer Rights and Responsibilities Following an OSHA Inspection." This document explains the responsibilities and courses of action available to the employer if a citation and fine are issued. The inspector shall then briefly discuss the information in the booklet and answer any questions. All matters discussed during the closing conference shall be documented in the inspector's case file.

During this closing conference, the employer may bring to the attention of the inspector any pertinent information regarding workplace conditions.

A closing conference does not need to be conducted immediately upon completion of the inspection. It may be held at a later date. Remember: OSHA has six (6) months to issue citations and fines for alleged violations. U.S.C.A. § 658(c).

Chapter 11

APPEAL OR NOT? AND APPEALING A CITATION OR PENALTY

Upon receipt of a Citation and Notification of Penalty from OSHA, your company is faced with a decision; perhaps it is your decision. Should you decide (or recommend) that an appeal be filed from the citation and/or the fine? This chapter is intended to give advice on whether or not to file such an appeal.

This chapter will discuss:

- Reasons to appeal
- Appealing a citation or penalty
- Informal conference

The time to decide whether or not to appeal an OSHA citation or fine is before receipt of such a document. You should establish a decision-making policy within the company regarding how such administrative agency actions are to be handled. Will the company automatically accept an adverse action without objection (as many do) or will each allegation of an administrative agency be reviewed on a case-by-case basis?

I. POSTING OF CITATION

Upon receipt of any citation, the employer must immediately post the citation or a copy at or near the place where the alleged violation occurred, unless such posting is impractical. If posting at the location of the alleged violation is no longer possible, the citation shall be posted in a prominent place, readily observable by company employees.

Where employees do not primarily work at or report to a single location, the citation may be posted at the location from which the employees operate to carry out their activities.

The citation or copy thereof must remain posted until the violation has been abated or for 3 workings days, *whichever is later.*

Filing an appeal from the citation does *not* affect this posting requirement.

II. REASONS TO APPEAL

If your company chooses to individually evaluate each proposed adverse administrative action, you should give consideration to at least the following factors:

- Existence of the violation
- Amount of civil fine
- Consequences *outside* of OSHA
- Citation improperly classified (e.g., not "serious" or not "willful")
- Possibility of a "repeat" violation
- Costs and likelihood of success
- Alienate OSHA: Yes or no?

A. Existence of the Violation

One legitimate reason for appealing an OSHA citation would be your belief that the violation did not exist. There will be occasions when a genuine factual dispute exists between you and the OSHA inspector as to the facts of an alleged violation: OSHA contends that the facts constitute a violation of a safety standard and your company disagrees.

An example of this type of situation may occur with a health standard such as 29 CFR 1910.95 whereby OSHA is alleging an employee has been exposed to a level of noise for a period of time exceeding the permissible exposure limit for such a noise level. Based on this belief, a citation (and fine) is issued to the company by OSHA. However, it is your opinion that the OSHA inspector did not perform the type of testing necessary to establish the existing noise level or did not accurately determine the length of time an employee was exposed to the alleged noise level. You believe that the citation was erroneous and that OSHA will be unable to carry *its burden* of proving a violation of the regulation.

Given such a situation, you must decide whether or not to file an appeal.

There may be occasions when OSHA has issued a citation which you believe alleges a violation of a safety regulation that did not apply to the circumstances. If you are familiar with the safety regulations, it may be your opinion that, not only did OSHA cite an improper safety order (that is, a safety regulation that was not violated), but OSHA will be unable to prove a violation of the safety regulation you believe properly applied to the existing circumstances. To prove your contention that the alleged violation did not exist, your only alternative is to file an appeal. Therefore, you are faced with the decision—appeal or not?

B. Amount of Civil Fine

Another reason for filing an appeal could be the amount of the penalties assessed as a result of the alleged violations. Penalties generally accompany a violation, and usually the more serious a condition, the higher the fine amount. It may be that the amount of the proposed penalty is too high given the circumstances or that it is excessive for your company and may pose an undue hardship on the viability of the company if upheld. The amount of the fine alone may justify the filing of an appeal.

While proposed OSHA fines are determined in accordance with a formula, the agency may not have afforded your company proper "credits" for all possible penalty reduction factors. If the credits had been computed in accordance with your contentions, the result could be a significant reduction in the amount of the fine.

In computing the amount of the fine, OSHA considers factors such as the size of your company's business, its OSHA "history" (any previous citations), its "good faith" (does it appear that you are trying to ensure safety on the job?), and other factors such as the gravity of the violation, how widespread the condition is (is every ladder defective, or only one of 100 ladders?), and the likelihood of an accident as a result of the unsafe condition.

These factors are all considered in computing the final amount of the penalty and generally result in reductions in the proposed penalty.

Also, if you are able to persuade an administrative law judge to modify a citation to a lesser category (for example "serious" to "other-than-serious"), the amount of the proposed penalty for the violation should be significantly reduced.

C. Consequences Outside of OSHA

It may be that an OSHA citation has repercussions outside of OSHA, repercussions that could be significant. For example, the violation of a safety regulation may support a criminal charge, perhaps civil litigation, a workers' compensation claim, as well as another administrative agency's allegations of wrongdoing. **Such consequences could outweigh all other factors!** You should verify whether any such consequences are possible in the state in which you are doing business or in which the violation allegedly occurred.

For example, if an OSHA citation can support a criminal charge, this possibility alone may trigger the need to appeal the OSHA citation.

D. Violation Improperly Characterized

One factor to consider in determining whether to file an appeal from an OSHA citation may be that the violation was improperly classified. It may be that while a violation of a safety order may have existed as alleged in a citation, you believe the classification of that violation as "serious" or "willful" or "repeated" is incorrect.

For example, perhaps OSHA has issued a "serious" citation to your company. A serious citation is deemed to exist "...if there is a substantial probability that death or serious physical harm could result from a condition which exists, or from one or more practices, means, methods, operations, or processes which have been adopted or are in use, in such place of employment unless the employer did not, and could not with the exercise of reasonable diligence, know of the presence of the violation." Title 29 U.S.C.A. § 666(k).

For OSHA to establish that a citation is properly classified as serious, it has the burden of proving *both* elements of the serious test. That is, the agency has to prove with substantial evidence that there was substantial probability of death or serious physical injury because of an existing condition or practice *and* that your company either knew of the condition or practice or, with the exercise of reasonable diligence, could have known of the condition or practice.

Perhaps a condition did exist which could have resulted in a serious injury. However, it is your belief that no management representative of the company had actual knowledge of the condition or, with the exercise of reasonable diligence, could have known of the condition or practice. You believe, therefore, that OSHA will be unable to prove the "knowledge" element of a serious violation. For this reason you may want to file an appeal of the citation. If you are successful, the citation, even though it may have existed, should be reduced from "serious" to an "other-than-serious" violation (generally with a significant reduction in the amount of any proposed fine).

E. Possibility of a Repeated Violation

It may be that you are dealing with a workplace practice or condition which is difficult to immediately correct or eliminate. You are working to correct the condition, but notwithstanding your efforts to eliminate or prevent the occurrence of the given condition or practice, it continues to exist. This ongoing practice or condition could result in repeated violations in the event of future OSHA inspections. In a case such as this, you may want to consider filing an appeal from a citation alleging a violation of such a condition or practice. If successful on appeal, you have avoided the possibility of that citation being used as a basis to support a future repeated violation.

For example, you have a noisy environment which may occasionally exceed the permissible sound level. You are unable to control the noise at its source; therefore, you have implemented an effective hearing conservation program. Unfortunately, no matter how hard you try, every time you walk into the plant, there is at least one employee who is failing to use hearing protection. These occasions always involve a different employee. While you are diligently working to ensure the use of hearing protection (which you provide without cost) by all of your employees at all times, you realize that you have not quite reached that level of compliance; therefore, there may be an occasional exposure by an employee to an excessive level of noise due to the failure of the employee to use the hearing protection provided by the company.

By failing to achieve a consistent 100% compliance by the employees with the company's hearing conservation program, it is possible that every time an OSHA inspection is conducted, your company could be cited for a violation for failing to effectively enforce its hearing conservation program.

Given these conditions, you may be well-advised to appeal from any citation alleging noncompliance with the requirement of the occupational noise exposure standard to use hearing protection. On appeal, it may turn out that no employee was exposed to an excessive noise level while not wearing proper hearing protection on the occasion(s) alleged by OSHA and that, therefore, the citation was, indeed, erroneous. In such an event, the citation would be rejected (if appealed) and could not, therefore, become the basis for a future repeated citation.

F. Costs and Likelihood of Success

In the company's determination of whether to file an appeal, you must consider the cost as well as the likelihood of success. In considering cost, you should consider not only the expense of an attorney, but also the time and cost of your own staff and employees in terms of preparing for and participating in the hearing.

You should also consider the likelihood of success of an appeal. If it appears that you do not have any realistic chance of success, it may be inadvisable to expend the time and effort necessary (and the cost) to prepare for and participate in the appeal hearing. The key to any likelihood of success is often the availability of possible defenses. Possible defenses could include one or more of the following:

- No employee exposure or access to the allegedly hazardous condition
- Employee negligence
- Wrong safety order cited
- Unreliable or missing evidence
- Impossibility of compliance

G. Alienate OSHA: Yes or No?

In determining whether to file an appeal, the question of whether such an action may alienate an OSHA inspector is often raised. Like it or not, that is a legitimate concern. The filing of an appeal from a citation should *not* and generally will not upset the inspector who conducted the inspection. Most OSHA inspectors understand that an appeal is an employer's right and simply consider such an action a part of their job.

The fact that an OSHA administrative law judge may subsequently issue a decision setting aside the citation will generally not change the fact that the inspector thinks he/she acted properly in the first place. OSHA inspectors are competent professionals and understand an employer's right to contest a citation and/or fine. Filing an appeal should not alienate an inspector or put your company at risk with OSHA in the future.

III. APPEALING A CITATION OR PENALTY

If, as a result of an OSHA inspection, your company has received a citation and proposed penalty which you have analyzed pursuant to company policy and have determined to appeal, you must satisfy the procedural steps in filing an appeal.

You may appeal a citation, any abatement requirements, or a civil penalty. You may initiate your appeal by notifying the OSHA Area Director *in writing* of your intention. This written notification is referred to as the "Notice of Contest."

There is *no particular format* necessary to initiate the Notice of Contest; a simple letter will suffice. It is advisable, however, to include a copy of the Citation(s) and Notification of Penalty with each appeal you send to the Area Director. The address of the Area Director who issued the citation should be set forth on the face of the Citation and Notification of Penalty.

It is also advisable (though not required) to send the Notice of Contest to the Area Director by certified or registered mail, return receipt requested. If you are not sending the appeal by registered or certified mail, it is advisable to include a *copy* of a Declaration of Proof of Service with the written correspondence requesting the appeal. The Declaration of Proof of Service should be signed and completed by the person depositing the appeal document(s) in the mail to ensure you are able to prove the date that the appeal was mailed to the Area Director. Retain the *original* declaration for company records.

While there is no particular format you must use to initiate the appeal, you must make sure that the written appeal is postmarked *within 15 working days* of the company's *receipt* of the citation and/or proposed penalty.

If you desire to appeal *only* the amount of any proposed penalty, since the fine is generally included on the face of the citation, you must still file your written appeal with the Area Director within 15 working days of the receipt of the citation.

Under OSHA, there is *no* provision allowing late appeals; any appeal must be served on the Area Director within 15 working days of the receipt of the citation and/or fine. 29 U.S.C.A. § 659(a).

Every Notice of Contest timely filed with the Area Director must clearly identify the scope of the company's appeal. For example, does the appeal include the citation as well as any proposed civil penalty? Is the appeal intended to contest issues of abatement?

You should also consider raising possible affirmative defenses in your Notice of Contest *whether or not* you eventually pursue such a defense. An affirmative defense is a defense which you must prove (such as employee negligence or impossibility of compliance). You may wait to identify affirmative defenses until such time as your answer is to be filed in response to the complaint which will be filed on behalf of OSHA.

Your Notice of Contest will be forwarded by OSHA to the OSHA Review Commission and will be assigned a docket (case) number. Upon receipt of the docketed Notice of Contest, you must post a copy of that document in a conspicuous place at the workplace. A copy of the docketed Notice of Contest must also be given to any of the affected employees (e.g., a union representative).

After filing your appeal, the Secretary of Labor will file a written complaint alleging that the citation and civil penalty were proper. You must file a timely written response to the complaint. The appeal will be scheduled for a hearing before an administrative law judge of the OSHA Review Commission. Pay attention to all documents and comply with all orders you receive from the Occupational Safety and Health Review Commission once an appeal has been filed.

A. Advice

If your company has been charged with more than one violation as a result of an inspection and you have decided to file an appeal, you would be well-advised to file an appeal from *all* of the violations, even if your concern is limited to only one of the violations. The reason that separate appeals should be filed from all of the violations is that you may reach a point in the appeals process when you are discussing the possibility of a settlement agreement with OSHA. You will have considerably more leverage in such a negotiation if all of the violations have been appealed.

For example, if OSHA has issued five citations to your company and you are really only concerned with Citation 2, by filing an appeal from all five of the citations you are in a better negotiating posture, because OSHA may be willing to modify or possibly withdraw Citation 2 if you agree to withdraw your appeals of Citations 1, 3, 4, and 5. However, if you have only appealed Citation 2, you are not in a good negotiating posture because you have nothing to give up in exchange for OSHA's considering the possibility of modifying or withdrawing Citation 2.

IV. INFORMAL CONFERENCE

In considering the appeal process, you may want to consider requesting an informal conference.

> "At the request of an affected employer, employee, or representative of employees, the Assistant Regional Director may hold an informal conference for the purpose of discussing any issues raised by an inspection, citation, notice of proposed penalty, or notice of intention to contest. ... No such conference or request for such conference shall operate as a stay of any 15-working day period for filing a notice of intention to contest a citation...." 29 CFR 1903.19.

Any request for an informal conference and the scheduling and completion of the conference do *not* operate as a stay of the appeal period; that is, the 15-day period to file a Notice of Contest *continues to run* even if an informal conference is scheduled!

Either the employer, an affected employee, or his/her representative may request an informal conference. 29 CFR 1903.19.*

The requesting party must notify all other parties of the request for the informal conference; that is, the employer must notify its employees and/or the representative(s) of the employees and vice versa.

If you request an informal conference, you may object to the presence of your employees or an employee representative, and separate informal conferences will be scheduled. Private discussions are permitted between you and the OSHA official presiding at such a conference if you so desire.

Area Directors have settlement authority, with the power to reclassify violations and modify or withdraw a penalty or citation.

---

* If you have already filed an appeal of the citation in issue, the informal conference may not be scheduled without prior approval of the Regional Solicitor.

A. Advice

Generally, you should not expect to have a citation set aside at an informal conference. If your intent is merely to accomplish a reduction in the amount of the proposed civil penalty or a reclassification of a citation (such as from "serious" to an "other-than-serious") you may be successful.

One word of advice! It is unusual for OSHA to withdraw a citation which has already been appealed. At an informal conference, your attempts to convince OSHA to consider your contentions may do more harm than good if your concerns are not resolved to your satisfaction, because you may end up providing OSHA with additional information which may then be used against you at a hearing. Always be prudent in your discussions in such a situation.

APPENDICES

Numbers at bottom of pages in appendices represent pages on which original material appeared.

Appendix 1A

U.S. Department of Labor, Occupational Safety and Health Administration, Regional and Area Offices

APPENDIX 1A

U.S. Department of Labor, Occupational Safety and Health Administration, Regional and Area Offices

Region I
(CT,* MA, ME, NH, RI, VT*)

133 Portland Street
1st Floor
Boston, MA 02114
Telephone: (617) 565-7164

Region II
(NJ, NY,* PR,* VI*)

201 Varick Street
Room 670
New York, NY 10014
Telephone: (212) 337-2378

Region III
(DC, DE, MD,* PA, VA,* WV)

Gateway Building, Suite 2100
3535 Market Street
Philadelphia, PA 19104
Telephone: (215) 596-1201

Region IV
(AL, FL, GA, KY,* MS, NC,* SC,* TN*)

1375 Peachtree Street, N.E.
Suite 587
Atlanta, GA 30367
Telephone: (404) 347-3573

Region V
(IL, IN,* MI,* MN,* OH, WI)

230 South Dearborn Street
Room 3244
Chicago, IL 60604
Telephone: (312) 353-2220

Region VI
(AR, LA, NM,* OK, TX)

525 Griffin Street
Room 602
Dallas, TX 75202
Telephone: (214) 767-4731

Region VII
(IA,* KS, MO, NE)

911 Walnut Street
Room 406
Kansas City, MO 64106
Telephone: (816) 426-5861

Region VIII
(CO, MT, ND, SD, UT,* WY*)

Federal Building, Room 1576
1961 Stout Street
Denver, CO 80294
Telephone: (303) 844-3061

Region IX
(American Samoa, AZ,* CA,* Guam, HI,* NV,* Trust Territories of the Pacific)

71 Stevenson Street, Room 415
San Francisco, CA 94105
Telephone: (415) 744-6670

Region X
(AK,* ID, OR,* WA*)

111 Third Avenue, Suite 715
Seattle, WA 98101-3212
Telephone: (206) 553-5930

* These states and territories operate their own OSHA-approved job safety and health programs (Connecticut and New York plans cover public employees only). States with approved programs must have a standard that is identical to, or at least as effective as, the federal standard.

Agencies preceded by an asterisk (*) are those in which a state safety and health plan under section 18(b) of the act is in operation. This agency may be contacted directly for specific information regarding regulations in the state.

Alabama Department of Labor
600 Administrative Building
Montgomery, AL 36130
Phone: (205) 261-3460

*Alaska Department of Labor
Research and Analysis Section
Post Office Box 1149
Juneau, AK 99802
Phone: (907) 465-4520

Territory of American Samoa
Department of Manpower
Resources
Government of American Samoa
Pago Pago, American Samoa 96799
Phone: 633-5849

*Individual Commission of Arizona
Division of Administration/
Research and Statistics Section
1601 W. Jefferson Street
Post Office Box 19070
Phoenix, AZ 85005
Phone: (602) 255-3739

Workers' Compensation Commission, OSH
Arkansas Department of Labor
OSH Research and Statistics
Room 502, 1022 High Street
Little Rock, AR 72202
Phone: (501) 371-2770

*California Department of Industrial
Relations
Labor Statistics and Research
Post Office Box 603
San Francisco, CA 94901
Phone: (415) 557-1466

*Colorado Department of Labor and
Employment
Division of Labor
1313 Sherman Street
Room 323
Denver, CO 80203
Phone: (303) 866-3748

*Connecticut Department of Labor
200 Folly Brook Boulevard
Wethersfield, CT 06109
Phone: (203) 566-4380

Delaware Department of Labor
Division of Industrial Affairs
820 N. French Street, 6th Floor
Wilmington, DE 19801
Phone: (302) 571-2888

Florida Department of Labor and
Employment Security
Division of Workers' Compensation
2551 Executive Center Circle West
Room 204
Tallahassee, FL 32301-5014
Phone: (904) 488-3044

Guam Department of Labor
Bureau of Labor Statistics
Post Office Box 23548
Guam Main Facility
Agana, Guam 96921
Phone: 477-9241

*State of Hawaii
Department of Labor and Industrial
Relations
Research and Statistics Office
Post Office Box 3680
Honolulu, HI 96811
Phone: (808) 548-7638

APPENDIX 1A

*Indiana Department of Labor
Research and Statistics Division
State Office Building—Room 1013
100 N. Senate Avenue
Indianapolis, IN 46204
Phone: (317) 232-2665

*Iowa Bureau of Labor
307 East 7th Street
Des Moines, IA 50319
Phone: (515) 281-5151

Kansas Department of Health and
Environment
Division of Policy and Planning
Occupational Safety and Health
Topeka, KS 66620
Phone: (913) 862-9360 Ext. 280

*Kentucky Labor Cabinet
Occupational Safety and Health
Program
U.S. 127 South Building
Frankfort, KY 40601
Phone: (502) 564-3100

Louisiana Department of Labor
Office of Employment
Security—OSH
1001 North 23rd and Fuqua
Baton Rouge, LA 70804
Phone: (504) 342-3126

Maine Building of Labor
Bureau of Labor Standards
Division of Research and Statistics
State Office Building
Augusta, ME 04330
Phone: (207) 289-3331

*Maryland Department of Licensing
and Regulation
Division of Labor and Industry
501 St. Paul Place
Baltimore, MD 21202
Phone: (301) 659-4202

Massachusetts Department of Labor
and Industries
Division of Industrial Safety
100 Cambridge Street
Boston, MS 02202
Phone: (617) 727-3593

*Michigan Department of Labor
7150 Harris Drive
Secondary Complex
Post Office Box 30015
Lansing, MI 48909
Phone: (517) 322-1848

*Minnesota Department of Labor and
Industry IMSD
444 Lafayette Road, 5th Floor
St. Paul, MN 55101
Phone: (612) 296-4893

Mississippi State Department of
Health
Office of Public Health Statistics
Post Office Box 1700
Jackson, MS 39215-1700
Phone: (601) 354-7233

Missouri Department of Labor and
Industrial Relations
Division of Workers' Compensation
Post Office Box 58
Jefferson City, Missouri 65102
Phone: (314) 751-4231

Montana Department of Labor and
Industry
Workers' Compensation Division
5 South Last Chance Gulch
Helena, MT 59601
Phone: (406) 444-6515

Nebraska Workmens' Compensation
Court
State Capitol, 12th Floor
Lincoln, NE 68509-4967
Phone: (402) 471-3547

*Nevada Department of Industrial
  Relations
 Division of Occupational Safety and
  Health
 1370 South Curry Street
 Carson City, NV 89710
 Phone: (702) 885-5240

New Jersey Department of Labor and
  Industry
 Division of Planning and Research
 C N 056
 Trenton, NJ 08625
 Phone: (609) 292-8997

*New Mexico Health and
  Environment Department
 Environmental Improvement
  Division
 Occupational Health and Safety
 P.O. Box 968 — Crown Building
 Sante Fe, NM 87504-0968
 Phone: (505) 827-5271 Ext. 230

New York Department of Labor
 Division of Research and Statistics
 2 World Trade Center
 New York, NY 10047
 Phone: (212) 488-4661

*North Carolina Department of Labor
 Research and Statistics Division
 214 West Jones Street
 Raleigh, NC 27603
 Phone: (919) 733-4940

Ohio Department of Industrial
  Relations
 OSHA Survey Office
 Post Office Box 12355
 Columbus, OH 43212
 Phone: (614) 466-7520

Oklahoma Department of Labor
 Supplemental Data Division
 315 North Broadway Place
 Oklahoma City, OK 73105
 Phone: (405) 235-1447

*Oregon Workers' Compensation
  Department
 Research and Statistics Section
 Labor and Industries Building
 Salem, OR 97310
 Phone: (503) 378-8254

Pennsylvania Department of Labor
  and Industry
 Office of Employment Security
 7th and Forster Streets
 Labor and Industry Building
 Harrisburg, PA 17121
 Phone: (717) 787-1918

*Puerto Rico Department of Labor
  and Human Resources
 Bureau of Labor Statistics
 505 Munoz Rivera Avenue
 San Juan, PR 00918
 Phone: (809) 754-5339

Rhode Island Department of Labor
 220 Elmwood Avenue
 Providence, RI 02907
 Phone: (401) 277-2731

*South Carolina Department of Labor
 Division of Technical Support
 Post Office Box 11329
 Columbia, SC 29211
 Phone: (803) 734-9652

*Tennessee Department of Labor
 Research and Statistics
 501 Union Building, 2nd Floor
 Nashville, TN 37219
 Phone: (615) 741-1748

Texas Department of Health
 Division of Occupational Safety
 1100 West 49th Street
 Austin, TX 78756
 Phone: (512) 458-7287

APPENDIX 1A **103**

*Utah Industrial Commission
  OSH Statistical Section
  160 East 300 South
  Salt Lake City, UT 84110-5800
  Phone: (801) 530-6827

*Vermont Department of Labor and
    Industry
  State Office Building
  Montpelier, VT 05602
  Phone: (802) 828-2765

*Virgin Islands Department of Labor
  Post Office Box 818
  St. Thomas, VI 00801
  Phone: (809) 776-3700

*Virginia Department of Labor and
    Industry
  Research and Statistics
  205 North 4th Street
  Post Office Box 12064
  Richmond, VA 23241
  Phone: (804) 786-2384

*State of Washington
  Department of Labor and Industries
  Division of Industrial Safety and
    Health
  Post Office Box 2589
  Olympia, WA 98504
  Phone: (206) 753-4013

West Virginia Department of Labor
  OSH Project Director
  Room 319, Bldg. 3
  Capitol Complex
  1800 Washington Street East
  Charleston, WV 25305
  Phone: (304) 348-7890

Wisconsin Department of Industry,
    Labor, and Human Resources
  Workers' Compensation Division/
    Research Section
  201 E. Washington Avenue
  Post Office Box 7901
  Madison, WI 53707
  Phone: (608) 266-7850

*Wyoming Department of Labor and
    Statistics
  Herschler Building
  Cheyenne, WY 82002
  Phone: (307) 777-6370

Offices of the Occupational Safety and Health Administration

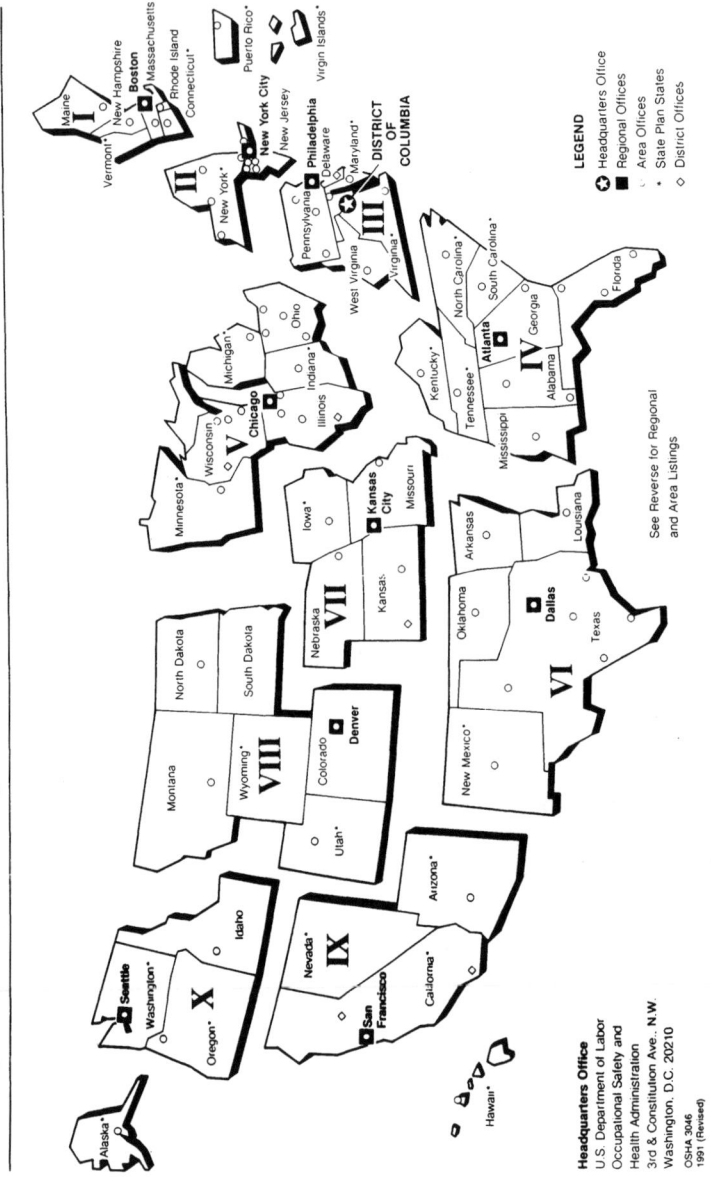

Appendix 2A
REGIONAL OFFICES OF THE BUREAU OF LABOR STATISTICS

U.S. Department of Labor
William E. Brock, Secretary

Bureau of Labor Statistics
Janet L. Norwood, Commissioner
June 1986

Regional Offices of the Bureau of Labor Statistics

Region I
Kennedy Federal Building
Suite 1603
Boston, MA 02203
Phone: (617) 565-2327

Region II
Room 808
201 Varick Street
New York, NY 10014
Phone: (212) 337-2400

Region III
3535 Market Street
P.O. Box 13309
Philadelphia, PA 19101
Phone: (215) 596-1154

Region IV
1371 Peachtree Street, N.E.
Atlanta, GA 30367
Phone: (404) 347-4416

Region V
9th Floor
Federal Office Building
230 S. Dearborn Street
Chicago, IL 60604
Phone: (312) 353-1880

Region VI
Federal Building
525 Griffin Street, Room 221
Dallas, TX 75202
Phone: (214) 767-6970

Regions VII and VIII
911 Walnut Street
Kansas City, MO 64106
Phone: (816) 426-2481

Regions IX and X
71 Stevenson Street
P.O. Box 3766
San Francisco, CA 94119
Phone: (415) 744-6600

Appendix 2B

A Brief Guide to Recordkeeping Requirements for Occupational Injuries and Illnesses

U.S. Department of Labor
Bureau of Labor Statistics
June 1986

The Occupational Safety and Health Act
of 1970 and 29 CFR 1904

O.M.B. No. 1220-0029

See OMB Disclosure
Statement on page i.

Effective April 1986

ATTENTION: OSHA RECORDKEEPER

IMPORTANT: DO NOT DISCARD. This booklet contains guidelines for keeping the occupational injury and illness records necessary to fulfill your recordkeeping obligation under the Occupational Safety and Health Act of 1970 (29 USC 651) and 29 CFR Part 1904, or equivalent State law.

Preface

The information in this pamphlet explains the requirements of the Occupational Safety and Health Act of 1970 and Title 29 of the *Code of Federal Regulations*, Part 1904 (29 CFR Part 1904) for recording and reporting occupational injuries and illnesses. The Occupational Safety and Health Act of 1970 and 29 CFR Part 1904 require employers to prepare and maintain records of occupational injuries and illnesses. The act made the Secretary of Labor responsible for the collection, compilation, and analysis of statistics of work-related injuries and illnesses. The Bureau of Labor Statistics (BLS) administers this recordkeeping and reporting system. In most States, a State agency cooperates with BLS in administering these programs.

Records of injuries and illnesses are necessary for carrying out the purposes of the act. They provide a basis for a statistical program which produces injury and illness data which are used by OSHA in measuring and directing the agency's efforts. The records are also helpful to employers and employees in identifying many of the factors which cause injuries or illnesses in the workplace. In addition, OSHA records are designed to assist safety and health compliance officers in making OSHA inspections.

This pamphlet summarizes the OSHA recordkeeping requirements of 29 CFR Part 1904, and provides basic instructions and guidelines to assist employers in fulfilling their recordkeeping and reporting obligations. Many specific standards and regulations of the Occupational Safety and Health Administration (OSHA) have additional requirements for the maintenance and retention of records of medical surveillance, exposure monitoring, inspections, accidents and other activities and incidents relevant to occupational safety and health, and for the reporting of certain information to employees and to OSHA. These additional requirements are not covered in this pamphlet. For information on these requirements, employers should refer directly to the OSHA standards or regulations or contact their OSHA Area Office.

Further information on the requirements outlined in this pamphlet is available in the free detailed report, *Recordkeeping Guidelines for Occupational Injuries and Illnesses*, which may be obtained by using the order form on page 18. Assistance can also be obtained by contacting the participating State agency or the BLS regional office for your area. The BLS regional offices are listed on the inside front cover. State agencies are listed at the end of this publication.

The following government agencies are involved in OSHA recordkeeping:

A. *The Occupational Safety and Health Administration, U.S. Department of Labor.* The Occupational Safety and Health Administration is responsible for developing, implementing, and enforcing safety and health standards and regulations. OSHA works with employers and employees to foster effective safety and health programs which reduce workplace hazards.

B. *Bureau of Labor Statistics, U.S. Department of Labor.* The Bureau of Labor Statistics is responsible for administering and maintaining the OSHA recordkeeping system, and for collecting, compiling, and analyzing work injury and illness statistics.

C. *State Agencies.* Many States cooperate with BLS in administering the OSHA recordkeeping and reporting programs. Some States have their own safety and health laws which may impose additional obligations. Employers should consult their State safety and health laws concerning these requirements.

These guidelines were prepared in the BLS Office of Occupational Safety and Health Statistics, by Stephen Newell, under the general direction of William M. Eisenberg, Associate Commissioner.

OMB DISCLOSURE STATEMENT

We estimate that the use of this supplementary instruction booklet will take an average of 6 minutes per reference, which is included in the estimate of time for completing and reviewing either a line entry on an OSHA Form No. 200 and/or an entire OSHA Form No. 101. If you have any comments regarding this estimate or any other aspect of this recordkeeping system, send them to the Bureau of Labor Statistics, Division of Management Systems (1220-0029), Washington, D.C. 20212 and to the Office of Management and Budget, Paperwork Reduction Project (1220-0029), Washington, D.C. 20503.

APPENDIX 2B

Contents

Chapters:		Page
I.	Employers subject to the recordkeeping requirements of the Occupational Safety and Health Act of 1970	1
II.	OSHA recordkeeping forms	3
III.	Location, retention, and maintenance of records	4
IV.	Deciding whether a case should be recorded and how to classify it	6
V.	Categories for evaluating the extent of recordable cases	12
VI.	Employer obligations for reporting occupational injuries and illnesses	13
VII.	Access to OSHA records and penalties for failure to comply with recordkeeping obligations	14

Glossary of terms	15
Order form	18
List of participating State agencies	18
BLS regional offices	inside front cover

Chapter I. Employers Subject to the Recordkeeping Requirements of the Occupational Safety and Health Act of 1970

The recordkeeping requirements of the Occupational Safety and Health Act of 1970 apply to private sector employers in all States, the District of Columbia, Puerto Rico, the Virgin Islands, American Samoa, Guam, and the Trust Territories of the Pacific Islands.

A. Employers who must keep OSHA records

Employers with 11 or more employees (at any one time in the previous calendar year) in the following industries must keep OSHA records. The industries are identified by name and by the appropriate Standard Industrial Classification (SIC) code:

- Agriculture, forestry, and fishing (SIC's 01-02 and 07-09)
- Oil and gas extraction (SIC 13 and 1477)
- Construction (SIC's 15-17)
- Manufacturing (SIC's 20-39)
- Transportation and public utilities (SIC's 41-42 and 44-49)
- Wholesale trade (SIC's 50-51)
- Building materials and garden supplies (SIC 52)
- General merchandise and food stores (SIC's 53 and 54)
- Hotels and other lodging places (SIC 70)
- Repair services (SIC's 75 and 76)
- Amusement and recreation services (SIC 79), and
- Health services (SIC 80).

If employers in any of the industries listed above have more than one establishment with combined employment of 11 or more employees, records must be kept for *each* individual establishment.

B. Employers who infrequently must keep OSHA records

Employers in the industries listed below are normally exempt from OSHA recordkeeping. However, each year a small rotating sample of these employers is required to keep records and participate in a mandatory statistical survey of occupational injuries and illnesses. Their participation is necessary to produce national estimates of occupational injuries and illnesses for *all* employers (both exempt and nonexempt) in the private sector. If an employer who is regularly exempt is selected to maintain records and participate in the Annual Survey of Occupational Injuries and Illnesses, he or she will be notified in advance and supplied with the necessary forms and instructions. Employers who normally do not have to keep OSHA records include:

1. All employers with no more than 10 full- or part-time employees *at any one time* in the previous calendar year.

2. Employers in the following retail trade, finance, insurance and real estate, and services industries (identified by SIC codes):

- Automotive dealers and gasoline service stations (SIC 55)
- Apparel and accessory stores (SIC 56)
- Furniture, home furnishings, and equipment stores (SIC 57)
- Eating and drinking places (SIC 58)
- Miscellaneous retail (SIC 59)
- Banking (SIC 60)
- Credit agencies other than banks (SIC 61)
- Security, commodity brokers, and services (SIC 62)
- Insurance (SIC 63)
- Insurance agents, brokers, and services (SIC 64)
- Real estate (SIC 65)
- Combined real estate, insurance, etc. (SIC 66)
- Holding and other investment offices (SIC 67)
- Personal services (SIC 72)
- Business services (SIC 73)
- Motion pictures (SIC 78)
- Legal services (SIC 81)
- Educational services (SIC 82)
- Social services (SIC 83)
- Museums, botanical, zoological gardens (SIC 84)
- Membership organizations (SIC 86)
- Private households (SIC 88), and
- Miscellaneous services (SIC 89).

Even though recordkeeping requirements are reduced for employers in these industries, they, like nonexempt employers, must comply with OSHA standards, display the OSHA poster, and report to OSHA within 48 hours any accident which results in one or more fatalities or the hospitalization of five of more employees. Also, some State safety and health laws may require regularly exempt employers to keep injury and illness records, and some States have more stringent catastrophic reporting requirements.

C. Employers and individuals who never keep OSHA records

The following employers and individuals do not have to keep OSHA injury and illness records:

- *Self-employed individuals;*
- *Partners with no employees;*
- *Employers of domestics* in the employers' private residence for the purposes of housekeeping or child care, or both; and
- *Employers engaged in religious activities* concerning the conduct of religious services or rites. Employees engaged in such activities include clergy, choir members, organists and other musicians, ushers, and the like. However, records of injuries and illnesses occurring to employees while performing secular activities must be kept. Recordkeeping is also required for employees of private hospitals and certain commercial establishments owned or operated by religious organizations.

State and local government agencies are usually exempt from OSHA recordkeeping. However, in certain States, agencies of State and local governments are required to keep injury and illness records in accordance with State regulations.

D. Employers subject to other Federal safety and health regulations

Employers subject to injury and illness recordkeeping requirements of other Federal safety and health regulations are not exempt from OSHA recordkeeping. However, records used to comply with other Federal recordkeeping obligations may also be used to satisfy the OSHA recordkeeping requirements. The forms used must be equivalent to the log and summary (OSHA No. 200) and the supplementary record (OSHA No. 101).

Chapter II. OSHA Recordkeeping Forms

Only two forms are used for OSHA recordkeeping. One form, the OSHA No. 200, serves as both the Log of Occupational Injuries and Illnesses, on which the occurrence and extent of cases are recorded during the year; and as the Summary of Occupational Injuries and Illnesses, which is used to summarize the log at the end of the year to satisfy employer posting obligations. The other form, the Supplementary Record of Occupational Injuries and Illnesses, OSHA No. 101, provides additional information on each of the cases that have been recorded on the log.

A. The Log and Summary of Occupational Injuries and Illnesses, OSHA No. 200

The log is used for recording and classifying occupational injuries and illnesses, and for noting the extent of each case. The log shows when the occupational injury or illness occurred, to whom, the regular job of the injured or ill person at the time of the injury or illness exposure, the department in which the person was employed, the kind of injury or illness, how much time was lost, whether the case resulted in a fatality, etc. The log consists of three parts: A descriptive section which identifies the employee and briefly describes the injury or illness; a section covering the extent of the injuries recorded; and a section on the type and extent of illnesses.

Usually, the OSHA No. 200 form is used by employers as their record of occupational injuries and illnesses. However, a private form equivalent to the log, such as a computer printout, may be used if it contains the same detail as the OSHA No. 200 and is as readable and comprehensible as the OSHA No. 200 to a person not familiar with the equivalent form. It is important that the columns of the equivalent form have the same identifying number as the corresponding columns of the OSHA No. 200 because the instructions for completing the survey of occupational injuries and illnesses refer to log columns by number. It is advisable that employers have private equivalents of the log form reviewed by BLS to insure compliance with the regulations.

The portion of the OSHA No. 200 to the right of the dotted vertical line is used to summarize injuries and illnesses in an establishment for the calendar year. Every nonexempt employer who is required to keep OSHA records must prepare an annual summary for each establishment based on the information contained in the log for each establishment. The summary is prepared by totaling the column entries on the log (or its equivalent) and signing and dating the certification portion of the form at the bottom of the page.

B. The Supplementary Record of Occupational Injuries and Illnesses, OSHA No. 101

For every injury or illness entered on the log, it is necessary to record additional information on the supplementary record, OSHA No. 101. The supplementary record describes how the accident or illness exposure occurred, lists the objects or substances involved, and indicates the nature of the injury or illness and the part(s) of the body affected.

The OSHA No. 101 is not the only form that can be used to satisfy this requirement. To eliminate duplicate recording, workers' compensation, insurance, or other reports may be used as supplementary records if they contain all of the items on the OSHA No. 101. If they do not, the missing items must be added to the substitute or included on a separate attachment.

Completed supplementary records must be present in the establishment within 6 workdays after the employer has received information that an injury or illness has occurred.

Chapter III. Location, Retention, and Maintenance of Records

Ordinarily, injury and illness records must be kept by employers for *each* of their establishments. This chapter describes what is considered to be an establishment for recordkeeping purposes, where the records must be located, how long they must be kept, and how they should be updated.

A. Establishments

If an employer has more than one establishment, a separate set of records must be maintained for *each* one. The recordkeeping regulations define an establishment as "a single physical location where business is conducted or where services or industrial operations are performed." Examples include a factory, mill, store, hotel, restaurant, movie theater, farm, ranch, sales office, warehouse, or central administrative office.

The regulations specify that distinctly separate activities performed at the same physical location (for example, contract construction activities operated from the same physical location as a lumber yard) shall each be treated as a separate establishment for recordkeeping purposes. Production of dissimilar products; different kinds of operational procedures; different facilities; and separate management, personnel, payroll, or support staff are all indicative of separate activities and separate establishments.

B. Location of records

Injury and illness records (the log, OSHA No. 200, and the supplementary record, OSHA No. 101) must be kept for every physical location where operations are performed. Under the regulations, the location of these records depends upon whether or not the employees are associated with a fixed establishment. The distinction between fixed and nonfixed establishments generally rests on the nature and duration of the operation and not on the type of structure in which the business is located. A nonfixed establishment usually operates at a single location for a relatively short period of time. A fixed establishment remains at a given location on a long-term or permanent basis. Generally, any operation at a given site for more than 1 year is considered a fixed establishment. Also, fixed establishments are generally places where clerical, administrative, or other business records are kept.

1. *Employees associated with fixed establishments.* Records for these employees should be located as follows:

   a. Records for employees working at fixed locations, such as factories, stores, restaurants, warehouses, etc., should be kept at the work location.
   b. Records for employees who report to a fixed location but work elsewhere should be kept at the place where the employees report each day. These employees are generally engaged in activities such as agriculture, construction, transportation, etc.
   c. Records for employees whose payroll or personnel records are maintained at a fixed location, but who do not report or work at a single establishment, should be maintained at the base from which they are paid or the base of their firm's personnel operations. This category includes generally unsupervised employees such as traveling salespeople, technicians, or engineers.

2. *Employees not associated with fixed establishments.* Some employees are subject to common supervision, but do not report or work at a fixed establishment on a regular basis. These employees are engaged in physically dispersed activities that occur in construction, installation, repair, or service operations. Records for these employees should be located as follows:

   a. Records may be kept at the field office or mobile base of operations.
   b. Records may also be kept at an established central location. If the records are maintained centrally: (1) The address and telephone number of the place where records are kept must be available at the worksite; and (2) there must be someone available at the central location during normal business hours to provide information from the records.

C. Location exception for the log (OSHA No. 200)

Although the supplementary record and the annual summary must be located as outlined in the previous section, it is possible to prepare and *maintain the log* at an alternate location or by means of data processing equipment, or both. Two requirements must be met: (1) Sufficient information must be available at the alternate location to complete the log within 6 workdays after receipt of information that a recordable case has occurred; and (2) a copy of the log updated to within 45 calendar days must be present at all times in the establishment. This location exception applies only to the log, and not to the other OSHA records. Also, it does not affect the employer's posting obligations.

D. Retention of OSHA records

The log and summary, OSHA No. 200, and the supplementary record, OSHA No. 101, must be retained in each establishment for 5 calendar years following the end of the year to which they relate. If an establishment changes ownership, the new employer must preserve the records for the remainder of the 5-year period. However, the new employer is not responsible for updating the records of the former owner.

E. Maintenance of the log (OSHA No. 200)

In addition to keeping the log on a calendar year basis, employers are required to update this form to include newly discovered cases and to reflect changes which occur in recorded cases after the end of the calendar year. Maintenance or updating of the log is different from the retention of records discussed in the previous section. Although all OSHA injury and illness records must be retained, only the log must be updated by the employer. If, during the 5-year retention period, there is a change in the extent or outcome of an injury or illness which affects an entry on a previous year's log, then the first entry should be lined out and a corrected entry made on that log. Also, new entries should be made for previously unrecorded cases that are discovered or for cases that initially weren't recorded but were found to be recordable after the end of the year in which the case occurred. The entire entry should be lined out for recorded cases that are later found nonrecordable. Log totals should also be modified to reflect these changes.

APPENDIX 2B

Chapter IV. Deciding Whether a Case Should Be Recorded and How To Classify It

This chapter presents guidelines for determining whether a case must be recorded under the OSHA recordkeeping requirements. These requirements should not be confused with recordkeeping requirements of various workers' compensation systems, internal industrial safety and health monitoring systems, the ANSI Z.16 standards for recording and measuring work injury and illness experience, and private insurance company rating systems. Reporting a case on the OSHA records should not affect recordkeeping determinations under these or other systems. Also—

Recording an injury or illness under the OSHA system does not necessarily imply that management was at fault, that the worker was at fault, that a violation of an OSHA standard has occurred, or that the injury or illness is compensable under workers' compensation or other systems.

A. Employees vs. other workers on site

Employers must maintain injury and illness records for their own employees at each of their establishments, but they are *not* responsible for maintaining records for employees of other firms or for independent contractors, even though these individuals may be working temporarily in their establishment or on one of their jobsites at the time an injury or illness exposure occurs. Therefore, before deciding whether a case is recordable an employment relationship needs to be determined.

Employee status generally exists for recordkeeping purposes when the employer supervises not only the output, product, or result to be accomplished by the person's work, but also the details, means, methods, and processes by which the work is accomplished. This means the employer who supervises the worker's day-to-day activities is responsible for recording his injuries and illnesses. Independent contractors are not considered employees; they are primarily subject to supervision by the using firm only in regard to the result to be accomplished or end product to be delivered. Independent contractors keep their own injury and illness records.

Other factors which may be considered in determining employee status are: (1) Whom the worker considers to be his or her employer; (2) who pays the worker's wages; (3) who withholds the worker's Social Security taxes; (4) who hired the worker; and (5) who has the authority to terminate the worker's employment.

B. Method used for case analysis

The decisionmaking process consists of five steps:

1. Determine whether a case occurred; that is, whether there was a death, illness, or an injury;
2. Establish that the case was work related; that it resulted from an event or exposure in the work environment;
3. Decide whether the case is an injury or an illness; and
4. If the case is an illness, record it and check the appropriate illness category on the log; or
5. If the case is an injury, decide if it is recordable based on a finding of medical treatment, loss of consciousness, restriction of work or motion, or transfer to another job.

Chart 1 presents this methodology in graphic form.

C. Determining whether a case occurred

The first step in the decisionmaking process is the determination of whether or not an injury or illness has occurred. Employers have nothing to record unless an employee has experienced a work-related injury or illness. In most instances, recognition of these injuries and illnesses is a fairly simple matter. However, some situations have troubled employers over the years. Two of these are:

1. *Hospitalization for observation.* If an employee goes to or is sent to a hospital for a brief period of time for observation, it is not recordable, provided no medical treatment was given, or no illness was recognized. The determining factor is not that the employee went to the hospital, but whether the incident is recordable as a work-related illness or as an injury requiring medical treatment or involving loss of consciousness, restriction of work or motion, or transfer to another job.

2. *Differentiating a new case from the recurrence of a previous injury or illness.* Employers are required to make new entries on their OSHA forms for each new recordable injury or illness. However, new entries should

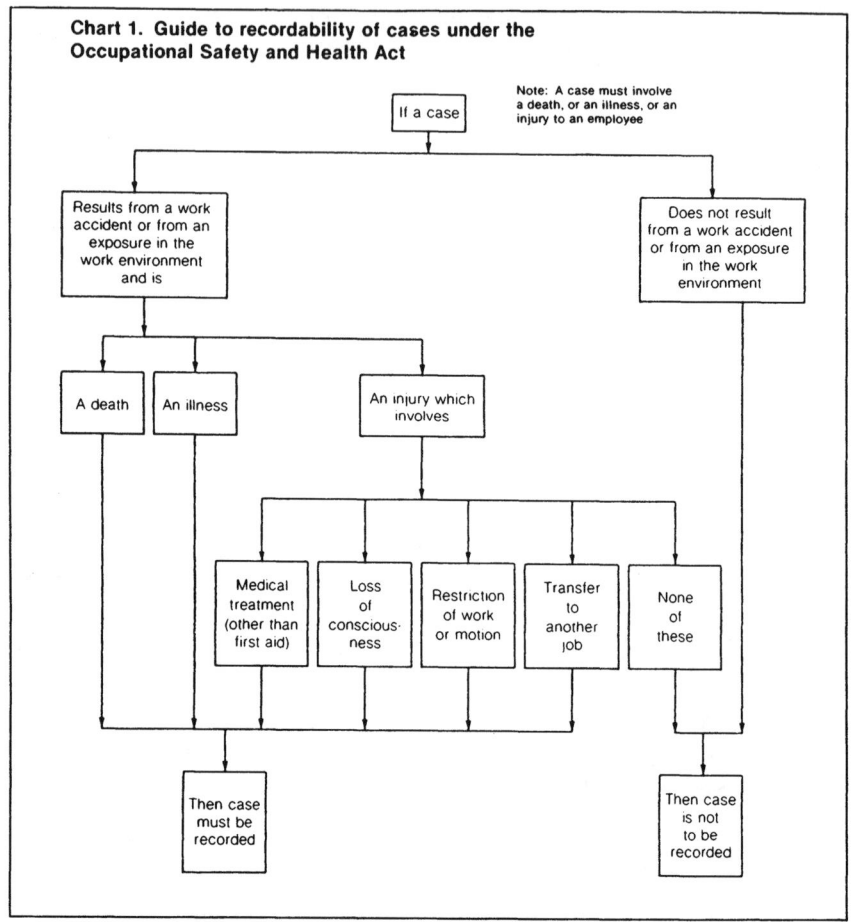

Chart 1. Guide to recordability of cases under the Occupational Safety and Health Act

not be made for the recurrence of symptoms from previous cases, and it is sometimes difficult to decide whether or not a situation is a new case or a recurrence. The following guidelines address this problem:

a. *Injuries.* The aggravation of a previous injury almost always results from some new incident involving the employee (such as a slip, trip, fall, sharp twist, etc.). Consequently, when work related, these new incidents should be recorded as new cases.
b. *Illnesses.* Generally, each occupational illness should be recorded with a separate entry on the OSHA No. 200. However, certain illnesses, such as silicosis, may have prolonged effects which recur over time. The recurrence of these symptoms should not be recorded as new cases on the OSHA forms. The recurrence of symptoms of previous illnesses may require adjustment of entries on the log for previously recorded illnesses to reflect possible changes in the extent or outcome of the particular case.

Some occupational illnesses, such as certain dermatitis or respiratory conditions, may recur as the result of new exposures to sensitizing agents, and should be recorded as new cases.

D. Establishing work relationship

The Occupational Safety and Health Act of 1970

requires employers to record only those injuries and illnesses that are work related. *Work relationship is established under the OSHA recordkeeping system when the injury or illness results from an event or exposure in the work environment. The work environment is primarily composed of: (1) The employer's premises, and (2) other locations where employees are engaged in work-related activities or are present as a condition of their employment.* When an employee is off the employer's premises, work relationship must be established; when on the premises, this relationship is presumed. The employer's premises encompass the total establishment, including not only the primary work facility, but also such areas as company storage facilities. In addition to physical locations, equipment or materials used in the course of an employee's work are also considered part of the employee's work environment.

1. *Injuries and illnesses resulting from events or exposures on the employer's premises.* Injuries and illnesses that result from an event or exposure on the employer's premises are generally considered work related. The employer's premises consist of the total establishment. They include the primary work facilities and other areas which are considered part of the employer's general work area.

The presumption of work relationship for activities on the employer's premises is rebuttable. Situations where the presumption would not apply include: (1) When a worker is on the employer's premises as a member of the general public and not as an employee, and (2) when employees have symptoms that merely surface on the employer's premises, but are the result of a nonwork-related event or exposure off the premises.

The following subjects warrant special mention:

a. Company restrooms, hallways, and cafeterias are all considered to be *part* of the employer's premises and constitute part of the work environment. Therefore, injuries occurring in these places are generally considered work related.

b. For OSHA recordkeeping purposes, the definition of work premises *excludes* all employer controlled ball fields, tennis courts, golf courses, parks, swimming pools, gyms, and other similar recreational facilities which are often apart from the workplace and used by employees on a voluntary basis for their own benefit, primarily during off-work hours. Therefore, injuries to employees in these recreational facilities are not recordable unless the employee was engaged in some work-related activity, or was required by the employer to participate.

c. Company parking facilities are generally *not* considered part of the employer's premises for OSHA recordkeeping purposes. Therefore, injuries to employees on these parking lots are not presumed to be work related, and are not recordable unless the employee was engaged in some work-related activity.

2. *Injuries and illnesses resulting from events or exposures off the employer's premises.* When an employee is off the employer's premises and suffers an injury or an illness exposure, work relationship must be established; it is not presumed. Injuries and illness exposures off premises are considered work related if the employee is engaged in a work activity or if they occur in the work environment. The work environment in these instances includes locations where employees are engaged in job tasks or work-related activities, or places where employees are present due to the nature of their job or as a condition of their employment.

Employees who travel on company business shall be considered to be engaged in work-related activities all the time they spend in the interest of the company, including, but not limited to, travel to and from customer contacts, and entertaining or being entertained for the purpose of transacting, discussing, or promoting business, etc. However, an injury/illness would not be recordable if it occurred during normal living activities (eating, sleeping, recreation); or if the employee deviates from a reasonably direct route of travel (side trip for vacation or other personal reasons). He would again be in the course of employment when he returned to the normal route of travel.

When a traveling employee checks into a hotel or motel, he establishes a "home away from home." Thereafter, his activities are evaluated in the same manner as for nontraveling employees. For example, if an employee on travel status is to report each day to a fixed worksite, then injuries sustained when traveling to this worksite would be considered off the job. The rationale is that an employee's normal commute from home to office would not be considered work related. However, there are situations where employees in travel status report to, or rotate among several different worksites after they establish their "home away from home" (such as a salesperson traveling to and from different customer contacts). In these situations, the injuries sustained when traveling to and from the sales locations would be considered job related.

Traveling sales personnel may establish only one base of operations (home or company office). A sales person with his home as an office is considered at work when he is in that office and when he leaves his premises in the interest of the company.

Chart 2 provides a guide for establishing the work relationship of cases.

E. Distinguishing between injuries and illnesses

Under the OSH Act, all work-related illnesses must be recorded, while injuries are recordable *only* when they require medical treatment (other than first aid), or involve loss of consciousness, restriction of work or motion, or transfer to another job. The distinction between injuries and illnesses, therefore, has significant recordkeeping implications.

Whether a case involves an injury or illness is determined by the nature of the original event or exposure

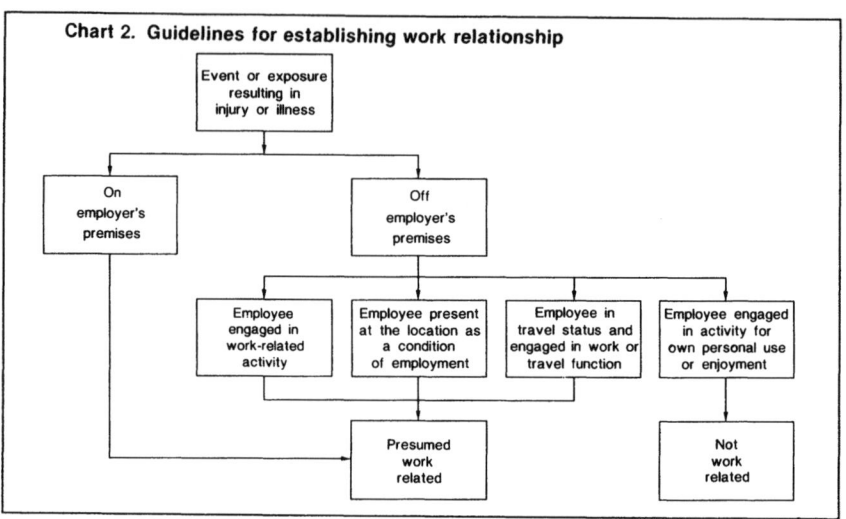

which caused the case, not by the resulting condition of the affected employee. Injuries are caused by instantaneous events in the work environment. Cases resulting from anything other than instantaneous events are considered illnesses. This concept of illnesses includes acute illnesses which result from exposures of relatively short duration.

Some conditions may be classified as either an injury or an illness (but not both), depending upon the nature of the event that produced the condition. For example, a loss of hearing resulting from an explosion (an instantaneous event) is classified as an injury; the same condition arising from exposure to industrial noise over a period of time would be classified as an occupational illness.

F. Recording occupational illnesses

Employers are required to record the occurrence of all occupational illnesses, which are defined in the instructions of the log and summary as:

> Any abnormal condition or disorder, other than one resulting from an occupational injury, caused by exposure to environmental factors associated with employment. It includes acute and chronic illnesses or diseases which may be caused by inhalation, absorption, ingestion, or direct contact.

The instructions also refer to recording illnesses which were "diagnosed or recognized." Illness exposures ultimately result in conditions of a chemical, physical, biological, or psychological nature.

Occupational illnesses must be diagnosed to be recordable. However, they do not necessarily have to be diagnosed by a physician or other medical personnel. Diagnosis may be by a physician, registered nurse, or a person who by training or experience is capable to make such a determination. Employers, employees, and others may be able to detect some illnesses such as skin diseases or disorders without the benefit of specialized medical training. However, a case more difficult to diagnose, such as silicosis, would require evaluation by properly trained medical personnel.

In addition to recording the occurrence of occupational illnesses, employers are required to record each illness case in 1 of the 7 categories on the front of the log. The back of the log form contains a listing of types of illnesses or disorders and gives examples for each illness category. These are only examples, however, and should not be considered as a complete list of types of illnesses under each category.

Recording and classifying occupational illnesses may be difficult for employers, especially the chronic and long term latent illnesses. Many illnesses are not easily detected; and once detected, it is often difficult to determine whether an illness is work related. Also, employees may not report illnesses because the symptoms may not be readily apparent, or because they do not think their illness is serious or work related.

The following material is provided to assist in detecting occupational illnesses and in establishing their work relationship:

1. *Detection and diagnosis of occupational illnesses.* An occupational illness is defined in the instructions on

APPENDIX 2B

the log as any work-related abnormal condition or disorder (other than an occupational injury). Detection of these abnormal conditions or disorders, the first step in recording illnesses, is often difficult. When an occupational illness is suspected, employers may want to consider the following:

a. A medical examination of the employee's physiological systems. For example:
   - Head and neck
   - Eyes, ears, nose, and throat
   - Endocrine
   - Genitourinary
   - Musculoskeletal
   - Neurological
   - Respiratory
   - Cardiovascular, and
   - Gastrointestinal;
b. Observation and evaluation of behavior related to emotional status, such as deterioration in job performance which cannot be explained;
c. Specific examination for health effects of suspected or possible disease agents by competent medical personnel;
d. Comparison of date of onset of symptoms with occupational history;
e. Evaluation of results of any past biological or medical monitoring (blood, urine, other sample analysis) and previous physical examinations;
f. Evaluation of laboratory tests: Routine (complete blood count, blood chemistry profile, urinalysis) and specific tests for suspected disease agents (e.g., blood and urine tests for specific agents, chest or other X-rays, liver function tests, pulmonary function tests); and
g. Reviewing the literature, such as Material Safety Data Sheets and other reference documents, to ascertain whether the levels to which the workers were exposed could have produced the ill effects.

2. *Determining whether the illness is occupationally related.* The instructions on the back of the log define occupational illnesses as those "caused by environmental factors associated with employment." In some cases, such as contact dermatitis, the relationship between an illness and work-related exposure is easy to recognize. In other cases, where the occupational cause is not direct and apparent, it may be difficult to determine accurately whether an employee's illness is occupational in nature. In these situations, it may help employers to ask the following questions:

a. Has an illness condition clearly been established?
b. Does it appear that the illness resulted from, or was aggravated by, suspected agents or other conditions in the work environment?
c. Are these suspected agents present (or have they been present) in the work environment?
d. Was the ill employee exposed to these agents in the work environment?
e. Was the exposure to a sufficient degree and/or duration to result in the illness condition?
f. Was the illness attributable solely to a nonoccupational exposure?

G. Deciding if work-related injuries are recordable

Although the OSH Act requires that all work-related deaths and illnesses be recorded, the recording of nonfatal injuries is limited to certain specific types of cases: Those which require medical treatment or involve loss of consciousness; restriction of work or motion; or transfer to another job. Minor injuries requiring only first aid treatment are *not* recordable.

1. *Medical treatment.* It is important to understand the distinction between medical treatment and first aid treatment since many work-related injuries are recordable only because medical treatment was given.

The regulations and the instructions on the back of the log and summary, OSHA No. 200, define medical treatment as any treatment, other than first aid treatment, administered to injured employees. Essentially, medical treatment involves the provision of medical or surgical care for injuries that are not minor through the application of procedures or systematic therapeutic measures.

The act also specifically states that work-related injuries which involve only first aid treatment should not be recorded. First aid is commonly thought to mean emergency treatment of injuries before regular medical care is available. However, first aid treatment has a different meaning for OSHA recordkeeping purposes. The regulations define first aid treatment as:

> ... any one-time treatment, and any followup visit for the purpose of observation, of minor scratches, cuts, burns, splinters, and so forth, which do not ordinarily require medical care. Such one-time treatment, and followup visit for the purpose of observation, is considered first aid even though provided by a physician or registered professional personnel.

The distinction between medical treatment and first aid depends not only on the treatment provided, but also on the severity of the injury being treated. First aid is: (1) Limited to one-time treatment and subsequent observation; *and* (2) involves treatment of only minor injuries, *not* emergency treatment of serious injuries. Injuries are *not* minor if:

a. They must be treated only by a physician or licensed medical personnel;
b. They impair bodily function (i.e., normal use of senses, limbs, etc.);
c. They result in damage to the physical structure of a nonsuperficial nature (e.g., fractures); or
d. They involve complications requiring followup medical treatment.

Physicians or registered medical professionals, working under the standing orders of a physician, routinely treat minor injuries. Such treatment may constitute first aid. Also, some visits to a doctor do not involve treatment at all. For example, a visit to a doctor for an examination or other diagnostic procedure to determine whether the employee has an injury does not constitute medical treatment. Conversely, medical treatment can be provided to employees by lay persons; i.e., someone other than a physician or registered medical personnel.

The following classifications list certain procedures as either medical treatment or first aid treatment.

Medical Treatment:

The following are generally considered medical treatment. Work-related injuries for which this type of treatment was provided or should have been provided are almost always recordable:

- Treatment of **INFECTION**
- Application of **ANTISEPTICS during second or subsequent visit** to medical personnel
- Treatment of **SECOND OR THIRD DEGREE BURN(S)**
- Application of **SUTURES** (stitches)
- Application of **BUTTERFLY ADHESIVE DRESSING(S) or STERI STRIP(S)** in lieu of sutures
- Removal of **FOREIGN BODIES EMBEDDED IN EYE**
- Removal of **FOREIGN BODIES FROM WOUND**; if procedure is **COMPLICATED** because of depth of embedment, size, or location
- Use of **PRESCRIPTION MEDICATIONS** (except a single dose administered on first visit for minor injury or discomfort)
- Use of hot or cold **SOAKING THERAPY during second or subsequent visit** to medical personnel
- Application of hot or cold **COMPRESS(ES) during second or subsequent visit** to medical personnel
- **CUTTING AWAY DEAD SKIN** (surgical debridement)
- Application of **HEAT THERAPY during second or subsequent visit** to medical personnel
- Use of **WHIRLPOOL BATH THERAPY during second or subsequent visit** to medical personnel
- **POSITIVE X-RAY DIAGNOSIS** (fractures, broken bones, etc.)
- **ADMISSION TO A HOSPITAL** or equivalent medical facility **FOR TREATMENT.**

First Aid Treatment:

The following are generally considered first aid treatment (e.g., one-time treatment and subsequent observation of minor injuries) and should not be recorded if the work-related injury does not involve loss of consciousness, restriction of work or motion, or transfer to another job:

- Application of **ANTISEPTICS during first visit** to medical personnel
- Treatment of **FIRST DEGREE BURN(S)**
- Application of **BANDAGE(S)** during any visit to medical personnel
- Use of **ELASTIC BANDAGE(S) during first visit** to medical personnel
- Removal of **FOREIGN BODIES NOT EMBEDDED IN EYE** if only irrigation is required
- Removal of **FOREIGN BODIES FROM WOUND**; if procedure is **UNCOMPLICATED**, and is, for example, by tweezers or other simple technique
- Use of **NONPRESCRIPTION MEDICATIONS AND** administration of **single dose of PRESCRIPTION MEDICATION** on first visit for minor injury or discomfort
- **SOAKING THERAPY on initial visit** to medical personnel or removal of bandages by **SOAKING**
- Application of hot or cold **COMPRESS(ES) during first visit** to medical personnel
- Application of **OINTMENTS** to abrasions to prevent drying or cracking
- Application of **HEAT THERAPY during first visit** to medical personnel
- Use of **WHIRLPOOL BATH THERAPY during first visit** to medical personnel
- **NEGATIVE X-RAY DIAGNOSIS**
- **OBSERVATION** of injury during visit to medical personnel.

The following procedure, by itself, is not considered medical treatment:

- Administration of **TETANUS SHOT(S) or BOOSTER(S).** However, these shots are often given in conjunction with more serious injuries; consequently, injuries requiring these shots may be recordable for other reasons.

2. *Loss of consciousness.* If an employee loses consciousness as the result of a work-related injury, the case must be recorded no matter what type of treatment was provided. The rationale behind this recording requirement is that loss of consciousness is generally associated with the more serious injuries.

3. *Restriction of work or motion.* Restricted work activity occurs when the employee, because of the impact of a job-related injury, is physically or mentally unable to perform all or any part of his or her normal assignment during all or any part of the workday or shift. The emphasis is on the employee's ability to perform normal job duties. Restriction of work or motion may result in either a lost worktime injury or a nonlost-worktime injury, depending upon whether the restriction extended beyond the day of injury.

4. *Transfer to another job.* Injuries requiring transfer of the employee to another job are also considered serious enough to be recordable regardless of the type of treatment provided. Transfers are seldom the sole criterion for recordability because injury cases are almost always recordable on other grounds, primarily medical treatment or restriction of work or motion.

APPENDIX 2B

Chapter V. Categories for Evaluating the Extent of Recordable Cases

Once the employer decides that a recordable injury or illness has occurred, the case must be evaluated to determine its extent or outcome. There are three categories of recordable cases: Fatalities, lost workday cases, and cases without lost workdays. Every recordable case must be placed in only one of these categories.

A. Fatalities

All work-related fatalities must be recorded, regardless of the time between the injury and the death, or the length of the illness.

B. Lost workday cases

Lost workday cases occur when the injured or ill employee experiences either days away from work, days of restricted work activity, or both. In these situations, the injured or ill employee is affected to such an extent that: (1) Days must be taken off from the job for medical treatment or recuperation; or (2) the employee is unable to perform his or her normal job duties over a normal work shift, even though the employee may be able to continue working.

1. Lost workday cases involving days away from work are cases resulting in days the employee would have worked but could not because of the job-related injury or illness. The focus of these cases is on the employee's inability, because of injury or illness, to be present in the work environment during his or her normal work shift.

2. Lost workday cases involving days of restricted work activity are those cases where, because of injury or illness, (1) the employee was assigned to another job on a temporary basis, or (2) the employee worked at a permanent job less than full time, or (3) the employee worked at his or her permanently assigned job but could not perform all the duties normally connected with it. Restricted work activity occurs when the employee, because of the job-related injury or illness, is physically or mentally unable to perform all or any part of his or her normal job duties over all or any part of his or her normal workday or shift. The emphasis is on the employee's inability to perform normal job duties over a normal work shift.

Injuries and illnesses are not considered lost workday cases unless they affect the employee beyond the day of injury or onset of illness. When counting the number of days away from work or days of restricted work activity, do not include the initial day of injury or onset of illness, or any days on which the employee would not have worked even though able to work (holidays, vacations, etc.).

C. Cases not resulting in death or lost workdays

These cases consist of the relatively less serious injuries and illnesses which satisfy the criteria for recordability but which do not result in death or require the affected employee to have days away from work or days of restricted work activity beyond the date of injury or onset of illness.

Chapter VI. Employer Obligations for Reporting Occupational Injuries and Illnesses

This chapter focuses on the requirements of Section 8(c)(2) of the Occupational Safety and Health Act of 1970 and Title 29, Part 1904, of the Code of Federal Regulations for employers to make reports of occupational injuries and illnesses. It does not include the reporting requirements of other standards or regulations of the Occupational Safety and Health Administration (OSHA) or of any other State or Federal agency.

A. The Annual Survey of Occupational Injuries and Illnesses

The survey is conducted on a sample basis, and firms required to submit reports of their injury and illness experience are contacted by BLS or a participating State agency. A firm not contacted by its State agency or BLS need not file a report of its injury and illness experience. Employers should note, however, that even if they are not selected to participate in the annual survey for a given year, they must still comply with the recordkeeping requirements listed in the preceding chapters as well as with the requirements for reporting fatalities and multiple hospitalization cases provided in the next section of this chapter.

Participants in the annual survey consist of two categories of employers: (1) Employers who maintain OSHA records on a regular basis; and (2) a small, rotating sample of employers who are regularly exempt from OSHA recordkeeping. The survey procedure is different for these two groups of employers.

1. *Participation of firms regularly maintaining OSHA records.* When employers regularly maintaining OSHA records are selected to participate in the Annual Survey of Occupational Injuries and Illnesses, they are mailed the survey questionnaire in February of the year following the reference calendar year of the survey. (A firm selected to participate in the 1985 survey would have been contacted in February of 1986.) The survey form, the Occupational Injuries and Illnesses Survey Questionnaire, OSHA No. 200-S, requests information about the establishment(s) included in the report and the injuries and illnesses experienced during the previous year. Information for the injury and illness portion of the report form usually can be copied directly from the totals on the log and summary, OSHA No. 200, which the employer should have completed and posted in the establishment by the time the questionnaire arrives. The survey form also requests summary information about the type of business activity and number of employees and hours worked at the reporting unit during the reference year.

2. *Participation of normally exempt small employers and employers in low-hazard industries.* A few regularly exempt employers (those with fewer than 11 employees in the previous calendar year and those in designated low-hazard industries) are also required to participate in the annual survey. Their participation is necessary for the production of injury and illness statistics that are comparable in coverage to the statistics published in years prior to the exemptions. These employers are notified prior to the reference calendar year of the survey that they must maintain injury and illness records for the coming year. (A firm selected to participate in the 1985 survey would have been contacted in December 1984.) At the time of notification, they are supplied with the necessary forms and instructions. During the reference calendar year, prenotified employers make entries on the log, OSHA No. 200, but are not required to complete a Supplementary Record of Occupational Injuries and Illnesses, OSHA No. 101, or post the summary of the OSHA No. 200 the following February (regularly participating employers do both).

B. Reporting fatalities and multiple hospitalizations

All employers are required to report accidents resulting in one or more fatalities or the hospitalization of five or more employees. (Some States have more stringent catastrophic reporting requirements.)

The report is made to the nearest office of the Area Director of the Occupational Safety and Health Administration, U.S. Department of Labor, unless the State in which the accident occurred is administering an approved State plan under Section 18(b) of the OSH Act. Those 18(b) States designate a State agency to which the report must be made.

The report must contain three pieces of information: (1) Circumstances surrounding the accident(s), (2) the number of fatalities, and (3) the extent of any injuries. If necessary, the OSHA Area Director may require additional information on the accident.

The report should be made within 48 hours after the occurrence of the accident or within 48 hours after the occurrence of the fatality, regardless of the time lapse between the occurrence of the accident and the death of the employee.

Chapter VII. Access to OSHA Records and Penalties for Failure To Comply With Recordkeeping Obligations

The preceding chapters describe recordkeeping and reporting requirements. This chapter covers subjects related to insuring the integrity of the OSH recordkeeping process—access to OSHA records and penalties for recordkeeping violations.

A. Access to OSHA records

All OSHA records, which are being kept by employers for the 5-year retention period, should be available for inspection and copying by authorized Federal and State government officials. Employees, former employees, and their representatives are provided access to only the log, OSHA No. 200.

Government officials with access to the OSHA records include: Representatives of the Department of Labor, including OSHA safety and health compliance officers and BLS representatives; representatives of the Department of Health and Human Services while carrying out that department's research responsibilities; and representatives of States accorded jurisdiction for inspections or statistical compilations. "Representatives" may include Department of Labor officials inspecting a workplace or gathering information, officials of the Department of Health and Human Services, or contractors working for the agencies mentioned above, depending on the provisions of the contract under which they work.

Employee access to the log is limited to the records of the establishment in which the employee currently works or formerly worked. All current logs and those being maintained for the 5-year retention period must be made available for inspection and copying by employees, former employees, and their representatives. An employee representative can be a member of a union representing the employee, or any person designated by the employee or former employee. Access to the log is to be provided in a reasonable manner and at a reasonable time. Redress for failure to comply with the access provisions of the regulations can be obtained through a complaint to OSHA.

B. Penalties for failure to comply with recordkeeping obligations

Employers committing recordkeeping and/or reporting violations are subject to the same sanctions as employers violating other OSHA requirements such as safety and health standards and regulations.

Glossary of Terms

Annual summary. Consists of a copy of the occupational injury and illness totals for the year from the OSHA No. 200, and the following information: The calendar year covered; company name; establishment address; certification signature, title, and date.

Annual survey. Each year, BLS conducts an annual survey of occupational injuries and illnesses to produce national statistics. The OSHA injury and illness records maintained by employers in their establishments serve as the basis for this survey.

Bureau of Labor Statistics (BLS). The Bureau of Labor Statistics is the agency responsible for administering and maintaining the OSHA recordkeeping system, and for collecting, compiling, and analyzing work injury and illness statistics.

Certification. The person who supervises the preparation of the Log and Summary of Occupational Injuries and Illnesses, OSHA No. 200, certifies that it is true and complete by signing the last page of, or by appending a statement to that effect to, the annual summary.

Cooperative program. A program jointly conducted by the States and the Federal Government to collect occupational injury and illness statistics.

Employee. One who is employed in the business of his or her employer affecting commerce.

Employee representative. Anyone designated by the employee for the purpose of gaining access to the employer's log of occupational injuries and illnesses.

Employer. Any person engaged in a business affecting commerce who has employees.

Establishment. A single physical location where business is conducted or where services or industrial operations are performed; the place where the employees report for work, operate from, or from which they are paid.

Exposure. The reasonable likelihood that a worker is or was subject to some effect, influence, or safety hazard; or in contact with a hazardous chemical or physical agent at a sufficient concentration and duration to produce an illness.

Federal Register. The official source of information and notification on OSHA's proposed rulemaking, standards, regulations, and other official matters, including amendments, corrections, insertions, or deletions.

First aid. Any one-time treatment and subsequent observation of minor scratches, cuts, burns, splinters, and so forth, which do not ordinarily require medical care. Such treatment and observation are considered first aid even though provided by a physician or registered professional personnel.

First report of injury. A workers' compensation form which may qualify as a substitute for the supplementary record, OSHA No. 101.

Incidence rate. The number of injuries, illnesses, or lost workdays related to a common exposure base of 100 full-time workers. The common exposure base enables one to make accurate interindustry comparisons, trend analysis over time, or comparisons among firms regardless of size. This rate is calculated as:

$$N/EH \times 200{,}000$$

where:

N = number of injuries and/or illnesses or lost workdays

EH = total hours worked by all employees during calendar year

$200{,}000$ = base for 100 full-time equivalent workers (working 40 hours per week, 50 weeks per year).

Log and Summary (OSHA No. 200). The OSHA recordkeeping form used to list injuries and illnesses and to note the extent of each case.

Lost workday cases. Cases which involve days away from work or days of restricted work activity, or both.

Lost workdays. The number of workdays (consecutive or not), beyond the day of injury or onset of illness, the

APPENDIX 2B

employee was away from work or limited to restricted work activity because of an occupational injury or illness.

(1) Lost workdays—away from work. The number of workdays (consecutive or not) on which the employee would have worked but could not because of occupational injury or illness.

(2) Lost workdays—restricted work activity. The number of workdays (consecutive or not) on which, because of injury or illness: (1) The employee was assigned to another job on a temporary basis; or (2) the employee worked at a permanent job less than full time; or (3) the employee worked at a permanently assigned job but could not perform all duties normally connected with it.

The number of days away from work or days of restricted work activity does not include the day of injury or onset of illness or any days on which the employee would not have worked even though able to work.

Low-hazard industries. Selected industries in retail trade; finance, insurance, and real estate; and services which are regularly exempt from OSHA recordkeeping. To be included in this exemption, an industry must fall within an SIC not targeted for general schedule inspections and must have an average lost workday case injury rate for a designated 3-year measurement period at or below 75 percent of the U.S. private sector average rate.

Medical treatment. Includes treatment of injuries administered by physicians, registered professional personnel, or lay persons (i.e., nonmedical personnel). Medical treatment does not include first aid treatment (one-time treatment and subsequent observation of minor scratches, cuts, burns, splinters, and so forth, which do not ordinarily require medical care) even though provided by a physician or registered professional personnel.

Occupational illness. Any abnormal condition or disorder, other than one resulting from an occupational injury, caused by exposure to environmental factors associated with employment. It includes acute and chronic illnesses or diseases which may be caused by inhalation, absorption, ingestion, or direct contact. The following categories should be used by employers to classify recordable occupational illnesses on the log in the columns indicated:

Column 7a. *Occupational skin diseases or disorders.*
Examples: Contact dermatitis, eczema, or rash caused by primary irritants and sensitizers or poisonous plants; oil acne; chrome ulcers; chemical burns or inflammations; etc.

Column 7b. *Dust diseases of the lungs (pneumoconioses).*
Examples: Silicosis, asbestosis, and other asbestos-related diseases, coal worker's pneumoconiosis, byssinosis, siderosis, and other pneumoconioses.

Column 7c. *Respiratory conditions due to toxic agents.*
Examples: Pneumonitis, pharyngitis, rhinitis or acute congestion due to chemicals, dusts, gases, or fumes; farmer's lung, etc.

Column 7d. *Poisoning (systemic effects of toxic materials).*
Examples: Poisoning by lead, mercury, cadmium, arsenic, or other metals; poisoning by carbon monoxide, hydrogen sulfide, or other gases; poisoning by benzol, carbon tetrachloride, or other organic solvents; poisoning by insecticide sprays such as parathion, lead arsenate; poisoning by other chemicals such as formaldehyde, plastics, and resins; etc.

Column 7e. *Disorders due to physical agents (other than toxic materials).*
Examples: Heatstroke, sunstroke, heat exhaustion, and other effects of environmental heat; freezing, frostbite, and effects of exposure to low temperatures; caisson disease; effects of ionizing radiation (isotopes, X-Rays, radium); effects of nonionizing radiation (welding flash, ultra-violet rays, microwaves, sunburn); etc.

Column 7f. *Disorders associated with repeated trauma.*
Examples: Noise-induced hearing loss; synovitis, tenosynovitis, and bursitis; Raynaud's phenomena; and other conditions due to repeated motion, vibration, or pressure.

Column 7g. *All other occupational illnesses.*
Examples: Anthrax, brucellosis, infectious hepatitis, malignant and benign tumors, food poisoning, histoplasmosis, coccidioidomycosis, etc.

Occupational injury. Any injury such as a cut, fracture, sprain, amputation, etc., which results from a work accident or from a single instantaneous exposure in the work environment.
Note: Conditions resulting from animal bites, such as insect or snake bites, and from one-time exposure to chemicals are considered to be injuries.

Occupational injuries and illnesses, extent and outcome. All recordable occupational injuries or illnesses result in either:
(1) Fatalities, regardless of the time between the injury, or the length of illness, and death;
(2) Lost workday cases, other than fatalities, that result in lost workdays; or
(3) Nonfatal cases without lost workdays.

Occupational Safety and Health Administration (OSHA). OSHA is responsible for developing, implementing, and enforcing safety and health standards and regulations. OSHA works with employers and employees to foster effective safety and health programs which reduce workplace hazards.

Posting. The annual summary of occupational injuries and illnesses must be posted at each establishment by February 1 and remain in place until March 1 to provide employees with the record of their establishment's injury and illness experience for the previous calendar year.

Premises, employer's. Consist of the employer's total establishment; they include the primary work facility and other areas in the employer's domain such as company storage facilities, cafeterias, and restrooms.

Recordable cases. All work-related deaths and illnesses, and those work-related injuries which result in: Loss of consciousness, restriction of work or motion, transfer to another job, or require medical treatment beyond first aid.

Recordkeeping system. Refers to the nationwide system for recording and reporting occupational injuries and illnesses mandated by the Occupational Safety and Health Act of 1970 and implemented by Title 29, Code of Federal Regulations, Part 1904. This system is the only source of national statistics on job-related injuries and illnesses for the private sector.

Regularly exempt employers. Employers regularly exempt from OSHA recordkeeping include: (A) All employers with no more than 10 full- or part-time employees at any one time in the previous calendar year; and (B) all employers in retail trade; finance, insurance, and real estate; and services industries; i.e., SIC's 52-89 (except building materials and garden supplies, SIC 52; general merchandise and food stores, SIC's 53 and 54; hotels and other lodging places, SIC 70; repair services, SIC's 75 and 76; amusement and recreation services, SIC 79; and health services, SIC 80). (Note: Some State safety and health laws may require these employers to keep OSHA records.)

Report form. Refers to survey form OSHA No. 200-S which is completed and returned by the surveyed reporting unit.

Restriction of work or motion. Occurs when the employee, because of the result of a job-related injury or illness, is physically or mentally unable to perform all or any part of his or her normal assignment during all or any part of the workday or shift.

Single dose (prescription medication). The measured quantity of a therapeutic agent to be taken at one time.

Small employers. Employers with no more than 10 full- and/or part-time employees among all the establishments of their firm at any one time during the previous calendar year.

Standard Industrial Classification (SIC). A classification system developed by the Office of Management and Budget, Executive Office of the President, for use in the classification of establishments by type of activity in which engaged. Each establishment is assigned an industry code for its major activity which is determined by the product manufactured or service rendered. Establishments may be classified in 2-, 3-, or 4-digit industries according to the degree of information available.

State (when mentioned alone). Refers to a State of the United States, the District of Columbia, and U.S. territories and jurisdictions.

State agency. State agency administering the OSHA recordkeeping and reporting system. Many States cooperate directly with BLS in administering the OSHA recordkeeping and reporting programs. Some States have their own safety and health laws which may impose additional obligations.

Supplementary Record (OSHA No. 101). The form (or equivalent) on which additional information is recorded for each injury and illness entered on the log.

Title 29 of the Code of Federal Regulations, Parts 1900-1999. The parts of the Code of Federal Regulations which contain OSHA regulations.

Volunteers. Workers who are not considered to be employees under the act when they serve of their own free will without compensation.

Work environment. Consists of the employer's premises and other locations where employees are engaged in work-related activities or are present as a condition of their employment. The work environment includes not only physical locations, but also the equipment or materials used by the employee during the course of his or her work.

Workers' compensation systems. State systems that provide medical benefits and/or indemnity compensation to victims of work-related injuries and illnesses.

APPENDIX 2B

ORDER FORM

Type or print

Please complete this form and mail it to the appropriate BLS regional office or participating State agency.

From:

Name _____

Firm _____

Street Address _____

City, State, Zip Code _____

Please send me the following items at no charge: Quantity

A Brief Guide to Recordkeeping Requirements for Occupational Injuries and Illnesses (18 pp.) .... _____

Recordkeeping Guidelines for Occupational Injuries and Illnesses (84 pp.) .... _____

OSHA No. 200 Forms (Log and Summary of Occupational Injuries and Illnesses) .... _____

OSHA No. 101 Forms (Supplementary Record of Occupational Injuries and Illnesses) ...... _____

ADDRESS LABEL

Name _____

Firm _____

Street Address _____

City, State, Zip Code _____

Participating State Agencies

Agencies preceded by an asterisk (*) have a State safety and health plan under section 18(b) of the act in operation and may be contacted directly for information regarding State regulations.

Alabama Department of Labor
651 Administrative Bldg.
Montgomery, AL 36130
Phone: 205-261-3460

*Alaska Department of Labor
Research and Analysis Section
P.O. Box 25501, Juneau, AK 99802
Phone: 907-465-4520

Government of American Samoa
Department of Manpower Resources
Division of Labor
Pago Pago, AS 96799
Phone: 633-5849

*Industrial Commission of Arizona
Division of Administration/Management
Research and Statistics Section
P.O. Box 19070, Phoenix, AZ 85005
Phone: 602-255-3739

Workers' Compensation Commission OSH
Arkansas Department of Labor
OSH Research and Statistics, Suite 219
1515 W. 7th St., Little Rock, AR 72201
Phone: 501-371-2770

*California Department of Industrial Relations, Labor Statistics and Research Division
P.O. Box 6880, San Francisco, CA 94101
Phone: 415-557-1466

Colorado Department of Labor and
Employment, Division of Labor
1313 Sherman St., Rm. 323
Denver, CO 80203
Phone: 303-866-3748

*Connecticut Department of Labor
200 Folly Brook Blvd.
Wethersfield, CT 06109
Phone: 203-566-4380

Delaware Department of Labor
Division of Industrial Affairs
820 N. French St., 6th Fl.
Wilmington, DE 19801
Phone: 302-571-2888

Florida Department of Labor and
Employment Security
Division of Worker's Compensation
2551 Executive Center
Circle West, Rm. 204
Tallahassee, FL 32301-5014
Phone: 904-488-3044

Guam Department of Labor
Bureau of Labor Statistics
Occupational Safety and Health Statistics
P.O. Box 23548, Guam Main Facility
Guam, M.I. 96921
Phone: 477-9241

*State of Hawaii
Department of Labor and Industrial
Relations, Research and Statistics
Office—OSHA
P.O. Box 3680, Honolulu, HI 96811
Phone: 808-548-7638

*Indiana Department of Labor
Research and Statistics Division
State Office Bldg.—Rm. 1013
100 N. Senate Ave.
Indianapolis, IN 46204
Phone: 317-232-2681

*Iowa Division of Labor Services
307 East 7th St., Des Moines, IA 50319
Phone: 515-281-3606

Kansas Department of Health and Environment
Division of Policy and Planning
Research and Analysis
Topeka, KS 66620
Phone: 913-862-9360 Ext. 280

*Kentucky Labor Cabinet
Occupational Safety and Health Program
U.S. 127 South Bldg., Frankfort, KY 40601
Phone: 502-564-3100

Louisiana Department of Labor
Office of Employment Security—OSH
P.O. Box 94094
Baton Rouge, LA 70804
Phone: 504-342-3126

Maine Department of Labor
Bureau of Labor Standards
Division of Research and Statistics
State Office Bldg., Augusta, ME 04330
Phone: 207-289-4311

*Maryland Department of Licensing and Regulation
Division of Labor and Industry
501 St. Paul Pl., Baltimore, MD 21202
Phone: 301-333-4202

Massachusetts Department of Labor and Industries
Division of Industrial Safety
100 Cambridge St., Boston, MA 02202
Phone: 617-727-3593

*Michigan Department of Labor
7150 Harris Dr., Secondary Complex
P.O. Box 30015, Lansing, MI 48909
Phone: 517-322-1848

*Minnesota Department of Labor
and Industry IMSD
444 Lafayette Rd., 5th Fl.
St. Paul, MN 55101
Phone: 612-296-4893

Mississippi State Department of Health
Office of Public Health Statistics
P.O. Box 1700
Jackson, MS 39215-1700
Phone: 601-354-7233

Missouri Department of Labor and Industrial Relations
Division of Workers' Compensation
P.O. Box 58, Jefferson City, MO 65102
Phone: 314-751-4231

Montana Department of Labor and Industry
Workers' Compensation Division
5 South Last Chance Gulch
Helena, MT 59601
Phone: 406-444-6515

Nebraska Workers' Compensation Court
State Capitol, 12th Fl.
Lincoln, NE 68509-4967
Phone: 402-471-3547

*Nevada Department of Industrial Relations
Division of Occupational Safety and Health
1370 South Curry St.
Carson City, NV 89710
Phone: 702-885-5240

New Jersey Department of Labor and Industry
Division of Planning and Research, CN 057
Trenton, NJ 08625
Phone: 609-292-8997

*New Mexico Health and Environment Department
Environmental Improvement Division
Occupational Health and Safety
P.O. Box 968
Sante Fe, NM 87504-0968
Phone: 505-827-2875

New York Department of Labor
Division of Research and Statistics
1 Main St., Rm 907
Brooklyn, NY 11201
Phone: 718-797-7701

*North Carolina Department of Labor
Research and Statistics Division
214 West Jones St.
Raleigh, NC 27603
Phone: 919-733-4940

Ohio Department of Industrial Relations
OSH Survey Office
P.O. Box 12355, Columbus, OH 43212
Phone: 614-466-7520

Oklahoma Department of Labor
Supplemental Data Division
1315 North Broadway Pl.
Oklahoma City, OK 73105
Phone: 405-235-1447

*Oregon Workers' Compensation Department
Research and Statistics Section
21 Labor and Industries Bldg.
Salem, OR 97310
Phone: 503-378-8254

Pennsylvania Department of Labor and Industry
Office of Employment Security
7th and Forster Sts.
Labor and Industry Bldg.
Harrisburg, PA 17121
Phone: 717-787-1918

*Puerto Rico Department of Labor and Human Resources
Bureau of Labor Statistics
505 Munoz Rivera Ave.
Hato Rey, PR 00918
Phone: 809-754-5339

Rhode Island Department of Labor
220 Elmwood Ave., Providence, RI 02907
Phone: 401-457-1852

*South Carolina Department of Labor
Division of Technical Support
P.O. Box 11329, Columbia, SC 29211
Phone: 803-734-9652

*Tennessee Department of Labor
Research and Statistics
501 Union Bldg., 6th Fl.
Nashville, TN 37219
Phone: 615-741-1748

Texas Department of Health
Division of Occupational Safety
1100 West 49th St., Austin, TX 78756
Phone: 512-458-7287

*Utah Industrial Commission
OSH Statistical Section
160 East 300 South
Salt Lake City, UT 84145-0580
Phone: 801-530-6827

*Vermont Department of Labor and Industry
State Office Bldg.
Montpelier, VT 05602
Phone: 802-828-2765

*Virgin Islands Department of Labor
P.O. Box 3359
St. Thomas, VI 00801
Phone: 809-776-3700

*Virginia Department of Labor and Industry
Planning and Research
205 North 4th St.
P.O. Box 12064, Richmond, VA 23241
Phone: 804-786-2384

*State of Washington
Department of Labor and Industries
Division of Industrial Safety and Health
P.O. Box 2589
Olympia, WA 98504
Phone: 206-753-4013

West Virginia Department of Labor
OSH Project Director
Rm. 319, Bldg. 3, Capitol Complex
1800 Washington St. East
Charleston, WV 25305
Phone: 304-348-7890

Wisconsin Department of Industry, Labor and Human Relations
Workers' Compensation Division
Research Section
201 E. Washington Ave.
P.O. Box 7901
Madison, WI 53707
Phone: 608-266-7850

*Wyoming Department of Labor and Statistics
Herschler Bldg., 2 East
Cheyenne, WY 82002
Phone: 307-777-6370

☆ U.S. GOVERNMENT PRINTING OFFICE: 1992 -- 312-410 / 54698

Appendix 2C
SIC
Code Exemptions

§ 1904.16 Establishments classified in Standard Industrial Classification Codes (SIC) 52–89, (except 52–54, 70, 75, 76, 79 and 80).

An employer whose establishment is classified in SIC's 52–89, (excluding 52–54, 70, 75, 76, 79 and 80) need not comply, for such establishment, with any of the requirements of this part except the following:

(a) Obligation to report under § 1904.8 concerning fatalities or multiple hospitalization accidents; and

(b) Obligation to maintain a log of occupational injuries and illnesses under § 1904.21, upon being notified in writing by the Bureau of Labor Statistics that the employer has been selected to participate in a statistical survey of occupational injuries and illnesses.

[47 FR 57702, Dec. 28, 1982]

Appendix 2D

SUPPLEMENTARY RECORDS OF OCCUPATIONAL INJURIES AND ILLNESSES

Bureau of Labor Statistics
Supplementary Record of
Occupational Injuries and Illnesses

U.S. Department of Labor

This form is required by Public Law 91-596 and must be kept in the establishment for 5 years. Failure to maintain can result in the issuance of citations and assessment of penalties.

Case or File No.

Form Approved
O.M.B. No. 1220-0029

Employer

1. Name

2. Mail address (No. and street, city or town, State, and zip code)

3. Location, if different from mail address

Injured or Ill Employee

4. Name (First, middle, and last)   Social Security No.

5. Home address (No. and street, city or town, State, and zip code)

6. Age   7. Sex: (Check one)   Male ☐   Female ☐

8. Occupation (Enter regular job title, not the specific activity he was performing at time of injury.)

9. Department (Enter name of department or division in which the injured person is regularly employed, even though he may have been temporarily working in another department at the time of injury.)

The Accident or Exposure to Occupational Illness

If accident or exposure occurred on employer's premises, give address of plant or establishment in which it occurred. Do not indicate department or division within the plant or establishment. If accident occurred outside employer's premises at an identifiable address, give that address. If it occurred on a public highway or at any other place which cannot be identified by number and street, please provide place references locating the place of injury as accurately as possible.

10. Place of accident or exposure (No. and street, city or town, State, and zip code)

11. Was place of accident or exposure on employer's premises?   Yes ☐   No ☐

12. What was the employee doing when injured? (Be specific. If he was using tools or equipment or handling material, name them and tell what he was doing with them.)

13. How did the accident occur? (Describe fully the events which resulted in the injury or occupational illness. Tell what happened and how it happened. Name any objects or substances involved and tell how they were involved. Give full details on all factors which led or contributed to the accident. Use separate sheet for additional space.)

Occupational Injury or Occupational Illness

14. Describe the injury or illness in detail and indicate the part of body affected. (E.g., amputation of right index finger at second joint; fracture of ribs; lead poisoning; dermatitis of left hand, etc.)

15. Name the object or substance which directly injured the employee. (For example, the machine or thing he struck against or which struck him; the vapor or poison he inhaled or swallowed; the chemical or radiation which irritated his skin; or in cases of strains, hernias, etc., the thing he was lifting, pulling, etc.)

16. Date of injury or initial diagnosis of occupational illness   17. Did employee die? (Check one)   Yes ☐   No ☐

Other

18. Name and address of physician

19. If hospitalized, name and address of hospital

Date of report   Prepared by   Official position

OSHA No. 101 (Feb. 1981)

Appendix 3A

29 CFR 1910.20

ACCESS TO EMPLOYEE EXPOSURE AND MEDICAL RECORDS

§ 1910.20 Access to employee exposure and medical records.

(a) *Purpose.* The purpose of this section is to provide employees and their designated representatives a right of access to relevant exposure and medical records; and to provide representatives of the Assistant Secretary a right of access to these records in order to fulfill responsibilities under the Occupational Safety and Health Act. Access by employees, their representatives, and the Assistant Secretary is necessary to yield both direct and indirect improvements in the detection, treatment, and prevention of occupational disease. Each employer is responsible for assuring compliance with this section, but the activities involved in complying with the access to medical records provisions can be carried out, on behalf of the employer, by the physician or other health care personnel in charge of employee medical records. Except as expressly provided, nothing in this section is intended to affect existing legal and ethical obligations concerning the maintenance and confidentiality of employee medical information, the duty to disclose information to a patient/employee or any other aspect of the medical-care relationship, or affect existing legal obligations concerning the protection of trade secret information.

(b) *Scope and application.* (1) This section applies to each general industry, maritime, and construction employer who makes, maintains, contracts for, or has access to employee exposure or medical records, or analyses thereof, pertaining to employees exposed to toxic substances or harmful physical agents.

(2) This section applies to all employee exposure and medical records, and analyses thereof, of such employees, whether or not the records are mandated by specific occupational safety and health standards.

(3) This section applies to all employee exposure and medical records, and analyses thereof, made or maintained in any manner, including on an in-house of contractual (e.g., fee-for-service) basis. Each employer shall assure that the preservation and access requirements of this section are complied with regardless of the manner in which the records are made or maintained.

(c) *Definitions.* (1) *Access* means the right and opportunity to examine and copy.

(2) *Analysis using exposure or medical records* means any compilation of data or any statistical study based at least in part on information collected from individual employee exposure or medical records or information collected from health insurance claims records, provided that either the analysis has been reported to the employer or no further work is currently being done by the person responsible for preparing the analysis.

(3) *Designated representative* means any individual or organization to whom an employee gives written authorization to exercise a right of access. For the purposes of access to employee exposure records and analyses using exposure or medical records, a recognized or certified collective bargaining agent shall be treated automatically as a designated representa-

Occupational Safety and Health Admin., Labor § 1910.20

tive without regard to written employee authorization.

(4) *Employee* means a current employee, a former employee, or an employee being assigned or transferred to work where there will be exposure to toxic substances or harmful physical agents. In the case of a deceased or legally incapacitated employee, the employee's legal representative may directly exercise all the employee's rights under this section.

(5) *Employee exposure record* means a record containing any of the following kinds of information:

(i) Environmental (workplace) monitoring or measuring of a toxic substance or harmful physical agent, including personal, area, grab, wipe, or other form of sampling, as well as related collection and analytical methodologies, calculations, and other background data relevant to interpretation of the results obtained;

(ii) Biological monitoring results which directly assess the absorption of a toxic substance or harmful physical agent by body systems (e.g., the level of a chemical in the blood, urine, breath, hair, fingernails, etc) but not including results which assess the biological effect of a substance or agent or which assess an employee's use of alcohol or drugs;

(iii) Material safety data sheets indicating that the material may pose a hazard to human health; or

(iv) In the absence of the above, a chemcial inventory or any other record which reveals where and when used and the identity (e.g., chemical, common, or trade name) of a toxic substance or harmful physical agent.

(6)(i) *Employee medical record* means a record concerning the health status of an employee which is made or maintained by a physician, nurse, or other health care personnel or technician, including:

(A) Medical and employment questionnaires or histories (including job description and occupational exposures),

(B) The results of medical examinations (pre-employment, pre-assignment, periodic, or episodic) and laboratory tests (including chest and other X-ray examinations taken for the purposes of establishing a base-line or detecting occupational illness, and all biological monitoring not defined as an "employee exposure record"),

(C) Medical opinions, diagnoses, progress notes, and recommendations,

(D) First aid records,

(E) Descriptions of treatments and prescriptions, and

(F) Employee medical complaints.

(ii) "Employee medical record" does not include medical information in the form of:

(A) Physical specimens (e.g., blood or urine samples) which are routinely discarded as a part of normal medical practice; or

(B) Records concerning health insurance claims if maintained separately from the employer's medical program and its records, and not accessible to the employer by employee name or other direct personal identifier (e.g., social security number, payroll number, etc.); or

(C) Records created solely in preparation for litigation which are privileged from discovery under the applicable rules of procedure or evidence; or

(D) Records concerning voluntary employee assistance programs (alcohol, drug abuse, or personal counseling programs) if maintained separately from the employer's medical program and its records.

(7) *Employer* means a current employer, a former employer, or a successor employer.

(8) *Exposure* or *exposed* means that an employee is subjected to a toxic substance or harmful physical agent in the course of employment through any route of entry (inhalation, ingestion, skin contact or absorption, etc.), and includes past exposure and potential (e.g., accidental or possible) exposure, but does not include situations where the employer can demonstrate that the toxic substance or harmful physical agent is not used, handled, stored, generated, or present in the workplace in any manner different from typical non-occupational situations.

(9) *Health Professional* means a physician, occupational health nurse, industrial hygienist, toxicologist, or epidemiologist, providing medical or other occupational health services to exposed employees.

§ 1910.20

(10) *Record* means any item, collection, or grouping of information regardless of the form or process by which it is maintained (e.g., paper document, microfiche, microfilm, X-ray film, or automated data processing).

(11) *Specific chemical identity* means the chemical name, Chemical Abstracts Service (CAS) Registry Number, or any other information that reveals the precise chemical designation of the substance.

(12)(i) *Specific written consent* means a written authorization containing the following:

(A) The name and signature of the employee authorizing the release of medical information,

(B) The date of the written authorization,

(C) The name of the individual or organization that is authorized to release the medical information,

(D) The name of the designated representative (individual or organization) that is authorized to receive the released information,

(E) A general description of the medical information that is authorized to be released,

(F) A general description of the purpose for the release of the medical information, and

(G) A date or condition upon which the written authorization will expire (if less than one year).

(ii) A written authorization does not operate to authorize the release of medical information not in existence on the date of written authorization, unless the release of future information is expressly authorized, and does not operate for more than one year from the date of written authorization.

(iii) A written authorization may be revoked in writing prospectively at any time.

(13) *Toxic substance or harmful physical agent* means any chemical substance, biological agent (bacteria, virus, fungus, etc.), or physical stress (noise, heat, cold, vibration, repetitive motion, ionizing and non-ionizing radiation, hypo—or hyperbaric pressure, etc.) which:

(i) Is listed in the least printed edition of the National Institute for Occupational Safety and Health (NIOSH) Registry of Toxic Effects of Chemical Substances (RTECS); or

(ii) Has yielded positive evidence of an acute or chronic health hazard in testing conducted by, or known to, the employer; or

(iii) Is the subject of a material safety data sheet kept by or known to the employer indicating that the material may pose a hazard to human health.

(14) *Trade secret* means any confidential formula, pattern, process, device, or information or compilation of information that is used in an employer's business and that gives the employer an opportunity to obtain an advantage over competitors who do not know or use it.

(d) *Preservation of records.* (1) Unless a specific occupational safety and health standard provides a different period of time, each employer shall assure the preservation and retention of records as follows:

(i) *Employee medical records.* The medical record for each employee shall be preserved and maintained for at least the duration of employment plus thirty (30) years, except that the following types of records need not be retained for any specified period:

(A) Health insurance claims records maintained separately from the employer's medical program and its records,

(B) First aid records (not including medical histories) of one-time treatment and subsequent observation of minor scratches, cuts, burns, splinters, and the like which do not involve medical treatment, loss of consciousness, restriction of work or motion, or transfer to another job, if made on-site by a non-physician and if maintained separately from the employer's medical program and its records, and

(C) The medical records of employees who have worked for less than (1) year for the employer need not be retained beyond the term of employment if they are provided to the employee upon the termination of employment.

(ii) *Employee exposure records.* Each employee exposure record shall be preserved and maintained for at least thirty (30) years, except that:

(A) Background data to environmental (workplace) monitoring or measuring, such as laboratory reports

Occupational Safety and Health Admin., Labor § 1910.20

and worksheets, need only be retained for one (1) year as long as the sampling results, the collection methodology (sampling plan), a description of the analytical and mathematical methods used, and a summary of other background data relevant to interpretation of the results obtained, are retained for at least thirty (30) years; and

(B) Material safety data sheets and paragraph (c)(5)(iv) records concerning the identity of a substance or agent need not be retained for any specified period as long as some record of the identity (chemical name if known) of the substance or agent, where it was used, and when it was used is retained for at least thirty (30) years;[1] and

(C) Biological monitoring results designated as exposure records by specific occupational safety and health standards shall be preserved and maintained as required by the specific standard.

(iii) *Analyses using exposure or medical records.* Each analysis using exposure or medial records shall be preserved and maintained for at least thirty (30) years.

(2) Nothing in this section is intended to mandate the form, manner, or process by which an employer preserves a record as long as the information contained in the record is preserved and retrievable, except that chest X-ray films shall be preserved in their original state.

(e) *Access to records*—(1) *General.* (i) Whenever an employee or designated representative requests access to a record, the employer shall assure that access is provided in a reasonable time, place, and manner. If the employer cannot reasonably provide access to the record within fifteen (15) working days, the employer shall within the fifteen (15) working days apprise the employee or designated representative requesting the record of the reason for the delay and the earliest date when the record can be made available.

(ii) The employer may require of the requester only such information as should be readily known to the requester and which may be necessary to locate or identify the records being requested (e.g. dates and locations where the employee worked during the time period in question).

(iii) Whenever an employee or designated representative requests a copy of a record, the employer shall assure that either:

(A) A copy of the record is provided without cost to the employee or representative,

(B) The necessary mechanical copying facilities (e.g., photocopying) are made available without cost to the employee or representative for copying the record, or

(C) The record is loaned to the employee or representative for a reasonable time to enable a copy to be made.

(iv) In the case of an original X-ray, the employer may restrict access to on-site examination or make other suitable arrangements for the temporary loan of the X-ray.

(v) Whenever a record has been previously provided without cost to an employee or designated representative, the employer may charge reasonable, non-discriminatory administrative costs (i.e., search and copying expenses but not including overhead expenses) for a request by the employee or designated representative for additional copies of the record, except that

(A) An employer shall not charge for an initial request for a copy of new information that has been added to a record which was previously provided; and

(B) An employer shall not charge for an initial request by a recognized or certified collective bargaining agent for a copy of an employee exposure record or an analysis using exposure or medical records.

(vi) Nothing in this section is intended to preclude employees and collective bargaining agents from collectively bargaining to obtain access to information in addition to that available under this section.

(2) *Employee and designated representative access*—(i) *Employee exposure records.* (A) Except as limited by paragraph (f) of this section, each employer shall, upon request, assure the access to each employee and designated representative to employee exposure records relevant to the employee. For

---

[1] Material safety data sheets must be kept for those chemicals currently in use that are effected by the Hazard Communication Standard in accordance with 29 CFR 1910.1200(g).

§ 1910.20

the purpose of this section, an exposure record relevant to the employee consists of:

(1) A record which measures or monitors the amount of a toxic substance or harmful physical agent to which the employee is or has been exposed;

(2) In the absence of such directly relevant records, such records of other employees with past or present job duties or working conditions related to or similar to those of the employee to the extent necessary to reasonably indicate the amount and nature of the toxic substances or harmful physical agents to which the employee is or has been subjected, and

(3) Exposure records to the extent necessary to reasonably indicate the amount and nature of the toxic substances or harmful physical agents at workplaces or under working conditions to which the employee is being assigned or transferred.

(B) Requests by designated representatives for unconsented access to employee exposure records shall be in writing and shall specify with reasonable particularity:

(1) The records requested to be disclosed; and

(2) The occupational health need for gaining access to these records.

(ii) *Employee medical records.* (A) Each employer shall, upon request, assure the access of each employee to employee medical records of which the employee is the subject, except as provided in paragraph (e)(2)(ii)(D) of this section.

(B) Each employer shall, upon request, assure the access of each designated representative to the employee medical records of any employee who has given the designated representative specific written consent. Appendix A to this section contains a sample form which may be used to establish specific written consent for access to employee medical records.

(C) Whenever access to employee medical records is requested, a physician representing the employer may recommend that the employee or designated representative:

(1) Consult with the physician for the purposes of reviewing and discussing the records requested,

(2) Accept a summary of material facts and opinions in lieu of the records requested, or

(3) Accept release of the requested records only to a physician or other designated representative.

(D) Whenever an employee requests access to his or her employee medical records, and a physician representing the employer believes that direct employee access to information contained in the records regarding a specific diagnosis of a terminal illness or a psychiatric condition could be detrimental to the employee's health, the employer may inform the employee that access will only be provided to a designated representative of the employee having specific written consent, and deny the employee's request for direct access to this information only. Where a designated representative with specific written consent requests access to information so withheld, the employer shall assure the access of the designated representative to this information, even when it is known that the designated representative will give the information to the employee.

(E) A physician, nurse, or other responsible health care personnel maintaining medical records may delete from requested medical records the identity of a family member, personal friend, or fellow employee who has provided confidential information concerning an employee's health status.

(iii) *Analyses using exposure or medical records.* (A) Each employee shall, upon request, assure the access of each employee and designated representative to each analysis using exposure or medical records concerning the employee's working conditions or workplace.

(B) Whenever access is requested to an analysis which reports the contents of employee medical records by either direct identifier (name, address, social security number, payroll number, etc.) or by information which could reasonably be used under the circumstances indirectly to identify specific employees (exact age, height, weight, race, sex, date of initial employment, job title, etc.), the employer shall assure that personal identifiers are removed before access is provided. If the employer can demonstrate that removal

Occupational Safety and Health Admin., Labor §1910.20

of personal identifiers from an analysis is not feasible, access to the personally identifiable portions of the analysis need not be provided.

(3) *OSHA access.* (i) Each employer shall, upon request, and without derogation of any rights under the Constitution or the Occupational Safety and Health Act of 1970, 29 U.S.C. 651 *et seq.*, that the employer chooses to exercise, assure the prompt access of representatives of the Assistant Secretary of Labor for Occupational Safety and Health to employee exposure and medical records and to analyses using exposure or medical records. Rules of agency practice and procedure governing OSHA access to employee medical records are contained in 29 CFR 1913.10.

(ii) Whenever OSHA seeks access to personally identifiable employee medical information by presenting to the employer a written access order pursuant to 29 CFR 1913.10(d), the employer shall prominently post a copy of the written access order and its accompanying cover letter for at least fifteen (15) working days.

(f) *Trade secrets.* (1) Except as provided in paragraph (f)(2) of this section, nothing in this section precludes an employer from deleting from records requested by a health professional, employee, or designated representative any trade secret data which discloses manufacturing processes, or discloses the percentage of a chemical substance in mixture, as long as the health professional, employee, or designated representative is notified that information has been deleted. Whenever deletion of trade secret information substantially impairs evaluation of the place where or the time when exposure to a toxic substance or harmful physical agent occurred, the employer shall provide alternative information which is sufficient to permit the requesting party to identify where and when exposure occurred.

(2) The employer may withhold the specific chemical identity, including the chemical name and other specific identification of a toxic substance from a disclosable record provided that:

(i) The claim that the information withheld is a trade secret can be supported;

(ii) All other available information on the properties and effects of the toxic substance is disclosed;

(iii) The employer informs the requesting party that the specific chemical identity is being withheld as a trade secret; and

(iv) The specific chemical identity is made available to health professionals, employees and designated representatives in accordance with the specific applicable provisions of this paragraph.

(3) Where a treating physician or nurse determines that a medical emergency exists and the specific chemical identity of a toxic substance is necessary for emergency or first-aid treatment, the employer shall immediately disclose the specific chemical identity of a trade secret chemical to the treating physician or nurse, regardless of the existence of a written statement of need or a confidentiality agreement. The employer may require a written statement of need and confidentiality agreement, in accordance with the provisions of paragraphs (f)(4) and (f)(5), as soon as circumstances permit.

(4) In non-emergency situations, an employer shall, upon request, disclose a specific chemical identity, otherwise permitted to be withheld under paragraph (f)(2) of this section, to a health professional, employee, or designated representative if:

(i) The request is in writing;

(ii) The request describes with reasonable detail one or more of the following occupational health needs for the information:

(A) To assess the hazards of the chemicals to which employees will be exposed;

(B) To conduct or assess sampling of the workplace atmosphere to determine employee exposure levels;

(C) To conduct pre-assignment or periodic medical surveillance of exposed employees;

(D) To provide medical treatment to exposed employees;

(E) To select or assess appropriate personal protective equipment for exposed employees;

(F) To design or assess engineering controls or other protective measures for exposed employees; and

(G) To conduct studies to determine the health effects of exposure.

85

§ 1910.20

(iii) The request explains in detail why the disclosure of the specific chemical identity is essential and that, in lieu thereof, the disclosure of the following information would not enable the health professional, employee or designated representative to provide the occupational health services described in paragraph (f)(4)(ii) of this section:

(A) The properties and effects of the chemical;

(B) Measures for controlling workers' exposure to the chemical;

(C) Methods of monitoring and analyzing worker exposure to the chemical; and,

(D) Methods of diagnosing and treating harmful exposures to the chemical;

(iv) The request includes a description of the procedures to be used to maintain the confidentiality of the disclosed information; and,

(v) The health professional, employee, or designated representative and the employer or contractor of the services of the health professional or designated representative agree in a written confidentiality agreement that the health professional, employee or designated representative will not use the trade secret information for any purpose other than the health need(s) asserted and agree not to release the information under any circumstances other than to OSHA, as provided in paragraph (f)(9) of this section, except as authorized by the terms of the agreement or by the employer.

(5) The confidentiality agreement authorized by paragraph (f)(4)(iv) of this section:

(i) May restrict the use of the information to the health purposes indicated in the written statement of need;

(ii) May provide for appropriate legal remedies in the event of a breach of the agreement, including stipulation of a reasonable pre-estimate of likely damages; and,

(iii) May not include requirements for the posting of a penalty bond.

(6) Nothing in this section is meant to preclude the parties from pursuing non-contractual remedies to the extent permitted by law.

(7) If the health professional, employee or designated representative receiving the trade secret information decides that there is a need to disclose it to OSHA, the employer who provided the information shall be informed by the health professional prior to, or at the same time as, such disclosure.

(8) If the employer denies a written request for disclosure of a specific chemical identity, the denial must:

(i) Be provided to the health professional, employee or designated representative within thirty days of the request;

(ii) Be in writing;

(iii) Include evidence to support the claim that the specific chemical identity is a trade secret;

(iv) State the specific reasons why the request is being denied; and,

(v) Explain in detail how alternative information may satisfy the specific medical or occupational health need without revealing the specific chemical identity.

(9) The health professional, employee, or designated representative whose request for information is denied under paragraph (f)(4) of this section may refer the request and the written denial of the request to OSHA for consideration.

(10) When a heath professional employee, or designated representative refers a denial to OSHA under paragraph (f)(9) of this section, OSHA shall consider the evidence to determine if:

(i) The employer has supported the claim that the specific chemical identity is a trade secret;

(ii) The health professional employee, or designated representative has supported the claim that there is a medical or occupational health need for the information; and

(iii) The health professional, employee or designated representative has demonstrated adequate means to protect the confidentiality.

(11)(i) If OSHA determines that the specific chemical identity requested under paragraph (f)(4) of this section is not a *bona fide* trade secret, or that it is a trade secret but the requesting health professional, employee or designated representatives has a legitimate medical or occupational health need for the information, has executed a written confidentiality agreement, and has shown adequate means for complying with the terms of such agreement, the employer will be subject to citation by OSHA.

(ii) If an employer demonstrates to OSHA that the execution of a confidentiality agreement would not provide sufficient protection against the potential harm from the unauthorized disclosure of a trade secret specific chemical identity, the Assistant Secretary may issue such orders or impose such additional limitations or conditions upon the disclosure of the requested chemical information as may be appropriate to assure that the occupational health needs are met without an undue risk of harm to the employer.

(12) Notwithstanding the existence of a trade secret claim, an employer shall, upon request, disclose to the Assistant Secretary any information which this section requires the employer to make available. Where there is a trade secret claim, such claim shall be made no later than at the time the information is provided to the Assistant Secretary so that suitable determinations of trade secret status can be made and the necessary protections can be implemented.

(13) Nothing in this paragraph shall be construed as requiring the disclosure under any circumstances of process or percentage of mixture information which is trade secret.

(g) *Employee information.* (1) Upon an employee's first entering into employment, and at least annually thereafter, each employer shall inform current employees covered by this section of the following:

(i) The existence, location, and availability of any records covered by this section;

(ii) The person responsible for maintaining and providing access to records; and

(iii) Each employee's rights of access to these records.

(2) Each employer shall keep a copy of this section and its appendices, and make copies readily available, upon request, to employees. The employer shall also distribute to current employees any informational materials concerning this section which are made available to the employer by the Assistant Secretary of Labor for Occupational Safety and Health.

(h) *Transfer of records.* (1) Whenever an employer is ceasing to do business, the employer shall transfer all records subject to this section to the successor employer. The successor employer shall receive and maintain these records.

(2) Whenever an employer is ceasing to do business and there is no successor employer to receive and maintain the records subject to this standard, the employer shall notify affected current employees of their rights of access to records at least three (3) months prior to the cessation of the employer's business.

(3) Whenever an employer either is ceasing to do business and there is no successor employer to receive and maintain the records, or intends to dispose of any records required to be preserved for at least thirty (30) years, the employer shall:

(i) Transfer the records to the Director of the National Institute for Occupational Safety and Health (NIOSH) if so required by a specific occupational safety and health standard; or

(ii) Notify the Director of NIOSH in writing of the impending disposal of records at least three (3) months prior to the disposal of the records.

(4) Where an employer regularly disposes of records required to be preserved for at least thirty (30) years, the employer may, with at least (3) months notice, notify the Director of NIOSH on an annual basis of the records intended to be disposed of in the coming year.

(i) *Appendices.* The information contained in appendices A and B to this section is not intended, by itself, to create any additional obligations not otherwise imposed by this section nor detract from any existing obligation.

(Approved by the Office of Management and Budget under control number 1218–0065)

APPENDIX A TO §1910.20—SAMPLE AUTHORIZATION LETTER FOR THE RELEASE OF EMPLOYEE MEDICAL RECORD INFORMATION TO A DESIGNATED REPRESENTATIVE (NON-MANDATORY)

I, ———— (full name of worker/patient), hereby authorize ———— (individual or organization holding the medical records) to release to ———— (individual or organization authorized to receive the medical in-

§ 1910.20

formation), the following medical information from my personal medical records:

___

(Describe generally the information desired to be released)

I give my permission for this medical information to be used for the following purpose:

___

but I do not give permission for any other use or re-disclosure of this information.

(NOTE: Several extra lines are provided below so that you can place additional restrictions on this authorization letter if you want to. You may, however, leave these lines blank. On the other hand, you may want to (1) specify a particular expiration date for this letter (if less than one year); (2) describe medical information to be created in the future that you intend to be covered by this authorization letter; or (3) describe portions of the medical information in your records which you do not intend to be released as a result of this letter.)

___

___

___

___

Full name of Employee or Legal Representative

___

Signature of Employee or Legal Representative

___

Date of Signature

APPENDIX B TO § 1910.20—AVAILABILITY OF NIOSH REGISTRY OF TOXIC EFFECTS OF CHEMICAL SUBSTANCES (RTECS) (NON-MANDATORY)

The final regulation, 29 CFR 1910.20, applies to all employee exposure and medical records, and analyses thereof, of employees exposed to toxic substances or harmful physical agents (paragraph (b)(2)). The term *toxic substance or harmful physical agent* is defined by paragraph (c)(13) to encompass chemical substances, biological agents, and physical stresses for which there is evidence of harmful health effects. The regulation uses the latest printed edition of the National Institute for Occupational Safety and Health (NIOSH) Registry of Toxic Effects of Chemical Substances (RTECS) as one of the chief sources of information as to whether evidence of harmful health effects exists. If a substance is listed in the latest printed RTECS, the regulation applies to exposure and medical records (and analyses of these records) relevant to employees exposed to the substance.

It is appropriate to note that the final regulation does not require that employers purchase a copy of RTECS, and many employers need not consult RTECS to ascertain whether their employee exposure or medical records are subject to the rule. Employers who do not currently have the latest printed edition of the NIOSH RTECS, however, may desire to obtain a copy. The RTECS is issued in an annual printed edition as mandated by section 20(a)(6) of the Occupational Safety and Health Act (29 U.S.C. 669(a)(6)).

The Introduction to the 1980 printed edition describes the RTECS as follows:

"The 1980 edition of the Registry of Toxic Effects of Chemical Substances, formerly known as the Toxic Substances list, is the ninth revision prepared in compliance with the requirements of Section 20(a)(6) of the Occupational Safety and Health Act of 1970 (Public Law 91-596). The original list was completed on June 28, 1971, and has been updated annually in book format. Beginning in October 1977, quarterly revisions have been provided in microfiche. This edition of the Registry contains 168,096 listings of chemical substances: 45,156 are names of different chemicals with their associated toxicity data and 122,940 are synonyms. This edition includes approximately 5,900 new chemical compounds that did not appear in the 1979 Registry. (p. xi)

"The Registry's purposes are many, and it serves a variety of users. It is a single source document for basic toxicity information and for other data, such as chemical identifiers ad information necessary for the preparation of safety directives and hazard evaluations for chemical substances. The various types of toxic effects linked to literature citations provide researchers and occupational health scientists with an introduction to the toxicological literature, making their own review of the toxic hazards of a given substance easier. By presenting data on the lowest reported doses that produce effects by several routes of entry in various species, the Registry furnishes valuable information to those responsible for preparing safety data sheets for chemical substances in the workplace. Chemical and production engineers can use the Registry to identify the hazards which may be associated with chemical intermediates in the development of final products, and thus can more readily select substitutes or alternative processes which may be less hazardous. Some organizations, including health agencies and chemical companies, have included the NIOSH Registry accession numbers with the listing of chemicals in their files to reference toxicity information associated with those chemicals. By including foreign language chemical names, a start has been made toward providing rapid identification of substances produced in other countries. (p. xi)

Occupational Safety and Health Admin., Labor § 1910.21

"In this edition of the Registry, the editors intend to identify "all known toxic substances" which may exist in the environment and to provide pertinent data on the toxic effects from known doses entering an organism by any route described. (p xi)

"It must be reemphasized that the entry of a substance in the Registry does not automatically mean that it must be avoided. A listing does mean, however, that the substance has the documented potential of being harmful if misused, and care must be exercised to prevent tragic consequences. Thus, the Registry lists many substances that are common in everyday life and are in nearly every household in the United States. One can name a variety of such dangerous substances: prescription and non-prescription drugs; food additives; pesticide concentrates, sprays, and dusts; fungicides; herbicides; paints; glazes, dyes; bleaches and other household cleaning agents; alkalies; and various solvents and diluents. The list is extensive because chemicals have become an integral part of our existence."

The RTECS printed edition may be purchased from the Superintendent of Documents, U.S. Government Printing Office (GPO), Washington, DC 20402 (202-783-3238).

Some employers may desire to subscribe to the quarterly update to the RTECS which is published in a microfiche edition. An annual subscription to the quarterly microfiche may be purchased from the GPO (Order the "Microfiche Edition, Registry of Toxic Effects of Chemical Substances"). Both the printed edition and the microfiche edition of RTECS are available for review at many university and public libraries throughout the country. The latest RTECS editions may also be examined at the OSHA Technical Data Center, Room N2439—Rear, United States Department of Labor, 200 Constitution Avenue, NW., Washington, DC 20210 (202-523-9700), or at any OSHA Regional or Area Office (*See*, major city telephone directories under United States Government-Labor Department).

[53 FR 38163, Sept. 29, 1988; 53 FR 49981, Dec. 13, 1988, as amended at 54 FR 24333, June 7, 1989; 55 FR 26431, June 28, 1990]

Appendix 3B

29 CFR 1910.38
EMPLOYEE EMERGENCY PLANS AND FIRE PREVENTION PLANS

§ 1910.38 Employee emergency plans and fire prevention plans.

(a) *Emergency action plan*—(1) *Scope and application.* This paragraph (a) applies to all emergency action plans required by a particular OSHA standard. The emergency action plan shall be in writing (except as provided in the last sentence of paragraph (a)(5)(iii) of this section) and shall cover those designated actions employers and employees must take to ensure employee safety from fire and other emergencies.

(2) *Elements.* The following elements, at a minimum, shall be included in the plan:

(i) Emergency escape procedures and emergency escape route assignments;

(ii) Procedures to be followed by employees who remain to operate critical plant operations before they evacuate;

(iii) Procedures to account for all employees after emergency evacuation has been completed;

(iv) Rescue and medical duties for those employees who are to perform them;

(v) The preferred means of reporting fires and other emergencies; and

(vi) Names or regular job titles of persons or departments who can be contacted for further information or explanation of duties under the plan.

(3) *Alarm system.* (i) The employer shall establish an employee alarm system which complies with § 1910.165.

(ii) If the employee alarm system is used for alerting fire brigade members, or for other purposes, a distinctive signal for each purpose shall be used.

(4) *Evacuation.* The employer shall establish in the emergency action plan the types of evacuation to be used in emergency circumstances.

(5) *Training.* (i) Before implementing the emergency action plan, the employer shall designate and train a sufficient number of persons to assist in the safe and orderly emergency evacuation of employees.

(ii) The employer shall review the plan with each employee covered by the plan at the following times:

(A) Initially when the plan is developed,

(B) Whenever the employee's responsibilities or designated actions under the plan change, and

(C) Whenever the plan is changed.

(iii) The employer shall review with each employee upon initial assignment those parts of the plan which the employee must know to protect the employee in the event of an emergency. The written plan shall be kept at the workplace and made available for employee review. For those employers with 10 or fewer employees the plan may be communicated orally to employees and the employer need not maintain a written plan.

(b) *Fire prevention plan*—(1) *Scope and application.* This paragraph (b) applies to all fire prevention plans required by a particular OSHA standard. The fire prevention plan shall be in writing, except as provided in the last sentence of paragraph (b)(4)(ii) of this section.

(2) *Elements.* The following elements, at a minimum, shall be included in the fire prevention plan:

(i) A list of the major workplace fire hazards and their proper handling and storage procedures, potential ignition sources (such as welding, smoking and others) and their control procedures, and the type of fire protection equipment or systems which can control a fire involving them;

(ii) Names or regular job titles of those personnel responsible for maintenance of equipment and systems installed to prevent or control ignitions or fires; and

(iii) Names or regular job titles of those personnel responsible for control of fuel source hazards.

(3) *Housekeeping.* The employer shall control accumulations of flammable and combustible waste materials and residues so that they do not contribute to a fire emergency. The housekeeping procedures shall be included in the written fire prevention plan.

(4) *Training.* (i) The employer shall apprise employees of the fire hazards of the materials and processes to which they are exposed.

(ii) The employer shall review with each employee upon initial assignment those parts of the fire prevention plan which the employee must know to protect the employee in the event of an emergency. The written plan shall be kept in the workplace and made available for employee review. For those employers with 10 or fewer employees, the plan may be communicated orally to employees and the employer need not maintain a written plan.

(5) *Maintenance.* The employer shall regularly and properly maintain, according to established procedures, equipment and systems installed on heat producing equipment to prevent accidental ignition of combustible materials. The maintenance procedures shall be included in the written fire prevention plan.

[45 FR 60703, Sept. 12, 1980]

Appendix 3C

29 CFR 1910.151 MEDICAL SERVICES AND FIRST AID; 29 CFR 1926.50 MEDICAL SERVICES AND FIRST AID

§ 1910.151 Medical services and first aid.

(a) The employer shall ensure the ready availability of medical personnel for advice and consultation on matters of plant health.

(b) In the absence of an infirmary, clinic, or hospital in near proximity to the workplace which is used for the treatment of all injured employees, a person or persons shall be adequately trained to render first aid. First aid supplies approved by the consulting physician shall be readily available.

(c) Where the eyes or body of any person may be exposed to injurious corrosive materials, suitable facilities for quick drenching or flushing of the eyes and body shall be provided within the work area for immediate emergency use.

§ 1926.50 Medical services and first aid.

(a) The employer shall insure the availability of medical personnel for advice and consultation on matters of occupational health.

(b) Provisions shall be made prior to commencement of the project for prompt medical attention in case of serious injury.

(c) In the absence of an infirmary, clinic, hospital, or physician, that is reasonably accessible in terms of time and distance to the worksite, which is available for the treatment of injured employees, a person who has a valid certificate in first-aid training from the U.S. Bureau of Mines, the American Red Cross, or equivalent training that can be verified by documentary evidence, shall be available at the worksite to render first aid.

(d)(1) First-aid supplies approved by the consulting physician shall be easily accessible when required.

(2) The first-aid kit shall consist of materials approved by the consulting physician in a weatherproof container with individual sealed packages for each type of item. The contents of the first-aid kit shall be checked by the employer before being sent out on each job and at least weekly on each job to ensure that the expended items are replaced.

(e) Proper equipment for prompt transportation of the injured person to a physician or hospital, or a communication system for contacting necessary ambulance service, shall be provided.

(f) The telephone numbers of the physicians, hospitals, or ambulances shall be conspicuously posted.

(g) Where the eyes or body of any person may be exposed to injurious corrosive materials, suitable facilities for quick drenching or flushing of the eyes and body shall be provided within the work area for immediate emergency use.

(The information collection requirements contained in paragraph (f) were approved by the Office of Management and Budget under control number 1218–0093.)

[44 FR 8577, Feb. 9, 1979; 44 FR 20940, Apr. 6, 1979, as amended at 49 FR 18295, Apr. 30, 1984; 58 FR 35084, June 30, 1993]

Appendix 3D

29 CFR 1910.22 General Requirements; 29 CFR 1910.176 Handling Materials—General; 29 CFR 1926.25 Housekeeping

§ 1910.22 General requirements.

This section applies to all permanent places of employment, except where domestic, mining, or agricultural work only is performed. Measures for the control of toxic materials are considered to be outside the scope of this section.

(a) *Housekeeping.* (1) All places of employment, passageways, storerooms, and service rooms shall be kept clean and orderly and in a sanitary condition.

(2) The floor of every workroom shall be maintained in a clean and, so far as possible, a dry condition. Where wet processes are used, drainage shall be maintained, and false floors, platforms, mats, or other dry standing places should be provided where practicable.

(3) To facilitate cleaning, every floor, working place, and passageway shall be kept free from protruding nails, splinters, holes, or loose boards.

(b) *Aisles and passageways.* (1) Where mechanical handling equipment is used, sufficient safe clearances shall be allowed for aisles, at loading docks, through doorways and wherever turns or passage must be made. Aisles and passageways shall be kept clear and in good repairs, with no obstruction across or in aisles that could create a hazard.

(2) Permanent aisles and passageways shall be appropriately marked.

(c) *Covers and guardrails.* Covers and/or guardrails shall be provided to protect personnel from the hazards of open pits, tanks, vats, ditches, etc.

(d) *Floor loading protection.* (1) In every building or other structure, or part thereof, used for mercantile, business, industrial, or storage purposes, the loads approved by the building official shall be marked on plates of approved design which shall be supplied and securely affixed by the owner of the building, or his duly authorized agent, in a conspicuous place in each space to which they relate. Such plates shall not be removed or defaced but, if lost, removed, or defaced, shall be replaced by the owner or his agent.

(2) It shall be unlawful to place, or cause, or permit to be placed, on any floor or roof of a building or other structure a load greater than that for which such floor or roof is approved by the building official.

§ 1910.176 Handling materials—general.

(a) *Use of mechanical equipment.* Where mechanical handling equipment is used, sufficient safe clearances shall be allowed for aisles, at loading docks, through doorways and wherever turns or passage must be made. Aisles and passageways shall be kept clear and in good repair, with no obstruction across or in aisles that could create a hazard. Permanent aisles and passageways shall be appropriately marked.

(b) *Secure storage.* Storage of material shall not create a hazard. Bags, containers, bundles, etc., stored in tiers shall be stacked, blocked, interlocked and limited in height so that they are stable and secure against sliding or collapse.

(c) *Housekeeping.* Storage areas shall be kept free from accumulation of materials that constitute hazards from tripping, fire, explosion, or pest harborage. Vegetation control will be exercised when necessary.

(d) [Reserved]

(e) *Clearance limits.* Clearance signs to warn of clearance limits shall be provided.

(f) *Rolling railroad cars.* Derail and/or bumper blocks shall be provided on spur railroad tracks where a rolling car could contact other cars being worked, enter a building, work or traffic area.

(g) *Guarding.* Covers and/or guardrails shall be provided to protect personnel from the hazards of open pits, tanks, vats, ditches, etc.

[39 FR 23052, June 27, 1974, as amended at 43 FR 49749, Oct. 24, 1978]

§ 1926.25 Housekeeping.

(a) During the course of construction, alteration, or repairs, form and scrap lumber with protruding nails, and all other debris, shall be kept cleared from work areas, passageways, and stairs, in and around buildings or other structures.

(b) Combustible scrap and debris shall be removed at regular intervals during the course of construction. Safe means shall be provided to facilitate such removal.

(c) Containers shall be provided for the collection and separation of waste, trash, oily and used rags, and other refuse. Containers used for garbage and other oily, flammable, or hazardous wastes, such as caustics, acids, harmful dusts, etc. shall be equipped with covers. Garbage and other waste shall be disposed of at frequent and regular intervals.

Appendix 3E
29 CFR 1910.1200 Hazard Communication

§ 1910.1200 Hazard communication.

(a) *Purpose.* (1) The purpose of this section is to ensure that the hazards of all chemicals produced or imported are evaluated, and that information concerning their hazards is transmitted to employers and employees. This transmittal of information is to be accomplished by means of comprehensive hazard communication programs, which are to include container labeling and other forms of warning, material safety data sheets and employee training.

(2) This occupational safety and health standard is intended to address comprehensively the issue of evaluating the potential hazards of chemicals, and communicating information concerning hazards and appropriate protective measures to employees, and to preempt any legal requirements of a state, or political subdivision of a state, pertaining to this subject. Evaluating the potential hazards of chemicals, and communicating information concerning hazards and appropriate protective measures to employees, may

Occupational Safety and Health Admin., Labor § 1910.1200

include, for example, but is not limited to, provisions for: developing and maintaining a written hazard communication program for the workplace, including lists of hazardous chemicals present; labeling of containers of chemicals in the workplace, as well as of containers of chemicals being shipped to other workplaces; preparation and distribution of material safety data sheets to employees and downstream employers; and development and implementation of employee training programs regarding hazards of chemicals and protective measures. Under section 18 of the Act, no state or political subdivision of a state may adopt or enforce, through any court or agency, any requirement relating to the issue addressed by this Federal standard, except pursuant to a Federally-approved state plan.

(b) *Scope and application.* (1) This section requires chemical manufacturers or importers to assess the hazards of chemicals which they produce or import, and all employers to provide information to their employees about the hazardous chemicals to which they are exposed, by means of a hazard communication program, labels and other forms of warning, material safety data sheets, and information and training. In addition, this section requires distributors to transmit the required information to employers. (Employers who do not produce or import chemicals need only focus on those parts of this rule that deal with establishing a workplace program and communicating information to their workers. Appendix E of this section is a general guide for such employers to help them determine their compliance obligations under the rule.)

(2) This section applies to any chemical which is known to be present in the workplace in such a manner that employees may be exposed under normal conditions of use or in a foreseeable emergency.

(3) This section applies to laboratories only as follows:

(i) Employers shall ensure that labels on incoming containers of hazardous chemicals are not removed or defaced;

(ii) Employers shall maintain any material safety data sheets that are received with incoming shipments of hazardous chemicals, and ensure that they are readily accessible during each workshift to laboratory employees when they are in their work areas;

(iii) Employers shall ensure that laboratory employees are provided information and training in accordance with paragraph (h) of this section, except for the location and availability of the written hazard communication program under paragraph (h)(2)(iii) of this section; and,

(iv) Laboratory employers that ship hazardous chemicals are considered to be either a chemical manufacturer or a distributor under this rule, and thus must ensure that any containers of hazardous chemicals leaving the laboratory are labeled in accordance with paragraph (f)(1) of this section, and that a material safety data sheet is provided to distributors and other employers in accordance with paragraphs (g)(6) and (g)(7) of this section.

(4) In work operations where employees only handle chemicals in sealed containers which are not opened under normal conditions of use (such as are found in marine cargo handling, warehousing, or retail sales), this section applies to these operations only as follows:

(i) Employers shall ensure that labels on incoming containers of hazardous chemicals are not removed or defaced;

(ii) Employers shall maintain copies of any material safety data sheets that are received with incoming shipments of the sealed containers of hazardous chemicals, shall obtain a material safety data sheet as soon as possible for sealed containers of hazardous chemicals received without a material safety data sheet if an employee requests the material safety data sheet, and shall ensure that the material safety data sheets are readily accessible during each work shift to employees when they are in their work area(s); and,

(iii) Employers shall ensure that employees are provided with information and training in accordance with paragraph (h) of this section (except for the location and availability of the written hazard communication program under paragraph (h)(2)(iii) of this section), to the extent necessary to protect them in the event of a spill or leak of a haz-

469

§ 1910.1200

ardous chemical from a sealed container.

(5) This section does not require labeling of the following chemicals:

(i) Any pesticide as such term is defined in the Federal Insecticide, Fungicide, and Rodenticide Act (7 U.S.C. 136 et seq.), when subject to the labeling requirements of that Act and labeling regulations issued under that Act by the Environmental Protection Agency;

(ii) Any chemical substance or mixture as such terms are defined in the Toxic Substances Control Act (15 U.S.C. 2601 et seq.), when subject to the labeling requirements of that Act and labeling regulations issued under that Act by the Environmental Protection Agency.

(iii) Any food, food additive, color additive, drug, cosmetic, or medical or veterinary device or product, including materials intended for use as ingredients in such products (e.g. flavors and fragrances), as such terms are defined in the Federal Food, Drug, and Cosmetic Act (21 U.S.C. 301 et seq.) or the Virus-Serum-Toxin Act of 1913 (21 U.S.C. 151 et seq.), and regulations issued under those Acts, when they are subject to the labeling requirements under those Acts by either the Food and Drug Administration or the Department of Agriculture;

(iv) Any distilled spirits (beverage alcohols), wine, or malt beverage intended for nonindustrial use, as such terms are defined in the Federal Alcohol Administration Act (27 U.S.C. 201 et seq.) and regulations issued under that Act, when subject to the labeling requirements of that Act and labeling regulations issued under that Act by the Bureau of Alcohol, Tobacco, and Firearms;

(v) Any consumer product or hazardous substance as those terms are defined in the Consumer Product Safety Act (15 U.S.C. 2051 et seq.) and Federal Hazardous Substances Act (15 U.S.C. 1261 et seq.) respectively, when subject to a consumer product safety standard or labeling requirement of those Acts, or regulations issued under those Acts by the Consumer Product Safety Commission; and,

(vi) Agricultural or vegetable seed treated with pesticides and labeled in accordance with the Federal Seed Act

29 CFR Ch. XVII (7-1-94 Edition)

(7 U.S.C. 1551 et seq.) and the labeling regulations issued under that Act by the Department of Agriculture.

(6) This section does not apply to: (i) Any hazardous waste as such term is defined by the Solid Waste Disposal Act, as amended by the Resource Conservation and Recovery Act of 1976, as amended (42 U.S.C. 6901 et seq.), when subject to regulations issued under that Act by the Environmental Protection Agency;

(ii) Any hazardous substance as such term is defined by the Comprehensive Environmental Response, Compensation, and Liability Act (CERCLA)(42 U.S.C. 9601 et seq.), when subject to regulations issued under that Act by the Environmental Protection Agency;

(iii) Tobacco or tobacco products;

(iv) Wood or wood products, including lumber which will not be processed, where the chemical manufacturer or importer can establish that the only hazard they pose to employees is the potential for flammability or combustibility (wood or wood products which have been treated with a hazardous chemical covered by this standard, and wood which may be subsequently sawed or cut, generating dust, are not exempted);

(v) Articles (as that term is defined in paragraph (c) of this section);

(vi) Food or alcoholic beverages which are sold, used, or prepared in a retail establishment (such as a grocery store, restaurant, or drinking place), and foods intended for personal consumption by employees while in the workplace;

(vii) Any drug, as that term is defined in the Federal Food, Drug, and Cosmetic Act (21 U.S.C. 301 et seq.), when it is in solid, final form for direct administration to the patient (e.g., tablets or pills); drugs which are packaged by the chemical manufacturer for sale to consumers in a retail establishment (e.g., over-the-counter drugs); and drugs intended for personal consumption by employees while in the workplace (e.g., first aid supplies);

(viii) Cosmetics which are packaged for sale to consumers in a retail establishment, and cosmetics intended for personal consumption by employees while in the workplace;

(ix) Any consumer product or hazardous substance, as those terms are defined in the Consumer Product Safety Act (15 U.S.C. 2051 et seq.) and Federal Hazardous Substances Act (15 U.S.C. 1261 et seq.) respectively, where the employer can show that it is used in the workplace for the purpose intended by the chemical manufacturer or importer of the product, and the use results in a duration and frequency of exposure which is not greater than the range of exposures that could reasonably be experienced by consumers when used for the purpose intended;

(x) Nuisance particulates where the chemical manufacturer or importer can establish that they do not pose any physical or health hazard covered under this section;

(xi) Ionizing and nonionizing radiation; and,

(xii) Biological hazards.

(c) *Definitions.*

Article means a manufactured item other than a fluid or particle: (i) which is formed to a specific shape or design during manufacture; (ii) which has end use function(s) dependent in whole or in part upon its shape or design during end use; and (iii) which under normal conditions of use does not release more than very small quantities, *e.g.*, minute or trace amounts of a hazardous chemical (as determined under paragraph (d) of this section), and does not pose a physical hazard or health risk to employees.

Assistant Secretary means the Assistant Secretary of Labor for Occupational Safety and Health, U.S. Department of Labor, or designee.

Chemical means any element, chemical compound or mixture of elements and/or compounds.

Chemical manufacturer means an employer with a workplace where chemical(s) are produced for use or distribution.

Chemical name means the scientific designation of a chemical in accordance with the nomenclature system developed by the International Union of Pure and Applied Chemistry (IUPAC) or the Chemical Abstracts Service (CAS) rules of nomenclature, or a name which will clearly identify the chemical for the purpose of conducting a hazard evaluation.

Combustible liquid means any liquid having a flashpoint at or above 100 °F (37.8 °C), but below 200 °F (93.3 °C), except any mixture having components with flashpoints of 200 °F (93.3 °C), or higher, the total volume of which make up 99 percent or more of the total volume of the mixture.

Commercial account means an arrangement whereby a retail distributor sells hazardous chemicals to an employer, generally in large quantities over time and/or at costs that are below the regular retail price.

Common name means any designation or identification such as code name, code number, trade name, brand name or generic name used to identify a chemical other than by its chemical name.

Compressed gas means:

(i) A gas or mixture of gases having, in a container, an absolute pressure exceeding 40 psi at 70 °F (21.1 °C); or

(ii) A gas or mixture of gases having, in a container, an absolute pressure exceeding 104 psi at 130 °F (54.4 °C) regardless of the pressure at 70 °F (21.1 °C); or

(iii) A liquid having a vapor pressure exceeding 40 psi at 100 °F (37.8 °C) as determined by ASTM D–323–72.

Container means any bag, barrel, bottle, box, can, cylinder, drum, reaction vessel, storage tank, or the like that contains a hazardous chemical. For purposes of this section, pipes or piping systems, and engines, fuel tanks, or other operating systems in a vehicle, are not considered to be containers.

Designated representative means any individual or organization to whom an employee gives written authorization to exercise such employee's rights under this section. A recognized or certified collective bargaining agent shall be treated automatically as a designated representative without regard to written employee authorization.

Director means the Director, National Institute for Occupational Safety and Health, U.S. Department of Health and Human Services, or designee.

Distributor means a business, other than a chemical manufacturer or importer, which supplies hazardous chemicals to other distributors or to employers.

Employee means a worker who may be exposed to hazardous chemicals under

471

§ 1910.1200   29 CFR Ch. XVII (7-1-94 Edition)

normal operating conditions or in foreseeable emergencies. Workers such as office workers or bank tellers who encounter hazardous chemicals only in non-routine, isolated instances are not covered.

Employer means a person engaged in a business where chemicals are either used, distributed, or are produced for use or distribution, including a contractor or subcontractor.

Explosive means a chemical that causes a sudden, almost instantaneous release of pressure, gas, and heat when subjected to sudden shock, pressure, or high temperature.

Exposure or *exposed* means that an employee is subjected in the course of employment to a chemical that is a physical or health hazard, and includes potential (*e.g.* accidental or possible) exposure. "Subjected" in terms of health hazards includes any route of entry (*e.g.* inhalation, ingestion, skin contact or absorption.)

Flammable means a chemical that falls into one of the following categories:

(i) *Aerosol, flammable* means an aerosol that, when tested by the method described in 16 CFR 1500.45, yields a flame projection exceeding 18 inches at full valve opening, or a flashback (a flame extending back to the valve) at any degree of valve opening;

(ii) *Gas, flammable* means: (A) A gas that, at ambient temperature and pressure, forms a flammable mixture with air at a concentration of thirteen (13) percent by volume or less; or

(B) A gas that, at ambient temperature and pressure, forms a range of flammable mixtures with air wider than twelve (12) percent by volume, regardless of the lower limit;

(iii) *Liquid, flammable* means any liquid having a flashpoint below 100°F (37.8°C), except any mixture having components with flashpoints of 100°F (37.8°C) or higher, the total of which make up 99 percent or more of the total volume of the mixture.

(iv) *Solid, flammable* means a solid, other than a blasting agent or explosive as defined in §1910.109(a), that is liable to cause fire through friction, absorption of moisture, spontaneous chemical change, or retained heat from manufacturing or processing, or which can be ignited readily and when ignited burns so vigorously and persistently as to create a serious hazard. A chemical shall be considered to be a flammable solid if, when tested by the method described in 16 CFR 1500.44, it ignites and burns with a self-sustained flame at a rate greater than one-tenth of an inch per second along its major axis.

Flashpoint means the minimum temperature at which a liquid gives off a vapor in sufficient concentration to ignite when tested as follows:

(i) Tagliabue Closed Tester (See American National Standard Method of Test for Flash Point by Tag Closed Tester, Z11.24-1979 (ASTM D 56-79)) for liquids with a viscosity of less than 45 Saybolt Universal Seconds (SUS) at 100°F (37.8°C), that do not contain suspended solids and do not have a tendency to form a surface film under test; or

(ii) Pensky-Martens Closed Tester (see American National Standard Method of Test for Flash Point by Pensky-Martens Closed Tester, Z11.7-1979 (ASTM D 93-79)) for liquids with a viscosity equal to or greater than 45 SUS at 100°F (37.8°C), or that contain suspended solids, or that have a tendency to form a surface film under test; or

(iii) Setaflash Closed Tester (see American National Standard Method of Test for Flash Point by Setaflash Closed Tester (ASTM D 3278-78)).

Organic peroxides, which undergo autoaccelerating thermal decomposition, are excluded from any of the flashpoint determination methods specified above.

Foreseeable emergency means any potential occurrence such as, but not limited to, equipment failure, rupture of containers, or failure of control equipment which could result in an uncontrolled release of a hazardous chemical into the workplace.

Hazardous chemical means any chemical which is a physical hazard or a health hazard.

Hazard warning means any words, pictures, symbols, or combination thereof appearing on a label or other appropriate form of warning which convey the specific physical or health hazard(s), including target organ effects, of the chemical(s) in the container(s). (See the definitions for "physical hazard" and "health hazard" to determine the hazards which must be covered.)

Health hazard means a chemical for which there is statistically significant evidence based on at least one study conducted in accordance with established scientific principles that acute or chronic health effects may occur in exposed employees. The term "health hazard" includes chemicals which are carcinogens, toxic or highly toxic agents, reproductive toxins, irritants, corrosives, sensitizers, hepatotoxins, nephrotoxins, neurotoxins, agents which act on the hematopoietic system, and agents which damage the lungs, skin, eyes, or mucous membranes. Appendix A provides further definitions and explanations of the scope of health hazards covered by this section, and Appendix B describes the criteria to be used to determine whether or not a chemical is to be considered hazardous for purposes of this standard.

Identity means any chemical or common name which is indicated on the material safety data sheet (MSDS) for the chemical. The identity used shall permit cross-references to be made among the required list of hazardous chemicals, the label and the MSDS.

Immediate use means that the hazardous chemical will be under the control of and used only by the person who transfers it from a labeled container and only within the work shift in which it is transferred.

Importer means the first business with employees within the Customs Territory of the United States which receives hazardous chemicals produced in other countries for the purpose of supplying them to distributors or employers within the United States.

Label means any written, printed, or graphic material displayed on or affixed to containers of hazardous chemicals.

Material safety data sheet (MSDS) means written or printed material concerning a hazardous chemical which is prepared in accordance with paragraph (g) of this section.

Mixture means any combination of two or more chemicals if the combination is not, in whole or in part, the result of a chemical reaction.

Organic peroxide means an organic compound that contains the bivalent -O-O-structure and which may be considered to be a structural derivative of hydrogen peroxide where one or both of the hydrogen atoms has been replaced by an organic radical.

Oxidizer means a chemical other than a blasting agent or explosive as defined in §1910.109(a), that initiates or promotes combustion in other materials, thereby causing fire either of itself or through the release of oxygen or other gases.

Physical hazard means a chemical for which there is scientifically valid evidence that it is a combustible liquid, a compressed gas, explosive, flammable, an organic peroxide, an oxidizer, pyrophoric, unstable (reactive) or water-reactive.

Produce means to manufacture, process, formulate, blend, extract, generate, emit, or repackage.

Pyrophoric means a chemical that will ignite spontaneously in air at a temperature of 130°F (54.4°C) or below.

Responsible party means someone who can provide additional information on the hazardous chemical and appropriate emergency procedures, if necessary.

Specific chemical identity means the chemical name, Chemical Abstracts Service (CAS) Registry Number, or any other information that reveals the precise chemical designation of the substance.

Trade secret means any confidential formula, pattern, process, device, information or compilation of information that is used in an employer's business, and that gives the employer an opportunity to obtain an advantage over competitors who do not know or use it. Appendix D sets out the criteria to be used in evaluating trade secrets.

Unstable (reactive) means a chemical which in the pure state, or as produced or transported, will vigorously polymerize, decompose, condense, or will become self-reactive under conditions of shocks, pressure or temperature.

Use means to package, handle, react, emit, extract, generate as a byproduct, or transfer.

Water-reactive means a chemical that reacts with water to release a gas that is either flammable or presents a health hazard.

Work area means a room or defined space in a workplace where hazardous chemicals are produced or used, and where employees are present.

Workplace means an establishment, job site, or project, at one geographical location containing one or more work areas.

(d) *Hazard determination.* (1) Chemical manufacturers and importers shall evaluate chemicals produced in their workplaces or imported by them to determine if they are hazardous. Employers are not required to evaluate chemicals unless they choose not to rely on the evaluation performed by the chemical manufacturer or importer for the chemical to satisfy this requirement.

(2) Chemical manufacturers, importers or employers evaluating chemicals shall identify and consider the available scientific evidence concerning such hazards. For health hazards, evidence which is statistically significant and which is based on at least one positive study conducted in accordance with established scientific principles is considered to be sufficient to establish a hazardous effect if the results of the study meet the definitions of health hazards in this section. Appendix A shall be consulted for the scope of health hazards covered, and Appendix B shall be consulted for the criteria to be followed with respect to the completeness of the evaluation, and the data to be reported.

(3) The chemical manufacturer, importer or employer evaluating chemicals shall treat the following sources as establishing that the chemicals listed in them are hazardous:

(i) 29 CFR part 1910, subpart Z, Toxic and Hazardous Substances, Occupational Safety and Health Administration (OSHA); or,

(ii) *Threshold Limit Values for Chemical Substances and Physical Agents in the Work Environment,* American Conference of Governmental Industrial Hygienists (ACGIH) (latest edition). The chemical manufacturer, importer, or employer is still responsible for evaluating the hazards associated with the chemicals in these source lists in accordance with the requirements of this standard.

(4) Chemical manufacturers, importers and employers evaluating chemicals shall treat the following sources as establishing that a chemical is a carcinogen or potential carcinogen for hazard communication purposes:

(i) National Toxicology Program (NTP), *Annual Report on Carcinogens* (latest edition);

(ii) International Agency for Research on Cancer (IARC) *Monographs* (latest editions); or

(iii) 29 CFR part 1910, subpart Z, Toxic and Hazardous Substances, Occupational Safety and Health Administration.

NOTE: The *Registry of Toxic Effects of Chemical Substances* published by the National Institute for Occupational Safety and Health indicates whether a chemical has been found by NTP or IARC to be a potential carcinogen.

(5) The chemical manufacturer, importer or employer shall determine the hazards of mixtures of chemicals as follows:

(i) If a mixture has been tested as a whole to determine its hazards, the results of such testing shall be used to determine whether the mixture is hazardous;

(ii) If a mixture has not been tested as a whole to determine whether the mixture is a health hazard, the mixture shall be assumed to present the same health hazards as do the components which comprise one percent (by weight or volume) or greater of the mixture, except that the mixture shall be assumed to present a carcinogenic hazard if it contains a component in concentrations of 0.1 percent or greater which is considered to be a carcinogen under paragraph (d)(4) of this section;

(iii) If a mixture has not been tested as a whole to determine whether the mixture is a physical hazard, the chemical manufacturer, importer, or employer may use whatever scientifically valid data is available to evaluate the physical hazard potential of the mixture; and,

(iv) If the chemical manufacturer, importer, or employer has evidence to indicate that a component present in the mixture in concentrations of less than one percent (or in the case of car-

Occupational Safety and Health Admin., Labor § 1910.1200

cinogens, less than 0.1 percent) could be released in concentrations which would exceed an established OSHA permissible exposure limit or ACGIH Threshold Limit Value, or could present a health risk to employees in those concentrations, the mixture shall be assumed to present the same hazard.

(6) Chemical manufacturers, importers, or employers evaluating chemicals shall describe in writing the procedures they use to determine the hazards of the chemical they evaluate. The written procedures are to be made available, upon request, to employees, their designated representatives, the Assistant Secretary and the Director. The written description may be incorporated into the written hazard communication program required under paragraph (e) of this section.

(e) *Written hazard communication program.* (1) Employers shall develop, implement, and maintain at each workplace, a written hazard communication program which at least describes how the criteria specified in paragraphs (f), (g), and (h) of this section for labels and other forms of warning, material safety data sheets, and employee information and training will be met, and which also includes the following:

(i) A list of the hazardous chemicals known to be present using an identity that is referenced on the appropriate material safety data sheet (the list may be compiled for the workplace as a whole or for individual work areas); and,

(ii) The methods the employer will use to inform employees of the hazards of non-routine tasks (for example, the cleaning of reactor vessels), and the hazards associated with chemicals contained in unlabeled pipes in their work areas.

(2) *Multi-employer workplaces.* Employers who produce, use, or store hazardous chemicals at a workplace in such a way that the employees of other employer(s) may be exposed (for example, employees of a construction contractor working on-site) shall additionally ensure that the hazard communication programs developed and implemented under this paragraph (e) include the following:

(i) The methods the employer will use to provide the other employer(s) on-site access to material safety data sheets for each hazardous chemical the other employer(s)' employees may be exposed to while working;

(ii) The methods the employer will use to inform the other employer(s) of any precautionary measures that need to be taken to protect employees during the workplace's normal operating conditions and in foreseeable emergencies; and,

(iii) The methods the employer will use to inform the other employer(s) of the labeling system used in the workplace.

(3) The employer may rely on an existing hazard communication program to comply with these requirements, provided that it meets the criteria established in this paragraph (e).

(4) The employer shall make the written hazard communication program available, upon request, to employees, their designated representatives, the Assistant Secretary and the Director, in accordance with the requirements of 29 CFR 1910.20 (e).

(5) Where employees must travel between workplaces during a workshift, i.e., their work is carried out at more than one geographical location, the written hazard communication program may be kept at the primary workplace facility.

(f) *Labels and other forms of warning.* (1) The chemical manufacturer, importer, or distributor shall ensure that each container of hazardous chemicals leaving the workplace is labeled, tagged or marked with the following information:

(i) Identity of the hazardous chemical(s);

(ii) Appropriate hazard warnings; and

(iii) Name and address of the chemical manufacturer, importer, or other responsible party.

(2)(i) For solid metal (such as a steel beam or a metal casting), solid wood, or plastic items that are not exempted as articles due to their downstream use, or shipments of whole grain, the required label may be transmitted to the customer at the time of the initial shipment, and need not be included with subsequent shipments to the same employer unless the information on the label changes;

§ 1910.1200

(ii) The label may be transmitted with the initial shipment itself, or with the material safety data sheet that is to be provided prior to or at the time of the first shipment; and,

(iii) This exception to requiring labels on every container of hazardous chemicals is only for the solid material itself, and does not apply to hazardous chemicals used in conjunction with, or known to be present with, the material and to which employees handling the items in transit may be exposed (for example, cutting fluids or pesticides in grains).

(3) Chemical manufacturers, importers, or distributors shall ensure that each container of hazardous chemicals leaving the workplace is labeled, tagged, or marked in accordance with this section in a manner which does not conflict with the requirements of the Hazardous Materials Transportation Act (49 U.S.C. 1801 et seq.) and regulations issued under that Act by the Department of Transportation.

(4) If the hazardous chemical is regulated by OSHA in a substance-specific health standard, the chemical manufacturer, importer, distributor or employer shall ensure that the labels or other forms of warning used are in accordance with the requirements of that standard.

(5) Except as provided in paragraphs (f)(6) and (f)(7) of this section, the employer shall ensure that each container of hazardous chemicals in the workplace is labeled, tagged or marked with the following information:

(i) Identity of the hazardous chemical(s) contained therein; and,

(ii) Appropriate hazard warnings, or alternatively, words, pictures, symbols, or combination thereof, which provide at least general information regarding the hazards of the chemicals, and which, in conjunction with the other information immediately available to employees under the hazard communication program, will provide employees with the specific information regarding the physical and health hazards of the hazardous chemical.

(6) The employer may use signs, placards, process sheets, batch tickets, operating procedures, or other such written materials in lieu of affixing labels to individual stationary process containers, as long as the alternative method identifies the containers to which it is applicable and conveys the information required by paragraph (f)(5) of this section to be on a label. The written materials shall be readily accessible to the employees in their work area throughout each work shift.

(7) The employer is not required to label portable containers into which hazardous chemicals are transferred from labeled containers, and which are intended only for the immediate use of the employee who performs the transfer. For purposes of this section, drugs which are dispensed by a pharmacy to a health care provider for direct administration to a patient are exempted from labeling.

(8) The employer shall not remove or deface existing labels on incoming containers of hazardous chemicals, unless the container is immediately marked with the required information.

(9) The employer shall ensure that labels or other forms of warning are legible, in English, and prominently displayed on the container. or readily available in the work area throughout each work shift. Employers having employees who speak other languages may add the information in their language to the material presented, as long as the information is presented in English as well.

(10) The chemical manufacturer, importer, distributor or employer need not affix new labels to comply with this section if existing labels already convey the required information.

(11) Chemical manufacturers, importers, distributors, or employers who become newly aware of any significant information regarding the hazards of a chemical shall revise the labels for the chemical within three months of becoming aware of the new information. Labels on containers of hazardous chemicals shipped after that time shall contain the new information. If the chemical is not currently produced or imported, the chemical manufacturer, importers, distributor, or employer shall add the information to the label before the chemical is shipped or introduced into the workplace again.

(g) *Material safety data sheets.* (1) Chemical manufacturers and importers shall obtain or develop a material safe-

Occupational Safety and Health Admin., Labor § 1910.1200

ty data sheet for each hazardous chemical they produce or import. Employers shall have a material safety data sheet in the workplace for each hazardous chemical which they use.

(2) Each material safety data sheet shall be in English (although the employer may maintain copies in other languages as well), and shall contain at least the following information:

(i) The identity used on the label, and, except as provided for in paragraph (i) of this section on trade secrets:

(A) If the hazardous chemical is a single substance, its chemical and common name(s);

(B) If the hazardous chemical is a mixture which has been tested as a whole to determine its hazards, the chemical and common name(s) of the ingredients which contribute to these known hazards, and the common name(s) of the mixture itself; or,

(C) If the hazardous chemical is a mixture which has not been tested as a whole:

(*1*) The chemical and common name(s) of all ingredients which have been determined to be health hazards, and which comprise 1% or greater of the composition, except that chemicals identified as carcinogens under paragraph (d) of this section shall be listed if the concentrations are 0.1% or greater; and,

(*2*) The chemical and common name(s) of all ingredients which have been determined to be health hazards, and which comprise less than 1% (0.1% for carcinogens) of the mixture, if there is evidence that the ingredient(s) could be released from the mixture in concentrations which would exceed an established OSHA permissible exposure limit or ACGIH Threshold Limit Value, or could present a health risk to employees; and,

(*3*) The chemical and common name(s) of all ingredients which have been determined to present a physical hazard when present in the mixture;

(ii) Physical and chemical characteristics of the hazardous chemical (such as vapor pressure, flash point);

(iii) The physical hazards of the hazardous chemical, including the potential for fire, explosion, and reactivity;

(iv) The health hazards of the hazardous chemical, including signs and symptoms of exposure, and any medical conditions which are generally recognized as being aggravated by exposure to the chemical;

(v) The primary route(s) of entry;

(vi) The OSHA permissible exposure limit, ACGIH Threshold Limit Value, and any other exposure limit used or recommended by the chemical manufacturer, importer, or employer preparing the material safety data sheet, where available;

(vii) Whether the hazardous chemical is listed in the National Toxicology Program (NTP) Annual Report on Carcinogens (latest edition) or has been found to be a potential carcinogen in the International Agency for Research on Cancer (IARC) Monographs (latest editions), or by OSHA;

(viii) Any generally applicable precautions for safe handling and use which are known to the chemical manufacturer, importer or employer preparing the material safety data sheet, including appropriate hygienic practices, protective measures during repair and maintenance of contaminated equipment, and procedures for clean-up of spills and leaks;

(ix) Any generally applicable control measures which are known to the chemical manufacturer, importer or employer preparing the material safety data sheet, such as appropriate engineering controls, work practices, or personal protective equipment;

(x) Emergency and first aid procedures;

(xi) The date of preparation of the material safety data sheet or the last change to it; and,

(xii) The name, address and telephone number of the chemical manufacturer, importer, employer or other responsible party preparing or distributing the material safety data sheet, who can provide additional information on the hazardous chemical and appropriate emergency procedures, if necessary.

(3) If no relevant information is found for any given category on the material safety data sheet, the chemical manufacturer, importer or employer preparing the material safety data sheet shall mark it to indicate

APPENDIX 3E

§ 1910.1200

that no applicable information was found.

(4) Where complex mixtures have similar hazards and contents (i.e. the chemical ingredients are essentially the same, but the specific composition varies from mixture to mixture), the chemical manufacturer, importer or employer may prepare one material safety data sheet to apply to all of these similar mixtures.

(5) The chemical manufacturer, importer or employer preparing the material safety data sheet shall ensure that the information recorded, accurately reflects the scientific evidence used in making the hazard determination. If the chemical manufacturer, importer or employer preparing the material safety data sheet becomes newly aware of any significant information regarding the hazards of a chemical, or ways to protect against the hazards, this new information shall be added to the material safety data sheet within three months. If the chemical is not currently being produced or imported the chemical manufacturer or importer shall add the information to the material safety data sheet before the chemical is introduced into the workplace again.

(6)(i) Chemical manufacturers or importers shall ensure that distributors and employers are provided an appropriate material safety data sheet with their initial shipment, and with the first shipment after a material safety data sheet is updated;

(ii) The chemical manufacturer or importer shall either provide material safety data sheets with the shipped containers or send them to the distributor or employer prior to or at the time of the shipment;

(iii) If the material safety data sheet is not provided with a shipment that has been labeled as a hazardous chemical, the distributor or employer shall obtain one from the chemical manufacturer or importer as soon as possible; and,

(iv) The chemical manufacturer or importer shall also provide distributors or employers with a material safety data sheet upon request.

(7)(i) Distributors shall ensure that material safety data sheets, and updated information, are provided to other distributors and employers with their initial shipment and with the first shipment after a material safety data sheet is updated;

(ii) The distributor shall either provide material safety data sheets with the shipped containers, or send them to the other distributor or employer prior to or at the time of the shipment;

(iii) Retail distributors selling hazardous chemicals to employers having a commercial account shall provide a material safety data sheet to such employers upon request, and shall post a sign or otherwise inform them that a material safety data sheet is available;

(iv) Wholesale distributors selling hazardous chemicals to employers over-the-counter may also, as an alternative to keeping a file of material safety data sheets for all hazardous chemicals they sell, provide material safety data sheets upon the request of the employer at the time of the over-the-counter purchase, and shall post a sign or otherwise inform such employers that a material safety data sheet is available;

(v) If an employer without a commercial account purchases a hazardous chemical from a retail distributor not required to have material safety data sheets on file (i.e., the retail distributor does not have commercial accounts and does not use the materials), the retail distributor shall provide the employer, upon request, with the name, address, and telephone number of the chemical manufacturer, importer, or distributor from which a material safety data sheet can be obtained;

(vi) Wholesale distributors shall also provide material safety data sheets to employers or other distributors upon request; and,

(vii) Chemical manufacturers, importers, and distributors need not provide material safety data sheets to retail distributors that have informed them that the retail distributor does not sell the product to commercial accounts or open the sealed container to use it in their own workplaces.

(8) The employer shall maintain in the workplace copies of the required material safety data sheets for each hazardous chemical, and shall ensure that they are readily accessible during each work shift to employees when

Occupational Safety and Health Admin., Labor § 1910.1200

they are in their work area(s). (Electronic access, microfiche, and other alternatives to maintaining paper copies of the material safety data sheets are permitted as long as no barriers to immediate employee access in each workplace are created by such options.)

(9) Where employees must travel between workplaces during a workshift, i.e., their work is carried out at more than one geographical location, the material safety data sheets may be kept at the primary workplace facility. In this situation, the employer shall ensure that employees can immediately obtain the required information in an emergency.

(10) Material safety data sheets may be kept in any form, including operating procedures, and may be designed to cover groups of hazardous chemicals in a work area where it may be more appropriate to address the hazards of a process rather than individual hazardous chemicals. However, the employer shall ensure that in all cases the required information is provided for each hazardous chemical, and is readily accessible during each work shift to employees when they are in in their work area(s).

(11) Material safety data sheets shall also be made readily available, upon request, to designated representatives and to the Assistant Secretary, in accordance with the requirements of 29 CFR 1910.20(e). The Director shall also be given access to material safety data sheets in the same manner.

(h) *Employee information and training.* (1) Employers shall provide employees with effective information and training on hazardous chemicals in their work area at the time of their initial assignment, and whenever a new physical or health hazard the employees have not previously been trained about is introduced into their work area. Information and training may be designed to cover categories of hazards (*e.g.*, flammability, carcinogenicity) or specific chemicals. Chemical-specific information must always be available through labels and material safety data sheets.

(2) *Information.* Employees shall be informed of:

(i) The requirements of this section;

(ii) Any operations in their work area where hazardous chemicals are present; and,

(iii) The location and availability of the written hazard communication program, including the required list(s) of hazardous chemicals, and material safety data sheets required by this section.

(3) *Training.* Employee training shall include at least:

(i) Methods and observations that may be used to detect the presence or release of a hazardous chemical in the work area (such as monitoring conducted by the employer, continuous monitoring devices, visual appearance or odor of hazardous chemicals when being released, etc.);

(ii) The physical and health hazards of the chemicals in the work area;

(iii) The measures employees can take to protect themselves from these hazards, including specific procedures the employer has implemented to protect employees from exposure to hazardous chemicals, such as appropriate work practices, emergency procedures, and personal protective equipment to be used; and,

(iv) The details of the hazard communication program developed by the employer, including an explanation of the labeling system and the material safety data sheet, and how employees can obtain and use the appropriate hazard information.

(i) *Trade secrets.* (1) The chemical manufacturer, importer, or employer may withhold the specific chemical identity, including the chemical name and other specific identification of a hazardous chemical, from the material safety data sheet, provided that:

(i) The claim that the information withheld is a trade secret can be supported;

(ii) Information contained in the material safety data sheet concerning the properties and effects of the hazardous chemical is disclosed;

(iii) The material safety data sheet indicates that the specific chemical identity is being withheld as a trade secret; and,

(iv) The specific chemical identity is made available to health professionals, employees, and designated representa-

§ 1910.1200

tives in accordance with the applicable provisions of this paragraph.

(2) Where a treating physician or nurse determines that a medical emergency exists and the specific chemical identity of a hazardous chemical is necessary for emergency or first-aid treatment, the chemical manufacturer, importer, or employer shall immediately disclose the specific chemical identity of a trade secret chemical to that treating physician or nurse, regardless of the existence of a written statement of need or a confidentiality agreement. The chemical manufacturer, importer, or employer may require a written statement of need and confidentiality agreement, in accordance with the provisions of paragraphs (i) (3) and (4) of this section, as soon as circumstances permit.

(3) In non-emergency situations, a chemical manufacturer, importer, or employer shall, upon request, disclose a specific chemical identity, otherwise permitted to be withheld under paragraph (i)(1) of this section, to a health professional (i.e. physician, industrial hygienist, toxicologist, epidemiologist, or occupational health nurse) providing medical or other occupational health services to exposed employee(s), and to employees or designated representatives, if:

(i) The request is in writing;

(ii) The request describes with reasonable detail one or more of the following occupational health needs for the information:

(A) To assess the hazards of the chemicals to which employees will be exposed;

(B) To conduct or assess sampling of the workplace atmosphere to determine employee exposure levels;

(C) To conduct pre-assignment or periodic medical surveillance of exposed employees;

(D) To provide medical treatment to exposed employees;

(E) To select or assess appropriate personal protective equipment for exposed employees;

(F) To design or assess engineering controls or other protective measures for exposed employees; and,

(G) To conduct studies to determine the health effects of exposure.

(iii) The request explains in detail why the disclosure of the specific chemical identity is essential and that, in lieu thereof, the disclosure of the following information to the health professional, employee, or designated representative, would not satisfy the purposes described in paragraph (i)(3)(ii) of this section:

(A) The properties and effects of the chemical;

(B) Measures for controlling workers' exposure to the chemical;

(C) Methods of monitoring and analyzing worker exposure to the chemical; and,

(D) Methods of diagnosing and treating harmful exposures to the chemical;

(iv) The request includes a description of the procedures to be used to maintain the confidentiality of the disclosed information; and,

(v) The health professional, and the employer or contractor of the services of the health professional (i.e. downstream employer, labor organization, or individual employee), employee, or designated representative, agree in a written confidentiality agreement that the health professional, employee, or designated representative, will not use the trade secret information for any purpose other than the health need(s) asserted and agree not to release the information under any circumstances other than to OSHA, as provided in paragraph (i)(6) of this section, except as authorized by the terms of the agreement or by the chemical manufacturer, importer, or employer.

(4) The confidentiality agreement authorized by paragraph (i)(3)(iv) of this section:

(i) May restrict the use of the information to the health purposes indicated in the written statement of need;

(ii) May provide for appropriate legal remedies in the event of a breach of the agreement, including stipulation of a reasonable pre-estimate of likely damages; and,

(iii) May not include requirements for the posting of a penalty bond.

(5) Nothing in this standard is meant to preclude the parties from pursuing non-contractual remedies to the extent permitted by law.

(6) If the health professional, employee, or designated representative re-

ceiving the trade secret information decides that there is a need to disclose it to OSHA, the chemical manufacturer, importer, or employer who provided the information shall be informed by the health professional, employee, or designated representative prior to, or at the same time as, such disclosure.

(7) If the chemical manufacturer, importer, or employer denies a written request for disclosure of a specific chemical identity, the denial must:

(i) Be provided to the health professional, employee, or designated representative, within thirty days of the request;

(ii) Be in writing;

(iii) Include evidence to support the claim that the specific chemical identity is a trade secret;

(iv) State the specific reasons why the request is being denied; and,

(v) Explain in detail how alternative information may satisfy the specific medical or occupational health need without revealing the specific chemical identity.

(8) The health professional, employee, or designated representative whose request for information is denied under paragraph (i)(3) of this section may refer the request and the written denial of the request to OSHA for consideration.

(9) When a health professional, employee, or designated representative refers the denial to OSHA under paragraph (i)(8) of this section, OSHA shall consider the evidence to determine if:

(i) The chemical manufacturer, importer, or employer has supported the claim that the specific chemical identity is a trade secret;

(ii) The health professional, employee, or designated representative has supported the claim that there is a medical or occupational health need for the information; and,

(iii) The health professional, employee or designated representative has demonstrated adequate means to protect the confidentiality.

(10)(i) If OSHA determines that the specific chemical identity requested under paragraph (i)(3) of this section is not a *bona fide* trade secret, or that it is a trade secret, but the requesting health professional, employee, or designated representative has a legitimate medical or occupational health need for the information, has executed a written confidentiality agreement, and has shown adequate means to protect the confidentiality of the information, the chemical manufacturer, importer, or employer will be subject to citation by OSHA.

(ii) If a chemical manufacturer, importer, or employer demonstrates to OSHA that the execution of a confidentiality agreement would not provide sufficient protection against the potential harm from the unauthorized disclosure of a trade secret specific chemical identity, the Assistant Secretary may issue such orders or impose such additional limitations or conditions upon the disclosure of the requested chemical information as may be appropriate to assure that the occupational health services are provided without an undue risk of harm to the chemical manufacturer, importer, or employer.

(11) If a citation for a failure to release specific chemical identity information is contested by the chemical manufacturer, importer, or employer, the matter will be adjudicated before the Occupational Safety and Health Review Commission in accordance with the Act's enforcement scheme and the applicable Commission rules of procedure. In accordance with the Commission rules, when a chemical manufacturer, importer, or employer continues to withhold the information during the contest, the Administrative Law Judge may review the citation and supporting documentation *in camera* or issue appropriate orders to protect the confidentiality of such matters.

(12) Notwithstanding the existence of a trade secret claim, a chemical manufacturer, importer, or employer shall, upon request, disclose to the Assistant Secretary any information which this section requires the chemical manufacturer, importer, or employer to make available. Where there is a trade secret claim, such claim shall be made no later than at the time the information is provided to the Assistant Secretary so that suitable determinations of trade secret status can be made and the necessary protections can be implemented.

§ 1910.1200, App. A

(13) Nothing in this paragraph shall be construed as requiring the disclosure under any circumstances of process or percentage of mixture information which is a trade secret.

(j) *Effective dates.* Chemical manufacturers, importers, distributors, and employers shall be in compliance with all provisions of this section by March 11, 1994.

NOTE: The effective date of the clarification that the exemption of wood and wood products from the Hazard Communication standard in paragraph (b)(6)(iv) only applies to wood and wood products including lumber which will not be processed, where the manufacturer or importer can establish that the only hazard they pose to employees is the potential for flammability or combustibility, and that the exemption does not apply to wood or wood products which have been treated with a hazardous chemical covered by this standard, and wood which may be subsequently sawed or cut generating dust has been stayed from March 11, 1994 to August 11, 1994.

APPENDIX A TO § 1910.1200—HEALTH HAZARD DEFINITIONS (MANDATORY)

Although safety hazards related to the physical characteristics of a chemical can be objectively defined in terms of testing requirements (e.g. flammability), health hazard definitions are less precise and more subjective. Health hazards may cause measurable changes in the body—such as decreased pulmonary function. These changes are generally indicated by the occurrence of signs and symptoms in the exposed employees—such as shortness of breath, a non-measurable, subjective feeling. Employees exposed to such hazards must be apprised of both the change in body function and the signs and symptoms that may occur to signal that change.

The determination of occupational health hazards is complicated by the fact that many of the effects or signs and symptoms occur commonly in non-occupationally exposed populations, so that effects of exposure are difficult to separate from normally occurring illnesses. Occasionally, a substance causes an effect that is rarely seen in the population at large, such as angiosarcomas caused by vinyl chloride exposure, thus making it easier to ascertain that the occupational exposure was the primary causative factor. More often, however, the effects are common, such as lung cancer. The situation is further complicated by the fact that most chemicals have not been adequately tested to determine their health hazard potential, and data do not exist to substantiate these effects.

There have been many attempts to categorize effects and to define them in various ways. Generally, the terms "acute" and "chronic" are used to delineate between effects on the basis of severity or duration. "Acute" effects usually occur rapidly as a result of short-term exposures, and are of short duration. "Chronic" effects generally occur as a result of long-term exposure, and are of long duration.

The acute effects referred to most frequently are those defined by the American National Standards Institute (ANSI) standard for Precautionary Labeling of Hazardous Industrial Chemicals (Z129.1–1988)—irritation, corrosivity, sensitization and lethal dose. Although these are important health effects, they do not adequately cover the considerable range of acute effects which may occur as a result of occupational exposure, such as, for example, narcosis.

Similarly, the term chronic effect is often used to cover only carcinogenicity, teratogenicity, and mutagenicity. These effects are obviously a concern in the workplace, but again, do not adequately cover the area of chronic effects, excluding, for example, blood dyscrasias (such as anemia), chronic bronchitis and liver atrophy.

The goal of defining precisely, in measurable terms, every possible health effect that may occur in the workplace as a result of chemical exposures cannot realistically be accomplished. This does not negate the need for employees to be informed of such effects and protected from them. Appendix B, which is also mandatory, outlines the principles and procedures of hazard assessment.

For purposes of this section, any chemicals which meet any of the following definitions, as determined by the criteria set forth in Appendix B are health hazards. However, this is not intended to be an exclusive categorization scheme. If there are available scientific data that involve other animal species or test methods, they must also be evaluated to determine the applicability of the HCS.7

1. *Carcinogen:* A chemical is considered to be a carcinogen if:

(a) It has been evaluated by the International Agency for Research on Cancer (IARC), and found to be a carcinogen or potential carcinogen; or

(b) It is listed as a carcinogen or potential carcinogen in the Annual Report on Carcinogens published by the National Toxicology Program (NTP) (latest edition); or,

(c) It is regulated by OSHA as a carcinogen.

2. *Corrosive:* A chemical that causes visible destruction of, or irreversible alterations in, living tissue by chemical action at the site of contact. For example, a chemical is considered to be corrosive if, when tested on the intact skin of albino rabbits by the method described by the U.S. Department of Transportation in appendix A to 49 CFR part 173,

Occupational Safety and Health Admin., Labor § 1910.1200, App. B

it destroys or changes irreversibly the structure of the tissue at the site of contact following an exposure period of four hours. This term shall not refer to action on inanimate surfaces.

3. *Highly toxic:* A chemical falling within any of the following categories:

(a) A chemical that has a median lethal dose (LD_{50}) of 50 milligrams or less per kilogram of body weight when administered orally to albino rats weighing between 200 and 300 grams each.

(b) A chemical that has a median lethal dose (LD_{50}) of 200 milligrams or less per kilogram of body weight when administered by continuous contact for 24 hours (or less if death occurs within 24 hours) with the bare skin of albino rabbits weighing between two and three kilograms each.

(c) A chemical that has a median lethal concentration (LC_{50}) in air of 200 parts per million by volume or less of gas or vapor, or 2 milligrams per liter or less of mist, fume, or dust, when administered by continuous inhalation for one hour (or less if death occurs within one hour) to albino rats weighing between 200 and 300 grams each.

4. *Irritant:* A chemical, which is not corrosive, but which causes a reversible inflammatory effect on living tissue by chemical action at the site of contact. A chemical is a skin irritant if, when tested on the intact skin of albino rabbits by the methods of 16 CFR 1500.41 for four hours exposure or by other appropriate techniques, it results in an empirical score of five or more. A chemical is an eye irritant if so determined under the procedure listed in 16 CFR 1500.42 or other appropriate techniques.

5. *Sensitizer:* A chemical that causes a substantial proportion of exposed people or animals to develop an allergic reaction in normal tissue after repeated exposure to the chemical.

6. *Toxic.* A chemical falling within any of the following categories:

(a) A chemical that has a median lethal dose (LD_{50}) of more than 50 milligrams per kilogram but not more than 500 milligrams per kilogram of body weight when administered orally to albino rats weighing between 200 and 300 grams each.

(b) A chemical that has a median lethal dose (LD_{50}) of more than 200 milligrams per kilogram but not more than 1,000 milligrams per kilogram of body weight when administered by continuous contact for 24 hours (or less if death occurs within 24 hours) with the bare skin of albino rabbits weighing between two and three kilograms each.

(c) A chemical that has a median lethal concentration (LC_{50}) in air of more than 200 parts per million but not more than 2,000 parts per million by volume of gas or vapor, or more than two milligrams per liter but not more than 20 milligrams per liter of mist, fume, or dust, when administered by continuous inhalation for one hour (or less if death occurs within one hour) to albino rats weighing between 200 and 300 grams each.

7. *Target organ effects.*

The following is a target organ categorization of effects which may occur, including examples of signs and symptoms and chemicals which have been found to cause such effects. These examples are presented to illustrate the range and diversity of effects and hazards found in the workplace, and the broad scope employers must consider in this area, but are not intended to be all-inclusive.

a. Hepatotoxins: Chemicals which produce liver damage3
 Signs & Symptoms: Jaundice; liver enlargement
 Chemicals: Carbon tetrachloride; nitrosamines
b. Nephrotoxins: Chemicals which produce kidney damage
 Signs & Symptoms: Edema; proteinuria
 Chemicals: Halogenated hydrocarbons; uranium
c. Neurotoxins: Chemicals which produce their primary toxic effects on the nervous system
 Signs & Symptoms: Narcosis; behavioral changes; decrease in motor functions
 Chemicals: Mercury; carbon disulfide
d. Agents which act on the blood or hematopoietic system: Decrease hemoglobin function; deprive the body tissues of oxygen
 Signs & Symptoms: Cyanosis; loss of consciousness
 Chemicals: Carbon monoxide; cyanides
e. Agents which damage the lung: Chemicals which irritate or damage pulmonary tissue
 Signs & Symptoms: Cough; tightness in chest; shortness of breath
 Chemicals: Silica; asbestos
f. Reproductive toxins: Chemicals which affect the reproductive capabilities including chromosomal damage (mutations) and effects on fetuses (teratogenesis)
 Signs & Symptoms: Birth defects; sterility
 Chemicals: Lead; DBCP
g. Cutaneous hazards: Chemicals which affect the dermal layer of the body
 Signs & Symptoms: Defatting of the skin; rashes; irritation.
 Chemicals: Ketones; chlorinated compounds
h. Eye hazards: Chemicals which affect the eye or visual capacity
 Signs & Symptoms: Conjunctivitis; corneal damage
 Chemicals: Organic solvents; acids

APPENDIX B TO § 1910.1200—HAZARD DETERMINATION (*Mandatory*)

The quality of a hazard communication program is largely dependent upon

§ 1910.1200, App. C

the adequacy and accuracy of the hazard determination. The hazard determination requirement of this standard is performance-oriented. Chemical manufacturers, importers, and employers evaluating chemicals are not required to follow any specific methods for determining hazards, but they must be able to demonstrate that they have adequately ascertained the hazards of the chemicals produced or imported in accordance with the criteria set forth in this Appendix.

Hazard evaluation is a process which relies heavily on the professional judgment of the evaluator, particularly in the area of chronic hazards. The performance-orientation of the hazard determination does not diminish the duty of the chemical manufacturer, importer or employer to conduct a thorough evaluation, examining all relevant data and producing a scientifically defensible evaluation. For purposes of this standard, the following criteria shall be used in making hazard determinations that meet the requirements of this standard.

1. *Carcinogenicity:* As described in paragraph (d)(4) of this section and Appendix A of this section, a determination by the National Toxicology Program, the International Agency for Research on Cancer, or OSHA that a chemical is a carcinogen or potential carcinogen will be considered conclusive evidence for purposes of this section. In addition, however, all available scientific data on carcinogenicity must be evaluated in accordance with the provisions of this Appendix and the requirements of the rule.

2. *Human data:* Where available, epidemiological studies and case reports of adverse health effects shall be considered in the evaluation.

3. *Animal data:* Human evidence of health effects in exposed populations is generally not available for the majority of chemicals produced or used in the workplace. Therefore, the available results of toxicological testing in animal populations shall be used to predict the health effects that may be experienced by exposed workers. In particular, the definitions of certain acute hazards refer to specific animal testing results (see Appendix A).

4. *Adequacy and reporting of data.* The results of any studies which are designed and conducted according to established scientific principles, and which report statistically significant conclusions regarding the health effects of a chemical, shall be a sufficient basis for a hazard determination and reported on any material safety data sheet. *In vitro* studies alone generally do not form the basis for a definitive finding of hazard under the HCS since they have a positive or negative result rather than a statistically significant finding.

The chemical manufacturer, importer, or employer may also report the results of other scientifically valid studies which tend to refute the findings of hazard.

APPENDIX C TO § 1910.1200—INFORMATION SOURCES (ADVISORY)

The following is a list of available data sources which the chemical manufacturer, importer, distributor, or employer may wish to consult to evaluate the hazards of chemicals they produce or import:

—Any information in their own company files, such as toxicity testing results or illness experience of company employees.

—Any information obtained from the supplier of the chemical, such as material safety data sheets or product safety bulletins.

—Any pertinent information obtained from the following source list (latest editions should be used):

Condensed Chemical Dictionary

Van Nostrand Reinhold Co., 135 West 50th Street, New York, NY 10020.

The Merck Index: An Encyclopedia of Chemicals and Drugs

Merck and Company, Inc., 126 E. Lincoln Ave., Rahway, NJ 07065.

IARC Monographs on the Evaluation of the Carcinogenic Risk of Chemicals to Man

Geneva: World Health Organization, International Agency for Research on Cancer, 1972–Present. (Multivolume work). Summaries are available in supplement volumes. 49 Sheridan Street, Albany, NY 12210.

Occupational Safety and Health Admin., Labor § 1910.1200, App. C

Industrial Hygiene and Toxicology, by F.A. Patty

John Wiley & Sons, Inc., New York, NY (Multivolume work).

Clinical Toxicology of Commercial Products

Gleason, Gosselin, and Hodge.

Casarett and Doull's Toxicology; The Basic Science of Poisons

Doull, Klaassen, and Amdur, Macmillan Publishing Co., Inc., New York, NY.

Industrial Toxicology, by Alice Hamilton and Harriet L. Hardy

Publishing Sciences Group, Inc., Acton, MA.

Toxicology of the Eye, by W. Morton Grant

Charles C. Thomas, 301–327 East Lawrence Avenue, Springfield, IL.

Recognition of Health Hazards in Industry

William A. Burgess, John Wiley and Sons, 605 Third Avenue, New York, NY 10158.

Chemical Hazards of the Workplace

Nick H. Proctor and James P. Hughes, J.P. Lipincott Company, 6 Winchester Terrace, New York, NY 10022.

Handbook of Chemistry and Physics

Chemical Rubber Company, 18901 Cranwood Parkway, Cleveland, OH 44128.

Threshold Limit Values for Chemical Substances and Physical Agents in the Work Environment and Biological Exposure Indices with Intended Changes

American Conference of Governmental Industrial Hygienists (ACGIH), 6500 Glenway Avenue, Bldg. D–5, Cincinnati, OH 45211.

Information on the physical hazards of chemicals may be found in publications of the National Fire Protection Association, Boston, MA.

NOTE: The following documents may be purchased from the Superintendent of Documents, U.S. Government Printing Office, Washington, DC 20402.

Occupational Health Guidelines

NIOSH/OSHA (NIOSH Pub. No. 81–123).

NIOSH Pocket Guide to Chemical Hazards

NIOSH Pub. No. 90–117.

Registry of Toxic Effects of Chemical Substances

(Latest edition)

Miscellaneous Documents published by the National Institute for Occupational Safety and Health:
Criteria documents.
Special Hazard Reviews.
Occupational Hazard Assessments.
Current Intelligence Bulletins.

OSHA's General Industry Standards (29 CFR Part 1910)

NTP Annual Report on Carcinogens and Summary of the Annual Report on Carcinogens.

National Technical Information Service (NTIS), 5285 Port Royal Road, Springfield, VA 22161; (703) 487–4650.

Bibliographic data bases service provider	File name
Bibliographic Retrieval Services (BRS), 1200 Route 7, Latham, NY 12110.	Biosis Previews CA Search Medlars NTIS Hazardline American Chemical Society Journal Excerpta Medica IRCS Medical Science Journal Pre-Med Intl Pharmaceutical Abstracts Paper Chem
Lockheed-DIALOG Information Service, Inc., 3460 Hillview Avenue, Palo Alto, CA 94304.	Biosis Prev. Files CA Search Files CAB Abstracts Chemical Exposure Chemname Chemsis Files Chemzero Embase Files Environmental Bibliographies Enviroline

485

APPENDIX 3E

§ 1910.1200, App. D   29 CFR Ch. XVII (7-1-94 Edition)

Bibliographic data bases service provider	File name
SDC-ORBIT, SDC Information Service, 2500 Colorado Avenue, Santa Monica, CA 90406.	Federal Research in Progress IRL Life Science Collection NTIS Occupational Safety and Health (NIOSH) Paper Chem CAS Files
National Library of Medicine .... Department of Health and Human Services, Public Health Service, National Institutes of Health, Bethesda, MD 20209.	Chemdex, 2, 3 NTIS Hazardous Substances Data Bank (NSDB) Medline Files
Pergamon International Information Corp., 1340 Old Chain Bridge Rd., McLean, VA 22101.	Toxline Files Cancerlit RTECS Chemline Laboratory Hazard Bulletin
Questel, Inc., 1625 Eye Street, NW, Suite 818, Washington, DC 20006.	CIS/ILO
Chemical Information System ICI (ICIS), Bureau of National Affairs, 1133 15th Street, NW, Suite 300, Washington, DC 20005.	Cancernet Structure and Nomenclature Search System (SANSS)
Occupational Health Services, 400 Plaza Drive, Secaucus, NJ 07094.	Acute Toxicity (RTECS) Clinical Toxicology of Commercial Products Oil and Hazardous Materials Technical Assistance Data System CCRIS CESARS MSDS Hazardline

APPENDIX D TO § 1910.1200—DEFINITION OF "TRADE SECRET" (MANDATORY)

The following is a reprint of the *Restatement of Torts* section 757, comment *b* (1939):

b. Definition of trade secret. A trade secret may consist of any formula, pattern, device or compilation of information which is used in one's business, and which gives him an opportunity to obtain an advantage over competitors who do not know or use it. It may be a formula for a chemical compound, a process of manufacturing, treating or preserving materials, a pattern for a machine or other device, or a list of customers. It differs from other secret information in a business (see s759 of the *Restatement of Torts* which is not included in this Appendix) in that it is not simply information as to single or ephemeral events in the conduct of the business, as, for example, the amount or other terms of a secret bid for a contract or the salary of certain employees, or the security investments made or contemplated, or the date fixed for the announcement of a new policy or for bringing out a new model or the like. A trade secret is a process or device for continuous use in the operations of the business. Generally it relates to the production of goods, as, for example, a machine or formula for the production of an article. It may, however, relate to the sale of goods or to other operations in the business, such as a code for determining discounts, rebates or other concessions in a price list or catalogue, or a list of specialized customers, or a method of bookkeeping or other office management.

Secrecy. The subject matter of a trade secret must be secret. Matters of public knowledge or of general knowledge in an industry cannot be appropriated by one as his secret. Matters which are completely disclosed by the goods which one markets cannot be his secret. Substantially, a trade secret is known only in the particular business in which it is used. It is not requisite that only the proprietor of the business know it. He may, without losing his protection, communicate it to employees involved in its use. He may likewise communicate it to others pledged to secrecy. Others may also know of it independently, as, for example, when they have discovered the process or formula by independent invention and are keeping it secret. Nevertheless, a substantial element of secrecy must exist, so that, except by the use of improper means, there would be difficulty in acquiring the information. An exact definition of a trade secret is not possible. Some factors to be considered in determining whether given information is one's trade secret are: (1) The extent to which the information is known outside of his business; (2) the extent to which it is known by employees and others involved in his business; (3) the extent of measures taken by him to

Occupational Safety and Health Admin., Labor § 1910.1200, App. E

guard the secrecy of the information; (4) the value of the information to him and his competitors; (5) the amount of effort or money expended by him in developing the information; (6) the ease or difficulty with which the information could be properly acquired or duplicated by others.

Novelty and prior art. A trade secret may be a device or process which is patentable; but it need not be that. It may be a device or process which is clearly anticipated in the prior art or one which is merely a mechanical improvement that a good mechanic can make. Novelty and invention are not requisite for a trade secret as they are for patentability. These requirements are essential to patentability because a patent protects against unlicensed use of the patented device or process even by one who discovers it properly through independent research. The patent monopoly is a reward to the inventor. But such is not the case with a trade secret. Its protection is not based on a policy of rewarding or otherwise encouraging the development of secret processes or devices. The protection is merely against breach of faith and reprehensible means of learning another's secret. For this limited protection it is not appropriate to require also the kind of novelty and invention which is a requisite of patentability. The nature of the secret is, however, an important factor in determining the kind of relief that is appropriate against one who is subject to liability under the rule stated in this Section. Thus, if the secret consists of a device or process which is a novel invention, one who acquires the secret wrongfully is ordinarily enjoined from further use of it and is required to account for the profits derived from his past use. If, on the other hand, the secret consists of mechanical improvements that a good mechanic can make without resort to the secret, the wrongdoer's liability may be limited to damages, and an injunction against future use of the improvements made with the aid of the secret may be inappropriate.

APPENDIX E TO § 1910.1200-(ADVISORY)— GUIDELINES FOR EMPLOYER COMPLIANCE

The Hazard Communication Standard (HCS) is based on a simple concept—that employees have both a need and a right to know the hazards and identities of the chemicals they are exposed to when working. They also need to know what protective measures are available to prevent adverse effects from occurring. The HCS is designed to provide employees with the information they need.

Knowledge acquired under the HCS will help employers provide safer workplaces for their employees. When employers have information about the chemicals being used, they can take steps to reduce exposures, substitute less hazardous materials, and establish proper work practices. These efforts will help prevent the occurrence of work-related illnesses and injuries caused by chemicals.

The HCS addresses the issues of evaluating and communicating hazards to workers. Evaluation of chemical hazards involves a number of technical concepts, and is a process that requires the professional judgment of experienced experts. That's why the HCS is designed so that employers who simply use chemicals, rather than produce or import them, are not required to evaluate the hazards of those chemicals. Hazard determination is the responsibility of the producers and importers of the materials. Producers and importers of chemicals are then required to provide the hazard information to employers that purchase their products.

Employers that don't produce or import chemicals need only focus on those parts of the rule that deal with establishing a workplace program and communicating information to their workers. This appendix is a general guide for such employers to help them determine what's required under the rule. It does not supplant or substitute for the regulatory provisions, but rather provides a simplified outline of the steps an average employer would follow to meet those requirements.

1. Becoming Familiar With The Rule.

OSHA has provided a simple summary of the HCS in a pamphlet entitled "Chemical Hazard Communication," OSHA Publication Number 3084. Some employers prefer to begin to become familiar with the rule's requirements by reading this pamphlet. A copy may be obtained from your local OSHA Area Office, or by contacting the OSHA Publications Office at (202) 523-9667.

The standard is long, and some parts of it are technical, but the basic concepts are simple. In fact, the requirements reflect what many employers have been doing for years. You may find that you are already largely in compliance with many of the provisions, and will simply have to modify your existing programs somewhat. If you are operating in an OSHA-approved State Plan State, you must comply with the State's requirements, which may be different than those of the Federal rule. Many of the State Plan States had hazard communication or "right-to-know" laws prior to promulgation of the Federal rule. Employers in State Plan States should contact their State OSHA offices for more information regarding applicable requirements.

The HCS requires information to be prepared and transmitted regarding all hazardous chemicals. The HCS covers both physical hazards (such as flammability), and health hazards (such as irritation, lung damage, and cancer). Most chemicals used in the workplace have some hazard potential, and thus will be covered by the rule.

§ 1910.1200, App. E

One difference between this rule and many others adopted by OSHA is that this one is performance-oriented. That means that you have the flexibility to adapt the rule to the needs of your workplace, rather than having to follow specific, rigid requirements. It also means that you have to exercise more judgment to implement an appropriate and effective program.

The standard's design is simple. Chemical manufacturers and importers must evaluate the hazards of the chemicals they produce or import. Using that information, they must then prepare labels for containers, and more detailed technical bulletins called material safety data sheets (MSDS).

Chemical manufacturers, importers, and distributors of hazardous chemicals are all required to provide the appropriate labels and material safety data sheets to the employers to which they ship the chemicals. The information is to be provided automatically. Every container of hazardous chemicals you receive must be labeled, tagged, or marked with the required information. Your suppliers must also send you a properly completed material safety data sheet (MSDS) at the time of the first shipment of the chemical, and with the next shipment after the MSDS is updated with new and significant information about the hazards.

You can rely on the information received from your suppliers. You have no independent duty to analyze the chemical or evaluate the hazards of it.

Employers that "use" hazardous chemicals must have a program to ensure the information is provided to exposed employees. "Use" means to package, handle, react, or transfer. This is an intentionally broad scope, and includes any situation where a chemical is present in such a way that employees may be exposed under normal conditions of use or in a foreseeable emergency.

The requirements of the rule that deal specifically with the hazard communication program are found in this section in paragraphs (e), written hazard communication program; (f), labels and other forms of warning; (g), material safety data sheets; and (h), employee information and training. The requirements of these paragraphs should be the focus of your attention. Concentrate on becoming familiar with them, using paragraphs (b), scope and application, and (c), definitions, as references when needed to help explain the provisions.

There are two types of work operations where the coverage of the rule is limited. These are laboratories and operations where chemicals are only handled in sealed containers (*e.g.*, a warehouse). The limited provisions for these workplaces can be found in paragraph (b) of this section, scope and application. Basically, employers having these types of work operations need only keep labels on containers as they are received;

29 CFR Ch. XVII (7-1-94 Edition)

maintain material safety data sheets that are received, and give employees access to them; and provide information and training for employees. Employers do not have to have written hazard communication programs and lists of chemicals for these types of operations.

The limited coverage of laboratories and sealed container operations addresses the obligation of an employer to the workers in the operations involved, and does not affect the employer's duties as a distributor of chemicals. For example, a distributor may have warehouse operations where employees would be protected under the limited sealed container provisions. In this situation, requirements for obtaining and maintaining MSDSs are limited to providing access to those received with containers while the substance is in the workplace, and requesting MSDSs when employees request access for those not received with the containers. However, as a distributor of hazardous chemicals, that employer will still have responsibilities for providing MSDSs to downstream customers at the time of the first shipment and when the MSDS is updated. Therefore, although they may not be required for the employees in the work operation, the distributor may, nevertheless, have to have MSDSs to satisfy other requirements of the rule.

2. Identify Responsible Staff

Hazard communication is going to be a continuing program in your facility. Compliance with the HCS is not a "one shot deal." In order to have a successful program, it will be necessary to assign responsibility for both the initial and ongoing activities that have to be undertaken to comply with the rule. In some cases, these activities may already be part of current job assignments. For example, site supervisors are frequently responsible for on-the-job training sessions. Early identification of the responsible employees, and involvement of them in the development of your plan of action, will result in a more effective program design. Evaluation of the effectiveness of your program will also be enhanced by involvement of affected employees.

For any safety and health program, success depends on commitment at every level of the organization. This is particularly true for hazard communication, where success requires a change in behavior. This will only occur if employers understand the program, and are committed to its success, and if employees are motivated by the people presenting the information to them.

3. Identify Hazardous Chemicals in the Workplace.

The standard requires a list of hazardous chemicals in the workplace as part of the written hazard communication program. The

Occupational Safety and Health Admin., Labor §1910.1200, App. E

list will eventually serve as an inventory of everything for which an MSDS must be maintained. At this point, however, preparing the list will help you complete the rest of the program since it will give you some idea of the scope of the program required for compliance in your facility.

The best way to prepare a comprehensive list is to survey the workplace. Purchasing records may also help, and certainly employers should establish procedures to ensure that in the future purchasing procedures result in MSDSs being received before a material is used in the workplace.

The broadest possible perspective should be taken when doing the survey. Sometimes people think of "chemicals" as being only liquids in containers. The HCS covers chemicals in all physical forms—liquids, solids, gases, vapors, fumes, and mists—whether they are "contained" or not. The hazardous nature of the chemical and the potential for exposure are the factors which determine whether a chemical is covered. If it's not hazardous, it's not covered. If there is no potential for exposure (e.g., the chemical is inextricably bound and cannot be released), the rule does not cover the chemical.

Look around. Identify chemicals in containers, including pipes, but also think about chemicals generated in the work operations. For example, welding fumes, dusts, and exhaust fumes are all sources of chemical exposures. Read labels provided by suppliers for hazard information. Make a list of all chemicals in the workplace that are potentially hazardous. For your own information and planning, you may also want to note on the list the location(s) of the products within the workplace, and an indication of the hazards as found on the label. This will help you as you prepare the rest of your program.

Paragraph (b) of this section, scope and application, includes exemptions for various chemicals or workplace situations. After compiling the complete list of chemicals, you should review paragraph (b) of this section to determine if any of the items can be eliminated from the list because they are exempted materials. For example, food, drugs, and cosmetics brought into the workplace for employee consumption are exempt. So rubbing alcohol in the first aid kit would not be covered.

Once you have compiled as complete a list as possible of the potentially hazardous chemicals in the workplace, the next step is to determine if you have received material safety data sheets for all of them. Check your files against the inventory you have just compiled. If any are missing, contact your supplier and request one. It is a good idea to document these requests, either by copy of a letter or a note regarding telephone conversations. If you have MSDSs for chemicals that are not on your list, figure out why. Maybe you don't use the chemical

anymore. Or maybe you missed it in your survey. Some suppliers do provide MSDSs for products that are not hazardous. These do not have to be maintained by you.

You should not allow employees to use any chemicals for which you have not received an MSDS. The MSDS provides information you need to ensure proper protective measures are implemented prior to exposure.

4. Preparing and Implementing a Hazard Communication Program

All workplaces where employees are exposed to hazardous chemicals must have a written plan which describes how the standard will be implemented in that facility. Preparation of a plan is not just a paper exercise—all of the elements must be implemented in the workplace in order to be in compliance with the rule. See paragraph (e) of this section for the specific requirements regarding written hazard communication programs. The only work operations which do not have to comply with the written plan requirements are laboratories and work operations where employees only handle chemicals in sealed containers. See paragraph (b) of this section, scope and application, for the specific requirements for these two types of workplaces.

The plan does not have to be lengthy or complicated. It is intended to be a blueprint for implementation of your program—an assurance that all aspects of the requirements have been addressed.

Many trade associations and other professional groups have provided sample programs and other assistance materials to affected employers. These have been very helpful to many employers since they tend to be tailored to the particular industry involved. You may wish to investigate whether your industry trade groups have developed such materials.

Although such general guidance may be helpful, you must remember that the written program has to reflect what you are doing in your workplace. Therefore, if you use a generic program it must be adapted to address the facility it covers. For example, the written plan must list the chemicals present at the site, indicate who is to be responsible for the various aspects of the program in your facility, and indicate where written materials will be made available to employees.

If OSHA inspects your workplace for compliance with the HCS, the OSHA compliance officer will ask to see your written plan at the outset of the inspection. In general, the following items will be considered in evaluating your program.

The written program must describe how the requirements for labels and other forms of warning, material safety data sheets, and employee information and training, are going to be met in your facility. The following discussion provides the type of informa-

489

§ 1910.1200, App. E

tion compliance officers will be looking for to decide whether these elements of the hazard communication program have been properly addressed:

A. Labels and Other Forms of Warning

In-plant containers of hazardous chemicals must be labeled, tagged, or marked with the identity of the material and appropriate hazard warnings. Chemical manufacturers, importers, and distributors are required to ensure that every container of hazardous chemicals they ship is appropriately labeled with such information and with the name and address of the producer or other responsible party. Employers purchasing chemicals can rely on the labels provided by their suppliers. If the material is subsequently transferred by the employer from a labeled container to another container, the employer will have to label that container unless it is subject to the portable container exemption. See paragraph (f) of this section for specific labeling requirements.

The primary information to be obtained from an OSHA-required label is an identity for the material, and appropriate hazard warnings. The identity is any term which appears on the label, the MSDS, and the list of chemicals, and thus links these three sources of information. The identity used by the supplier may be a common or trade name ("Black Magic Formula"), or a chemical name (1,1,1,-trichloroethane). The hazard warning is a brief statement of the hazardous effects of the chemical ("flammable," "causes lung damage"). Labels frequently contain other information, such as precautionary measures ("do not use near open flame"), but this information is provided voluntarily and is not required by the rule. Labels must be legible, and prominently displayed. There are no specific requirements for size or color, or any specified text.

With these requirements in mind, the compliance officer will be looking for the following types of information to ensure that labeling will be properly implemented in your facility:
1. Designation of person(s) responsible for ensuring labeling of in-plant containers;
2. Designation of person(s) responsible for ensuring labeling of any shipped containers;
3. Description of labeling system(s) used;
4. Description of written alternatives to labeling of in-plant containers (if used); and,
5. Procedures to review and update label information when necessary.

Employers that are purchasing and using hazardous chemicals—rather than producing or distributing them—will primarily be concerned with ensuring that every purchased container is labeled. If materials are transferred into other containers, the employer must ensure that these are labeled as well, unless they fall under the portable container exemption (paragraph (f)(7) of this section).

In terms of labeling systems, you can simply choose to use the labels provided by your suppliers on the containers. These will generally be verbal text labels, and do not usually include numerical rating systems or symbols that require special training. The most important thing to remember is that this is a continuing duty—all in-plant containers of hazardous chemicals must always be labeled. Therefore, it is important to designate someone to be responsible for ensuring that the labels are maintained as required on the containers in your facility, and that newly purchased materials are checked for labels prior to use.

B. Material Safety Data Sheets

Chemical manufacturers and importers are required to obtain or develop a material safety data sheet for each hazardous chemical they produce or import. Distributors are responsible for ensuring that their customers are provided a copy of these MSDSs. Employers must have an MSDS for each hazardous chemical which they use. Employers may rely on the information received from their suppliers. The specific requirements for material safety data sheets are in paragraph (g) of this section.

There is no specified format for the MSDS under the rule, although there are specific information requirements. OSHA has developed a non-mandatory format, OSHA Form 174, which may be used by chemical manufacturers and importers to comply with the rule. The MSDS must be in English. You are entitled to receive from your supplier a data sheet which includes all of the information required under the rule. If you do not receive one automatically, you should request one. If you receive one that is obviously inadequate, with, for example, blank spaces that are not completed, you should request an appropriately completed one. If your request for a data sheet or for a corrected data sheet does not produce the information needed, you should contact your local OSHA Area Office for assistance in obtaining the MSDS.

The role of MSDSs under the rule is to provide detailed information on each hazardous chemical, including its potential hazardous effects, its physical and chemical characteristics, and recommendations for appropriate protective measures. This information should be useful to you as the employer responsible for designing protective programs, as well as to the workers. If you are not familiar with material safety data sheets and with chemical terminology, you may need to learn to use them yourself. A glossary of MSDS terms may be helpful in this regard. Generally speaking, most employers using hazardous chemicals will primarily be concerned with MSDS information regarding hazardous effects and recommended protective measures. Focus on the sections of the MSDS that are applicable to your situation.

MSDSs must be readily accessible to employees when they are in their work areas during their workshifts. This may be accomplished in many different ways. You must decide what is appropriate for your particular workplace. Some employers keep the MSDSs in a binder in a central location (e.g., in the pick-up truck on a construction site). Others, particularly in workplaces with large numbers of chemicals, computerize the information and provide access through terminals. As long as employees can get the information when they need it, any approach may be used. The employees must have access to the MSDSs themselves—simply having a system where the information can be read to them over the phone is only permitted under the mobile worksite provision, paragraph (g)(9) of this section, when employees must travel between workplaces during the shift. In this situation, they have access to the MSDSs prior to leaving the primary worksite, and when they return, so the telephone system is simply an emergency arrangement.

In order to ensure that you have a current MSDS for each chemical in the plant as required, and that employee access is provided, the compliance officers will be looking for the following types of information in your written program:

1. Designation of person(s) responsible for obtaining and maintaining the MSDSs;
2. How such sheets are to be maintained in the workplace (e.g., in notebooks in the work area(s) or in a computer with terminal access), and how employees can obtain access to them when they are in their work area during the work shift;
3. Procedures to follow when the MSDS is not received at the time of the first shipment;
4. For producers, procedures to update the MSDS when new and significant health information is found; and,
5. Description of alternatives to actual data sheets in the workplace, if used.

For employers using hazardous chemicals, the most important aspect of the written program in terms of MSDSs is to ensure that someone is responsible for obtaining and maintaining the MSDSs for every hazardous chemical in the workplace. The list of hazardous chemicals required to be maintained as part of the written program will serve as an inventory. As new chemicals are purchased, the list should be updated. Many companies have found it convenient to include on their purchase orders the name and address of the person designated in their company to receive MSDSs.

C. Employee Information and Training

Each employee who may be "exposed" to hazardous chemicals when working must be provided information and trained prior to initial assignment to work with a hazardous chemical, and whenever the hazard changes. "Exposure" or "exposed" under the rule means that "an employee is subjected to a hazardous chemical in the course of employment through any route of entry (inhalation, ingestion, skin contact or absorption, etc.) and includes potential (e.g., accidental or possible) exposure." See paragraph (h) of this section for specific requirements. Information and training may be done either by individual chemical, or by categories of hazards (such as flammability or carcinogenicity). If there are only a few chemicals in the workplace, then you may want to discuss each one individually. Where there are large numbers of chemicals, or the chemicals change frequently, you will probably want to train generally based on the hazard categories (e.g., flammable liquids, corrosive materials, carcinogens). Employees will have access to the substance-specific information on the labels and MSDSs.

Information and training is a critical part of the hazard communication program. Information regarding hazards and protective measures are provided to workers through written labels and material safety data sheets. However, through effective information and training, workers will learn to read and understand such information, determine how it can be obtained and used in their own workplaces, and understand the risks of exposure to the chemicals in their workplaces as well as the ways to protect themselves. A properly conducted training program will ensure comprehension and understanding. It is not sufficient to either just read material to the workers, or simply hand them material to read. You want to create a climate where workers feel free to ask questions. This will help you to ensure that the information is understood. You must always remember that the underlying purpose of the HCS is to reduce the incidence of chemical source illnesses and injuries. This will be accomplished by modifying behavior through the provision of hazard information and information about protective measures. If your program works, you and your workers will better understand the chemical hazards within the workplace. The procedures you establish regarding, for example, purchasing, storage, and handling of these chemicals will improve, and thereby reduce the risks posed to employees exposed to the chemical hazards involved. Furthermore, your workers' comprehension will also be increased, and proper work practices will be followed in your workplace.

If you are going to do the training yourself, you will have to understand the material and be prepared to motivate the workers to learn. This is not always an easy task, but the benefits are worth the effort. More information regarding appropriate training can be found in OSHA Publication No. 2254 which

§ 1910.1200, App. E

contains voluntary training guidelines prepared by OSHA's Training Institute. A copy of this document is available from OSHA's Publications Office at (202) 219-4667.

In reviewing your written program with regard to information and training, the following items need to be considered:

1. Designation of person(s) responsible for conducting training;
2. Format of the program to be used (audiovisuals, classroom instruction, etc.);
3. Elements of the training program (should be consistent with the elements in paragraph (h) of this section); and,
4. Procedure to train new employees at the time of their initial assignment to work with a hazardous chemical, and to train employees when a new hazard is introduced into the workplace.

The written program should provide enough details about the employer's plans in this area to assess whether or not a good faith effort is being made to train employees. OSHA does not expect that every worker will be able to recite all of the information about each chemical in the workplace. In general, the most important aspects of training under the HCS are to ensure that employees are aware that they are exposed to hazardous chemicals, that they know how to read and use labels and material safety data sheets, and that, as a consequence of learning this information, they are following the appropriate protective measures established by the employer. OSHA compliance officers will be talking to employees to determine if they have received training, if they know they are exposed to hazardous chemicals, and if they know where to obtain substance-specific information on labels and MSDSs.

The rule does not require employers to maintain records of employee training, but many employers choose to do so. This may help you monitor your own program to ensure that all employees are appropriately trained. If you already have a training program, you may simply have to supplement it with whatever additional information is required under the HCS. For example, construction employers that are already in compliance with the construction training standard (29 CFR 1926.21) will have little extra training to do.

An employer can provide employees information and training through whatever means are found appropriate and protective. Although there would always have to be some training on-site (such as informing employees of the location and availability of the written program and MSDSs), employee training may be satisfied in part by general training about the requirements of the HCS and about chemical hazards on the job which is provided by, for example, trade associations, unions, colleges, and professional schools. In addition, previous training, education and experience of a worker may relieve the employer of some of the burdens of informing and training that worker. Regardless of the method relied upon, however, the employer is always ultimately responsible for ensuring that employees are adequately trained. If the compliance officer finds that the training is deficient, the employer will be cited for the deficiency regardless of who actually provided the training on behalf of the employer.

D. Other Requirements

In addition to these specific items, compliance officers will also be asking the following questions in assessing the adequacy of the program:

Does a list of the hazardous chemicals exist in each work area or at a central location?

Are methods the employer will use to inform employees of the hazards of non-routine tasks outlined?

Are employees informed of the hazards associated with chemicals contained in unlabeled pipes in their work areas?

On multi-employer worksites, has the employer provided other employers with information about labeling systems and precautionary measures where the other employers have employees exposed to the initial employer's chemicals?

Is the written program made available to employees and their designated representatives?

If your program adequately addresses the means of communicating information to employees in your workplace, and provides answers to the basic questions outlined above, it will be found to be in compliance with the rule.

5. Checklist for Compliance

The following checklist will help to ensure you are in compliance with the rule:
Obtained a copy of the rule. _____
Read and understood the requirements. _____
Assigned responsibility for tasks. _____
Prepared an inventory of chemicals. _____
Ensured containers are labeled. _____
Obtained MSDS for each chemical. _____
Prepared written program. _____
Made MSDSs available to workers. _____
Conducted training of workers. _____
Established procedures to maintain current program. _____
Established procedures to evaluate effectiveness. _____

6. Further Assistance

If you have a question regarding compliance with the HCS, you should contact your local OSHA Area Office for assistance. In addition, each OSHA Regional Office has a Hazard Communication Coordinator who can answer your questions. Free consultation services are also available to assist employers, and information regarding these services can be obtained through the Area and Regional offices as well.

The telephone number for the OSHA office closest to you should be listed in your local telephone directory. If you are not able to obtain this information, you may contact OSHA's Office of Information and Consumer Affairs at (202) 219–8151 for further assistance in identifying the appropriate contacts.

[59 FR 6170, Feb. 9, 1994, as amended at 59 FR 17479, Apr. 13, 1994]

Appendix 4A

29 CFR 1910.132 GENERAL REQUIREMENTS; 29 CFR 1910.133 EYE AND FACE PROTECTION; 29 CFR 1910.134 RESPIRATORY PROTECTION

§ 1910.132 General requirements.

(a) *Application.* Protective equipment, including personal protective equipment for eyes, face, head, and extremities, protective clothing, respiratory devices, and protective shields and barriers, shall be provided, used, and maintained in a sanitary and reliable condition wherever it is necessary by reason of hazards of processes or environment, chemical hazards, radiological hazards, or mechanical irritants encountered in a manner capable of causing injury or impairment in the function of any part of the body through absorption, inhalation or physical contact.

(b) *Employee-owned equipment.* Where employees provide their own protective equipment, the employer shall be responsible to assure its adequacy, including proper maintenance, and sanitation of such equipment.

(c) *Design.* All personal protective equipment shall be of safe design and construction for the work to be performed.

(d) *Hazard assessment and equipment selection.* (1) The employer shall assess the workplace to determine if hazards are present, or are likely to be present, which necessitate the use of personal protective equipment (PPE). If such hazards are present, or likely to be present, the employer shall:

(i) Select, and have each affected employee use, the types of PPE that will protect the affected employee from the

Occupational Safety and Health Admin., Labor §1910.133

hazards identified in the hazard assessment;

(ii) Communicate selection decisions to each affected employee; and,

(iii) Select PPE that properly fits each affected employee.

Note: Non-mandatory Appendix B contains an example of procedures that would comply with the requirement for a hazard assessment.

(2) The employer shall verify that the required workplace hazard assessment has been performed through a written certification that identifies the workplace evaluated; the person certifying that the evaluation has been performed; the date(s) of the hazard assessment; and, which identifies the document as a certification of hazard assessment.

(e) *Defective and damaged equipment.* Defective or damaged personal protective equipment shall not be used.

(f) *Training.* (1) The employer shall provide training to each employee who is required by this section to use PPE. Each such employee shall be trained to know at least the following:

(i) When PPE is necessary;

(ii) What PPE is necessary;

(iii) How to properly don, doff, adjust, and wear PPE;

(iv) The limitations of the PPE; and,

(v) The proper care, maintenance, useful life and disposal of the PPE.

(2) Each affected employee shall demonstrate an understanding of the training specified in paragraph (f)(1) of this section, and the ability to use PPE properly, before being allowed to perform work requiring the use of PPE.

(3) When the employer has reason to believe that any affected employee who has already been trained does not have the understanding and skill required by paragraph (f)(2) of this section, the employer shall retrain each such employee. Circumstances where retraining is required include, but are not limited to, situations where:

(i) Changes in the workplace render previous training obsolete; or

(ii) Changes in the types of PPE to be used render previous training obsolete; or

(iii) Inadequacies in an affected employee's knowledge or use of assigned PPE indicate that the employee has not retained the requisite understanding or skill.

(4) The employer shall verify that each affected employee has received and understood the required training through a written certification that contains the name of each employee trained, the date(s) of training, and that identifies the subject of the certification.

(g) Paragraphs (d) and (f) of this section apply only to §§1910.133, 1910.135, 1910.136, and 1910.138. Paragraphs (d) and (f) of this section do not apply to §§1910.134 and 1910.137.

[39 FR 23502, June 27, 1974, as amended at 59 FR 16334, Apr. 6, 1994, 59 FR 33910, July 1, 1994]

EFFECTIVE DATE NOTE: At 59 FR 16360, April 6, 1994, paragraphs (d) through (f) were added to §1910.132, effective July 5, 1994. On July 1, 1994. At 59 FR 33910, July 1, 1994, paragraph (g) was added, effective July 5, 1994.

§1910.133 Eye and face protection.

(a) *General requirements.* (1) Each affected employee shall use appropriate eye or face protection when exposed to eye or face hazards from flying particles, molten metal, liquid chemicals, acids or caustic liquids, chemical gases or vapors, or potentially injurious light radiation.

(2) Each affected employee shall use eye protection that provides side protection when there is a hazard from flying objects. Detachable side protectors (e.g. clip-on or slide-on side shields) meeting the pertinent requirements of this section are acceptable.

(3) Each affected employee who wears prescription lenses while engaged in operations that involve eye hazards shall wear eye protection that incorporates the prescription in its design, or shall wear eye protection that can be worn over the prescription lenses without disturbing the proper position of the prescription lenses or the protective lenses.

(4) Eye and face PPE shall be distinctly marked to facilitate identification of the manufacturer.

(5) Each affected employee shall use equipment with filter lenses that have a shade number appropriate for the work being performed for protection from injurious light radiation. The following is a listing of appropriate shade numbers for various operations.

411

APPENDIX 4A

§1910.133   29 CFR Ch. XVII (7-1-94 Edition)

Filter Lenses for Protection Against Radiant Energy

Operations	Electrode Size 1/32 in.	Arc Current	Minimum* Protective Shade
Shielded metal arc welding	Less than 3	Less than 60	7
	3-5	60-160	8
	5-8	160-250	10
	More than 8	250-550	11
Gas metal arc welding and flux cored arc welding		less than 60	7
		60-160	10
		160-250	10
		250-500	10
Gas Tungsten arc welding		less than 50	8
		50-150	8
		150-500	10
Air carbon	(Light)	less than 500	10
Arc cutting	(Heavy)	500-1000	11
Plasma arc welding		less than 20	6
		20-100	8
		100-400	10
		400-800	11
Plasma arc cutting	(light)**	less than 300	8
	(medium)**	300-400	9
	(heavy)**	400-800	10
Torch brazing			3
Torch soldering			2
Carbon arc welding			14

Filter Lenses for Protection Against Radiant Energy

Operations	Plate thickness—inches	Plate thickness—mm	Minimum* Protective Shade
Gas Welding:			
Light	Under 1/8	Under 3.2	4
Medium	1/8 to 1/2	3.2 to 12.7	5
Heavy	Over 1/2	Over 12.7	6
Oxygen cutting:			
Light	Under 1	Under 25	3
Medium	1 to 6	25 to 150	4
Heavy	Over 6	Over 150	5

* As a rule of thumb, start with a shade that is too dark to see the weld zone. Then go to a lighter shade which gives sufficient view of the weld zone without going below the minimum. In oxyfuel gas welding or cutting where the torch produces a high yellow light, it is desirable to use a filter lens that absorbs the yellow or sodium line in the visible light of the (spectrum) operation.

** These values apply where the actual arc is clearly seen. Experience has shown that lighter filters may be used when the arc is hidden by the workpiece.

Occupational Safety and Health Admin., Labor § 1910.134

(b) *Criteria for protective eye and face devices.* (1) Protective eye and face devices purchased after July 5, 1994 shall comply with ANSI Z87.1–1989, "American National Standard Practice for Occupational and Educational Eye and Face Protection," which is incorporated by reference, or shall be demonstrated by the employer to be equally effective. This incorporation by reference was approved by the Director of the Federal Register in accordance with 5 U.S.C. 552(a) and 1 CFR part 51. Copies may be obtained from the American National Standards Institute. Copies may be inspected at the Docket Office, Occupational Safety and Health Administration, U.S. Department of Labor, 200 Constitution Ave., N.W. room N2634, Washington, D.C. or at the Office of the Federal Register, 800 North Capitol Street NW., suite 700, Washington, DC.

(2) Eye and face protective devices purchased before July 5, 1994 shall comply with the ANSI "USA standard for Occupational and Educational Eye and Face Protection," Z87.1–1968 or shall be demonstrated by the employer to be equally effective. This incorporation by reference was approved by the Director of the Federal Register in accordance with 5 U.S.C. 552(a) and 1 CFR part 51. Copies may be inspected at the Docket Office, Occupational Safety and Health Administration, U.S. Department of Labor, 200 Constitution Ave., N.W. room N2634, Washington, D.C. or at the Office of the Federal Register, 800 North Capitol Street NW., suite 700, Washington, DC.

[59 FR 16360, Apr. 6, 1994; 59 FR 33911, July 1, 1994]

EFFECTIVE DATE NOTE: At 59 FR 16360, April 6, 1994, § 1910.133 was revised, effective July 5, 1994. At 59 FR 33911, July 1, 1994, in the table "Filter Lenses for Protection Against Radiant Energy", the column heading "Electric Size 1/32 in." is corrected to read "Electrode Size 1/32 in.", effective July 5, 1994. For the convenience of the user, the superseded text appears below:

§ 1910.133   Eye and face protection.

(a) *General.* (1) Protective eye and face equipment shall be required where there is a rasonable probability of injury that can be prevented by such equipment. In such cases, employees shall make conveniently available a type of protector suitable for the work to be proformed, and employees shall use such protectors. No unprotected person shall knowingly be subjected to a hazardous environmental condition. Suitable eye protectors shall be provided where machines or operations prosent the hazard of flying objects, glare, liquids, injurious radiation, or a combination of these hazards.

(2) Protectors shaall meet the following minimum requirements:

(i) They shall provide adequate protection against the particular haards for which they are designed.

(ii) They shall be reasonalby cpmfortable when worn under the designated conditions.

(iii) They shall fit snugly and shall not unduly interfere with the movements of the wearer.

(iv) They shall be durable.

(v) They shall be capable of being disinfected.

(vi) They shall be easily cleanable.

(vii) Protectors shall be kept clean and in good repair.

(3) Persons whose vision requires the use of corrective lenses in spectacles, and who are required by this standard tp wear eye protection, shall wear goggles or spectacles of one of the following types:

(i) Spectacles whose protective lenses provide optical correction.

(ii) Goggles that can be worn over corrective spectacles without disturbing the adjustment of the spectacles.

(iii) Goggles that incorporate corrective lenses mounted behind the prootective lenses.

(4) Every protector shall be distinctly marked to facilitate identification only of the manufacturer.

(5) When limitations or precautions are indicated by the manufacturer, they shall be transmitted to the user and care taken to see that such limitations and precautions are strictly observed.

(6) Design, construction, testing, and use of devices for eye and face protection shaall be in accordance with American Naational Standard for Occupational and Educaational Eye and Face Protection, Z87.1-1968.

§ 1910.134   Respiratory protection.

(a) *Permissible practice.* (1) In the control of those occupational diseases caused by breathing air contaminated with harmful dusts, fogs, fumes, mists, gases, smokes, sprays, or vapors, the primary objective shall be to prevent atmospheric contamination. This shall be accomplished as far as feasible by accepted engineering control measures (for example, enclosure or confinement of the operation, general and local ventilation, and substitution of less toxic materials). When effective engineering

§ 1910.134

controls are not feasible, or while they are being instituted, appropriate respirators shall be used pursuant to the following requirements.

(2) Respirators shall be provided by the employer when such equipment is necessary to protect the health of the employee. The employer shall provide the respirators which are applicable and suitable for the purpose intended. The employer shall be responsible for the establishment and maintenance of a respiratory protective program which shall include the requirements outlined in paragraph (b) of this section.

(3) The employee shall use the provided respiratory protection in accordance with instructions and training received.

(b) *Requirements for a minimal acceptable program.* (1) Written standard operating procedures governing the selection and use of respirators shall be established.

(2) Respirators shall be selected on the basis of hazards to which the worker is exposed.

(3) The user shall be instructed and trained in the proper use of respirators and their limitations.

(4) [Reserved]

(5) Respirators shall be regularly cleaned and disinfected. Those used by more than one worker shall be thoroughly cleaned and disinfected after each use.

(6) Respirators shall be stored in a convenient, clean, and sanitary location.

(7) Respirators used routinely shall be inspected during cleaning. Worn or deteriorated parts shall be replaced. Respirators for emergency use such as self-contained devices shall be thoroughly inspected at least once a month and after each use.

(8) Appropriate surveillance of work area conditions and degree of employee exposure or stress shall be maintained.

(9) There shall be regular inspection and evaluation to determine the continued effectiveness of the program.

(10) Persons should not be assigned to tasks requiring use of respirators unless it has been determined that they are physically able to perform the work and use the equipment. The local physician shall determine what health and physical conditions are pertinent. The respirator user's medical status should be reviewed periodically (for instance, annually).

(11) Respirators shall be selected from among those jointly approved by the Mine Safety and Health Administration and the National Institute for Occupational Safety and Health under the provisions of 30 CFR part 11.

(c) *Selection of respirators.* Proper selection of respirators shall be made according to the guidance of American National Standard Practices for Respiratory Protection Z88.2-1969.

(d) *Air quality.* (1) Compressed air, compressed oxygen, liquid air, and liquid oxygen used for respiration shall be of high purity. Oxygen shall meet the requirements of the United States Pharmacopoeia for medical or breathing oxygen. Breathing air shall meet at least the requirements of the specification for Grade D breathing air as described in Compressed Gas Association Commodity Specification G-7.1-1966. Compressed oxygen shall not be used in supplied-air respirators or in open circuit self-contained breathing apparatus that have previously used compressed air. Oxygen must never be used with air line respirators.

(2) Breathing air may be supplied to respirators from cylinders or air compressors.

(i) Cylinders shall be tested and maintained as prescribed in the Shipping Container Specification Regulations of the Department of Transportation (49 CFR part 178).

(ii) The compressor for supplying air shall be equipped with necessary safety and standby devices. A breathing air-type compressor shall be used. Compressors shall be constructed and situated so as to avoid entry of contaminated air into the system and suitable in-line air purifying sorbent beds and filters installed to further assure breathing air quality. A receiver of sufficient capacity to enable the respirator wearer to escape from a contaminated atmosphere in event of compressor failure, and alarms to indicate compressor failure and overheating shall be installed in the system. If an oil-lubricated compressor is used, it shall have a high-temperature or carbon monoxide alarm, or both. If only a

Occupational Safety and Health Admin., Labor § 1910.134

high-temperature alarm is used, the air from the compressor shall be frequently tested for carbon monoxide to insure that it meets the specifications in paragraph (d)(1) of this section.

(3) Air line couplings shall be incompatible with outlets for other gas systems to prevent inadvertent servicing of air line respirators with nonrespirable gases or oxygen.

(4) Breathing gas containers shall be marked in accordance with American National Standard Method of Marking Portable Compressed Gas Containers to Identify the Material Contained, Z48.1–1954; Federal Specification BB–A–1034a, June 21, 1968, Air, Compressed for Breathing Purposes; or Interim Federal Specification GG–B–00675b, April 27, 1965, Breathing Apparatus, Self-Contained.

(e) *Use of respirators.* (1) Standard procedures shall be developed for respirator use. These should include all information and guidance necessary for their proper selection, use, and care. Possible emergency and routine uses of respirators should be anticipated and planned for.

(2) The correct respirator shall be specified for each job. The respirator type is usually specified in the work procedures by a qualified individual supervising the respiratory protective program. The individual issuing them shall be adequately instructed to insure that the correct respirator is issued.

(3) Written procedures shall be prepared covering safe use of respirators in dangerous atmospheres that might be encountered in normal operations or in emergencies. Personnel shall be familiar with these procedures and the available respirators.

(i) In areas where the wearer, with failure of the respirator, could be overcome by a toxic or oxygen-deficient atmosphere, at least one additional man shall be present. Communications (visual, voice, or signal line) shall be maintained between both or all individuals present. Planning shall be such that one individual will be unaffected by any likely incident and have the proper rescue equipment to be able to assist the other(s) in case of emergency.

(ii) When self-contained breathing apparatus or hose masks with blowers are used in atmospheres immediately dangerous to life or health, standby men must be present with suitable rescue equipment.

(iii) Persons using air line respirators in atmospheres immediately hazardous to life or health shall be equipped with safety harnesses and safety lines for lifting or removing persons from hazardous atmospheres or other and equivalent provisions for the rescue of persons from hazardous atmospheres shall be used. A standby man or men with suitable self-contained breathing apparatus shall be at the nearest fresh air base for emergency rescue.

(4) Respiratory protection is no better than the respirator in use, even though it is worn conscientiously. Frequent random inspections shall be conducted by a qualified individual to assure that respirators are properly selected, used, cleaned, and maintained.

(5) For safe use of any respirator, it is essential that the user be properly instructed in its selection, use, and maintenance. Both supervisors and workers shall be so instructed by competent persons. Training shall provide the men an opportunity to handle the respirator, have it fitted properly, test its face-piece-to-face seal, wear it in normal air for a long familiarity period, and, finally, to wear it in a test atmosphere.

(i) Every respirator wearer shall receive fitting instructions including demonstrations and practice in how the respirator should be worn, how to adjust it, and how to determine if it fits properly. Respirators shall not be worn when conditions prevent a good face seal. Such conditions may be a growth of beard, sideburns, a skull cap that projects under the facepiece, or temple pieces on glasses. Also, the absence of one or both dentures can seriously affect the fit of a facepiece. The worker's diligence in observing these factors shall be evaluated by periodic check. To assure proper protection, the facepiece fit shall be checked by the wearer each time he puts on the respirator. This may be done by following the manufacturer's facepiece fitting instructions.

(ii) Providing respiratory protection for individuals wearing corrective glasses is a serious problem. A proper

415

seal cannot be established if the temple bars of eye glasses extend through the sealing edge of the full facepiece. As a temporary measure, glasses with short temple bars or without temple bars may be taped to the wearer's head. Wearing of contact lenses in contaminated atmospheres with a respirator shall not be allowed. Systems have been developed for mounting corrective lenses inside full facepieces. When a workman must wear corrective lenses as part of the facepiece, the facepiece and lenses shall be fitted by qualified individuals to provide good vision, comfort, and a gas-tight seal.

(iii) If corrective spectacles or goggles are required, they shall be worn so as not to affect the fit of the facepiece. Proper selection of equipment will minimize or avoid this problem.

(f) *Maintenance and care of respirators.* (1) A program for maintenance and care of respirators shall be adjusted to the type of plant, working conditions, and hazards involved, and shall include the following basic services:

(i) Inspection for defects (including a leak check),

(ii) Cleaning and disinfecting,

(iii) Repair,

(iv) Storage

Equipment shall be properly maintained to retain its original effectiveness.

(2) (i) All respirators shall be inspected routinely before and after each use. A respirator that is not routinely used but is kept ready for emergency use shall be inspected after each use and at least monthly to assure that it is in satisfactory working condition.

(ii) Self-contained breathing apparatus shall be inspected monthly. Air and oxygen cylinders shall be fully charged according to the manufacturer's instructions. It shall be determined that the regulator and warning devices function properly.

(iii) Respirator inspection shall include a check of the tightness of connections and the condition of the facepiece, headbands, valves, connecting tube, and canisters. Rubber or elastomer parts shall be inspected for pliability and signs of deterioration. Stretching and manipulating rubber or elastomer parts with a massaging action will keep them pliable and flexible and prevent them from taking a set during storage.

(iv) A record shall be kept of inspection dates and findings for respirators maintained for emergency use.

(3) Routinely used respirators shall be collected, cleaned, and disinfected as frequently as necessary to insure that proper protection is provided for the wearer. Respirators maintained for emergency use shall be cleaned and disinfected after each use.

(4) Replacement or repairs shall be done only by experienced persons with parts designed for the respirator. No attempt shall be made to replace components or to make adjustment or repairs beyond the manufacturer's recommendations. Reducing or admission valves or regulators shall be returned to the manufacturer or to a trained technician for adjustment or repair.

(5) (i) After inspection, cleaning, and necessary repair, respirators shall be stored to protect against dust, sunlight, heat, extreme cold, excessive moisture, or damaging chemicals. Respirators placed at stations and work areas for emergency use should be quickly accessible at all times and should be stored in compartments built for the purpose. The compartments should be clearly marked. Routinely used respirators, such as dust respirators, may be placed in plastic bags. Respirators should not be stored in such places as lockers or tool boxes unless they are in carrying cases or cartons.

(ii) Respirators should be packed or stored so that the facepiece and exhalation valve will rest in a normal position and function will not be impaired by the elastomer setting in an abnormal position.

(iii) Instructions for proper storage of emergency respirators, such as gas masks and self-contained breathing apparatus, are found in "use and care" instructions usually mounted inside the carrying case lid.

(g) *Identification of gas mask canisters.* (1) The primary means of identifying a gas mask canister shall be by means of properly worded labels. The secondary means of identifying a gas mask canister shall be by a color code.

(2) All who issue or use gas masks falling within the scope of this section

Occupational Safety and Health Admin., Labor §1910.134

shall see that all gas mask canisters purchased or used by them are properly labeled and colored in accordance with these requirements before they are placed in service and that the labels and colors are properly maintained at all times thereafter until the canisters have completely served their purpose.

(3) On each canister shall appear in bold letters the following:

(i)—
Canister for ———————————————
(Name for atmospheric contaminant)

or

Type N Gas Mask Canister

(ii) In addition, essentially the following wording shall appear beneath the appropriate phrase on the canister label: "For respiratory protection in atmospheres containing not more than ————————— percent by volume of ————————."
(Name of atmospheric contaminant)

(4) Canisters having a special high-efficiency filter for protection against radionuclides and other highly toxic particulates shall be labeled with a statement of the type and degree of protection afforded by the filter. The label shall be affixed to the neck end of, or to the gray stripe which is around and near the top of, the canister. The degree of protection shall be marked as the percent of penetration of the canister by a 0.3–micron-diameter dioctyl phthalate (DOP) smoke at a flow rate of 85 liters per minute.

(5) Each canister shall have a label warning that gas masks should be used only in atmospheres containing sufficient oxygen to support life (at least 16 percent by volume), since gas mask canisters are only designed to neutralize or remove contaminants from the air.

(6) Each gas mask canister shall be painted a distinctive color or combination of colors indicated in Table I–1. All colors used shall be such that they are clearly identifiable by the user and clearly distinguishable from one another. The color coating used shall offer a high degree of resistance to chipping, scaling, peeling, blistering, fading, and the effects of the ordinary atmospheres to which they may be exposed under normal conditions of storage and use. Appropriately colored pressure sensitive tape may be used for the stripes.

TABLE I–1

Atmospheric contaminants to be protected against	Colors assigned [1]
Acid gases	White.
Hydrocyanic acid gas	White with ½-inch green stripe completely around the canister near the bottom.
Chlorine gas	White with ½-inch yellow stripe completely around the canister near the bottom.
Organic vapors	Black.
Ammonia gas	Green.
Acid gases and ammonia gas	Green with ½-inch white stripe completely around the canister near the bottom.
Carbon monoxide	Blue.
Acid gases and organic vapors	Yellow.
Hydrocyanic acid gas and chloropicrin vapor	Yellow with ½-inch blue stripe completely around the canister near the bottom.
Acid gases, organic vapors, and ammonia gases	Brown.
Radioactive materials, excepting tritium and noble gases	Purple (Magenta).
Particulates (dusts, fumes, mists, fogs, or smokes) in combination with any of the above gases or vapors.	Canister color for contaminant, as designated above, with ½-inch gray stripe completely around the canister near the top.
All of the above atmospheric contaminants	Red with ½-inch gray stripe completely around the canister near the top.

[1] Gray shall not be assigned as the main color for a canister designed to remove acids or vapors.
NOTE: Orange shall be used as a complete body, or stripe color to represent gases not included in this table. The user will need to refer to the canister label to determine the degree of protection the canister will afford.

(Approved by the Office of Management and Budget under control number 1218–0099)

[39 FR 23502, June 27, 1974, as amended at 43 FR 49748, Oct. 24, 1978; 49 FR 5322, Feb. 10, 1984; 49 FR 18295, Apr. 30, 1984; 58 FR 35309, June 30, 1993]

Appendix 4B

29 CFR 1910.146
PERMIT REQUIRED CONFINED SPACES

§ 1910.146 Permit-required confined spaces.

(a) *Scope and application.* This section contains requirements for practices and procedures to protect employees in general industry from the hazards of entry into permit-required confined spaces. This section does not apply to agriculture, to construction, or to shipyard employment (Parts 1928, 1926, and 1915 of this chapter, respectively).

(b) *Definitions.*

Acceptable entry conditions means the conditions that must exist in a permit space to allow entry and to ensure that employees involved with a permit-required confined space entry can safely enter into and work within the space.

Attendant means an individual stationed outside one or more permit spaces who monitors the authorized entrants and who performs all attendant's duties assigned in the employer's permit space program.

Authorized entrant means an employee who is authorized by the employer to enter a permit space.

Blanking or blinding means the absolute closure of a pipe, line, or duct by the fastening of a solid plate (such as a spectacle blind or a skillet blind) that completely covers the bore and that is capable of withstanding the maximum pressure of the pipe, line, or duct with no leakage beyond the plate.

Confined space means a space that:
(1) Is large enough and so configured that an employee can bodily enter and perform assigned work; and
(2) Has limited or restricted means for entry or exit (for example, tanks, vessels, silos, storage bins, hoppers, vaults, and pits are spaces that may have limited means of entry.); and
(3) Is not designed for continuous employee occupancy.

Double block and bleed means the closure of a line, duct, or pipe by closing and locking or tagging two in-line valves and by opening and locking or tagging a drain or vent valve in the line between the two closed valves.

Emergency means any occurrence (including any failure of hazard control or monitoring equipment) or event internal or external to the permit space that could endanger entrants.

Engulfment means the surrounding and effective capture of a person by a liquid or finely divided (flowable) solid substance that can be aspirated to cause death by filling or plugging the respiratory system or that can exert enough force on the body to cause death by strangulation, constriction, or crushing.

Entry means the action by which a person passes through an opening into

§ 1910.146

a permit-required confined space. Entry includes ensuing work activities in that space and is considered to have occurred as soon as any part of the entrant's body breaks the plane of an opening into the space.

Entry permit (permit) means the written or printed document that is provided by the employer to allow and control entry into a permit space and that contains the information specified in paragraph (f) of this section.

Entry supervisor means the person (such as the employer, foreman, or crew chief) responsible for determining if acceptable entry conditions are present at a permit space where entry is planned, for authorizing entry and overseeing entry operations, and for terminating entry as required by this section.

NOTE: An entry supervisor also may serve as an attendant or as an authorized entrant, as long as that person is trained and equipped as required by this section for each role he or she fills. Also, the duties of entry supervisor may be passed from one individual to another during the course of an entry operation.

Hazardous atmosphere means an atmosphere that may expose employees to the risk of death, incapacitation, impairment of ability to self-rescue (that is, escape unaided from a permit space), injury, or acute illness from one or more of the following causes:

(1) Flammable gas, vapor, or mist in excess of 10 percent of its lower flammable limit (LFL);

(2) Airborne combustible dust at a concentration that meets or exceeds its LFL;

NOTE: This concentration may be approximated as a condition in which the dust obscures vision at a distance of 5 feet (1.52 m) or less.

(3) Atmospheric oxygen concentration below 19.5 percent or above 23.5 percent;

(4) Atmospheric concentration of any substance for which a dose or a permissible exposure limit is published in Subpart G, *Occupational Health and Environmental Control*, or in Subpart Z, *Toxic and Hazardous Substances*, of this part and which could result in employee exposure in excess of its dose or permissible exposure limit;

NOTE: An atmospheric concentration of any substance that is not capable of causing death, incapacitation, impairment of ability to self-rescue, injury, or acute illness due to its health effects is not covered by this provision.

(5) Any other atmospheric condition that is immediately dangerous to life or health.

NOTE: For air contaminants for which OSHA has not determined a dose or permissible exposure limit, other sources of information, such as Material Safety Data Sheets that comply with the Hazard Communication Standard, §1910.1200 of this part, published information, and internal documents can provide guidance in establishing acceptable atmospheric conditions.

Hot work permit means the employer's written authorization to perform operations (for example, riveting, welding, cutting, burning, and heating) capable of providing a source of ignition.

Immediately dangerous to life or health (IDLH) means any condition that poses an immediate or delayed threat to life or that would cause irreversible adverse health effects or that would interfere with an individual's ability to escape unaided from a permit space.

NOTE: Some materials—hydrogen fluoride gas and cadmium vapor, for example—may produce immediate transient effects that, even if severe, may pass without medical attention, but are followed by sudden, possibly fatal collapse 12–72 hours after exposure. The victim "feels normal" from recovery from transient effects until collapse. Such materials in hazardous quantities are considered to be "immediately" dangerous to life or health.

Inerting means the displacement of the atmosphere in a permit space by a noncombustible gas (such as nitrogen) to such an extent that the resulting atmosphere is noncombustible.

NOTE: This procedure produces an IDLH oxygen-deficient atmosphere.

Isolation means the process by which a permit space is removed from service and completely protected against the release of energy and material into the space by such means as: blanking or blinding; misaligning or removing sections of lines, pipes, or ducts; a double block and bleed system; lockout or tagout of all sources of energy; or blocking or disconnecting all mechanical linkages.

Occupational Safety and Health Admin., Labor § 1910.146

Line breaking means the intentional opening of a pipe, line, or duct that is or has been carrying flammable, corrosive, or toxic material, an inert gas, or any fluid at a volume, pressure, or temperature capable of causing injury.

Non-permit confined space means a confined space that does not contain or, with respect to atmospheric hazards, have the potential to contain any hazard capable of causing death or serious physical harm.

Oxygen deficient atmosphere means an atmosphere containing less than 19.5 percent oxygen by volume.

Oxygen enriched atmosphere means an atmosphere containing more than 23.5 percent oxygen by volume.

Permit-required confined space (permit space) means a confined space that has one or more of the following characteristics:

(1) Contains or has a potential to contain a hazardous atmosphere;

(2) Contains a material that has the potential for engulfing an entrant;

(3) Has an internal configuration such that an entrant could be trapped or asphyxiated by inwardly converging walls or by a floor which slopes downward and tapers to a smaller cross- section; or

(4) Contains any other recognized serious safety or health hazard.

Permit-required confined space program (permit space program) means the employer's overall program for controlling, and, where appropriate, for protecting employees from, permit space hazards and for regulating employee entry into permit spaces.

Permit system means the employer's written procedure for preparing and issuing permits for entry and for returning the permit space to service following termination of entry.

Prohibited condition means any condition in a permit space that is not allowed by the permit during the period when entry is authorized.

Rescue service means the personnel designated to rescue employees from permit spaces.

Retrieval system means the equipment (including a retrieval line, chest or full-body harness, wristlets, if appropriate, and a lifting device or anchor) used for non-entry rescue of persons from permit spaces.

Testing means the process by which the hazards that may confront entrants of a permit space are identified and evaluated. Testing includes specifying the tests that are to be performed in the permit space.

NOTE: Testing enables employers both to devise and implement adequate control measures for the protection of authorized entrants and to determine if acceptable entry conditions are present immediately prior to, and during, entry.

(c) *General requirements.* (1) The employer shall evaluate the workplace to determine if any spaces are permit- required confined spaces.

NOTE: Proper application of the decision flow chart in Appendix A to §1910.146 would facilitate compliance with this requirement.

(2) If the workplace contains permit spaces, the employer shall inform exposed employees, by posting danger signs or by any other equally effective means, of the existence and location of and the danger posed by the permit spaces.

NOTE: A sign reading "DANGER—PERMIT-REQUIRED CONFINED SPACE, DO NOT ENTER" or using other similar language would satisfy the requirement for a sign.

(3) If the employer decides that its employees will not enter permit spaces, the employer shall take effective measures to prevent its employees from entering the permit spaces and shall comply with paragraphs (c)(1), (c)(2), (c)(6), and (c)(8) of this section.

(4) If the employer decides that its employees will enter permit spaces, the employer shall develop and implement a written permit space program that complies with this section. The written program shall be available for inspection by employees and their authorized representatives.

(5) An employer may use the alternate procedures specified in paragraph (c)(5)(ii) of this section for entering a permit space under the conditions set forth in paragraph (c)(5)(i) of this section.

(i) An employer whose employees enter a permit space need not comply with paragraphs (d) through (f) and (h) through (k) of this section, provided that:

(A) The employer can demonstrate that the only hazard posed by the per-

§ 1910.146

mit space is an actual or potential hazardous atmosphere;

(B) The employer can demonstrate that continuous forced air ventilation alone is sufficient to maintain that permit space safe for entry;

(C) The employer develops monitoring and inspection data that supports the demonstrations required by paragraphs (c)(5)(i)(A) and (c)(5)(i)(B) of this section;

(D) If an initial entry of the permit space is necessary to obtain the data required by paragraph (c)(5)(i)(C) of this section, the entry is performed in compliance with paragraphs (d) through (k) of this section;

(E) The determinations and supporting data required by paragraphs (c)(5)(i)(A), (c)(5)(i)(B), and (c)(5)(i)(C) of this section are documented by the employer and are made available to each employee who enters the permit space under the terms of paragraph (c)(5) of this section; and

(F) Entry into the permit space under the terms of paragraph (c)(5)(i) of this section is performed in accordance with the requirements of paragraph (c)(5)(ii) of this section.

NOTE: See paragraph (c)(7) of this section for reclassification of a permit space after all hazards within the space have been eliminated.

(ii) The following requirements apply to entry into permit spaces that meet the conditions set forth in paragraph (c)(5)(i) of this section.

(A) Any conditions making it unsafe to remove an entrance cover shall be eliminated before the cover is removed.

(B) When entrance covers are removed, the opening shall be promptly guarded by a railing, temporary cover, or other temporary barrier that will prevent an accidental fall through the opening and that will protect each employee working in the space from foreign objects entering the space.

(C) Before an employee enters the space, the internal atmosphere shall be tested, with a calibrated direct-reading instrument, for the following conditions in the order given:

(*1*) Oxygen content,

(*2*) Flammable gases and vapors, and

(*3*) Potential toxic air contaminants.

(D) There may be no hazardous atmosphere within the space whenever any employee is inside the space.

(E) Continuous forced air ventilation shall be used, as follows:

(*1*) An employee may not enter the space until the forced air ventilation has eliminated any hazardous atmosphere;

(*2*) The forced air ventilation shall be so directed as to ventilate the immediate areas where an employee is or will be present within the space and shall continue until all employees have left the space;

(*3*) The air supply for the forced air ventilation shall be from a clean source and may not increase the hazards in the space.

(F) The atmosphere within the space shall be periodically tested as necessary to ensure that the continuous forced air ventilation is preventing the accumulation of a hazardous atmosphere.

(G) If a hazardous atmosphere is detected during entry:

(*1*) Each employee shall leave the space immediately;

(*2*) The space shall be evaluated to determine how the hazardous atmosphere developed; and

(*3*) Measures shall be implemented to protect employees from the hazardous atmosphere before any subsequent entry takes place.

(H) The employer shall verify that the space is safe for entry and that the pre-entry measures required by paragraph (c)(5)(ii) of this section have been taken, through a written certification that contains the date, the location of the space, and the signature of the person providing the certification. The certification shall be made before entry and shall be made available to each employee entering the space.

(6) When there are changes in the use or configuration of a non-permit confined space that might increase the hazards to entrants, the employer shall reevaluate that space and, if necessary, reclassify it as a permit-required confined space.

(7) A space classified by the employer as a permit-required confined space may be reclassified as a non-permit confined space under the following procedures:

Occupational Safety and Health Admin., Labor § 1910.146

(i) If the permit space poses no actual or potential atmospheric hazards and if all hazards within the space are eliminated without entry into the space, the permit space may be reclassified as a non-permit confined space for as long as the non-atmospheric hazards remain eliminated.

(ii) If it is necessary to enter the permit space to eliminate hazards, such entry shall be performed under paragraphs (d) through (k) of this section. If testing and inspection during that entry demonstrate that the hazards within the permit space have been eliminated, the permit space may be reclassified as a non-permit confined space for as long as the hazards remain eliminated.

NOTE: Control of atmospheric hazards through forced air ventilation does not constitute elimination of the hazards. Paragraph (c)(5) covers permit space entry where the employer can demonstrate that forced air ventilation alone will control all hazards in the space.

(iii) The employer shall document the basis for determining that all hazards in a permit space have been eliminated, through a certification that contains the date, the location of the space, and the signature of the person making the determination. The certification shall be made available to each employee entering the space.

(iv) If hazards arise within a permit space that has been declassified to a non-permit space under paragraph (c)(7) of this section, each employee in the space shall exit the space. The employer shall then reevaluate the space and determine whether it must be reclassified as a permit space, in accordance with other applicable provisions of this section.

(8) When an employer (host employer) arranges to have employees of another employer (contractor) perform work that involves permit space entry, the host employer shall:

(i) Inform the contractor that the workplace contains permit spaces and that permit space entry is allowed only through compliance with a permit space program meeting the requirements of this section;

(ii) Apprise the contractor of the elements, including the hazards identified and the host employer's experience with the space, that make the space in question a permit space;

(iii) Apprise the contractor of any precautions or procedures that the host employer has implemented for the protection of employees in or near permit spaces where contractor personnel will be working;

(iv) Coordinate entry operations with the contractor, when both host employer personnel and contractor personnel will be working in or near permit spaces, as required by paragraph (d)(11) of this section; and

(v) Debrief the contractor at the conclusion of the entry operations regarding the permit space program followed and regarding any hazards confronted or created in permit spaces during entry operations.

(9) In addition to complying with the permit space requirements that apply to all employers, each contractor who is retained to perform permit space entry operations shall:

(i) Obtain any available information regarding permit space hazards and entry operations from the host employer;

(ii) Coordinate entry operations with the host employer, when both host employer personnel and contractor personnel will be working in or near permit spaces, as required by paragraph (d)(11) of this section; and

(iii) Inform the host employer of the permit space program that the contractor will follow and of any hazards confronted or created in permit spaces, either through a debriefing or during the entry operation.

(d) *Permit-required confined space program* (permit space program). Under the permit space program required by paragraph (c)(4) of this section, the employer shall:

(1) Implement the measures necessary to prevent unauthorized entry;

(2) Identify and evaluate the hazards of permit spaces before employees enter them;

(3) Develop and implement the means, procedures, and practices necessary for safe permit space entry operations, including, but not limited to, the following:

(i) Specifying acceptable entry conditions;

(ii) Isolating the permit space;

§ 1910.146

(iii) Purging, inerting, flushing, or ventilating the permit space as necessary to eliminate or control atmospheric hazards;

(iv) Providing pedestrian, vehicle, or other barriers as necessary to protect entrants from external hazards; and

(v) Verifying that conditions in the permit space are acceptable for entry throughout the duration of an authorized entry.

(4) Provide the following equipment (specified in paragraphs (d)(4)(i) through (d)(4)(ix) of this section) at no cost to employees, maintain that equipment properly, and ensure that employees use that equipment properly:

(i) Testing and monitoring equipment needed to comply with paragraph (d)(5) of this section;

(ii) Ventilating equipment needed to obtain acceptable entry conditions;

(iii) Communications equipment necessary for compliance with paragraphs (h)(3) and (i)(5) of this section;

(iv) Personal protective equipment insofar as feasible engineering and work practice controls do not adequately protect employees;

(v) Lighting equipment needed to enable employees to see well enough to work safely and to exit the space quickly in an emergency;

(vi) Barriers and shields as required by paragraph (d)(3)(iv) of this section;

(vii) Equipment, such as ladders, needed for safe ingress and egress by authorized entrants;

(viii) Rescue and emergency equipment needed to comply with paragraph (d)(9) of this section, except to the extent that the equipment is provided by rescue services; and

(ix) Any other equipment necessary for safe entry into and rescue from permit spaces.

(5) Evaluate permit space conditions as follows when entry operations are conducted:

(i) Test conditions in the permit space to determine if acceptable entry conditions exist before entry is authorized to begin, except that, if isolation of the space is infeasible because the space is large or is part of a continuous system (such as a sewer), pre-entry testing shall be performed to the extent feasible before entry is authorized and, if entry is authorized, entry conditions shall be continuously monitored in the areas where authorized entrants are working;

(ii) Test or monitor the permit space as necessary to determine if acceptable entry conditions are being maintained during the course of entry operations; and

(iii) When testing for atmospheric hazards, test first for oxygen, then for combustible gases and vapors, and then for toxic gases and vapors.

NOTE: Atmospheric testing conducted in accordance with Appendix B to § 1910.146 would be considered as satisfying the requirements of this paragraph. For permit space operations in sewers, atmospheric testing conducted in accordance with Appendix B, as supplemented by Appendix E to § 1910.146, would be considered as satisfying the requirements of this paragraph.

(6) Provide at least one attendant outside the permit space into which entry is authorized for the duration of entry operations;

NOTE: Attendants may be assigned to monitor more than one permit space provided the duties described in paragraph (i) of this section can be effectively performed for each permit space that is monitored. Likewise, attendants may be stationed at any location outside the permit space to be monitored as long as the duties described in paragraph (i) of this section can be effectively performed for each permit space that is monitored.

(7) If multiple spaces are to be monitored by a single attendant, include in the permit program the means and procedures to enable the attendant to respond to an emergency affecting one or more of the permit spaces being monitored without distraction from the attendant's responsibilities under paragraph (i) of this section;

(8) Designate the persons who are to have active roles (as, for example, authorized entrants, attendants, entry supervisors, or persons who test or monitor the atmosphere in a permit space) in entry operations, identify the duties of each such employee, and provide each such employee with the training required by paragraph (g) of this section;

(9) Develop and implement procedures for summoning rescue and emergency services, for rescuing entrants from permit spaces, for providing nec-

APPENDIX 4B

Occupational Safety and Health Admin., Labor §1910.146

essary emergency services to rescued employees, and for preventing unauthorized personnel from attempting a rescue;

(10) Develop and implement a system for the preparation, issuance, use, and cancellation of entry permits as required by this section;

(11) Develop and implement procedures to coordinate entry operations when employees of more than one employer are working simultaneously as authorized entrants in a permit space, so that employees of one employer do not endanger the employees of any other employer;

(12) Develop and implement procedures (such as closing off a permit space and canceling the permit) necessary for concluding the entry after entry operations have been completed;

(13) Review entry operations when the employer has reason to believe that the measures taken under the permit space program may not protect employees and revise the program to correct deficiencies found to exist before subsequent entries are authorized; and

NOTE: Examples of circumstances requiring the review of the permit space program are: any unauthorized entry of a permit space, the detection of a permit space hazard not covered by the permit, the detection of a condition prohibited by the permit, the occurrence of an injury or near-miss during entry, a change in the use or configuration of a permit space, and employee complaints about the effectiveness of the program.

(14) Review the permit space program, using the canceled permits retained under paragraph (e)(6) of this section within 1 year after each entry and revise the program as necessary, to ensure that employees participating in entry operations are protected from permit space hazards.

NOTE: Employers may perform a single annual review covering all entries performed during a 12-month period. If no entry is performed during a 12-month period, no review is necessary.

Appendix C to §1910.146 presents examples of permit space programs that are considered to comply with the requirements of paragraph (d) of this section.

(e) *Permit system.* (1) Before entry is authorized, the employer shall document the completion of measures required by paragraph (d)(3) of this section by preparing an entry permit.

NOTE: Appendix D to §1910.146 presents examples of permits whose elements are considered to comply with the requirements of this section.

(2) Before entry begins, the entry supervisor identified on the permit shall sign the entry permit to authorize entry.

(3) The completed permit shall be made available at the time of entry to all authorized entrants, by posting it at the entry portal or by any other equally effective means, so that the entrants can confirm that pre-entry preparations have been completed.

(4) The duration of the permit may not exceed the time required to complete the assigned task or job identified on the permit in accordance with paragraph (f)(2) of this section.

(5) The entry supervisor shall terminate entry and cancel the entry permit when:

(i) The entry operations covered by the entry permit have been completed; or

(ii) A condition that is not allowed under the entry permit arises in or near the permit space.

(6) The employer shall retain each canceled entry permit for at least 1 year to facilitate the review of the permit-required confined space program required by paragraph (d)(14) of this section. Any problems encountered during an entry operation shall be noted on the pertinent permit so that appropriate revisions to the permit space program can be made.

(f) *Entry permit.* The entry permit that documents compliance with this section and authorizes entry to a permit space shall identify:

(1) The permit space to be entered;

(2) The purpose of the entry;

(3) The date and the authorized duration of the entry permit;

(4) The authorized entrants within the permit space, by name or by such other means (for example, through the use of rosters or tracking systems) as will enable the attendant to determine quickly and accurately, for the duration of the permit, which authorized entrants are inside the permit space;

§ 1910.146

NOTE: This requirement may be met by inserting a reference on the entry permit as to the means used, such as a roster or tracking system, to keep track of the authorized entrants within the permit space.

(5) The personnel, by name, currently serving as attendants;

(6) The individual, by name, currently serving as entry supervisor, with a space for the signature or initials of the entry supervisor who originally authorized entry;

(7) The hazards of the permit space to be entered;

(8) The measures used to isolate the permit space and to eliminate or control permit space hazards before entry;

NOTE: Those measures can include the lockout or tagging of equipment and procedures for purging, inerting, ventilating, and flushing permit spaces.

(9) The acceptable entry conditions;

(10) The results of initial and periodic tests performed under paragraph (d)(5) of this section, accompanied by the names or initials of the testers and by an indication of when the tests were performed;

(11) The rescue and emergency services that can be summoned and the means (such as the equipment to use and the numbers to call) for summoning those services;

(12) The communication procedures used by authorized entrants and attendants to maintain contact during the entry;

(13) Equipment, such as personal protective equipment, testing equipment, communications equipment, alarm systems, and rescue equipment, to be provided for compliance with this section;

(14) Any other information whose inclusion is necessary, given the circumstances of the particular confined space, in order to ensure employee safety; and

(15) Any additional permits, such as for hot work, that have been issued to authorize work in the permit space.

(g) *Training.* (1) The employer shall provide training so that all employees whose work is regulated by this section acquire the understanding, knowledge, and skills necessary for the safe performance of the duties assigned under this section.

(2) Training shall be provided to each affected employee:

(i) Before the employee is first assigned duties under this section;

(ii) Before there is a change in assigned duties;

(iii) Whenever there is a change in permit space operations that presents a hazard about which an employee has not previously been trained;

(iv) Whenever the employer has reason to believe either that there are deviations from the permit space entry procedures required by paragraph (d)(3) of this section or that there are inadequacies in the employee's knowledge or use of these procedures.

(3) The training shall establish employee proficiency in the duties required by this section and shall introduce new or revised procedures, as necessary, for compliance with this section.

(4) The employer shall certify that the training required by paragraphs (g)(1) through (g)(3) of this section has been accomplished. The certification shall contain each employee's name, the signatures or initials of the trainers, and the dates of training. The certification shall be available for inspection by employees and their authorized representatives.

(h) *Duties of authorized entrants.* The employer shall ensure that all authorized entrants:

(1) Know the hazards that may be faced during entry, including information on the mode, signs or symptoms, and consequences of the exposure;

(2) Properly use equipment as required by paragraph (d)(4) of this section;

(3) Communicate with the attendant as necessary to enable the attendant to monitor entrant status and to enable the attendant to alert entrants of the need to evacuate the space as required by paragraph (i)(6) of this section;

(4) Alert the attendant whenever:

(i) The entrant recognizes any warning sign or symptom of exposure to a dangerous situation, or

(ii) The entrant detects a prohibited condition; and

(5) Exit from the permit space as quickly as possible whenever:

(i) An order to evacuate is given by the attendant or the entry supervisor,

Occupational Safety and Health Admin., Labor § 1910.146

(ii) The entrant recognizes any warning sign or symptom of exposure to a dangerous situation,

(iii) The entrant detects a prohibited condition, or

(iv) An evacuation alarm is activated.

(i) *Duties of attendants.* The employer shall ensure that each attendant:

(1) Knows the hazards that may be faced during entry, including information on the mode, signs or symptoms, and consequences of the exposure;

(2) Is aware of possible behavioral effects of hazard exposure in authorized entrants;

(3) Continuously maintains an accurate count of authorized entrants in the permit space and ensures that the means used to identify authorized entrants under paragraph (f)(4) of this section accurately identifies who is in the permit space;

(4) Remains outside the permit space during entry operations until relieved by another attendant;

NOTE: When the employer's permit entry program allows attendant entry for rescue, attendants may enter a permit space to attempt a rescue if they have been trained and equipped for rescue operations as required by paragraph (k)(1) of this section and if they have been relieved as required by paragraph (i)(4) of this section.

(5) Communicates with authorized entrants as necessary to monitor entrant status and to alert entrants of the need to evacuate the space under paragraph (i)(6) of this section;

(6) Monitors activities inside and outside the space to determine if it is safe for entrants to remain in the space and orders the authorized entrants to evacuate the permit space immediately under any of the following conditions:

(i) If the attendant detects a prohibited condition;

(ii) If the attendant detects the behavioral effects of hazard exposure in an authorized entrant;

(iii) If the attendant detects a situation outside the space that could endanger the authorized entrants; or

(iv) If the attendant cannot effectively and safely perform all the duties required under paragraph (i) of this section;

(7) Summon rescue and other emergency services as soon as the attendant determines that authorized entrants may need assistance to escape from permit space hazards;

(8) Takes the following actions when unauthorized persons approach or enter a permit space while entry is underway:

(i) Warn the unauthorized persons that they must stay away from the permit space;

(ii) Advise the unauthorized persons that they must exit immediately if they have entered the permit space; and

(iii) Inform the authorized entrants and the entry supervisor if unauthorized persons have entered the permit space;

(9) Performs non-entry rescues as specified by the employer's rescue procedure; and

(10) Performs no duties that might interfere with the attendant's primary duty to monitor and protect the authorized entrants.

(j) *Duties of entry supervisors.* The employer shall ensure that each entry supervisor:

(1) Knows the hazards that may be faced during entry, including information on the mode, signs or symptoms, and consequences of the exposure;

(2) Verifies, by checking that the appropriate entries have been made on the permit, that all tests specified by the permit have been conducted and that all procedures and equipment specified by the permit are in place before endorsing the permit and allowing entry to begin;

(3) Terminates the entry and cancels the permit as required by paragraph (e)(5) of this section;

(4) Verifies that rescue services are available and that the means for summoning them are operable;

(5) Removes unauthorized individuals who enter or who attempt to enter the permit space during entry operations; and

(6) Determines, whenever responsibility for a permit space entry operation is transferred and at intervals dictated by the hazards and operations performed within the space, that entry operations remain consistent with terms of the entry permit and that acceptable entry conditions are maintained.

§ 1910.146

(k) *Rescue and emergency services.* (1) The following requirements apply to employers who have employees enter permit spaces to perform rescue services.

(i) The employer shall ensure that each member of the rescue service is provided with, and is trained to use properly, the personal protective equipment and rescue equipment necessary for making rescues from permit spaces.

(ii) Each member of the rescue service shall be trained to perform the assigned rescue duties. Each member of the rescue service shall also receive the training required of authorized entrants under paragraph (g) of this section.

(iii) Each member of the rescue service shall practice making permit space rescues at least once every 12 months, by means of simulated rescue operations in which they remove dummies, manikins, or actual persons from the actual permit spaces or from representative permit spaces. Representative permit spaces shall, with respect to opening size, configuration, and accessibility, simulate the types of permit spaces from which rescue is to be performed.

(iv) Each member of the rescue service shall be trained in basic first-aid and in cardiopulmonary resuscitation (CPR). At least one member of the rescue service holding current certification in first aid and in CPR shall be available.

(2) When an employer (host employer) arranges to have persons other than the host employer's employees perform permit space rescue, the host employer shall:

(i) Inform the rescue service of the hazards they may confront when called on to perform rescue at the host employer's facility, and

(ii) Provide the rescue service with access to all permit spaces from which rescue may be necessary so that the rescue service can develop appropriate rescue plans and practice rescue operations.

(3) To facilitate non-entry rescue, retrieval systems or methods shall be used whenever an authorized entrant enters a permit space, unless the retrieval equipment would increase the overall risk of entry or would not contribute to the rescue of the entrant. Retrieval systems shall meet the following requirements.

(i) Each authorized entrant shall use a chest or full body harness, with a retrieval line attached at the center of the entrant's back near shoulder level, or above the entrant's head. Wristlets may be used in lieu of the chest or full body harness if the employer can demonstrate that the use of a chest or full body harness is infeasible or creates a greater hazard and that the use of wristlets is the safest and most effective alternative.

(ii) The other end of the retrieval line shall be attached to a mechanical device or fixed point outside the permit space in such a manner that rescue can begin as soon as the rescuer becomes aware that rescue is necessary. A mechanical device shall be available to retrieve personnel from vertical type permit spaces more than 5 feet (1.52 m) deep.

(4) If an injured entrant is exposed to a substance for which a Material Safety Data Sheet (MSDS) or other similar written information is required to be kept at the worksite, that MSDS or written information shall be made available to the medical facility treating the exposed entrant.

[58 FR 4549, Jan. 14, 1993; 58 FR 34885, June 29, 1993, as amended at 59 FR 26114, May 19, 1994]

APPENDICES TO § 1910.146—PERMIT-REQUIRED CONFINED SPACES

NOTE: Appendices A through E serve to provide information and non-mandatory guidelines to assist employers and employees in complying with the appropriate requirements of this section.

APPENDIX 4B

Occupational Safety and Health Admin., Labor § 1910.146

APPENDIX A TO § 1910.146—PERMIT-REQUIRED CONFINED SPACE DECISION FLOW CHART

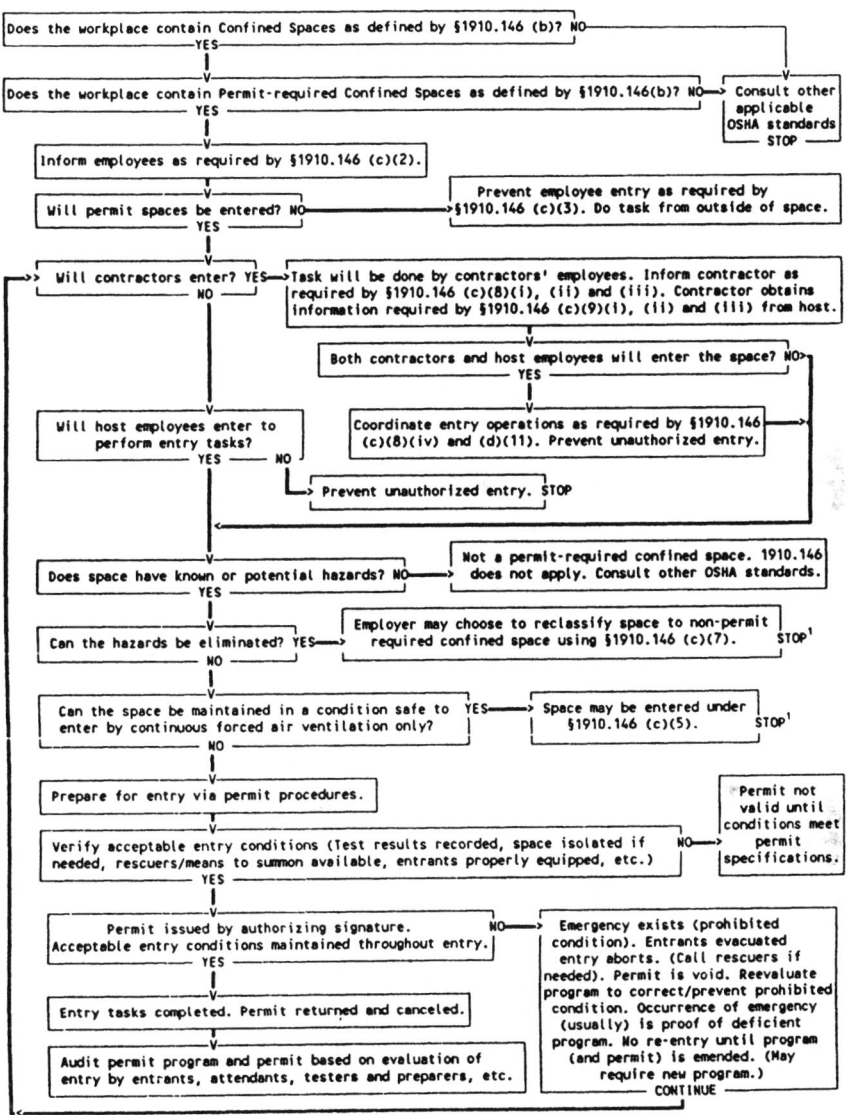

[1] Spaces may have to be evacuated and re-evaluated if hazards arise during entry

[58 FR 4549, Jan. 14, 1993; 58 FR 34846, June 29, 1993]

§ 1910.146

APPENDIX B TO § 1910.146—PROCEDURES FOR ATMOSPHERIC TESTING

Atmospheric testing is required for two distinct purposes: evaluation of the hazards of the permit space and verification that acceptable entry conditions for entry into that space exist.

(1) *Evaluation testing.* The atmosphere of a confined space should be analyzed using equipment of sufficient sensitivity and specificity to identify and evaluate any hazardous atmospheres that may exist or arise, so that appropriate permit entry procedures can be developed and acceptable entry conditions stipulated for that space. Evaluation and interpretation of these data, and development of the entry procedure, should be done by, or reviewed by, a technically qualified professional (e.g., OSHA consultation service, or certified industrial hygienist, registered safety engineer, certified safety professional, certified marine chemist, etc.) based on evaluation of all serious hazards.

(2) *Verification testing.* The atmosphere of a permit space which may contain a hazardous atmosphere should be tested for residues of all contaminants identified by evaluation testing using permit specified equipment to determine that residual concentrations at the time of testing and entry are within the range of acceptable entry conditions. Results of testing (i.e., actual concentration, etc.) should be recorded on the permit in the space provided adjacent to the stipulated acceptable entry condition.

(3) *Duration of testing.* Measurement of values for each atmospheric parameter should be made for at least the minimum response time of the test instrument specified by the manufacturer.

(4) *Testing stratified atmospheres.* When monitoring for entries involving a descent into atmospheres that may be stratified, the atmospheric envelope should be tested a distance of approximately 4 feet (1.22 m) in the direction of travel and to each side. If a sampling probe is used, the entrant's rate of progress should be slowed to accommodate the sampling speed and detector response.

(5) *Order of testing.* A test for oxygen is performed first because most combustible gas meters are oxygen dependent and will not provide reliable readings in an oxygen deficient atmosphere. Combustible gasses are tested for next because the threat of fire or explosion is both more immediate and more life threatening, in most cases, than exposure to toxic gasses and vapors. If tests for toxic gasses and vapors are necessary, they are performed last.

APPENDIX C TO § 1910.146—EXAMPLES OF PERMIT-REQUIRED CONFINED SPACE PROGRAMS

Example 1.

Workplace. Sewer entry.

Potential hazards. The employees could be exposed to the following:

Engulfment.

Presence of toxic gases. Equal to or more than 10 ppm hydrogen sulfide measured as an 8-hour time-weighted average. If the presence of other toxic contaminants is suspected, specific monitoring programs will be developed.

Presence of explosive/flammable gases. Equal to or greater than 10% of the lower flammable limit (LFL).

Oxygen Deficiency. A concentration of oxygen in the atmosphere equal to or less than 19.5% by volume.

A. *Entry Without Permit/Attendant*

Certification. Confined spaces may be entered without the need for a written permit or attendant provided that the space can be maintained in a safe condition for entry by mechanical ventilation alone, as provided in §1910.146(c)(5). All spaces shall be considered permit-required confined spaces until the pre-entry procedures demonstrate otherwise. Any employee required or permitted to pre-check or enter an enclosed/confined space shall have successfully completed, -as a minimum, the training as required by the following sections of these procedures. *A written copy of operating and rescue procedures as required by these procedures shall be at the work site for the duration of the job.* The Confined Space Pre-Entry Check List must be completed by the LEAD WORKER before entry into a confined space. This list verifies completion of items listed below. This check list shall be kept at the job site for duration of the job. If circumstances dictate an interruption in the work, the permit space must be re-evaluated and a new check list must be completed.

Control of atmospheric and engulfment hazards.

Pumps and Lines. All pumps and lines which may reasonably cause contaminants to flow into the space shall be disconnected, blinded and locked out, or effectively isolated by other means to prevent development of dangerous air contamination or engulfment. Not all laterals to sewers or storm drains require blocking. However, where experience or knowledge of industrial use indicates there is a reasonable potential for contamination of air or engulfment into an occupied sewer, then all affected laterals shall be blocked. If blocking and/or isolation requires entry into the space the provisions for entry into a permit- required confined space must be implemented.

Surveillance. The surrounding area shall be surveyed to avoid hazards such as drifting vapors from the tanks, piping, or sewers.

Testing. The atmosphere within the space will be tested to determine whether dangerous air contamination and/or oxygen defi-

APPENDIX 4B

Occupational Safety and Health Admin., Labor § 1910.146

ciency exists. Detector tubes, alarm only gas monitors and explosion meters are examples of monitoring equipment that may be used to test permit space atmospheres. Testing shall be performed by the LEAD WORKER who has successfully completed the Gas Detector training for the monitor he will use. The minimum parameters to be monitored are oxygen deficiency, LFL, and hydrogen sulfide concentration. A written record of the pre-entry test results shall be made and kept at the work site for the duration of the job. The supervisor will certify in writing, based upon the results of the pre-entry testing, that all hazards have been eliminated. Affected employees shall be able to review the testing results. The most hazardous conditions shall govern when work is being performed in two adjoining, connecting spaces.

Entry Procedures. If there are no non-atmospheric hazards present and if the pre-entry tests show there is no dangerous air contamination and/or oxygen deficiency within the space and there is no reason to believe that any is likely to develop, entry into and work within may proceed. Continuous testing of the atmosphere in the immediate vicinity of the workers within the space shall be accomplished. The workers will immediately leave the permit space when any of the gas monitor alarm set points are reached as defined. Workers will not return to the area until a SUPERVISOR who has completed the gas detector training has used a direct reading gas detector to evaluate the situation and has determined that it is safe to enter.

Rescue. Arrangements for rescue services are not required where there is no attendant. See the rescue portion of section B., below, for instructions regarding rescue planning where an entry permit is required.

B. *Entry Permit Required*

Permits. Confined Space Entry Permit. All spaces shall be considered permit-required confined spaces until the pre-entry procedures demonstrate otherwise. Any employee required or permitted to pre-check or enter a permit-required confined space shall have successfully completed, as a minimum, the training as required by the following sections of these procedures. *A written copy of operating and rescue procedures as required by these procedures shall be at the work site for the duration of the job.* The Confined Space Entry Permit must be completed before approval can be given to enter a permit-required confined space. This permit verifies completion of items listed below. This permit shall be kept at the job site for the duration of the job. If circumstances cause an interruption in the work or a change in the alarm conditions for which entry was approved, a new Confined Space Entry Permit must be completed.

Control of atmospheric and engulfment hazards.

Surveillance. The surrounding area shall be surveyed to avoid hazards such as drifting vapors from tanks, piping or sewers.

Testing. The confined space atmosphere shall be tested to determine whether dangerous air contamination and/or oxygen deficiency exists. A direct reading gas monitor shall be used. Testing shall be performed by the SUPERVISOR who has successfully completed the gas detector training for the monitor he will use. The minimum parameters to be monitored are oxygen deficiency, LFL and hydrogen sulfide concentration. A written record of the pre-entry test results shall be made and kept at the work site for the duration of the job. Affected employees shall be able to review the testing results. The most hazardous conditions shall govern when work is being performed in two adjoining, connected spaces.

Space Ventilation. Mechanical ventilation systems, where applicable, shall be set at 100% outside air. Where possible, open additional manholes to increase air circulation. Use portable blowers to augment natural circulation if needed. After a suitable ventilating period, repeat the testing. Entry may not begin until testing has demonstrated that the hazardous atmosphere has been eliminated.

Entry Procedures. The following procedure shall be observed under any of the following conditions: 1.) Testing demonstrates the existence of dangerous or deficient conditions and additional ventilation cannot reduce concentrations to safe levels; 2.) The atmosphere tests as safe but unsafe conditions can reasonably be expected to develop; 3.) It is not feasible to provide for ready exit from spaces equipped with automatic fire suppression systems and it is not practical or safe to deactivate such systems; or 4.) An emergency exists and it is not feasible to wait for pre-entry procedures to take effect.

All personnel must be trained. A self contained breathing apparatus shall be worn by any person entering the space. At least one worker shall stand by the outside of the space ready to give assistance in case of emergency. The standby worker shall have a self contained breathing apparatus available for immediate use. There shall be at least one additional worker within sight or call of the standby worker. Continuous powered communications shall be maintained between the worker within the confined space and standby personnel.

If at any time there is any questionable action or non- movement by the worker inside, a verbal check will be made. If there is no response, the worker will be moved immediately. *Exception:* If the worker is disabled due to falling or impact, he/she shall not be removed from the confined space unless there is immediate danger to his/her life. Local fire department rescue personnel shall

447

§ 1910.146

be notified immediately. The standby worker may only enter the confined space in case of an emergency (wearing the self contained breathing apparatus) and only after being relieved by another worker. Safety belt or harness with attached lifeline shall be used by all workers entering the space with the free end of the line secured outside the entry opening. The standby worker shall attempt to remove a disabled worker via his lifeline before entering the space.

When practical, these spaces shall be entered through side openings—those within 3 1/2 feet (1.07 m) of the bottom. When entry must be through a top opening, the safety belt shall be of the harness type that suspends a person upright and a hoisting device or similar apparatus shall be available for lifting workers out of the space.

In any situation where their use may endanger the worker, use of a hoisting device or safety belt and attached lifeline may be discontinued.

When dangerous air contamination is attributable to flammable and/or explosive substances, lighting and electrical equipment shall be Class 1, Division 1 rated per National Electrical Code and no ignition sources shall be introduced into the area.

Continuous gas monitoring shall be performed during all confined space operations. If alarm conditions change adversely, entry personnel shall exit the confined space and a new confined space permit issued.

Rescue. Call the fire department services for rescue. Where immediate hazards to injured personnel are present, workers at the site shall implement emergency procedures to fit the situation.

Example 2.

Workplace. Meat and poultry rendering plants.

Cookers and dryers are either batch or continuous in their operation. Multiple batch cookers are operated in parallel. When one unit of a multiple set is shut down for repairs, means are available to isolate that unit from the others which remain in operation.

Cookers and dryers are horizontal, cylindrical vessels equipped with a center, rotating shaft and agitator paddles or discs. If the inner shell is jacketed, it is usually heated with steam at pressures up to 150 psig (1034.25 kPa). The rotating shaft assembly of the continuous cooker or dryer is also steam heated.

Potential Hazards. The recognized hazards associated with cookers and dryers are the risk that employees could be:
1. Struck or caught by rotating agitator;
2. Engulfed in raw material or hot, recycled fat;
3. Burned by steam from leaks into the cooker/dryer steam jacket or the condenser duct system if steam valves are not properly closed and locked out;
4. Burned by contact with hot metal surfaces, such as the agitator shaft assembly, or inner shell of the cooker/dryer;
5. Heat stress caused by warm atmosphere inside cooker/dryer;
6. Slipping and falling on grease in the cooker/dryer;
7. Electrically shocked by faulty equipment taken into the cooker/dryer;
8. Burned or overcome by fire or products of combustion; or
9. Overcome by fumes generated by welding or cutting done on grease covered surfaces.

Permits. The supervisor in this case is always present at the cooker/dryer or other permit entry confined space when entry is made. The supervisor must follow the pre-entry isolation procedures described in the entry permit in preparing for entry, and ensure that the protective clothing, ventilating equipment and any other equipment required by the permit are at the entry site.

Control of hazards. Mechanical. Lock out main power switch to agitator motor at main power panel. Affix tag to the lock to inform others that a permit entry confined space entry is in progress.

Engulfment. Close all valves in the raw material blow line. Secure each valve in its closed position using chain and lock. Attach a tag to the valve and chain warning that a permit entry confined space entry is in progress. The same procedure shall be used for securing the fat recycle valve.

Burns and heat stress. Close steam supply valves to jacket and secure with chains and tags. Insert solid blank at flange in cooker vent line to condenser manifold duct system. Vent cooker/dryer by opening access door at discharge end and top center door to allow natural ventilation throughout the entry. If faster cooling is needed, use an portable ventilation fan to increase ventilation. Cooling water may be circulated through the jacket to reduce both outer and inner surface temperatures of cooker/dryers faster. Check air and inner surface temperatures in cooker/dryer to assure they are within acceptable limits before entering, or use proper protective clothing.

Fire and fume hazards. Careful site preparation, such as cleaning the area within 4 inches (10.16 cm) of all welding or torch cutting operations, and proper ventilation are the preferred controls. All welding and cutting operations shall be done in accordance with the requirements of 29 CFR Part 1910, Subpart Q, OSHA's welding standard. Proper ventilation may be achieved by local exhaust ventilation, or the use of portable ventilation fans, or a combination of the two practices.

APPENDIX 4B

Occupational Safety and Health Admin., Labor § 1910.146

Electrical shock. Electrical equipment used in cooker/dryers shall be in serviceable condition.

Slips and falls. Remove residual grease before entering cooker/dryer.

Attendant. The supervisor shall be the attendant for employees entering cooker/dryers.

Permit. The permit shall specify how isolation shall be done and any other preparations needed before making entry. This is especially important in parallel arrangements of cooker/dryers so that the entire operation need not be shut down to allow safe entry into one unit.

Rescue. When necessary, the attendant shall call the fire department as previously arranged.

Example 3.

Workplace. Workplaces where tank cars, trucks, and trailers, dry bulk tanks and trailers, railroad tank cars, and similar portable tanks are fabricated or serviced.

A. *During fabrication.* These tanks and drybulk carriers are entered repeatedly throughout the fabrication process. These products are not configured identically, but the manufacturing processes by which they are made are very similar.

Sources of hazards. In addition to the mechanical hazards arising from the risks that an entrant would be injured due to contact with components of the tank or the tools being used, there is also the risk that a worker could be injured by breathing fumes from welding materials or mists or vapors from materials used to coat the tank interior. In addition, many of these vapors and mists are flammable, so the failure to properly ventilate a tank could lead to a fire or explosion.

Control of hazards.

Welding. Local exhaust ventilation shall be used to remove welding fumes once the tank or carrier is completed to the point that workers may enter and exit only through a manhole. (Follow the requirements of 29 CFR 1910, Subpart Q, OSHA's welding standard, at all times.) Welding gas tanks may never be brought into a tank or carrier that is a permit entry confined space.

Application of interior coatings/linings. Atmospheric hazards shall be controlled by forced air ventilation sufficient to keep the atmospheric concentration of flammable materials below 10% of the lower flammable limit (LFL) (or lower explosive limit (LEL), whichever term is used locally). The appropriate respirators are provided and shall be used in addition to providing forced ventilation if the forced ventilation does not maintain acceptable respiratory conditions.

Permits. Because of the repetitive nature of the entries in these operations, an "Area Entry Permit" will be issued for a 1 month period to cover those production areas where tanks are fabricated to the point that entry and exit are made using manholes.

Authorization. Only the area supervisor may authorize an employee to enter a tank within the permit area. The area supervisor must determine that conditions in the tank trailer, dry bulk trailer or truck, etc. meet permit requirements before authorizing entry.

Attendant. The area supervisor shall designate an employee to maintain communication by employer specified means with employees working in tanks to ensure their safety. The attendant may not enter any permit entry confined space to rescue an entrant or for any other reason, unless authorized by the rescue procedure and, and even then, only after calling the rescue team and being relieved by as attendant by another worker.

Communications and observation. Communications between attendant and entrant(s) shall be maintained throughout entry. Methods of communication that may be specified by the permit include voice, voice powered radio, tapping or rapping codes on tank walls, signalling tugs on a rope, and the attendant's observation that work activities such as chipping, grinding, welding, spraying, etc., which require deliberate operator control continue normally. These activities often generate so much noise that the necessary hearing protection makes communication by voice difficult.

Rescue procedures. Acceptable rescue procedures include entry by a team of employee-rescuers, use of public emergency services, and procedures for breaching the tank. The area permit specifies which procedures are available, but the area supervisor makes the final decision based on circumstances. (Certain injuries may make it necessary to breach the tank to remove a person rather than risk additional injury by removal through an existing manhole. However, the supervisor must ensure that no breaching procedure used for rescue would violate terms of the entry permit. For instance, if the tank must be breached by cutting with a torch, the tank surfaces to be cut must be free of volatile or combustible coatings within 4 inches (10.16 cm) of the cutting line and the atmosphere within the tank must be below the LFL.

Retrieval line and harnesses. The retrieval lines and harnesses generally required under this standard are usually impractical for use in tanks because the internal configuration of the tanks and their interior baffles and other structures would prevent rescuers from hauling out injured entrants. However, unless the rescue procedure calls for breaching the tank for rescue, the rescue team shall be

§ 1910.146

trained in the use of retrieval lines and harnesses for removing injured employees through manholes.

B. *Repair or service of "used" tanks and bulk trailers.*

Sources of hazards. In addition to facing the potential hazards encountered in fabrication or manufacturing, tanks or trailers which have been in service may contain residues of dangerous materials, whether left over from the transportation of hazardous cargoes or generated by chemical or bacterial action on residues of non-hazardous cargoes.

Control of atmospheric hazards. A "used" tank shall be brought into areas where tank entry is authorized only after the tank has been emptied, cleansed (without employee entry) of any residues, and purged of any potential atmospheric hazards.

Welding. In addition to tank cleaning for control of atmospheric hazards, coating and surface materials shall be removed 4 inches (10.16 cm) or more from any surface area where welding or other torch work will be done and care taken that the atmosphere within the tank remains well below the LFL. (Follow the requirements of 29 CFR 1910, Subpart Q, OSHA's welding standard, at all times.)

Permits. An entry permit valid for up to 1 year shall be issued prior to authorization of entry into used tank trailers, dry bulk trailers or trucks. In addition to the pre-entry cleaning requirement, this permit shall require the employee safeguards specified for new tank fabrication or construction permit areas.

Authorization. Only the area supervisor may authorize an employee to enter a tank trailer, dry bulk trailer or truck within the permit area. The area supervisor must determine that the entry permit requirements have been met before authorizing entry.

APPENDIX 4B

Occupational Safety and Health Admin., Labor §1910.146

APPENDIX D TO §1910.146—SAMPLE PERMITS

```
                        Appendix D - 1
                  Confined Space Entry Permit
    Date & Time Issued: _____     Date and Time Expires: _____
    Job site/Space I.D.: _____     Job Supervisor: _____
    Equipment to be worked on: _____     Work to be performed: _____
    Stand-by personnel: _____

 1. Atmospheric Checks:   Time _____
                          Oxygen _____ %
                          Explosive ___ % L.F.L.
                          Toxic _____ PPM

 2. Tester's signature: _____

 3. Source isolation (No Entry):        N/A    Yes    No
        Pumps or lines blinded,         ( )    ( )    ( )
        disconnected, or blocked        ( )    ( )    ( )

 4. Ventilation Modification:           N/A    Yes    No
        Mechanical                      ( )    ( )    ( )
        Natural Ventilation only        ( )    ( )    ( )

 5. Atmospheric check after
    isolation and ventilation:
        Oxygen      _____ %       > 19.5 %
        Explosive   _____ % L.F.L. < 10 %
        Toxic       _____ PPM     < 10 PPM $H_2S$
        Time        _____
        Testers signature: _____

 6. Communication procedures: _____

 7. Rescue procedures: _____

 8. Entry, standby, and back up persons:       Yes    No
        Successfully completed required
        training?                              ( )    ( )
        Is it current?                         ( )    ( )

 9. Equipment:                              N/A    Yes    No
        Direct reading gas monitor -
            tested                          ( )    ( )    ( )
        Safety harnesses and lifelines
            for entry and standby persons   ( )    ( )    ( )
        Hoisting equipment                  ( )    ( )    ( )
        Powered communications              ( )    ( )    ( )
        SCBA's for entry and standby
            persons                         ( )    ( )    ( )
        Protective Clothing                 ( )    ( )    ( )
        All electric equipment listed
            Class I, Division I, Group D
            and Non-sparking tools          ( )    ( )    ( )

10. Periodic atmospheric tests:
        Oxygen _____ %  Time _____   Oxygen _____ %  Time _____
        Oxygen _____ %  Time _____   Oxygen _____ %  Time _____
        Explosive __ %  Time _____   Explosive __ %  Time _____
        Explosive __ %  Time _____   Explosive __ %  Time _____
        Toxic _____ %   Time _____   Toxic _____ %   Time _____
        Toxic _____ %   Time _____   Toxic _____ %   Time _____
```

We have reviewed the work authorized by this permit and the information contained here-in. Written instructions and safety procedures have been received and are understood. Entry cannot be approved if any squares are marked in the "No" column. This permit is not valid unless all appropriate items are completed.
Permit Prepared By: (Supervisor) _____
Approved By: (Unit Supervisor) _____
Reviewed By (Cs Operations Personnel): _____
                                          (printed name)   (signature)

This permit to be kept at job site. Return job site copy to Safety office following job completion.
Copies: White Original (Safety Office)   Yellow (Unit Supervisor)   Hard(Job site)

§ 1910.146   29 CFR Ch. XVII (7-1-94 Edition)

Appendix D - 2   ENTRY PERMIT

PERMIT VALID FOR 8 HOURS ONLY. ALL PERMIT COPIES REMAIN AT SITE UNTIL JOB COMPLETED
DATE: - -   SITE LOCATION/DESCRIPTION
PURPOSE OF ENTRY
SUPERVISOR(S) in charge of crews   Type of Crew Phone #

COMMUNICATION PROCEDURES
RESCUE PROCEDURES (PHONE NUMBERS AT BOTTOM)

* BOLD DENOTES MINIMUM REQUIREMENTS TO BE COMPLETED AND REVIEWED PRIOR TO ENTRY*
REQUIREMENTS COMPLETED   DATE TIME   REQUIREMENTS COMPLETED   DATE TIME
Lock Out/De-energize/Try-out _____   Full Body Harness w/"D" ring _____
Line(s) Broken-Capped-Blank   _____   Emergency Escape Retrieval Eq _____
Purge-Flush and Vent   _____   Lifelines   _____
Ventilation   _____   Fire Extinguishers   _____
Secure Area (Post and Flag)   _____   Lighting (Explosive Proof)   _____
Breathing Apparatus   _____   Protective Clothing   _____
Resuscitator - Inhalator   _____   Respirator(s) (Air Purifying) _____
Standby Safety Personnel   _____   Burning and Welding Permit   _____
Note: Items that do not apply enter N/A in the blank.

                                 ** RECORD CONTINUOUS MONITORING RESULTS EVERY 2 HOURS **
CONTINUOUS MONITORING**   Permissible
TEST(S) TO BE TAKEN   Entry Level
PERCENT OF OXYGEN   19.5% to 23.5%   _____
LOWER FLAMMABLE LIMIT   Under 10%   _____
CARBON MONOXIDE   +35 PPM   _____
Aromatic Hydrocarbon   + 1 PPM * 5PPM   _____
Hydrogen Cyanide   (Skin) * 4PPM   _____
Hydrogen Sulfide   +10 PPM *15PPM   _____
Sulfur Dioxide   + 2 PPM * 5PPM   _____
Ammonia   *35PPM   _____

* Short-term exposure limit:Employee can work in the area up to 15 minutes.
+ 8 hr. Time Weighted Avg.:Employee can work in area 8 hrs (longer with appropriate respiratory protection).
REMARKS:
GAS TESTER NAME & CHECK #   INSTRUMENT(S) USED MODEL &/OR TYPE   SERIAL &/OR UNIT #

                SAFETY STANDBY PERSON IS REQUIRED FOR ALL CONFINED SPACE WORK
SAFETY STANDBY PERSON(S) CHECK #   CONFINED SPACE ENTRANT(S) CHECK # CONFINED SPACE ENTRANT(S) CHECK #

SUPERVISOR AUTHORIZATION - ALL CONDITIONS SATISFIED _____ DEPARTMENT/PHONE
AMBULANCE 2800 FIRE 2900   Safety   4901   Gas Coordinator 4529/5387

Occupational Safety and Health Admin., Labor § 1910.147

APPENDIX E TO § 1910.146—SEWER SYSTEM ENTRY

Sewer entry differs in three vital respects from other permit entries; first, there rarely exists any way to completely isolate the space (a section of a continuous system) to be entered; second, because isolation is not complete, the atmosphere may suddenly and unpredictably become lethally hazardous (toxic, flammable or explosive) from causes beyond the control of the entrant or employer, and third, experienced sewer workers are especially knowledgeable in entry and work in their permit spaces because of their frequent entries. Unlike other employments where permit space entry is a rare and exceptional event, sewer workers' usual work environment is a permit space.

(1) *Adherence to procedure.* The employer should designate as entrants only employees who are thoroughly trained in the employer's sewer entry procedures and who demonstrate that they follow these entry procedures exactly as prescribed when performing sewer entries.

(2) *Atmospheric monitoring.* Entrants should be trained in the use of, and be equipped with, atmospheric monitoring equipment which sounds an audible alarm, in addition to its visual readout, whenever one of the following conditions are encountered: Oxygen concentration less than 19.5 percent; flammable gas or vapor at 10 percent or more of the lower flammable limit (LFL); or hydrogen sulfide or carbon monoxide at or above 10 ppm or 35 ppm, respectively, measured as an 8-hour time-weighted average. Atmospheric monitoring equipment needs to be calibrated according to the manufacturer's instructions. The oxygen sensor/broad range sensor is best suited for initial use in situations where the actual or potential contaminants have not been identified, because broad range sensors, unlike substance-specific sensors, enable employers to obtain an overall reading of the hydrocarbons (flammables) present in the space. However, such sensors only indicate that a hazardous threshold of a class of chemicals has been exceeded. They do not measure the levels of contamination of specific substances. Therefore, substance-specific devices, which measure the actual levels of specific substances, are best suited for use where actual and potential contaminants have been identified. The measurements obtained with substance-specific devices are of vital importance to the employer when decisions are made concerning the measures necessary to protect entrants (such as ventilation or personal protective equipment) and the setting and attainment of appropriate entry conditions. However, the sewer environment may suddenly and unpredictably change, and the substance-specific devices may not detect the potentially lethal atmospheric hazards which may enter the sewer environment.

Although OSHA considers the information and guidance provided above to be appropriate and useful in most sewer entry situations, the Agency emphasizes that each employer must consider the unique circumstances, including the predictability of the atmosphere, of the sewer permit spaces in the employer's workplace in preparing for entry. Only the employer can decide, based upon his or her knowledge of, and experience with permit spaces in sewer systems, what the best type of testing instrument may be for any specific entry operation.

The selected testing instrument should be carried and used by the entrant in sewer line work to monitor the atmosphere in the entrant's environment, and in advance of the entrant's direction of movement, to warn the entrant of any deterioration in atmospheric conditions. Where several entrants are working together in the same immediate location, one instrument, used by the lead entrant, is acceptable.

(3) *Surge flow and flooding.* Sewer crews should develop and maintain liaison, to the extent possible, with the local weather bureau and fire and emergency services in their area so that sewer work may be delayed or interrupted and entrants withdrawn whenever sewer lines might be suddenly flooded by rain or fire suppression activities, or whenever flammable or other hazardous materials are released into sewers during emergencies by industrial or transportation accidents.

(4) *Special Equipment.* Entry into large bore sewers may require the use of special equipment. Such equipment might include such items as atmosphere monitoring devices with automatic audible alarms, escape self-contained breathing apparatus (ESCBA) with at least 10 minute air supply (or other NIOSH approved self-rescuer), and waterproof flashlights, and may also include boats and rafts, radios and rope stand-offs for pulling around bends and corners as needed.

[58 FR 4549, Jan. 14, 1993; 58 FR 34845, June 29, 1993, as amended at 59 FR 26114, May 19, 1994]

§ 1910.147 The control of hazardous energy (lockout/tagout).

(a) *Scope, application and purpose*—(1) *Scope.* (i) This standard covers the servicing and maintenance of machines and equipment in which the *unexpected* energization or start up of the machines or equipment, or release of stored energy could cause injury to employees. This standard establishes minimum performance requirements for the control of such hazardous energy.

(ii) This standard does not cover the following:

Appendix 4C

29 CFR 1910.95
OCCUPATIONAL NOISE EXPOSURE

§ 1910.95 Occupational noise exposure.

(a) Protection against the effects of noise exposure shall be provided when the sound levels exceed those shown in Table G-16 when measured on the A scale of a standard sound level meter at slow response. When noise levels are determined by octave band analysis, the equivalent A-weighted sound level may be determined as follows:

(b)(1) When employees are subjected to sound exceeding those listed in Table G-16, feasible administrative or engineering controls shall be utilized. If such controls fail to reduce sound levels within the levels of Table G-16, personal protective equipment shall be

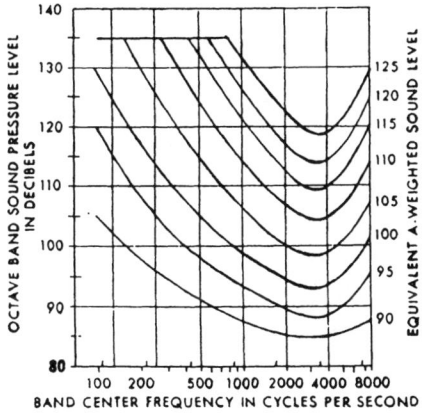

FIGURE G-9

Equivalent sound level contours. Octave band sound pressure levels may be converted to the equivalent A-weighted sound level by plotting them on this graph and noting the A-weighted sound level corresponding to the point of highest penetration into the sound level contours. This equivalent A-weighted sound level, which may differ from the actual A-weighted sound level of the noise, is used to determine exposure limits from Table 1.G-16.

Occupational Safety and Health Admin., Labor §1910.95

provided and used to reduce sound levels within the levels of the table.

(2) If the variations in noise level involve maxima at intervals of 1 second or less, it is to be considered continuous.

TABLE G–16—PERMISSIBLE NOISE EXPOSURES [1]

Duration per day, hours	Sound level dBA slow response
8	90
6	92
4	95
3	97
2	100
1½	102
1	105
½	110
¼ or less	115

[1] When the daily noise exposure is composed of two or more periods of noise exposure of different levels, their combined effect should be considered, rather than the individual effect of each. If the sum of the following fractions: $C_1/T_1 + C_2/T_2 \ldots C_n/T_n$ exceeds unity, then, the mixed exposure should be considered to exceed the limit value. Cn indicates the total time of exposure at a specified noise level, and Tn indicates the total time of exposure permitted at that level.

Exposure to impulsive or impact noise should not exceed 140 dB peak sound pressure level.

(c) *Hearing conservation program.* (1) The employer shall administer a continuing, effective hearing conservation program, as described in paragraphs (c) through (o) of this section, whenever employee noise exposures equal or exceed an 8-hour time-weighted average sound level (TWA) of 85 decibels measured on the A scale (slow response) or, equivalently, a dose of fifty percent. For purposes of the hearing conservation program, employee noise exposures shall be computed in accordance with appendix A and Table G–16a, and without regard to any attenuation provided by the use of personal protective equipment.

(2) For purposes of paragraphs (c) through (n) of this section, an 8-hour time-weighted average of 85 decibels or a dose of fifty percent shall also be referred to as the action level.

(d) *Monitoring.* (1) When information indicates that any employee's exposure may equal or exceed an 8-hour time-weighted average of 85 decibels, the employer shall develop and implement a monitoring program.

(i) The sampling strategy shall be designed to identify employees for inclusion in the hearing conservation program and to enable the proper selection of hearing protectors.

(ii) Where circumstances such as high worker mobility, significant variations in sound level, or a significant component of impulse noise make area monitoring generally inappropriate, the employer shall use representative personal sampling to comply with the monitoring requirements of this paragraph unless the employer can show that area sampling produces equivalent results.

(2)(i) All continuous, intermittent and impulsive sound levels from 80 decibels to 130 decibels shall be integrated into the noise measurements.

(ii) Instruments used to measure employee noise exposure shall be calibrated to ensure measurement accuracy.

(3) Monitoring shall be repeated whenever a change in production, process, equipment or controls increases noise exposures to the extent that:

(i) Additional employees may be exposed at or above the action level; or

(ii) The attenuation provided by hearing protectors being used by employees may be rendered inadequate to meet the requirements of paragraph (j) of this section.

(e) *Employee notification.* The employer shall notify each employee exposed at or above an 8-hour time-weighted average of 85 decibels of the results of the monitoring.

(f) *Observation of monitoring.* The employer shall provide affected employees or their representatives with an opportunity to observe any noise measurements conducted pursuant to this section.

(g) *Audiometric testing program.* (1) The employer shall establish and maintain an audiometric testing program as provided in this paragraph by making audiometric testing available to all employees whose exposures equal or exceed an 8-hour time-weighted average of 85 decibels.

(2) The program shall be provided at no cost to employees.

(3) Audiometric tests shall be performed by a licensed or certified audiologist, otolaryngologist, or other physician, or by a technician who is certified by the Council of Accreditation in Occupational Hearing Conservation, or who has satisfactorily demonstrated competence in administering

§ 1910.95

audiometric examinations, obtaining valid audiograms, and properly using, maintaining and checking calibration and proper functioning of the audiometers being used. A technician who operates microprocessor audiometers does not need to be certified. A technician who performs audiometric tests must be responsible to an audiologist, otolaryngologist or physician.

(4) All audiograms obtained pursuant to this section shall meet the requirements of Appendix C: *Audiometric Measuring Instruments.*

(5) *Baseline audiogram.* (i) Within 6 months of an employee's first exposure at or above the action level, the employer shall establish a valid baseline audiogram against which subsequent audiograms can be compared.

(ii) *Mobile test van exception.* Where mobile test vans are used to meet the audiometric testing obligation, the employer shall obtain a valid baseline audiogram within 1 year of an employee's first exposure at or above the action level. Where baseline audiograms are obtained more than 6 months after the employee's first exposure at or above the action level, employees shall wearing hearing protectors for any period exceeding six months after first exposure until the baseline audiogram is obtained.

(iii) Testing to establish a baseline audiogram shall be preceded by at least 14 hours without exposure to workplace noise. Hearing protectors may be used as a substitute for the requirement that baseline audiograms be preceded by 14 hours without exposure to workplace noise.

(iv) The employer shall notify employees of the need to avoid high levels of non-occupational noise exposure during the 14-hour period immediately preceding the audiometric examination.

(6) *Annual audiogram.* At least annually after obtaining the baseline audiogram, the employer shall obtain a new audiogram for each employee exposed at or above an 8-hour time-weighted average of 85 decibels.

(7) *Evaluation of audiogram.* (i) Each employee's annual audiogram shall be compared to that employee's baseline audiogram to determine if the audiogram is valid and if a standard threshold shift as defined in paragraph (g)(10) of this section has occurred. This comparison may be done by a technician.

(ii) If the annual audiogram shows that an employee has suffered a standard threshold shift, the employer may obtain a retest within 30 days and consider the results of the retest as the annual audiogram.

(iii) The audiologist, otolaryngologist, or physician shall review problem audiograms and shall determine whether there is a need for further evaluation. The employer shall provide to the person performing this evaluation the following information:

(A) A copy of the requirements for hearing conservation as set forth in paragraphs (c) through (n) of this section;

(B) The baseline audiogram and most recent audiogram of the employee to be evaluated;

(C) Measurements of background sound pressure levels in the audiometric test room as required in Appendix D: Audiometric Test Rooms.

(D) Records of audiometer calibrations required by paragraph (h)(5) of this section.

(8) *Follow-up procedures.* (i) If a comparison of the annual audiogram to the baseline audiogram indicates a standard threshold shift as defined in paragraph (g)(10) of this section has occurred, the employee shall be informed of this fact in writing, within 21 days of the determination.

(ii) Unless a physician determines that the standard threshold shift is not work related or aggravated by occupational noise exposure, the employer shall ensure that the following steps are taken when a standard threshold shift occurs:

(A) Employees not using hearing protectors shall be fitted with hearing protectors, trained in their use and care, and required to use them.

(B) Employees already using hearing protectors shall be refitted and retrained in the use of hearing protectors and provided with hearing protectors offering greater attenuation if necessary.

(C) The employee shall be referred for a clinical audiological evaluation or an otological examination, as appropriate, if additional testing is necessary or if

Occupational Safety and Health Admin., Labor § 1910.95

the employer suspects that a medical pathology of the ear is caused or aggravated by the wearing of hearing protectors.

(D) The employee is informed of the need for an otological examination if a medical pathology of the ear that is unrelated to the use of hearing protectors is suspected.

(iii) If subsequent audiometric testing of an employee whose exposure to noise is less than an 8-hour TWA of 90 decibels indicates that a standard threshold shift is not persistent, the employer:

(A) Shall inform the employee of the new audiometric interpretation; and

(B) May discontinue the required use of hearing protectors for that employee.

(9) *Revised baseline.* An annual audiogram may be substituted for the baseline audiogram when, in the judgment of the audiologist, otolaryngologist or physician who is evaluating the audiogram:

(i) The standard threshold shift revealed by the audiogram is persistent; or

(ii) The hearing threshold shown in the annual audiogram indicates significant improvement over the baseline audiogram.

(10) *Standard threshold shift.* (i) As used in this section, a standard threshold shift is a change in hearing threshold relative to the baseline audiogram of an average of 10 dB or more at 2000, 3000, and 4000 Hz in either ear.

(ii) In determining whether a standard threshold shift has occurred, allowance may be made for the contribution of aging (presbycusis) to the change in hearing level by correcting the annual audiogram according to the procedure described in Appendix F: *Calculation and Application of Age Correction to Audiograms.*

(h) *Audiometric test requirements.* (1) Audiometric tests shall be pure tone, air conduction, hearing threshold examinations, with test frequencies including as a minimum 500, 1000, 2000, 3000, 4000, and 6000 Hz. Tests at each frequency shall be taken separately for each ear.

(2) Audiometric tests shall be conducted with audiometers (including microprocessor audiometers) that meet the specifications of, and are maintained and used in accordance with, American National Standard Specification for Audiometers, S3.6-1969.

(3) Pulsed-tone and self-recording audiometers, if used, shall meet the requirements specified in Appendix C: *Audiometric Measuring Instruments.*

(4) Audiometric examinations shall be administered in a room meeting the requirements listed in Appendix D: *Audiometric Test Rooms.*

(5) *Audiometer calibration.* (i) The functional operation of the audiometer shall be checked before each day's use by testing a person with known, stable hearing thresholds, and by listening to the audiometer's output to make sure that the output is free from distorted or unwanted sounds. Deviations of 10 decibels or greater require an acoustic calibration.

(ii) Audiometer calibration shall be checked acoustically at least annually in accordance with Appendix E: *Acoustic Calibration of Audiometers.* Test frequencies below 500 Hz and above 6000 Hz may be omitted from this check. Deviations of 15 decibels or greater require an exhaustive calibration.

(iii) An exhaustive calibration shall be performed at least every two years in accordance with sections 4.1.2; 4.1.3.; 4.1.4.3; 4.2; 4.4.1; 4.4.2; 4.4.3; and 4.5 of the American National Standard Specification for Audiometers, S3.6-1969. Test frequencies below 500 Hz and above 6000 Hz may be omitted from this calibration.

(i) *Hearing protectors.* (1) Employers shall make hearing protectors available to all employees exposed to an 8-hour time-weighted average of 85 decibels or greater at no cost to the employees. Hearing protectors shall be replaced as necessary.

(2) Employers shall ensure that hearing protectors are worn:

(i) By an employee who is required by paragraph (b)(1) of this section to wear personal protective equipment; and

(ii) By any employee who is exposed to an 8-hour time-weighted average of 85 decibels or greater, and who:

(A) Has not yet had a baseline audiogram established pursuant to paragraph (g)(5)(ii); or

(B) Has experienced a standard threshold shift.

§ 1910.95

(3) Employees shall be given the opportunity to select their hearing protectors from a variety of suitable hearing protectors provided by the employer.

(4) The employer shall provide training in the use and care of all hearing protectors provided to employees.

(5) The employer shall ensure proper initial fitting and supervise the correct use of all hearing protectors.

(j) *Hearing protector attenuation.* (1) The employer shall evaluate hearing protector attenuation for the specific noise environments in which the protector will be used. The employer shall use one of the evaluation methods described in Appendix B: *Methods for Estimating the Adequacy of Hearing Protection Attenuation.*

(2) Hearing protectors must attenuate employee exposure at least to an 8-hour time-weighted average of 90 decibels as required by paragraph (b) of this section.

(3) For employees who have experienced a standard threshold shift, hearing protectors must attenuate employee exposure to an 8-hour time-weighted average of 85 decibels or below.

(4) The adequacy of hearing protector attenuation shall be re-evaluated whenever employee noise exposures increase to the extent that the hearing protectors provided may no longer provide adequate attenuation. The employer shall provide more effective hearing protectors where necessary.

(k) *Training program.* (1) The employer shall institute a training program for all employees who are exposed to noise at or above an 8-hour time-weighted average of 85 decibels, and shall ensure employee participation in such program.

(2) The training program shall be repeated annually for each employee included in the hearing conservation program. Information provided in the training program shall be updated to be consistent with changes in protective equipment and work processes.

(3) The employer shall ensure that each employee is informed of the following:

(i) The effects of noise on hearing;

(ii) The purpose of hearing protectors, the advantages, disadvantages, and attenuation of various types, and instructions on selection, fitting, use, and care; and

(iii) The purpose of audiometric testing, and an explanation of the test procedures.

(l) *Access to information and training materials.* (1) The employer shall make available to affected employees or their representatives copies of this standard and shall also post a copy in the workplace.

(2) The employer shall provide to affected employees any informational materials pertaining to the standard that are supplied to the employer by the Assistant Secretary.

(3) The employer shall provide, upon request, all materials related to the employer's training and education program pertaining to this standard to the Assistant Secretary and the Director.

(m) *Recordkeeping*—(1) *Exposure measurements.* The employer shall maintain an accurate record of all employee exposure measurements required by paragraph (d) of this section.

(2) *Audiometric tests.* (i) The employer shall retain all employee audiometric test records obtained pursuant to paragraph (g) of this section:

(ii) This record shall include:

(A) Name and job classification of the employee;

(B) Date of the audiogram;

(C) The examiner's name;

(D) Date of the last acoustic or exhaustive calibration of the audiometer; and

(E) Employee's most recent noise exposure assessment.

(F) The employer shall maintain accurate records of the measurements of the background sound pressure levels in audiometric test rooms.

(3) *Record retention.* The employer shall retain records required in this paragraph (m) for at least the following periods.

(i) Noise exposure measurement records shall be retained for two years.

(ii) Audiometric test records shall be retained for the duration of the affected employee's employment.

(4) *Access to records.* All records required by this section shall be provided upon request to employees, former employees, representatives designated by the individual employee, and the As-

Occupational Safety and Health Admin., Labor § 1910.95

sistant Secretary. The provisions of 29 CFR 1910.20 (a)–(e) and (g)–(i) apply to access to records under this section.

(5) *Transfer of records.* If the employer ceases to do business, the employer shall transfer to the successor employer all records required to be maintained by this section, and the successor employer shall retain them for the remainder of the period prescribed in paragraph (m) (3) of this section.

(n) *Appendices.* (1) Appendices A, B, C, D, and E to this section are incorporated as part of this section and the contents of these appendices are mandatory.

(2) Appendices F and G to this section are informational and are not intended to create any additional obligations not otherwise imposed or to detract from any existing obligations.

(o) *Exemptions.* Paragraphs (c) through (n) of this section shall not apply to employers engaged in oil and gas well drilling and servicing operations.

(p) *Startup date.* Baseline audiograms required by paragraph (g) of this section shall be completed by March 1, 1984.

(Approved by the Office of Management and Budget under control number 1218–0048)

APPENDIX A TO § 1910.95—NOISE EXPOSURE COMPUTATION

This Appendix is Mandatory

I. Computation of Employee Noise Exposure

(1) Noise dose is computed using Table G–16a as follows:

(i) When the sound level, L, is constant over the entire work shift, the noise dose, D, in percent, is given by: D=100 C/T where C is the total length of the work day, in hours, and T is the reference duration corresponding to the measured sound level, L, as given in Table G–16a or by the formula shown as a footnote to that table.

(ii) When the workshift noise exposure is composed of two or more periods of noise at different levels, the total noise dose over the work day is given by:

$D = 100 \ (C_1/T_1 + C_2/T_2 + \ldots + C_n/T_n)$,

where C_n indicates the total time of exposure at a specific noise level, and T_n indicates the reference duration for that level as given by Table G–16a.

(2) The eight-hour time-weighted average sound level (TWA), in decibels, may be computed from the dose, in percent, by means of the formula: TWA=16.61 $\log_{10}$ (D/100)+90. For an eight-hour workshift with the noise level constant over the entire shift, the TWA is equal to the measured sound level.

(3) A table relating dose and TWA is given in Section II.

TABLE G–16a

A-weighted sound level, L (decibel)	Reference duration, T (hour)
80	32
81	27.9
82	24.3
83	21.1
84	18.4
85	16
86	13.9
87	12.1
88	10.6
89	9.2
90	8
91	7.0
92	6.1
93	5.3
94	4.6
95	4
96	3.5
97	3.0
98	2.6
99	2.3
100	2
101	1.7
102	1.5
103	1.3
104	1.1
105	1
106	0.87
107	0.76
108	0.66
109	0.57
110	0.5
111	0.44
112	0.38
113	0.33
114	0.29
115	0.25
116	0.22
117	0.19
118	0.16
119	0.14
120	0.125
121	0.11
122	0.095
123	0.082
124	0.072
125	0.063
126	0.054
127	0.047
128	0.041
129	0.036
130	0.031

In the above table the reference duration, T, is computed by

$$T = \frac{8}{2^{(L-90)/5}}$$

where L is the measured A-weighted sound level.

APPENDIX 4C

§ 1910.95

II. Conversion Between "Dose" and "8-Hour Time-Weighted Average" Sound Level

Compliance with paragraphs (c)–(r) of this regulation is determined by the amount of exposure to noise in the workplace. The amount of such exposure is usually measured with an audiodosimeter which gives a read-out in terms of "dose." In order to better understand the requirements of the amendment, dosimeter readings can be converted to an "8-hour time-weighted average sound level." (TWA).

In order to convert the reading of a dosimeter into TWA, see Table A-1, below. This table applies to dosimeters that are set by the manufacturer to calculate dose or percent exposure according to the relationships in Table G–16a. So, for example, a dose of 91 percent over an eight hour day results in a TWA of 89.3 dB, and, a dose of 50 percent corresponds to a TWA of 85 dB.

If the dose as read on the dosimeter is less than or greater than the values found in Table A-1, the TWA may be calculated by using the formula: TWA=16.61 log$_{10}$ (D/100)+90 where TWA=8-hour time-weighted average sound level and D=accumulated dose in percent exposure.

TABLE A-1—CONVERSION FROM "PERCENT NOISE EXPOSURE" OR "DOSE" TO "8-HOUR TIME-WEIGHTED AVERAGE SOUND LEVEL" (TWA)

Dose or percent noise exposure	TWA
10	73.4
15	76.3
20	78.4
25	80.0
30	81.3
35	82.4
40	83.4
45	84.2
50	85.0
55	85.7
60	86.3
65	86.9
70	87.4
75	87.9
80	88.4
81	88.5
82	88.6
83	88.7
84	88.7
85	88.8
86	88.9
87	89.0
88	89.1
89	89.2
90	89.2
91	89.3
92	89.4
93	89.5
94	89.6
95	89.6
96	89.7
97	89.8
98	89.9
99	89.9
100	90.0

TABLE A-1—CONVERSION FROM "PERCENT NOISE EXPOSURE" OR "DOSE" TO "8-HOUR TIME-WEIGHTED AVERAGE SOUND LEVEL" (TWA)—Continued

Dose or percent noise exposure	TWA
101	90.1
102	90.1
103	90.2
104	90.3
105	90.4
106	90.4
107	90.5
108	90.6
109	90.6
110	90.7
111	90.8
112	90.8
113	90.9
114	90.9
115	91.1
116	91.1
117	91.1
118	91.2
119	91.3
120	91.3
125	91.6
130	91.9
135	92.2
140	92.4
145	92.7
150	92.9
155	93.2
160	93.4
165	93.6
170	93.8
175	94.0
180	94.2
185	94.4
190	94.6
195	94.8
200	95.0
210	95.4
220	95.7
230	96.0
240	96.3
250	96.6
260	96.9
270	97.2
280	97.4
290	97.7
300	97.9
310	98.2
320	98.4
330	98.6
340	98.8
350	99.0
360	99.2
370	99.4
380	99.6
390	99.8
400	100.0
410	100.2
420	100.4
430	100.5
440	100.7
450	100.8
460	101.0
470	101.2
480	101.3
490	101.5
500	101.6
510	101.8
520	101.9

Occupational Safety and Health Admin., Labor §1910.95

TABLE A-1—CONVERSION FROM "PERCENT NOISE EXPOSURE" OR "DOSE" TO "8-HOUR TIME-WEIGHTED AVERAGE SOUND LEVEL" (TWA)—Continued

Dose or percent noise exposure	TWA
530	102.0
540	102.2
550	102.3
560	102.4
570	102.6
580	102.7
590	102.8
600	102.9
610	103.0
620	103.2
630	103.3
640	103.4
650	103.5
660	103.6
670	103.7
680	103.8
690	103.9
700	104.0
710	104.1
720	104.2
730	104.3
740	104.4
750	104.5
760	104.6
770	104.7
780	104.8
790	104.9
800	105.0
810	105.1
820	105.2
830	105.3
840	105.4
850	105.4
860	105.5
870	105.6
880	105.7
890	105.8
900	105.8
910	105.9
920	106.0
930	106.1
940	106.2
950	106.2
960	106.3
970	106.4
980	106.5
990	106.5
999	106.6

APPENDIX B TO §1910.95—METHODS FOR ESTIMATING THE ADEQUACY OF HEARING PROTECTOR ATTENUATION

This Appendix is Mandatory

For employees who have experienced a significant threshold shift, hearing protector attenuation must be sufficient to reduce employee exposure to a TWA of 85 dB. Employers must select one of the following methods by which to estimate the adequacy of hearing protector attenuation.

The most convenient method is the Noise Reduction Rating (NRR) developed by the Environmental Protection Agency (EPA). According to EPA regulation, the NRR must be shown on the hearing protector package. The NRR is then related to an individual worker's noise environment in order to assess the adequacy of the attenuation of a given hearing protector. This appendix describes four methods of using the NRR to determine whether a particular hearing protector provides adequate protection within a given exposure environment. Selection among the four procedures is dependent upon the employer's noise measuring instruments.

Instead of using the NRR, employers may evaluate the adequacy of hearing protector attenuation by using one of the three methods developed by the National Institute for Occupational Safety and Health (NIOSH), which are described in the "List of Personal Hearing Protectors and Attenuation Data," HEW Publication No. 76-120, 1975, pages 21-37. These methods are known as NIOSH methods #1, #2 and #3. The NRR described below is a simplification of NIOSH method #2. The most complex method is NIOSH method #1, which is probably the most accurate method since it uses the largest amount of spectral information from the individual employee's noise environment. As in the case of the NRR method described below, if one of the NIOSH methods is used, the selected method must be applied to an individual's noise environment to assess the adequacy of the attenuation. Employers should be careful to take a sufficient number of measurements in order to achieve a representative sample for each time segment.

NOTE: The employer must remember that calculated attenuation values reflect realistic values only to the extent that the protectors are properly fitted and worn.

When using the NRR to assess hearing protector adequacy, one of the following methods must be used:

(i) When using a dosimeter that is capable of C-weighted measurements:

(A) Obtain the employee's C-weighted dose for the entire workshift, and convert to TWA (see appendix A, II).

(B) Subtract the NRR from the C-weighted TWA to obtain the estimated A-weighted TWA under the ear protector.

(ii) When using a dosimeter that is not capable of C-weighted measurements, the following method may be used:

(A) Convert the A-weighted dose to TWA (see appendix A).

(B) Subtract 7 dB from the NRR.

(C) Subtract the remainder from the A-weighted TWA to obtain the estimated A-weighted TWA under the ear protector.

(iii) When using a sound level meter set to the A-weighting network:

(A) Obtain the employee's A-weighted TWA.

(B) Subtract 7 dB from the NRR, and subtract the remainder from the A-weighted

APPENDIX 4C

§ 1910.95

TWA to obtain the estimated A-weighted TWA under the ear protector.

(iv) When using a sound level meter set on the C-weighting network:

(A) Obtain a representative sample of the C-weighted sound levels in the employee's environment.

(B) Subtract the NRR from the C-weighted average sound level to obtain the estimated A-weighted TWA under the ear protector.

(v) When using area monitoring procedures and a sound level meter set to the A-weighing network:

(A) Obtain a representative sound level for the area in question.

(B) Subtract 7 dB from the NRR and subtract the remainder from the A-weighted sound level for that area.

(vi) When using area monitoring procedures and a sound level meter set to the C-weighting network:

(A) Obtain a representative sound level for the area in question.

(B) Subtract the NRR from the C-weighted sound level for that area.

APPENDIX C TO § 1910.95—AUDIOMETRIC MEASURING INSTRUMENTS

This Appendix is Mandatory

1. In the event that pulsed-tone audiometers are used, they shall have a tone on-time of at least 200 milliseconds.

2. Self-recording audiometers shall comply with the following requirements:

(A) The chart upon which the audiogram is traced shall have lines at positions corresponding to all multiples of 10 dB hearing level within the intensity range spanned by the audiometer. The lines shall be equally spaced and shall be separated by at least ¼ inch. Additional increments are optional. The audiogram pen tracings shall not exceed 2 dB in width.

(B) It shall be possible to set the stylus manually at the 10-dB increment lines for calibration purposes.

(C) The slewing rate for the audiometer attenuator shall not be more than 6 dB/sec except that an initial slewing rate greater than 6 dB/sec is permitted at the beginning of each new test frequency, but only until the second subject response.

(D) The audiometer shall remain at each required test frequency for 30 seconds (± 3 seconds). The audiogram shall be clearly marked at each change of frequency and the actual frequency change of the audiometer shall not deviate from the frequency boundaries marked on the audiogram by more than ± 3 seconds.

(E) It must be possible at each test frequency to place a horizontal line segment parallel to the time axis on the audiogram, such that the audiometric tracing crosses the line segment at least six times at that test frequency. At each test frequency the

29 CFR Ch. XVII (7-1-94 Edition)

threshold shall be the average of the midpoints of the tracing excursions.

APPENDIX D TO § 1910.95—AUDIOMETRIC TEST ROOMS

This Appendix is Mandatory

Rooms used for audiometric testing shall not have background sound pressure levels exceeding those in Table D-1 when measured by equipment conforming at least to the Type 2 requirements of American National Standard Specification for Sound Level Meters, S1.4–1971 (R1976), and to the Class II requirements of American National Standard Specification for Octave, Half-Octave, and Third-Octave Band Filter Sets, S1.11–1971 (R1976).

TABLE D-1—MAXIMUM ALLOWABLE OCTAVE-BAND SOUND PRESSURE LEVELS FOR AUDIOMETRIC TEST ROOMS

Octave-band center frequency (Hz)	500	1000	2000	4000	8000
Sound pressure level (dB)	40	40	47	57	62

APPENDIX E TO § 1910.95—ACOUSTIC CALIBRATION OF AUDIOMETERS

This Appendix is Mandatory

Audiometer calibration shall be checked acoustically, at least annually, according to the procedures described in this appendix. The equipment necessary to perform these measurements is a sound level meter, octave-band filter set, and a National Bureau of Standards 9A coupler. In making these measurements, the accuracy of the calibrating equipment shall be sufficient to determine that the audiometer is within the tolerances permitted by American Standard Specification for Audiometers, S3.6–1969.

(1) Sound Pressure Output Check

A. Place the earphone coupler over the microphone of the sound level meter and place the earphone on the coupler.

B. Set the audiometer's hearing threshold level (HTL) dial to 70 dB.

C. Measure the sound pressure level of the tones at each test frequency from 500 Hz through 6000 Hz for each earphone.

D. At each frequency the readout on the sound level meter should correspond to the levels in Table E-1 or Table E-2, as appropriate, for the type of earphone, in the column entitled "sound level meter reading."

(2) Linearity Check

A. With the earphone in place, set the frequency to 1000 Hz and the HTL dial on the audiometer to 70 dB.

B. Measure the sound levels in the coupler at each 10-dB decrement from 70 dB to 10 dB, noting the sound level meter reading at each setting.

206

Occupational Safety and Health Admin., Labor § 1910.95

C. For each 10-dB decrement on the audiometer the sound level meter should indicate a corresponding 10 dB decrease.

D. This measurement may be made electrically with a voltmeter connected to the earphone terminals.

(3) Tolerances

When any of the measured sound levels deviate from the levels in Table E–1 or Table E–2 by ± 3 dB at any test frequency between 500 and 3000 Hz, 4 dB at 4000 Hz, or 5 dB at 6000 Hz, an exhaustive calibration is advised. An exhaustive calibration is required if the deviations are greater than 15 dB or greater at any test frequency.

TABLE E–1—REFERENCE THRESHOLD LEVELS FOR TELEPHONICS—TDH–39 EARPHONES

Frequency, Hz	Reference threshold level for TDH–39 earphones, dB	Sound level meter reading, dB
500	11.5	81.5
1000	7	77
2000	9	79
3000	10	80
4000	9.5	79.5
6000	15.5	85.5

TABLE E–2—REFERENCE THRESHOLD LEVELS FOR TELEPHONICS—TDH–49 EARPHONES

Frequency, Hz	Reference threshold level for TDH–49 earphones, dB	Sound level meter reading, dB
500	13.5	83.5
1000	7.5	77.5
2000	11	81.0
3000	9.5	79.5
4000	10.5	80.5
6000	13.5	83.5

APPENDIX F TO § 1910.95—CALCULATIONS AND APPLICATION OF AGE CORRECTIONS TO AUDIOGRAMS

This Appendix Is Non-Mandatory

In determining whether a standard threshold shift has occurred, allowance may be made for the contribution of aging to the change in hearing level by adjusting the most recent audiogram. If the employer chooses to adjust the audiogram, the employer shall follow the procedure described below. This procedure and the age correction tables were developed by the National Institute for Occupational Safety and Health in the criteria document entitled "Criteria for a Recommended Standard . . . Occupational Exposure to Noise," ((HSM)–11001).

For each audiometric test frequency;

(i) Determine from Tables F–1 or F–2 the age correction values for the employee by:

(A) Finding the age at which the most recent audiogram was taken and recording the corresponding values of age corrections at 1000 Hz through 6000 Hz;

(B) Finding the age at which the baseline audiogram was taken and recording the corresponding values of age corrections at 1000 Hz through 6000 Hz.

(ii) Subtract the values found in step (i)(B) from the value found in step (i)(A).

(iii) The differences calculated in step (ii) represented that portion of the change in hearing that may be due to aging.

EXAMPLE: Employee is a 32-year-old male. The audiometric history for his right ear is shown in decibels below.

Employee's age	Audiometric test frequency (Hz)				
	1000	2000	3000	4000	6000
26	10	5	5	10	5
*27	0	0	0	5	5
28	0	0	0	10	5
29	5	0	5	15	5
30	0	5	10	20	10
31	5	10	20	15	15
*32	5	10	10	25	20

The audiogram at age 27 is considered the baseline since it shows the best hearing threshold levels. Asterisks have been used to identify the baseline and most recent audiogram. A threshold shift of 20 dB exists at 4000 Hz between the audiograms taken at ages 27 and 32.

(The threshold shift is computed by subtracting the hearing threshold at age 27, which was 5, from the hearing threshold at age 32, which is 25.) A retest audiogram has confirmed this shift. The contribution of aging to this change in hearing may be estimated in the following manner:

Go to Table F–1 and find the age correction values (in dB) for 4000 Hz at age 27 and age 32.

	Frequency (Hz)				
	1000	2000	3000	4000	6000
Age 32	6	5	7	10	14
Age 27	5	4	6	7	11
Difference	1	1	1	3	3

The difference represents the amount of hearing loss that may be attributed to aging in the time period between the baseline audiogram and the most recent audiogram. In this example, the difference at 4000 Hz is 3 dB. This value is subtracted from the hearing level at 4000 Hz, which in the most recent audiogram is 25, yielding 22 after adjustment. Then the hearing threshold in the baseline audiogram at 4000 Hz (5) is subtracted from the adjusted annual audiogram

APPENDIX 4C

§ 1910.95

hearing threshold at 4000 Hz (22). Thus the age-corrected threshold shift would be 17 dB (as opposed to a threshold shift of 20 dB without age correction).

TABLE F–1—AGE CORRECTION VALUES IN DECIBELS FOR MALES

Years	Audiometric Test Frequencies (Hz)				
	1000	2000	3000	4000	6000
20 or younger	5	3	4	5	8
21	5	3	4	5	8
22	5	3	4	5	8
23	5	3	4	6	9
24	5	3	5	6	9
25	5	3	5	7	10
26	5	4	5	7	10
27	5	4	6	7	11
28	6	4	6	8	11
29	6	4	6	8	12
30	6	4	6	9	12
31	6	4	7	9	13
32	6	5	7	10	14
33	6	5	7	10	14
34	6	5	8	11	15
35	7	5	8	11	15
36	7	5	9	12	16
37	7	6	9	12	17
38	7	6	9	13	17
39	7	6	10	14	18
40	7	6	10	14	19
41	7	6	10	14	20
42	8	7	11	16	20
43	8	7	12	16	21
44	8	7	12	17	22
45	8	7	13	18	23
46	8	8	13	19	24
47	8	8	14	19	24
48	9	8	14	20	25
49	9	9	15	21	26
50	9	9	16	22	27
51	9	9	16	23	28
52	9	10	17	24	29
53	9	10	18	25	30
54	10	10	18	26	31
55	10	11	19	27	32
56	10	11	20	28	34
57	10	11	21	29	35
58	10	12	22	31	36
59	11	12	22	32	37
60 or older	11	13	23	33	38

TABLE F–2—AGE CORRECTION VALUES IN DECIBELS FOR FEMALES

Years	Audiometric Test Frequencies (Hz)				
	1000	2000	3000	4000	6000
20 or younger	7	4	3	3	6
21	7	4	4	3	6
22	7	4	4	4	6
23	7	5	4	4	7
24	7	5	4	4	7
25	8	5	4	4	7
26	8	5	5	4	8
27	8	5	5	5	8
28	8	5	5	5	8
29	8	5	5	5	9
30	8	6	5	5	9
31	8	6	6	5	9
32	9	6	6	6	10
33	9	6	6	6	10

TABLE F–2—AGE CORRECTION VALUES IN DECIBELS FOR FEMALES—Continued

Years	Audiometric Test Frequencies (Hz)				
	1000	2000	3000	4000	6000
34	9	6	6	6	10
35	9	6	7	7	11
36	9	7	7	7	11
37	9	7	7	7	12
38	10	7	7	7	12
39	10	7	8	8	12
40	10	7	8	8	13
41	10	8	8	8	13
42	10	8	9	9	13
43	11	8	9	9	14
44	11	8	9	9	14
45	11	8	10	10	15
46	11	9	10	10	15
47	11	9	10	11	16
48	12	9	11	11	16
49	12	9	11	11	16
50	12	10	11	12	17
51	12	10	12	12	17
52	12	10	12	13	18
53	13	10	13	13	18
54	13	11	13	14	19
55	13	11	14	14	19
56	13	11	14	15	20
57	13	11	15	15	20
58	14	12	15	16	21
59	14	12	16	16	21
60 or older	14	12	16	17	22

APPENDIX G TO § 1910.95—MONITORING NOISE LEVELS NON-MANDATORY INFORMATIONAL APPENDIX

This appendix provides information to help employers comply with the noise monitoring obligations that are part of the hearing conservation amendment.

WHAT IS THE PURPOSE OF NOISE MONITORING?

This revised amendment requires that employees be placed in a hearing conservation program if they are exposed to average noise levels of 85 dB or greater during an 8 hour workday. In order to determine if exposures are at or above this level, it may be necessary to measure or monitor the actual noise levels in the workplace and to estimate the noise exposure or "dose" received by employees during the workday.

WHEN IS IT NECESSARY TO IMPLEMENT A NOISE MONITORING PROGRAM?

It is not necessary for every employer to measure workplace noise. Noise monitoring or measuring must be conducted only when exposures are at or above 85 dB. Factors which suggest that noise exposures in the workplace may be at this level include employee complaints about the loudness of noise, indications that employees are losing their hearing, or noisy conditions which make normal conversation difficult. The employer should also consider any information available regarding noise emitted from specific machines. In addition, actual workplace noise measurements can suggest whether or not a monitoring program should be initiated.

HOW IS NOISE MEASURED?

Basically, there are two different instruments to measure noise exposures: the sound level meter and the dosimeter. A sound level meter is a device that measures the intensity of sound at a given moment. Since sound level meters provide a measure of sound intensity at only one point in time, it is generally necessary to take a number of measurements at different times during the day to estimate noise exposure over a workday. If noise levels fluctuate, the amount of time noise remains at each of the various measured levels must be determined.

To estimate employee noise exposures with a sound level meter it is also generally necessary to take several measurements at different locations within the workplace. After appropriate sound level meter readings are obtained, people sometimes draw "maps" of the sound levels within different areas of the workplace. By using a sound level "map" and information on employee locations throughout the day, estimates of individual exposure levels can be developed. This measurement method is generally referred to as *area* noise monitoring.

A dosimeter is like a sound level meter except that it stores sound level measurements and integrates these measurements over time, providing an average noise exposure reading for a given period of time, such as an 8-hour workday. With a dosimeter, a microphone is attached to the employee's clothing and the exposure measurement is simply read at the end of the desired time period. A reader may be used to read-out the dosimeter's measurements. Since the dosimeter is worn by the employee, it measures noise levels in those locations in which the employee travels. A sound level meter can also be positioned within the immediate vicinity of the exposed worker to obtain an individual exposure estimate. Such procedures are generally referred to as *personal* noise monitoring.

Area monitoring can be used to estimate noise exposure when the noise levels are relatively constant and employees are not mobile. In workplaces where employees move about in different areas or where the noise intensity tends to fluctuate over time, noise exposure is generally more accurately estimated by the personal monitoring approach.

In situations where personal monitoring is appropriate, proper positioning of the microphone is necessary to obtain accurate measurements. With a dosimeter, the microphone is generally located on the shoulder and remains in that position for the entire workday. With a sound level meter, the microphone is stationed near the employee's head, and the instrument is usually held by an individual who follows the employee as he or she moves about.

Manufacturer's instructions, contained in dosimeter and sound level meter operating manuals, should be followed for calibration and maintenance. To ensure accurate results, it is considered good professional practice to calibrate instruments before and after each use.

HOW OFTEN IS IT NECESSARY TO MONITOR NOISE LEVELS?

The amendment requires that when there are significant changes in machinery or production processes that may result in increased noise levels, remonitoring must be conducted to determine whether additional employees need to be included in the hearing conservation program. Many companies choose to remonitor periodically (once every year or two) to ensure that all exposed employees are included in their hearing conservation programs.

WHERE CAN EQUIPMENT AND TECHNICAL ADVICE BE OBTAINED?

Noise monitoring equipment may be either purchased or rented. Sound level meters cost about $500 to $1,000, while dosimeters range in price from about $750 to $1,500. Smaller companies may find it more economical to rent equipment rather than to purchase it. Names of equipment suppliers may be found in the telephone book (Yellow Pages) under headings such as: "Safety Equipment," "Industrial Hygiene," or "Engineers-Acoustical." In addition to providing information on obtaining noise monitoring equipment, many companies and individuals included under such listings can provide professional advice on how to conduct a valid noise monitoring program. Some audiological testing firms and industrial hygiene firms also provide noise monitoring services. Universities with audiology, industrial hygiene, or acoustical engineering departments may also provide information or may be able to help employers meet their obligations under this amendment.

Free, on-site assistance may be obtained from OSHA-supported state and private consultation organizations. These safety and health consultative entities generally give priority to the needs of small businesses. See the attached directory for a listing of organizations to contact for aid.

OSHA ONSITE CONSULTATION PROJECT DIRECTORY

State	Office and address	Contact
Alabama	Alabama Consultation Program, P.O. Box 6005, University, Alabama 35486.	(205) 348–7136, Mr. William Weems, Director.

APPENDIX 4C

§ 1910.95

29 CFR Ch. XVII (7-1-94 Edition)

OSHA ONSITE CONSULTATION PROJECT DIRECTORY—Continued

State	Office and address	Contact
Alaska	State of Alaska, Department of Labor, Occupational Safety & Health, 3301 Eagle St., Pouch 7–022, Anchorage, Alaska 99510.	(907) 276–5013, Mr. Stan Godsoe, Project Manager (Air Mail).
American Samoa	Service not yet available.	
Arizona	Consultation and Training, Arizona Division of Occupational Safety and Health, P.O. Box 19070, 1624 W. Adams, Phoenix, AZ 85005.	(602) 255–5795, Mr. Thomas Ramaley, Manager.
Arkansas	OSHA Consultation, Arkansas Department of Labor, 1022 High St., Little Rock, Ark. 72202.	(501) 371–2992, Mr. George Smith, Project Director.
California	CAL/OSHA Consultation Service, 2nd Floor, 525 Golden Gate Avenue, San Francisco, CA 94102.	(415) 557–2870, Mr. Emmett Jones, Chief.
Colorado	Occupational Safety & Health Section, Colorado State University, Institute of Rural Environmental Health, 110 Veterinary Science Building, Fort Collins, CO 80523.	(303) 491–6151, Dr. Roy M. Buchan, Project Director.
Connecticut	Division of Occupational Safety & Health, Connecticut Department of Labor, 200 Folly Brook Boulevard, Wethersfield, Conn. 06109.	(203) 566–4550, Mr. Leo Alix, Director.
Delaware	Delaware Department of Labor, Division of Industrial Affairs, 820 North French Street, 6th Floor, Wilmington, DE 19801.	(302) 571–3908, Mr. Bruno Salvadori, Director.
District of Columbia	Occupational Safety & Health Division, District of Columbia, Department Employment Services, Office of Labor Standards, 2900 Newton Street NE., Washington, DC 20018.	(202) 832–1230, Mr. Lorenzo M. White, Acting Associate Director.
Florida	Department of Labor & Employment Security, Bureau of Industrial Safety and Health, LaFayette Building, Room 204, 2551 Executive Center Circle West, Tallahassee, FL 32301.	(904) 488–3044, Mr. John C. Glenn, Administrator.
Georgia	Economic Development Division, Technology and Development Laboratory, Engineering Experiment Station, Georgia Institute of Technology, Atlanta, GA 30332.	(404) 894–3806, Mr. William C. Howard, Assistant to Director, Mr. James Burson, Project Manager.
Guam	Department of Labor, Government of Guam, 23548 Guam Main Facility, Agana, Guam 96921.	(671) 772–6291, Joe R. San Agustin, Director.
Hawaii	Education and Information Branch, Division of Occupational Safety and Health, Suite 910, 677 Ala Moana, Honolulu, HI 96813.	(808) 548–2511, Mr. Don Alper, Manager (Air Mail).
Idaho	OSHA Onsite Consultation Program, Boise State University, Community and Environmental Health, 1910 University Drive, Boise, ID 83725.	(208) 385–3929, Dr. Eldon Edmundson, Director.
Illinois	Division of Industrial Services, Dept. of Commerce and Community Affairs, 310 S. Michigan Avenue, 10 Floor, Chicago, IL 60601.	(800) 972–4140/4216 (Toll-free in State), (312) 793–3270, Mr. Stan Czwinski, Assistant Director.
Iowa	Bureau of Labor, 307 E. Seventh Street, Des Moines, IA 50319.	(515) 281–3606, Mr. Allen J. Meier, Commissioner.
Indiana	Bureau of Safety, Education and Training, Indiana Division of Labor, 1013 State Office Building, Indianapolis, IN 46204.	(317) 633–5845, Mr. Harold Mills, Director.
Kansas	Kansas Dept. of Human Resources, 401 Topeka Ave., Topeka, KS 66603.	(913) 296–4086, Mr. Jerry Abbott, Secretary.
Kentucky	Education and Training, Occupational Safety and Health, Kentucky Department of Labor, 127 Building, 127 South, Frankfort, KY 40601.	(502) 564–6895, Mr. Larry Potter, Director.
Louisiana	No services available as yet (Pending FY 83).	
Maine	Division of Industrial Safety, Maine Dept. of Labor, Labor Station 45, State Office Building, Augusta, ME 04333.	(207) 289–3331, Mr. Lester Wood, Director.
Maryland	Consultation Services, Division of Labor & Industry, 501 St. Paul Place, Baltimore, Maryland 21202.	(301) 659–4210, Ms. Ileana O'Brien, Project Manager, 7(c)(1) Agreement.
Massachusetts	Division of Industrial Safety, Massachusetts Department of Labor and Industries, 100 Cambridge Street, Boston, MA 02202.	(617) 727–3567, Mr. Edward Noseworthy, Project Director.
Michigan (Health)	Special Programs Section, Division of Occupational Health, Michigan Dept. of Public Health, 3500 N. Logan, Lansing, MI 48909.	(517) 373–1410, Mr. Irving Davis, Chief.
Michigan (Safety)	Safety Education & Training Division Bureau of Safety and Regulation, Michigan Department of Labor, 7150 Harris Drive, Box 30015, Lansing, Michigan 48909.	(517) 322–1809, Mr. Alan Harvie, Chief.

Occupational Safety and Health Admin., Labor § 1910.95

OSHA ONSITE CONSULTATION PROJECT DIRECTORY—Continued

State	Office and address	Contact
Minnesota	Training and Education Unit, Department of Labor and Industry, 5th Floor, 444 Lafayette Road, St. Paul, MN 55101.	(612) 296-2973, Mr. Timothy Tierney, Project Manager.
Mississippi	Division of Occupational Safety and Health, Mississippi State Board of Health, P.O. Box 1700, Jackson, MS 39205.	(601) 982-6315, Mr. Henry L. Laird, Director.
Missouri	Missouri Department of Labor and Industrial Relations, 722 Jefferson Street, Jefferson City, MO 65101.	1-(800) 392-0208, (314) 751-3403, Ms. Paula Smith, Mr. Jim Brake.
Montana	Montana Bureau of Safety & Health, Division of Workers Compensation, 815 Front Street, Helena, MT 59601.	(406) 449-3402, Mr. Ed Gatzemeier, Chief.
Nebraska	Nebraska Department of Labor, State House Station, State Capitol, P.O. Box 94600, Lincoln, NB 68509.	475-8451 Ext. 258, Mr. Joseph Carroll, Commissioner.
Nevada	Department of Occupational Safety and Health, Nevada Industrial Commission, 515 E. Muffer Street, Carson City, NV 89714.	(702) 885-5240, Mr. Allen Traenkner, Director.
New Hampshire	For information contact	Office of Consultation Programs, Room N3472 200 Constitution Avenue, NW. Washington, DC 20210, Phone: (202) 523-8985.
New Jersey	New Jersey Department of Labor and Industry Division of Work Place Standards, CN-054, Trenton, NJ 08625.	(609) 292-2313, FTS-8-477-2313, Mr. William Clark, Assistant Commissioner.
New Mexico	OSHA Consultation, Health and Environment Department, Environmental Improvement Division, Occupational Health & Safety Section, 4215 Montgomery Boulevard, NE., Albuquerque, NM 87109.	(505) 842-3387, Mr. Albert M. Stevens, Project Manager.
New York	Division of Safety and Health, New York State Department of Labor, 2 World Trade Center, Room 6995, New York, NY 10047.	(212) 488-7746/7, Mr. Joseph Alleva, Project Manager, DOSH.
North Carolina	Consultation Services, North Carolina Department of Labor, 4 West Edenton Street, Raleigh, NC 27601.	(919) 733-4885, Mr. David Pierce, Director.
North Dakota	Division of Environmental Research, Department of Health, Missouri Office Building, 1200 Missouri Avenue, Bismarck, ND 58505.	(701) 224-2348, Mr. Jay Crawford, Director.
Ohio	Department of Industrial Relations, Division of Onsite Consultation, P.O. Box 825, 2323 5th Avenue, Columbus, OH 43216.	(800) 282-1425 (Toll-free in State), (614) 466-7485, Mr. Andrew Doehrel, Project Manager.
Oklahoma	OSHA Division, Oklahoma Department of Labor, State Capitol, Suite 118, Oklahoma City, OK 73105.	(405) 521-2461, Mr. Charles W. McGlon, Director.
Oregon	Consultative Section, Department of Workers' Compensation, Accident Prevention Division, Room 102, Building 1, 2110 Front Street NE., Salem, OR 97310.	(503) 378-2890, Mr. Jack Buckland, Supervisor.
Pennsylvania	For information contact	Office of Consultation Programs, Room N3472, 200 Constitution Avenue NW., Washington, DC 20210, Phone: (202) 523-8985.
Puerto Rico	Occupational Safety & Health, Puerto Rico Department of Labor and Human Resources, 505 Munoz Rivera Ave., 21st Floor, Hato Rey, Puerto Rico 00919.	(809) 754-2134, Mr. John Cinque, Assistant Secretary, (Air Mail).
Rhode Island	Division of Occupational Health, Rhode Island Department of Health, The Cannon Building, 206 Health Department Building, Providence, RI 02903.	(401) 277-2438, Mr. James E. Hickey, Chief.
South Carolina	Consultation and Monitoring, South Carolina Department of Labor, P.O. Box 11329, Columbia, SC 29211.	(803) 758-8921, Mr. Robert Peck, Director, 7(c)(1), Project.
South Dakota	South Dakota Consultation Program, South Dakota State University, S.T.A.T.E.-Engineering Extension, 201 Pugsley Center-SDSO, Brookings, SD 57007.	(605) 688-4101, Mr. James Ceglian, Director.
Tennessee	OSHA Consultative Services, Tennessee Department of Labor, 2nd Floor, 501 Union Building, Nashville, TN 37219.	(615) 741-2793, Mr. L. H. Craig Director.
Texas	Division of Occupational Safety and State Safety Engineer, Texas Department of Health and Resources, 1100 West 49th Street, Austin, TX 78756.	(512) 458-7287, Mr. Walter G. Martin, P.E. Director.
Trust Territories	Service not yet available.	
Utah	Utah Job Safety and Health Consultation Service, Suite 4004, Crane Building, 307 West 200 South, Salt Lake City, UT 84101.	(801) 533-7927/8/9, Mr. H. M. Bergeson, Project Director.
Vermont	Division of Occupational Safety and Health, Vermont Department of Labor and Industry, 118 State Street, Montpelier, VT 05602.	(802) 828-2765, Mr. Robert Mcleod, Project Director.

APPENDIX 4C

§ 1910.95 29 CFR Ch. XVII (7-1-94 Edition)

OSHA ONSITE CONSULTATION PROJECT DIRECTORY—Continued

State	Office and address	Contact
Virginia	Department of Labor and Industry, P.O. Box 12064, 205 N. 4th Street, Richmond, Va. 23241.	(804) 786-5875, Mr. Robert Beard, Commissioner.
Virgin Islands	Division of Occupational Safety and Health, Virgin Islands Department of Labor, Lagoon Street, Room 207, Frederiksted, Virgin Islands 00840.	(809) 772-1315, Mr. Louis Llanos, Deputy Director-DOSH.
Washington	Department of Labor and Industry, P.O. Box 207, Olympia, WA 98504.	(206) 753-6500, Mr. James Sullivan, Assistant Director.
West Virginia	West Virginia Department of Labor, Room 451B, State Capitol, 1900 Washington Street, Charleston, WV 25305.	FTS 8-885-7890, Mr. Lawrence Barker, Commissioner.
Wisconsin (Health)	Section of Occupational Health, Department of Health and Social Services, P.O. Box 309, Madison, WI 53701.	(608) 266-0417, Ms. Patricia Natzke, Acting Chief.
Wisconsin (Safety)	Division of Safety and Buildings, Department of Industry, Labor and Human Relations, 1570 E. Moreland Blvd., Waukesha, WI 53186.	(414) 544-8686, Mr. Richard Michalski, Supervisor.
Wyoming	Wyoming Occupational Health and Safety Department, 200 East 8th Avenue, Cheyenne, Wyo. 82002.	(307) 777-7786, Mr. Donald Owsley, Health and Safety Administrator.

APPENDIX H TO § 1910.95—AVAILABILITY OF REFERENCED DOCUMENTS

Paragraphs (c) through (o) of 29 CFR 1910.95 and the accompanying appendices contain provisions which incorporate publications by reference. Generally, the publications provide criteria for instruments to be used in monitoring and audiometric testing. These criteria are intended to be mandatory when so indicated in the applicable paragraphs of § 1910.95 and appendices.

It should be noted that OSHA does not require that employers purchase a copy of the referenced publications. Employers, however, may desire to obtain a copy of the referenced publications for their own information.

The designation of the paragraph of the standard in which the referenced publications appear, the titles of the publications, and the availability of the publications are as follows:

Paragraph designation	Referenced publication	Available from—
Appendix B	"List of Personal Hearing Protectors and Attenuation Data," HEW Pub. No. 76-120, 1975. NTIS-PB267461.	National Technical Information Service, Port Royal Road, Springfield, VA 22161.
Appendix D	"Specification for Sound Level Meters," S1.4-1971 (R1976).	American National Standards Institute, Inc., 1430 Broadway, New York, NY 10018.
§ 1910.95(k)(2), appendix E	"Specifications for Audiometers," S3.6-1969.	American National Standards Institute, Inc., 1430 Broadway, New York, NY 10018.
Appendix D	"Specification for Octave, Half-Octave and Third-Octave Band Filter Sets," S1.11-1971 (R1976).	Back Numbers Department, Dept. STD, American Institute of Physics, 333 E. 45th St., New York, NY 10017; American National Standards Institute, Inc., 1430 Broadway, New York, NY 10018.

The referenced publications (or a microfiche of the publications) are available for review at many universities and public libraries throughout the country. These publications may also be examined at the OSHA Technical Data Center, Room N2439, United States Department of Labor, 200 Constitution Avenue, NW., Washington, DC 20210, (202) 523-9700 or at any OSHA Regional Office (see telephone directories under United States Government--Labor Department).

APPENDIX I TO § 1910.95—DEFINITIONS

These definitions apply to the following terms as used in paragraphs (c) through (n) of 29 CFR 1910.95.

Action level—An 8-hour time-weighted average of 85 decibels measured on the A-scale, slow response, or equivalently, a dose of fifty percent.

Audiogram—A chart, graph, or table resulting from an audiometric test showing an individual's hearing threshold levels as a function of frequency.

Audiologist—A professional, specializing in the study and rehabilitation of hearing, who is certified by the American Speech-Language-Hearing Association or licensed by a state board of examiners.

Baseline audiogram—The audiogram against which future audiograms are compared.

Occupational Safety and Health Admin., Labor § 1910.96

Criterion sound level—A sound level of 90 decibels.

Decibel (dB)—Unit of measurement of sound level.

Hertz (Hz)—Unit of measurement of frequency, numerically equal to cycles per second.

Medical pathology—A disorder or disease. For purposes of this regulation, a condition or disease affecting the ear, which should be treated by a physician specialist.

Noise dose—The ratio, expressed as a percentage, of (1) the time integral, over a stated time or event, of the 0.6 power of the measured SLOW exponential time-averaged, squared A-weighted sound pressure and (2) the product of the criterion duration (8 hours) and the 0.6 power of the squared sound pressure corresponding to the criterion sound level (90 dB).

Noise dosimeter—An instrument that integrates a function of sound pressure over a period of time in such a manner that it directly indicates a noise dose.

Otolaryngologist—A physician specializing in diagnosis and treatment of disorders of the ear, nose and throat.

Representative exposure—Measurements of an employee's noise dose or 8-hour time-weighted average sound level that the employers deem to be representative of the exposures of other employees in the workplace.

Sound level—Ten times the common logarithm of the ratio of the square of the measured A-weighted sound pressure to the square of the standard reference pressure of 20 micropascals. Unit: decibels (dB). For use with this regulation, SLOW time response, in accordance with ANSI S1.4–1971 (R1976), is required.

Sound level meter—An instrument for the measurement of sound level.

Time-weighted average sound level—That sound level, which if constant over an 8-hour exposure, would result in the same noise dose as is measured.

[39 FR 23502, June 27, 1974, as amended at 46 FR 4161, Jan. 16, 1981; 46 FR 62845, Dec. 29, 1981; 48 FR 9776, Mar. 8, 1983; 48 FR 29687, June 28, 1983; 54 FR 24333, June 7, 1989]

Appendix 4D
29 CFR 1910.1000–1910.1001
Air Contaminants

§ 1910.1000 Air contaminants.

An employee's exposure to any substance listed in Tables Z–1, Z–2, or Z–3 of this section shall be limited in accordance with the requirements of the following paragraphs of this section.

(a) *Table Z–1.* (1) *Substances with limits preceded by "C"—Ceiling Values.* An employee's exposure to any substance in Table Z–1, the exposure limit of which is preceded by a "C", shall at no time exceed the exposure limit given for that substance. If instantaneous monitoring is not feasible, then the ceiling shall be assessed as a 15-minute time weighted average exposure which shall not be exceeded at any time during the working day.

(2) *Other substances—8-hour Time Weighted Averages.* An employee's exposure to any substance in Table Z–1, the exposure limit of which is not preceded by a "C", shall not exceed the 8-hour Time Weighted Average given for that substance in any 8-hour work shift of a 40-hour work week.

(b) *Table Z–2.* An employee's exposure to any substance listed in Table Z–2 shall not exceed the exposure limits specified as follows:

(1) *8-hour time weighted averages.* An employee's exposure to any substance listed in Table Z–2, in any 8-hour work shift of a 40-hour work week, shall not exceed the 8-hour time weighted average limit given for that substance in Table Z–2.

(2) *Acceptable ceiling concentrations.* An employee's exposure to a substance listed in Table Z–2 shall not exceed at any time during an 8-hour shift the ac-

Occupational Safety and Health Admin., Labor § 1910.1000

ceptable ceiling concentration limit given for the substance in the table, except for a time period, and up to a concentration not exceeding the maximum duration and concentration allowed in the column under "acceptable maximum peak above the acceptable ceiling concentration for an 8-hour shift."

(3) *Example.* During an 8-hour work shift, an employee may be exposed to a concentration of Substance A (with a 10 ppm TWA, 25 ppm ceiling and 50 ppm peak) above 25 ppm (but never above 50 ppm) only for a maximum period of 10 minutes. Such exposure must be compensated by exposures to concentrations less than 10 ppm so that the cumulative exposure for the entire 8-hour work shift does not exceed a weighted average of 10 ppm.

(c) *Table Z-3.* An employee's exposure to any substance listed in Table Z-3, in any 8-hour work shift of a 40-hour work week, shall not exceed the 8-hour time weighted average limit given for that substance in the table.

(d) *Computation formulae.* The computation formula which shall apply to employee exposure to more than one substance for which 8-hour time weighted averages are listed in subpart Z of 29 CFR part 1910 in order to determine whether an employee is exposed over the regulatory limit is as follows:

(1)(i) The cumulative exposure for an 8-hour work shift shall be computed as follows:

$E=(C_aT_a+C_bT_b+...C_nT_n)\div 8$

Where:

E is the equivalent exposure for the working shift.
C is the concentration during any period of time T where the concentration remains constant.
T is the duration in hours of the exposure at the concentration C.

The value of E shall not exceed the 8-hour time weighted average specified in subpart Z of 29 CFR part 1910 for the substance involved.

(ii) To illustrate the formula prescribed in paragraph (d)(1)(i) of this section, assume that Substance A has an 8-hour time weighted average limit of 100 ppm noted in Table Z-1. Assume that an employee is subject to the following exposure:

Two hours exposure at 150 ppm
Two hours exposure at 75 ppm
Four hours exposure at 50 ppm

Substituting this information in the formula, we have

$(2\times 150+2\times 75+4\times 50)\div 8=81.25$ ppm

Since 81.25 ppm is less than 100 ppm, the 8-hour time weighted average limit, the exposure is acceptable.

(2)(i) in case of a mixture of air contaminants an employer shall compute the equivalent exposure as follows:

$E_m=(C_1+L_1+C_2+L_2)+...(C_n+L_n)$

Where:

E_m is the equivalent exposure for the mixture.
C is the concentration of a particular contaminant.
L is the exposure limit for that substance specified in subpart Z of 29 CFR part 1910.

The value of E_m shall not exceed unity (1).

(ii) To illustrate the formula prescribed in paragraph (d)(2)(i) of this section, consider the following exposures:

Substance	Actual concentration of 8-hour exposure (ppm)	8-hour TWA PEL (ppm)
B	500	1,000
C	45	200
D	40	200

Substituting in the formula, we have:

$E_m=500\div 1,000+45\div 200+40\div 200$
$E_m=0.500+0.225+0.200$
$E_m=0.925$

Since E_m is less than unity (1), the exposure combination is within acceptable limits.

(e) To achieve compliance with paragraphs (a) through (d) of this section, administrative or engineering controls must first be determined and implemented whenever feasible. When such controls are not feasible to achieve full compliance, protective equipment or any other protective measures shall be used to keep the exposure of employees to air contaminants within the limits prescribed in this section. Any equipment and/or technical measures used for this purpose must be approved for each particular use by a competent industrial hygienist or other technically qualified person. Whenever respirators are used, their use shall comply with 1910.134.

(f) *Effective dates.* The exposure limits specified have been in effect with the

APPENDIX 4D

§ 1910.1000   29 CFR Ch. XVII (7-1-94 Edition)

method of compliance specified in paragraph (e) of this section since May 29, 1971.

TABLE Z-1.—LIMITS FOR AIR CONTAMINANTS

Substance	CAS No. (c)	ppm (a)[1]	mg/m³ (b)[1]	Skin designation
Acetaldehyde	75-07-0	200	360	
Acetic acid	64-19-7	10	25	
Acetic anhydride	108-24-7	5	20	
Acetone	67-64-1	1000	2400	
Acetonitrile	75-05-8	40	70	
2-Acetylaminofluorine; see 1910.1014	53-96-3			
Acetylene dichloride; see 1,2-Dichloroethylene.				
Acetylene tetrabromide	79-27-6	1	14	
Acrolein	107-02-8	0.1	0.25	
Acrylamide	79-06-1		0.3	X
Acrylonitrile; see 1910.1045	107-13-1			
Aldrin	309-00-2		0.25	X
Allyl alcohol	107-18-6	2	5	X
Allyl chloride	107-05-1	1	3	
Allyl glycidyl ether (AGE)	106-92-3	(C)10	(C)45	
Allyl propyl disulfide	2179-59-1	2	12	
alpha-Alumina	1344-28-1			
Total dust			15	
Respirable fraction			5	
Aluminum, metal (as Al)	7429-90-5			
Total dust			15	
Respirable fraction			5	
4-Aminodiphenyl; see 1910.1011	92-67-1			
2-Aminoethanol; see Ethanolamine.				
2-Aminopyridine	504-29-0	0.5	2	
Ammonia	7664-41-7	50	35	
Ammonium sulfamate	7773-06-0			
Total dust			15	
Respirable fraction			5	
n-Amyl acetate	628-63-7	100	525	
sec-Amyl acetate	626-38-0	125	650	
Aniline and homologs	62-53-3	5	19	X
Anisidine (o-, p-isomers)	29191-52-4		0.5	X
Antimony and compounds (as Sb)	7440-36-0		0.5	
ANTU (alpha Naphthylthiourea)	86-88-4		0.3	
Arsenic, inorganic compounds (as As); see 1910.1018.	7440-38-2			
Arsenic, organic compounds (as As)	7440-38-2		0.5	
Arsine	7784-42-1	0.05	0.2	
Asbestos; see 1910.1001	(4)			
Azinphos-methyl	86-50-0		0.2	X
Barium, soluble compounds (as Ba)	7440-39-3		0.5	
Barium sulfate	7727-43-7			
Total dust			15	
Respirable fraction			5	
Benomyl	17804-35-2			
Total dust			15	
Respirable fraction			5	
Benzene; see 1910.1028	71-43-2			
See Table Z-2 for the limits applicable in the operations or sectors excluded in 1910.1028[d]				
Benzidine; see 1910.1010	92-87-5			
p-Benzoquinone; see Quinone.				
Benzo(a)pyrene; see Coal tar pitch volatiles..				
Benzoyl peroxide	94-36-0		5	
Benzyl chloride	100-44-7	1	5	
Beryllium and beryllium compounds (as Be).	7440-41-7		(²)	
Biphenyl; see Diphenyl.				
Bismuth telluride, Undoped	1304-82-1			
Total dust			15	
Respirable fraction			5	
Boron oxide	1303-86-2			
Total dust			15	

Occupational Safety and Health Admin., Labor § 1910.1000

TABLE Z-1.—LIMITS FOR AIR CONTAMINANTS—Continued

Substance	CAS No. (c)	ppm (a)[1]	mg/m^3 (b)[1]	Skin designation
Boron trifluoride	7637-07-2	(C)1	(C)3	
Bromine	7726-95-6	0.1	0.7	
Bromoform	75-25-2	0.5	5	X
Butadiene (1,3-Butadiene)	106-99-0	1000	2200	
Butanethiol; see Butyl mercaptan.				
2-Butanone (Methyl ethyl ketone)	78-93-3	200	590	
2-Butoxyethanol	111-76-2	50	240	X
n-Butyl-acetate	123-86-4	150	710	
sec-Butyl acetate	105-46-4	200	950	
tert-Butyl acetate	540-88-5	200	950	
n-Butyl alcohol	71-36-3	100	300	
sec-Butyl alcohol	78-92-2	150	450	
tert-Butyl alcohol	75-65-0	100	300	
Butylamine	109-73-9	(C)5	(C)15	X
tert-Butyl chromate (as CrO$_3$)	1189-85-1		(C)0.1	X
n-Butyl glycidyl ether (BGE)	2426-08-6	50	270	
Butyl mercaptan	109-79-5	10	35	
p-tert-Butyltoluene	98-51-1	10	60	
Cadmium (as Cd); see 1910.1027	7440-43-9			
Calcium carbonate	1317-65-3			
Total dust			15	
Respirable fraction			5	
Calcium hydroxide	1305-62-0			
Total dust			15	
Respirable fraction			5	
Calcium oxide	1305-78-8		5	
Calcium silicate	1344-95-2			
Total dust			15	
Respirable fraction			5	
Calcium sulfate	7778-18-9			
Total dust			15	
Respirable fraction			5	
Camphor, synthetic	76-22-2		2	
Carbaryl (Sevin)	63-25-2		5	
Carbon black	1333-86-4		3.5	
Carbon dioxide	124-38-9	5000	9000	
Carbon disulfide	75-15-0		(^{2})	
Carbon monoxide	630-08-0	50	55	
Carbon tetrachloride	56-23-5		(^{2})	
Cellulose	9004-34-6			
Total dust			15	
Respirable fraction			5	
Chlordane	57-74-9		0.5	X
Chlorinated camphene	8001-35-2		0.5	X
Chlorinated diphenyl oxide	55720-99-5		0.5	
Chlorine	7782-50-5	(C)1	(C)3	
Chlorine dioxide	10049-04-4	0.1	0.3	
Chlorine trifluoride	7790-91-2	(C)0.1	(C)0.4	
Chloroacetaldehyde	107-20-0	(C)1	(C)3	
a-Chloroacetophenone (Phenacyl chloride).	532-27-4	0.05	0.3	
Chlorobenzene	108-90-7	75	350	
o-Chlorobenzylidene malononitrile	2698-41-1	0.05	0.4	
Chlorobromomethane	74-97-5	200	1050	
2-Chloro-1,3-butadiene; see beta-Chloroprene.				
Chlorodiphenyl (42% Chlorine) (PCB)	53469-21-9		1	X
Chlorodiphenyl (54% Chlorine) (PCB)	11097-69-1		0.5	X
1-Chloro-2,3-epoxypropane; see Epichlorohydrin.				
2-Chloroethanol; see Ethylene chlorohydrin.				
Chloroethylene; see Vinyl chloride.				
Chloroform (Trichloromethane)	67-66-3	(C)50	(C)240	
bis(Chloromethyl) ether; see 1910.1008.	542-88-1			
Chloromethyl methyl ether; see 1910.1006.	107-30-2			
1-Chloro-1-nitropropane	600-25-9	20	100	
Chloropicrin	76-06-2	0.1	0.7	
beta-Chloroprene	126-99-8	25	90	X
2-Chloro-6-(trichloromethyl) pyridine	1929-82-4			

APPENDIX 4D

§ 1910.1000   29 CFR Ch. XVII (7-1-94 Edition)

TABLE Z-1.—LIMITS FOR AIR CONTAMINANTS—Continued

Substance	CAS No. (c)	ppm (a)[1]	mg/m³ (b)[1]	Skin designation
Total dust			15	
Respirable fraction			5	
Chromic acid and chromates (as CrO_3)	([4])		([2])	
Chromium (II) compounds. (as Cr)	7440-47-3		0.5	
Chromium (III) compounds. (as Cr)	7440-47-3		0.5	
Chromium metal and insol. salts (as Cr).	7440-47-3		1	
Chrysene; see Coal tar pitch volatiles.				
Clopidol	2971-90-6			
Total dust			15	
Respirable fraction			5	
Coal dust (less than 5% SiO_2), respirable fraction.			([3])	
Coal dust (greater than or equal to 5% SiO_2), respirable fraction.			([3])	
Coal tar pitch volatiles (benzene soluble fraction), anthracene, BaP, phenanthrene, acridine, chrysene, pyrene.	65966-93-2		0.2	
Cobalt metal, dust, and fume (as Co)	7440-48-4		0.1	
Coke oven emissions; see 1910.1029.				
Copper	7440-50-8			
Fume (as Cu)			0.1	
Dusts and mists (as Cu)			1	
Cotton dust[e]; see 1910.1043			1	
Crag herbicide (Sesone)	136-78-7			
Total dust			15	
Respirable fraction			5	
Cresol, all isomers	1319-77-3	5	22	X
Crotonaldehyde	123-73-9; 4170-30-3	2	6	
Cumene	98-82-8	50	245	X
Cyanides (as CN)	([4])		5	
Cyclohexane	110-82-7	300	1050	
Cyclohexanol	108-93-0	50	200	
Cyclohexanone	108-94-1	50	200	
Cyclohexene	110-83-8	300	1015	
Cyclopentadiene	542-92-7	75	200	
2,4-D (Dichlorophenoxyacetic acid)	94-75-7		10	
Decaborane	17702-41-9	0.05	0.3	X
Demeton (Systox)	8065-48-3		0.1	X
Diacetone alcohol (4-Hydroxy-4-methyl-2-pentanone).	123-42-2	50	240	
1,2-Diaminoethane; see Ethylenediamine.				
Diazomethane	334-88-3	0.2	0.4	
Diborane	19287-45-7	0.1	0.1	
1,2-Dibromo-3-chloropropane (CBCP); see 1910.1044.	96-12-8			
1,2-Dibromoethane; see Ethylene dibromide.				
Dibutyl phosphate	107-66-4	1	5	
Dibutyl phthalate	84-74-2		5	
o-Dichlorobenzene	95-50-1	(C)50	(C)300	
p-Dichlorobenzene	106-46-7	75	450	
3,3'-Dichlorobenzidine; see 1910.1007	91-94-1			
Dichlorodifluoromethane	75-71-8	1000	4950	
1,3-Dichloro-5,5-dimethyl hydantoin	118-52-5		0.2	
Dichlorodiphenyltrichloroethane (DDT)	50-29-3		1	X
1,1-Dichloroethane	75-34-3	100	400	
1,2-Dichloroethane; see Ethylene dichloride.				
1,2-Dichloroethylene	540-59-0	200	790	
Dichloroethyl ether	111-44-4	(C)15	(C)90	X
Dichloromethane; see Methylene chloride.				
Dichloromonofluoromethane	75-43-4	1000	4200	
1,1-Dichloro-1-nitroethane	594-72-9	(C)10	(C)60	
1,2-Dichloropropane; see Propylene dichloride.				
Dichlorotetrafluoroethane	76-14-2	1000	7000	

Occupational Safety and Health Admin., Labor § 1910.1000

TABLE Z-1.—LIMITS FOR AIR CONTAMINANTS—Continued

Substance	CAS No. (c)	ppm (a)[1]	mg/m³ (b)[1]	Skin designation
Dichlorvos (DDVP)	62-73-7		1	X
Dicyclopentadienyl iron	102-54-5			
Total dust			15	
Respirable fraction			5	
Dieldrin	60-57-1		0.25	X
Diethylamine	109-89-7	25	75	
2-Diethylaminoethanol	100-37-8	10	50	X
Diethyl ether; see Ethyl ether.				
Difluorodibromomethane	75-61-6	100	860	
Diglycidyl ether (DGE)	2238-07-5	(C)0.5	(C)2.8	
Dihydroxybenzene; see Hydroquinone.				
Diisobutyl ketone	108-83-8	50	290	
Diisopropylamine	108-18-9	5	20	X
4-Dimethylaminoazobenzene; see 1910.1015.	60-11-7			
Dimethoxymethane; see Methylal.				
Dimethyl acetamide	127-19-5	10	35	X
Dimethylamine	124-40-3	10	18	
Dimethylaminobenzene; see Xylidine.				
Dimethylaniline (N,N-Dimethylaniline)	121-69-7	5	25	X
Dimethylbenzene; see Xylene.				
Dimethyl-1,2-dibromo-2,2-dichloroethyl phosphate.	300-76-5		3	
Dimethylformamide	68-12-2	10	30	X
2,6-Dimethyl-4-heptanone; see Diisobutyl ketone.				
1,1-Dimethylhydrazine	57-14-7	0.5	1	X
Dimethylphthalate	131-11-3		5	
Dimethyl sulfate	77-78-1	1	5	X
Dinitrobenzene (all isomers)			1	X
(ortho)	528-29-0			
(meta)	99-65-0			
(para)	100-25-4			
Dinitro-o-cresol	534-52-1		0.2	X
Dinitrotoluene	25321-14-6		1.5	X
Dioxane (Diethylene dioxide)	123-91-1	100	360	X
Diphenyl (Biphenyl)	92-52-4	0.2	1	
Diphenylmethane diisocyanate; see Methylene bisphenyl isocyanate.				
Dipropylene glycol methyl ether	34590-94-8	100	600	X
Di-sec octyl phthalate (Di-(2-ethylhexyl) phthalate).	117-81-7		5	
Emery	12415-34-8			
Total dust			15	
Respirable fraction			5	
Endosulfan	115-29-7		0.1	X
Endrin	72-20-8		0.1	X
Epichlorohydrin	106-89-8	5	19	X
EPN	2104-64-5		0.5	X
1,2-Epoxypropane; see Propylene oxide.				
2,3-Epoxy-1-propanol; see Glycidol.				
Ethanethiol; see Ethyl mercaptan.				
Ethanolamine	141-43-5	3	6	
2-Ethoxyethanol (Cellosolve)	110-80-5	200	740	X
2-Ethoxyethyl acetate (Cellosolve acetate).	111-15-9	100	540	X
Ethyl acetate	141-78-6	400	1400	
Ethyl acrylate	140-88-5	25	100	X
Ethyl alcohol (Ethanol)	64-17-5	1000	1900	
Ethylamine	75-04-7	10	18	
Ethyl amyl ketone (5-Methyl-3-heptanone).	541-85-5	25	130	
Ethyl benzene	100-41-4	100	435	
Ethyl bromide	74-96-4	200	890	
Ethyl butyl ketone (3-Heptanone)	106-35-4	50	230	
Ethyl chloride	75-00-3	1000	2600	
Ethyl ether	60-29-7	400	1200	
Ethyl formate	109-94-4	100	300	
Ethyl mercaptan	75-08-1	(C)10	(C)25	
Ethyl silicate	78-10-4	100	850	
Ethylene chlorohydrin	107-07-3	5	16	X

11

APPENDIX 4D

§ 1910.1000   29 CFR Ch. XVII (7-1-94 Edition)

TABLE Z-1.—LIMITS FOR AIR CONTAMINANTS—Continued

Substance	CAS No. (c)	ppm (a)[1]	mg/m³ (b)[1]	Skin designation
Ethylenediamine	107-15-3	10	25	
Ethylene dibromide	106-93-4		([2])	
Ethylene dichloride (1,2-Dichloroethane).	107-06-2		([2])	
Ethylene glycol dinitrate	628-96-6	(C)0.2	(C)1	X
Ethylene glycol methyl acetate; see Methyl cellosolve acetate.				
Ethyleneimine; see 1910.1012	151-56-4			
Ethylene oxide; see 1910.1047	75-21-8			
Ethylidene chloride; see 1,1-Dichloroethane.				
N-Ethylmorpholine	100-74-3	20	94	X
Ferbam	14484-64-1			
Total dust			15	
Ferrovanadium dust	12604-58-9		1	
Fluorides (as F)	([4])		2.5	
Fluorine	7782-41-4	0.1	0.2	
Fluorotrichloromethane (Trichlorofluoromethane).	75-69-4	1000	5600	
Formaldehyde; see 1910.1048	50-00-0			
Formic acid	64-18-6	5	9	
Furfural	98-01-1	5	20	X
Furfuryl alcohol	98-00-0	50	200	
Grain dust (oat, wheat, barley)			10	
Glycerin (mist)	56-81-5			
Total dust			15	
Respirable fraction			5	
Glycidol	556-52-5	50	150	
Glycol monoethyl ether; see 2-Ethoxyethanol.				
Graphite, natural, respirable dust	7782-42-5		([3])	
Graphite, synthetic				
Total dust			15	
Respirable fraction			5	
Guthion; see Azinphos methyl.				
Gypsum	13397-24-5			
Total dust			15	
Respirable fraction			5	
Hafnium	7440-58-6		0.5	
Heptachlor	76-44-8		0.5	X
Heptane (n-Heptane)	142-82-5	500	2000	
Hexachloroethane	67-72-1	1	10	X
Hexachloronaphthalene	1335-87-1		0.2	X
n-Hexane	110-54-3	500	1800	
2-Hexanone (Methyl n-butyl ketone)	591-78-6	100	410	
Hexone (Methyl isobutyl ketone)	108-10-1	100	410	
sec-Hexyl acetate	108-84-9	50	300	
Hydrazine	302-01-2	1	1.3	X
Hydrogen bromide	10035-10-6	3	10	
Hydrogen chloride	7647-01-0	(C)5	(C)7	
Hydrogen cyanide	74-90-8	10	11	X
Hydrogen fluoride (as F)	7664-39-3		([2])	
Hydrogen peroxide	7722-84-1	1	1.4	
Hydrogen selenide (as Se)	7783-07-5	0.05	0.2	
Hydrogen sulfide	7783-06-4		([2])	
Hydroquinone	123-31-9		2	
Iodine	7553-56-2	(C)0.1	(C)1	
Iron oxide fume	1309-37-1		10	
Isoamyl acetate	123-92-2	100	525	
Isoamyl alcohol (primary and secondary).	123-51-3	100	360	
Isobutyl acetate	110-19-0	150	700	
Isobutyl alcohol	78-83-1	100	300	
Isophorone	78-59-1	25	140	
Isopropyl acetate	108-21-4	250	950	
Isopropyl alcohol	67-63-0	400	980	
Isopropylamine	75-31-0	5	12	
Isopropyl ether	108-20-3	500	2100	
Isopropyl glycidyl ether (IGE)	4016-14-2	50	240	
Kaolin	1332-58-7			
Total dust			15	
Respirable fraction			5	

12

Occupational Safety and Health Admin., Labor § 1910.1000

TABLE Z-1.—LIMITS FOR AIR CONTAMINANTS—Continued

Substance	CAS No. (c)	ppm (a)[1]	mg/m³ (b)[1]	Skin designation
Ketene	463-51-4	0.5	0.9	
Lead, inorganic (as Pb); see 1910.1025.	7439-92-1			
Limestone	1317-65-3			
Total dust			15	
Respirable fraction			5	
Lindane	58-89-9		0.5	X
Lithium hydride	7580-67-8		0.025	
L.P.G. (Liquefied petroleum gas)	68476-85-7	1000	1800	
Magnesite	546-93-0			
Total dust			15	
Respirable fraction			5	
Magnesium oxide fume	1309-48-4			
Total particulate			15	
Malathion	121-75-5			
Total dust			15	X
Maleic anhydride	108-31-6	0.25	1	
Manganese compounds (as Mn)	7439-96-5		(C)5	
Manganese fume (as Mn)	7439-96-5		(C)5	
Marble	1317-65-3			
Total dust			15	
Respirable fraction			5	
Mercury (aryl and inorganic) (as Hg)	7439-97-6		(²)	
Mercury (organo) alkyl compounds (as Hg).	7439-97-6		(²)	
Mercury (vapor) (as Hg)	7439-97-6		(²)	
Mesityl oxide	141-79-7	25	100	
Methanethiol; see Methyl mercaptan.				
Methoxychlor	72-43-5			
Total dust			15	
2-Methoxyethanol (Methyl cellosolve)	109-86-4	25	80	X
2-Methoxyethyl acetate (Methyl cellosolve acetate).	110-49-6	25	120	X
Methyl acetate	79-20-9	200	610	
Methyl acetylene (Propyne)	74-99-7	1000	1650	
Methyl acetylene-propadiene mixture (MAPP).		1000	1800	
Methyl acrylate	96-33-3	10	35	X
Methylal (Dimethoxy-methane)	109-87-5	1000	3100	
Methyl alcohol	67-56-1	200	260	
Methylamine	74-89-5	10	12	
Methyl amyl alcohol; see Methyl isobutyl carbinol.				
Methyl n-amyl ketone	110-43-0	100	465	
Methyl bromide	74-83-9	(C)20	(C)80	X
Methyl butyl ketone; see 2-Hexanone.				
Methyl cellosolve; see 2-Methoxyethanol.				
Methyl cellosolve acetate; see 2-Methoxyethyl acetate.				
Methyl chloride	74-87-3		(²)	
Methyl chloroform (1,1,1-Trichloroethane).	71-55-6	350	1900	
Methylcyclohexane	108-87-2	500	2000	
Methylcyclohexanol	25639-42-3	100	470	
o-Methylcyclohexanone	583-60-8	100	460	X
Methylene chloride	75-09-2		(²)	
Methyl ethyl ketone (MEK); see 2-Butanone.				
Methyl formate	107-31-3	100	250	
Methyl hydrazine (Monomethyl hydrazine).	60-34-4	(C)0.2	(C)0.35	X
Methyl iodide	74-88-4	5	28	X
Methyl isoamyl ketone	110-12-3	100	475	
Methyl isobutyl carbinol	108-11-2	25	100	X
Methyl isobutyl ketone; see Hexone.				
Methyl isocyanate	624-83-9	0.02	0.05	X
Methyl mercaptan	74-93-1	(C)10	(C)20	
Methyl methacrylate	80-62-6	100	410	
Methyl propyl ketone; see 2-Pentanone.				
alpha-Methyl styrene	98-83-9	(C)100	(C)480	

§ 1910.1000

TABLE Z-1.—LIMITS FOR AIR CONTAMINANTS—Continued

Substance	CAS No. (c)	ppm (a)[1]	mg/m³ (b)[1]	Skin designation
Methylene bisphenyl isocyanate (MDI)	101-68-8	(C)0.02	(C)0.2	
Mica; see Silicates.				
Molybdenum (as Mo)	7439-98-7			
Soluble compounds			5	
Insoluble compounds.				
Total dust			15	
Monomethyl aniline	100-61-8	2	9	X
Monomethyl hydrazine; see Methyl hydrazine.				
Morpholine	110-91-8	20	70	X
Naphtha (Coal tar)	8030-30-6	100	400	
Naphthalene	91-20-3	10	50	
alpha-Naphthylamine; see 1910.1004	134-32-7			
beta-Naphthylamine; see 1910.1009	91-59-8			
Nickel carbonyl (as Ni)	13463-39-3	0.001	0.007	
Nickel, metal and insoluble compounds (as Ni).	7440-02-0		1	
Nickel, soluble compounds (as Ni)	7440-02-0		1	
Nicotine	54-11-5		0.5	X
Nitric acid	7697-37-2	2	5	
Nitric oxide	10102-43-9	25	30	
p-Nitroaniline	100-01-6	1	6	X
Nitrobenzene	98-95-3	1	5	X
p-Nitrochlorobenzene	100-00-5		1	X
4-Nitrodiphenyl; see 1910.1003	92-93-3			
Nitroethane	79-24-3	100	310	
Nitrogen dioxide	10102-44-0	(C)5	(C)9	
Nitrogen trifluoride	7783-54-2	10	29	
Nitroglycerin	55-63-0	(C)0.2	(C)2	X
Nitromethane	75-52-5	100	250	
1-Nitropropane	108-03-2	25	90	
2-Nitropropane	79-46-9	25	90	
N-Nitrosodimethylamine; see 1910.1016.				
Nitrotoluene (all isomers)		5	30	X
o-isomer	88-72-2			
m-isomer	99-08-1			
p-isomer	99-99-0			
Nitrotrichloromethane; see Chloropicrin.				
Octachloronaphthalene	2234-13-1		0.1	X
Octane	111-65-9	500	2350	
Oil mist, mineral	8012-95-1		5	
Osmium tetroxide (as Os)	20816-12-0		0.002	
Oxalic acid	144-62-7		1	
Oxygen difluoride	7783-41-7	0.05	0.1	
Ozone	10028-15-6	0.1	0.2	
Paraquat, respirable dust	4685-14-7; 1910-42-5; 2074-50-2		0.5	X
Parathion	56-38-2		0.1	X
Particulates not otherwise regulated (PNOR)[f].				
Total dust			15	
Respirable fraction			5	
PCB; see Chlorodiphenyl (42% and 54% chlorine).				
Pentaborane	19624-22-7	0.005	0.01	
Pentachloronaphthalene	1321-64-8		0.5	X
Pentachlorophenol	87-86-5		0.5	X
Pentaerythritol	115-77-5			
Total dust			15	
Respirable fraction			5	
Pentane	109-66-0	1000	2950	
2-Pentanone (Methyl propyl ketone)	107-87-9	200	700	
Perchloroethylene (Tetrachloroethylene).	127-18-4		([2])	
Perchloromethyl mercaptan	594-42-3	0.1	0.8	
Perchloryl fluoride	7616-94-6	3	13.5	
Perlite	93763-70-3			
Total dust			15	
Respirable fraction			5	

Occupational Safety and Health Admin., Labor § 1910.1000

TABLE Z-1.—LIMITS FOR AIR CONTAMINANTS—Continued

Substance	CAS No. (c)	ppm (a)[1]	mg/m³ (b)[1]	Skin designation
Petroleum distillates (Naphtha) (Rubber Solvent).		500	2000	
Phenol	108-95-2	5	19	X
p-Phenylene diamine	106-50-3		0.1	X
Phenyl ether, vapor	101-84-8	1	7	
Phenyl ether-biphenyl mixture, vapor		1	7	
Phenylethylene; see Styrene.				
Phenyl glycidyl ether (PGE)	122-60-1	10	60	
Phenylhydrazine	100-63-0	5	22	X
Phosdrin (Mevinphos)	7786-34-7		0.1	X
Phosgene (Carbonyl chloride)	75-44-5	0.1	0.4	
Phosphine	7803-51-2	0.3	0.4	
Phosphoric acid	7664-38-2		1	
Phosphorus (yellow)	7723-14-0		0.1	
Phosphorus pentachloride	10026-13-8		1	
Phosphorus pentasulfide	1314-80-3		1	
Phosphorus trichloride	7719-12-2	0.5	3	
Phthalic anhydride	85-44-9	2	12	
Picloram	1918-02-1			
Total dust			15	
Respirable fraction			5	
Picric acid	88-89-1		0.1	X
Pindone (2-Pivalyl-1,3-indandione)	83-26-1		0.1	
Plaster of Paris	26499-65-0			
Total dust			15	
Respirable fraction			5	
Platinum (as Pt)	7440-06-4			
Metal				
Soluble salts			0.002	
Portland cement	65997-15-1			
Total dust			15	
Respirable fraction			5	
Propane	74-98-6	1000	1800	
beta-Propriolactone; see 1910.1013	57-57-8			
n-Propyl acetate	109-60-4	200	840	
n-Propyl alcohol	71-23-8	200	500	
n-Propyl nitrate	627-13-4	25	110	
Propylene dichloride	78-87-5	75	350	
Propylene imine	75-55-8	2	5	X
Propylene oxide	75-56-9	100	240	
Propyne; see Methyl acetylene.				
Pyrethrum	8003-34-7		5	
Pyridine	110-86-1	5	15	
Quinone	106-51-4	0.1	0.4	
RDX; see Cyclonite.				
Rhodium (as Rh), metal fume and insoluble compounds.	7440-16-6		0.1	
Rhodium (as Rh), soluble compounds	7440-16-6		0.001	
Ronnel	299-84-3		15	
Rotenone	83-79-4		5	
Rouge				
Total dust			15	
Respirable fraction			5	
Selenium compounds (as Se)	7782-49-2		0.2	
Selenium hexafluoride (as Se)	7783-79-1	0.05	0.4	
Silica, amorphous, precipitated and gel	112926-00-8		([3])	
Silica, amorphous, diatomaceous earth, containing less than 1% crystalline silica.	61790-53-2		([3])	
Silica, crystalline cristobalite, respirable dust.	14464-46-1		([3])	
Silica, crystalline quartz, respirable dust.	14808-60-7		([3])	
Silica, crystalline tripoli (as quartz), respirable dust.	1317-95-9		([3])	
Silica, crystalline tridymite, respirable dust.	15468-32-3		([3])	
Silica, fused, respirable dust	60676-86-0		([3])	
Silicates (less than 1% crystalline silica).				
Mica (respirable dust)	12001-26-2		([3])	
Soapstone, total dust			([3])	

APPENDIX 4D

§ 1910.1000   29 CFR Ch. XVII (7-1-94 Edition)

TABLE Z-1.—LIMITS FOR AIR CONTAMINANTS—Continued

Substance	CAS No. (c)	ppm (a)[1]	mg/m³ (b)[1]	Skin designation
Soapstone, respirable dust			([3])	
Talc (containing asbestos); use asbestos limit; see 29 CFR 1910.1001.			([3])	
Talc (containing no asbestos), respirable dust.	14807-96-6		([3])	
Tremolite, asbestiform; see 1910.1001.				
Silicon	7440-21-3			
Total dust			15	
Respirable fraction			5	
Silicon carbide	409-21-2			
Total dust			15	
Respirable fraction			5	
Silver, metal and soluble compounds (as Ag).	7440-22-4		0.01	
Soapstone; see Silicates.				
Sodium fluoroacetate	62-74-8		0.05	X
Sodium hydroxide	1310-73-2		2	
Starch	9005-25-8			
Total dust			15	
Respirable fraction			5	
Stibine	7803-52-3	0.1	0.5	
Stoddard solvent	8052-41-3	500	2900	
Strychnine	57-24-9		0.15	
Styrene	100-42-5		([2])	
Sucrose	57-50-1			
Total dust			15	
Respirable fraction			5	
Sulfur dioxide	7446-09-5	5	13	
Sulfur hexafluoride	2551-62-4	1000	6000	
Sulfuric acid	7664-93-9		1	
Sulfur monochloride	10025-67-9	1	6	
Sulfur pentafluoride	5714-22-7	0.025	0.25	
Sulfuryl fluoride	2699-79-8	5	20	
Systox; see Demeton.				
2,4,5-T (2,4,5-trichlorophenoxyacetic acid).	93-76-5		10	
Talc; see Silicates.				
Tantalum, metal and oxide dust	7440-25-7		5	
TEDP (Sulfotep)	3689-24-5		0.2	X
Tellurium and compounds (as Te)	13494-80-9		0.1	
Tellurium hexafluoride (as Te)	7783-80-4	0.02	0.2	
Temephos	3383-96-8			
Total dust			15	
Respirable fraction			5	
TEPP (Tetraethyl pyrophosphate)	107-49-3		0.05	X
Terphenyls	26140-60-3	(C)1	(C)9	
1,1,1,2-Tetrachloro-2,2-difluoroethane	76-11-9	500	4170	
1,1,2,2-Tetrachloro-1,2-difluoroethane	76-12-0	500	4170	
1,1,2,2-Tetrachloroethane	79-34-5	5	35	X
Tetrachloroethylene; see Perchloroethylene.				
Tetrachloromethane; see Carbon tetrachloride.				
Tetrachloronaphthalene	1335-88-2		2	X
Tetraethyl lead (as Pb)	78-00-2		0.075	X
Tetrahydrofuran	109-99-9	200	590	
Tetramethyl lead (as Pb)	75-74-1		0.075	X
Tetramethyl succinonitrile	3333-52-6	0.5	3	X
Tetranitromethane	509-14-8	1	8	
Tetryl (2,4,6-Trinitrophenylmethylnitramine).	479-45-8		1.5	X
Thallium, soluble compounds (as Tl)	7440-28-0		0.1	X
4,4'-Thiobis (6-tert, Butyl-m-cresol)	96-69-5			
Total dust			15	
Respirable fraction			5	
Thiram	137-26-8		5	
Tin, inorganic compounds (except oxides) (as Sn).	7440-31-5		2	
Tin, organic compounds (as Sn)	7440-31-5		0.1	
Titanium dioxide	13463-67-7			

Occupational Safety and Health Admin., Labor § 1910.1000

TABLE Z-1.—LIMITS FOR AIR CONTAMINANTS—Continued

Substance	CAS No. (c)	ppm (a)[1]	mg/m³ (b)[1]	Skin designation
Total dust			15	
Toluene	108-88-3		([2])	
Toluene-2,4-diisocyanate (TDI)	584-84-9	(C)0.02	(C)0.14	
o-Toluidine	95-53-4	5	22	X
Toxaphene; see Chlorinated camphene.				
Tremolite; see Silicates.				
Tributyl phosphate	126-73-8		5	
1,1,1-Trichloroethane; see Methyl chloroform.				
1,1,2-Trichloroethane	79-00-5	10	45	X
Trichloroethylene	79-01-6		([2])	
Trichloromethane; see Chloroform.				
Trichloronaphthalene	1321-65-9		5	X
1,2,3-Trichloropropane	96-18-4	50	300	
1,1,2-Trichloro-1,2,2-trifluoroethane	76-13-1	1000	7600	
Triethylamine	121-44-8	25	100	
Trifluorobromomethane	75-63-8	1000	6100	
2,4,6-Trinitrophenyl; see Picric acid.				
2,4,6-Trinitrophenylmethylnitramine; see Tetryl.				
2,4,6-Trinitrotoluene (TNT)	118-96-7		1.5	X
Triorthocresyl phosphate	78-30-8		0.1	
Triphenyl phosphate	115-86-6		3	
Turpentine	8006-64-2	100	560	
Uranium (as U)	7440-61-1			
Soluble compounds			0.05	
Insoluble compounds			0.05	
Vanadium	1314-62-1			
Respirable dust (as V_2O_5)			(C)0.5	
Fume (as V_2O_5)			(C)0.1	
Vegetable oil mist				
Total dust			15	
Respirable fraction			5	
Vinyl benzene; see Styrene.				
Vinyl chloride; see 1910.1017	75-01-4			
Vinyl cyanide; see Acrylonitrile.				
Vinyl toluene	25013-15-4	100	480	
Warfarin	81-81-2		0.1	
Xylenes (o-, m-, p-isomers)	1330-20-7	100	435	
Xylidine	1300-73-8	5	25	X
Yttrium	7440-65-5		1	
Zinc chloride fume	7646-85-7		1	
Zinc oxide fume	1314-13-2		5	
Zinc oxide	1314-13-2			
Total dust			15	
Respirable fraction			5	
Zinc stearate	557-05-1			
Total dust			15	
Respirable fraction			5	
Zirconium compounds (as Zr)	7440-67-7		5	

[1] The PELs are 8-hour TWAs unless otherwise noted; a (C) designation denotes a ceiling limit. They are to be determined from breathing-zone air samples.
  (a) Parts of vapor or gas per million parts of contaminated air by volume at 25 °C and 760 torr.
  (b) Milligrams of substance per cubic meter of air. When entry is in this column only, the value is exact; when listed with a ppm entry, it is approximate.
  (c) The CAS number is for information only. Enforcement is based on the substance name. For an entry covering more than one metal compound, measured as the metal, the CAS number for the metal is given—not CAS numbers for the individual compounds.
  (d) The final benzene standard in 1910.1028 applies to all occupational exposures to benzene except in some circumstances the distribution and sale of fuels, sealed containers and pipelines, coke production, oil and gas drilling and production, natural gas processing, and the percentage exclusion for liquid mixtures; for the excepted subsegments, the benzene limits in Table Z-2 apply. See 1910.1028 for specific circumstances.
  (e) This 8-hour TWA applies to respirable dust as measured by a vertical elutriator cotton dust sampler or equivalent instrument. The time-weighted average applies to the cottom waste processing operations of waste recycling (sorting, blending, cleaning and willowing) and garnetting. See also 1910.1043 for cotton dust limits applicable to other sectors.
  (f) All inert or nuisance dusts, whether mineral, inorganic, or organic, not listed specifically by substance name are covered by the Particulates Not Otherwise Regulated (PNOR) limit which is the same as the inert or nuisance dust limit of Table Z-3.
[2] See Table Z-2.
[3] See Table Z-3.
[4] Varies with compound.

APPENDIX 4D

§ 1910.1000 29 CFR Ch. XVII (7-1-94 Edition)

TABLE Z-2

Substance	8-hour time weighted average	Acceptable ceiling concentration	Acceptable maximum peak above the acceptable ceiling concentration for an 8-hr shift	
			Concentration	Maximum duration
Benzene[a] (Z37.40-1969)	10 ppm	25 ppm	50 ppm	10 minutes.
Beryllium and beryllium compounds (Z37.29-1970)	2 µg/m³	5 µg/m³	25 µg/m³	30 minutes.
Cadmium fume[b] (Z37.5-1970)	0.1 mg/m³	0.3 mg/m³		
Cadmium dust[b] (Z37.5-1970)	0.2 mg/m³	0.6 mg/m³.		
Carbon disulfide (Z37.3-1968)	20 ppm	30 ppm	100 ppm	30 minutes.
Carbon tetrachloride (Z37.17-1967)	10 ppm	25 ppm	200 ppm	5 min. in any 4 hrs.
Chromic acid and chromates (Z37.7-1971)		1 mg/10m³.		
Ethylene dibromide (Z37.31-1970)	20 ppm	30 ppm	50 ppm	5 minutes.
Ethylene dichloride (Z37.21-1969)	50 ppm	100 ppm	200 ppm	5 min. in any 3 hrs.
Fluoride as dust (Z37.28-1969)	2.5 mg/m³			
Formaldehyde; see 1910.1048				
Hydrogen fluoride (Z37.28-1969)	3 ppm			
Hydrogen sulfide (Z37.2-1966)		20 ppm	50 ppm	10 mins. once, only if no other meas. exp. occurs.
Mercury (Z37.8-1971)		1 mg/10m³		
Methyl chloride (Z37.18-1969)	100 ppm	200 ppm	300 ppm	5 mins. in any 3 hrs.
Methylene chloride (Z37.23-1969)	500 ppm	1,000 ppm	2,000 ppm	5 mins. in any 2 hrs.
Organo (alkyl) mercury (Z37.30-1969)	0.01 mg/m³	0.04 mg/m³		
Styrene (Z37.15-1969)	100 ppm	200 ppm	600 ppm	5 mins. in any 3 hrs.
Tetrachloroethylene (Z37.22-1967)	100 ppm	200 ppm	300 ppm	5 mins. in any 3 hrs.
Toluene (Z37.12-1967)	200 ppm	300 ppm	500 ppm	10 minutes.
Trichloroethylene (Z37.19-1967)	100 ppm	200 ppm	300 ppm	5 mins. in any 2 hrs.

[a] This standard applies to the industry segments exempt from the 1 ppm 8-hour TWA and 5 ppm STEL of the benzene standard at 1910.1028.
[b] This standard applies to any operations or sectors for which the Cadmium standard, 1910.1027, is stayed or otherwise not in effect.

TABLE Z-3 MINERAL DUSTS

Substance	mppcf[a]	mg/m³
Silica:		
Crystalline		
Quartz (Respirable)	250[b] / (%SiO$_2$+5)	10 mg/m³ [c] / (% SiO$_2$ + 2)
Quartz (Total Dust)		30 mg/m³ / (% SiO$_2$ + 2)
Cristobalite: Use ½ the value calculated from the count or mass formulae for quartz		
Tridymite: Use ½ the value calculated from the formulae for quartz		
Amorphous, including natural diatomaceous earth	20	80 mg/m³ / %SiO$_2$
Silicates (less than 1% crystalline silica):		
Mica	20	
Soapstone	20	
Talc (not containing asbestos)	20[c]	
Talc (containing asbestos) Use asbestos limit.		

Occupational Safety and Health Admin., Labor § 1910.1001

TABLE Z-3 MINERAL DUSTS—Continued

Substance	mppcf [a]	mg/m³
Tremolite, asbestiform (see 29 CFR 1910.1001). Portland cement	50	
Graphite (Natural)	15	
Coal Dust:		
Respirable fraction less than 5% SiO_2		2.4 mg/m³ [e]
		$\%SiO_2+2$
Respirable fraction greater than 5% SiO_2		10 mg/m³ [e]
		$\%SiO_2+2$
Inert or Nuisance Dust: [d]		
Respirable fraction	15	5 mg/m³
Total dust	50	15 mg/m³

Note—Conversion factors - mppcf X 35.3 = million particles per cubic meter = particles per c.c.

[a] Millions of particles per cubic foot of air, based on impinger samples counted by light-field techniques.
[b] The percentage of crystalline silica in the formula is the amount determined from airborne samples, except in those instances in which other methods have been shown to be applicable.
[c] Containing less than 1% quartz; if 1% quartz or more, use quartz limit.
[d] All inert or nuisance dusts, whether mineral, inorganic, or organic, not listed specifically by substance name are covered by this limit, which is the same as the Particulates Not Otherwise Regulated (PNOR) limit in Table Z-1.
[e] Both concentration and percent quartz for the application of this limit are to be determined from the fraction passing a size-selector with the following characteristics:

Aerodynamic diameter (unit density sphere)	Percent passing selector
2	90
2.5	75
3.5	50
5.0	25
10	0

The measurements under this note refer to the use of an AEC (now NRC) instrument. The respirable fraction of coal dust is determined with an MRE; the figure corresponding to that of 2.4 mg/m³ in the table for coal dust is 4.5 mg/m³ᴹᴿᴱ.

[58 FR 35340, June 30. 1993; 58 FR 40191, July 27, 1993]

§ 1910.1001 Asbestos.

(a) *Scope and application.* (1) This section applies to all occupational exposures to asbestos in all industries covered by the Occupational Safety and Health Act, except as provided in paragraph (a)(2) of this section.

(2) This section does not apply to construction work as defined in 29 CFR 1910.12(b). [Exposure to asbestos in construction work is covered by 29 CFR 1926.58.]

(b) *Definitions. Action level* means an airborne concentration of asbestos, of 0.1 fiber per cubic centimeter (f/cc) of air calculated as an eight (8)—hour time-weighted average.

Asbestos includes chrysotile, amosite, crocidolite, tremolite asbestos, anthophyllite asbestos, actinolite asbestos, and any of these minerals that have been chemically treated and/or altered.

Assistant Secretary means the Assistant Secretary of Labor for Occupational Safety and Health, U.S. Department of Labor, or designee.

Authorized person means any person authorized by the employer and required by work duties to be present in regulated areas.

Director means the Director of the National Institute for Occupational Safety and Health, U.S. Department of

APPENDIX 4D

§ 1910.1001

Health and Human Services, or designee.

Employee exposure means that exposure to airborne asbestos that would occur if the employee were not using respiratory protective equipment.

Fiber means a particulate form of asbestos, 5 micrometers or longer, with a length-to-diameter ratio of at least 3 to 1.

High-efficiency particulate air (HEPA) filter means a filter capable of trapping and retaining at least 99.97 percent of 0.3 micrometer diameter mono-disperse particles.

Regulated area means an area established by the employer to demarcate areas where airborne concentrations of asbestos exceed, or can reasonably be expected to exceed, the permissible exposure limit.

(c) *Permissible exposure limits (PELS)*—(1) *Time-weighted average limit (TWA).* The employer shall ensure that no employee is exposed to an airborne concentration of asbestos in excess of 0.2 fiber per cubic centimeter of air as an eight (8)-hour time-weighted average (TWA) as determined by the method prescribed in Appendix A of this section, or by an equivalent method.

(2) *Excursion limit.* The employer shall ensure that no employee is exposed to an airborne concentration of asbestos in excess of 1.0 fiber per cubic centimeter of air (1 f/cc) as averaged over a sampling period of thirty (30) minutes.

(d) *Exposure monitoring*—(1) *General.* (i) Determinations of employee exposure shall be made from breathing zone air samples that are representative of the 8-hour TWA and 30-minute short-term exposures of each employee.

(ii) Representative 8-hour TWA employee exposures shall be determined on the basis of one or more samples representing full-shift exposures for each shift for each employee in each job classification in each work area. Representative 30-minute short-term employee exposures shall be determined on the basis of one or more samples representing 30 minute exposures associated with operations that are most likely to produce exposures above the excursion limit for each shift for each job classification in each work area.

(2) *Initial monitoring.* (i) Each employer who has a workplace or work operation covered by this standard, except as provided for in paragraphs (d)(2)(ii) and (d)(2)(iii) of this section, shall perform initial monitoring of employees who are, or may reasonably be expected to be exposed to airborne concentrations at or above the action level and/or excursion limit.

(ii) Where the employer has monitored after December 20, 1985, for the TWA and after March 14, 1988, for the excursion limit, and the monitoring satisfies all other requirements of this section, the employer may rely on such earlier monitoring results to satisfy the requirements of paragraph (d)(2)(i) of this section.

(iii) Where the employer has relied upon objective data that demonstrates that asbestos is not capable of being released in airborne concentrations at or above the action level and/or excursion limit under the expected conditions of processing, use, or handling, then no initial monitoring is required.

(3) *Monitoring frequency (periodic monitoring) and patterns.* After the initial determinations required by paragraph (d)(2)(i) of this section, samples shall be of such frequency and pattern as to represent with reasonable accuracy the levels of exposure of the employees. In no case shall sampling be at intervals greater than six months for employees whose exposures may reasonably be foreseen to exceed the action level and/ or excursion limit.

(4) *Changes in monitoring frequency.* If either the initial or the periodic monitoring required by paragraphs (d)(2) and (d)(3) of this section statistically indicates that employee exposures are below the action level and/or excursion limit, the employer may discontinue the monitoring for those employees whose exposures are represented by such monitoring.

(5) *Additional monitoring.* Notwithstanding the provisions of paragraphs (d)(2)(ii) and (d)(4) of this section, the employer shall institute the exposure monitoring required under paragraphs (d)(2)(i) and (d)(3) of this section whenever there has been a change in the production, process, control equipment, personnel or work practices that may result in new or additional expo-

sures above the action level and/or excursion limit or when the employer has any reason to suspect that a change may result in new or additional exposures above the action level and/or excursion limit.

(6) *Method of monitoring.* (i) All samples taken to satisfy the monitoring requirements of paragraph (d) shall be personal samples collected following the procedures specified in Appendix A.

(ii) All samples taken to satisfy the monitoring requirements of paragraph (d) shall be evaluated using the OSHA Reference Method (ORM) specified in Appendix A of this section, or an equivalent counting method.

(iii) If an equivalent method to the ORM is used, the employer shall ensure that the method meets the following criteria:

(A) Replicate exposure data used to establish equivalency are collected in side-by-side field and laboratory comparisons; and

(B) The comparison indicates that 90% of the samples collected in the range 0.5 to 2.0 times the permissible limit have an accuracy range of plus or minus 25 percent of the ORM results with a 95% confidence level as demonstrated by a statistically valid protocol; and

(C) The equivalent method is documented and the results of the comparison testing are maintained.

(iv) To satisfy the monitoring requirements of paragraph (d) of this section, employers must use the results of monitoring analysis performed by laboratories which have instituted quality assurance programs that include the elements as prescribed in Appendix A.

(7) *Employee notification of monitoring results.* (i) The employer shall, within 15 working days after the receipt of the results of any monitoring performed under the standard, notify the affected employees of these results in writing either either individually or by posting of results in an appropriate location that is accessible to affected employees.

(ii) The written notification required by paragraph (d)(7)(i) of this section shall contain the corrective action being taken by the employer to reduce employee exposure to or below the TWA and/or excursion limit, wherever monitoring results indicated that the TWA and/or excursion limit had been exceeded.

(e) *Regulated Areas*—(1) *Establishment.* The employer shall establish regulated areas wherever airborne concentrations of asbestos are in excess of the TWA and/or excursion limit prescribed in paragraph (c) of this section.

(2) *Demarcation.* Regulated areas shall be demarcated from the rest of the workplace in any manner that minimizes the number of persons who will be exposed to asbestos.

(3) *Access.* Access to regulated areas shall be limited to authorized persons or to persons authorized by the Act or regulations issued pursuant thereto.

(4) *Provision of respirators.* Each person entering a regulated area shall be supplied with and required to use a respirator, selected in accordance with paragraph (g)(2) of this section.

(5) *Prohibited activities.* The employer shall ensure that employees do not eat, drink, smoke, chew tobacco or gum, or apply cosmetics in the regulated areas.

(f) *Methods of compliance*—(1) *Engineering controls and work practices.* (i) The employer shall institute engineering controls and work practices to reduce and maintain employee exposure to or below the TWA and/or excursion limit, prescribed in paragraph (c) of this section, except to the extent that such controls are not feasible.

(ii) Wherever the feasible engineering controls and work practices that can be instituted are not sufficient to reduce employee exposure to or below the TWA and/or excursion limit prescribed in paragraph (c) of this section, the employer shall use them to reduce employee exposure to the lowest levels achievable by these controls and shall supplement them by the use of respiratory protection that complies with the requirements of paragraph (g) of this section.

(iii) For the following operations, wherever feasible engineering controls and work practices that can be instituted are not sufficient to reduce the employee exposure to or below the TWA and/or excursion limit, prescribed in paragraph (c) of this section, the employer shall use them to reduce employee exposure to or below 0.5 fiber per cubic centimeter of air (as an

APPENDIX 4D

§ 1910.1001

eight-hour time-weighted average) or 2.5 fibers/cc for 30 minutes (short-term exposure) and shall supplement them by the use of any combination of respiratory protection that complies with the requirements of paragraph (g) of this section, work practices and feasible engineering controls that will reduce employee exposure to or below the TWA and to or below the excursion limit prescribed in paragraph (c) of this section: Coupling cutoff in primary asbestos cement pipe manufacturing; sanding in primary and secondary asbestos cement sheet manufacturing; grinding in primary and secondary friction product manufacturing; carding and spinning in dry textile processes; and grinding and sanding in primary plastics manufacturing.

(iv) *Local exhaust ventilation.* Local exhaust ventilation and dust collection systems shall be designed, constructed, installed, and maintained in accordance with good practices such as those found in the American National Standard Fundamentals Governing the Design and Operation of Local Exhaust Systems, ANSI Z9.2–1979.

(v) *Particular tools.* All hand-operated and power-operated tools with would produce or release fibers of asbestos so as to expose employees to levels in excess of the TWA and/or excursion limit prescribed in paragraph (c) of this section, such as, but not limited to saws, scorers, abrasive wheels, and drills, shall be provided with local exhaust ventilation systems which comply with paragraph (f)(1)(iv) of this section.

(vi) *Wet methods.* Insofar as practicable, asbestos shall be handled, mixed, applied, removed, cut, scored, or otherwise worked in a wet state sufficient to prevent the emission of airborne fibers so as to expose employees to levels in excess of the TWA and/or excursion limit, prescribed in paragraph (c) of this section, unless the usefulness of the product would be diminished thereby.

(vii) [Reserved]

(viii) *Particular products and operations.* No asbestos cement, mortar, coating, grout, plaster, or similar material containing asbestos shall be removed from bags, cartons, or other containers in which they are shipped, without being either wetted, or en-

29 CFR Ch. XVII (7-1-94 Edition)

closed, or ventilated so as to prevent effectively the release of airborne fibers of asbestos so as to expose employees to levels in excess of the TWA and/or excursion limit prescribed in paragraph (c) of this section.

(ix) *Compressed air.* Compressed air shall not be used to remove asbestos or materials containing asbestos, unless the compressed air is used in conjunction with a ventilation system designed to capture the dust cloud created by the compressed air.

(2) *Compliance program.* (i) Where the TWA and/or excursion limit is exceeded, the employer shall establish and implement a written program to reduce employee exposure to or below the TWA and to or below the excursion limit by means of engineering and work practice controls as required by paragraph (f)(1) of this section, and by the use of respiratory protection where required or permitted under this section.

(ii) Such programs shall be reviewed and updated as necessary to reflect significant changes in the status of the employer's compliance program.

(iii) Written programs shall be submitted upon request for examination and copying to the Assistant Secretary, the Director, affected employees and designated employee representatives.

(iv) The employer shall not use employee rotation as a means of compliance with the TWA and/or excursion limit.

(g) *Respiratory protection*—(1) *General.* The employer shall provide respirators, and ensure that they are used, where required by this section. Respirators shall be used in the following circumstances:

(i) During the interval necessary to install or implement feasible engineering and work practice controls;

(ii) In work operations, such as maintenance and repair activities, or other activities for which engineering and work practice controls are not feasible;

(iii) In work situations where feasible engineering and work practice controls are not yet sufficient to reduce exposure to or below the TWA and/or excursion limit; and

(iv) In emergencies.

Occupational Safety and Health Admin., Labor § 1910.1001

(2) *Respirator selection.* (i) Where respirators are required under this section, the employer shall select and provide, at no cost to the employee, the appropriate respirator as specified in Table 1. The employer shall select respirators from among those jointly approved as being acceptable for protection by the Mine Safety and Health Administration (MSHA) and by the National Institute for Occupational Safety and Health (NIOSH) under the provisions of 30 CFR Part 11.

(ii) The employer shall provide a powered, air-purifying respirator in lieu of any negative pressure respirator specified in Table 1 whenever:

(A) An employee chooses to use this type of respirator; and

(B) This respirator will provide adequate protection to the employee.

TABLE 1—RESPIRATORY PROTECTION FOR ASBESTOS FIBERS

Airborne concentration of asbestos	Required respirator
Not in excess of 2 f/cc (10 X PEL).	1. Half-mask air-purifying respirator, other than a disposable respirator, equipped with high-efficiency filters.
Not in excess of 10 f/cc (50 X PEL).	1. Full facepiece air-purifying respirator equipped with high-efficiency filters.
Not in excess of 20 f/cc (100 X PEL).	1. Any powered air-purifying respirator equipped with high-efficiency filters. 2. Any supplied-air respirator operated in continuous flow mode.
Not in excess of 200 f/cc (1000 X PEL).	1. Full facepiece supplied-air respirator operated in pressure demand mode.
Greater than 200 f/cc (> 1,000 X PEL) or unknown concentration.	1. Full facepiece supplied air respirator operated in pressure demand mode equipped with an auxiliary positive pressure self-contained breathing apparatus.

NOTE: a. Respirators assigned for higher environmental concentrations may be used at lower concentrations.
b. A high-efficiency filter means a filter that is at least 99.97 percent efficient against mono-dispersed particles of 0.3 micrometers or larger.

(3) *Respirator program.* (i) Where respiratory protection is required, the employer shall institute a respirator program in accordance with 29 CFR 1910.134(b), (d), (e), and (f).

(ii) The employer shall permit each employee who uses a filter respirator to change the filter elements whenever an increase in breathing resistance is detected and shall maintain an adequate supply of filter elements for this purpose.

(iii) Employees who wear respirators shall, be permitted to leave the regulated area to wash their faces and respirator facepieces whenever necessary to prevent skin irritation associated with respirator use.

(iv) No employee shall be assigned to tasks requiring the use of respirators if, based upon his or her most recent examination, an examining physician determines that the employee will be unable to function normally wearing a respirator, or that the safety or health of the employee or other employees will be impaired by the use of a respirator. Such employee shall be assigned to another job or given the opportunity to transfer to a different position whose duties he or she is able to perform with the same employer, in the same geographical area and with the same seniority, status, and rate of pay the employee had just prior to such transfer, if such a different position is available.

(4) *Respirator fit testing.* (i) The employer shall ensure that the respirator issued to the employee exhibits the least possible facepiece leakage and that the respirator is fitted properly.

(ii) For each employee wearing negative pressure respirators, employers shall perform either quantitative or qualitative face fit tests at the time of initial fitting and at least every six months thereafter. The qualitative fit tests may be used only for testing the fit of half-mask respirators where they are permitted to be worn, and shall be conducted in accordance with Appendix C. The tests shall be used to select facepieces that provide the required protection as prescribed in Table I.

(h) *Protective work clothing and equipment*—(1) *Provision and use.* If an employee is exposed to asbestos above the TWA and/or excursion limit, or where the possibility of eye irritation exists, the employer shall provide at no cost to the employee and ensure that the employee uses appropriate work clothing and equipment such as, but not limited to:

(i) **Coveralls** or similar full-body work clothing;

(ii) **Gloves**, head coverings, and foot coverings; and

(iii) **Face** shields, vented goggles, or other appropriate protective equipment which complies with § 1910.133 of this Part.

23

150-116 O—94——2

§ 1910.1001

(2) *Removal and storage.* (i) The employer shall ensure that employees remove work clothing contaminated with asbestos only in change rooms provided in accordance with paragraph (i)(1) of this section.

(ii) The employer shall ensure that no employee takes contaminated work clothing out of the change room, except those employees authorized to do so for the purpose of laundering, maintenance, or disposal.

(iii) Contaminated work clothing shall be placed and stored in closed containers which prevent dispersion of the asbestos outside the container.

(iv) Containers of contaminated protective devices or work clothing which are to be taken out of change rooms or the workplace for cleaning, maintenance or disposal, shall bear labels in accordance with paragraph (j)(2) of this section.

(3) *Cleaning and replacement.* (i) The employer shall clean, launder, repair, or replace protective clothing and equipment required by this paragraph to maintain their effectiveness. The employer shall provide clean protective clothing and equipment at least weekly to each affected employee.

(ii) The employer shall prohibit the removal of asbestos from protective clothing and equipment by blowing or shaking.

(iii) Laundering of contaminated clothing shall be done so as to prevent the release of airborne fibers of asbestos in excess of the permissible exposure limits prescribed in paragraph (c) of this section.

(iv) Any employer who gives contaminated clothing to another person for laundering shall inform such person of the requirement in paragraph (h)(3)(iii) of this section to effectively prevent the release of asbestos in excess of the permissible exposure limits.

(v) The employer shall inform any person who launders or cleans protective clothing or equipment contaminated with asbestos of the potentially harmful effects of exposure to asbestos.

(vi) Contaminated clothing shall be transported in sealed impermeable bags, or other closed, impermeable containers, and labeled in accordance with paragraph (j) of this seciton.

(i) *Hygiene facilities and practices*—(1) *Change rooms.* (i) The employer shall provide clean change rooms for employees who work in areas where their airborne exposure to asbestos is above the TWA and/or excursion limit.

(ii) The employer shall ensure that change rooms are in accordance with § 1910.141(e) of this part, and are equipped with two separate lockers or storage facilities, so separated as to prevent contamination of the employee's street clothes from his protective work clothing and equipment.

(2) *Showers.* (i) The employer shall ensure that employees who work in areas where their airborne exposure is above the TWA and/or excursion limit shower at the end of the work shift.

(ii) The employer shall provide shower facilities which comply with § 1910.141(d)(3) of this part.

(iii) The employer shall ensure that employees who are required to shower pursuant to paragraph (i)(2)(i) of this section do not leave the workplace wearing any clothing or equipment worn during the work shift.

(3) *Lunchrooms.* (i) The employer shall provide lunchroom facilities for employees who work in areas where their airborne exposure is above the TWA and/or excursion limit.

(ii) The employer shall ensure that lunchroom facilities have a positive pressure, filtered air supply, and are readily accessible to employees.

(iii) The employer shall ensure that employees who work in areas where their airborne exposure is above the TWA and/or excursion limit wash their hands and faces prior to eating, drinking or smoking.

(iv) The employer shall ensure that employees do not enter lunchroom facilities with protective work clothing or equipment unless surface asbestos fibers have been removed from the clothing or equipment by vacuuming or other method that removes dust without causing the asbestos to become airborne.

(4) *Smoking in work areas.* The employer shall ensure that employees do not smoke in work areas where they are occupationally exposed to asbestos because of activities in that work area.

(j) *Communication of hazards to employees*—(1) *Warning signs.* (i) Posting.

Occupational Safety and Health Admin., Labor § 1910.1001

Warning signs shall be provided and displayed at each regulated area. In addition, warning signs shall be posted at all approaches to regulated areas so that an employee may read the signs and take necessary protective steps before entering the area.

(ii) *Sign specifications.* The warning signs required by paragraph (j)(1)(i) of this section shall bear the following information:

DANGER
ASBESTOS
CANCER AND LUNG DISEASE HAZARD
AUTHORIZED PERSONNEL ONLY
RESPIRATORS AND PROTECTIVE CLOTHING
ARE REQUIRED IN THIS AREA

(iii) [Reserved]

(iv) The employer shall ensure that employees working in and contiguous to regulated areas comprehend the warning signs required to be posted by paragraph (j)(1)(i) of this section. Means to ensure employee comprehension may include the use of foreign languages, pictographs and graphics.

(2) *Warning labels.* (i) Labeling. Warning labels shall be affixed to all raw materials, mixtures, scrap, waste, debris, and other products containing asbestos fibers, or to their containers.

(ii) *Label specifications.* The labels shall comply with the requirements of 29 CFR 1910.1200(f) of OSHA's Hazard Communication standard, and shall include the following information:

DANGER
CONTAINS ASBESTOS FIBERS
AVOID CREATING DUST
CANCER AND LUNG DISEASE HAZARD

(3) *Material safety data sheets.* Employers who are manufacturers or importers of asbestos or asbestos products shall comply with the requirements regarding development of material safety data sheets as specified in 29 CFR 1910.1200(g) of OSHA's Hazard Communication standard, except as provided by paragraph (j)(4) of this section.

(4) The provisions for labels required by paragraph (j)(2) or for material safety data sheets required by paragraph (j)(3) do not apply where:

(i) Asbestos fibers have been modified by a bonding agent, coating, binder, or other material provided that the manufacturer can demonstrate that during any reasonably foreseeable use, handling, storage, disposal, processing, or transportation, no airborne concentrations of fibers of asbestos in excess of the action level and/or excursion limit will be released or

(ii) Asbestos is present in a product in concentrations less than 0.1%.

(5) *Employee information and training.*
(i) The employer shall institute a training program for all employees who are exposed to airborne concentrations of asbestos at or above the action level and/or excursion limit and ensure their participation in the program.

(ii) Training shall be provided prior to or at the time of initial assignment and at least annually thereafter.

(iii) The training program shall be conducted in a manner which the employee is able to understand. The employer shall ensure that each employee is informed of the following:

(A) The health effects associated with asbestos exposure;

(B) The relationship between smoking and exposure to asbestos in producing lung cancer:

(C) The quantity, location, manner of use, release, and storage of asbestos, and the specfic nature of operations which could result in exposure to asbestos;

(D) The engineering controls and work practices associated with the employee's job assignment;

(E) The specific procedures implemented to protect employees from exposure to asbestos, such as appropriate work practices, emergency and clean-up procedures, and personal protective equipment to be used;

(F) The purpose, proper use, and limitations of respirators and protective clothing;

(G) The purpose and a description of the medical surveillance program required by paragraph (l) of this section;

(H) The content of this standard, including appendices.

(I) The names, addresses and phone numbers of public health organizations which provide information, materials, and/or conduct programs concerning smoking cessation. The employer may distribute the list of such organiza-

§ 1910.1001

tions contained in Appendix I, to comply with this requirement.

(J) The requirements for posting signs and affixing labels and the meaning of the required legends for such signs and labels.

(iv) Access to information and training materials.

(A) The employer shall make a copy of this standard and its appendices readily available without cost to all affected employees.

(B) The employer shall provide, upon request, all materials relating to the employee information and training program to the Assistant Secretary and the training program to the Assistant Secretary and the Director.

(C) The employer shall inform all employees concerning the availability of self-help smoking cessation program material. Upon employee request, the employer shall distribute such material, consisting of NIH Publication No. 89-1647, or equivalent self-help material, which is approved or published by a public health organization listed in appendix I.

(k) *Housekeeping.* (1) All surfaces shall be maintained as free as practicable of accumulations of dusts and waste containing asbestos.

(2) All spills and sudden releases of material containing asbestos shall be cleaned up as soon as possible.

(3) Surfaces contaminated with asbestos may not be cleaned by the use of compressed air.

(4) Vacuuming. HEPA-filtered vacuuming equipment shall be used for vacuuming. The equipment shall be used and emptied in a manner which minimizes the reentry of asbestos into the workplace.

(5) Shoveling, dry sweeping and dry clean-up of asbestos may be used only where vacuuming and/or wet cleaning are not feasible.

(6) Waste disposal. Waste, scrap, debris, bags, containers, equipment, and clothing contaminated with asbestos consigned for disposal, shall be collected and disposed of in sealed impermeable bags, or other closed, impermeable containers.

(l) *Medical surveillance*—(1) *General.* (i) The employer shall institute a medical surveillance program for all employees who are or will be exposed to airborne concentrations of asbestos at or above the action level and/or excursion limit.

(ii) *Examination by a physician.* (A) The employer shall ensure that all medical examinations and procedures are performed by or under the supervision of a licensed physician, and shall be provided without cost to the employee and at a reasonable time and place.

(B) Persons other than licensed physicians, who administer the pulmonary function testing required by this section, shall complete a training course in spirometry sponsored by an appropriate academic or professional institution.

(2) *Preplacement examinations.* (i) Before an employee is assigned to an occupation exposed to airborne concentrations of asbestos fibers, a preplacement medical examination shall be provided or made available by the employer.

(ii) Such examination shall include, as a minimum, a medical and work history; a complete physical examination of all systems with emphasis on the respiratory system, the cardiovascular system and digestive tract; completion of the respiratory disease standardized questionnaire in Appendix D, Part 1; a chest roentgenogram (posterior-anterior 14x17 inches); pulmonary function tests to include forced vital capacity (FVC) and forced expiratory volume at 1 second ($FEV_{1.0}$); and any additional tests deemed appropriate by the examining physician. Interpretation and classification of chest roentgenograms shall be conducted in accordance with Appendix E.

(3) *Periodic examinations.* (i) Periodic medical examinations shall be made available annually.

(ii) The scope of the medical examination shall be in conformance with the protocol established in paragraph (l)(2)(ii) of this section, except that the frequency of chest roentgenograms shall be conducted in accordance with Table 2, and the abbreviated standardized questionnaire contained in Appendix D, Part 2, shall be administered to the employee.

Occupational Safety and Health Admin., Labor § 1910.1001

TABLE 2—FREQUENCY OF CHEST ROENTGENOGRAMS

Years since first exposure	Age of employee		
	15 to 35	35+ to 45	45+
0 to 10	Every 5 years	Every 5 years	Every 5 years.
10+	Every 5 years	Every 2 years	Every 1 year.

(4) *Termination of employment examinations.* (i) The employer shall provide, or make available, a termination of employment medical examination for any employee who has been exposed to airborne concentrations of fibers of asbestos at or above the action level and/or excursion limit.

(ii) The medical examination shall be in accordance with the requirements of the periodic examinations stipulated in paragraph (1)(3) of this section, and shall be given within 30 calendar days before or after the date of termination of employment.

(5) *Recent examinations.* No medical examination is required of any employee, if adequate records show that the employee has been examined in accordance with any of the preceding paragraphs [(l)(2)–(l)(4)] within the past 1 year period.

(6) *Information provided to the physician.* The employer shall provide the following information to the examining physician:

(i) A copy of this standard and Appendices D and E.

(ii) A description of the affected employee's duties as they relate to the employee's exposure.

(iii) The employee's representative exposure level or anticipated exposure level.

(iv) A description of any personal protective and respiratory equipment used or to be used.

(v) Information from previous medical examinations of the affected employee that is not otherwise available to the examining physician.

(7) *Physician's written opinion.* (i) The employer shall obtain a written signed opinion from the examining physician. This written opinion shall contain the results of the medical examination and shall include:

(A) The physician's opinion as to whether the employee has any detected medical conditions that would place the employee at an increased risk of material health impairment from exposure to asbestos;

(B) Any recommended limitations on the employee or upon the use of personal protective equipment such as clothing or respirators; and

(C) A statement that the employee has been informed by the physician of the results of the medical examination and of any medical conditions resulting from asbestos exposure that require further explanation or treatment.

(D) A statement that the employee has been informed by the physician of the increased risk of lung cancer attributable to the combined effect of smoking and asbestos exposure.

(ii) The employer shall instruct the physician not to reveal in the written opinion given to the employer specific findings or diagnoses unrelated to occupational exposure to asbestos.

(iii) The employer shall provide a copy of the physician's written opinion to the affected employee within 30 days from its receipt.

(m) *Recordkeeping*—(1) *Exposure measurements.* (i) The employer shall keep an accurate record of all measurements taken to monitor employee exposure to asbestos as prescribed in paragraph (d) of this section.

(ii) This record shall include at least the following information:

(A) The date of measurement;

(B) The operation involving exposure to asbestos which is being monitored;

(C) Sampling and analytical methods used and evidence of their accuracy;

(D) Number, duration, and results of samples taken;

(E) Type of respiratory protective devices worn, if any; and

(F) Name, social security number and exposure of the employees whose exposure are represented.

(iii) The employer shall maintain this record for at least thirty (30) years, in accordance with 29 CFR 1910.20.

§ 1910.1001

(2) *Objective data for exempted operations.* (i) Where the processing, use, or handling of products made from or containing asbestos is exempted from other requirements of this section under paragraph (d)(2)(iii) of this section, the employer shall establish and maintain an accurate record of objective data reasonably relied upon in support of the exemption.

(ii) The record shall include at least the following:

(A) The product qualifying for exemption;

(B) The source of the objective data;

(C) The testing protocol, results of testing, and/or analysis of the material for the release of asbestos;

(D) A description of the operation exempted and how the data support the exemption; and

(E) Other data relevant to the operations, materials, processing, or employee exposures covered by the exemption.

(iii) The employer shall maintain this record for the duration of the employer's reliance upon such objective data.

NOTE: The employer may utilize the services of competent organizations such as industry trade associations and employee associations to maintain the records required by this section.

(3) *Medical surveillance.* (i) The employer shall establish and maintain an accurate record for each employee subject to medical surveillance by paragraph (l)(1)(i) of this section, in accordance with 29 CFR 1910.20.

(ii) The record shall include at least the following information:

(A) The name and social security number of the employee;

(B) Physician's written opinions;

(C) Any employee medical complaints related to exposure to asbestos; and

(D) A copy of the information provided to the physician as required by paragraph (l)(6) of this section.

(iii) The employer shall ensure that this record is maintained for the duration of employment plus thirty (30) years, in accordance with 29 CFR 1910.20.

(4) *Training.* The employer shall maintain all employee training records for one (1) year beyond the last date of employment of that employee.

(5) *Availability.* (i) The employer, upon written request, shall make all records required to be maintained by this section available to the Assistant Secretary and the Director for examination and copying.

(ii) The employer, upon request shall make any exposure records required by paragraph (m)(1) of this section available for examination and copying to affected employees, former employees, designated representatives and the Assistant Secretary, in accordance with 29 CFR 1910.20 (a)–(e) and (g)–(i).

(iii) The employer, upon request, shall make employee medical records required by paragraph (m)(2) of this section available for examination and copying to the subject employee, to anyone having the specific written consent of the subject employee, and the Assistant Secretary, in accordance with 29 CFR 1910.20.

(6) *Transfer of records.* (i) The employer shall comply with the requirements concerning transfer of records set forth in 29 CFR 1910.20(h).

(ii) Whenever the employer ceases to do business and there is no successor employer to receive and retain the records for the prescribed period, the employer shall notify the Director at least 90 days prior to disposal of records and, upon request, transmit them to the Director.

(n) *Observation of monitoring*—(1) *Employee observation.* The employer shall provide affected employees or their designated representatives an opportunity to observe any monitoring of employee exposure to asbestos conducted in accordance with paragraph (d) of this section.

(2) *Observation procedures.* When observation of the monitoring of employee exposure to asbestos requires entry into an area where the use of protective clothing or equipment is required, the observer shall be provided with and be required to use such clothing and equipment and shall comply with all other applicable safety and health procedures.

(o) *Dates*—(1) *Effective date.* This standard shall become effective July 21, 1986. The requirements in the amended paragraphs in this section

Occupational Safety and Health Admin., Labor § 1910.1001, App. A

which pertain only to or are triggered by the excursion limit shall become effective October 14, 1988.

(2) *Start-up dates.* All obligations of this standard commence on the effective date except as follows:

(i) *Exposure monitoring.* Initial monitoring required by paragraph (d)(2) of this section shall be completed as soon as possible but no later than October 20, 1986.

(ii) *Regulated areas.* Regulated areas required to be established by paragraph (e) of this section as a result of initial monitoring shall be set up as soon as possible after the results of that monitoring are known and not later than November 17, 1986.

(iii) *Respiratory protection.* Respiratory protection required by paragraph (g) of this section shall be provided as soon as possible but no later than the following schedule:

(A) Employees whose 8-hour TWA exposure exceeds 2 fibers/cc—July 21, 1986.

(B) Employees whose 8-hour TWA exposure exceeds the PEL but is less than 2 fibers/cc—November 17, 1986.

(C) Powered air-purifying respirators provided under paragraph (g)(2)(ii)—January 16, 1987.

(iv) *Hygiene and lunchroom facilities.* Construction plans for changerooms, showers, lavatories, and lunchroom facilities shall be completed no later than January 16, 1987; and these facilities shall be constructed and in use no later than July 20, 1987. However, if as part of the compliance plan it is predicted by an independent engineering firm that engineering controls and work practices will reduce exposures below the permissible exposure limit by July 20, 1988, for affected employees, then such facilities need not be completed until 1 year after the engineering controls are completed, if such controls have not in fact succeeded in reducing exposure to below the permissible exposure limit.

(v) *Employee information and training.* Employee information and training required by paragraph (j)(5) of this section shall be provided as soon as possible but no later than October 20, 1986.

(vi) *Medical surveillance.* Medical examinations required by paragraph (l) of this section shall be provided as soon as possible but no later than November 17, 1986.

(vii) *Compliance program.* Written compliance programs required by paragraph (f)(2) of this section as a result of initial monitoring shall be completed and available for inspection and copying as soon as possible but no later than July 20, 1987.

(viii) *Methods of compliance.* The engineering and work practice controls as required by paragraph (f)(1) shall be implemented as soon as possible but no later than July 20, 1988.

(3) *Start-up dates for excursion limit.* Compliance with the excursion limit requirements in this section shall be as follows:

(i) Paragraphs (c), (d), (e), (g), (h), (j), (k), (l), (m) of this section, shall be complied with by December 13, 1988.

(ii) Paragraph (f) of this section, shall be complied with by March 13, 1989.

(iii) Paragraph (i) of this section, shall be complied with by September 14, 1989.

(4) *Compliance date.* The requirements of paragraphs (i)(4), (j)(1)(iv), (j)(5)(iii)(I), (j)(5)(iii)(J), (j)(5)(iv)(C), and (l)(7)(i)(D) shall be complied with by May 7, 1990.

(p) *Appedices.* (1) Appendices A, C, D, and E to this section are incorporated as part of this section and the contents of these Appendices are mandatory.

(2) Appendices B, F, G, H, and I to this section are informational and are not intended to create any additional obligation not otherwise imposed or to detract from any existing obligation.

APPENDIX A TO § 1910.1001—OSHA REFERENCE METHOD—MANDATORY

This mandatory appendix specifies the procedure for analyzing air samples for asbestos and specifies quality control procedures that must be implemented by laboratories performing the analysis. The sampling and analytical methods described below represent the elements of the available monitoring methods (such as the NIOSH 7400 method) which OSHA considers to be essential to achieve adequate employee exposure monitoring while allowing employers to use methods that are already established within their organizations. All employers who are required to conduct air monitoring under paragraph (d) of the standard are required to utilize analytical laboratories that use this

§ 1910.1001, App. A

procedure, or an equivalent method, for collecting and analyzing samples.

Sampling and Analytical Procedure

1. The sampling medium for air samples shall be mixed cellulose ester filter membranes. These shall be designated by the manufacturer as suitable for asbestos counting. See below for rejection of blanks.

2. The preferred collection device shall be the 25-mm diameter cassette with an open-faced 50-mm electrically conductive extension cowl. The 37-mm cassette may be used if necessary but only if written justification for the need to use the 37-mm filter cassette accompanies the sample results in the employee's exposure monitoring record.

3. An air flow rate between 0.5 liter/min and 2.5 liters/min shall be selected for the 25-mm cassette. If the 37-mm cassette is used, an air flow rate between 1 liter/min and 2.5 liters/min shall be selected.

4. Where possible, a sufficient air volume for each air sample shall be collected to yield between 100 and 1,300 fibers per square millimeter on the membrane filter. If a filter darkens in appearance or if loose dust is seen on the filter, a second sample shall be started.

5. Ship the samples in a rigid container with sufficient packing material to prevent dislodging the collected fibers. Packing material that has a high electrostatic charge on its surface (e.g., expanded polystyrene) cannot be used because such material can cause loss of fibers to the sides of the cassette.

6. Calibrate each personal sampling pump before and after use with a representative filter cassette installed between the pump and the calibration devices.

7. Personal samples shall be taken in the "breathing zone" of the employee (i.e., attached to or near the collar or lapel near the worker's face).

8. Fiber counts shall be made by positive phase contrast using a microscope with an 8 to 10 X eyepiece and a 40 to 45 X objective for a total magnification of approximately 400 X and a numerical aperture of 0.65 to 0.75. The microscope shall also be fitted with a green or blue filter.

9. The microscope shall be fitted with a Walton-Beckett eyepiece graticule calibrated for a field diameter of 100 micrometers (+/−2 micrometers).

10. The phase-shift detection limit of the microscope shall be about 3 degrees measured using the HSE phase shift test slide as outlined below.

a. Place the test slide on the microscope stage and center it under the phase objective.

b. Bring the blocks of grooved lines into focus.

NOTE: The slide consists of seven sets of grooved lines (ca. 20 grooves to each block) in descending order of visibility from sets 1 to 7, seven being the least visible. The requirements for asbestos counting are that the microscope optics must resolve the grooved lines in set 3 completely, although they may appear somewhat faint, and that the grooved lines in sets 6 and 7 must be invisible. Sets 4 and 5 must be at least partially visible but may vary slightly in visibility between microscopes. A microscope that fails to meet these requirements has either too low or too high a resolution to be used for asbestos counting.

c. If the image deteriorates, clean and adjust the microscope optics. If the problem persists, consult the microscope manufacturer.

11. Each set of samples taken will include 10 percent blanks or a minimum of 2 blanks. The blank results shall be averaged and subtracted from the analytical results before reporting. Any samples represented by a blank having a fiber count in excess of 7 fibers/100 fields shall be rejected.

12. The samples shall be mounted by the acetone/triacetin method or a method with an equivalent index of refraction and similar clarity.

13. Observe the following counting rules.

a. Count only fibers equal to or longer than 5 micrometers. Measure the length of curved fibers along the curve.

b. In the absence of other information, count all particles as asbesto that have a length-to-width ratio (aspect ratio) of 3:1 or greater.

c. Fibers lying entirely within the boundary of the Walton-Beckett graticule field shall receive a count of 1. Fibers crossing the boundary once, having one end within the circle, shall receive the count of one half (½). Do not count any fiber that crosses the graticule boundary more than once. Reject and do not count any other fibers even though they may be visible outside the graticule area.

d. Count bundles of fibers as one fiber unless individual fibers can be identified by observing both ends of an individual fiber.

e. Count enough graticule fields to yield 100 fibers. Count a minimum of 20 fields; stop counting at 100 fields regardless of fiber count.

14. Blind recounts shall be conducted at the rate of 10 percent.

Quality Control Procedures

1. Intralaboratory program. Each laboratory and/or each company with more than one microscopist counting slides shall establish a statistically designed quality assurance program involving blind recounts and comparisons between microscopists to monitor the variability of counting by each microscopist and between microscopists. In a company with more than one laboratory, the program shall include all laboratories and

Occupational Safety and Health Admin., Labor § 1910.1001, App. B

shall also evaluate the laboratory-to-laboratory variability.

2. Interlaboratory program. Each laboratory analyzing asbestos samples for compliance determination shall implement an interlaboratory quality assurance program that as a minimum includes participation of at least two other independent laboratories. Each laboratory shall participate in round robin testing at least once every 6 months with at least all the other laboratories in its interlaboratory quality assurance group. Each laboratory shall submit slides typical of its own work load for use in this program. The round robin shall be designed and results analyzed using appropriate statistical methodology.

3. All individuals performing asbestos analysis must have taken the NIOSH course for sampling and evaluating airborne asbestos dust or an equalivalent course.

4. When the use of different microscopes contributes to differences between counters and laboratories, the effect of the different microscope shall be evaluated and the microscope shall be replaced, as necessary.

5. Current results of these quality assurance programs shall be posted in each laboratory to keep the microscopists informed.

APPENDIX B TO § 1910.1001—DETAILED PROCEDURE FOR ASBESTOS SAMPLING AND ANALYSIS—NON-MANDATORY

This appendix contains a detailed procedure for sampling and analysis and includes those critical elements specified in Appendix A. Employers are not required to use this procedure, but they are required to use Appendix A. The purpose of Appendix B is to provide a detailed step-by-step sampling and analysis procedure that conforms to the elements specified in Appendix A. Since this procedure may also standardize the analysis and reduce variability, OSHA encourages employers to use this appendix.

Asbestos Sampling and Analysis Method

Technique: Microscopy, Phase Contrast
Analyte: Fibers (manual count)
Sample Preparation: Acetone/triacetin method
Calibration: Phase-shift detection limit about 3 degrees
Range: 100 to 1300 fibers/mm^2 filter area
Estimated limit of detection: 7 fibers/mm^2 filter area
Sampler: Filter (0.8–1.2 um mixed cellulose ester membrane, 25-mm diameter)
Flow rate: 0.5 L/min to 2.5 L/min (25-mm cassette) 1.0 L/min to 2.5 L/min (37-mm cassette)
Sample volume: Adjust to obtain 100 to 1300 fibers/mm^2
Shipment: Routine
Sample stability: Indefinite
Blanks: 10% of samples (minimum 2)
Standard analytical error: 0.25.

Applicability: The working range is 0.02 f/cc (1920–L air sample) to 1.25 f/cc (400–L air sample). The method gives an index of airborne asbestos fibers but may be used for other materials such as fibrous glass by inserting suitable parameters into the counting rules. The method does not differentiate between asbestos and other fibers. Asbestos fibers less than ca. 0.25 um diameter will not be detected by this method.

Interferences: Any other airborne fiber may interfere since all particles meeting the counting criteria are counted. Chainlike particles may appear fibrous. High levels of nonfibrous dust particles may obscure fibers in the field of view and raise the detection limit.

Reagents: 1. Acetone. 2. Triacetin (glycerol triacetate), reagent grade

Special precautions: Acetone is an extremely flammable liquid and precautions must be taken not to ignite it. Heating of acetone must be done in a ventilated laboratory fume hood using a flameless, spark-free heat source.

Equipment: 1. Collection device: 25-mm cassette with 50-mm electrically conductive extension cowl with cellulose ester filter, 0.8 to 1.2 mm pore size and backup pad.

NOTE: Analyze representative filters for fiber background before use and discard the filter lot if more than 5 fibers/100 fields are found.

2. Personal sampling pump, greater than or equal to 0.5 L/min. with flexible connecting tubing.

3. Microscope, phase contrast, with green or blue filter, 8 to 10X eyepiece, and 40 to 45X phase objective (total magnification ca 400X; numerical aperture = 0.65 to 0.75.

4. Slides, glass, single-frosted, pre-cleaned, 25 x 75 mm.

5. Cover slips, 25 x 25 mm, no. 1½ unless otherwise specified by microscope manufacturer.

6. Knife, No. 1 surgical steel, curved blade.

7. Tweezers.

8. Flask, Guth-type, insulated neck, 250 to 500 mL (with single-holed rubber stopper and elbow-jointed glass tubing, 16 to 22 cm long).

9. Hotplate, spark-free, stirring type; heating mantle; or infrared lamp and magnetic stirrer.

10. Syringe, hypodermic, with 22-gauge needle.

11. Graticule, Walton-Beckett type with 100 um diameter circular field at the specimen plane (area = 0.00785 mm^2). (Type G-22).

NOTE: the graticule is custom-made for each microscope.

12. HSE/NPL phase contrast test slide, Mark II.

13. Telescope, ocular phase-ring centering.

14. Stage micrometer (0.01 mm divisions).

§ 1910.1001, App. B

Sampling

1. Calibrate each personal sampling pump with a representative sampler in line.
2. Fasten the sampler to the worker's lapel as close as possible to the worker's mouth. Remove the top cover from the end of the cowl extension (open face) and orient face down. Wrap the joint between the extender and the monitor's body with shrink tape to prevent air leaks.
3. Submit at least two blanks (or 10% of the total samples, whichever is greater) for each set of samples. Remove the caps from the field blank cassettes and store the caps and cassettes in a clean area (bag or box) during the sampling period. Replace the caps in the cassettes when sampling is completed.
4. Sample at 0.5 L/min or greater. Do not exceed 1 mg total dust loading on the filter. Adjust sampling flow rate, Q (L/min), and time to produce a fiber density, E (fibers/mm^2), of 100 to 1300 fibers/m^2 [3.85×10^4 to 5×10^5 fibers per 25-mm filter with effective collection area (A_c=385 mm^2)] for optimum counting precision (see step 21 below). Calculate the minimum sampling time, $t_{minimum}$ (min) at the action level (one-half of the current standard), L (f/cc) of the fibrous aerosol being sampled:

$$t_{minimum} = \frac{(Ac)(E)}{(Q)(L)10^3}$$

5. Remove the field monitor at the end of sampling, replace the plastic top cover and small end caps, and store the monitor.
6. Ship the samples in a rigid container with sufficient packing material to prevent jostling or damage.

NOTE: Do not use polystyrene foam in the shipping container because of electrostatic forces which may cause fiber loss from the sample filter.

Sample Preparation

NOTE: The object is to produce samples with a smooth (non-grainy) background in a medium with a refractive index equal to or less than 1.46. The method below collapses the filter for easier focusing and produces permanent mounts which are useful for quality control and interlaboratory comparison. Other mounting techniques meeting the above criteria may also be used, e.g., the nonpermanent field mounting technique used in P & CAM 239.

7. Ensure that the glass slides and cover slips are free of dust and fibers.
8. Place 40 to 60 ml of acetone into a Guth-type flask. Stopper the flask with a single-hole rubber stopper through which a glass tube extends 5 to 8 cm into the flask. The portion of the glass tube that exits the top of the stopper (8 to 10 cm) is bent downward in an elbow that makes an angle of 20 to 30 degrees with the horizontal.
9. Place the flask in a stirring hotplate or wrap in a heating mantle. Heat the acetone gradually to its boiling temperature (ca. 58 °C).

CAUTION.—The acetone vapor must be generated in a ventilated fume hood away from all open flames and spark sources. Alternate heating methods can be used, providing no open flame or sparks are present.

10. Mount either the whole sample filter or a wedge cut from the sample filter on a clean glass slide.
    a. Cut wedges of ca. 25 percent of the filter area with a curved-blade steel surgical knife using a rocking motion to prevent tearing.
    b. Place the filter or wedge, dust side up, on the slide. Static electricity will usually keep the filter on the slide until it is cleared.
    c. Hold the glass slide supporting the filter approximately 1 to 2 cm from the glass tube port where the acetone vapor is escaping from the heated flask. The acetone vapor stream should cause a condensation spot on the glass slide ca. 2 to 3 cm in diameter. Move the glass slide gently in the vapor stream. The filter should clear in 2 to 5 sec. If the filter curls, distorts, or is otherwise rendered unusable, the vapor stream is probably not strong enough. Periodically wipe the outlet port with tissue to prevent liquid acetone dripping onto the filter.
    d. Using the hypodermic syringe with a 22-gauge needle, place 1 to 2 drops of triacetin on the filter. Gently lower a clean 25-mm square cover slip down onto the filter at a slight angle to reduce the possibility of forming bubbles. If too many bubbles form or the amount of triacetin is insufficient, the cover slip may become detached within a few hours.
    e. Glue the edges of the cover slip to the glass slide using a lacquer or nail polish.

NOTE: If clearing is slow, the sample preparation may be heated on a hotplate (surface temperature 50 °C) for 15 min to hasten clearing. Counting may proceed immediately after clearing and mounting are completed.

Calibration and Quality Control

11. Calibration of the Walton-Beckett graticule. The diameter, d_c(mm), of the circular counting area and the disc diameter must be specified when ordering the graticule.
    a. Insert any available graticule into the eyepiece and focus so that the graticule lines are sharp and clear.
    b. Set the appropriate interpupillary distance and, if applicable, reset the binocular head adjustment so that the magnification remains constant.
    c. Install the 40 to 45X phase objective.
    d. Place a stage micrometer on the microscope object stage and focus the microscope on the graduated lines.

e. Measure the magnified grid length, L_o(mm), using the stage micrometer.

f. Remove the graticule from the microscope and measure its actual grid length, L_a(mm). This can best be accomplished by using a stage fitted with verniers.

g. Calculate the circle diameter, d_c(mm), for the Walton-Beckett graticule:

$$d_c = \frac{L_a \times D}{L_o}$$

EXAMPLE.—If L_o = 108 um, L_a = 2.93 mm and D = 100 um, then d_c = 2.71 mm.

h. Check the field diameter, D(acceptable range 100 mm ± 2 mm) with a stage micrometer upon receipt of the graticule from the manufacturer. Determine field area (mm²).

12. Microscope adjustments. Follow the manufacturer's instructions and also the following:

a. Adjust the light source for even illumination across the field of view at the condenser iris.

NOTE: Kohler illumination is preferred, where available.

b. Focus on the particulate material to be examined.

c. Make sure that the field iris is in focus, centered on the sample, and open only enough to fully illuminate the field of view.

d. Use the telescope ocular supplied by the manufacturer to ensure that the phase rings (annular diaphragm and phase-shifting elements) are concentric.

13. Check the phase-shift detection limit of the microscope periodically.

a. Remove the HSE/NPL phase-contrast test slide from its shipping container and center it under the phase objective.

b. Bring the blocks of grooved lines into focus.

NOTE: The slide consists of seven sets of grooves (ca. 20 grooves to each block) in descending order of visibility from sets 1 to 7. The requirements for counting are that the microscope optics must resolve the grooved lines in set 3 completely, although they may appear somewhat faint, and that the grooved lines in sets 6 to 7 must be invisible. Sets 4 and 5 must be at least partially visible but may vary slightly in visibility between microscopes. A microscope which fails to meet these requirements has either too low or too high a resolution to be used for asbestos counting.

c. If the image quality deteriorates, clean the microscope optics and, if the problem persists, consult the microscope manufacturer.

14. Quality control of fiber counts.

a. Prepare and count field blanks along with the field samples. Report the counts on each blank. Calculate the mean of the field blank counts and subtract this value from each sample count before reporting the results.

NOTE 1: The identity of the blank filters should be unknown to the counter until all counts have been completed.

NOTE 2: If a field blank yields fiber counts greater than 7 fibers/100 fields, report possible contamination of the samples.

b. Perform blind recounts by the same counter on 10 percent of filters counted (slides relabeled by a person other than the counter).

15. Use the following test to determine whether a pair of counts on the same filter should be rejected because of possible bias. This statistic estimates the counting repeatability at the 95% confidence level. Discard the sample if the difference between the two counts exceeds 2.77(F)s_r, where F=average of the two fiber counts and s_r=relative standard deviation, which should be derived by each laboratory based on historical in-house data.

NOTE: If a pair of counts is rejected as a result of this test, recount the remaining samples in the set and test the new counts against the first counts. Discard all rejected paired counts.

16. Enroll each new counter in a training course that compares performance of counters on a variety of samples using this procedure.

NOTE: To ensure good reproducibility, all laboratories engaged in asbestos counting are required to participate in the Proficiency Analytical Testing (PAT) Program and should routinely participate with other asbestos fiber counting laboratories in the exchange of field samples to compare performance of counters.

Measurement

17. Place the slide on the mechanical stage of the calibrated microscope with the center of the filter under the objective lens. Focus the microscope on the plane of the filter.

18. Regularly check phase-ring alignment and Kohler illumination.

19. The following are the counting rules:

a. Count only fibers longer than 5 um. Measure the length of curved fibers along the curve.

b. Count only fibers with a length-to-width ratio equal to or greater than 3:1.

c. For fibers that cross the boundary of the graticule field, do the following:

1. Count any fiber longer tha 5 um that lies entirely within the graticule area.

2. Count as ½ fiber any fiber with only one end lying within the graticule area.

3. Do not count any fiber that crosses the graticule boundary more than once.

4. Reject and do not count all other fibers.

d. Count bundles of fibers as one fiber unless individual fibers can be identified by observing both ends of a fiber.

§ 1910.1001, App. C

e. Count enough graticule fields to yield 100 fibers. Count a minimum of 20 fields. Stop at 100 fields regardless of fiber count.

20. Start counting from one end of the filter and progress along a radial line to the other end, shift either up or down on the filter, and continue in the reverse direction. Select fields randomly by looking away from the eyepiece briefly while advancing the mechanical stage. When an agglomerate covers ca. ⅙ or more of the field of view, reject the field and select another. Do not report rejected fields in the number of total fields counted.

NOTE: When counting a field, continuously scan a range of focal planes by moving the fine focus knob to detect very fine fibers which have become embedded in the filter. The small-diameter fibers will be very faint but are an important contribution to the total count.

Calculations

21. Calculate and report fiber density on the filter, E (fibers/mm^2); by dividing the total fiber count, F; minus the mean field blank count, B, by the number of fields, n; and the field area, A_f (0.00785 mm^2 for a properly calibrated Walton-Beckett graticule):

$$E = \frac{(F/n_f) - (B/n_b)}{A_f} \text{ fibers/mm}^2$$

where:
n_f = number of fields in submission sample
n_b = number of fields in blank sample

22. Calculate the concentration, C (f/cc), of fibers in the air volume sampled, V (L), using the effective collection area of the filter, A_c (385 mm^2 for a 25-mm filter):

$$C = \frac{(E)(A_c)}{V(10^3)}$$

NOTE: Periodically check and adjust the value of A_c, if necessary.

APPENDIX C TO § 1910.1001—QUALITATIVE AND QUANTITATIVE FIT TESTING PROCEDURES—MANDATORY

QUALITATIVE FIT TEST PROTOCOLS

I. Isoamyl Acetate Protocol.

A. Odor Threshold Screening

1. Three 1-liter glass jars with metal lids (e.g. Mason or Bell jars) are required.
2. Odor-free water (e.g. distilled or spring water) at approximately 25°C shall be used for the solutions.
3. The isoamyl acetate (IAA) (also known as isopentyl acetate) stock solution is prepared by adding 1 cc of pure IAA to 800 cc of odor free water in a 1-liter jar and shaking for 30 seconds. This solution shall be prepared new at least weekly.
4. The screening test shall be conducted in a room separate from the room used for actual fit testing. The two rooms shall be well ventilated but shall not be connected to the same recirculating ventilation system.
5. The odor test solution is prepared in a second jar by placing 0.4 cc of the stock solution into 500 cc of odor free water using a clean dropper or pipette. Shake for 30 seconds and allow to stand for two to three minutes so that the IAA concentration above the liquid may reach equilibrium. This solution may be used for only one day.
6. A test blank is prepared in a third jar by adding 500 cc of odor free water.
7. The odor test and test blank jars shall be labelled 1 and 2 for jar identification. If the labels are put on the lids they can be periodically peeled, dried off and switched to maintain the integrity of the test.
8. The following instructions shall be typed on a card and placed on the table in front of the two test jars (i.e. 1 and 2): "The purpose of this test is to determine if you can smell banana oil at a low concentration. The two bottles in front of you contain water. One of these bottles also contains a small amount of banana oil. Be sure the covers are on tight, then shake each bottle for two seconds. Unscrew the lid of each bottle, one at a time, and sniff at the mouth of the bottle. Indicate to the test conductor which bottle contains banana oil."
9. The mixtures used in the IAA odor detection test shall be prepared in an area separate from where the test is performed, in order to prevent olfactory fatigue in the subject.
10. If the test subject is unable to correctly identify the jar containing the odor test solution, the IAA qualitative fit test may not be used.
11. If the test subject correctly identifies the jar containing the odor test solution, the test subject may proceed to respirator selection and fit testing.

B. Respirator Selection

1. The test subject shall be allowed to pick the most comfortable respirator from a selection including respirators of various sizes from different manufacturers. The selection shall include at least five sizes of elastomeric half facepieces, from at least two manufacturers.
2. The selection process shall be conducted in a room separate from the fit-test chamber to prevent odor fatigue. Prior to the selection process, the test subject shall be shown how to put on a respirator, how it should be positioned on the face, how to set strap tension and how to determine a "comfortable" respirator. A mirror shall be available to as-

Occupational Safety and Health Admin., Labor § 1910.1001, App. C

sist the subject in evaluating the fit and positioning of the respirator. This instruction may not constitute the subject's formal training on respirator use, as it is only a review.

3. The test subject should understand that the employee is being asked to select the respirator which provides the most comfortable fit. Each respirator represents a different size and shape and, if fit properly and used properly will provide adequate protection.

4. The test subject holds each facepiece up to the face and eliminates those which obviously do not give a comfortable fit. Normally, selection will begin with a half-mask and if a good fit cannot be found, the subject will be asked to test the full facepiece respirators. (A small percentage of users will not be able to wear any half-mask.)

5. The more comfortable facepieces are noted; the most comfortable mask is donned and *worn at least five minutes* to assess comfort. All donning and adjustments of the facepiece shall be performed by the test subject without assistance from the test conductor or other person. Assistance in assessing comfort can be given by discussing the points in #6 below. If the test subject is not familiar with using a particular respirator, the test subject shall be directed to don the mask several times and to adjust the straps each time to become adept at setting proper tension on the straps.

6. Assessment of comfort shall include reviewing the following points with the test subject and allowing the test subject adequate time to determine the comfort of the respirator:
- Positioning of mask on nose.
- Room for eye protection.
- Room to talk.
- Positioning mask on face and cheeks.

7. The following criteria shall be used to help determine the adequacy of the respirator fit:
- Chin properly placed.
- Strap tension.
- Fit across nose bridge.
- Distance from nose to chin.
- Tendency to slip.
- Self-observation in mirror.

8. The test subject shall conduct the conventional negative and positive-pressure fit checks (e.g. see ANSI Z88.2-1980). Before conducting the negative- or positive-pressure test the subject shall be told to "seat" the mask by rapidly moving the head from side-to-side and up and down, while taking a few deep breaths.

9. The test subject is now ready for fit testing.

10. After passing the fit test, the test subject shall be questioned again regarding the comfort of the respirator. If it has become uncomfortable, another model of respirator shall be tried.

11. The employee shall be given the opportunity to select a different facepiece and be retested if the chosen facepiece becomes increasingly uncomfortable at any time.

C. Fit Test

1. The fit test chamber shall be similar to a clear 55 gal drum liner suspended inverted over a 2 foot diameter frame, so that the top of the chamber is about 6 inches above the test subject's head. The inside top center of the chamber shall have a small hook attached.

2. Each respirator used for the fitting and fit testing shall be equipped with organic vapor cartridges or offer protection against organic vapors. The cartridges or masks shall be changed at least weekly.

3. After selecting, donning, and properly adjusting a respirator, the test subject shall wear it to the fit testing room. This room shall be separate from the room used for odor threshold screening and respirator selection, and shall be well ventilated, as by an exhaust fan or lab hood, to prevent general room contamination.

4. A copy of the following test exercises and rainbow passage shall be taped to the inside of the test chamber:

Test Exercises

i. Breathe normally.

ii. Breathe deeply. Be certain breaths are *deep* and *regular*.

iii. Turn head all the way from one side to the other. Inhale on each side. Be certain movement is complete. Do not bump the respirator against the shoulders.

iv. Nod head up-and-down. Inhale when head is in the full up position (looking toward ceiling). Be certain motions are complete and made about every second. Do not bump the respirator on the chest.

v. Talking. Talk aloud and slowly for several minutes. The following paragraph is called the Rainbow Passage. Reading it will result in a wide range of facial movements, and thus be useful to satisfy this requirement. Alternative passages which serve the same purpose may also be used.

vi. Jogging in place.

vii. Breathe normally.

Rainbow Passage

When the sunlight strikes raindrops in the air, they act like a prism and form a rainbow. The rainbow is a division of white light into many beautiful colors. These take the shape of a long round arch, with its path high above, and its two ends apparently beyond the horizon. There is, according to legend, a boiling pot of gold at one end. People look but no one ever finds it. When a man looks for something beyond reach, his friends say he is looking for the pot of gold at the end of the rainbow.

35

§ 1910.1001, App. C

5. Each test subject shall wear the respirator for at least 10 minutes before starting the fit test.

6. Upon entering the test chamber, the test subject shall be given a 6 inch by 5 inch piece of paper towel or other porous absorbent single ply material, folded in half and wetted with three-quarters of one cc of pure IAA. The test subject shall hang the wet towel on the hook at the top of the chamber.

7. Allow two minutes for the IAA test concentration to be reached before starting the fit-test exercises. This would be an appropriate time to talk with the test subject, to explain the fit test, the importance of cooperation, the purpose for the head exercises, or to demonstrate some of the exercises.

8. Each exercise described in #4 above shall be performed for at least one minute.

9. If at any time during the test, the subject detects the banana-like odor of IAA, the test has failed. The subject shall quickly exit from the test chamber and leave the test area to avoid olfactory fatigue.

10. If the test is failed, the subject shall return to the selection room and remove the respirator, repeat the odor sensitivity test, select and put on another respirator, return to the test chamber, and again begin the procedure described in the c(4) through c(8) above. The process continues until a respirator that fits well has been found. Should the odor sensitivity test be failed, the subject shall wait about 5 minutes before retesting. Odor sensitivity will usually have returned by this time.

11. If a person cannot pass the fit test described above wearing a half-mask respirator from the available selection, full facepiece models must be used.

12. When a respirator is found that passes the test, the subject breaks the faceseal and takes a breath before exiting the chamber. This is to assure that the reason the test subject is not smelling the IAA is the good fit of the respirator facepiece seal and not olfactory fatigue.

13. When the test subject leaves the chamber, the subject shall remove the saturated towel and return it to the person conducting the test. To keep the area from becoming contaminated, the used towels shall be kept in a self-sealing bag so there is no significant IAA concentration buildup in the test chamber during subsequent tests.

14. At least two facepieces shall be selected for the IAA test protocol. The test subject shall be given the opportunity to wear them for one week to choose the one which is more comfortable to wear.

15. Persons who have successfully passed this fit test with a half-mask respirator may be assigned the use of the test respirator in atmospheres with up to 10 times the PEL of airborne asbestos.

16. The test shall not be conducted if there is any hair growth between the skin the facepiece sealing surface.

17. If hair growth or apparel interfere with a satisfactory fit, then they shall be altered or removed so as to eliminate interference and allow a satisfactory fit. If a satisfactory fit is still not attained, the test subject must use a positive-pressure respirator such as powered air-purifying respirators, supplied air respirator, or self-contained breathing apparatus.

18. If a test subject exhibits difficulty in breathing during the tests, she or he shall be referred to a physician trained in respirator diseases or pulmonary medicine to determine whether the test subject can wear a respirator while performing her or his duties.

19. Qualitative fit testing shall be repeated at least every six months.

20. In addition, because the sealing of the respirator may be affected, qualitative fit testing shall be repeated immediately when the test subject has a:
(1) Weight change of 20 pounds or more,
(2) Significant facial scarring in the area of the facepiece seal,
(3) Significant dental changes; i.e., multiple extractions without prothesis, or acquiring dentures,
(4) Reconstructive or cosmetic surgery, or
(5) Any other condition that may interfere with facepiece sealing.

D. Recordkeeping

A summary of all test results shall be maintained in each office for 3 years. The summary shall include:
(1) Name of test subject.
(2) Date of testing.
(3) Name of the test conductor.
(4) Respirators selected (indicate manufacturer, model, size and approval number).
(5) Testing agent.

II. Saccharin Solution Aerosol Protocol

A. Respirator Selection

Respirators shall be selected as described in section IB (respirator selection) above, except that each respirator shall be equipped with a particulate filter.

B. Taste Threshold Screening

1. An enclosure about head and shoulders shall be used for threshold screening (to determine if the individual can taste saccharin) and for fit testing. The enclosure shall be approximately 12 inches in diameter by 14 inches tall with at least the front clear to allow free movement of the head when a respirator is worn.

2. The test enclosure shall have a three-quarter inch hole in front of the test subject's nose and mouth area to accommodate the nebulizer nozzle.

3. The entire screening and testing procedure shall be explained to the test subject prior to conducting the screening test.

4. During the threshold screening test, the test subject shall don the test enclosure and breathe with open mouth with tongue extended.

5. Using a DeVilbiss Model 40 Inhalation Medication Nebulizer or equivalent, the test conductor shall spray the threshold check solution into the enclosure. This nebulizer shall be clearly marked to distinguish it from the fit test solution nebulizer.

6. The threshold check solution consists of 0.83 grams of sodium saccharin, USP in water. It can be prepared by putting 1 cc of the test solution (see C 7 below) in 100 cc of water.

7. To produce the aerosol, the nebulizer bulb is firmly squeezed so that it collapses completely, then is released and allowed to fully expand.

8. Ten squeezes of the nebulizer bulb are repeated rapidly and then the test subject is asked whether the saccharin can be tasted.

9. If the first response is negative, ten more squeezes of the nebulizer bulb are repeated rapidly and the test subject is again asked whether the saccharin can be tasted.

10. If the second response is negative ten more squeezes are repeated rapidly and the test subject is again asked whether the saccharin can be tasted.

11. The test conductor will take note of the number of squeezes required to elicit a taste response.

12. If the saccharin is not tasted after 30 squeezes (Step 10), the saccharin fit test cannot be performed on the test subject.

13. If a taste response is elicited, the test subject shall be asked to take note of the taste for reference in the fit test.

14. Correct use of the nebulizer means that approximately 1 cc of liquid is used at a time in the nebulizer body.

15. The nebulizer shall be thoroughly rinsed in water, shaken dry, and refilled at least every four hours.

C. Fit Test

1. The test subject shall don and adjust the respirator without the assistance from any person.

2. The fit test uses the same enclosure described in IIB above.

3. Each test subject shall wear the respirator for at least 10 minutes before starting the fit test.

4. The test subject shall don the enclosure while wearing the respirator selected in section 1B above. This respirator shall be properly adjusted and equipped with a particulate filter.

5. The test subject may not eat, drink (except plain water), or chew gum for 15 minutes before the test.

6. A second DeVilbiss Model 40 Inhalation Medication Nebulizer is used to spray the fit test solution into the enclosure. This nebulizer shall be clearly marked to distinguish it from the screening test solution nebulizer.

7. The fit test solution is prepared by adding 83 grams of sodium saccharin to 100 cc of warm water.

8. As before, the test subject shall breathe with mouth open and tongue extended.

9. The nebulizer is inserted into the hole in the front of the enclosure and the fit test solution is sprayed into the enclosure using the same technique as for the taste threshold screening and the same number of squeezes required to elicit a taste response in the screening. (See B8 through B10 above).

10. After generation of the aerosol read the following instructions to the test subject. The test subject shall perform the exercises for one minute each.

  i. Breathe normally.

  ii. Breathe deeply. Be certain breaths are *deep* and *regular*.

  iii. Turn head all the way from one side *to the other*. Be certain movement is complete. Inhale on each side. Do not bump the respirator against the shoulders.

  iv. Nod head up-and-down. Be certain motions are complete. Inhale when head is in the full up position (when looking toward the ceiling). Do not bump the respirator on the chest.

  v. Talking. Talk aloud and slowly for several minutes. The following paragraph is called the Rainbow Passage. Reading it will result in a wide range of facial movements, and thus be useful to satisfy this requirement. Alternative passages which serve the same purpose may also be used.

  vi. Jogging in place.

  vii. Breathe normally.

Rainbow Passage

When the sunlight strikes raindrops in the air, they act like a prism and form a rainbow. The rainbow is a division of white light into many beautiful colors. These take the shape of a long round arch, with its path high above, and its two ends apparently beyond the horizon. There is, according to legend, a boiling pot of gold at one end. People look, but no one ever finds it. When a man looks for something beyond his reach, his friends say he is looking for the pot of gold at the end of the rainbow.

11. At the beginning of each exercise, the aerosol concentration shall be replenished using one-half the number of squeezes as initially described in C9.

12. The test subject shall indicate to the test conductor if at any time during the fit test the taste of saccharin is detected.

13. If the saccharin is detected the fit is deemed unsatisfactory and a different respirator shall be tried.

APPENDIX 4D

§ 1910.1001, App. C

14. At least two facepieces shall be selected by the saccharin solution aerosol test protocol. The test subject shall be given the opportunity to wear them for one week to choose the one which is more comfortable to wear.

15. Successful completion of the test protocol shall allow the use of the half mask tested respirator in contaminated atmospheres up to 10 times the PEL of asbestos. In other words this protocol may be used to assign protection factors no higher than ten.

16. The test shall not be conducted if there is any hair growth between the skin and the facepiece sealing surface.

17. If hair growth or apparel interfere with a satisfactory fit, then they shall be altered or removed so as to eliminate interference and allow a satisfactory fit. If a satisfactory fit is still not attained, the test subject must use a positive-pressure respirator such as powered air-purifying respirators, supplied air respirator, or self-contained breathing apparatus.

18. If a test subject exhibits difficulty in breathing during the tests, she or he shall be referred to a physician trained in respirator diseases or pulmonary medicine to determine whether the test subject can wear a respirator while performing her or his duties.

19. Qualitative fit testing shall be repeated at least every six months.

20. In addition, because the sealing of the respirator may be affected, qualitative fit testing shall be repeated immediately when the test subject has a:

(1) Weight change of 20 pounds or more,
(2) Significant facial scarring in the area of the facepiece seal,
(3) Significant dental changes; i.e.; multiple extractions without prothesis, or acquiring dentures,
(4) Reconstructive or cosmetic surgery, or
(5) Any other condition that may interfere with facepiece sealing.

D. Recordkeeping

A summary of all test results shall be maintained in each office for 3 years. The summary shall include:

(1) Name of test subject.
(2) Date of testing.
(3) Name of test conductor.
(4) Respirators selected (indicate manufacturer, model, size and approval number).
(5) Testing agent.

III. Irritant Fume Protocol

A. Respirator selection

Respirators shall be selected as described in section IB above, except that each respirator shall be equipped with a high-efficiency cartridge.

29 CFR Ch. XVII (7-1-94 Edition)

B. Fit test

1. The test subject shall be allowed to smell a weak concentration of the irritant smoke to familiarize the subject with the characteristic odor.

2. The test subject shall properly don the respirator selected as above, and wear it for at least 10 minutes before starting the fit test.

3. The test conductor shall review this protocol with the test subject before testing.

4. The test subject shall perform the conventional positive pressure and negative pressure fit checks (see ANSI Z88.2 1980). Failure of either check shall be cause to select an alternate respirator.

5. Break both ends of a ventilation smoke tube containing stannic oxychloride, such as the MSA part #5645, or equivalent. Attach a short length of tubing to one end of the smoke tube. Attach the other end of the smoke tube to a low pressure air pump set to deliver 200 milliliters per minute.

6. Advise the test subject that the smoke can be irritating to the eyes and instruct the subject to keep the eyes closed while the test is performed.

7. The test conductor shall direct the stream of irritant smoke from the tube towards the faceseal area of the test subject. The person conducting the test shall begin with the tube at least 12 inches from the facepiece and gradually move to within one inch, moving around the whole perimeter of the mask.

8. The test subject shall be instructed to do the following exercises while the respirator is being challenged by the smoke. Each exercise shall be performed for one minute.

 i. Breathe normally.
 ii. Breathe deeply. Be certain breaths are *deep* and *regular*.
 iii. Turn head all the way from one side to the other. Be certain movement is complete. Inhale on each side. Do not bump the respirator against the shoulders.
 iv. Nod head up-and-down. Be certain motions are complete and made every second. Inhale when head is in the full up position (looking toward ceiling). Do not bump the respirator against the chest.
 v. Talking. Talk aloud and slowly for several minutes. The following paragraph is called the Rainbow Passage. Repeating it after the test conductor (keeping eyes closed) will result in a wide range of facial movements, and thus be useful to satisfy this requirement. Alternative passages which serve the same purpose may also be used.

Rainbow Passage

When the sunlight strikes raindrops in the air, they act like a prism and form a rainbow. The rainbow is a division of white light into many beautiful colors. These take the

Occupational Safety and Health Admin., Labor §1910.1001, App. C

shape of a long round arch, with its path high above, and its two ends apparently beyond the horizon. There is, according to legend, a boiling pot of gold at one end. People look, but no one ever finds it. When a man looks for something beyond his reach, his friends say he is looking for the pot of gold at the end of the rainbow.

vi. Jogging in Place.

vii. Breathe normally.

9. The test subject shall indicate to the test conductor if the irritant smoke is detected. If smoke is detected, the test conductor shall stop the test. In this case, the tested respirator is rejected and another respirator shall be selected.

10. Each test subject passing the smoke test (i.e. without detecting the smoke) shall be given a sensitivity check of smoke from the same tube to determine if the test subject reacts to the smoke. Failure to evoke a response shall void the fit test.

11. Steps B4, B9, B10 of this fit test protocol be performed in a location with exhaust ventilation sufficient to prevent general contamination of the testing area by the test agents.

12. At least two facepieces shall be selected by the irritant fume test protocol. The test subject shall be given the opportunity to wear them for one week to choose the one which is more comfortable to wear.

13. Respirators successfully tested by the protocol may be used in contaminated atmospheres up to ten times the PEL of asbestos.

14. The test shall not be conducted if there is any hair growth between the skin and the facepiece sealing surface.

15. If hair growth or apparel interfere with a satisfactory fit, then they shall be altered or removed so as to eliminate interference and allow a satisfactory fit. If a satisfactory fit is still not attained, the test subject must use a positive-pressure respirator such as powered air-purifying respirators, supplied air respirator, or self-contained breathing apparatus.

16. If a test subject exhibits difficulty in breathing during the tests, she or he shall be referred to a physician trained in respirator diseases or pulmonary medicine to determine whether the test subject can wear a respirator while performing her or his duties.

17. Qualitative fit testing shall be repeated at least every six months.

18. In addition, because the sealing of the respirator may be affected, qualitative fit testing shall be repeated immediately when the test subject has a:

(1) Weight change of 20 pounds or more,

(2) Significant facial scarring in the area of the facepiece seal,

(3) Significant dental changes; i.e.; multiple extractions without prothesis, or acquiring dentures,

(4) Reconstructive or cosmetic surgery, or

(5) Any other condition that may interfere with facepiece sealing.

C. Recordkeeping

A summary of all test results shall be maintained in each office for 3 years. The summary shall include:

(1) Name of test subject.

(2) Date of testing.

(3) Name of test conductor.

(4) Respirators selected (indicate manufacturer, model, size and approval number).

(5) Testing agent

Quantitative Fit Test Procedures

1. General.

a. The method applies to the negative-pressure nonpowered air-purifying respirators only.

b. The employer shall assign one individual who shall assume the full responsibility for implementing the respirator quantitative fit test program.

2. *Definition.*

a. *Quantitative Fit Test* means the measurement of the effectiveness of a respirator seal in excluding the ambient atmosphere. The test is performed by dividing the measured concentration of challenge agent in a test chamber by the measured concentration of the challenge agent inside the respirator facepiece when the normal air purifying element has been replaced by an essentially perfect purifying element.

b. *Challenge Agent* means the air contaminant introduced into a test chamber so that its concentration inside and outside the respirator may be compared.

c. *Test Subject* means the person wearing the respirator for quantitative fit testing.

d. *Normal Standing Position* means standing erect and straight with arms down along the sides and looking straight ahead.

e. *Fit Factor* means the ratio of challenge agent concentration outside with respect to the inside of a respirator inlet covering (facepiece or enclosure).

3. *Apparatus.*

a. *Instrumentation.* Corn oil, sodium chloride or other appropriate aerosol generation, dilution, and measurement systems shall be used for quantitative fit test.

b. *Test chamber.* The test chamber shall be large enough to permit all test subjects to freely perform all required exercises without distributing the challenge agent concentration or the measurement apparatus. The test chamber shall be equipped and constructed so that the challenge agent is effectively isolated from the ambient air yet uniform in concentration throughout the chamber.

c. When testing air-purifying respirators, the normal filter or cartridge element shall be replaced with a high-efficiency particulate filter supplied by the same manufacturer.

APPENDIX 4D

§ 1910.1001, App. C   29 CFR Ch. XVII (7-1-94 Edition)

d. The sampling instrument shall be selected so that a strip chart record may be made of the test showing the rise and fall of challenge agent concentration with each inspiration and expiration at fit factors of at least 2,000.

e. The combination of substitute air-purifying elements (if any), challenge agent, and challenge agent concentration in the test chamber shall be such that the test subject is not exposed in excess of PEL to the challenge agent at any time during the testing process.

f. The sampling port on the test specimen respirator shall be placed and constructed so that there is no detectable leak around the port, a free air flow is allowed into the sampling line at all times and so there is no interference with the fit or performance of the respirator.

g. The test chamber and test set-up shall permit the person administering the test to observe one test subject inside the chamber during the test.

h. The equipment generating the challenge atmosphere shall maintain the concentration of challenge agent constant within a 10 percent variation for the duration of the test.

i. The time lag (interval between an event and its being recorded on the strip chart) of the instrumentation may not exceed 2 seconds.

j. The tubing for the test chamber atmosphere and for the respirator sampling port shall be the same diameter, length and material. It shall be kept as short as possible. The smallest diameter tubing recommended by the manufacturer shall be used.

k. The exhaust flow from the test chamber shall pass through a high-efficiency filter before release to the room.

l. When sodium chloride aerosol is used, the relative humidity inside the test chamber shall not exceed 50 percent.

4. *Procedural Requirements.*

a. The fitting of half-mask respirators should be started with those having multiple sizes and a variety of interchangeable cartridges and canisters such as the MSA Comfo II-M, North M. Survivair M, A-O M, or Scott-M. Use either of the tests outlined below to assure that the facepiece is properly adjusted.

(1) *Positive pressure test.* With the exhaust port(s) blocked, the negative pressure of slight inhalation should remain constant for several seconds.

(2) *Negative pressure test.* With the intake port(s) blocked, the negative pressure slight inhalation should remain constant for several seconds.

b. After a facepiece is adjusted, the test subject shall wear the facepiece for at least 5 minutes before conducting a qualitive test by using either of the methods described below and using the exercise regime described in 5.a., b., c., d, and e.

(1) *Isoamyl acetate test.* When using organic vapor cartridges, the test subject who can smell the odor should be unable to detect the odor of isoamyl acetate squirted into the air near the most vulnerable portions of the facepiece seal. In a location which is separated from the test area, the test subject shall be instructed to close her/his eyes during the test period. A combination cartridge or canister with organic vapor and high-efficiency filters shall be used when available for the particular mask being tested. The test subject shall be given an opportunity to smell the odor of isoamyl acetate before the test is conducted.

(2) *Irritant fume test.* When using high-efficiency filters, the test subject should be unable to detect the odor of irritant fume (stannic chloride or titanium tetrachloride ventilation smoke tubes) squirted into the air near the most vulnerable portions of the facepiece seal. The test subject shall be instructed to close her/his eyes during the test period.

c. The test subject may enter the quantitative testing chamber only if she or he has obtained a satisfactory fit as stated in 4.b. of this Appendix.

d. Before the subject enters the test chamber, a reasonably stable challenge agent concentration shall be measured in the test chamber.

e. Immediately after the subject enters the test chamber, the challenge agent concentration inside the respirator shall be measured to ensure that the peak penetration does not exceed 5 percent for a half-mask and 1 percent for a full facepiece.

f. A stable challenge agent concentration shall be obtained prior to the actual start of testing.

(1) Respirator restraining straps may not be overtightened for testing. The straps shall be adjusted by the wearer to give a reasonably comfortable fit typical of normal use.

5. *Exercise Regime.* Prior to entering the test chamber, the test subject shall be given complete instructions as to her/his part in the test procedures. The test subject shall perform the following exercises, in the order given, for each independent test.

a. *Normal Breathing (NB).* In the normal standing position, without talking, the subject shall breathe normally for at least one minute.

b. *Deep Breathing (DB).* In the normal standing position the subject shall do deep breathing for at least one minute pausing so as not to hyperventilate.

c. *Turning head side to side (SS).* Standing in place the subject shall slowly turn his/her head from side between the extreme positions to each side. The head shall be held at each extreme position for at least 5 seconds. Perform for at least three complete cycles.

Occupational Safety and Health Admin., Labor § 1910.1001, App. C

d. *Moving head up and down (UD)*. Standing in place, the subject shall slowly move his/her head up and down between the extreme position straight up and the extreme position straight down. The head shall be held at each extreme position for at least 5 seconds. Perform for at least three complete cycles.

e. *Reading (R)*. The test subject (keeping eyes closed) shall repeat after the test conductor the 'rainbow passage' at the end of this section. The subject shall talk slowly and aloud so as to be heard clearly by the test conductor or monitor.

f. *Grimace (G)*. The test subject shall grimace, smile, frown, and generally contort the face using the facial muscles. Continue for at least 15 seconds.

g. *Bend over and touch toes (B)*. The test subject shall bend at the waist and touch toes and return to upright position. Repeat for at least 30 seconds.

h. *Jogging in place (J)*. The test subject shall perform jog in place for at least 30 seconds.

i. *Normal Breathing (NB)*. Same as exercise a.

Rainbow Passage

When the sunlight strikes raindrops in the air, they act like a prism and form a rainbow. The rainbow is a division of white light into many beautiful colors. These take the shape of a long round arch, with its path high above, and its two ends apparently beyond the horizon. There is, according to legend, a boiling pot of gold at one end. People look, but no one ever finds it. When a man looks for something beyond reach, his friends say he is looking for the pot of gold at the end of the rainbow.

6. The test shall be terminated whenever any single peak penetration exceeds 5 percent for half-masks and 1 percent for full facepieces. The test subject may be refitted and retested. If two of the three required tests are terminated, the fit shall be deemed inadequate.

7. *Calculation of Fit Factors.*

a. The fit factor determined by the quantitative fit test equals the average concentration inside the respirator.

b. The average test chamber concentration is the arithmetic average of the test chamber concentration at the beginning and of the end of the test.

c. The average peak concentration of the challenge agent inside the respirator shall be the arithmetic average peak concentrations for each of the nine exercises of the test which are computed as the arithmetic average of the peak concentrations found for each breath during the exercise.

d. The average peak concentration for an exercise may be determined graphically if there is not a great variation in the peak concentrations during a single exercise.

8. *Interpretation of Test Results.* The fit factor measured by the quantitative fit testing shall be the lowest of the three protection factors resulting from three independent tests.

9. *Other Requirements.*

a. The test subject shall not be permitted to wear a half-mask or full facepiece mask if the minimum fit factor of 100 or 1,000, respectively, cannot be obtained. If hair growth or apparel interfere with a satisfactory fit, then they shall be altered or removed so as to eliminate interference and allow a satisfactory fit. If a satisfactory fit is still not attained, the test subject must use a positive-pressure respirator such as powered air-purifying respirators, supplied air respirator, or self-contained breathing apparatus.

b. The test shall not be conducted if there is any hair growth between the skin and the facepiece sealing surface.

c. If a test subject exhibits difficulty in breathing during the tests, she or he shall be referred to a physician trained in respirator diseases or pulmonary medicine to determine whether the test subject can wear a respirator while performing her or his duties.

d. The test subject shall be given the opportunity to wear the assigned respirator for one week. If the respirator does not provide a satisfactory fit during actual use, the test subject may request another QNFT which shall be performed immediately.

e. A respirator fit factor card shall be issued to the test subject with the following information:

(1) Name.

(2) Date of fit test.

(3) Protection factors obtained through each manufacturer, model and approval number of respirator tested.

(4) Name and signature of the person that conducted the test.

f. Filters used for qualitative or quantitative fit testing shall be replaced weekly, whenever increased breathing resistance is encountered, or when the test agent has altered the integrity of the filter media. Organic vapor cartridges/canisters shall be replaced daily or sooner if there is any indication of breakthrough by the test agent.

10. In addition, because the sealing of the respirator may be affected, quantitative fit testing shall be repeated immediately when the test subject has a:

(1) Weight change of 20 pounds or more,

(2) Significant facial scarring in the area of the facepiece seal,

(3) Significant dental changes; i.e., multiple extractions without prothesis, or acquiring dentures.

(4) Reconstructive or cosmetic surgery, or

(5) Any other condition that may interfere with facepiece sealing.

11. *Recordkeeping.*

§ 1910.1001, App. D

A summary of all test results shall be maintained for 3 years. The summary shall include:
(1) Name of test subject.
(2) Date of testing.
(3) Name of the test conductor.
(4) Fit factors obtained from every respirator tested (indicate manufacturer, model, size and approval number).

APPENDIX D TO § 1910.1001—MEDICAL QUESTIONNAIRES; MANDATORY

This mandatory appendix contains the medical questionnaires that must be administered to all employees who are exposed to asbestos above the action level, and who will therefore be included in their employer's medical surveillance program. Part 1 of the appendix contains the Initial Medical Questionnaire, which must be obtained for all new hires who will be covered by the medical surveillance requirements. Part 2 includes the abbreviated Periodical Medical Questionnaire, which must be administered to all employees who are provided periodic medical examinations under the medical surveillance provisions of the standard.

Occupational Safety and Health Admin., Labor § 1910.1001, App. D

Part 1
INITIAL MEDICAL QUESTIONNAIRE

1. NAME _____

2. SOCIAL SECURITY # ___ ___ ___ ___ ___ ___ ___ ___ ___
                                    1 2 3 4 5 6 7 8 9

3. CLOCK NUMBER ___ ___ ___ ___ ___ ___
                        10 11 12 13 14 15

4. PRESENT OCCUPATION _____

5. PLANT _____

6. ADDRESS _____

7. _____
                        (Zip Code)

8. TELEPHONE NUMBER _____

9. INTERVIEWER _____

10. DATE _____ ___ ___ ___ ___ ___ ___
                                16 17 18 19 20 21

11. Date of Birth ___ ___ ___ ___ ___ ___ ___ ___ ___
                   Month Day Year 22 23 24 25 26 27

12. Place of Birth _____

13. Sex   1. Male ___
                             2. Female ___

14. What is your marital status?   1. Single ___   4. Separated/
                                           2. Married ___   Divorced ___
                                           3. Widowed ___

15. Race   1. White ___ 4. Hispanic ___
                             2. Black ___ 5. Indian ___
                             3. Asian ___ 6. Other ___

16. What is the highest grade completed in school? _____
    (For example 12 years is completion of high school)

OCCUPATIONAL HISTORY

17A. Have you ever worked full time (30 hours   1. Yes ___ 2. No ___
     per week or more) for 6 months or more?

    IF YES TO 17A:

  B. Have you ever worked for a year or more in   1. Yes ___ 2. No ___
     any dusty job?   3. Does Not Apply ___

APPENDIX 4D

§ 1910.1001, App. D   **29 CFR Ch. XVII (7-1-94 Edition)**

    Specify job/industry _____ Total Years Worked ____

    Was dust exposure: 1. Mild ___ 2. Moderate ___ 3. Severe ___

C. Have you even been exposed to gas or   1. Yes ___ 2. No ___
chemical fumes in your work?
Specify job/industry _____ Total Years Worked ___

    Was exposure: 1. Mild ___ 2. Moderate ___ 3. Severe ___

D. What has been your usual occupation or job--the one you have worked at the longest?

    1. Job occupation _____

    2. Number of years employed in this occupation _____

    3. Position/job title _____

    4. Business, field or industry _____

(Record on lines the years in which you have worked in any of these industries, e.g. 1960-1969)

Have you ever worked:

		YES	NO
E.	In a mine?...........................	[__]	[__]
F.	In a quarry?.........................	[__]	[__]
G.	In a foundry?........................	[__]	[__]
H.	In a pottery?........................	[__]	[__]
I.	In a cotton, flax or hemp mill?......	[__]	[__]
J.	With asbestos?.......................	[__]	[__]

18. **PAST MEDICAL HISTORY**

	YES	NO
A. Do you consider yourself to be in good health?	[__]	[__]

    If "NO" state reason _____

B. Have you any defect of vision?............... [__]   [__]

    If "YES" state nature of defect _____

C. Have you any hearing defect?................. [__]   [__]

    If "YES" state nature of defect _____

44

Occupational Safety and Health Admin., Labor § 1910.1001, App. D

D. Are you suffering from or have you ever suffered from:

    a. Epilepsy (or fits, seizures, convulsions)? [__] [__]

    b. Rheumatic fever? [__] [__]

    c. Kidney disease? [__] [__]

    d. Bladder disease? [__] [__]

    e. Diabetes? [__] [__]

    f. Jaundice? [__] [__]

19. CHEST COLDS AND CHEST ILLNESSES

19A. If you get a cold, does it <u>usually</u> go to your chest? (Usually means more than 1/2 the time)   1. Yes __   2. No __   3. Don't get colds __

20A. During the past 3 years, have you had any chest illnesses that have kept you off work, indoors at home, or in bed?   1. Yes __   2. No __

    IF YES TO 20A:
  B. Did you produce phlegm with any of these chest illnesses?   1. Yes __   2. No __   3. Does Not Apply __

  C. In the last 3 years, how many such illnesses with (increased) phlegm did you have which lasted a week or more?   Number of illnesses __   No such illnesses __

21. Did you have any lung trouble before the age of 16?   1. Yes __   2. No __

22. Have you ever had any of the following?

    1A. Attacks of bronchitis?   1. Yes __   2. No __

      IF YES TO 1A:
    B. Was it confirmed by a doctor?   1. Yes __   2. No __   3. Does Not Apply __

    C. At what age was your first attack?   Age in Years __   Does Not Apply __

    2A. Pneumonia (include bronchopneumonia)?   1. Yes __   2. No __

      IF YES TO 2A:
    B. Was it confirmed by a doctor?   1. Yes __   2. No __   3. Does Not Apply __

    C. At what age did you first have it?   Age in Years __   Does Not Apply __

APPENDIX 4D

§ 1910.1001, App. D   29 CFR Ch. XVII (7-1-94 Edition)

```
    3A. Hay Fever?                                  1. Yes ___    2. No ___

        IF YES TO 3A:
     B. Was it confirmed by a doctor?               1. Yes ___    2. No ___
                                                    3. Does Not Apply ___

     C. At what age did it start?                   Age in Years      ___
                                                    Does Not Apply    ___

   23A. Have you ever had chronic bronchitis?       1. Yes ___    2. No ___

        IF YES TO 23A:
     B. Do you still have it?                       1. Yes ___    2. No ___
                                                    3. Does Not Apply ___

     C. Was it confirmed by a doctor?               1. Yes ___    2. No ___
                                                    3. Does Not Apply ___

     D. At what age did it start?                   Age in Years      ___
                                                    Does Not Apply    ___

   24A. Have you ever had emphysema?                1. Yes ___    2. No ___

        IF YES TO 24A:
     B. Do you still have it?                       1. Yes ___    2. No ___
                                                    3. Does Not Apply ___

     C. Was it confirmed by a doctor?               1. Yes ___    2. No ___
                                                    3. Does Not Apply ___

     D. At what age did it start?                   Age in Years      ___
                                                    Does Not Apply    ___

   25A. Have you ever had asthma?                   1. Yes ___    2. No ___

        IF YES TO 25A:
     B. Do you still have it?                       1. Yes ___    2. No ___
                                                    3. Does Not Apply ___

     C. Was it confirmed by a doctor?               1. Yes ___    2. No ___
                                                    3. Does Not Apply ___

     D. At what age did it start?                   Age in Years      ___
                                                    Does Not Apply    ___

     E. If you no longer have it, at what age did it   Age stopped    ___
        stop?                                          Does Not Apply ___

    26. Have you ever had:

     A. Any other chest illness?                    1. Yes ___    2. No ___

        If yes, please specify _____
```

Occupational Safety and Health Admin., Labor §1910.1001, App. D

B. Any chest operations?   1. Yes ___   2. No ___

    If yes, please specify _____

C. Any chest injuries?   1. Yes ___   2. No ___

    If yes, please specify _____

27A. Has a doctor ever told you that you had heart trouble?   1. Yes ___   2. No ___

   IF YES TO 27A:
B. Have you ever had treatment for heart trouble in the past 10 years?   1. Yes ___   2. No ___
    3. Does Not Apply ___

28A. Has a doctor ever told you that you had high blood pressure?   1. Yes ___   2. No ___

   IF YES TO 28A:
B. Have you had any treatment for high blood pressure (hypertension) in the past 10 years?   1. Yes ___   2. No ___
    3. Does Not Apply ___

29. When did you last have your chest X-rayed? (Year) ___ ___ ___ ___
                                                                                     25   26   27   28

30. Where did you last have your chest X-rayed (if known)? _____

    What was the outcome? _____

FAMILY HISTORY

31. Were either of your natural parents ever told by a doctor that they had a chronic lung condition such as:

	FATHER			MOTHER		
	1. Yes	2. No	3. Don't Know	1. Yes	2. No	3. Don't Know
A. Chronic Bronchitis?	___	___	___	___	___	___
B. Emphysema?	___	___	___	___	___	___
C. Asthma?	___	___	___	___	___	___
D. Lung cancer?	___	___	___	___	___	___
E. Other chest conditions	___	___	___	___	___	___
F. Is parent currently alive?	___	___	___	___	___	___
G. Please Specify	___ Age if Living ___ Age at Death ___ Don't Know			___ Age if Living ___ Age at Death ___ Don't Know		

APPENDIX 4D

§ 1910.1001, App. D   29 CFR Ch. XVII (7-1-94 Edition)

H. Please specify cause of death _____   _____

COUGH

32A. Do you usually have a cough? (Count   1. Yes ___   2. No ___
     a cough with first smoke or on first
     going out of doors. Exclude clearing
     of throat.) [If no, skip to question
     32C.]

  B. Do you usually cough as much as 4 to   1. Yes ___   2. No ___
     6 times a day 4 or more days out of
     the week?

  C. Do you usually cough at all on getting 1. Yes ___   2. No ___
     up or first thing in the morning?

  D. Do you usually cough at all during the 1. Yes ___   2. No ___
     rest of the day or at night?

IF YES TO ANY OF ABOVE (32A, B, C, or D), ANSWER THE FOLLOWING. IF NO
TO ALL, CHECK <u>DOES NOT APPLY</u> AND SKIP TO NEXT PAGE

  E. Do you usually cough like this on most 1. Yes ___   2. No ___
     days for 3 consecutive months or more   3. Does not apply ___
     during the year?

  F. For how many years have you had the cough?   Number of years ___
                                                  Does not apply ___

33A. Do you usually bring up phlegm from your   1. Yes ___   2. No ___
     chest?
     (Count phlegm with the first smoke or
     on first going out of doors. Exclude
     phlegm from the nose. Count swallowed
     phlegm.) (If no, skip to 33C)

  B. Do you usually bring up phlegm like this   1. Yes ___   2. No ___
     as much as twice a day 4 or more days
     out of the week?

  C. Do you usually bring up phlegm at all on   1. Yes ___   2. No ___
     getting up or first thing in the morning?

  D. Do you usually bring up phlegm at all   1. Yes ___   2. No ___
     during the rest of the day or at night?

IF YES TO ANY OF THE ABOVE (33A, B, C, or D), ANSWER THE FOLLOWING:
IF NO TO ALL, CHECK <u>DOES NOT APPLY</u> AND SKIP TO 34A.

  E. Do you bring up phlegm like this on most   1. Yes ___   2. No ___
     days for 3 consecutive months or more   3. Does not apply ___
     during the year?

Occupational Safety and Health Admin., Labor § 1910.1001, App. D

F. For how many years have you had trouble with phlegm?   Number of years __   Does not apply __

EPISODES OF COUGH AND PHLEGM

34A. Have you had periods or episodes of (increased*) cough and phlegm lasting for 3 weeks or more each year?   1. Yes __   2. No __
*(For persons who usually have cough and/or phlegm)

If YES TO 34A
B. For how long have you had at least 1 such episode per year?   Number of years __   Does not apply __

WHEEZING

35A. Does your chest ever sound wheezy or whistling
    1. When you have a cold?   1. Yes __   2. No __
    2. Occasionally apart from colds?   1. Yes __   2. No __
    3. Most days or nights?   1. Yes __   2. No __

IF YES TO 1, 2, or 3 in 35A
B. For how many years has this been present?   Number of years __   Does not apply __

36A. Have you ever had an attack of wheezing that has made you feel short of breath?   1. Yes __   2. No __

IF YES TO 36A
B. How old were you when you had your first such attack?   Age in years __   Does not apply __

C. Have you had 2 or more such episodes?   1. Yes __   2. No __   3. Does not apply __

D. Have you ever required medicine or treatment for the(se) attack(s)?   1. Yes __   2. No __   3. Does not apply __

BREATHLESSNESS

37. If disabled from walking by any condition other than heart or lung disease, please describe and proceed to question 39A.
Nature of condition(s)_____

38A. Are you troubled by shortness of breath when hurrying on the level or walking up a slight hill?   1. Yes __   2. No __

§ 1910.1001, App. D   29 CFR Ch. XVII (7-1-94 Edition)

IF YES TO 38A

B. Do you have to walk slower than people of your age on the level because of breathlessness?
   1. Yes ___   2. No ___
   3. Does not apply ___

C. Do you ever have to stop for breath when walking at your own pace on the level?
   1. Yes ___   2. No ___
   3. Does not apply ___

D. Do you ever have to stop for breath after walking about 100 yards (or after a few minutes) on the level?
   1. Yes ___   2. No ___
   3. Does not apply ___

E. Are you too breathless to leave the house or breathless on dressing or climbing one flight of stairs?
   1. Yes ___   2. No ___
   3. Does not apply ___

TOBACCO SMOKING

39A. Have you ever smoked cigarettes? (No means less than 20 packs of cigarettes or 12 oz. of tobacco in a lifetime or less than 1 cigarette a day for 1 year.)
   1. Yes ___   2. No ___

IF YES TO 39A

B. Do you now smoke cigarettes (as of one month ago)
   1. Yes ___   2. No ___
   3. Does not apply ___

C. How old were you when you first started regular cigarette smoking?
   Age in years ___
   Does not apply ___

D. If you have stopped smoking cigarettes completely, how old were you when you stopped?
   Age stopped ___
   Check if still smoking ___
   Does not apply ___

E. How many cigarettes do you smoke per day now?
   Cigarettes per day ___
   Does not apply ___

F. On the average of the entire time you smoked, how many cigarettes did you smoke per day?
   Cigarettes per day ___
   Does not apply ___

G. Do or did you inhale the cigarette smoke?
   1. Does not apply ___
   2. Not at all ___
   3. Slightly ___
   4. Moderately ___
   5. Deeply ___

40A. Have you ever smoked a pipe regularly? (Yes means more than 12 oz. of tobacco in a lifetime.)
   1. Yes ___   2. No ___

50

Occupational Safety and Health Admin., Labor §1910.1001, App. D

IF YES TO 40A:
FOR PERSONS WHO HAVE EVER SMOKED A PIPE

B. 1. How old were you when you started to smoke a pipe regularly?   Age ___

    2. If you have stopped smoking a pipe completely, how old were you when you stopped?
Age stopped ___
Check if still smoking pipe ___
Does not apply ___

C. On the average over the entire time you smoked a pipe, how much pipe tobacco did you smoke per week?
___ oz. per week (a standard pouch of tobacco contains 1 1/2 oz.)
___ Does not apply

D. How much pipe tobacco are you smoking now?
oz. per week ___
Not currently smoking a pipe ___

E. Do you or did you inhale the pipe smoke?
1. Never smoked ___
2. Not at all ___
3. Slightly ___
4. Moderately ___
5. Deeply ___

41A. Have you ever smoked cigars regularly? (Yes means more than 1 cigar a week for a year)   1. Yes ___   2. No ___

IF YES TO 41A
FOR PERSONS WHO HAVE EVER SMOKED CIGARS

B. 1. How old were you when you started smoking cigars regularly?   Age ___

    2. If you have stopped smoking cigars completely, how old were you when you stopped.
Age stopped ___
Check if still smoking cigars ___
Does not apply ___

C. On the average over the entire time you smoked cigars, how many cigars did you smoke per week?
Cigars per week ___
Does not apply ___

D. How many cigars are you smoking per week now?
Cigars per week ___
Check if not smoking cigars currently ___

E. Do or did you inhale the cigar smoke?
1. Never smoked ___
2. Not at all ___
3. Slightly ___
4. Moderately ___
5. Deeply ___

Signature _____   Date _____

APPENDIX 4D

§ 1910.1001, App. D   29 CFR Ch. XVII (7-1-94 Edition)

Part 2
PERIODIC MEDICAL QUESTIONNAIRE

1. NAME _____

2. SOCIAL SECURITY # __ __ __ __ __ __ __ __ __ __
                       1 2 3 4 5 6 7 8 9

3. CLOCK NUMBER   __ __ __ __ __ __ __
                                     10 11 12 13 14 15

4. PRESENT OCCUPATION _____

5. PLANT _____

6. ADDRESS _____

7. _____
                    (Zip Code)

8. TELEPHONE NUMBER _____

9. INTERVIEWER _____

10. DATE _____ __ __ __ __ __ __ __
                                         16 17 18 19 20 21

11. What is your marital status?   1. Single ___   4. Separated/
                                    2. Married ___   Divorced ___
                                    3. Widowed ___

12. OCCUPATIONAL HISTORY

12A. In the past year, did you work   1. Yes ___   2. No ___
     full time (30 hours per week
     or more) for 6 months or more?

     IF YES TO 12A:

12B. In the past year, did you work   1. Yes ___   2. No ___
     in a dusty job?   3. Does Not Apply ___

12C. Was dust exposure: 1. Mild ___   2. Moderate ___   3. Severe ___

12D. In the past year, were you   1. Yes ___   2. No ___
     exposed to gas or chemical
     fumes in your work?

12E. Was exposure: 1. Mild ___   2. Moderate ___   3. Severe ___

12F. In the past year,
     what was your: 1. Job/occupation? _____
                           2. Position/job title? _____

52

Occupational Safety and Health Admin., Labor § 1910.1001, App. D

13. **RECENT MEDICAL HISTORY**

   13A. Do you consider yourself to
   be in good health?   Yes ___   No ___

   If NO, state reason _____

   13B. In the past year, have you
   developed: Yes   No
                        Epilepsy?   ___   ___
                        Rheumatic fever?   ___   ___
                        Kidney disease?   ___   ___
                        Bladder disease?   ___   ___
                        Diabetes?   ___   ___
                        Jaundice?   ___   ___
                        Cancer?   ___   ___

14. **CHEST COLDS AND CHEST ILLNESSES**

   14A. If you get a cold, does it <u>usually</u> go to your chest?
   (Usually means more than 1/2 the time)
                                          1. Yes ___   2. No ___
                                          3. Don't get colds ___

   15A. During the past year, have you had
   any chest illnesses that have kept you   1. Yes ___   2. No ___
   off work, indoors at home, or in bed?   3. Does Not Apply ___

   IF YES TO 15A:

   15B. Did you produce phlegm with any   1. Yes ___   2. No ___
   of these chest illnesses?   3. Does Not Apply ___

   15C. In the past year, how many such   Number of illnesses ___
   illnesses with (increased) phlegm   No such illnesses ___
   did you have which lasted a week
   or more?

16. **RESPIRATORY SYSTEM**

   In the past year have you had:

                         Yes or No   <u>Further Comment on Positive</u>
                                               <u>Answers</u>
   Asthma   _____

   Bronchitis   _____

   Hay Fever   _____

   Other Allergies   _____

53

APPENDIX 4D

§ 1910.1001, App. D **29 CFR Ch. XVII (7-1-94 Edition)**

	Yes or No	Further Comment on Positive Answers
Pneumonia	_____	
Tuberculosis	_____	
Chest Surgery	_____	
Other Lung Problems	_____	
Heart Disease	_____	

Do you have:

	Yes or No	Further Comment on Positive Answers
Frequent colds	_____	
Chronic cough	_____	
Shortness of breath when walking or climbing one flight or stairs	_____	

Do you:

	Yes or No	
Wheeze	_____	
Cough up phlegm	_____	
Smoke cigarettes	_____	Packs per day ___ How many years ___

Date _____   Signature _____

Occupational Safety and Health Admin., Labor § 1910.1001, App. F

APPENDIX E TO § 1910.1001—INTERPRETATION AND CLASSIFICATION OF CHEST ROENTGENOGRAMS—MANDATORY

(a) Chest roentgenograms shall be interpreted and classified in accordance with a professionally accepted Classification system and recorded on an interpretation form following the format of the CDC/NIOSH (M) 2.8 form. As a minimum, the content within the bold lines of this form (items 1 though 4) shall be included. This form is not to be submitted to NIOSH.

(b) Roentgenograms shall be interpreted and classified only by a B-reader, a board eligible/certified radiologist, or an experienced physician with known expertise in pneumoconioses.

(c) All interpreters, whenever interpreting chest roentgenograms made under this section, shall have immediately available for reference a complete set of the ILO–U/C International Classification of Radiographs for Pneumoconioses, 1980.

APPENDIX F TO § 1910.1001—WORK PRACTICES AND ENGINEERING CONTROLS FOR AUTOMOTIVE BRAKE REPAIR OPERATIONS—NON-MANDATORY

This appendix is intended as guidance for employers in the automotive brake and clutch repair industry who wish to reduce their employees' asbestos exposures during repair operations to levels below the new standard's action level (0.1 f/cc). OSHA believes that employers in this industry sector are likely to be able to reduce their employees' exposures to asbestos by employing the engineering and work practice controls described in Sections A and B of this appendix. Those employers who choose to use these controls and who achieve exposures below the action level will thus be able to avoid any burden that might be imposed by complying with such requirements as medical surveillance, recordkeeping, training, respiratory protection, and regulated areas, which are triggered when employee exposures exceed the action level or PEL.

Asbestos exposure in the automotive brake and clutch repair industry occurs primarily during the replacement of clutch plates and brake pads, shoes, and linings. Asbestos fibers may become airborne when an automotive mechanic removes the asbestos-containing residue that has been deposited as brakes and clutches wear. Employee exposures to asbestos occur during the cleaning of the brake drum or clutch housing.

Based on evidence in the rulemaking record (Exs. 84–74, 84–263, 90–148), OSHA believes that employers engaged in brake repair operations who implement any of the work practices and engineering controls described in Sections A and B of this appendix may be able to reduce their employees' exposures to levels below the action level (0.1 fiber/cc). These control methods and the relevant record evidence on these and other methods are described in the following sections.

A. Enclosed Cylinder/HEPA Vacuum System Method

The enclosed cylinder-vacuum system used in one of the facilities visited by representatives of the National Institute for Occupational Safety and Health (NIOSH) during a health hazard evaluation of brake repair facilities (Ex. 84–263) consists of three components:

(1) A wheel-shaped cylinder designed to cover and enclose the wheel assembly;

(2) A compressed-air hose and nozzle that fits into a port in the cylinder; and

(3) A HEPA-filtered vacuum used to evacuate airborne dust generated within the cylinder by the compressed air.

To operate the system, the brake assembly is enclosed in a cylinder that has viewing ports to provide visibility and cotton sleeves through which the mechanic can handle the brake assembly parts. The cylinder effectively isolates asbestos dust in the drum from the mechanic's breathing zone. One company manufactures the brake assembly isolation cylinder in two sizes to fit brake drums in the 7-to-12-inch size range common to automobiles and light trucks and the 12-to-19-inch size range common to large commercial vehicles. The cylinder is equipped with built-in compressed-air guns and a connection for a vacuum cleaner equipped with a High Efficiency Particulate Air (HEPA) filter. This type of filter is capable of removing all particles greater than 0.3 microns from the air. When the vacuum cleaner's filter is full, it must be replaced according to the manufacturer's instruction, and appropriate HEPA-filtered dual cartridge respirators should be worn during the process. The filter of the vacuum cleaner is assumed to be contaminated with asbestos fibers and should be handled carefully, wetted with a fine mist of water, placed immediately in a labelled plastic bag, and disposed of properly. When the cylinder is in place around the brake assembly and the HEPA vacuum is connected, compressed air is blown into the cylinder to loosen the residue from the brake assembly parts. The vacuum then evacuates the loosened material from within the cylinder, capturing the airborne material on the HEPA filter.

The HEPA vacuum system can be disconnected from the brake assembly isolation cylinder when the cylinder is not being used. The HEPA vacuum can then be used for clutch facing work, grinding, or other routine cleaning.

§ 1910.1001, App. F

B. Compressed Air/Solvent System Method

A compressed-air hose fitted at the end with a bottle of solvent can be used to loosen the asbestos-containing residue and to capture the resulting airborne particles in the solvent mist. The mechanic should begin spraying the asbestos-contaminated parts with the solvent at a sufficient distance to ensure that the asbestos particles are not dislodged by the velocity of the solvent spray. After the asbestos particles are thoroughly wetted, the spray may be brought closer to the parts and the parts may be sprayed as necessary to remove grease and other material. The automotive parts sprayed with the mist are then wiped with a rag, which must then be disposed of appropriately. Rags should be placed in a labelled plastic bag or other container while they are still wet. This ensures that the asbestos fibers will not become airborne after the brake and clutch parts have been cleaned. (If cleanup rags are laundered rather than disposed of, they must be washed using methods appropriate for the laundering of asbestos-contaminated materials.)

OSHA believes that a variant of this compressed-air/solvent mist process offers advantages over the compressed-air/solvent mist technique discussed above, both in terms of costs and employee protection. The variant involves the use of spray cans filled with any of several solvent cleaners commercially available from auto supply stores. Spray cans of solvent are inexpensive, readily available, and easy to use. These cans will also save time, because no solvent delivery system has to be asembled, i.e., no compressed-air hose/mister ensemble. OSHA believes that a spray can will deliver solvent to the parts to be cleaned with considerably less force than the alternative compressed-air delivery system described above, and will thus generate fewer airborne asbestos fibers than the compressed-air method. The Agency therefore believes that the exposure levels of automotive repair mechanics using the spray can/solvent mist process will be even lower than the exposures reported by NIOSH (Ex. 84-263) for the compressed-air/solvent mist system (0.08 f/cc).

C. Information on the Effectiveness of Various Control Measures

The amount of airborne asbestos generated during brake and clutch repair operations depends on the work practices and engineering controls used during the repair or removal activity. Data in the rulemaking record document the 8-hour time-weighted average (TWA$_8$) asbestos exposure levels associated with various methods of brake and clutch repair and removal.

NIOSH submitted a report to the record entitled "Health Hazard Evaluation for Automotive Brake Repair" (Ex. 84-263). In addition, Exhibits 84-74 and 90-148 provided exposure data for comparing the airborne concentrations of asbestos generated by the use of various work practices during brake repair operations. These reports present exposure data for brake repair operations involving a variety of controls and work practices, including:

• Use of compressed air to blow out the brake drums;
• Use of a brush, without a wetting agent, to remove the asbestos-containing residue;
• Use of a brush dipped in water or a solvent to remove the asbestos-containing residue;
• Use of an enclosed vacuum cleaning system to capture the asbestos-containing residue; and
• Use of a solvent mixture applied with compressed air to remove the residue.

Prohibited Methods

The use of compressed air to blow the asbestos-containing residue off the surface of the brake drum removes the residue effectively but simultaneously produces an airborne cloud of asbestos fibers. According to NIOSH (Ex. 84-263), the peak exposures of mechanics using this technique were as high as 15 fibers/cc, and 8-hour TWA exposures ranged from 0.03 to 0.19 f/cc.

Dr. William J. Nicholson of the Mount Sinai School of Medicine (Ex. 84-74) cited data from Knight and Hickish (1970) that indicated that the concentration of asbestos ranged from 0.84 to 5.35 f/cc over a 60-minute sampling period when compressed air was being used to blow out the asbestos-containing residue from the brake drum. In the same study, a peak concentration of 87 f/cc was measured for a few seconds during brake cleaning performed with compressed air. Rohl et al. (1976) (Ex. 90-148) measured area concentrations (of unspecified duration) within 3-5 feet of operations involving the cleaning of brakes with compressed air and obtained readings ranging from 6.6 to 29.8 f/cc. Because of the high exposure levels that result from cleaning brake and clutch parts using compressed air, OSHA has prohibited this practice in the revised standard.

Ineffective Methods

When dry brushing was used to remove the asbestos-containing residue from the brake drums and wheel assemblies, peak exposures measured by NIOSH ranged from 0.61 to 0.81 f/cc, while 8-hour TWA levels were at the new standard's permissible exposure limit (PEL) of 0.2 f/cc (Ex. 84-263). Rohl and his colleagues (Ex. 90-148) collected area samples 1-3 feet from a brake cleaning operation being performed with a dry brush, and measured concentrations ranging from 1.3 to 3.6 f/cc; however, sampling times and TWA concentrations were not presented in the Rohl et al. study.

When a brush wetted with water, gasoline, or Stoddart solvent was used to clean the asbestos-containing residue from the affected parts, exposure levels (8-hour TWAs) measured by NIOSH also exceeded the new 0.2 f/cc PEL, and peak exposures ranged as high as 2.62 f/cc (Ex. 84-263).

Preferred Methods

Use of an engineering control system involving a cylinder that completely encloses the brake shoe assembly and a High Efficiency Particulate Air (HEPA) filter-equipped vacuum produced 8-hour TWA employee exposures of 0.01 f/cc and peak exposures ranging from nondetectable to 0.07 f/cc (Ex. 84-263). (Because this system achieved exposure levels below the standard's action level, it is described in detail above.) Data collected by the Mount Sinai Medical Center (Ex. 90-148) for Nilfisk of America, Inc., the manufacturer of the brake assembly enclosure system, showed that for two of three operations sampled, the exposure of mechanics to airborne asbestos fibers was nondetectable. For the third operator sampled by Mt. Sinai researchers, the exposure was 0.5 f/cc, which the authors attributed to asbestos that had contaminated the operator's clothing in the course of previous brake repair operations performed without the enclosed cylinder/vacuum system.

Some automotive repair facilities use a compressed-air hose to apply a solvent mist to remove the asbestos-containing residue from the brake drums before repair. The NIOSH data (Ex. 84-263) indicated that mechanics employing this method experienced exposures (8-hour TWAs) of 0.8 f/cc, with peaks of 0.25 to 0.68 f/cc. This technique, and a variant of it that OSHA believes is both less costly and more effective in reducing employee exposures, is described in greater detail above in Sections A and B.

D. Summary

In conclusion, OSHA believes that it is likely that employers in the brake and clutch repair industry will be able to avail themselves of the action level trigger built into the revised standard if they conscientiously employ one of the three control methods described above: the enclosed cylinder/HEPA vacuum system, the compressed air/solvent method, or the spray can/solvent mist system.

APPENDIX G TO §1910.1001—SUBSTANCE TECHNICAL INFORMATION FOR ASBESTOS—NON-MANDATORY

I. Substance Identification

A. Substance: "Asbestos" is the name of a class of magnesium-silicate minerals that occur in fibrous form. Minerals that are included in this group are chrysotile, crocidolite, amosite, tremolite asbestos, anthophyllite asbestos, and actinolite asbestos.

B. Asbestos is used in the manufacture of heat-resistant clothing, automative brake and clutch linings, and a variety of building materials including floor tiles, roofing felts, ceiling tiles, asbestos-cement pipe and sheet, and fire-resistant drywall. Asbestos is also present in pipe and boiler insulation materials, and in sprayed-on materials located on beams, in crawlspaces, and between walls.

C. The potential for a product containing asbestos to release breatheable fibers depends on its degree of friability. Friable means that the material can be crumbled with hand pressure and is therefore likely to emit fibers. The fibrous or fluffy sprayed-on materials used for fireproofing, insulation, or sound proofing are considered to be friable, and they readily release airborne fibers if disturbed. Materials such as vinyl-asbestos floor tile or roofing felts are considered nonfriable and generally do not emit airborne fibers unless subjected to sanding or sawing operations. Asbestos-cement pipe or sheet can emit airborne fibers if the materials are cut or sawed, or if they are broken during demolition operations.

D. Permissible exposure: Exposure to airborne asbestos fibers may not exceed 0.2 fibers per cubic centimeter of air (0.2 f/cc) averaged over the 8-hour workday.

II. Health Hazard Data

A. Asbestos can cause disabling respiratory disease and various types of cancers if the fibers are inhaled. Inhaling or ingesting fibers from contaminated clothing or skin can also result in these diseases. The symptoms of these diseases generally do not appear for 20 or more years after initial exposure.

B. Exposure to asbestos has been shown to cause lung cancer, mesothelioma, and cancer of the stomach and colon. Mesothelioma is a rare cancer of the thin membrane lining of the chest and abdomen. Symptoms of mesothelioma include shortness of breath, pain in the walls of the chest, and/or abdominal pain.

III. Respirators and Protective Clothing

A. Respirators: You are required to wear a respirator when performing tasks that result in asbestos exposure that exceeds the permissible exposure limit (PEL) of 0.2 f/cc. These conditions can occur while your employer is in the process of installing engineering controls to reduce asbestos exposure, or where engineering controls are not feasible to reduce asbestos exposure. Air-purifying respirators equipped with a high-efficiency particulate air (HEPA) filter can be used where airborne asbestos fiber con-

§ 1910.1001, App. H

centrations do not exceed 2 f/cc; otherwise, air-supplied, positive-pressure, full facepiece respirators must be used. Disposable respirators or dust masks are not permitted to be used for asbestos work. For effective protection, respirators must fit your face and head snugly. Your employer is required to conduct fit tests when you are first assigned a respirator and every 6 months thereafter. Respirators should not be loosened or removed in work situations where their use is required.

B. Protective Clothing: You are required to wear protective clothing in work areas where asbestos fiber concentrations exceed the permissible exposure limit (PEL) of 0.2 f/cc to prevent contamination of the skin. Where protective clothing is required, your employer must provide you with clean garments. Unless you are working on a large asbestos removal or demolition project, your employer must also provide a change room and separate lockers for your street clothes and contaminated work clothes. If you are working on a large asbestos removal or demolition project, and where it is feasible to do so, your employer must provide a clean room, shower, and decontamination room contiguous to the work area. When leaving the work area, you must remove contaminated clothing before proceeding to the shower. If the shower is not adjacent to the work area, you must vacuum your clothing before proceeding to the change room and shower. To prevent inhaling fibers in contaminated change rooms and showers, leave your respirator on until you leave the shower and enter the clean change room.

IV. Disposal Procedures and Cleanup

A. Wastes that are generated by processes where asbestos is present include:
1. Empty asbestos shipping containers.
2. Process wastes such as cuttings, trimmings, or reject material.
3. Housekeeping waste from sweeping or vacuuming.
4. Asbestos fireproofing or insulating material that is removed from buildings.
5. Building products that contain asbestos removed during building renovation or demolition.
6. Contaminated disposable protective clothing.

B. Empty shipping bags can be flattened under exhaust hoods and packed into air-tight containers for disposal. Empty shipping drums are difficult to clean and should be sealed.

C. Vacuum bags or disposable paper filters should not be cleaned, but should be sprayed with a fine water mist and placed into a labeled waste container.

D. Process waste and housekeeping waste should be wetted with water or a mixture of water and surfactant prior to packaging in disposable containers.

29 CFR Ch. XVII (7-1-94 Edition)

E. Material containing asbestos that is removed from buildings must be disposed of in leak-tight 6-mil thick plastic bags, plastic-lined cardboard containers, or plastic-lined metal containers. These wastes, which are removed while wet, should be sealed in containers before they dry out to minimize the release of asbestos fibers during handling.

V. Access to Information

A. Each year, your employer is required to inform you of the information contained in this standard and appendices for asbestos. In addition, your employer must instruct you in the proper work practices for handling materials containing asbestos, and the correct use of protective equipment.

B. Your employer is required to determine whether you are being exposed to asbestos. You or your representative has the right to observe employee measurements and to record the results obtained. Your employer is required to inform you of your exposure, and, if you are exposed above the permissible limit, he or she is required to inform you of the actions that are being taken to reduce your exposure to within the permissible limit.

C. Your employer is required to keep records of your exposures and medical examinations. These exposure records must be kept for at least thirty (30) years. Medical records must be kept for the period of your employment plus thirty (30) years.

D. Your employer is required to release your exposure and medical records to your physician or designated representative upon your written request.

APPENDIX H TO § 1910.1001—MEDICAL SURVEILLANCE GUIDELINES FOR ASBESTOS NON-MANDATORY

I. Route of Entry Inhalation, Ingestion

II. Toxicology

Clinical evidence of the adverse effects associated with exposure to asbestos is present in the form of several well-conducted epidemiological studies of occupationally exposed workers, family contacts of workers, and persons living near asbestos mines. These studies have shown a definite association between exposure to asbestos and an increased incidence of lung cancer, pleural and peritoneal mesothelioma, gastrointestinal cancer, and asbestosis. The latter is a disabling fibrotic lung disease that is caused only by exposure to asbestos. Exposure to asbestos has also been associated with an increased incidence of esophageal, kidney, laryngeal, pharyngeal, and buccal cavity cancers. As with other known chronic occupational diseases, disease associated with asbestos generally appears about 20 years following the first occurrence of exposure: There are no known acute effects associated with exposure to asbestos.

Epidemiological studies indicate that the risk of lung cancer among exposed workers who smoke cigarettes is greatly increased over the risk of lung cancer among non-exposed smokers or exposed nonsmokers. These studies suggest that cessation of smoking will reduce the risk of lung cancer for a person exposed to asbestos but will not reduce it to the same level of risk as that existing for an exposed worker who has never smoked.

III. Signs and Symptoms of Exposure-Related Disease

The signs and symptoms of lung cancer or gastrointestinal cancer induced by exposure to asbestos are not unique, except that a chest X-ray of an exposed patient with lung cancer may show pleural plaques, pleural calcification, or pleural fibrosis. Symptoms characteristic of mesothelioma include shortness of breath, pain in the walls of the chest, or abdominal pain. Mesothelioma has a much longer latency period compared with lung cancer (40 years versus 15–20 years), and mesothelioma is therefore more likely to be found among workers who were first exposed to asbestos at an early age. Mesothelioma is always fatal.

Asbestosis is pulmonary fibrosis caused by the accumulation of asbestos fibers in the lungs. Symptoms include shortness of breath, coughing, fatigue, and vague feelings of sickness. When the fibrosis worsens, shortness of breath occurs even at rest. The diagnosis of asbestosis is based on a history of exposure to asbestos, the presence of characteristic radiologic changes, end-inspiratory crackles (rales), and other clinical features of fibrosing lung disease. Pleural plaques and thickening are observed on X-rays taken during the early stages of the disease. Asbestosis is often a progressive disease even in the absence of continued exposure, although this appears to be a highly individualized characteristic. In severe cases, death may be caused by respiratory or cardiac failure.

IV. Surveillance and Preventive Considerations

As noted above, exposure to asbestos has been linked to an increased risk of lung cancer, mesothelioma, gastrointestinal cancer, and asbestosis among occupationally exposed workers. Adequate screening tests to determine an employee's potential for developing serious chronic diseases, such as cancer, from exposure to asbestos do not presently exist. However, some tests, particularly chest X-rays and pulmonary function tests, may indicate that an employee has been overexposed to asbestos increasing his or her risk of developing exposure-related chronic diseases. It is important for the physician to become familiar with the operating conditions in which occupational exposure to asbestos is likely to occur. This is particularly important in evaluating medical and work histories and in conducting physical examinations. When an active employee has been identified as having been overexposed to asbestos, measures taken by the employer to eliminate or mitigate further exposure should also lower the risk of serious long-term consequences.

The employer is required to institute a medical surveillance program for all employees who are or will be exposed to asbestos at or above the action level (0.1 fiber per cubic centimeter of air). All examinations and procedures must be performed by or under the supervision of a licensed physician, at a reasonable time and place, and at no cost to the employee.

Although broad latitude is given to the physician in prescribing specific tests to be included in the medical surveillance program, OSHA requires inclusion of the following elements in the routine examination:

(i) Medical and work histories with special emphasis directed to symptoms of the respiratory system, cardiovascular system, and digestive tract.

(ii) Completion of the respiratory disease questionnaire contained in Appendix D.

(iii) A physical examination including a chest roentgenogram and pulmonary function test that includes measurement of the employee's forced vital capacity (FVC) and forced expiratory volume at one second (FEV_1).

(iv) Any laboratory or other test that the examining physician deems by sound medical practice to be necessary.

The employer is required to make the prescribed tests available at least annually to those employees covered; more often than specified if recommended by the examining physician; and upon termination of employment.

The employer is required to provide the physician with the following information: A copy of this standard and appendices; a description of the mployee's duties as they relate to asbestos exposure; the employee's representative level of exposure to asbestos; a description of any personal protective and respiratory equipment used; and information from previous medical examinations of the affected employee that is not otherwise available to the physician. Making this information available to the physician will aid in the evaluation of the employee's health in relation to assigned duties and fitness to wear personal protective equipment, if required.

The employer is required to obtain a written opinion from the examining physician containing the results of the medical examination; the physician's opinion as to whether the employee has any detected medical

§ 1910.1001, App. I

conditions that would place the employee at an increased risk of exposure-related disease; any recommended limitations on the employee or on the use of personal protective equipment; and a statement that the employee has been informed by the physician of the results of the medical examination and of any medical conditions related to asbestos exposure that require further explanation or treatment. This written opinion must not reveal specific findings or diagnoses unrelated to exposure to asbestos, and a copy of the opinion must be provided to the affected employee.

APPENDIX I TO § 1910.1001—SMOKING CESSATION PROGRAM INFORMATION FOR ASBESTOS—NON-MANDATORY

The following organizations provide smoking cessation information and program material.

1. The National Cancer Institute operates a toll-free Cancer Information Service (CIS) with trained personnel to help you. Call 1-800-4-CANCER* to reach the CIS office serving your area, or write: Office of Cancer Communications, National Cancer Institute, National Institutes of Health, Building 31, Room 10A24, Bethesda, Maryland 20892.

2. American Cancer Society, 3340 Peachtree Road, NE., Atlanta, Georgia 30062, (404) 320-3333.

The American Cancer Society (ACS) is a voluntary organization composed of 58 divisions and 3,100 local units. Through "The Great American Smokeout" in November, the annual Cancer Crusade in April, and numerous educational materials, ACS helps people learn about the health hazards of smoking and become successful ex-smokers.

3. American Heart Association, 7320 Greenville Avenue, Dallas, Texas 75231, (214) 750-5300.

The American Heart Association (AHA) is a voluntary organization with 130,000 members (physicians, scientists, and laypersons) in 55 state and regional groups. AHA produces a variety of publications and audiovisual materials about the effects of smoking on the heart. AHA also has developed a guidebook for incorporating a weight-control component into smoking cessation programs.

4. American Lung Association, 1740 Broadway, New York, New York 10019, (212) 245-8000.

A voluntary organization of 7,500 members (physicians, nurses, and laypersons), the American Lung Association (ALA) conducts numerous public information programs about the health effect of smoking. ALA has 59 state and 85 local units. The organization actively supports legislation and information campaigns for non-smokers' rights and provides help for smokers who want to quit, for example, through "Freedom From Smoking," a self-help smoking cessation program.

29 CFR Ch. XVII (7-1-94 Edition)

5. Office on Smoking and Health, U.S. Department of Health and, Human Services, 5600 Fishers Lane, Park Building, Room 110, Rockville, Maryland 20857.

The Office on Smoking and Health (OSH) is the Department of Health and Human Services' lead agency in smoking control. OSH has sponsored distribution of publications on smoking-realted topics, such as free flyers on relapse after initial quitting, helping a friend or family member quit smoking, the health hazards of smoking, and the effects of parental smoking on teenagers.

*In Hawaii, on Oahu call 524-1234 (call collect from neighboring islands),

Spanish-speaking staff members are available during daytime hours to callers from the following areas: California, Florida, Georgia, Illinois, New Jersey (area code 210), New York, and Texas. Consult your local telephone directory for listings of local chapters.

(Reporting and recordkeeping requirements in paragraphs (d)(2), (3), (5), and (7), (f)(2) and (3)(i), (j)(5), (l), and (m) as they apply to the excursion limit have been approved by the Office of Management and Budget under control numbers 1218-0133 and 1218-0134. The OMB clearance expires on February 29, 1992.)

(Reporting and recordkeeping requirements in paragraph (j)(5)(iv)(C) have received OMB paperwork clearance under OMB clearance number 1218-0133. The OMB clearance expires on April 30, 1993.)

(Approved by the Office of Management and Budget under control number 1218-0133)

[51 FR 22733, June 20, 1986, as amended at 51 FR 37004, Oct. 17, 1986; 52 FR 17754, 17755, May 12, 1987; 53 FR 35625, September 14, 1988; 54 FR 24334, June 7, 1989; 54 FR 29546, July 13, 1989; 54 FR 52027, Dec. 20, 1989, 55 FR 3731, Feb. 5, 1990; 55 FR 34710, Aug. 24, 1990; 57 FR 24330, June 8, 1992]

§ 1910.1002 Coal tar pitch volatiles; interpretation of term.

As used in § 1910.1000 (Table Z-1), coal tar pitch volatiles include the fused polycyclic hydrocarbons which volatilize from the distillation residues of coal, petroleum (excluding asphalt), wood, and other organic matter. Asphalt (CAS 8052-42-4, and CAS 64742-93-4) is not covered under the "coal tar pitch volatiles" standard.

[48 FR 2768, Jan. 21, 1983]

§ 1910.1003 4-Nitrobiphenyl.

(a) *Scope and application.* (1) This section applies to any area in which 4-Nitrobiphenyl, Chemical Abstracts Service Registry Number 92933 is man-

Appendix 4E

29 CFR 1910.1030 BLOODBORNE PATHOGENS

§ 1910.1030 Bloodborne pathogens.

(a) *Scope and Application.* This section applies to all occupational exposure to blood or other potentially infectious materials as defined by paragraph (b) of this section.

(b) *Definitions.* For purposes of this section, the following shall apply:

Assistant Secretary means the Assistant Secretary of Labor for Occupational Safety and Health, or designated representative.

Blood means human blood, human blood components, and products made from human blood.

Bloodborne Pathogens means pathogenic microorganisms that are present in human blood and can cause disease in humans. These pathogens include, but are not limited to, hepatitis B virus (HBV) and human immunodeficiency virus (HIV).

Clinical Laboratory means a workplace where diagnostic or other screening procedures are performed on blood or other potentially infectious materials.

Contaminated means the presence or the reasonably anticipated presence of blood or other potentially infectious materials on an item or surface.

Contaminated Laundry means laundry which has been soiled with blood or other potentially infectious materials or may contain sharps.

Contaminated Sharps means any contaminated object that can penetrate the skin including, but not limited to, needles, scalpels, broken glass, broken capillary tubes, and exposed ends of dental wires.

Decontamination means the use of physical or chemical means to remove, inactivate, or destroy bloodborne pathogens on a surface or item to the point where they are no longer capable of transmitting infectious particles and the surface or item is rendered safe for handling, use, or disposal.

Director means the Director of the National Institute for Occupational Safety and Health, U.S. Department of Health and Human Services, or designated representative.

Engineering Controls means controls (e.g., sharps disposal containers, self-sheathing needles) that isolate or remove the bloodborne pathogens hazard from the workplace.

Exposure Incident means a specific eye, mouth, other mucous membrane, non-intact skin, or parenteral contact with blood or other potentially infectious materials that results from the performance of an employee's duties.

Handwashing Facilities means a facility providing an adequate supply of running potable water, soap and single use towels or hot air drying machines.

Licensed Healthcare Professional is a person whose legally permitted scope of practice allows him or her to independently perform the activities required by paragraph (f) Hepatitis B Vaccination and Post-exposure Evaluation and Follow-up.

HBV means hepatitis B virus.

HIV means human immunodeficiency virus.

Occupational Exposure means reasonably anticipated skin, eye, mucous membrane, or parenteral contact with blood or other potentially infectious materials that may result from the performance of an employee's duties.

Other Potentially Infectious Materials means

(1) The following human body fluids: semen, vaginal secretions, cerebrospinal fluid, synovial fluid, pleural fluid, pericardial fluid, peritoneal fluid, amniotic fluid, saliva in dental procedures, any body fluid that is visibly contaminated with blood, and all body fluids in situations where it is difficult or impossible to differentiate between body fluids;

(2) Any unfixed tissue or organ (other than intact skin) from a human (living or dead); and

(3) HIV-containing cell or tissue cultures, organ cultures, and HIV- or HBV-containing culture medium or other solutions; and blood, organs, or other tissues from experimental animals infected with HIV or HBV.

Parenteral means piercing mucous membranes or the skin barrier through such events as needlesticks, human bites, cuts, and abrasions.

Personal Protective Equipment is specialized clothing or equipment worn by an employee for protection against a hazard. General work clothes (e.g., uniforms, pants, shirts or blouses) not intended to function as protection against a hazard are not considered to be personal protective equipment.

Production Facility means a facility engaged in industrial-scale, large-volume or high concentration production of HIV or HBV.

Regulated Waste means liquid or semi-liquid blood or other potentially infectious materials; contaminated items that would release blood or other potentially infectious materials in a liquid or semi-liquid state if compressed; items that are caked with dried blood or other potentially infectious materials and are capable of releasing these materials during handling; contaminated sharps; and pathological and microbiological wastes containing blood or other potentially infectious materials.

Research Laboratory means a laboratory producing or using research-lab-

APPENDIX 4E

§ 1910.1030

29 CFR Ch. XVII (7-1-94 Edition)

oratory-scale amounts of HIV or HBV. Research laboratories may produce high concentrations of HIV or HBV but not in the volume found in production facilities.

Source Individual means any individual, living or dead, whose blood or other potentially infectious materials may be a source of occupational exposure to the employee. Examples include, but are not limited to, hospital and clinic patients; clients in institutions for the developmentally disabled; trauma victims; clients of drug and alcohol treatment facilities; residents of hospices and nursing homes; human remains; and individuals who donate or sell blood or blood components.

Sterilize means the use of a physical or chemical procedure to destroy all microbial life including highly resistant bacterial endospores.

Universal Precautions is an approach to infection control. According to the concept of Universal Precautions, all human blood and certain human body fluids are treated as if known to be infectious for HIV, HBV, and other bloodborne pathogens.

Work Practice Controls means controls that reduce the likelihood of exposure by altering the manner in which a task is performed (e.g., prohibiting recapping of needles by a two-handed technique).

(c) *Exposure control*—(1) *Exposure Control Plan.* (i) Each employer having an employee(s) with occupational exposure as defined by paragraph (b) of this section shall establish a written Exposure Control Plan designed to eliminate or minimize employee exposure.

(ii) The Exposure Control Plan shall contain at least the following elements:

(A) The exposure determination required by paragraph(c)(2),

(B) The schedule and method of implementation for paragraphs (d) Methods of Compliance, (e) HIV and HBV Research Laboratories and Production Facilities, (f) Hepatitis B Vaccination and Post-Exposure Evaluation and Follow-up, (g) Communication of Hazards to Employees, and (h) Recordkeeping, of this standard, and

(C) The procedure for the evaluation of circumstances surrounding exposure incidents as required by paragraph (f)(3)(i) of this standard.

(iii) Each employer shall ensure that a copy of the Exposure Control Plan is accessible to employees in accordance with 29 CFR 1910.20(e).

(iv) The Exposure Control Plan shall be reviewed and updated at least annually and whenever necessary to reflect new or modified tasks and procedures which affect occupational exposure and to reflect new or revised employee positions with occupational exposure.

(v) The Exposure Control Plan shall be made available to the Assistant Secretary and the Director upon request for examination and copying.

(2) *Exposure determination.* (i) Each employer who has an employee(s) with occupational exposure as defined by paragraph (b) of this section shall prepare an exposure determination. This exposure determination shall contain the following:

(A) A list of all job classifications in which all employees in those job classifications have occupational exposure;

(B) A list of job classifications in which some employees have occupational exposure, and

(C) A list of all tasks and procedures or groups of closely related task and procedures in which occupational exposure occurs and that are performed by employees in job classifications listed in accordance with the provisions of paragraph (c)(2)(i)(B) of this standard.

(ii) This exposure determination shall be made without regard to the use of personal protective equipment.

(d) *Methods of compliance*—(1) *General*—Universal precautions shall be observed to prevent contact with blood or other potentially infectious materials. Under circumstances in which differentiation between body fluid types is difficult or impossible, all body fluids shall be considered potentially infectious materials.

(2) *Engineering and work practice controls.* (i) Engineering and work practice controls shall be used to eliminate or minimize employee exposure. Where occupational exposure remains after institution of these controls, personal protective equipment shall also be used.

(ii) Engineering controls shall be examined and maintained or replaced on

318

Occupational Safety and Health Admin., Labor § 1910.1030

a regular schedule to ensure their effectiveness.

(iii) Employers shall provide handwashing facilities which are readily accessible to employees.

(iv) When provision of handwashing facilities is not feasible, the employer shall provide either an appropriate antiseptic hand cleanser in conjunction with clean cloth/paper towels or antiseptic towelettes. When antiseptic hand cleansers or towelettes are used, hands shall be washed with soap and running water as soon as feasible.

(v) Employers shall ensure that employees wash their hands immediately or as soon as feasible after removal of gloves or other personal protective equipment.

(vi) Employers shall ensure that employees wash hands and any other skin with soap and water, or flush mucous membranes with water immediately or as soon as feasible following contact of such body areas with blood or other potentially infectious materials.

(vii) Contaminated needles and other contaminated sharps shall not be bent, recapped, or removed except as noted in paragraphs (d)(2)(vii)(A) and (d)(2)(vii)(B) below. Shearing or breaking of contaminated needles is prohibited.

(A) Contaminated needles and other contaminated sharps shall not be bent, recapped or removed unless the employer can demonstrate that no alternative is feasible or that such action is required by a specific medical or dental procedure.

(B) Such bending, recapping or needle removal must be accomplished through the use of a mechanical device or a one-handed technique.

(viii) Immediately or as soon as possible after use, contaminated reusable sharps shall be placed in appropriate containers until properly reprocessed. These containers shall be:

(A) Puncture resistant;

(B) Labeled or color-coded in accordance with this standard;

(C) Leakproof on the sides and bottom; and

(D) In accordance with the requirements set forth in paragraph (d)(4)(ii)(E) for reusable sharps.

(ix) Eating, drinking, smoking, applying cosmetics or lip balm, and handling contact lenses are prohibited in work areas where there is a reasonable likelihood of occupational exposure.

(x) Food and drink shall not be kept in refrigerators, freezers, shelves, cabinets or on countertops or benchtops where blood or other potentially infectious materials are present.

(xi) All procedures involving blood or other potentially infectious materials shall be performed in such a manner as to minimize splashing, spraying, spattering, and generation of droplets of these substances.

(xii) Mouth pipetting/suctioning of blood or other potentially infectious materials is prohibited.

(xiii) Specimens of blood or other potentially infectious materials shall be placed in a container which prevents leakage during collection, handling, processing, storage, transport, or shipping.

(A) The container for storage, transport, or shipping shall be labeled or color-coded according to paragraph (g)(1)(i) and closed prior to being stored, transported, or shipped. When a facility utilizes Universal Precautions in the handling of all specimens, the labeling/color-coding of specimens is not necessary provided containers are recognizable as containing specimens. This exemption only applies while such specimens/containers remain within the facility. Labeling or color-coding in accordance with paragraph (g)(1)(i) is required when such specimens/containers leave the facility.

(B) If outside contamination of the primary container occurs, the primary container shall be placed within a second container which prevents leakage during handling, processing, storage, transport, or shipping and is labeled or color-coded according to the requirements of this standard.

(C) If the specimen could puncture the primary container, the primary container shall be placed in a secondary container which is puncture-resistant in addition to the above characteristics.

(xiv) Equipment which may become contaminated with blood or other potentially infectious materials shall be examined prior to servicing or shipping and shall be decontaminated as necessary, unless the employer can dem-

§ 1910.1030

onstrate that decontamination of such equipment or portions of such equipment is not feasible.

(A) A readily observable label in accordance with paragraph (g)(1)(i)(H) shall be attached to the equipment stating which portions remain contaminated.

(B) The employer shall ensure that this information is conveyed to all affected employees, the servicing representative, and/or the manufacturer, as appropriate, prior to handling, servicing, or shipping so that appropriate precautions will be taken.

(3) *Personal protective equipment*—(i) Provision. When there is occupational exposure, the employer shall provide, at no cost to the employee, appropriate personal protective equipment such as, but not limited to, gloves, gowns, laboratory coats, face shields or masks and eye protection, and mouthpieces, resuscitation bags, pocket masks, or other ventilation devices. Personal protective equipment will be considered "appropriate" only if it does not permit blood or other potentially infectious materials to pass through to or reach the employee's work clothes, street clothes, undergarments, skin, eyes, mouth, or other mucous membranes under normal conditions of use and for the duration of time which the protective equipment will be used.

(ii) Use. The employer shall ensure that the employee uses appropriate personal protective equipment unless the employer shows that the employee temporarily and briefly declined to use personal protective equipment when, under rare and extraordinary circumstances, it was the employee's professional judgment that in the specific instance its use would have prevented the delivery of health care or public safety services or would have posed an increased hazard to the safety of the worker or co-worker. When the employee makes this judgement, the circumstances shall be investigated and documented in order to determine whether changes can be instituted to prevent such occurences in the future.

(iii) Accessibility. The employer shall ensure that appropriate personal protective equipment in the appropriate sizes is readily accessible at the worksite or is issued to employees. Hypoallergenic gloves, glove liners, powderless gloves, or other similar alternatives shall be readily accessible to those employees who are allergic to the gloves normally provided.

(iv) Cleaning, Laundering, and Disposal. The employer shall clean, launder, and dispose of personal protective equipment required by paragraphs (d) and (e) of this standard, at no cost to the employee.

(v) Repair and Replacement. The employer shall repair or replace personal protective equipment as needed to maintain its effectiveness, at no cost to the employee.

(vi) If a garment(s) is penetrated by blood or other potentially infectious materials, the garment(s) shall be removed immediately or as soon as feasible.

(vii) All personal protective equipment shall be removed prior to leaving the work area.

(viii) When personal protective equipment is removed it shall be placed in an appropriately designated area or container for storage, washing, decontamination or disposal.

(ix) Gloves. Gloves shall be worn when it can be reasonably anticipated that the employee may have hand contact with blood, other potentially infectious materials, mucous membranes, and non-intact skin; when performing vascular access procedures except as specified in paragraph (d)(3)(ix)(D); and when handling or touching contaminated items or surfaces.

(A) Disposable (single use) gloves such as surgical or examination gloves, shall be replaced as soon as practical when contaminated or as soon as feasible if they are torn, punctured, or when their ability to function as a barrier is compromised.

(B) Disposable (single use) gloves shall not be washed or decontaminated for re-use.

(C) Utility gloves may be decontaminated for re-use if the integrity of the glove is not compromised. However, they must be discarded if they are cracked, peeling, torn, punctured, or exhibit other signs of deterioration or when their ability to function as a barrier is compromised.

(D) If an employer in a volunteer blood donation center judges that routine gloving for all phlebotomies is not necessary then the employer shall:

(*1*) Periodically reevaluate this policy;

(*2*) Make gloves available to all employees who wish to use them for phlebotomy;

(*3*) Not discourage the use of gloves for phlebotomy; and

(*4*) Require that gloves be used for phlebotomy in the following circumstances:

(i) When the employee has cuts, scratches, or other breaks in his or her skin;

(ii) When the employee judges that hand contamination with blood may occur, for example, when performing phlebotomy on an uncooperative source individual; and

(iii) When the employee is receiving training in phlebotomy.

(x) Masks, Eye Protection, and Face Shields. Masks in combination with eye protection devices, such as goggles or glasses with solid side shields, or chin-length face shields, shall be worn whenever splashes, spray, spatter, or droplets of blood or other potentially infectious materials may be generated and eye, nose, or mouth contamination can be reasonably anticipated.

(xi) Gowns, Aprons, and Other Protective Body Clothing. Appropriate protective clothing such as, but not limited to, gowns, aprons, lab coats, clinic jackets, or similar outer garments shall be worn in occupational exposure situations. The type and characteristics will depend upon the task and degree of exposure anticipated.

(xii) Surgical caps or hoods and/or shoe covers or boots shall be worn in instances when gross contamination can reasonably be anticipated (e.g., autopsies, orthopaedic surgery).

(4) *Housekeeping.* (i) General. Employers shall ensure that the worksite is maintained in a clean and sanitary condition. The employer shall determine and implement an appropriate written schedule for cleaning and method of decontamination based upon the location within the facility, type of surface to be cleaned, type of soil present, and tasks or procedures being performed in the area.

(ii) All equipment and environmental and working surfaces shall be cleaned and decontaminated after contact with blood or other potentially infectious materials.

(A) Contaminated work surfaces shall be decontaminated with an appropriate disinfectant after completion of procedures; immediately or as soon as feasible when surfaces are overtly contaminated or after any spill of blood or other potentially infectious materials; and at the end of the work shift if the surface may have become contaminated since the last cleaning.

(B) Protective coverings, such as plastic wrap, aluminum foil, or imperviously-backed absorbent paper used to cover equipment and environmental surfaces, shall be removed and replaced as soon as feasible when they become overtly contaminated or at the end of the workshift if they may have become contaminated during the shift.

(C) All bins, pails, cans, and similar receptacles intended for reuse which have a reasonable likelihood for becoming contaminated with blood or other potentially infectious materials shall be inspected and decontaminated on a regularly scheduled basis and cleaned and decontaminated immediately or as soon as feasible upon visible contamination.

(D) Broken glassware which may be contaminated shall not be picked up directly with the hands. It shall be cleaned up using mechanical means, such as a brush and dust pan, tongs, or forceps.

(E) Reusable sharps that are contaminated with blood or other potentially infectious materials shall not be stored or processed in a manner that requires employees to reach by hand into the containers where these sharps have been placed.

(iii) Regulated Waste.

(A) Contaminated Sharps Discarding and Containment. (*1*) Contaminated sharps shall be discarded immediately or as soon as feasible in containers that are:

(i) Closable;

(ii) Puncture resistant;

(iii) Leakproof on sides and bottom; and

§ 1910.1030

(*iv*) Labeled or color-coded in accordance with paragraph (g)(1)(i) of this standard.

(2) During use, containers for contaminated sharps shall be:

(*i*) Easily accessible to personnel and located as close as is feasible to the immediate area where sharps are used or can be reasonably anticipated to be found (e.g., laundries);

(*ii*) Maintained upright throughout use; and

(*iii*) Replaced routinely and not be allowed to overfill.

(3) When moving containers of contaminated sharps from the area of use, the containers shall be:

(*i*) Closed immediately prior to removal or replacement to prevent spillage or protrusion of contents during handling, storage, transport, or shipping;

(*ii*) Placed in a secondary container if leakage is possible. The second container shall be:

(*A*) Closable;

(*B*) Constructed to contain all contents and prevent leakage during handling, storage, transport, or shipping; and

(*C*) Labeled or color-coded according to paragraph (g)(1)(i) of this standard.

(4) Reusable containers shall not be opened, emptied, or cleaned manually or in any other manner which would expose employees to the risk of percutaneous injury.

(B) Other Regulated Waste Containment. (*1*) Regulated waste shall be placed in containers which are:

(*i*) Closable;

(*ii*) Constructed to contain all contents and prevent leakage of fluids during handling, storage, transport or shipping;

(*iii*) Labeled or color-coded in accordance with paragraph (g)(1)(i) this standard; and

(*iv*) Closed prior to removal to prevent spillage or protrusion of contents during handling, storage, transport, or shipping.

(*2*) If outside contamination of the regulated waste container occurs, it shall be placed in a second container. The second container shall be:

(*i*) Closable;

(*ii*) Constructed to contain all contents and prevent leakage of fluids dur-

ing handling, storage, transport or shipping;

(*iii*) Labeled or color-coded in accordance with paragraph (g)(1)(i) of this standard; and

(*iv*) Closed prior to removal to prevent spillage or protrusion of contents during handling, storage, transport, or shipping.

(C) Disposal of all regulated waste shall be in accordance with applicable regulations of the United States, States and Territories, and political subdivisions of States and Territories.

(iv) Laundry.

(A) Contaminated laundry shall be handled as little as possible with a minimum of agitation. (1) Contaminated laundry shall be bagged or containerized at the location where it was used and shall not be sorted or rinsed in the location of use.

(2) Contaminated laundry shall be placed and transported in bags or containers labeled or color-coded in accordance with paragraph (g)(1)(i) of this standard. When a facility utilizes Universal Precautions in the handling of all soiled laundry, alternative labeling or color-coding is sufficient if it permits all employees to recognize the containers as requiring compliance with Universal Precautions.

(3) Whenever contaminated laundry is wet and presents a reasonable likelihood of soak-through of or leakage from the bag or container, the laundry shall be placed and transported in bags or containers which prevent soak-through and/or leakage of fluids to the exterior.

(B) The employer shall ensure that employees who have contact with contaminated laundry wear protective gloves and other appropriate personal protective equipment.

(C) When a facility ships contaminated laundry off-site to a second facility which does not utilize Universal Precautions in the handling of all laundry, the facility generating the contaminated laundry must place such laundry in bags or containers which are labeled or color-coded in accordance with paragraph (g)(1)(i).

(e) *HIV and HBV Research Laboratories and Production Facilities.* (1) This paragraph applies to research laboratories and production facilities engaged in the culture, production, concentration, experimentation, and manipulation of HIV and HBV. It does not apply to clinical or diagnostic laboratories engaged solely in the analysis of blood, tissues, or organs. These requirements apply in addition to the other requirements of the standard.

(2) Research laboratories and production facilities shall meet the following criteria:

(i) Standard microbiological practices. All regulated waste shall either be incinerated or decontaminated by a method such as autoclaving known to effectively destroy bloodborne pathogens.

(ii) Special practices.

(A) Laboratory doors shall be kept closed when work involving HIV or HBV is in progress.

(B) Contaminated materials that are to be decontaminated at a site away from the work area shall be placed in a durable, leakproof, labeled or color-coded container that is closed before being removed from the work area.

(C) Access to the work area shall be limited to authorized persons. Written policies and procedures shall be established whereby only persons who have been advised of the potential biohazard, who meet any specific entry requirements, and who comply with all entry and exit procedures shall be allowed to enter the work areas and animal rooms.

(D) When other potentially infectious materials or infected animals are present in the work area or containment module, a hazard warning sign incorporating the universal biohazard symbol shall be posted on all access doors. The hazard warning sign shall comply with paragraph (g)(1)(ii) of this standard.

(E) All activities involving other potentially infectious materials shall be conducted in biological safety cabinets or other physical-containment devices within the containment module. No work with these other potentially infectious materials shall be conducted on the open bench.

(F) Laboratory coats, gowns, smocks, uniforms, or other appropriate protective clothing shall be used in the work area and animal rooms. Protective clothing shall not be worn outside of the work area and shall be decontaminated before being laundered.

(G) Special care shall be taken to avoid skin contact with other potentially infectious materials. Gloves shall be worn when handling infected animals and when making hand contact with other potentially infectious materials is unavoidable.

(H) Before disposal all waste from work areas and from animal rooms shall either be incinerated or decontaminated by a method such as autoclaving known to effectively destroy bloodborne pathogens.

(I) Vacuum lines shall be protected with liquid disinfectant traps and high-efficiency particulate air (HEPA) filters or filters of equivalent or superior efficiency and which are checked routinely and maintained or replaced as necessary.

(J) Hypodermic needles and syringes shall be used only for parenteral injection and aspiration of fluids from laboratory animals and diaphragm bottles. Only needle-locking syringes or disposable syringe-needle units (i.e., the needle is integral to the syringe) shall be used for the injection or aspiration of other potentially infectious materials. Extreme caution shall be used when handling needles and syringes. A needle shall not be bent, sheared, replaced in the sheath or guard, or removed from the syringe following use. The needle and syringe shall be promptly placed in a puncture-resistant container and autoclaved or decontaminated before reuse or disposal.

(K) All spills shall be immediately contained and cleaned up by appropriate professional staff or others properly trained and equipped to work with potentially concentrated infectious materials.

(L) A spill or accident that results in an exposure incident shall be immediately reported to the laboratory director or other responsible person.

(M) A biosafety manual shall be prepared or adopted and periodically reviewed and updated at least annually or more often if necessary. Personnel shall be advised of potential hazards, shall be required to read instructions on practices and procedures, and shall be required to follow them.

§ 1910.1030

(iii) *Containment equipment.* (A) Certified biological safety cabinets (Class I, II, or III) or other appropriate combinations of personal protection or physical containment devices, such as special protective clothing, respirators, centrifuge safety cups, sealed centrifuge rotors, and containment caging for animals, shall be used for all activities with other potentially infectious materials that pose a threat of exposure to droplets, splashes, spills, or aerosols.

(B) Biological safety cabinets shall be certified when installed, whenever they are moved and at least annually.

(3) HIV and HBV research laboratories shall meet the following criteria:

(i) Each laboratory shall contain a facility for hand washing and an eye wash facility which is readily available within the work area.

(ii) An autoclave for decontamination of regulated waste shall be available.

(4) HIV and HBV production facilities shall meet the following criteria:

(i) The work areas shall be separated from areas that are open to unrestricted traffic flow within the building. Passage through two sets of doors shall be the basic requirement for entry into the work area from access corridors or other contiguous areas. Physical separation of the high-containment work area from access corridors or other areas or activities may also be provided by a double-doored clothes-change room (showers may be included), airlock, or other access facility that requires passing through two sets of doors before entering the work area.

(ii) The surfaces of doors, walls, floors and ceilings in the work area shall be water resistant so that they can be easily cleaned. Penetrations in these surfaces shall be sealed or capable of being sealed to facilitate decontamination.

(iii) Each work area shall contain a sink for washing hands and a readily available eye wash facility. The sink shall be foot, elbow, or automatically operated and shall be located near the exit door of the work area.

(iv) Access doors to the work area or containment module shall be self-closing.

(v) An autoclave for decontamination of regulated waste shall be available within or as near as possible to the work area.

(vi) A ducted exhaust-air ventilation system shall be provided. This system shall create directional airflow that draws air into the work area through the entry area. The exhaust air shall not be recirculated to any other area of the building, shall be discharged to the outside, and shall be dispersed away from occupied areas and air intakes. The proper direction of the airflow shall be verified (i.e., into the work area).

(5) *Training Requirements.* Additional training requirements for employees in HIV and HBV research laboratories and HIV and HBV production facilities are specified in paragraph (g)(2)(ix).

(f) *Hepatitis B vaccination and post-exposure evaluation and follow-up*—(1) *General.* (i) The employer shall make available the hepatitis B vaccine and vaccination series to all employees who have occupational exposure, and post-exposure evaluation and follow-up to all employees who have had an exposure incident.

(ii) The employer shall ensure that all medical evaluations and procedures including the hepatitis B vaccine and vaccination series and post-exposure evaluation and follow-up, including prophylaxis, are:

(A) Made available at no cost to the employee;

(B) Made available to the employee at a reasonable time and place;

(C) Performed by or under the supervision of a licensed physician or by or under the supervision of another licensed healthcare professional; and

(D) Provided according to recommendations of the U.S. Public Health Service current at the time these evaluations and procedures take place, except as specified by this paragraph (f).

(iii) The employer shall ensure that all laboratory tests are conducted by an accredited laboratory at no cost to the employee.

(2) *Hepatitis B Vaccination.* (i) Hepatitis B vaccination shall be made available after the employee has received the training required in paragraph (g)(2)(vii)(I) and within 10 working days

of initial assignment to all employees who have occupational exposure unless the employee has previously received the complete hepatitis B vaccination series, antibody testing has revealed that the employee is immune, or the vaccine is contraindicated for medical reasons.

(ii) The employer shall not make participation in a prescreening program a prerequisite for receiving hepatitis B vaccination.

(iii) If the employee initially declines hepatitis B vaccination but at a later date while still covered under the standard decides to accept the vaccination, the employer shall make available hepatitis B vaccination at that time.

(iv) The employer shall assure that employees who decline to accept hepatitis B vaccination offered by the employer sign the statement in appendix A.

(v) If a routine booster dose(s) of hepatitis B vaccine is recommended by the U.S. Public Health Service at a future date, such booster dose(s) shall be made available in accordance with section (f)(1)(ii).

(3) *Post-exposure Evaluation and Follow-up.* Following a report of an exposure incident, the employer shall make immediately available to the exposed employee a confidential medical evaluation and follow-up, including at least the following elements:

(i) Documentation of the route(s) of exposure, and the circumstances under which the exposure incident occurred;

(ii) Identification and documentation of the source individual, unless the employer can establish that identification is infeasible or prohibited by state or local law;

(A) The source individual's blood shall be tested as soon as feasible and after consent is obtained in order to determine HBV and HIV infectivity. If consent is not obtained, the employer shall establish that legally required consent cannot be obtained. When the source individual's consent is not required by law, the source individual's blood, if available, shall be tested and the results documented.

(B) When the source individual is already known to be infected with HBV or HIV, testing for the source individual's known HBV or HIV status need not be repeated.

(C) Results of the source individual's testing shall be made available to the exposed employee, and the employee shall be informed of applicable laws and regulations concerning disclosure of the identity and infectious status of the source individual.

(iii) Collection and testing of blood for HBV and HIV serological status;

(A) The exposed employee's blood shall be collected as soon as feasible and tested after consent is obtained.

(B) If the employee consents to baseline blood collection, but does not give consent at that time for HIV serologic testing, the sample shall be preserved for at least 90 days. If, within 90 days of the exposure incident, the employee elects to have the baseline sample tested, such testing shall be done as soon as feasible.

(iv) Post-exposure prophylaxis, when medically indicated, as recommended by the U.S. Public Health Service;

(v) Counseling; and

(vi) Evaluation of reported illnesses.

(4) *Information Provided to the Healthcare Professional.* (i) The employer shall ensure that the healthcare professional responsible for the employee's Hepatitis B vaccination is provided a copy of this regulation.

(ii) The employer shall ensure that the healthcare professional evaluating an employee after an exposure incident is provided the following information:

(A) A copy of this regulation;

(B) A description of the exposed employee's duties as they relate to the exposure incident;

(C) Documentation of the route(s) of exposure and circumstances under which exposure occurred;

(D) Results of the source individual's blood testing, if available; and

(E) All medical records relevant to the appropriate treatment of the employee including vaccination status which are the employer's responsibility to maintain.

(5) *Healthcare Professional's Written Opinion.* The employer shall obtain and provide the employee with a copy of the evaluating healthcare professional's written opinion within 15 days of the completion of the evaluation.

§ 1910.1030

(i) The healthcare professional's written opinion for Hepatitis B vaccination shall be limited to whether Hepatitis B vaccination is indicated for an employee, and if the employee has received such vaccination.

(ii) The healthcare professional's written opinion for post-exposure evaluation and follow-up shall be limited to the following information:

(A) That the employee has been informed of the results of the evaluation; and

(B) That the employee has been told about any medical conditions resulting from exposure to blood or other potentially infectious materials which require further evaluation or treatment.

(iii) All other findings or diagnoses shall remain confidential and shall not be included in the written report.

(6) *Medical recordkeeping.* Medical records required by this standard shall be maintained in accordance with paragraph (h)(1) of this section.

(g) *Communication of hazards to employees*—(1) *Labels and signs.* (i) Labels. (A) Warning labels shall be affixed to containers of regulated waste, refrigerators and freezers containing blood or other potentially infectious material; and other containers used to store, transport or ship blood or other potentially infectious materials, except as provided in paragraph (g)(1)(i)(E), (F) and (G).

(B) Labels required by this section shall include the following legend:

BIOHAZARD

(C) These labels shall be fluorescent orange or orange-red or predominantly so, with lettering and symbols in a contrasting color.

(D) Labels shall be affixed as close as feasible to the container by string, wire, adhesive, or other method that prevents their loss or unintentional removal.

(E) Red bags or red containers may be substituted for labels.

(F) Containers of blood, blood components, or blood products that are labeled as to their contents and have been released for transfusion or other clinical use are exempted from the labeling requirements of paragraph (g).

(G) Individual containers of blood or other potentially infectious materials that are placed in a labeled container during storage, transport, shipment or disposal are exempted from the labeling requirement.

(H) Labels required for contaminated equipment shall be in accordance with this paragraph and shall also state which portions of the equipment remain contaminated.

(I) Regulated waste that has been decontaminated need not be labeled or color-coded.

(ii) Signs. (A) The employer shall post signs at the entrance to work areas specified in paragraph (e), HIV and HBV Research Laboratory and Production Facilities, which shall bear the following legend:

BIOHAZARD

(Name of the Infectious Agent)
(Special requirements for entering the area)
(Name, telephone number of the laboratory director or other responsible person.)

(B) These signs shall be fluorescent orange-red or predominantly so, with lettering and symbols in a contrasting color.

(2) *Information and Training.* (i) Employers shall ensure that all employees with occupational exposure participate in a training program which must be provided at no cost to the employee and during working hours.

(ii) Training shall be provided as follows:

(A) At the time of initial assignment to tasks where occupational exposure may take place;
(B) Within 90 days after the effective date of the standard; and
(C) At least annually thereafter.

(iii) For employees who have received training on bloodborne pathogens in the year preceding the effective date of the standard, only training with respect to the provisions of the standard which were not included need be provided.

(iv) Annual training for all employees shall be provided within one year of their previous training.

(v) Employers shall provide additional training when changes such as modification of tasks or procedures or institution of new tasks or procedures affect the employee's occupational exposure. The additional training may be limited to addressing the new exposures created.

(vi) Material appropriate in content and vocabulary to educational level, literacy, and language of employees shall be used.

(vii) The training program shall contain at a minimum the following elements:
(A) An accessible copy of the regulatory text of this standard and an explanation of its contents;
(B) A general explanation of the epidemiology and symptoms of bloodborne diseases;
(C) An explanation of the modes of transmission of bloodborne pathogens;
(D) An explanation of the employer's exposure control plan and the means by which the employee can obtain a copy of the written plan;
(E) An explanation of the appropriate methods for recognizing tasks and other activities that may involve exposure to blood and other potentially infectious materials;
(F) An explanation of the use and limitations of methods that will prevent or reduce exposure including appropriate engineering controls, work practices, and personal protective equipment;
(G) Information on the types, proper use, location, removal, handling, decontamination and disposal of personal protective equipment;
(H) An explanation of the basis for selection of personal protective equipment;
(I) Information on the hepatitis B vaccine, including information on its efficacy, safety, method of administration, the benefits of being vaccinated, and that the vaccine and vaccination will be offered free of charge;
(J) Information on the appropriate actions to take and persons to contact in an emergency involving blood or other potentially infectious materials;
(K) An explanation of the procedure to follow if an exposure incident occurs, including the method of reporting the incident and the medical follow-up that will be made available;
(L) Information on the post-exposure evaluation and follow-up that the employer is required to provide for the employee following an exposure incident;
(M) An explanation of the signs and labels and/or color coding required by paragraph (g)(1); and
(N) An opportunity for interactive questions and answers with the person conducting the training session.

(viii) The person conducting the training shall be knowledgeable in the subject matter covered by the elements contained in the training program as it relates to the workplace that the training will address.

(ix) Additional Initial Training for Employees in HIV and HBV Laboratories and Production Facilities. Employees in HIV or HBV research laboratories and HIV or HBV production facilities shall receive the following initial training in addition to the above training requirements.
(A) The employer shall assure that employees demonstrate proficiency in standard microbiological practices and techniques and in the practices and operations specific to the facility before being allowed to work with HIV or HBV.
(B) The employer shall assure that employees have prior experience in the handling of human pathogens or tissue cultures before working with HIV or HBV.
(C) The employer shall provide a training program to employees who have no prior experience in handling human pathogens. Initial work activi-

§ 1910.1030

ties shall not include the handling of infectious agents. A progression of work activities shall be assigned as techniques are learned and proficiency is developed. The employer shall assure that employees participate in work activities involving infectious agents only after proficiency has been demonstrated.

(h) *Recordkeeping*—(1) *Medical Records.* (i) The employer shall establish and maintain an accurate record for each employee with occupational exposure, in accordance with 29 CFR 1910.20.

(ii) This record shall include:

(A) The name and social security number of the employee;

(B) A copy of the employee's hepatitis B vaccination status including the dates of all the hepatitis B vaccinations and any medical records relative to the employee's ability to receive vaccination as required by paragraph (f)(2);

(C) A copy of all results of examinations, medical testing, and follow-up procedures as required by paragraph (f)(3);

(D) The employer's copy of the healthcare professional's written opinion as required by paragraph (f)(5); and

(E) A copy of the information provided to the healthcare professional as required by paragraphs (f)(4)(ii)(B)(C) and (D).

(iii) *Confidentiality.* The employer shall ensure that employee medical records required by paragraph (h)(1) are:

(A) Kept confidential; and

(B) Not disclosed or reported without the employee's express written consent to any person within or outside the workplace except as required by this section or as may be required by law.

(iv) The employer shall maintain the records required by paragraph (h) for at least the duration of employment plus 30 years in accordance with 29 CFR 1910.20.

(2) *Training Records.* (i) Training records shall include the following information:

(A) The dates of the training sessions;

(B) The contents or a summary of the training sessions;

(C) The names and qualifications of persons conducting the training; and

(D) The names and job titles of all persons attending the training sessions.

(ii) Training records shall be maintained for 3 years from the date on which the training occurred.

(3) *Availability.* (i) The employer shall ensure that all records required to be maintained by this section shall be made available upon request to the Assistant Secretary and the Director for examination and copying.

(ii) Employee training records required by this paragraph shall be provided upon request for examination and copying to employees, to employee representatives, to the Director, and to the Assistant Secretary.

(iii) Employee medical records required by this paragraph shall be provided upon request for examination and copying to the subject employee, to anyone having written consent of the subject employee, to the Director, and to the Assistant Secretary in accordance with 29 CFR 1910.20.

(4) *Transfer of Records.* (i) The employer shall comply with the requirements involving transfer of records set forth in 29 CFR 1910.20(h).

(ii) If the employer ceases to do business and there is no successor employer to receive and retain the records for the prescribed period, the employer shall notify the Director, at least three months prior to their disposal and transmit them to the Director, if required by the Director to do so, within that three month period.

(i) *Dates*—(1) *Effective Date.* The standard shall become effective on March 6, 1992.

(2) The Exposure Control Plan required by paragraph (c) of this section shall be completed on or before May 5, 1992.

(3) Paragraph (g)(2) Information and Training and (h) Recordkeeping shall take effect on or before June 4, 1992.

(4) Paragraphs (d)(2) Engineering and Work Practice Controls, (d)(3) Personal Protective Equipment, (d)(4) Housekeeping, (e) HIV and HBV Research Laboratories and Production Facilities, (f) Hepatitis B Vaccination and Post-Exposure Evaluation and Follow-

Occupational Safety and Health Admin., Labor § 1910.1043

up, and (g) (1) Labels and Signs, shall take effect July 6, 1992.

APPENDIX A TO SECTION 1910.1030—HEPATITIS B VACCINE DECLINATION (MANDATORY)

I understand that due to my occupational exposure to blood or other potentially infectious materials I may be at risk of acquiring hepatitis B virus (HBV) infection. I have been given the opportunity to be vaccinated with hepatitis B vaccine, at no charge to myself. However, I decline hepatitis B vaccination at this time. I understand that by declining this vaccine, I continue to be at risk of acquiring hepatitis B, a serious disease. If in the future I continue to have occupational exposure to blood or other potentially infectious materials and I want to be vaccinated with hepatitis B vaccine, I can receive the vaccination series at no charge to me.

(Apporved by the Office of Management and Budget under control number 1218–0180)

[56 FR 64175, Dec. 6, 1991, as amended at 57 FR 12717, Apr. 13, 1992; 57 FR 29206, July 1, 1992]

Appendix 4F

29 CFR 1910.1450
OCCUPATIONAL EXPOSURE TO HAZARDOUS CHEMICALS IN LABORATORIES

§ 1910.1450 **Occupational exposure to hazardous chemicals in laboratories.**

(a) *Scope and application.* (1) This section shall apply to all employers engaged in the laboratory use of hazardous chemicals as defined below.

(2) Where this section applies, it shall supersede, for laboratories, the requirements of all other OSHA health standards in 29 CFR part 1910, subpart Z, except as follows:

(i) For any OSHA health standard, only the requirement to limit employee exposure to the specific permissible exposure limit shall apply for laboratories, unless that particular standard states otherwise or unless the conditions of paragraph (a)(2)(iii) of this section apply.

(ii) Prohibition of eye and skin contact where specified by any OSHA health standard shall be observed.

(iii) Where the action level (or in the absence of an action level, the permissible exposure limit) is routinely exceeded for an OSHA regulated substance with exposure monitoring and medical surveillance requirements, paragraphs (d) and (g)(1)(ii) of this section shall apply.

(3) This section shall not apply to:

(i) Uses of hazardous chemicals which do not meet the definition of laboratory use, and in such cases, the employer shall comply with the relevant standard in 29 CFR part 1910, subpart Z, even if such use occurs in a laboratory.

(ii) Laboratory uses of hazardous chemicals which provide no potential for employee exposure. Examples of such conditions might include:

(A) Procedures using chemically-impregnated test media such as Dip-and-Read tests where a reagent strip is dipped into the specimen to be tested and the results are interpreted by comparing the color reaction to a color chart supplied by the manufacturer of the test strip; and

(B) Commercially prepared kits such as those used in performing pregnancy tests in which all of the reagents needed to conduct the test are contained in the kit.

(b) *Definitions—*

Action level means a concentration designated in 29 CFR part 1910 for a specific substance, calculated as an eight (8)-hour time-weighted average, which initiates certain required activities such as exposure monitoring and medical surveillance.

Assistant Secretary means the Assistant Secretary of Labor for Occupational Safety and Health, U.S. Department of Labor, or designee.

Carcinogen (see *select carcinogen*).

Chemical Hygiene Officer means an employee who is designated by the employer, and who is qualified by training or experience, to provide technical guidance in the development and implementation of the provisions of the Chemical Hygiene Plan. This definition is not intended to place limitations on the position description or job classification that the designated indvidual shall hold within the employer's organizational structure.

Chemical Hygiene Plan means a written program developed and implemented by the employer which sets forth procedures, equipment, personal protective equipment and work practices that (i) are capable of protecting employees from the health hazards presented by hazardous chemicals used in that particular workplace and (ii) meets the requirements of paragraph (e) of this section.

Combustible liquid means any liquid having a flashpoint at or above 100 °F (37.8 °C), but below 200 °F (93.3 °C), except any mixture having components with flashpoints of 200 °F (93.3 °C), or higher, the total volume of which make up 99 percent or more of the total volume of the mixture.

Compressed gas means:

(i) A gas or mixture of gases having, in a container, an absolute pressure exceeding 40 psi at 70 °F (21.1 °C); or

(ii) A gas or mixture of gases having, in a container, an absolute pressure ex-

§ 1910.1450

ceeding 104 psi at 130 °F (54.4 °C) regardless of the pressure at 70 °F (21.1 °C); or

(iii) A liquid having a vapor pressure exceeding 40 psi at 100 °F (37.8 °C) as determined by ASTM D-323-72.

Designated area means an area which may be used for work with "select carcinogens," reproductive toxins or substances which have a high degree of acute toxicity. A designated area may be the entire laboratory, an area of a laboratory or a device such as a laboratory hood.

Emergency means any occurrence such as, but not limited to, equipment failure, rupture of containers or failure of control equipment which results in an uncontrolled release of a hazardous chemical into the workplace.

Employee means an individual employed in a laboratory workplace who may be exposed to hazardous chemicals in the course of his or her assignments.

Explosive means a chemical that causes a sudden, almost instantaneous release of pressure, gas, and heat when subjected to sudden shock, pressure, or high temperature.

Flammable means a chemical that falls into one of the following categories:

(i) *Aerosol, flammable* means an aerosol that, when tested by the method described in 16 CFR 1500.45, yields a flame protection exceeding 18 inches at full valve opening, or a flashback (a flame extending back to the valve) at any degree of valve opening;

(ii) *Gas, flammable* means:

(A) A gas that, at ambient temperature and pressure, forms a flammable mixture with air at a concentration of 13 percent by volume or less; or

(B) A gas that, at ambient temperature and pressure, forms a range of flammable mixtures with air wider than 12 percent by volume, regardless of the lower limit.

(iii) *Liquid, flammable* means any liquid having a flashpoint below 100 °F (37.8 °C), except any mixture having components with flashpoints of 100 °F (37.8 °C) or higher, the total of which make up 99 percent or more of the total volume of the mixture.

(iv) *Solid, flammable* means a solid, other than a blasting agent or explosive as defined in §1910.109(a), that is liable to cause fire through friction, absorption of moisture, spontaneous chemical change, or retained heat from manufacturing or processing, or which can be ignited readily and when ignited burns so vigorously and persistently as to create a serious hazard. A chemical shall be considered to be a flammable solid if, when tested by the method described in 16 CFR 1500.44, it ignites and burns with a self-sustained flame at a rate greater than one-tenth of an inch per second along its major axis.

Flashpoint means the minimum temperature at which a liquid gives off a vapor in sufficient concentration to ignite when tested as follows:

(i) Tagliabue Closed Tester (See American National Standard Method of Test for Flash Point by Tag Closed Tester, Z11.24-1979 (ASTM D 56-79))-for liquids with a viscosity of less than 45 Saybolt Universal Seconds (SUS) at 100 °F (37.8 °C), that do not contain suspended solids and do not have a tendency to form a surface film under test; or

(ii) Pensky-Martens Closed Tester (see American National Standard Method of Test for Flash Point by Pensky-Martens Closed Tester, Z11.7-1979 (ASTM D 93-79))-for liquids with a viscosity equal to or greater than 45 SUS at 100 °F (37.8 °C), or that contain suspended solids, or that have a tendency to form a surface film under test; or

(iii) Setaflash Closed Tester (see American National Standard Method of Test for Flash Point by Setaflash Closed Tester (ASTM D 3278-78)).

Organic peroxides, which undergo autoaccelerating thermal decomposition, are excluded from any of the flashpoint determination methods specified above.

Hazardous chemical means a chemical for which there is statistically significant evidence based on at least one study conducted in accordance with established scientific principles that acute or chronic health effects may occur in exposed employees. The term *health hazard* includes chemicals which are carcinogens, toxic or highly toxic agents, reproductive toxins, irritants, corrosives, sensitizers, hepatotoxins, nephrotoxins, neurotoxins, agents which act on the hematopoietic systems, and agents which damage the

Occupational Safety and Health Admin., Labor § 1910.1450

lungs, skin, eyes, or mucous membranes.

Appendices A and B of the Hazard Communication Standard (29 CFR 1910.1200) provide further guidance in defining the scope of health hazards and determining whether or not a chemical is to be considered hazardous for purposes of this standard.

Laboratory means a facility where the "laboratory use of hazardous chemicals" occurs. It is a workplace where relatively small quantities of hazardous chemicals are used on a non-production basis.

Laboratory scale means work with substances in which the containers used for reactions, transfers, and other handling of substances are designed to be easily and safely manipulated by one person. "Laboratory scale" excludes those workplaces whose function is to produce commercial quantities of materials.

Laboratory-type hood means a device located in a laboratory, enclosure on five sides with a moveable sash or fixed partial enclosed on the remaining side; constructed and maintained to draw air from the laboratory and to prevent or minimize the escape of air contaminants into the laboratory; and allows chemical manipulations to be conducted in the enclosure without insertion of any portion of the employee's body other than hands and arms.

Walk-in hoods with adjustable sashes meet the above definition provided that the sashes are adjusted during use so that the airflow and the exhaust of air contaminants are not compromised and employees do not work inside the enclosure during the release of airborne hazardous chemicals.

Laboratory use of hazardous chemicals means handling or use of such chemicals in which all of the following conditions are met:

(i) Chemical manipulations are carried out on a "laboratory scale;"

(ii) Multiple chemical procedures or chemicals are used;

(iii) The procedures involved are not part of a production process, nor in any way simulate a production process; and

(iv) "Protective laboratory practices and equipment" are available and in common use to minimize the potential for employee exposure to hazardous chemicals.

Medical consultation means a consultation which takes place between an employee and a licensed physician for the purpose of determining what medical examinations or procedures, if any, are appropriate in cases where a significant exposure to a hazardous chemical may have taken place.

Organic peroxide means an organic compound that contains the bivalent –O–O– structure and which may be considered to be a structural derivative of hydrogen peroxide where one or both of the hydrogen atoms has been replaced by an organic radical.

Oxidizer means a chemical other than a blasting agent or explosive as defined in § 1910.109(a), that initiates or promotes combustion in other materials, thereby causing fire either of itself or through the release of oxygen or other gases.

Physical hazard means a chemical for which there is scientifically valid evidence that it is a combustible liquid, a compressed gas, explosive, flammable, an organic peroxide, an oxidizer, pyrophoric, unstable (reactive) or water-reactive.

Protective laboratory practices and equipment means those laboratory procedures, practices and equipment accepted by laboratory health and safety experts as effective, or that the employer can show to be effective, in minimizing the potential for employee exposure to hazardous chemicals.

Reproductive toxins means chemicals which affect the reproductive capabilities including chromosomal damage (mutations) and effects on fetuses (teratogenesis)

Select carcinogen means any substance which meets one of the following criteria:

(i) It is regulated by OSHA as a carcinogen; or

(ii) It is listed under the category, "known to be carcinogens," in the Annual Report on Carcinogens published by the National Toxicology Program (NTP) (latest edition); or

(iii) It is listed under Group 1 ("carcinogenic to humans") by the International Agency for Research on Cancer Monographs (IARC) (latest editions); or

§ 1910.1450

(iv) It is listed in either Group 2A or 2B by IARC or under the category, "reasonably anticipated to be carcinogens" by NTP, and causes statistically significant tumor incidence in experimental animals in accordance with any of the following criteria:

(A) After inhalation exposure of 6–7 hours per day, 5 days per week, for a significant portion of a lifetime to dosages of less than 10 mg/m^3;

(B) After repeated skin application of less than 300 (mg/kg of body weight) per week; or

(C) After oral dosages of less than 50 mg/kg of body weight per day.

Unstable (reactive) means a chemical which is the pure state, or as produced or transported, will vigorously polymerize, decompose, condense, or will become self-reactive under conditions of shocks, pressure or temperature.

Water-reactive means a chemical that reacts with water to release a gas that is either flammable or presents a health hazard.

(c) *Permissible exposure limits.* For laboratory uses of OSHA regulated substances, the employer shall assure that laboratory employees' exposures to such substances do not exceed the permissible exposure limits specified in 29 CFR part 1910, subpart Z.

(d) *Employee exposure determination*—(1) *Initial monitoring.* The employer shall measure the employee's exposure to any substance regulated by a standard which requires monitoring if there is reason to believe that exposure levels for that substance routinely exceed the action level (or in the absence of an action level, the PEL).

(2) *Periodic monitoring.* If the initial monitoring prescribed by paragraph (d)(1) of this section discloses employee exposure over the action level (or in the absence of an action level, the PEL), the employer shall immediately comply with the exposure monitoring provisions of the relevant standard.

(3) *Termination of monitoring.* Monitoring may be terminated in accordance with the relevant standard.

(4) *Employee notification of monitoring results.* The employer shall, within 15 working days after the receipt of any monitoring results, notify the employee of these results in writing either individually or by posting results in an appropriate location that is accessible to employees.

(e) *Chemical hygiene plan—General.* (Appendix A of this section is non-mandatory but provides guidance to assist employers in the development of the Chemical Hygiene Plan.)

(1) Where hazardous chemicals as defined by this standard are used in the workplace, the employer shall develop and carry out the provisions of a written Chemical Hygiene Plan which is:

(i) Capable of protecting employees from health hazards associated with hazardous chemicals in that laboratory and

(ii) Capable of keeping exposures below the limits specified in paragraph (c) of this section.

(2) The Chemical Hygiene Plan shall be readily available to employees, employee representatives and, upon request, to the Assistant Secretary.

(3) The Chemical Hygiene Plan shall include each of the following elements and shall indicate specific measures that the employer will take to ensure laboratory employee protection:

(i) Standard operating procedures relevant to safety and health considerations to be followed when laboratory work involves the use of hazardous chemicals;

(ii) Criteria that the employer will use to determine and implement control measures to reduce employee exposure to hazardous chemicals including engineering controls, the use of personal protective equipment and hygiene practices; particular attention shall be given to the selection of control measures for chemicals that are known to be extremely hazardous;

(iii) A requirement that fume hoods and other protective equipment are functioning properly and specific measures that shall be taken to ensure proper and adequate performance of such equipment;

(iv) Provisions for employee information and training as prescribed in paragraph (f) of this section;

(v) The circumstances under which a particular laboratory operation, procedure or activity shall require prior approval from the employer or the employer's designee before implementation;

Occupational Safety and Health Admin., Labor § 1910.1450

(vi) Provisions for medical consultation and medical examinations in accordance with paragraph (g) of this section;

(vii) Designation of personnel responsible for implementation of the Chemical Hygiene Plan including the assignment of a Chemical Hygiene Officer and, if appropriate, establishment of a Chemical Hygiene Committee; and

(viii) Provisions for additional employee protection for work with particularly hazardous substances. These include "select carcinogens," reproductive toxins and substances which have a high degree of acute toxicity. Specific consideration shall be given to the following provisions which shall be included where appropriate:

(A) Establishment of a designated area;

(B) Use of containment devices such as fume hoods or glove boxes;

(C) Procedures for safe removal of contaminated waste; and

(D) Decontamination procedures.

(4) The employer shall review and evaluate the effectiveness of the Chemical Hygiene Plan at least annually and update it as necessary.

(f) *Employee information and training.* (1) The employer shall provide employees with information and training to ensure that they are apprised of the hazards of chemicals present in their work area.

(2) Such information shall be provided at the time of an employee's initial assignment to a work area where hazardous chemicals are present and prior to assignments involving new exposure situations. The frequency of refresher information and training shall be determined by the employer.

(3) *Information.* Employees shall be informed of:

(i) The contents of this standard and its appendices which shall be made available to employees;

(ii) The location and availability of the employer's Chemical Hygiene Plan;

(iii) The permissible exposure limits for OSHA regulated substances or recommended exposure limits for other hazardous chemicals where there is no applicable OSHA standard;

(iv) Signs and symptoms associated with exposures to hazardous chemicals used in the laboratory; and

(v) The location and availability of known reference material on the hazards, safe handling, storage and disposal of hazardous chemicals found in the laboratory including, but not limited to, Material Safety Data Sheets received from the chemical supplier.

(4) *Training.* (i) Employee training shall include:

(A) Methods and observations that may be used to detect the presence or release of a hazardous chemical (such as monitoring conducted by the employer, continuous monitoring devices, visual appearance or odor of hazardous chemicals when being released, etc.);

(B) The physical and health hazards of chemicals in the work area; and

(C) The measures employees can take to protect themselves from these hazards, including specific procedures the employer has implemented to protect employees from exposure to hazardous chemicals, such as appropriate work practices, emergency procedures, and personal protective equipment to be used.

(ii) The employee shall be trained on the applicable details of the employer's written Chemical Hygiene Plan.

(g) *Medical consultation and medical examinations.* (1) The employer shall provide all employees who work with hazardous chemicals an opportunity to receive medical attention, including any follow-up examinations which the examining physician determines to be necessary, under the following circumstances:

(i) Whenever an employee develops signs or symptoms associated with a hazardous chemical to which the employee may have been exposed in the laboratory, the employee shall be provided an opportunity to receive an appropriate medical examination.

(ii) Where exposure monitoring reveals an exposure level routinely above the action level (or in the absence of an action level, the PEL) for an OSHA regulated substance for which there are exposure monitoring and medical surveillance requirements, medical surveillance shall be established for the affected employee as prescribed by the particular standard.

(iii) Whenever an event takes place in the work area such as a spill, leak, explosion or other occurrence resulting

§ 1910.1450

in the likelihood of a hazardous exposure, the affected employee shall be provided an opportunity for a medical consultation. Such consultation shall be for the purpose of determining the need for a medical examination.

(2) All medical examinations and consultations shall be performed by or under the direct supervision of a licensed physician and shall be provided without cost to the employee, without loss of pay and at a reasonable time and place.

(3) *Information provided to the physician.* The employer shall provide the following information to the physician:

(i) The identity of the hazardous chemical(s) to which the employee may have been exposed;

(ii) A description of the conditions under which the exposure occurred including quantitative exposure data, if available; and

(iii) A description of the signs and symptoms of exposure that the employee is experiencing, if any.

(4) *Physician's written opinion.* (i) For examination or consultation required under this standard, the employer shall obtain a written opinion from the examining physician which shall include the following:

(A) Any recommendation for further medical follow-up;

(B) The results of the medical examination and any associated tests;

(C) Any medical condition which may be revealed in the course of the examination which may place the employee at increased risk as a result of exposure to a hazardous chemical found in the workplace; and

(D) A statement that the employee has been informed by the physician of the results of the consultation or medical examination and any medical condition that may require further examination or treatment.

(ii) The written opinion shall not reveal specific findings of diagnoses unrelated to occupational exposure.

(h) *Hazard identification.* (1) With respect to labels and material safety data sheets:

(i) Employers shall ensure that labels on incoming containers of hazardous chemicals are not removed or defaced.

(ii) Employers shall maintain any material safety data sheets that are received with incoming shipments of hazardous chemicals, and ensure that they are readily accessible to laboratory employees.

(2) The following provisions shall apply to chemical substances developed in the laboratory:

(i) If the composition of the chemical substance which is produced exclusively for the laboratory's use is known, the employer shall determine if it is a hazardous chemical as defined in paragraph (b) of this section. If the chemical is determined to be hazardous, the employer shall provide appropriate training as required under paragraph (f) of this section.

(ii) If the chemical produced is a by-product whose composition is not known, the employer shall assume that the substance is hazardous and shall implement paragraph (e) of this section.

(iii) If the chemical substance is produced for another user outside of the laboratory, the employer shall comply with the Hazard Communication Standard (29 CFR 1910.1200) including the requirements for preparation of material safety data sheets and labeling.

(i) *Use of respirators.* Where the use of respirators is necessary to maintain exposure below permissible exposure limits, the employer shall provide, at no cost to the employee, the proper respiratory equipment. Respirators shall be selected and used in accordance with the requirements of 29 CFR 1910.134.

(j) *Recordkeeping.* (1) The employer shall establish and maintain for each employee an accurate record of any measurements taken to monitor employee exposures and any medical consultation and examinations including tests or written opinions required by this standard.

(2) The employer shall assure that such records are kept, transferred, and made available in accordance with 29 CFR 1910.20.

(k) *Dates*—(1) *Effective date.* This section shall become effective May 1, 1990.

(2) *Start-up dates.* (i) Employers shall have developed and implemented a written Chemical Hygiene Plan no later than January 31, 1991.

Occupational Safety and Health Admin., Labor § 1910.1450, App. A

(ii) Paragraph (a)(2) of this section shall not take effect until the employer has developed and implemented a written Chemical Hygiene Plan.

(l) *Appendices.* The information contained in the appendices is not intended, by itself, to create any additional obligations not otherwise imposed or to detract from any existing obligation.

[55 FR 3327, Jan. 31, 1990, 55 FR 7967, Mar. 6, 1990, 55 FR 12111, Mar. 30, 1990]

APPENDIX A TO §1910.1450—NATIONAL RESEARCH COUNCIL RECOMMENDATIONS CONCERNING CHEMICAL HYGIENE IN LABORATORIES (NON-MANDATORY)

TABLE OF CONTENTS

Foreword

Corresponding Sections of the Standard and This Appendix

A. General Principles

1. Minimize all Chemical Exposures
2. Avoid Underestimation of Risk
3. Provide Adequate Ventilation
4. Institute a Chemical Hygiene Program
5. Observe the PELs and TLVs

B. Responsibilities

1. Chief Executive Officer
2. Supervisor of Administrative Unit
3. Chemical Hygiene Officer
4. Laboratory Supervisor
5. Project Director
6. Laboratory Worker

C. The Laboratory Facility

1. Design
2. Maintenance
3. Usage
4. Ventilation

D. Components of the Chemical Hygiene Plan

1. Basic Rules and Procedures
2. Chemical Procurement, Distribution, and Storage
3. Environmental Monitoring
4. Housekeeping, Maintenance and Inspections
5. Medical Program
6. Personal Protective Apparel and Equipment
7. Records
8. Signs and Labels
9. Spills and Accidents
10. Training and Information
11. Waste Disposal

E. General Procedures for Working With Chemicals

1. General Rules for all Laboratory Work with Chemicals
2. Allergens and Embryotoxins
3. Chemicals of Moderate Chronic or High Acute Toxicity
4. Chemicals of High Chronic Toxicity
5. Animal Work with Chemicals of High Chronic Toxicity

F. Safety Recommendations

G. Material Safety Data Sheets

Foreword

As guidance for each employer's development of an appropriate laboratory Chemical Hygiene Plan, the following non-mandatory recommendations are provided. They were extracted from "Prudent Practices for Handling Hazardous Chemicals in Laboratories" (referred to below as "Prudent Practices"), which was published in 1981 by the National Research Council and is available from the National Academy Press, 2101 Constitution Ave., NW., Washington DC 20418.

"Prudent Practices" is cited because of its wide distribution and acceptance and because of its preparation by members of the laboratory community through the sponsorship of the National Research Council. However, none of the recommendations given here will modify any requirements of the laboratory standard. This Appendix merely presents pertinent recommendations from "Prudent Practices", organized into a form convenient for quick reference during operation of a laboratory facility and during development and application of a Chemical Hygiene Plan. Users of this appendix should consult "Prudent Practices" for a more extended presentation and justification for each recommendation.

"Prudent Practices" deals with both safety and chemical hazards while the laboratory standard is concerned primarily with chemical hazards. Therefore, only those recommendations directed primarily toward control of toxic exposures are cited in this appendix, with the term "chemical hygiene" being substituted for the word "safety". However, since conditions producing or threatening physical injury often pose toxic risks as well, page references concerning major categories of safety hazards in the laboratory are given in section F.

The recommendations from "Prudent Practices" have been paraphrased, combined, or otherwise reorganized, and headings have been added. However, their sense has not been changed.

499

§ 1910.1450, App. A

Corresponding Sections of the Standard and this Appendix

The following table is given for the convenience of those who are developing a Chemical Hygiene Plan which will satisfy the requirements of paragraph (e) of the standard. It indicates those sections of this appendix which are most pertinent to each of the sections of paragraph (e) and related paragraphs.

Paragraph and topic in laboratory standard	Relevant appendix section
(e)(3)(i) Standard operating procedures for handling toxic chemicals.	C, D, E
(e)(3)(ii) Criteria to be used for implementation of measures to reduce exposures.	D
(e)(3)(iii) Fume hood performance	C4b
(e)(3)(iv) Employee information and training (including emergency procedures).	D10, D9
(e)(3)(v) Requirements for prior approval of laboratory activities.	E2b, E4b
(e)(3)(vi) Medical consultation and medical examinations.	D5, E4f
(e)(3)(vii) Chemical hygiene responsibilities ...	B
(e)(3)(viii) Special precautions for work with particularly hazardous substances.	E2, E3, E4

In this appendix, those recommendations directed primarily at administrators and supervisors are given in sections A–D. Those recommendations of primary concern to employees who are actually handling laboratory chemicals are given in section E. (Reference to page numbers in "Prudent Practices" are given in parentheses.)

A. General Principles for Work with Laboratory Chemicals

In addition to the more detailed recommendations listed below in sections B–E, "Prudent Practices" expresses certain general principles, including the following:

1. *It is prudent to minimize all chemical exposures.* Because few laboratory chemicals are without hazards, general precautions for handling all laboratory chemicals should be adopted, rather than specific guidelines for particular chemicals (2, 10). Skin contact with chemicals should be avoided as a cardinal rule (198).

2. *Avoid underestimation of risk.* Even for substances of no known significant hazard, exposure should be minimized; for work with substances which present special hazards, special precautions should be taken (10, 37, 38). One should assume that any mixture will be more toxic than its most toxic component (30, 103) and that all substances of unknown toxicity are toxic (3, 34).

3. *Provide adequate ventilation.* The best way to prevent exposure to airborne substances is to prevent their escape into the working atmosphere by use of hoods and other ventilation devices (32, 198).

4. *Institute a chemical hygiene program.* A mandatory chemical hygiene program designed to minimize exposures is needed; it should be a regular, continuing effort, not merely a standby or short-term activity (6, 11). Its recommendations should be followed in academic teaching laboratories as well as by full-time laboratory workers (13).

5. *Observe the PELs, TLVs.* The Permissible Exposure Limits of OSHA and the Threshold Limit Values of the American Conference of Governmental Industrial Hygienists should not be exceeded (13).

B. Chemical Hygiene Responsibilities

Responsibility for chemical hygiene rests at all levels (6, 11, 21) including the:

1. *Chief executive officer,* who has ultimate responsibility for chemical hygiene within the institution and must, with other administrators, provide continuing support for institutional chemical hygiene (7, 11).

2. *Supervisor of the department or other administrative unit,* who is responsible for chemical hygiene in that unit (7).

3. *Chemical hygiene officer(s),* whose appointment is essential (7) and who must:

(a) Work with administrators and other employees to develop and implement appropriate chemical hygiene policies and practices (7);

(b) Monitor procurement, use, and disposal of chemicals used in the lab (8);

(c) See that appropriate audits are maintained (8);

(d) Help project directors develop precautions and adequate facilities (10);

(e) Know the current legal requirements concerning regulated substances (50); and

(f) Seek ways to improve the chemical hygiene program (8, 11).

4. *Laboratory supervisor,* who has overall responsibility for chemical hygiene in the laboratory (21) including responsibility to:

(a) Ensure that workers know and follow the chemical hygiene rules, that protective equipment is available and in working order, and that appropriate training has been provided (21, 22);

(b) Provide regular, formal chemical hygiene and housekeeping inspections including routine inspections of emergency equipment (21, 171);

(c) Know the current legal requirements concerning regulated substances (50, 231);

(d) Determine the required levels of protective apparel and equipment (156, 160, 162); and

(e) Ensure that facilities and training for use of any material being ordered are adequate (215).

5. *Project director or director of other specific operation,* who has primary responsibility for chemical hygiene procedures for that operation (7).

6. *Laboratory worker,* who is responsible for:

(a) Planning and conducting each operation in accordance with the institutional

Occupational Safety and Health Admin., Labor § 1910.1450, App. A

chemical hygiene procedures (7, 21, 22, 230); and

(b) Developing good personal chemical hygiene habits (22).

C. The Laboratory Facility

1. *Design.* The laboratory facility should have:

(a) An appropriate general ventilation system (see C4 below) with air intakes and exhausts located so as to avoid intake of contaminated air (194);

(b) Adequate, well-ventilated stockrooms/storerooms (218, 219);

(c) Laboratory hoods and sinks (12, 162);

(d) Other safety equipment including eyewash fountains and drench showers (162, 169); and

(e) Arrangements for waste disposal (12, 240).

2. *Maintenance.* Chemical-hygiene-related equipment (hoods, incinerator, etc.) should undergo continuing appraisal and be modified if inadequate (11, 12).

3. *Usage.* The work conducted (10) and its scale (12) must be appropriate to the physical facilities available and, especially, to the quality of ventilation (13).

4. *Ventilation*—(a) *General laboratory ventilation.* This system should: Provide a source of air for breathing and for input to local ventilation devices (199); it should not be relied on for protection from toxic substances released into the laboratory (198); ensure that laboratory air is continually replaced, preventing increase of air concentrations of toxic substances during the working day (194); direct air flow into the laboratory from non-laboratory areas and out to the exterior of the building (194).

(b) *Hoods.* A laboratory hood with 2.5 linear feet of hood space per person should be provided for every 2 workers if they spend most of their time working with chemicals (199); each hood should have a continuous monitoring device to allow convenient confirmation of adequate hood performance before use (200, 209). If this is not possible, work with substances of unknown toxicity should be avoided (13) or other types of local ventilation devices should be provided (199). See pp. 201–206 for a discussion of hood design, construction, and evaluation.

(c) *Other local ventilation devices.* Ventilated storage cabinets, canopy hoods, snorkels, etc. should be provided as needed (199). Each canopy hood and snorkel should have a separate exhaust duct (207).

(d) *Special ventilation areas.* Exhaust air from glove boxes and isolation rooms should be passed through scrubbers or other treatment before release into the regular exhaust system (208). Cold rooms and warm rooms should have provisions for rapid escape and for escape in the event of electrical failure (209).

(e) *Modifications.* Any alteration of the ventilation system should be made only if thorough testing indicates that worker protection from airborne toxic substances will continue to be adequate (12, 193, 204).

(f) *Performance.* Rate: 4–12 room air changes/hour is normally adequate general ventilation if local exhaust systems such as hoods are used as the primary method of control (194).

(g) *Quality.* General air flow should not be turbulent and should be relatively uniform throughout the laboratory, with no high velocity or static areas (194, 195); airflow into and within the hood should not be excessively turbulent (200); hood face velocity should be adequate (typically 60–100 lfm) (200, 204).

(h) *Evaluation.* Quality and quantity of ventilation should be evaluated on installation (202), regularly monitored (at least every 3 months) (6, 12, 14, 195), and reevaluated whenever a change in local ventilation devices is made (12, 195, 207). See pp. 195–198 for methods of evaluation and for calculation of estimated airborne contaminant concentrations.

D. Components of the Chemical Hygiene Plan

1. Basic Rules and Procedures (Recommendations for these are given in section E, below)

2. Chemical Procurement, Distribution, and Storage

(a) *Procurement.* Before a substance is received, information on proper handling, storage, and disposal should be known to those who will be involved (215, 216). No container should be accepted without an adequate identifying label (216). Preferably, all substances should be received in a central location (216).

(b) *Stockrooms/storerooms.* Toxic substances should be segregated in a well-identified area with local exhaust ventilation (221). Chemicals which are highly toxic (227) or other chemicals whose containers have been opened should be in unbreakable secondary containers (219). Stored chemicals should be examined periodically (at least annually) for replacement, deterioration, and container integrity (218–19).

Stockrooms/storerooms should not be used as preparation or repackaging areas, should be open during normal working hours, and should be controlled by one person (219).

(c) *Distribution.* When chemicals are hand carried, the container should be placed in an outside container or bucket. Freight-only elevators should be used if possible (223).

(d) *Laboratory storage.* Amounts permitted should be as small as practical. Storage on bench tops and in hoods is inadvisable. Exposure to heat or direct sunlight should be avoided. Periodic inventories should be con-

§ 1910.1450, App. A

ducted, with unneeded items being discarded or returned to the storeroom/stockroom (225-6, 229).

3. Environmental Monitoring

Regular instrumental monitoring of airborne concentrations is not usually justified or practical in laboratories but may be appropriate when testing or redesigning hoods or other ventilation devices (12) or when a highly toxic substance is stored or used regularly (e.g., 3 times/week) (13).

4. Housekeeping, Maintenance, and Inspections

(a) *Cleaning.* Floors should be cleaned regularly (24).

(b) *Inspections.* Formal housekeeping and chemical hygiene inspections should be held at least quarterly (6, 21) for units which have frequent pesonnel changes and semiannually for others; informal inspections should be continual (21).

(c) *Maintenance.* Eye wash fountains should be inspected at intervals of not less than 3 months (6). Respirators for routine use should be inspected periodically by the laboratory supervisor (169). Safety showers should be tested routinely (169). Other safety equipment should be inspected regularly. (e.g., every 3-6 months) (6, 24, 171). Procedures to prevent restarting of out-of-service equipment should be established (25).

(d) *Passageways.* Stairways and hallways should not be used as storage areas (24). Access to exits, emergency equipment, and utility controls should never be blocked (24).

5. Medical Program

(a) *Compliance with regulations.* Regular medical surveillance should be established to the extent required by regulations (12).

(b) *Routine surveillance.* Anyone whose work involves regular and frequent handling of toxicologically significant quantities of a chemical should consult a qualified physician to determine on an individual basis whether a regular schedule of medical surveillance is desirable (11, 50).

(c) *First aid.* Personnel trained in first aid should be available during working hours and an emergency room with medical personnel should be nearby (173). See pp. 176-178 for description of some emergency first aid procedures.

6. Protective Apparel and Equipment

These should include for each laboratory:
(a) Protective apparel compatible with the required degree of protection for substances being handled (158-161);
(b) An easily accessible drench-type safety shower (162, 169);
(c) An eyewash fountain (162);
(d) A fire extinguisher (162-164);

29 CFR Ch. XVII (7-1-94 Edition)

(e) Respiratory protection (164-9), fire alarm and telephone for emergency use (162) should be available nearby; and
(f) Other items designated by the laboratory supervisor (156, 160).

7. Records

(a) Accident records should be written and retained (174).
(b) Chemical Hygiene Plan records should document that the facilities and precautions were compatible with current knowledge and regulations (7).
(c) Inventory and usage records for high-risk substances should be kept as specified in sections E3e below.
(d) Medical records should be retained by the institution in accordance with the requirements of state and federal regulations (12).

8. Signs and Labels

Prominent signs and labels of the following types should be posted:
(a) Emergency telephone numbers of emergency personnel/facilities, supervisors, and laboratory workers (28);
(b) Identity labels, showing contents of containers (including waste receptacles) and associated hazards (27, 48);
(c) Location signs for safety showers, eyewash stations, other safety and first aid equipment, exits (27) and areas where food and beverage consumption and storage are permitted (24); and
(d) Warnings at areas or equipment where special or unusual hazards exist (27).

9. Spills and Accidents

(a) A written emergency plan should be established and communicated to all personnel; it should include procedures for ventilation failure (200), evacuation, medical care, reporting, and drills (172).
(b) There should be an alarm system to alert people in all parts of the facility including isolation areas such as cold rooms (172).
(c) A spill control policy should be developed and should include consideration of prevention, containment, cleanup, and reporting (175).
(d) All accidents or near accidents should be carefully analyzed with the results distributed to all who might benefit (8, 28).

10. Information and Training Program

(a) Aim: To assure that all individuals at risk are adequately informed about the work in the laboratory, its risks, and what to do if an accident occurs (5, 15).
(b) Emergency and Personal Protection Training: Every laboratory worker should know the location and proper use of available protective apparel and equipment (154, 169).

Occupational Safety and Health Admin., Labor § 1910.1450, App. A

Some of the full-time personnel of the laboratory should be trained in the proper use of emergency equipment and procedures (6).

Such training as well as first aid instruction should be available to (154) and encouraged for (176) everyone who might need it.

(c) Receiving and stockroom/storeroom personnel should know about hazards, handling equipment, protective apparel, and relevant regulations (217).

(d) Frequency of Training: The training and education program should be a regular, continuing activity—not simply an annual presentation (15).

(e) Literature/Consultation: Literature and consulting advice concerning chemical hygiene should be readily available to laboratory personnel, who should be encouraged to use these information resources (14).

11. *Waste Disposal Program.*

(a) Aim: To assure that minimal harm to people, other organisms, and the environment will result from the disposal of waste laboratory chemicals (5).

(b) Content (14, 232, 233, 240): The waste disposal program should specify how waste is to be collected, segregated, stored, and transported and include consideration of what materials can be incinerated. Transport from the institution must be in accordance with DOT regulations (244).

(c) Discarding Chemical Stocks: Unlabeled containers of chemicals and solutions should undergo prompt disposal; if partially used, they should not be opened (24, 27).

Before a worker's employment in the laboratory ends, chemicals for which that person was responsible should be discarded or returned to storage (226).

(d) Frequency of Disposal: Waste should be removed from laboratories to a central waste storage area at least once per week and from the central waste storage area at regular intervals (14).

(e) Method of Disposal: Incineration in an environmentally acceptable manner is the most practical disposal method for combustible laboratory waste (14, 238, 241).

Indiscriminate disposal by pouring waste chemicals down the drain (14, 231, 242) or adding them to mixed refuse for landfill burial is unacceptable (14).

Hoods should not be used as a means of disposal for volatile chemicals (40, 200).

Disposal by recycling (233, 243) or chemical decontamination (40, 230) should be used when possible.

E. *Basic Rules and Procedures for Working with Chemicals*

The Chemical Hygiene Plan should require that laboratory workers know and follow its rules and procedures. In addition to the procedures of the sub programs mentioned above, these should include the rules listed below.

1. General Rules

The following should be used for essentially all laboratory work with chemicals:

(a) *Accidents and spills*—Eye Contact: Promptly flush eyes with water for a prolonged period (15 minutes) and seek medical attention (33, 172).

Ingestion: Encourage the victim to drink large amounts of water (178).

Skin Contact: Promptly flush the affected area with water (33, 172, 178) and remove any contaminated clothing (172, 178). If symptoms persist after washing, seek medical attention (33).

Clean-up. Promptly clean up spills, using appropriate protective apparel and equipment and proper disposal (24 33). See pp. 233-237 for specific clean-up recommendations.

(b) *Avoidance of "routine" exposure:* Develop and encourage safe habits (23); avoid unnecessary exposure to chemicals by any route (23);

Do not smell or taste chemicals (32). Vent apparatus which may discharge toxic chemicals (vacuum pumps, distillation columns, etc.) into local exhaust devices (199).

Inspect gloves (157) and test glove boxes (208) before use.

Do not allow release of toxic substances in cold rooms and warm rooms, since these have contained recirculated atmospheres (209).

(c) *Choice of chemicals:* Use only those chemicals for which the quality of the available ventilation system is appropriate (13).

(d) *Eating, smoking, etc.:* Avoid eating, drinking, smoking, gum chewing, or application of cosmetics in areas where laboratory chemicals are present (22, 24, 32, 40); wash hands before conducting these activities (23, 24).

Avoid storage, handling or consumption of food or beverages in storage areas, refrigerators, glassware or utensils which are also used for laboratory operations (23, 24, 226).

(e) *Equipment and glassware:* Handle and store laboratory glassware with care to avoid damage; do not use damaged glassware (25). Use extra care with Dewar flasks and other evacuated glass apparatus; shield or wrap them to contain chemicals and fragments should implosion occur (25). Use equipment only for its designed purpose (23, 26).

(f) *Exiting:* Wash areas of exposed skin well before leaving the laboratory (23).

(g) *Horseplay:* Avoid practical jokes or other behavior which might confuse, startle or distract another worker (23).

(h) *Mouth suction:* Do not use mouth suction for pipeting or starting a siphon (23, 32).

(i) *Personal apparel:* Confine long hair and loose clothing (23, 158). Wear shoes at all

§ 1910.1450, App. A

times in the laboratory but do not wear sandals, perforated shoes, or sneakers (158).

(j) *Personal housekeeping:* Keep the work area clean and uncluttered, with chemicals and equipment being properly labeled and stored; clean up the work area on completion of an operation or at the end of each day (24).

(k) *Personal protection:* Assure that appropriate eye protection (154–156) is worn by all persons, including visitors, where chemicals are stored or handled (22, 23, 33, 154).

Wear appropriate gloves when the potential for contact with toxic materials exists (157); inspect the gloves before each use, wash them before removal, and replace them periodically (157). (A table of resistance to chemicals of common glove materials is given p. 159).

Use appropriate (164–168) respiratory equipment when air contaminant concentrations are not sufficiently restricted by engineering controls (164–5), inspecting the respirator before use (169).

Use any other protective and emergency apparel and equipment as appropriate (22, 157–162).

Avoid use of contact lenses in the laboratory unless necessary; if they are used, inform supervisor so special precautions can be taken (155).

Remove laboratory coats immediately on significant contamination (161).

(l) *Planning:* Seek information and advice about hazards (7), plan appropriate protective procedures, and plan positioning of equipment before beginning any new operation (22, 23).

(m) *Unattended operations:* Leave lights on, place an appropriate sign on the door, and provide for containment of toxic substances in the event of failure of a utility service (such as cooling water) to an unattended operation (27, 128).

(n) *Use of hood:* Use the hood for operations which might result in release of toxic chemical vapors or dust (198–9).

As a rule of thumb, use a hood or other local ventilation device when working with any appreciably volatile substance with a TLV of less than 50 ppm (13).

Confirm adequate hood performance before use; keep hood closed at all times except when adjustments within the hood are being made (200); keep materials stored in hoods to a minimum and do not allow them to block vents or air flow (200).

Leave the hood "on" when it is not in active use if toxic substances are stored in it or if it is uncertain whether adequate general laboratory ventilation will be maintained when it is "off" (200).

(o) *Vigilance:* Be alert to unsafe conditions and see that they are corrected when detected (22).

(p) *Waste disposal:* Assure that the plan for each laboratory operation includes plans and training for waste disposal (230).

29 CFR Ch. XVII (7-1-94 Edition)

Deposit chemical waste in appropriately labeled receptacles and follow all other waste disposal procedures of the Chemical Hygiene Plan (22, 24).

Do not discharge to the sewer concentrated acids or bases (231); highly toxic, malodorous, or lachrymatory substances (231); or any substances which might interfere with the biological activity of waste water treatment plants, create fire or explosion hazards, cause structural damage or obstruct flow (242).

(q) *Working alone:* Avoid working alone in a building; do not work alone in a laboratory if the procedures being conducted are hazardous (28).

2. Working with Allergens and Embryotoxins

(a) *Allergens* (examples: diazomethane, isocyanates, bichromates): Wear suitable gloves to prevent hand contact with allergens or substances of unknown allergenic activity (35).

(b) *Embryotoxins* (34–5) (examples: organomercurials, lead compounds, formamide): If you are a woman of childbearing age, handle these substances only in a hood whose satisfactory performance has been confirmed, using appropriate protective apparel (especially gloves) to prevent skin contact.

Review each use of these materials with the research supervisor and review continuing uses annually or whenever a procedural change is made.

Store these substances, properly labeled, in an adequately ventilated area in an unbreakable secondary container.

Notify supervisors of all incidents of exposure or spills; consult a qualified physician when appropriate.

3. Work with Chemicals of Moderate Chronic or High Acute Toxicity

EXAMPLES: diisopropylflurophosphate (41), hydrofluoric acid (43), hydrogen cyanide (45).

Supplemental rules to be followed in addition to those mentioned above (Procedure B of "Prudent Practices", pp. 39–41):

(a) *Aim:* To minimize exposure to these toxic substances by any route using all reasonable precautions (39).

(b) *Applicability:* These precautions are appropriate for substances with moderate chronic or high acute toxicity used in significant quantities (39).

(c) *Location:* Use and store these substances only in areas of restricted access with special warning signs (40, 229).

Always use a hood (previously evaluated to confirm adequate performance with a face velocity of at least 60 linear feet per minute) (40) or other containment device for procedures which may result in the generation of aerosols or vapors containing the substance

Occupational Safety and Health Admin., Labor § 1910.1450, App. A

(39); trap released vapors to prevent their discharge with the hood exhaust (40).

(d) *Personal protection:* Always avoid skin contact by use of gloves and long sleeves (and other protective apparel as appropriate) (39). Always wash hands and arms immediately after working with these materials (40).

(e) *Records:* Maintain records of the amounts of these materials on hand, amounts used, and the names of the workers involved (40, 229).

(f) *Prevention of spills and accidents:* Be prepared for accidents and spills (41).

Assure that at least 2 people are present at all times if a compound in use is highly toxic or of unknown toxicity (39).

Store breakable containers of these substances in chemically resistant trays; also work and mount apparatus above such trays or cover work and storage surfaces with removable, absorbent, plastic backed paper (40).

If a major spill occurs outside the hood, evacuate the area; assure that cleanup personnel wear suitable protective apparel and equipment (41).

(g) *Waste:* Thoroughly decontaminate or incinerate contaminated clothing or shoes (41). If possible, chemically decontaminate by chemical conversion (40).

Store contaminated waste in closed, suitably labeled, impervious containers (for liquids, in glass or plastic bottles half-filled with vermiculite) (40).

4. Work with Chemicals of High Chronic Toxicity

(Examples: dimethylmercury and nickel carbonyl (48), benzo-a-pyrene (51), N-nitrosodiethylamine (54), other human carcinogens or substances with high carcinogenic potency in animals (38).)

Further supplemental rules to be followed, in addition to all these mentioned above, for work with substances of known high chronic toxicity (in quantities above a few milligrams to a few grams, depending on the substance) (47). (Procedure A of "Prudent Practices" pp. 47–50).

(a) *Access:* Conduct all transfers and work with these substances in a "controlled area": a restricted access hood, glove box, or portion of a lab, designated for use of highly toxic substances, for which all people with access are aware of the substances being used and necessary precautions (48).

(b) *Approvals:* Prepare a plan for use and disposal of these materials and obtain the approval of the laboratory supervisor (48).

(c) *Non-contamination/Decontamination:* Protect vacuum pumps against contamination by scrubbers or HEPA filters and vent them into the hood (49). Decontaminate vacuum pumps or other contaminated equipment, including glassware, in the hood before removing them from the controlled area (49, 50).

Decontaminate the controlled area before normal work is resumed there (50).

(d) *Exiting:* On leaving a controlled area, remove any protective apparel (placing it in an appropriate, labeled container) and thoroughly wash hands, forearms, face, and neck (49).

(e) *Housekeeping:* Use a wet mop or a vacuum cleaner equipped with a HEPA filter instead of dry sweeping if the toxic substance was a dry powder (50).

(f) *Medical surveillance:* If using toxicologically significant quantities of such a substance on a regular basis (*e.g.*, 3 times per week), consult a qualified physician concerning desirability of regular medical surveillance (50).

(g) *Records:* Keep accurate records of the amounts of these substances stored (229) and used, the dates of use, and names of users (48).

(h) *Signs and labels:* Assure that the controlled area is conspicuously marked with warning and restricted access signs (49) and that all containers of these substances are appropriately labeled with identity and warning labels (48).

(i) *Spills:* Assure that contingency plans, equipment, and materials to minimize exposures of people and property in case of accident are available (233–4).

(j) *Storage:* Store containers of these chemicals only in a ventilated, limited access (48, 227, 229) area in appropriately labeled, unbreakable, chemically resistant, secondary containers (48, 229).

(k) *Glove boxes:* For a negative pressure glove box, ventilation rate must be at least 2 volume changes/hour and pressure at least 0.5 inches of water (48). For a positive pressure glove box, thoroughly check for leaks before each use (49). In either case, trap the exit gases or filter them through a HEPA filter and then release them into the hood (49).

(l) *Waste:* Use chemical decontamination whenever possible; ensure that containers of contaminated waste (including washings from contaminated flasks) are transferred from the controlled area in a secondary container under the supervision of authorized personnel (49, 50, 233).

5. Animal Work with Chemicals of High Chronic Toxicity

(a) *Access:* For large scale studies, special facilities with restricted access are preferable (56).

(b) *Administration of the toxic substance:* When possible, administer the substance by injection or gavage instead of in the diet. If administration is in the diet, use a caging system under negative pressure or under laminar air flow directed toward HEPA filters (56).

(c) *Aerosol suppression:* Devise procedures which minimize formation and dispersal of contaminated aerosols, including those from

APPENDIX 4F

§ 1910.1450, App. B

food, urine, and feces (e.g., use HEPA filtered vacuum equipment for cleaning, moisten contaminated bedding before removal from the cage, mix diets in closed containers in a hood) (55, 56).

(d) *Personal protection:* When working in the animal room, wear plastic or rubber gloves, fully buttoned laboratory coat or jumpsuit and, if needed because of incomplete suppression of aerosols, other apparel and equipment (shoe and head coverings, respirator) (56).

(e) *Waste disposal:* Dispose of contaminated animal tissues and excreta by incineration if the available incinerator can convert the contaminant to non-toxic products (238); otherwise, package the waste appropriately for burial in an EPA-approved site (239).

F. Safety Recommendations

The above recommendations from "Prudent Practices" do not include those which are directed primarily toward prevention of physical injury rather than toxic exposure. However, failure of precautions against injury will often have the secondary effect of causing toxic exposures. Therefore, we list below page references for recommendations concerning some of the major categories of safety hazards which also have implications for chemical hygiene:

1. Corrosive agents: (35–6)
2. Electrically powered laboratory apparatus: (179–92)
3. Fires, explosions: (26, 57–74, 162–4, 174–5, 219–20, 226–7)
4. Low temperature procedures: (26, 88)
5. Pressurized and vacuum operations (including use of compressed gas cylinders): (27, 75–101)

G. Material Safety Data Sheets

Material safety data sheets are presented in "Prudent Practices" for the chemicals listed below. (Asterisks denote that comprehensive material safety data sheets are provided).

*Acetyl peroxide (105)
*Acrolein (106)
*Acrylonilrile (107)
Ammonia (anhydrous) (91)
*Aniline (109)
*Benzene (110)
*Benzo[a]pyrene (112)
*Bis(chloromethyl) ether (113)
Boron trichloride (91)
Boron trifluoride (92)
Bromine (114)
*Tert-butyl hydroperoxide (148)
*Carbon disulfide (116)
Carbon monoxide (92)
*Carbon tetrachloride (118)
*Chlorine (119)
Chlorine trifluoride (94)
*Chloroform (121)
Chloromethane (93)
*Diethyl ether (122)
Diisopropyl fluorophosphate (41)
*Dimethylformamide (123)
*Dimethyl sulfate (125)
*Dioxane (126)
*Ethylene dibromide (128)
*Fluorine (95)
*Formaldehyde (130)
*Hydrazine and salts (132)
Hydrofluoric acid (43)
Hydrogen bromide (98)
Hydrogen chloride (98)
*Hydrogen cyanide (133)
*Hydrogen sulfide (135)
Mercury and compounds (52)
*Methanol (137)
*Morpholine (138)
*Nickel carbonyl (99)
*Nitrobenzene (139)
Nitrogen dioxide (100)
N-nitrosodiethylamine (54)
*Peracetic acid (141)
*Phenol (142)
*Phosgene (143)
*Pyridine (144)
*Sodium azide (145)
*Sodium cyanide (147)
Sulfur dioxide (101)
*Trichloroethylene (149)
*Vinyl chloride (150)

APPENDIX B TO § 1910 1450—REFERENCES (NON-MANDATORY)

The following references are provided to assist the employer in the development of a Chemical Hygiene Plan. The materials listed below are offered as non-mandatory guidance. References listed here do not imply specific endorsement of a book, opinion, technique, policy or a specific solution for a safety or health problem. Other references not listed here may better meet the needs of a specific laboratory. (a) Materials for the development of the Chemical Hygiene Plan:

1. American Chemical Society, Safety in Academic Chemistry Laboratories, 4th edition, 1985.

2. Fawcett, H.H. and W. S. Wood, Safety and Accident Prevention in Chemical Operations, 2nd edition, Wiley-Interscience, New York, 1982.

3. Flury, Patricia A., Environmental Health and Safety in the Hospital Laboratory, Charles C. Thomas Publisher, Springfield IL, 1978.

4. Green, Michael E. and Turk, Amos, Safety in Working with Chemicals, Macmillan Publishing Co., NY, 1978.

5. Kaufman, James A., Laboratory Safety Guidelines, Dow Chemical Co., Box 1713, Midland, MI 48640, 1977.

6. National Institutes of Health, NIH Guidelines for the Laboratory use of Chemical Carcinogens, NIH Pub. No. 81-2385, GPO, Washington, DC 20402, 1981.

7. National Research Council, Prudent Practices for Disposal of Chemicals from

Occupational Safety and Health Admin., Labor § 1910.1500

Laboratories, National Academy Press, Washington, DC, 1983.

8. National Research Council, Prudent Practices for Handling Hazardous Chemicals in Laboratories, National Academy Press, Washington, DC, 1981.

9. Renfrew, Malcolm, Ed., Safety in the Chemical Laboratory, Vol. IV, *J. Chem. Ed.*, American Chemical Society, Easlon, PA, 1981.

10. Steere, Norman V., Ed., Safety in the Chemical Laboratory, *J. Chem. Ed.* American Chemical Society, Easlon, PA, 18042, Vol. I, 1967, Vol. II, 1971, Vol. III 1974.

11. Steere, Norman V., Handbook of Laboratory Safety, the Chemical Rubber Company Cleveland, OH, 1971.

12. Young, Jay A., Ed., Improving Safety in the Chemical Laboratory, John Wiley & Sons, Inc. New York, 1987.

(b) Hazardous Substances Information:

1. American Conference of Governmental Industrial Hygienists, Threshold Limit Values for Chemical Substances and Physical Agents in the Workroom Environment with Intended Changes, 6500 Glenway Avenue, Bldg. D–7 Cincinnati, OH 45211–4438 (latest edition).

2. Annual Report on Carcinogens, National Toxicology Program U.S. Department of Health and Human Services, Public Health Service. U.S. Government Printing Office, Washington, DC, (latest edition).

3. Best Company, Best Safety Directory, Vols. I and II, Oldwick, N.J., 1981.

4. Bretherick, L., Handbook of Reactive Chemical Hazards, 2nd edition, Butterworths, London, 1979.

5. Bretherick, L., Hazards in the Chemical Laboratory, 3rd edition, Royal Society of Chemistry, London, 1986.

6. Code of Federal Regulations, 29 CFR part 1910 subpart Z. U.S. Govt. Printing Office, Washington, DC 20402 (latest edition).

7. IARC Monographs on the Evaluation of the Carcinogenic Risk of Chemicals to Man, World Health Organization Publications Center, 49 Sheridan Avenue, Albany, New York 12210 (latest editions).

8. NIOSH/OSHA Pocket Guide to Chemical Hazards. NIOSH Pub. No. 85–114, U.S. Government Printing Office, Washington, DC, 1985 (or latest edition).

9. Occupational Health Guidelines, NIOSH/OSHA NIOSH Pub. No. 81–123 U.S. Government Printing Office, Washington, DC, 1981.

10. Patty, F.A., Industrial Hygiene and Toxicology, John Wiley & Sons, Inc., New York, NY (Five Volumes).

11. Registry of Toxic Effects of Chemical Substances, U.S. Department of Health and Human Services, Public Health Service, Centers for Disease Control, National Institute for Occupational Safety and Health, Revised Annually, for sale from Superintendent of Documents U.S. Govt. Printing Office, Washington, DC 20402.

12. The Merck Index: An Encyclopedia of Chemicals and Drugs. Merck and Company Inc. Rahway, N.J., 1976 (or latest edition).

13. Sax, N.I. Dangerous Properties of Industrial Materials, 5th edition, Van Nostrand Reinhold, NY., 1979.

14. Sittig, Marshall, Handbook of Toxic and Hazardous Chemicals, Noyes Publications, Park Ridge, NJ, 1981.

(c) Information on Ventilation:

1. American Conference of Governmental Industrial Hygienists Industrial Ventilation (latest edition), 6500 Glenway Avenue, Bldg. D–7, Cincinnati, Ohio 45211–4438.

2. American National Standards Institute, Inc. American National Standards Fundamentals Governing the Design and Operation of Local Exhaust Systems ANSI Z 9.2–1979 American National Standards Institute, N.Y. 1979.

3. Imad, A.P. and Watson, C.L. Ventilation Index: An Easy Way to Decide about Hazardous Liquids, Professional Safety pp 15–18, April 1980.

4. National Fire Protection Association, Fire Protection for Laboratories Using Chemicals NFPA–45, 1982.

Safety Standard for Laboratories in Health Related Institutions, NFPA, 56c, 1980.

Fire Protection Guide on Hazardous Materials, 7th edition, 1978.

National Fire Protection Association, Batterymarch Park, Quincy, MA 02269.

5. Scientific Apparatus Makers Association (SAMA), Standard for Laboratory Fume Hoods, SAMA LF7–1980, 1101 16th Street, NW., Washington, DC 20036.

(d) Information on Availability of Referenced Material:

1. American National Standards Institute (ANSI), 1430 Broadway, New York, NY 10018.

2. American Society for Testing and Materials (ASTM), 1916 Race Street, Philadelphia, PA 19103.

(Approved by the Office of Management and Budget under control number 1218–0131)

[55 FR 3327, Jan. 31, 1990; 55 FR 7967, Mar. 6, 1990; 57 FR 29204, July 1, 1992]

Appendix 5A

Workplace Injury & Illness Prevention Sample Programs

Workplace Injury & Illness Prevention Sample Programs

with sample record forms

CS-1A revised January 1993 Cal/OSHA Consultation Service
State of California—Department of Industrial Relations—Division of Occupational Safety & Health

Cal/OSHA Consultation Service Offices

Headquarters
455 Golden Gate Avenue, Room 5246
San Francisco, CA 94102

Fresno
1901 North Gateway Blvd, Suite 102
Fresno, CA 93727
Telephone (209) 454-1295

Sacramento
2424 Arden Way, Suite 410
Sacramento, CA 95825
Telephone (916) 263-2855

San Diego
7827 Convoy Court, Suite 406
San Diego, CA 92111
Telephone (619) 279-3771

San Mateo
3 Waters Park Drive, Suite 230
San Mateo, CA 94403
Telephone (415) 573-3862

Santa Fe Springs
10350 Heritage Park Drive, Suite 201
Santa Fe Springs, CA 90670
Telephone (310) 944-9366

This publication (CS-1A) can be ordered from:

Department of Industrial Relations
Cal/OSHA Publications
Post Office Box 420603
San Francisco, CA 94142-0603

State of California
Pete Wilson, Governor
Lloyd W. Aubry Jr,
Director of Industrial Relations

Table of Contents

About These Sample Programs	2
Sample Injury & Illness Prevention Program for Less Complex Operations	3
Sample Injury & Illness Prevention Program for More Complex Operations	5
Employee Communication & Compliance	10
Sample: Safety & Health Compliance Process	10
Sample: Acknowledgment of Receipt & Review of Code of Safe Practices	10
Construction Safety Orders Code of Safe Practices	11
General Industry Safety Orders Code of Safe Practices	13
General Office Code of Safe Practices	15
Report of Safety Hazard sample form	16
Hazard Evaluation & Abatement	17
Hazard Checklist sample form	17
Sample: Hazard Assessment Form	22
Sample: Hazard Abatement Record	23
Accident Investigation	24
Basic Rules for Accident Investigation	24
Accident/Exposure Investigation Report sample forms	25
Training	28
Sample: Employee Safety Checklist	28
Sample: Request for Training	29
Sample: Employee Safety Meeting Attendance	29
Employee Safety Training Verification sample form	30
Training Requirements in California Code of Regulations Title 8	31

About These Sample Programs

California Senate Bill 198 of 1989 requires every employer in the state, regardless of size or industry, to implement an Injury and Illness Prevention Program (IIPP). It must be a written plan that describes the procedures to be put into practice.

These sample programs—the first for employers whose operations are not complex, and the second for employers who require a more complex IIPP—can be used as a guide for employers to follow in developing their own specific program. The samples were assembled from a variety of plans reviewed by Cal/OSHA Consultation Service staff.

All the required elements of Title 8 (T8) Section 3203 of the *California Code of Regulations* (CCR) are addressed in both samples.

Since each sample was written for a broad spectrum of employers, it may not match your facility exactly. However, it does provide the essential framework needed to customize an Injury and Illness Prevention Program.

The format is not rigid—what is essential is that you have all the required elements in your individual program. You need to develop and carry out specific procedures to transform the sample program into an IIPP that is effective in your workplace.

We have included a sampling of forms that you are welcome to use or revise according to your own needs.

The scope of this program is limited to satisfying the employer's requirement for an IIPP. T8 CCR contains a multitude of other safety and health standards that employers need to learn about and comply with.

Also, employers who have collective bargaining relationships should note that they may have an obligation to bargain over portions of an IIPP.

If you desire further assistance, please contact one of the Cal/OSHA Consultation offices listed on the inside front cover.

2

Sample Injury & Illness Prevention Program for Less Complex Operations

Policy

_____
(Company name)
will institute and administer a comprehensive and continuous occupational Injury and Illness Prevention Program (IIPP) for all employees. The health and safety of the individual employee, whether in the field, factory or office, takes precedence over all other concerns. Management's goal is to prevent accidents, to reduce personal injury and occupational illness, and to comply with all safety and health standards.

Responsibility

The program administrator, _____
(Name)
_____, has the authority and is responsible for overall management and administration of the Injury and Illness Prevention Program. All supervisors are responsible for carrying out the IIPP in their work areas. A copy of the IIPP shall be available from each supervisor, who can answer employee questions about the program.

Employee Compliance

Employees who follow safe and healthful work practices will have this fact recognized and documented on their performance reviews.

Employees who are unaware of correct safety and health procedures will be trained or retrained (see *Training* section).

Willful violations of safe work practices (see *Safety & Health Compliance Process*) may result in disciplinary action in accordance with company policies.

Communication

Matters concerning occupational safety and health will be communicated to employees by means of written documentation, staff meetings, formal and informal training and posting.

Exception: Employers with fewer than 10 employees shall be permitted to communicate to and instruct employees orally in general safe work practices, with specific instructions regarding hazards unique to the employees' job assignments.

Communication from employees to supervisors and/or safety representatives about unsafe or unhealthy conditions is encouraged and may be verbal or written, as the employee chooses. The employee may use the *Report of Safety Hazard* form and remain anonymous.

No employee shall be retaliated against for reporting hazards or potential hazards, or for making suggestions related to safety.

The results of the investigation of any employee safety suggestion or report of hazard will be distributed to all employees affected by the hazard, or posted on appropriate bulletin boards.

Inspections

Each supervisor and/or safety representative will conduct inspections/investigations to identify unsafe work conditions and practices:

1. _____
(Frequency)
in all work areas.

2. Whenever new substances, processes, procedures or equipment introduced into the workplace present a new occupational safety and health hazard.

3. Whenever the supervisor/safety representative is made aware of a new or previously unrecognized hazard.

The *Hazard Checklist* or *Hazard Assessment Form* will be used to document these inspections/investigations.

Injury/Illness Investigation

Occupational injuries and illness will be investigated in accordance with established procedures and documented, as described in *Basic Rules for Accident Investigation*.

Correction of Unsafe or Unhealthful Conditions

Whenever an unsafe or unhealthful condition, practice or procedure is observed, discovered or reported, the program administrator or designee will take appropriate corrective measures in a timely manner based upon the severity of the hazard. Employees will be informed of the hazard, and interim protective measures taken until the hazard is corrected.

Employees may not enter an imminent hazard area without appropriate protective equipment, training, and prior specific approval given by the program administrator or designee.

Training

The program administrator or designee shall assure that supervisors receive training on recognizing the safety and health hazards to which employees under their immediate direction and control may be exposed.

Supervisors are responsible for seeing that those under their direction receive training on general workplace safety, and specific instructions regarding hazards unique to any job assignment.

This training is provided:
1. To all employees and those given new job assignments for which training was not previously received—the *Employee Safety Checklist* should be used to document this training.
2. Whenever new substances, processes, procedures or equipment introduced to the workplace present a new hazard.
3. Whenever the employer is made aware of a new or previously unrecognized hazard.

When supervisors are unable to provide the required training themselves, they should request that the training be given by others through notifying the program administrator or designee. The *Request for Training* form should be used.

(A list of specific requirements for employee instruction or training contained in Title 8 of the *California Code of Regulations* is given at the end of this guide.)

Recordkeeping

The program administrator or designee shall keep records of inspections, including the name of the person(s) conducting the inspection, the unsafe conditions and work practices identified, and action taken to correct these identified unsafe conditions and work practices. The records shall be maintained for three (3) years.

Exception: Employers with fewer than 10 employees may elect to maintain the inspection records only until the hazard is corrected.

The program administrator or designee shall also keep documentation of safety and health training attended by each employee, including employee name or other identifier, training dates, type(s) of training, and training providers. This documentation shall be maintained for three (3) years.

Exception: Employers with fewer than 10 employees can substantially comply with the documentation provision by maintaining a log of the instructions given the employee regarding hazards unique to the employee's job assignment when first hired or assigned new duties.

(The *Training* section contains a variety of sample forms for documentation of training/communication.)

APPENDIX 5A

Sample Injury & Illness Prevention Program for More Complex Operations

Policy

(Company name) believes that everyone benefits from a safe and healthful work environment. We are committed to maintaining an injury-free and illness-free workplace, and to complying with applicable laws and regulations governing workplace safety.

To achieve this goal the Company has adopted an Injury and Illness Prevention Program (IIPP). This program is everyone's responsibility as we work together to identify and eliminate conditions and practices that reduce the benefits of a safe and healthful work environment.

Responsibility

All employees are expected to work conscientiously to implement and maintain the IIPP program. _(Name)_, the program administrator, has the authority and responsibility for implementing the provisions of this program. Any questions regarding the program should be directed to the program administrator.

Senior Management

Senior management must set policy and provide leadership by participation, example, and a demonstrated interest in the program.

Responsibilities include:
- developing policy
- allocating adequate resources
- ensuring responsibility
- reviewing and evaluating results.

IIPP Program Administrator

The program administrator is responsible for ensuring that all provisions of the IIPP are implemented.

Responsibilities include:
- advising senior management on safety and health policy issues
- maintaining current information on local, state and federal safety and health regulations
- acting as liaison with government agencies
- planning, organizing and coordinating safety training
- preparing and distributing company policies and procedures on workplace safety and health issues
- developing a code of safe practices and inspection guidelines
- arranging safety and health inspections and followup to ensure that necessary corrective action is completed
- making sure that an adequate supply of personal protective equipment is available
- establishing accident report and investigation procedures, and maintaining injury and illness records (OSHA log 200)
- reviewing injury and illness trends
- establishing a system for maintaining records of inspection, hazard abatement, and training.

Supervisors

Supervisors are responsible for ensuring that employees know and abide by the Company policy and procedures on safety. They are expected to do everything within their control to assure a safe workplace in their area.

Responsibilities include:
- keeping abreast of safety and health regulations affecting operations they supervise
- ensuring that each subordinate is able to and understands how to complete each assigned task safely
- conducting on-the-job safety training of those they supervise

- advising the program administrator of training needs of subordinates
- making sure equipment and machines are in safe operating condition
- ascertaining that subordinates follow safe work practices and health regulations
- ensuring that employees under their direction wear required protective equipment
- correcting unsafe and unhealthful conditions within their power
- investigating accidents to discover cause(s) and identifying corrective action to prevent future occurrences
- conducting periodic inspections of their work areas according to the appropriate inspection checklist(s).

Compliance

Management is responsible for ensuring that Company safety and health policies and procedures are clearly communicated and understood by all employees. Managers and supervisors are expected to enforce the rules fairly and uniformly.

All employees are responsible for using safe work practices, for following all directives, policies and procedures, and for assisting in maintaining a safe work environment.

As part of an employee's regular performance review, the employee will be evaluated on his/her compliance with safe work practices.

Employees who make a significant contribution to the maintenance of a safe workplace, as determined by the program administrator, will receive written acknowledgment that is maintained in the employee's personnel file.

Employees who are unaware of correct safety and health procedures will be trained or retrained (see *Training* section).

Employees who deliberately fail to follow safe work practices and/or procedures, or who violate the Company's safety rules or directives, will be subject to disciplinary action, up to and including termination (see *Safety & Health Compliance Process*).

Communication

The Company recognizes that open, two-way communication between management and staff on health and safety issues is essential to an injury-free, productive workplace. The following system of communication is designed to facilitate a continuous flow of safety and health information between management and staff in a form that is readily understandable.

1. The new-employee orientation will include review of the Company's IIPP and a discussion of policy and procedures that the employee is expected to follow (see *Employee Communication & Compliance* section).

2. The Company will schedule a time at general employee meetings when safety is freely and openly discussed by all present. Such meetings will be regularly scheduled and announced to all employees, so that maximum participation can occur.

3. From time to time, the Company will post and/or distribute written safety notifications. Employees should check Company bulletin boards regularly for such posting(s).

Safety-related memos and documents are to be read promptly. Questions about the meaning or implementation of this information should be directed to the supervisor.

4. Other methods of communicating pertinent health and safety information include electronic mail or a safety committee.

5. All employees are encouraged to inform their supervisor, the program administrator or designee of any matter which they perceive to be a workplace hazard and/or a potential workplace hazard. Employees are also encouraged to make safety suggestions and safety training suggestions.

If an employee so wishes, he/she may make such notification anonymously by depositing it in the program administrator's mailbox. A *Report of Safety Hazard* form may be used by the employee.

6. *No employee shall be retaliated against for reporting hazards or potential hazards, or for making suggestions related to safety.*

APPENDIX 5A

7. All suggestions will be reviewed by the program administrator or designee, who will initiate an investigation of each report of a hazard, potential hazard or safety suggestion in accordance with Company procedures for hazard control.

8. Any directives issued as a result of the investigation shall be distributed to all employees affected by the hazard, or shall be posted on appropriate bulletin boards.

Workplace Hazard Evaluation and Abatement

Hazard control is the heart of an effective IIPP program. The Company's hazard control procedure is: identify hazards that exist or develop in the workplace, describe how to correct those hazards, and initiate steps to prevent their recurrence.

Assessment of Hazards

Inspection of the workplace is our primary tool used to identify unsafe conditions and practices. While we encourage all employees to continuously identify and correct hazards and poor safety practices, certain situations require formal evaluation and documentation.

Along with each inspection/investigation, the program administrator or designee shall evaluate the severity of the hazard identified, and if it can not be abated immediately, suggest priority for corrective action. The *Hazard Checklist* or *Hazard Assessment Form* is to be used to document inspections/investigations.

The program administrator or designee will conduct an inspection or investigation whenever any of the following occur:

1. Routinely in each work area, ——————————— the time and frequency of (daily, monthly, weekly) inspection will be set by the program administrator or designee according to the type of work being performed in each worksite.

Prior to the periodic inspection, the inspector should review workplace injury reports and inspection reports which have been filed since the last investigation or inspection.

The *Hazard Checklist* for the appropriate work area is to be used by the inspector(s).

2. The introduction of new substances, processes, procedures or equipment present a new safety/health hazard.

Each supervisor is responsible for promptly reporting to the program administrator or designee whenever a new substance (such as a chemical or solvent), new work procedure or technique, and/or new equipment is introduced which may pose a safety risk. A *Report of Safety Hazard* form shall be used by the supervisor.

Each supervisor's report should include an evaluation of the potential hazard(s), training and/or other steps to be taken to provide abatement solutions for any potential hazard(s).

Based upon the information, the program administrator or designee will conduct an inspection and issue any directive that may be necessary.

3. The program administrator becomes aware of a new or previously unrecognized hazard, either independently or by receipt of information from an employee, including receipt of a *Report of Safety Hazard* form.

4. An occupational injury, occupational illness, or near-miss accident occurs (see *Accident Investigation* section).

5. From time to time, the program administrator or designee may conduct unannounced inspections.

All investigations and findings shall be fully documented on the *Hazard Assessment Form* and filed as directed in *Recordkeeping*.

Abatement of Hazards

It is the Company's intention to eliminate all hazards and unsafe work practices immediately. Some corrective actions require more time. Priority will be given to severe and imminent hazards.

The *Hazard Checklist / Hazard Assessment* forms completed during the inspection/investigation will be used by the program administrator or designee to describe measures taken to abate the hazard or correct the unsafe work practice. Actions to be taken may include, but are not limited to:
- fixing or replacing defective equipment
- implementing safer procedures
- installing guards, modifying equipment
- employee training
- posting warning notices.

All such actions taken and the dates they are completed shall be documented on the appropriate forms.

When corrective action involves multiple steps or cannot be completed promptly, an action plan needs to be developed. The *Hazard Abatement Record* is to be used for this purpose and filed as directed in *Recordkeeping*.

While corrective action is in progress, necessary precautions are to be taken to protect or remove employees from exposure to the hazard.

Employees shall not enter an imminent hazard area without prior specific approval of the program administrator or designee. Employees expected to correct the imminent hazard shall be properly trained and provided with necessary safeguards.

Accident Investigation

The purpose of an accident investigation is to find the cause of an accident and prevent further occurrences—not to assign blame.

A thorough and properly completed accident investigation is necessary to obtain facts. The investigation should focus on causes and hazards. Analysis of what happened and why it happened is aimed at determining how it can be prevented in the future.

Injury and Illness

The occurrence of an occupational injury and/or illness precipitates a document called *Employer's Report of Injury*. This report is completed by the injured employee's supervisor, and a copy of the report is to be sent to the program administrator or designee within 24 hours of the occurrence. Upon receipt, the program administrator:

1. Reports fatalities and serious injuries or illness ***immediately*** by phone or FAX to the nearest office of the Division of Occupational Safety and Health (CCR Title 8, Section 342).

2. Investigates the incident by visiting the site and interviewing the victim and witnesses.

Accidents

The majority of accidents do not cause injury or illness, yet result in property damage and/or lost time. Such mishaps usually indicate an unsafe act, faulty procedure or hidden hazard. Investigations of these occurrences are conducted at the discretion of the supervisor, program administrator or designee.

All investigation facts, findings and recommendations shall be fully documented on the *Accident/Exposure Investigation Report* form. This report is filed in accordance with the instructions in *Recordkeeping*.

Training

Training is essential to maximizing the skills and knowledge of employees. It is the key to productivity.

The Company has a duty to include safety as an integral part of employee training. Employees need to work safely as well as productively and efficiently. The supervisor is the essential link in ensuring the proper outcome.

Supervisors must know how to perform a designated job, and be aware of safety and health hazards facing employees under their immediate supervision. Supervisors are responsible for ensuring that they themselves and those under their direction receive training on general workplace safety, as well as on safety and health issues specific to each job.

With this in mind, training will be conducted with the following considerations:

Supervisors

The program administrator or designee will consult with department administrators

APPENDIX 5A

or supervisors to determine training topics and needs of supervisors—these include human relations, trainer skills, production/process skills, and familiarization with hazards and risks faced by employees.

Supervisors who recognize their own need for training are encouraged to submit a direct request for training in any area in which they feel deficient.

Employees

Supervisors are expected to assess training needs of all employees under their direction. They are to train those they supervise in general workplace safety and give them specific instructions regarding hazards unique to any job assignment, to the extent that such information was not already covered in other trainings (see *Employee Safety Checklist*).

The Company recognizes that continuing safety and health training is needed for:

1. Employees given a job assignment for which they have not previously received training. If the position is supervisory, such training shall include familiarization with hazards and risks faced by the employees under the supervisor's direction.

2. Whenever new substances, processes, procedures or equipment pose a new hazard.

3. Whenever the supervisor, program administrator or designee becomes aware of a previously unrecognized hazard.

4. All employees in periodic refresher safety training involving general workplace safety, job-specific hazards, and/or hazardous materials as applicable.

All training shall be documented on one of the training record forms and filed as directed in *Recordkeeping*. (A list of specific requirements for employee instruction or training contained in Title 8 of the *California Code of Regulations* is given at the end of this guide.)

Recordkeeping

No operation can be successful without recordkeeping that enables the Company to learn from past experience and make corrections for future operations. In addition, the IIPP regulation requires records to be kept of the steps taken to establish and maintain the Company's Injury and Illness Prevention Program.

Injury and Illness Prevention Program Records

Each supervisor will maintain an updated copy of the Company's IIPP. The program administrator will retain the following records on file for at least three (3) years:

- master copy of IIPP, changes/updates
- documents verifying that the Company has maintained ongoing two-way communication with employees, such as —

  —memos, letters to employees on safety and health issues

  —new employee safety orientation session acknowledgment form

  —employee suggestions and Company response

- all records of inspections/investigations—including date, name of person who performed the inspection/investigation, unsafe conditions and work practices identified, corrective action taken and date of correction—forms covered in this category include:

  —*Report of Safety Hazard*

  —*Hazard Checklist*

  —*Hazard Assessment Form*

  —*Hazard Abatement Record*

  —*Accident/Exposure Investigation Report*

- records of safety and health training received by employees—containing the employee's name, training date, type of training and identification of trainer—examples are:

  —*Employee Safety Meeting Attendance*

  —*Employee Safety Checklist*

  —*Employee Safety Training Verification*

Employee Communication & Compliance

Sample :

Safety & Health Compliance Process

Disciplinary measures are progressive and involve four steps:

1. Should a safety and health violation be noted, the supervisor is to informally discuss the behavior with the employee—stating the potential dangerous result and outlining the correct procedure—then to retrain the employee to ensure understanding.

2. A second violation should generate either a formal verbal warning or a written warning to the employee, depending on the severity of the violation.

3. A third infraction results in a formal written warning or employee suspension.

4. A fourth violation may lead to employee termination.

These suggested disciplinary measures should be reviewed in the context of any collective bargaining agreement which may exist.

Sample :

Acknowledgment of Receipt & Review of Code of Safe Practices

TO ALL EMPLOYEES:

Attached is a copy of the code of safe practices. These guidelines are provided for your safety.

It is the responsibility of

_____
(Name)
to provide and review this code with each employee.

It is the employee's responsibility to read and comply with this code.

The attached copy of the code of safe practices is for you to keep.

Please sign and date below and return *only* this page to:

_____
(Name)

I have read and understand the code of safe practices.

Date _____

Signed _____
(Employee)

10

APPENDIX 5A

Employee Communication & Compliance

Construction Safety Orders
Code of Safe Practices

This is a suggested format, general in nature, intended as a basis for preparing a code of safe practices that is tailored to fit the contractor's operations.

General

1. All persons shall follow these safe practices rules, render every possible aid to safe operations, and report all unsafe conditions or practices to the foreman or superintendent.

2. Foremen shall insist on employees observing and obeying every applicable Company, state or federal regulation and order necessary to the safe conduct of the work, and take action as necessary to obtain compliance.

3. All employees shall be given frequent accident prevention instruction. Instruction shall be given at least every 10 working days.

4. Anyone known to be under the influence of drugs or intoxicating substances, which impair the employee's ability to safely perform assigned duties, shall not be allowed on the job while in that condition.

5. Horseplay, scuffling, or other acts that tend to adversely influence the safety or well-being of the employees shall be prohibited.

6. Work shall be well planned and supervised to prevent injuries in materials handling and working together with equipment.

7. No employees shall knowingly be permitted or required to work while their ability or alertness is so impaired by fatigue, illness, or other causes that they might unnecessarily expose themselves or others to injury.

8. Employees shall not enter manholes, underground vaults, chambers, tanks, silos, or other similar places receiving little ventilation, unless these places are determined safe to enter.

9. Employees shall be instructed to ensure that all guards and other protective devices are in the proper places and adjusted, and shall report deficiencies promptly to the foreman or superintendent.

10. Crowding or pushing when boarding or leaving any vehicle or other conveyance shall be prohibited.

11. Workers shall not handle or tamper with any electrical equipment, machinery, or air or water lines in a manner not within the scope of their duties, unless they receive instructions from their foreman.

12. All injuries shall be reported promptly to the foreman or superintendent so arrangements can be made for medical or first aid treatment.

13. When lifting heavy objects, the large muscles of the leg instead of the smaller muscles of the back shall be used.

14. Inappropriate footwear or shoes with thin or badly worn soles must not be worn.

15. Materials, tools, or other objects shall not be thrown from buildings or structures until proper precautions are taken to protect others from the falling objects.

16. Employees shall cleanse themselves thoroughly after handling hazardous substances, and follow special instructions from authorized sources.

17. Hod carriers should avoid using extension ladders when carrying loads. Though such ladders may provide adequate strength, the

rung position and rope arrangement make climbing difficult and hazardous for this trade.

18. Work shall be arranged so that employees are able to face a ladder and use both hands while climbing.

19. Gasoline shall not be used for cleaning purposes.

20. No burning, welding, or other source of ignition shall be applied to any enclosed tank or vessel, even if there are some openings, until it has first been determined that no possibility of explosion exists, and authority for the work is obtained from the foreman or superintendent.

21. Any damage to scaffolds, falsework, or other supporting structures shall be immediately reported to the foreman and repaired before use.

Use of Tools & Equipment

22. All tools and equipment shall be maintained in good condition.

23. Damaged tools or equipment shall be removed from service and tagged "DEFECTIVE."

24. Pipe or Stillson wrenches shall not be used as a substitute for other wrenches.

25. Only appropriate tools shall be used for a specific job.

26. Wrenches shall not be altered by the addition of handle-extensions or "cheaters."

27. Files shall be equipped with handles and not used to punch or pry.

28. Screwdrivers shall not be used as chisels.

29. Wheelbarrows shall not be pushed with handles in an upright position.

30. Portable electric tools shall not be lifted or lowered by means of the power cord. Ropes shall be used.

31. Electric cords shall not be exposed to damage by vehicles.

32. In locations where using a portable power tool is difficult, the tool shall be supported by means of a rope or similar support of adequate strength.

Machinery & Vehicles

33. Only authorized persons shall operate machinery or equipment.

34. Loose or frayed clothing, long hair, dangling ties, or finger rings shall not be worn around moving machinery or other places where they may become entangled.

35. Machinery shall not be serviced, repaired or adjusted while in operation, nor shall oiling of moving parts be attempted, except on equipment designed or fitted with safeguards to protect the person performing the work.

36. Where appropriate, lock-out procedures shall be used.

37. Employees shall not work under vehicles supported by jacks or chain hoists without protective blocking to prevent injury if jacks or hoists should fail.

38. Air hoses shall not be disconnected at compressors until the hose line has been bled.

39. All excavations shall be visually inspected before backfilling to ensure that it is safe to backfill.

40. Excavating equipment shall not be operated near tops of cuts, banks, or cliffs if employees are working below.

41. Tractors, bulldozers, scrapers and carryalls shall not operate where there is a possibility of overturning in dangerous areas like edges of deep fills, cut banks and steep slopes.

42. When loading where there is a probability of dangerous slides or movement of material, the wheels or treads of loading equipment, other than that riding on rails, should be turned in the direction which will facilitate escape in case of danger, except in a situation where this position of the wheels or treads would cause a greater operational hazard.

12

Employee Communication & Compliance

General Industry Safety Orders Code of Safe Practices

This is a suggested format, general in nature, intended as a basis for preparing a code of safe practices that is tailored to fit the employer's operations.

It is our policy that everything possible will be done to protect employees, customers and visitors from accidents. Safety is a cooperative undertaking that requires participation by every employee. Failure by any employee to comply with safety rules will be grounds for corrective discipline. Supervisors shall insist that employees observe all applicable Company, state and federal safety rules and practices, and take action as necessary to obtain compliance.

To carry out this policy:

1. Employees shall report all unsafe conditions and equipment to the supervisor or safety coordinator.

2. Employees shall report immediately all accidents, injuries and illnesses to the supervisor or safety coordinator.

3. Anyone known to be under the influence of intoxicating liquor or drugs shall not be allowed on the job while in that condition.

4. Horseplay, scuffling, or other acts that tend to adversely influence the safety or well-being of the employees are prohibited.

5. Means of egress shall be kept unblocked, well lighted and unlocked during work hours.

6. In the event of fire, sound the alarm and evacuate.

7. Upon hearing a fire alarm, stop work and proceed to the nearest clear exit. Gather at the designated location.

8. Only workers trained for it may attempt to respond to a fire or other emergency.

9. Exit doors must comply with fire safety regulations during business hours.

10. Keep stairways clear of items that can be tripped over. All areas under stairways that are egress routes should not be used to store combustibles.

11. Materials and equipment will not be stored against doors or exits, fire ladders or fire extinguisher stations.

12. Aisles must be kept clear at all times.

13. Work areas should be maintained in a neat, orderly manner. Throw trash and refuse into proper waste containers.

14. All spills shall be wiped up promptly.

15. Always use the correct lifting technique. Never attempt to lift or push an object that is too heavy. Contact the supervisor when help is needed to move a heavy object.

16. Never stack material precariously on top of lockers, file cabinets or other high places.

17. When carrying objects, use caution in watching for and avoiding obstructions or loose material.

18. Do not stack material in an unstable manner.

19. Report exposed wiring and cords that are frayed or have deteriorated insulation, so that they can be repaired promptly.

20. Never use a metal ladder where it could come in contact with energized parts of equipment, fixtures or circuit conductors.

21. Maintain sufficient access and working space around all electrical equipment for ready and safe operations and maintenance.

22. Do not use any portable electrical equipment or tools that are not grounded or double insulated.

23. Plug all electrical equipment into appropriate wall receptacles, or into an extension of only one cord of similar size and capacity. Three-pronged plugs should be used to ensure continuity of ground.

24. All cords running into walk areas must be taped down or inserted through rubber protectors to prevent tripping hazards.

25. Inspect motorized vehicles and other mechanized equipment daily or prior to use.

26. Shut off engine, set brakes and block wheels prior to loading or unloading vehicles.

27. Inspect pallets and their loads for integrity and stability before loading or moving.

28. Do not store compressed gas cylinders in areas that are exposed to heat sources, electric arcs or high temperature lines.

29. Do not use compressed air for cleaning off clothing unless pressure is less than 10 psi.

30. Identify contents of pipelines prior to initiating any work that affects the integrity of the pipe.

31. Wear hearing protection in all areas identified as having high noise exposure.

32. Goggles or face shields must be worn when grinding.

33. Do not use any faulty or worn hand tools.

34. Guard floor openings by a cover, guardrail, or equivalent.

35. Do not enter into a confined space unless tests for toxic substances, explosive concentrations, and oxygen deficiency have been taken.

36. Always keep flammable or toxic chemicals in closed containers when not in use.

37. Do not eat in areas where hazardous chemicals are present.

38. Be aware of potential hazards involving various chemicals stored or used in the workplace.

39. Cleaning supplies should be stored away from edible items on kitchen shelves.

40. Store cleaning solvents and flammable liquids in appropriate containers.

41. Keep solutions that may be poisonous or are not intended for consumption in well labeled containers.

42. When working with a VDT, have all furniture adjusted, positioned and arranged to minimize strain on all parts of the body.

43. Never leave lower desk or cabinet drawers open, a tripping hazard. Use care when opening and closing drawers to avoid pinching fingers.

44. Do not open more than one upper drawer at a time, particularly the top two drawers on tall file cabinets.

45. Keep individual heaters at work areas clear of combustible materials such as drapes or waste from wastebaskets. Use newer heaters that are equipped with tip-over switches.

46. Keep appliances such as coffeepots or microwave ovens in working order and inspect them for signs of wear, heat or frayed cords.

47. Fans used in work areas should be guarded, and guards must not allow fingers to be inserted through the mesh. Newer fans are equipped with proper guards.

14

APPENDIX 5A

Employee Communication & Compliance

General Office Code of Safe Practices

This is a suggested format, general in nature, intended as a basis for preparing a code of safe practices that is tailored to fit the employer's operations.

It is our policy that everything possible will be done to protect employees, customers and visitors from accidents. Safety is a cooperative undertaking that requires participation by every employee. Failure by any employee to comply with safety rules will be grounds for corrective discipline. Supervisors shall insist that employees observe all applicable Company, state and federal safety rules and practices, and take action as necessary to obtain compliance.

To carry out this policy:

1. Employees shall report all unsafe conditions and equipment to the supervisor or safety coordinator.

2. Employees shall report immediately all accidents, injuries and illnesses to the supervisor or safety coordinator.

3. Means of egress shall be kept unblocked, well lighted and unlocked during work hours.

4. In the event of fire, sound the alarm and evacuate.

5. Upon hearing a fire alarm, stop work and proceed to the nearest clear exit. Gather at the designated location.

6. Only workers trained for it may attempt to respond to a fire or other emergency.

7. Exit doors must comply with fire safety regulations during business hours.

8. Keep stairways clear of items that can be tripped over. All areas under stairways that are egress routes should not be used to store combustibles.

9. Do not store materials and equipment against doors or exits, fire ladders or fire extinguisher stations.

10. Keep aisles clear at all times.

11. Maintain work areas in a neat, orderly manner. Throw trash and refuse into proper waste containers.

12. Wipe up all spills promptly.

13. Store files and supplies in a manner that prevents damage to supplies or injury to personnel when they are moved. Store heaviest items closest to the floor and lightweight items above.

14. All cords running into walk areas must be taped down or inserted through rubber protectors to prevent tripping hazards.

15. Never stack material precariously on top of lockers, file cabinets or other high places.

16. Never leave lower desk or cabinet drawers open, a tripping hazard. Use care when opening and closing drawers to avoid pinching fingers.

17. Do not open more than one upper drawer at a time, particularly the top two drawers on tall file cabinets.

18. Always use the correct lifting technique. Never attempt to lift or push an object that is too heavy. Contact the supervisor when help is needed to move a heavy object.

19. When carrying objects, use caution in watching for and avoiding obstructions or loose material.

20. Plug all electrical equipment into appropriate wall receptacles, or into an extension of only one cord of similar size and capacity. Three-pronged plugs should be used to ensure continuity of ground.

21. Keep individual heaters at work areas clear of combustible materials such as drapes or waste from wastebaskets. Use newer heaters that are equipped with tip-over switches.

22. Keep appliances such as coffeepots or microwave ovens in working order and inspect them for signs of wear, heat or frayed cords.

23. Fans used in work areas should be guarded, and guards must not allow fingers to be inserted through the mesh. Newer fans are equipped with proper guards.

24. Use equipment such as scissors or staplers for their intended purposes only, and do not misuse them as hammers, pry bars, screwdrivers. Misuse can cause damage to the equipment and possible injury to the user.

25. Store cleaning supplies away from edible items on kitchen shelves.

26. Store cleaning solvents and flammable liquids in appropriate containers.

27. Keep solutions that may be poisonous or are not intended for consumption in well labeled containers.

Employee Communication & Compliance

Report of Safety Hazard

Name (optional)		Date	Year	Number
			Supervisor's Name	

Describe Substance, Equipment, Process, Practice or Workplace Condition	Health and/or Safety Hazard	Suggestions for Minimizing or Abating Hazard — or for Training	Action

Make additional copies of this form as needed.

APPENDIX 5A

Hazard Evaluation & Abatement

Hazard Checklist		**Company/Entity Name & Location**
Inspected by	**Date**	

Rating evaluations: S=Satisfactory   U=Unsatisfactory   NA=Not applicable
If Unsatisfactory, prioritize by severity:
U1=Immediate   U2=Within 48 hours   U3=Within 2 weeks   U4=Abatement plan needed

Checklist Item	S	U	NA	Corrective Action Taken & Date
Employer Posting				
Is the Cal/OSHA poster "Safety and Health Protection on the Job" displayed in a prominent location where all employees are likely to see it?				
Are emergency telephone numbers posted where they can be easily found in case of emergency?				
Where employees may be exposed to any toxic substances or harmful physical agents, has appropriate information on employee access to medical and exposure records and Material Safety Data Sheets been posted or otherwise made easily available?				
Are signs posted where appropriate to inform of building exits, room capacities, floor loading, and exposure to x-ray, microwave, or other harmful radiation or substances?				
Are other California posters properly displayed— • Industrial Welfare Commission orders regulating wages, hours, and working conditions?				
• Discrimination in employment prohibited by law?				
• Notice to employees of unemployment and disability insurance?				
• Payday notice?				
Emergency Action Plan				
Are alarm systems properly maintained and tested regularly?				
Is the emergency action plan reviewed and revised periodically?				
Do employees know their responsibilities— • For reporting emergencies?				
• During an emergency?				
• For conducting rescue and medical duties?				

Make additional copies of this form as needed.

17

Hazard Evaluation & Abatement

Hazard Checklist			Company/Entity Name & Location		
Inspected by		**Date**			

Rating evaluations: S=Satisfactory   U=Unsatisfactory   NA=Not applicable
If Unsatisfactory, prioritize by severity:
U1=Immediate U2=Within 48 hours U3=Within 2 weeks U4=Abatement plan needed

Checklist Item	S	U	NA	Corrective Action Taken & Date
Fire Protection				
Do you have a fire prevention plan?				
Does your plan describe the type of fire protection equipment and/or system?				
Have you established practices and procedures to control potential fire hazards and ignition sources?				
Is your local fire department well acquainted with your facilities, location and specific hazards?				
If you have a fire alarm system, is it certified as required?				
If you have a fire alarm system, is it tested at least annually?				
Are fire doors and shutters in good operating condition?				
Are automatic sprinkler system water control valves, air and water pressures checked weekly/periodically as required?				
Is maintenance of automatic sprinkler systems assigned to responsible persons, or to a sprinkler contractor?				

Make additional copies of this form as needed.

18

Hazard Evaluation & Abatement

Hazard Checklist		**Company/Entity Name & Location**
Inspected by	**Date**	

Rating evaluations: S=Satisfactory   U=Unsatisfactory   NA=Not applicable
If Unsatisfactory, prioritize by severity:
U1=Immediate   U2=Within 48 hours   U3=Within 2 weeks   U4=Abatement plan needed

Checklist Item	S	U	NA	Corrective Action Taken & Date
Exiting or Egress				
Are all exits marked with an exit sign and illuminated by a reliable light source?				
Are the directions to exits, when not immediately apparent, marked with visible signs?				
Are doors, passageways or stairways, which are neither exits nor access to exits, and which could be mistaken for exits, appropriately marked "NOT AN EXIT", "TO BASEMENT", "STOREROOM", or in such a way that they will not be mistaken for exits?				
Are all exits kept free of obstructions?				
Are there sufficient exits to permit prompt escape in case of emergency?				
Are special precautions taken to protect employees during construction and repair operations?				
Where exiting will be through frameless glass doors or glass exit doors, are the doors of fully tempered glass and do they meet the safety requirements for human impact?				

Make additional copies of this form as needed.

19

Hazard Evaluation & Abatement

Hazard Checklist

Inspected by	Date	Company/Entity Name & Location

Rating evaluations: S=Satisfactory   U=Unsatisfactory   NA=Not applicable
If Unsatisfactory, prioritize by severity:
U1=Immediate   U2=Within 48 hours   U3=Within 2 weeks   U4=Abatement plan needed

Checklist Item	S	U	NA	Corrective Action Taken & Date
General Work Environment Are all worksites clean and orderly?				
Are work surfaces kept dry, or appropriate means taken to assure the surfaces are slip-resistant?				
Are all spilled materials or liquids cleaned up immediately?				
Are the minimum number of toilets and washing facilities provided?				
Are all toilets and washing facilities clean and sanitary?				
Are all work areas adequately illuminated?				
Walkways Are aisles and passageways kept clear?				
Are aisles and walkways marked as appropriate?				
Are wet surfaces covered with non-slip materials?				
Are holes in the floor, sidewalk or other walking surface repaired properly, covered or otherwise made safe?				

Make additional copies of this form as needed.

20

APPENDIX 5A

Hazard Evaluation & Abatement

Hazard Checklist

| Inspected by | Date | Company/Entity Name & Location |

Rating evaluations: S=Satisfactory U=Unsatisfactory NA=Not applicable
If Unsatisfactory, prioritize by severity:
U1=Immediate U2=Within 48 hours U3=Within 2 weeks U4=Abatement plan needed

Checklist Item	S	U	NA	Corrective Action Taken & Date
Medical Services & First Aid				
If medical and first aid facilities are not in proximity of your workplace, is at least one employee on each shift currently qualified to render first aid?				
Are medical personnel readily available for advice and consultation on matters of employee health?				
Are emergency phone numbers posted?				
Are first aid kits easily accessible to each work area, with necessary supplies available, periodically inspected and replenished as needed?				
Have first aid kit supplies been approved by a physician, indicating they are adequate for a particular area or operation?				
Miscellaneous (Note to Employer/Inspector: Please add applicable questions below.)				

Make additional copies of this form as needed.

Hazard Evaluation & Abatement

Sample :

Hazard Assessment Form
Investigation/Inspection & Abatement Record

Date of Investigation/Inspection

Reason for Inspection:

☐ New Equipment/Substance
Explain:

☐ New Process
Explain:

☐ New or Revised Procedure
Explain:

Name of Person(s) Conducting Investigation:

Name of Person(s) Consulted:

Description of Investigation: (attach additional sheets as necessary)

Findings—Including Identification of Hazard & Severity: (attach additional sheets as necessary)

Steps Taken to Abate Hazard & Date of These Steps: (attach additional sheets as necessary)

22

APPENDIX 5A

Hazard Evaluation & Abatement

Sample :

Hazard Abatement Record

Safety/Health items identified during ―――(Date)――― inspection/investigation will be submitted to ―――(Name)――― for review, and an action plan will be developed to resolve each specific safety/health item (such as hazards, needed policies) by a fixed completion date, and by those assigned responsibility. This form will be used to document identified problems, steps to be taken, and completion deadline.

Overall Action Plan

Major action steps to be taken:	Priority assign each step a number	Projected Completion Date	Date Completed
1.			
2.			
3.			
4.			
5.			

Accident Investigation

Basic Rules for Accident Investigation

Every employer shall report *immediately* — within 24 hours—by telephone or telegraph to the nearest district office of the California Division of Occupational Safety and Health—any serious injury or illness or death of an employee, occuring in a place of employment or in connection with any employment (see CCR Title 8, Section 342).

- The purpose of an investigation is to find the cause of an accident and prevent further occurrences, *not* to fix blame. An unbiased approach is necessary for obtaining objective findings.

- Visit the accident scene as soon as possible while the facts are fresh, and before witnesses forget important details.

- If possible, interview the injured worker at the scene of the accident and "walk" him or her through a mock re-enactment.

- All interviews should be conducted as privately as possible. Interview witnesses one at a time. Talk with everyone who has knowledge of the accident, even if they did not actually witness it.

- Consider taking signed statements in cases where facts are unclear or there is an element of controversy.

- Document details graphically. Use sketches, diagrams and photos as needed, and take measurements when appropriate.

- Focus on causes and hazards. Develop an analysis of what happened, how it happened and how it could have been prevented. Determine what caused the accident itself, not just the injury.

- Every investigation should include an action plan. How will you prevent such accidents in the future?

- If a third party or defective product contributed to the accident, save any evidence. It could be critical to the recovery of claims costs.

APPENDIX 5A

Accident Investigation

Accident/Exposure Investigation Report

Company	**Date**
Investigation Team	
Employee's Name & ID	
Sex Age Job Description	
Department & Location	
Accident Date & Time	
Date & Time Accident Reported to Supervisor	
Nature of Incident	
Nature of Injury	
Referred to Medical Facility/Doctor Yes No	
Employee Returned to Work Yes Date/Time No	
Injured Employee Interview/Statement—Attached	
Witnesses	
Witnesses Interviews/Statements—Attached	
Photographs of Site—Attached	
Diagrams of Site—Attached	
Equipment Records—Attached—Reviewed Yes No	
Accident/Exposure Incident Description	

Make additional copies of this form as needed. (form provided courtesy of Safety Publications of California © 1990)

25

Accident Investigation

Accident/Exposure Investigation Report

Accident Description

Date & Time **Location**

Employees Involved

Preventive Action Recommendations

Corrective Actions Completed	Manager Responsible	Date Completed

—Employee Lost Time—Temporary Help—Cleanup—Repair—Discussion—

Accident Cost Analysis	Investigation	Compliance	Total Cost
Medical			
Production Loss			

Report Prepared By	**Date Completed**
Safety Committee Review Yes	No
Corrective Action	Date Started
Safety Communication Notice Prepared	Date
Safety Director Signature	

Make additional copies of this form as needed. (form provided courtesy of Safety Publications of California © 1990)

26

APPENDIX 5A

Accident Investigation

Accident/Exposure Investigation Report

Accident Description

Date & Time   **Location**

Employees Involved

Employee Interview/Statement—Injured Employee—Witness

Employee Name

Interviewed By

Accident Diagram/Photographs

Make additional copies of this form as needed. (form provided courtesy of Safety Publications of California © 1990)

Training

Sample :

Employee Safety Checklist

This report is to be completed by the supervisor and new or reassigned employee within _____ days after employment or reassignment and filed with _____.
_(Name)

Employee Name

_____
(print)   First   Middle   Last Name)

Date Employed or Reassigned	Date Checklist Completed

Department Assigned _____

Type of Work _____

Outline employee's past work experience
_____
_____

Ask employee: Do you have any physical conditions or handicaps which might limit your ability to perform this job? If so, what reasonable accommodation can be made by us?

Did employee have a pre-placement physical?
Yes ____ No ____
If yes, any work restrictions indicated? _____

The supervisor and new employee are to review the following safety concerns, check and discuss those which apply:

☐ Applicable Company, state and federal safety policies and programs
☐ Applicable Company, state and federal safety rules, general and specific to job assignment
☐ Company safety rule enforcement procedures
☐ Company policy on medical treatment for work-related injuries
☐ Use of tools and equipment
☐ Proper guarding of equipment

☐ Proper work shoes and other personal protective equipment, as needed
☐ Handling of product
☐ Use of specific lifting equipment, such as hoists, hand truck
☐ How, when and where to report injuries
☐ Importance of housekeeping
☐ Special hazards of job
☐ When and where to report unsafe conditions
☐ Emergency procedures
☐ Employee responsibility for the prevention of accidents
☐ Training on any toxic material which employee might be exposed to
☐ Fire safety
☐ Safe operation of vehicle(s)
☐ Employee is to receive special additional instruction and guidance
☐ Supervisor will adequately and frequently review performance of new employee: superior behavior will be rewarded, substandard behavior will be corrected
☐ Probationary period
☐ Supervisor will formally review employee's performance on (mark calendar)
☐ Employee agrees to fully cooperate with the safety efforts of the employer, follow all safety rules and use good judgment concerning safe work behavior

Supervisor signature	Employee signature

28

APPENDIX 5A

Training

Sample :

Request for Training

Employees must be given safety training on the performance of their duties.

Name _____

Department _____

The employee has been given the safety indoctrination, advised of Company safety rules, and needs additional training indicated below:

Training Topic	Must be Trained by Date	Date Training Completed	Initials Trainer	Employee

Sample :

Employee Safety Meeting Attendance

Date & Time _____
Conducted By _____ (Name & title) _____
Subject Discussed _____

Signatures of Employees

_____ _____ _____
_____ _____ _____
_____ _____ _____
_____ _____ _____

Approved By _____ (Manager) _____ Date _____

Make meetings brief, 15 to 20 minutes. Cover only one specific subject. Use an object to focus the attention of the employees. Involve them in the talk.

29

Training

Employee Safety Training Verification

Company

Employee's Name & ID

Hire Date **Job Description**

Training Program	Date Completed	Instructor	Comments

Make additional copies of this form as needed. (form provided courtesy of Safety Publications of California © 1990)

APPENDIX 5A   337

Training Requirements in California Code of Regulations Title 8, January 1993

Specific requirements for employee instruction or training are contained in Title 8, Division 1, Chapter 4 of the *California Code of Regulations*, and are listed sequentially here by their subject titles.

CCR T8 Construction Safety Orders

1509 (a) & (e) Injury and Illness Prevention Program
1510 (a) & (c) Safety Instructions for Employees
1512 (b),(d) & (j) Emergency Medical Service
1529 (o)(1)(A) Asbestos
1531 (c) Respiratory Protective Equipment
1532 Confined Space (see CCR T8, 5157 General Industry Safety Orders)
1637 (k)(1) Scaffold Erection and Dismantling
1662 (a) Boatswains Chairs
1585 (a)(1) Powder Actuated Tools, Operator and Instructor
1585 (b)(1) Qualifications
1599 (f) Vehicle Traffic Control, Flaggers, Barricades and Warning Signs
1740 (k)(l) Use of Fuel Gas (Liquid Propane)
1801 (a) Ionizing Radiation, High Voltage Electrical Safety Orders
2940 Work Procedures (Inspection of Safety Devices)

CCR T8 General Industry Safety Orders

3203 (a)(1) Injury and Illness Prevention Program
3220 (g) Emergency Action Plan
3221 (d) Fire Prevention Plan
3282 (f) Window Cleaning Operations
3286 (f)(2) Boatswains Chairs
3314 (a) Cleaning, Repairing, Servicing and Adjusting Prime Movers, Machinery and Equipment
3326 (c) Servicing Single, Split and Multi-piece Rims or Wheels
3333 (d) Blue Stop Signs (Railcars)
3400 (b) Medical Service and First Aid
3411 (c) Private Fire Brigades
3421 (c), (f) & (j) Tree-work Maintenance and Removal
3439 (b) Agricultural Operations, First Aid
3441 (a) Operation of Agricultural Equipment, Operating Instructions Marine Terminal Operations
3463 (b)(5)(A) Respiratory Protective Equipment (reference to 5144)
3464 (a)(1) Accident Prevention and First Aid
3472 (b)(1) Qualifications of Machinery Operation
3638 (d) Elevating Work Platform
3648 (l)(7) Aerial Devices (Towering)
3657 (h) Elevating Employees with Lift Trucks
3664 (a)(1) Operating Rules (Industrial Trucks)
4203 (b) Power Press Operation
4243 (a)(6) Forging Machinery and Equipment
4355 (a)(2) Operating Rules for Compaction Equipment
4402 Pulp and Paper Mills
4445 (3) Hand-fed Engraving Press
4494 (a) Operating Rules, Laundry and Dry Cleaning
4799 (a) Training of Operators, Gas Systems and for Welding and Cutting
4848 (a)(21) Fire Prevention and Suppression Procedure
5006 (a) Crane, Hoists, Derrick Operators Qualifications
5099 (a) Control of Noise Exposure
5144 (c) Respiratory Protective Equipment
5154 (j)(1) Open Surface Tank Operations
5157 (b) Confined Spaces
5166 (a) Cleaning, Repairing or Altering Containers
5185 (a) Changing and Charging Storage Batteries
5189 (g) Process Safety Management of Acutely Hazardous Materials
5190 (i) Cotton Dust
5191 (f) Occupational Exposure to Hazardous Chemicals in Laboratories
5192 (e) & (l)(3)(D) Hazardous Waste Operations and Emergency Response—Uncontrolled Waste Site Operations

31

5192 (p)(2), (p)(7) & (p)(8)(C) Hazardous Waste Operations and Emergency Response—RCRA Operations
5192 (q)(6) Hazardous Waste Operations and Emergency Response—Emergency Response Operations
5193 (c)(5) & (g)(2) Bloodborne Pathogens
5194 (b)(1) Hazard Communication, Employee Information and Training
5208 (o)(1) Asbestos
5208.1 (n)(1)(B) Non Asbestiform Minerals
5209 (e)(5) Carcinogens
5210 (j) Vinyl Chloride
5211 (t)(1) Coke Oven Emissions
5212 (r)(1) 1, 2 Dibromo-3 Chloropropane (DBCP)
5213 (o)(1) Acrylonitrile (AN)
5214 (m)(1) Inorganic Arsenic
5215 (j)(1) 4, 4'-Methylenebis (2-Chloroaniline), MBOCA
5216 (l)(1) Lead
5217 (n) Formaldehyde
5218 (j)(3) Benzene
5219 (j) Ethylene Dibromide
5220 (i)(1) Ethylene Oxide (EtO)
5221 (c) Fumigation: General
5229 Protection (Labels)
5239 Handle or Transport Explosives
5322 Manufacture of Explosives and Fireworks
5571 (g) Service Stations (Portable Fire Extinguishers)
6052 (d)(1) Diving Operations (Dive Team Training)

Fire Protection
6151 (g)(1) Portable Fire Extinguishers
6165 (f)(2)(F) Standpipe and Hose Systems
6175 (a)(10) Fixed Extinguishers Systems

Logging and Sawmills
6251 (d) First Aid Training

Petroleum Safety Orders: Drilling and Production
6507 (A) Safety Training and Instruction

Petroleum Safety Orders: Refining, Transportation, Handling
6760 (A) Safety Training and Instruction

Mine Safety Orders and Instruction
6963 Safety Training and Instruction
6967 Certification of Safety Representative at Underground Mines
6968 (a), (b) & (c) First Aid Training
7074 (d) Emergency Plan (Underground)
7083 (c) Mine Rescue Stations
7085 (a) Mine Rescue Training and Procedure
7150 (d) Qualified Hoistmen (Persons)
7201 Explosives

Ship Building, Ship Repairing and Ship Breaking Safety Orders
8355 (b) Hazardous Work
8397.1(b) Radioactive Material

Tunnel Safety Orders
8407 Safety Instructions for New Employees
8421 (a) First Aid Training
8430 (a) Rescue Apparatus (Trained Rescue Crew)
8455 (a) Mechanical Tunneling Methods and Equipment
8499 (b) Hoisting Engineers
8506 Explosives

Tunnel Safety Orders Appendix B—Labor Code Excerpts Part 9 Tunnel and Mine Safety
7952 Trained DOSH Safety Engineers
7958 Trained Rescue Crews
7990 Explosives Blasters Licensed
7999 Gas Testers and Safety Representatives

Telecommunication Orders
8603 Training

Elevator Safety Orders
3003 (c) Certified Elevator Inspectors

Aerial Passenger Tramway Safety Orders
3157.1(c)(2) Operator Experience and Training

Appendix 6A

29 CFR 1926.21
SAFETY TRAINING AND EDUCATION

§ 1926.21 Safety training and education.

(a) *General requirements.* The Secretary shall, pursuant to section 107(f) of the Act, establish and supervise programs for the education and training of employers and employees in the recognition, avoidance and prevention of unsafe conditions in employments covered by the act.

(b) *Employer responsibility.* (1) The employer should avail himself of the safety and health training programs the Secretary provides.

(2) The employer shall instruct each employee in the recognition and avoidance of unsafe conditions and the regulations applicable to his work environment to control or eliminate any hazards or other exposure to illness or injury.

(3) Employees required to handle or use poisons, caustics, and other harmful substances shall be instructed regarding the safe handling and use, and be made aware of the potential hazards, personal hygiene, and personal protective measures required.

(4) In job site areas where harmful plants or animals are present, employees who may be exposed shall be instructed regarding the potential hazards, and how to avoid injury, and the first aid procedures to be used in the event of injury.

(5) Employees required to handle or use flammable liquids, gases, or toxic materials shall be instructed in the safe handling and use of these materials and made aware of the specific requirements contained in subparts D, F, and other applicable subparts of this part.

(6)(i) All employees required to enter into confined or enclosed spaces shall be instructed as to the nature of the hazards involved, the necessary precautions to be taken, and in the use of protective and emergency equipment required. The employer shall comply with any specific regulations that apply to work in dangerous or potentially dangerous areas.

(ii) For purposes of paragraph (b)(6)(i) of this section, "confined or enclosed space" means any space having a limited means of egress, which is subject to the accumulation of toxic or flammable contaminants or has an oxygen deficient atmosphere. Confined or enclosed spaces include, but are not limited to, storage tanks, process vessels, bins, boilers, ventilation or exhaust ducts, sewers, underground utility vaults, tunnels, pipelines, and open top spaces more than 4 feet in depth such as pits, tubs, vaults, and vessels.

Appendix 6B

29 CFR 1910.120
HAZARDOUS WASTE OPERATIONS AND EMERGENCY RESPONSE

§ 1910.120 Hazardous waste operations and emergency response.

(a) *Scope, application, and definitions*—(1) *Scope.* This section covers the following operations, unless the employer can demonstrate that the operation does not involve employee exposure or the reasonable possibility for employee exposure to safety or health hazards:

(i) Clean-up operations required by a governmental body, whether Federal, state, local or other involving hazardous substances that are conducted at uncontrolled hazardous waste sites (including, but not limited to, the EPA's National Priority Site List (NPL), state priority site lists, sites recommended for the EPA NPL, and initial investigations of government identified sites which are conducted before the presence or absence of hazardous substances has been ascertained);

(ii) Corrective actions involving clean-up operations at sites covered by the Resource Conservation and Recovery Act of 1976 (RCRA) as amended (42 U.S.C. 6901 *et seq.*);

(iii) Voluntary clean-up operations at sites recognized by Federal, state, local or other governmental bodies as uncontrolled hazardous waste sites;

(iv) Operations involving hazardous wastes that are conducted at treatment, storage, and disposal (TSD) facilities regulated by 40 CFR parts 264 and 265 pursuant to RCRA; or by agencies under agreement with U.S.E.P.A. to implement RCRA regulations; and

(v) Emergency response operations for releases of, or substantial threats of releases of, hazardous substances without regard to the location of the hazard.

(2) *Application.* (i) All requirements of part 1910 and part 1926 of title 29 of the Code of Federal Regulations apply pursuant to their terms to hazardous waste and emergency response operations whether covered by this section or not. If there is a conflict or overlap, the provision more protective of em-

Occupational Safety and Health Admin., Labor § 1910.120

ployee safety and health shall apply without regard to 29 CFR 1910.5(c)(1).

(ii) Hazardous substance clean-up operations within the scope of paragraphs (a)(1)(i) through (a)(1)(iii) of this section must comply with all paragraphs of this section except paragraphs (p) and (q).

(iii) Operations within the scope of paragraph (a)(1)(iv) of this section must comply only with the requirements of paragraph (p) of this section.

Notes and Exceptions: (A) All provisions of paragraph (p) of this section cover any treatment, storage or disposal (TSD) operation regulated by 40 CFR parts 264 and 265 or by state law authorized under RCRA, and required to have a permit or interim status from EPA pursuant to 40 CFR 270.1 or from a state agency pursuant to RCRA.

(B) Employers who are not required to have a permit or interim status because they are conditionally exempt small quantity generators under 40 CFR 261.5 or are generators who qualify under 40 CFR 262.34 for exemptions from regulation under 40 CFR parts 264, 265 and 270 ("excepted employers") are not covered by paragraphs (p)(1) through (p)(7) of this section. Excepted employers who are required by the EPA or state agency to have their employees engage in emergency response or who direct their employees to engage in emergency response are covered by paragraph (p)(8) of this section, and cannot be exempted by (p)(8)(i) of this section. Excepted employers who are not required to have employees engage in emergency response, who direct their employees to evacuate in the case of such emergencies and who meet the requirements of paragraph (p)(8)(i) of this section are exempt from the balance of paragraph (p)(8) of this section.

(C) If an area is used primarily for treatment, storage or disposal, any emergency response operations in that area shall comply with paragraph (p)(8) of this section. In other areas not used primarily for treatment, storage, or disposal, any emergency response operations shall comply with paragraph (q) of this section. Compliance with the requirements of paragraph (q) of this section shall be deemed to be in compliance with the requirements of paragraph (p)(8) of this section.

(iv) Emergency response operations for releases of, or substantial threats of releases of, hazardous substances which are not covered by paragraphs (a)(1)(i) through (a)(1)(iv) of this section must only comply with the requirements of paragraph (q) of this section.

(3) *Definitions*—"*Buddy system* means a system of organizing employees into work groups in such a manner that each employee of the work group is designated to be observed by at least one other employee in the work group. The purpose of the buddy system is to provide rapid assistance to employees in the event of an emergency.

Clean-up operation means an operation where hazardous substances are removed, contained, incinerated, neutralized, stabilized, cleared-up, or in any other manner processed or handled with the ultimate goal of making the site safer for people or the environment.

Decontamination means the removal of hazardous substances from employees and their equipment to the extent necessary to preclude the occurrence of foreseeable adverse health affects.

Emergency response or responding to emergencies means a response effort by employees from outside the immediate release area or by other designated responders (i.e., mutual-aid groups, local fire departments, etc.) to an occurrence which results, or is likely to result, in an uncontrolled release of a hazardous substance. Responses to incidental releases of hazardous substances where the substance can be absorbed, neutralized, or otherwise controlled at the time of release by employees in the immediate release area, or by maintenance personnel are not considered to be emergency responses within the scope of this standard. Responses to releases of hazardous substances where there is no potential safety or health hazard (i.e., fire, explosion, or chemical exposure) are not considered to be emergency responses.

Facility means (A) any building, structure, installation, equipment, pipe or pipeline (including any pipe into a sewer or publicly owned treatment works), well, pit, pond, lagoon, impoundment, ditch, storage container, motor vehicle, rolling stock, or aircraft, or (B) any site or area where a hazardous substance has been deposited, stored, disposed of, or placed, or otherwise come to be located; but does not include any consumer product in consumer use or any water-borne vessel.

Hazardous materials response (HAZMAT) team means an organized group of employees, designated by the

377

§ 1910.120

employer, who are expected to perform work to handle and control actual or potential leaks or spills of hazardous substances requiring possible close approach to the substance. The team members perform responses to releases or potential releases of hazardous substances for the purpose of control or stabilization of the incident. A HAZMAT team is not a fire brigade nor is a typical fire brigade a HAZMAT team. A HAZMAT team, however, may be a separate component of a fire brigade or fire department.

Hazardous substance means any substance designated or listed under paragraphs (A) through (D) of this definition, exposure to which results or may result in adverse affects on the health or safety of employees:

(A) Any substance defined under section 101(14) of CERCLA;

(B) Any biological agent and other disease-causing agent which after release into the environment and upon exposure, ingestion, inhalation. or assimilation into any person, either directly from the environment or indirectly by ingestion through food chains, will or may reasonably be anticipated to cause death, disease, behavioral abnormalities, cancer, genetic mutation, physiological malfunctions (including malfunctions in reproduction) or physical deformations in such persons or their offspring;

(C) Any substance listed by the U.S. Department of Transportation as hazardous materials under 49 CFR 172.101 and appendices; and

(D) Hazardous waste as herein defined.

Hazardous waste means—

(A) A waste or combination of wastes as defined in 40 CFR 261.3, or

(B) Those substances defined as hazardous wastes in 49 CFR 171.8.

Hazardous waste operation means any operation conducted within the scope of this standard.

Hazardous waste site or *Site* means any facility or location within the scope of this standard at which hazardous waste operations take place.

Health hazard means a chemical, mixture of chemicals or a pathogen for which there is statistically significant evidence based on at least one study conducted in accordance with established scientific principles that acute or chronic health effects may occur in exposed employees. The term "health hazard" includes chemicals which are carcinogens, toxic or highly toxic agents, reproductive toxins, irritants, corrosives, sensitizers, heptaotoxins, nephrotoxins, neurotoxins, agents which act on the hematopoietic system, and agents which damage the lungs, skin, eyes, or mucous membranes. It also includes stress due to temperature extremes. Further definition of the terms used above can be found in appendix A to 29 CFR 1910.1200.

IDLH or *Immediately dangerous to life or health* means an atmospheric concentration of any toxic, corrosive or asphyxiant substance that poses an immediate threat to life or would cause irreversible or delayed adverse health effects or would interfere with an individual's ability to escape from a dangerous atmosphere.

Oxygen deficiency means that concentration of oxygen by volume below which atmosphere supplying respiratory protection must be provided. It exists in atmospheres where the percentage of oxygen by volume is less than 19.5 percent oxygen.

Permissible exposure limit means the exposure, inhalation or dermal permissible exposure limit specified in 29 CFR part 1910, subparts G and Z.

Published exposure level means the exposure limits published in "NIOSH Recommendations for Occupational Health Standards" dated 1986 incorporated by reference, or if none is specified, the exposure limits published in the standards specified by the American Conference of Governmental Industrial Hygienists in their publication "Threshold Limit Values and Biological Exposure Indices for 1987–88" dated 1987 incorporated by reference.

Post emergency response means that portion of an emergency response performed after the immediate threat of a release has been stabilized or eliminated and clean-up of the site has begun. If post emergency response is performed by an employer's own employees who were part of the initial emergency response, it is considered to be part of the initial response and not post emergency response. However, if a group of an employer's own employees, separate from the group providing initial response, performs the clean-up operation, then the separate group of employees would be considered to be performing post-emergency response and subject to paragraph (q)(11) of this section.

Qualified person means a person with specific training, knowledge and experience in the area for which the person has the responsibility and the authority to control.

Site safety and health supervisor (or official) means the individual located on a hazardous waste site who is responsible to the employer and has the authority and knowledge necessary to implement the site safety and health plan and verify compliance with applicable safety and health requirements.

Small quantity qenerator means a generator of hazardous wastes who in any calendar month generates no more than 1,000 kilograms (2,205 pounds) of hazardous waste in that month.

Uncontrolled hazardous waste site, means an area identified as an uncontrolled hazardous waste site by a governmental body, whether Federal, state, local or other where an accumulation of hazardous substances creates a threat to the health and safety of individuals or the environment or both. Some sites are found on public lands such as those created by former municipal, county or state landfills where illegal or poorly managed waste disposal has taken place. Other sites are found on private property, often belonging to generators or former generators of hazardous substance wastes. Examples of such sites include, but are not limited to, surface impoundments, landfills, dumps, and tank or drum farms. Normal operations at TSD sites are not covered by this definition.

(b) *Safety and health program.*

NOTE TO (b): Safety and health programs developed and implemented to meet other Federal, state, or local regulations are considered acceptable in meeting this requirement if they cover or are modified to cover the topics required in this paragraph. An additional or separate safety and health program is not required by this paragraph.

(1) *General.* (i) Employers shall develop and implement a written safety and health program for their employees involved in hazardous waste operations. The program shall be designed to identify, evaluate, and control safety and health hazards, and provide for emergency response for hazardous waste operations.

(ii) The written safety and health program shall incorporate the following:

(A) An organizational structure;

(B) A comprehensive workplan;

(C) A site-specific safety and health plan which need not repeat the employer's standard operating procedures required in paragraph (b)(1)(ii)(F) of this section;

(D) The safety and health training program;

(E) The medical surveillance program;

(F) The employer's standard operating procedures for safety and health; and

(G) Any necessary interface between general program and site specific activities.

(iii) *Site excavation.* Site excavations created during initial site preparation or during hazardous waste operations shall be shored or sloped as appropriate to prevent accidental collapse in accordance with subpart P of 29 CFR part 1926.

(iv) *Contractors and sub-contractors.* An employer who retains contractor or sub-contractor services for work in hazardous waste operations shall inform those contractors, sub-contractors, or their representatives of the site emergency response procedures and any potential fire, explosion, health, safety or other hazards of the hazardous waste operation that have been identified by the employer, including those identified in the employer's information program.

(v) *Program availability.* The written safety and health program shall be made available to any contractor or subcontractor or their representative who will be involved with the hazardous waste operation; to employees; to employee designated representatives; to OSHA personnel, and to personnel of other Federal, state, or local agencies with regulatory authority over the site.

(2) *Organizational structure part of the site program*—(i) The organizational structure part of the program shall es-

§ 1910.120

tablish the specific chain of command and specify the overall responsibilities of supervisors and employees. It shall include, at a minimum, the following elements:

(A) A general supervisor who has the responsibility and authority to direct all hazardous waste operations.

(B) A site safety and health supervisor who has the responsibility and authority to develop and implement the site safety and health plan and verify compliance.

(C) All other personnel needed for hazardous waste site operations and emergency response and their general functions and responsibilities.

(D) The lines of authority, responsibility, and communication.

(ii) The organizational structure shall be reviewed and updated as necessary to reflect the current status of waste site operations.

(3) *Comprehensive workplan part of the site program.* The comprehensive workplan part of the program shall address the tasks and objectives of the site operations and the logistics and resources required to reach those tasks and objectives.

(i) The comprehensive workplan shall address anticipated clean-up activities as well as normal operating procedures which need not repeat the employer's procedures available elsewhere.

(ii) The comprehensive workplan shall define work tasks and objectives and identify the methods for accomplishing those tasks and objectives.

(iii) The comprehensive workplan shall establish personnel requirements for implementing the plan.

(iv) The comprehensive workplan shall provide for the implementation of the training required in paragraph (e) of this section.

(v) The comprehensive workplan shall provide for the implementation of the required informational programs required in paragraph (i) of this section.

(vi) The comprehensive workplan shall provide for the implementation of the medical surveillance program described in paragraph (f) of this section.

(4) *Site-specific safety and health plan part of the program*—(i) *General.* The site safety and health plan, which must be kept on site, shall address the safety and health hazards of each phase of site operation and include the requirements and procedures for employee protection.

(ii) *Elements.* The site safety and health plan, as a minimum, shall address the following:

(A) A safety and health risk or hazard analysis for each site task and operation found in the workplan.

(B) Employee training assignments to assure compliance with paragraph (e) of this section.

(C) Personal protective equipment to be used by employees for each of the site tasks and operations being conducted as required by the personal protective equipment program in paragraph (g)(5) of this section.

(D) Medical surveillance requirements in accordance with the program in paragraph (f) of this section.

(E) Frequency and types of air monitoring, personnel monitoring, and environmental sampling techniques and instrumentation to be used, including methods of maintenance and calibration of monitoring and sampling equipment to be used.

(F) Site control measures in accordance with the site control program required in paragraph (d) of this section.

(G) Decontamination procedures in accordance with paragraph (k) of this section.

(H) An emergency response plan meeting the requirements of paragraph (l) of this section for safe and effective responses to emergencies, including the necessary PPE and other equipment.

(I) Confined space entry procedures.

(J) A spill containment program meeting the requirements of paragraph (j) of this section.

(iii) *Pre-entry briefing.* The site specific safety and health plan shall provide for pre-entry briefings to be held prior to initiating any site activity, and at such other times as necessary to ensure that employees are apprised of the site safety and health plan and that this plan is being followed. The information and data obtained from site characterization and analysis work required in paragraph (c) of this section shall be used to prepare and update the site safety and health plan.

(iv) *Effectiveness of site safety and health plan.* Inspections shall be conducted by the site safety and health supervisor or, in the absence of that individual, another individual who is knowledgeable in occupational safety and health, acting on behalf of the employer as necessary to determine the effectiveness of the site safety and health plan. Any deficiencies in the effectiveness of the site safety and health plan shall be corrected by the employer.

(c) *Site characterization and analysis*—(1) *General.* Hazardous waste sites shall be evaluated in accordance with this paragraph to identify specific site hazards and to determine the appropriate safety and health control procedures needed to protect employees from the identified hazards.

(2) *Preliminary evaluation.* A preliminary evaluation of a site's characteristics shall be performed prior to site entry by a qualified person in order to aid in the selection of appropriate employee protection methods prior to site entry. Immediately after initial site entry, a more detailed evaluation of the site's specific characteristics shall be performed by a qualified person in order to further identify existing site hazards and to further aid in the selection of the appropriate engineering controls and personal protective equipment for the tasks to be performed.

(3) *Hazard identification.* All suspected conditions that may pose inhalation or skin absorption hazards that are immediately dangerous to life or health (IDLH), or other conditions that may cause death or serious harm, shall be identified during the preliminary survey and evaluated during the detailed survey. Examples of such hazards include, but are not limited to, confined space entry, potentially explosive or flammable situations, visible vapor clouds, or areas where biological indicators such as dead animals or vegetation are located.

(4) *Required information.* The following information to the extent available shall be obtained by the employer prior to allowing employees to enter a site:

(i) Location and approximate size of the site.

(ii) Description of the response activity and/or the job task to be performed.

(iii) Duration of the planned employee activity.

(iv) Site topography and accessibility by air and roads.

(v) Safety and health hazards expected at the site.

(vi) Pathways for hazardous substance dispersion.

(vii) Present status and capabilities of emergency response teams that would provide assistance to hazardous waste clean-up site employees at the time of an emergency.

(viii) Hazardous substances and health hazards involved or expected at the site, and their chemical and physical properties.

(5) *Personal protective equipment.* Personal protective equipment (PPE) shall be provided and used during initial site entry in accordance with the following requirements:

(i) Based upon the results of the preliminary site evaluation, an ensemble of PPE shall be selected and used during initial site entry which will provide protection to a level of exposure below permissible exposure limits and published exposure levels for known or suspected hazardous substances and health hazards, and which will provide protection against other known and suspected hazards identified during the preliminary site evaluation. If there is no permissible exposure limit or published exposure level, the employer may use other published studies and information as a guide to appropriate personal protective equipment.

(ii) If positive-pressure self-contained breathing apparatus is not used as part of the entry ensemble, and if respiratory protection is warranted by the potential hazards identified during the preliminary site evaluation, an escape self-contained breathing apparatus of at least five minute's duration shall be carried by employees during initial site entry.

(iii) If the preliminary site evaluation does not produce sufficient information to identify the hazards or suspected hazards of the site, an ensemble providing protection equivalent to Level B PPE shall be provided as minimum protection, and direct reading instruments shall be used as appropriate for identifying IDLH conditions. (See appendix B for a description of Level B

§ 1910.120

hazards and the recommendations for Level B protective equipment.)

(iv) Once the hazards of the site have been identified, the appropriate PPE shall be selected and used in accordance with paragraph (g) of this section.

(6) *Monitoring.* The following monitoring shall be conducted during initial site entry when the site evaluation produces information that shows the potential for ionizing radiation or IDLH conditions, or when the site information is not sufficient reasonably to eliminate these possible conditions:

(i) Monitoring with direct reading instruments for hazardous levels of ionizing radiation.

(ii) Monitoring the air with appropriate direct reading test equipment (i.e., combustible gas meters, detector tubes) for IDLH and other conditions that may cause death or serious harm (combustible or explosive atmospheres, oxygen deficiency, toxic substances).

(iii) Visually observing for signs of actual or potential IDLH or other dangerous conditions.

(iv) An ongoing air monitoring program in accordance with paragraph (h) of this section shall be implemented after site characterization has determined the site is safe for the start-up of operations.

(7) *Risk identification.* Once the presence and concentrations of specific hazardous substances and health hazards have been established, the risks associated with these substances shall be identified. Employees who will be working on the site shall be informed of any risks that have been identified. In situations covered by the Hazard Communication Standard, 29 CFR 1910.1200, training required by that standard need not be duplicated.

NOTE TO (c)(7).—Risks to consider include, but are not limited to:

(a) Exposures exceeding the permissible exposure limits and published exposure levels.
(b) IDLH concentrations.
(c) Potential skin absorption and irritation sources.
(d) Potential eye irritation sources.
(e) Explosion sensitivity and flammability ranges.
(f) Oxygen deficiency.

(8) *Employee notification.* Any information concerning the chemical, physical, and toxicologic properties of each substance known or expected to be present on site that is available to the employer and relevant to the duties an employee is expected to perform shall be made available to the affected employees prior to the commencement of their work activities. The employer may utilize information developed for the hazard communication standard for this purpose.

(d) *Site control*—(1) *General.* Appropriate site control procedures shall be implemented to control employee exposure to hazardous substances before clean-up work begins.

(2) *Site control program.* A site control program for protecting employees which is part of the employer's site safety and health program required in paragraph (b) of this section shall be developed during the planning stages of a hazardous waste clean-up operation and modified as necessary as new information becomes available.

(3) *Elements of the site control program.* The site control program shall, as a minimum, include: A site map; site work zones; the use of a "buddy system"; site communications including alerting means for emergencies; the standard operating procedures or safe work practices; and, identification of the nearest medical assistance. Where these requirements are covered elsewhere they need not be repeated.

(e) *Training*—(1) *General.* (i) All employees working on site (such as but not limited to equipment operators, general laborers and others) exposed to hazardous substances, health hazards, or safety hazards and their supervisors and management responsible for the site shall receive training meeting the requirements of this paragraph before they are permitted to engage in hazardous waste operations that could expose them to hazardous substances, safety, or health hazards, and they shall receive review training as specified in this paragraph.

(ii) Employees shall not be permitted to participate in or supervise field activities until they have been trained to a level required by their job function and responsibility.

(2) *Elements to be covered.* The training shall thoroughly cover the following:

(i) Names of personnel and alternates responsible for site safety and health;

(ii) Safety, health and other hazards present on the site;

(iii) Use of personal protective equipment;

(iv) Work practices by which the employee can minimize risks from hazards;

(v) Safe use of engineering controls and equipment on the site;

(vi) Medical surveillance requirements, including recognition of symptoms and signs which might indicate overexposure to hazards; and

(vii) The contents of paragraphs (G) through (J) of the site safety and health plan set forth in paragraph (b)(4)(ii) of this section.

(3) *Initial training.* (i) General site workers (such as equipment operators, general laborers and supervisory personnel) engaged in hazardous substance removal or other activities which expose or potentially expose workers to hazardous substances and health hazards shall receive a minimum of 40 hours of instruction off the site, and a minimum of three days actual field experience under the direct supervision of a trained, experienced supervisor.

(ii) Workers on site only occasionally for a specific limited task (such as, but not limited to, ground water monitoring, land surveying, or geo-physical surveying) and who are unlikely to be exposed over permissible exposure limits and published exposure limits shall receive a minimum of 24 hours of instruction off the site, and the minimum of one day actual field experience under the direct supervision of a trained, experienced supervisor.

(iii) Workers regularly on site who work in areas which have been monitored and fully characterized indicating that exposures are under permissible exposure limits and published exposure limits where respirators are not necessary, and the characterization indicates that there are no health hazards or the possibility of an emergency developing, shall receive a minimum of 24 hours of instruction off the site and the minimum of one day actual field experience under the direct supervision of a trained, experienced supervisor.

(iv) Workers with 24 hours of training who are covered by paragraphs (e)(3)(ii) and (e)(3)(iii) of this section, and who become general site workers or who are required to wear respirators, shall have the additional 16 hours and two days of training necessary to total the training specified in paragraph (e)(3)(i).

(4) *Management and supervisor training.* On-site management and supervisors directly responsible for, or who supervise employees engaged in, hazardous waste operations shall receive 40 hours initial training, and three days of supervised field experience (the training may be reduced to 24 hours and one day if the only area of their responsibility is employees covered by paragraphs (e)(3)(ii) and (e)(3)(iii)) and at least eight additional hours of specialized training at the time of job assignment on such topics as, but not limited to, the employer's safety and health program and the associated employee training program, personal protective equipment program, spill containment program, and health hazard monitoring procedure and techniques.

(5) *Qualifications for trainers.* Trainers shall be qualified to instruct employees about the subject matter that is being presented in training. Such trainers shall have satisfactorily completed a training program for teaching the subjects they are expected to teach, or they shall have the academic credentials and instructional experience necessary for teaching the subjects. Instructors shall demonstrate competent instructional skills and knowledge of the applicable subject matter.

(6) *Training certification.* Employees and supervisors that have received and successfully completed the training and field experience specified in paragraphs (e)(1) through (e)(4) of this section shall be certified by their instructor or the head instructor and trained supervisor as having successfully completed the necessary training. A written certificate shall be given to each person so certified. Any person who has not been so certified or who does not meet the requirements of paragraph (e)(9) of this section shall be prohibited from engaging in hazardous waste operations.

(7) *Emergency response.* Employees who are engaged in responding to hazardous emergency situations at hazardous waste clean-up sites that may expose them to hazardous substances

§ 1910.120

shall be trained in how to respond to such expected emergencies.

(8) *Refresher training.* Employees specified in paragraph (e)(1) of this section, and managers and supervisors specified in paragraph (e)(4) of this section, shall receive eight hours of refresher training annually on the items specified in paragraph (e)(2) and/or (e)(4) of this section, any critique of incidents that have occurred in the past year that can serve as training examples of related work, and other relevant topics.

(9) *Equivalent training.* Employers who can show by documentation or certification that an employee's work experience and/or training has resulted in training equivalent to that training required in paragraphs (e)(1) through (e)(4) of this section shall not be required to provide the initial training requirements of those paragraphs to such employees and shall provide a copy of the certification or documentation to the employee upon request. However, certified employees or employees with equivalent training new to a site shall receive appropriate, site specific training before site entry and have appropriate supervised field experience at the new site. Equivalent training includes any academic training or the training that existing employees might have already received from actual hazardous waste site work experience.

(f) *Medical surveillance*—(1) *General.* Employers engaged in operations specified in paragraphs (a)(1)(i) through (a)(1)(iv) of this section and not covered by (a)(2)(iii) exceptions and employers of employees specified in paragraph (q)(9) shall institute a medical surveillance program in accordance with this paragraph.

(2) *Employees covered.* The medical surveillance program shall be instituted by the employer for the following employees:

(i) All employees who are or may be exposed to hazardous substances or health hazards at or above the permissible exposure limits or, if there is no permissible exposure limit, above the published exposure levels for these substances, without regard to the use of respirators, for 30 days or more a year;

(ii) All employees who wear a respirator for 30 days or more a year or as required by § 1910.134;

(iii) All employees who are injured, become ill or develop signs or symptoms due to possible overexposure involving hazardous substances or health hazards from an emergency response or hazardous waste operation; and

(iv) Members of HAZMAT teams.

(3) *Frequency of medical examinations and consultations.* Medical examinations and consultations shall be made available by the employer to each employee covered under paragraph (f)(2) of this section on the following schedules:

(i) For employees covered under paragraphs (f)(2)(i), (f)(2)(ii), and (f)(2)(iv):

(A) Prior to assignment;

(B) At least once every twelve months for each employee covered unless the attending physician believes a longer interval (not greater than biennially) is appropriate;

(C) At termination of employment or reassignment to an area where the employee would not be covered if the employee has not had an examination within the last six months;

(D) As soon as possible upon notification by an employee that the employee has developed signs or symptoms indicating possible overexposure to hazardous substances or health hazards, or that the employee has been injured or exposed above the permissible exposure limits or published exposure levels in an emergency situation;

(E) At more frequent times, if the examining physician determines that an increased frequency of examination is medically necessary.

(ii) For employees covered under paragraph (f)(2)(iii) and for all employees including those of employers covered by paragraph (a)(1)(v) who may have been injured, received a health impairment, developed signs or symptoms which may have resulted from exposure to hazardous substances resulting from an emergency incident, or exposed during an emergency incident to hazardous substances at concentrations above the permissible exposure limits or the published exposure levels without the necessary personal protective equipment being used:

(A) As soon as possible following the emergency incident or development of signs or symptoms;

(B) At additional times, if the examining physician determines that follow-up examinations or consultations are medically necessary.

(4) *Content of medical examinations and consultations.* (i) Medical examinations required by paragraph (f)(3) of this section shall include a medical and work history (or updated history if one is in the employee's file) with special emphasis on symptoms related to the handling of hazardous substances and health hazards, and to fitness for duty including the ability to wear any required PPE under conditions (i.e., temperature extremes) that may be expected at the work site.

(ii) The content of medical examinations or consultations made available to employees pursuant to paragraph (f) shall be determined by the attending physician. The guidelines in the *Occupational Safety and Health Guidance Manual for Hazardous Waste Site Activities* (See appendix D, Reference #10) should be consulted.

(5) *Examination bv a physician and costs.* All medical examinations and procedures shall be performed by or under the supervision of a licensed physician, preferably one knowledgeable in occupational medicine, and shall be provided without cost to the employee, without loss of pay, and at a reasonable time and place.

(6) *Information provided to the physician.* The employer shall provide one copy of this standard and its appendices to the attending physician, and in addition the following for each employee:

(i) A description of the employee's duties as they relate to the employee's exposures.

(ii) The employee's exposure levels or anticipated exposure levels.

(iii) A description of any personal protective equipment used or to be used.

(iv) Information from previous medical examinations of the employee which is not readily available to the examining physician.

(v) Information required by § 1910.134.

(7) *Physician's written opinion.* (i) The employer shall obtain and furnish the employee with a copy of a written opinion from the attending physician containing the following:

(A) The physician's opinion as to whether the employee has any detected medical conditions which would place the employee at increased risk of material impairment of the employee's health from work in hazardous waste operations or emergency response, or from respirator use.

(B) The physician's recommended limitations upon the employee's assigned work.

(C) The results of the medical examination and tests if requested by the employee.

(D) A statement that the employee has been informed by the physician of the results of the medical examination and any medical conditions which require further examination or treatment.

(ii) The written opinion obtained by the employer shall not reveal specific findings or diagnoses unrelated to occupational exposures.

(8) *Recordkeeping.* (i) An accurate record of the medical surveillance required by paragraph (f) of this section shall be retained. This record shall be retained for the period specified and meet the criteria of 29 CFR 1910.20.

(ii) The record required in paragraph (f)(8)(i) of this section shall include at least the following information:

(A) The name and social security number of the employee;

(B) Physician's written opinions, recommended limitations, and results of examinations and tests;

(C) Any employee medical complaints related to exposure to hazardous substances;

(D) A copy of the information provided to the examining physician by the employer, with the exception of the standard and its appendices.

(g) *Engineering controls, work practices, and personal protective equipment for employee protection.* Engineering controls, work practices, personal protective equipment, or a combination of these shall be implemented in accordance with this paragraph to protect employees from exposure to hazardous substances and safety and health hazards.

APPENDIX 6B

§ 1910.120

(1) *Engineering controls, work practices and PPE for substances regulated in subparts G and Z.* (i) Engineering controls and work practices shall be instituted to reduce and maintain employee exposure to or below the permissible exposure limits for substances regulated by 29 CFR part 1910, to the extent required by subpart Z, except to the extent that such controls and practices are not feasible.

NOTE TO (g)(1)(i): Engineering controls which may be feasible include the use of pressurized cabs or control booths on equipment, and/or the use of remotely operated material handling equipment. Work practices which may be feasible are removing all non-essential employees from potential exposure during opening of drums, wetting down dusty operations and locating employees upwind of possible hazards.

(ii) Whenever engineering controls and work practices are not feasible or not required, any reasonable combination of engineering controls, work practices and PPE shall be used to reduce and maintain employee exposures to or below the permissible exposure limits or dose limits for substances regulated by 29 CFR part 1910, subpart Z.

(iii) The employer shall not implement a schedule of employee rotation as a means of compliance with permissible exposure limits or dose limits except when there is no other feasible way of complying with the airborne or dermal dose limits for ionizing radiation.

(iv) The provisions of 29 CFR, subpart G, shall be followed.

(2) *Engineering controls, work practices, and PPE for substances not regulated in subparts G and Z.* An appropriate combination of engineering controls, work practices and personal protective equipment shall be used to reduce and maintain employee exposure to or below published exposure levels for hazardous substances and health hazards not regulated by 29 CFR part 1910, subparts G and Z. The employer may use the published literature and MSDS as a guide in making the employer's determination as to what level of protection the employer believes is appropriate for hazardous substances and health hazards for which there is no permissible exposure limit or published exposure limit.

29 CFR Ch. XVII (7-1-94 Edition)

(3) *Personal protective equipment selection.* (i) Personal protective equipment (PPE) shall be selected and used which will protect employees from the hazards and potential hazards they are likely to encounter as identified during the site characterization and analysis.

(ii) Personal protective equipment selection shall be based on an evaluation of the performance characteristics of the PPE relative to the requirements and limitations of the site, the task-specific conditions and duration, and the hazards and potential hazards identified at the site.

(iii) Positive pressure self-contained breathing apparatus, or positive pressure air-line respirators equipped with an escape air supply, shall be used when chemical exposure levels present will create a substantial possibility of immediate death, immediate serious illness or injury, or impair the ability to escape.

(iv) Totally-encapsulating chemical protective suits (protection equivalent to Level A protection as recommended in appendix B) shall be used in conditions where skin absorption of a hazardous substance may result in a substantial possibility of immediate death, immediate serious illness or injury, or impair the ability to escape.

(v) The level of protection provided by PPE selection shall be increased when additional information on site conditions indicates that increased protection is necessary to reduce employee exposures below permissible exposure limits and published exposure levels for hazardous substances and health hazards. (See appendix B for guidance on selecting PPE ensembles.)

NOTE TO (g)(3): The level of employee protection provided may be decreased when additional information or site conditions show that decreased protection will not result in hazardous exposures to employees.

(vi) Personal protective equipment shall be selected and used to meet the requirements of 29 CFR part 1910, subpart I, and additional requirements specified in this section.

(4) *Totally-encapsulating chemical protective suits.* (i) Totally-encapsulating suits shall protect employees from the particular hazards which are identified

Occupational Safety and Health Admin., Labor § 1910.120

during site characterization and analysis.

(ii) Totally-encapsulating suits shall be capable of maintaining positive air pressure. (See appendix A for a test method which may be used to evaluate this requirement.)

(iii) Totally-encapsulating suits shall be capable of preventing inward test gas leakage of more than 0.5 percent. (See appendix A for a test method which may be used to evaluate this requirement.)

(5) *Personal protective equipment (PPE) program.* A written personal protective equipment program, which is part of the employer's safety and health program required in paragraph (b) of this section or required in paragraph (p)(1) of this section and which is also a part of the site-specific safety and health plan shall be established. The PPE program shall address the elements listed below. When elements, such as donning and doffing procedures, are provided by the manufacturer of a piece of equipment and are attached to the plan, they need not be rewritten into the plan as long as they adequately address the procedure or element.

(i) PPE selection based upon site hazards,

(ii) PPE use and limitations of the equipment,

(iii) Work mission duration,

(iv) PPE maintenance and storage,

(v) PPE decontamination and disposal,

(vi) PPE training and proper fitting,

(vii) PPE donning and doffing procedures,

(viii) PPE inspection procedures prior to, during, and after use,

(ix) Evaluation of the effectiveness of the PPE program, and

(x) Limitations during temperature extremes, heat stress, and other appropriate medical considerations.

(h) *Monitoring*—(1) *General.* (i) Monitoring shall be performed in accordance with this paragraph where there may be a question of employee exposure to hazardous concentrations of hazardous substances in order to assure proper selection of engineering controls, work practices and personal protective equipment so that employees are not exposed to levels which exceed permissible exposure limits, or published exposure levels if there are no permissible exposure limits, for hazardous substances.

(ii) Air monitoring shall be used to identify and quantify airborne levels of hazardous substances and safety and health hazards in order to determine the appropriate level of employee protection needed on site.

(2) *Initial entry.* Upon initial entry, representative air monitoring shall be conducted to identify any IDLH condition, exposure over permissible exposure limits or published exposure levels, exposure over a radioactive material's dose limits or other dangerous condition such as the presence of flammable atmospheres or oxygen-deficient environments.

(3) *Periodic monitoring.* Periodic monitoring shall be conducted when the possibility of an IDLH condition or flammable atmosphere has developed or when there is indication that exposures may have risen over permissible exposure limits or published exposure levels since prior monitoring. Situations where it shall be considered whether the possibility that exposures have risen are as follows:

(i) When work begins on a different portion of the site.

(ii) When contaminants other than those previously identified are being handled.

(iii) When a different type of operation is initiated (e.g., drum opening as opposed to exploratory well drilling).

(iv) When employees are handling leaking drums or containers or working in areas with obvious liquid contamination (e.g., a spill or lagoon).

(4) *Monitoring of high-risk employees.* After the actual clean-up phase of any hazardous waste operation commences; for example, when soil, surface water or containers are moved or disturbed; the employer shall monitor those employees likely to have the highest exposures to hazardous substances and health hazards likely to be present above permissible exposure limits or published exposure levels by using personal sampling frequently enough to characterize employee exposures. If the employees likely to have the highest exposure are over permissible exposure limits or published exposure limits, then monitoring shall continue to de-

§ 1910.120

termine all employees likely to be above those limits. The employer may utilize a representative sampling approach by documenting that the employees and chemicals chosen for monitoring are based on the criteria stated above.

NOTE TO (h): It is not required to monitor employees engaged in site characterization operations covered by paragraph (c) of this section.

(i) *Informational programs.* Employers shall develop and implement a program, which is part of the employer's safety and health program required in paragraph (b) of this section, to inform employees, contractors, and subcontractors (or their representative) actually engaged in hazardous waste operations of the nature, level and degree of exposure likely as a result of participation in such hazardous waste operations. Employees, contractors and subcontractors working outside of the operations part of a site are not covered by this standard.

(j) *Handling drums and containers*—(1) *General.* (i) Hazardous substances and contaminated soils, liquids, and other residues shall be handled, transported, labeled, and disposed of in accordance with this paragraph.

(ii) Drums and containers used during the clean-up shall meet the appropriate DOT, OSHA, and EPA regulations for the wastes that they contain.

(iii) When practical, drums and containers shall be inspected and their integrity shall be assured prior to being moved. Drums or containers that cannot be inspected before being moved because of storage conditions (i.e., buried beneath the earth, stacked behind other drums, stacked several tiers high in a pile, etc.) shall be moved to an accessible location and inspected prior to further handling.

(iv) Unlabelled drums and containers shall be considered to contain hazardous substances and handled accordingly until the contents are positively identified and labeled.

(v) Site operations shall be organized to minimize the amount of drum or container movement.

(vi) Prior to movement of drums or containers, all employees exposed to the transfer operation shall be warned of the potential hazards associated with the contents of the drums or containers.

(vii) U.S. Department of Transportation specified salvage drums or containers and suitable quantities of proper absorbent shall be kept available and used in areas where spills, leaks, or ruptures may occur.

(viii) Where major spills may occur, a spill containment program, which is part of the employer's safety and health program required in paragraph (b) of this section, shall be implemented to contain and isolate the entire volume of the hazardous substance being transferred.

(ix) Drums and containers that cannot be moved without rupture, leakage, or spillage shall be emptied into a sound container using a device classified for the material being transferred.

(x) A ground-penetrating system or other type of detection system or device shall be used to estimate the location and depth of buried drums or containers.

(xi) Soil or covering material shall be removed with caution to prevent drum or container rupture.

(xii) Fire extinguishing equipment meeting the requirements of 29 CFR part 1910, subpart L, shall be on hand and ready for use to control incipient fires.

(2) *Opening drums and containers.* The following procedures shall be followed in areas where drums or containers are being opened:

(i) Where an airline respirator system is used, connections to the source of air supply shall be protected from contamination and the entire system shall be protected from physical damage.

(ii) Employees not actually involved in opening drums or containers shall be kept a safe distance from the drums or containers being opened.

(iii) If employees must work near or adjacent to drums or containers being opened, a suitable shield that does not interfere with the work operation shall be placed between the employee and the drums or containers being opened to protect the employee in case of accidental explosion.

(iv) Controls for drum or container opening equipment, monitoring equipment, and fire suppression equipment

Occupational Safety and Health Admin., Labor § 1910.120

shall be located behind the explosion-resistant barrier.

(v) When there is a reasonable possibility of flammable atmospheres being present, material handling equipment and hand tools shall be of the type to prevent sources of ignition.

(vi) Drums and containers shall be opened in such a manner that excess interior pressure will be safely relieved. If pressure can not be relieved from a remote location, appropriate shielding shall be placed between the employee and the drums or containers to reduce the risk of employee injury.

(vii) Employees shall not stand upon or work from drums or containers.

(3) *Material handling equipment.* Material handling equipment used to transfer drums and containers shall be selected, positioned and operated to minimize sources of ignition related to the equipment from igniting vapors released from ruptured drums or containers.

(4) *Radioactive wastes.* Drums and containers containing radioactive wastes shall not be handled until such time as their hazard to employees is properly assessed.

(5) *Shock sensitive wastes.* As a minimum, the following special precautions shall be taken when drums and containers containing or suspected of containing shock-sensitive wastes are handled:

(i) All non-essential employees shall be evacuated from the area of transfer.

(ii) Material handling equipment shall be provided with explosive containment devices or protective shields to protect equipment operators from exploding containers.

(iii) An employee alarm system capable of being perceived above surrounding light and noise conditions shall be used to signal the commencement and completion of explosive waste handling activities.

(iv) Continuous communications (i.e., portable radios, hand signals, telephones, as appropriate) shall be maintained between the employee-in-charge of the immediate handling area and both the site safety and health supervisor and the command post until such time as the handling operation is completed. Communication equipment or methods that could cause shock sensitive materials to explode shall not be used.

(v) Drums and containers under pressure, as evidenced by bulging or swelling, shall not be moved until such time as the cause for excess pressure is determined and appropriate containment procedures have been implemented to protect employees from explosive relief of the drum.

(vi) Drums and containers containing packaged laboratory wastes shall be considered to contain shock-sensitive or explosive materials until they have been characterized.

CAUTION: Shipping of shock sensitive wastes may be prohibited under U.S. Department of Transportation regulations. Employers and their shippers should refer to 49 CFR 173.21 and 173.50.

(6) *Laboratory waste packs.* In addition to the requirements of paragraph (j)(5) of this section, the following precautions shall be taken, as a minimum, in handling laboratory waste packs (lab packs):

(i) Lab packs shall be opened only when necessary and then only by an individual knowledgeable in the inspection, classification, and segregation of the containers within the pack according to the hazards of the wastes.

(ii) If crystalline material is noted on any container, the contents shall be handled as a shock-sensitive waste until the contents are identified.

(7) *Sampling of drum and container contents.* Sampling of containers and drums shall be done in accordance with a sampling procedure which is part of the site safety and health plan developed for and available to employees and others at the specific worksite.

(8) *Shipping and transport.* (i) Drums and containers shall be identified and classified prior to packaging for shipment.

(ii) Drum or container staging areas shall be kept to the minimum number necessary to identify and classify materials safely and prepare them for transport.

(iii) Staging areas shall be provided with adequate access and egress routes.

(iv) Bulking of hazardous wastes shall be permitted only after a thorough characterization of the materials has been completed.

§ 1910.120

(9) *Tank and vault procedures.* (i) Tanks and vaults containing hazardous substances shall be handled in a manner similar to that for drums and containers, taking into consideration the size of the tank or vault.

(ii) Appropriate tank or vault entry procedures as described in the employer's safety and health plan shall be followed whenever employees must enter a tank or vault.

(k) *Decontamination*—(1) *General.* Procedures for all phases of decontamination shall be developed and implemented in accordance with this paragraph.

(2) *Decontamination procedures.* (i) A decontamination procedure shall be developed, communicated to employees and implemented before any employees or equipment may enter areas on site where potential for exposure to hazardous substances exists.

(ii) Standard operating procedures shall be developed to minimize employee contact with hazardous substances or with equipment that has contacted hazardous substances.

(iii) All employees leaving a contaminated area shall be appropriately decontaminated; all contaminated clothing and equipment leaving a contaminated area shall be appropriately disposed of or decontaminated.

(iv) Decontamination procedures shall be monitored by the site safety and health supervisor to determine their effectiveness. When such procedures are found to be ineffective, appropriate steps shall be taken to correct any deficiencies.

(3) *Location.* Decontamination shall be performed in geographical areas that will minimize the exposure of uncontaminated employees or equipment to contaminated employees or equipment.

(4) *Equipment and solvents.* All equipment and solvents used for decontamination shall be decontaminated or disposed of properly.

(5) *Personal protective clothing and equipment.* (i) Protective clothing and equipment shall be decontaminated, cleaned, laundered, maintained or replaced as needed to maintain their effectiveness.

(ii) Employees whose non-impermeable clothing becomes wetted with hazardous substances shall immediately remove that clothing and proceed to shower. The clothing shall be disposed of or decontaminated before it is removed from the work zone.

(6) *Unauthorized employees.* Unauthorized employees shall not remove protective clothing or equipment from change rooms.

(7) *Commercial laundries or cleaning establishments.* Commercial laundries or cleaning establishments that decontaminate protective clothing or equipment shall be informed of the potentially harmful effects of exposures to hazardous substances.

(8) *Showers and change rooms.* Where the decontamination procedure indicates a need for regular showers and change rooms outside of a contaminated area, they shall be provided and meet the requirements of 29 CFR 1910.141. If temperature conditions prevent the effective use of water, then other effective means for cleansing shall be provided and used.

(l) *Emergency response by employees at uncontrolled hazardous waste sites*—(1) *Emergency response plan.* (i) An emergency response plan shall be developed and implemented by all employers within the scope of paragraphs (a)(1)(i)–(ii) of this section to handle anticipated emergencies prior to the commencement of hazardous waste operations. The plan shall be in writing and available for inspection and copying by employees, their representatives, OSHA personnel and other governmental agencies with relevant responsibilities.

(ii) Employers who will evacuate their employees from the danger area when an emergency occurs, and who do not permit any of their employees to assist in handling the emergency, are exempt from the requirements of this paragraph if they provide an emergency action plan complying with § 1910.38(a) of this part.

(2) *Elements of an emergency response plan.* The employer shall develop an emergency response plan for emergencies which shall address, as a minimum, the following:

(i) Pre-emergency planning.

(ii) Personnel roles, lines of authority, and communication.

(iii) Emergency recognition and prevention.
(iv) Safe distances and places of refuge.
(v) Site security and control.
(vi) Evacuation routes and procedures.
(vii) Decontamination procedures which are not covered by the site safety and health plan.
(viii) Emergency medical treatment and first aid.
(ix) Emergency alerting and response procedures.
(x) Critique of response and follow-up.
(xi) PPE and emergency equipment.

(3) *Procedures for handling emergency incidents.* (i) In addition to the elements for the emergency response plan required in paragraph (1)(2) of this section, the following elements shall be included for emergency response plans:

(A) Site topography, layout, and prevailing weather conditions.
(B) Procedures for reporting incidents to local, state, and federal governmental agencies.
(ii) The emergency response plan shall be a separate section of the Site Safety and Health Plan.
(iii) The emergency response plan shall be compatible and integrated with the disaster, fire and/or emergency response plans of local, state, and federal agencies.
(iv) The emergency response plan shall be rehearsed regularly as part of the overall training program for site operations.
(v) The site emergency response plan shall be reviewed periodically and, as necessary, be amended to keep it current with new or changing site conditions or information.
(vi) An employee alarm system shall be installed in accordance with 29 CFR 1910.165 to notify employees of an emergency situation; to stop work activities if necessary; to lower background noise in order to speed communication; and to begin emergency procedures.
(vii) Based upon the information available at time of the emergency, the employer shall evaluate the incident and the site response capabilities and proceed with the appropriate steps to implement the site emergency response plan.

(m) *Illumination.* Areas accessible to employees shall be lighted to not less than the minimum illumination intensities listed in the following Table H-120.1 while any work is in progress:

TABLE H-120.1—MINIMUM ILLUMINATION INTENSITIES IN FOOT-CANDLES

Foot-candles	Area or operations
5	General site areas.
3	Excavation and waste areas, accessways, active storage areas, loading platforms, refueling, and field maintenance areas.
5	Indoors: Warehouses, corridors, hallways, and exitways.
5	Tunnels, shafts, and general underground work areas. (Exception: Minimum of 10 foot-candles is required at tunnel and shaft heading during drilling mucking, and scaling. Mine Safety and Health Administration approved cap lights shall be acceptable for use in the tunnel heading.)
10	General shops (e.g., mechanical and electrical equipment rooms, active storerooms, barracks or living quarters, locker or dressing rooms, dining areas, and indoor toilets and workrooms.)
30	First aid stations, infirmaries, and offices.

(n) *Sanitation at temporary workplaces*—(1) *Potable water.* (i) An adequate supply of potable water shall be provided on the site.
(ii) Portable containers used to dispense drinking water shall be capable of being tightly closed, and equipped with a tap. Water shall not be dipped from containers.
(iii) Any container used to distribute drinking water shall be clearly marked as to the nature of its contents and not used for any other purpose.
(iv) Where single service cups (to be used but once) are supplied, both a sanitary container for the unused cups and a receptacle for disposing of the used cups shall be provided.
(2) *Nonpotable water.* (i) Outlets for nonpotable water, such as water for firefighting purposes, shall be identified to indicate clearly that the water is unsafe and is not to be used for drinking, washing, or cooking purposes.
(ii) There shall be no cross-connection, open or potential, between a system furnishing potable water and a system furnishing nonpotable water.
(3) *Toilet facilities.* (i) Toilets shall be provided for employees according to the following Table H-120.2.

§ 1910.120

TABLE H–120.2—TOILET FACILITIES

Number of employees	Minimum number of facilities
20 or fewer	One.
More than 20, fewer than 200	One toilet seat and one urinal per 40 employees.
More than 200	One toilet seat and one urinal per 50 employees.

(ii) Under temporary field conditions, provisions shall be made to assure that at least one toilet facility is available.

(iii) Hazardous waste sites not provided with a sanitary sewer shall be provided with the following toilet facilities unless prohibited by local codes:

(A) Chemical toilets;
(B) Recirculating toilets;
(C) Combustion toilets; or
(D) Flush toilets.

(iv) The requirements of this paragraph for sanitation facilities shall not apply to mobile crews having transportation readily available to nearby toilet facilities.

(v) Doors entering toilet facilities shall be provided with entrance locks controlled from inside the facility.

(4) *Food handling.* All food service facilities and operations for employees shall meet the applicable laws, ordinances, and regulations of the jurisdictions in which they are located.

(5) *Temporary sleeping quarters.* When temporary sleeping quarters are provided, they shall be heated, ventilated, and lighted.

(6) *Washing facilities.* The employer shall provide adequate washing facilities for employees engaged in operations where hazardous substances may be harmful to employees. Such facilities shall be in near proximity to the worksite; in areas where exposures are below permissible exposure limits and published exposure levels and which are under the controls of the employer; and shall be so equipped as to enable employees to remove hazardous substances from themselves.

(7) *Showers and change rooms.* When hazardous waste clean-up or removal operations commence on a site and the duration of the work will require six months or greater time to complete, the employer shall provide showers and change rooms for all employees exposed to hazardous substances and health hazards involved in hazardous waste clean-up or removal operations.

(i) Showers shall be provided and shall meet the requirements of 29 CFR 1910.141(d)(3).

(ii) Change rooms shall be provided and shall meet the requirements of 29 CFR 1910.141(e). Change rooms shall consist of two separate change areas separated by the shower area required in paragraph (n)(7)(i) of this section. One change area, with an exit leading off the worksite, shall provide employees with a clean area where they can remove, store, and put on street clothing. The second area, with an exit to the worksite, shall provide employees with an area where they can put on, remove and store work clothing and personal protective equipment.

(iii) Showers and change rooms shall be located in areas where exposures are below the permissible exposure limits and published exposure levels. If this cannot be accomplished, then a ventilation system shall be provided that will supply air that is below the permissible exposure limits and published exposure levels.

(iv) Employers shall assure that employees shower at the end of their work shift and when leaving the hazardous waste site.

(o) *New technology programs.* (1) The employer shall develop and implement procedures for the introduction of effective new technologies and equipment developed for the improved protection of employees working with hazardous waste clean-up operations, and the same shall be implemented as part of the site safety and health program to assure that employee protection is being maintained.

(2) New technologies, equipment or control measures available to the industry, such as the use of foams, absorbents, adsorbents, neutralizers, or other means to suppress the level of air contaminates while excavating the site or for spill control, shall be evaluated by employers or their representatives. Such an evaluation shall be done to determine the effectiveness of the new methods, materials, or equipment before implementing their use on a large scale for enhancing employee protection. Information and data from manufacturers or suppliers may be used as

part of the employer's evaluation effort. Such evaluations shall be made available to OSHA upon request.

(p) *Certain Operations Conducted Under the Resource Conservation and Recovery Act of 1976 (RCRA).* Employers conducting operations at treatment, storage and disposal (TSD) facilities specified in paragraph (a)(1)(iv) of this section shall provide and implement the programs specified in this paragraph. See the "Notes and Exceptions" to paragraph (a)(2)(iii) of this section for employers not covered.)".

(1) *Safety and health program.* The employer shall develop and implement a written safety and health program for employees involved in hazardous waste operations that shall be available for inspection by employees, their representatives and OSHA personnel. The program shall be designed to identify, evaluate and control safety and health hazards in their facilities for the purpose of employee protection, to provide for emergency response meeting the requirements of paragraph (p)(8) of this section and to address as appropriate site analysis, engineering controls, maximum exposure limits, hazardous waste handling procedures and uses of new technologies.

(2) *Hazard communication program.* The employer shall implement a hazard communication program meeting the requirements of 29 CFR 1910.1200 as part of the employer's safety and program.

NOTE TO 1910.120—The exemption for hazardous waste provided in § 1910.1200 is applicable to this section.

(3) *Medical surveillance program.* The employer shall develop and implement a medical surveillance program meeting the requirements of paragraph (f) of this section.

(4) *Decontamination program.* The employer shall develop and implement a decontamination procedure meeting the requirements of paragraph (k) of this section.

(5) *New technology program.* The employer shall develop and implement procedures meeting the requirements of paragraph (o) of this section for introducing new and innovative equipment into the workplace.

(6) *Material handling program.* Where employees will be handling drums or containers, the employer shall develop and implement procedures meeting the requirements of paragraphs (j)(1) (ii) through (viii) and (xi) of this section, as well as (j)(3) and (j)(8) of this section prior to starting such work.

(7) *Training program*—(i) *New employees.* The employer shall develop and implement a training program, which is part of the employer's safety and health program, for employees exposed to health hazards or hazardous substances at TSD operations to enable the employees to perform their assigned duties and functions in a safe and healthful manner so as not endanger themselves or other employees. The initial training shall be for 24 hours and refresher training shall be for eight hours annually. Employees who have received the initial training required by this paragraph shall be given a written certificate attesting that they have successfully completed the necessary training.

(ii) *Current employees.* Employers who can show by an employee's previous work experience and/or training that the employee has had training equivalent to the initial training required by this paragraph, shall be considered as meeting the initial training requirements of this paragraph as to that employee. Equivalent training includes the training that existing employees might have already received from actual site work experience. Current employees shall receive eight hours of refresher training annually.

(iii) *Trainers.* Trainers who teach initial training shall have satisfactorily completed a training course for teaching the subjects they are expected to teach or they shall have the academic credentials and instruction experience necessary to demonstrate a good command of the subject matter of the courses and competent instructional skills.

(8) *Emergency response program*—(i) *Emergency response plan.* An emergency response plan shall be developed and implemented by all employers. Such plans need not duplicate any of the subjects fully addressed in the employer's contingency planning required by permits, such as those issued by the U.S. Environmental Protection Agency, provided that the contingency plan

§ 1910.120

is made part of the emergency response plan. The emergency response plan shall be a written portion of the employers safety and health program required in paragraph (p)(1) of this section. Employers who will evacuate their employees from the worksite location when an emergency occurs and who do not permit any of their employees to assist in handling the emergency are exempt from the requirements of paragraph (p)(8) if they provide an emergency action plan complying with § 1910.38(a) of this part.

(ii) *Elements of an emergency response plan.* The employer shall develop an emergency response plan for emergencies which shall address, as a minimum, the following areas to the extent that they are not addressed in any specific program required in this paragraph:

(A) Pre-emergency planning and co-ordination with outside parties.
(B) Personnel roles, lines of authority, and communication.
(C) Emergency recognition and prevention.
(D) Safe distances and places of refuge.
(E) Site security and control.
(F) Evacuation routes and procedures.
(G) Decontamination procedures.
(H) Emergency medical treatment and first aid.
(I) Emergency alerting and response procedures.
(J) Critique of response and follow-up.
(K) PPE and emergency equipment.

(iii) *Training.* (A) Training for emergency response employees shall be completed before they are called upon to perform in real emergencies. Such training shall include the elements of the emergency response plan, standard operating procedures the employer has established for the job, the personal protective equipment to be worn and procedures for handling emergency incidents.

Exception #1: An employer need not train all employees to the degree specified if the employer divides the work force in a manner such that a sufficient number of employees who have responsibility to control emergencies have the training specified, and all other employees, who may first respond to an emergency incident, have sufficient awareness training to recognize that an emergency response situation exists and that they are instructed in that case to summon the fully trained employees and not attempt control activities for which they are not trained.

Exception #2: An employer need not train all employees to the degree specified if arrangements have been made in advance for an outside fully-trained emergency response team to respond in a reasonable period and all employees, who may come to the incident first, have sufficient awareness training to recognize that an emergency response situation exists and they have been instructed to call the designated outside fully-trained emergency response team for assistance.

(B) Employee members of TSD facility emergency response organizations shall be trained to a level of competence in the recognition of health and safety hazards to protect themselves and other employees. This would include training in the methods used to minimize the risk from safety and health hazards; in the safe use of control equipment; in the selection and use of appropriate personal protective equipment; in the safe operating procedures to be used at the incident scene; in the techniques of coordination with other employees to minimize risks; in the appropriate response to over exposure from health hazards or injury to themselves and other employees; and in the recognition of subsequent symptoms which may result from over exposures.

(C) The employer shall certify that each covered employee has attended and successfully completed the training required in paragraph (p)(8)(iii) of this section, or shall certify the employee's competency at least yearly. The method used to demonstrate competency for certification of training shall be recorded and maintained by the employer.

(iv) *Procedures for handling emergency incidents.* (A) In addition to the elements for the emergency response plan required in paragraph (p)(8)(ii) of this section, the following elements shall be included for emergency response plans to the extent that they do not repeat any information already contained in the emergency response plan:

(*1*) Site topography, layout, and prevailing weather conditions.

(2) Procedures for reporting incidents to local, state, and federal governmental agencies.

(B) The emergency response plan shall be compatible and integrated with the disaster, fire and/or emergency response plans of local, state, and federal agencies.

(C) The emergency response plan shall be rehearsed regularly as part of the overall training program for site operations.

(D) The site emergency response plan shall be reviewed periodically and, as necessary, be amended to keep it current with new or changing site conditions or information.

(E) An employee alarm system shall be installed in accordance with 29 CFR 1910.165 to notify employees of an emergency situation; to stop work activities if necessary; to lower background noise in order to speed communication; and to begin emergency procedures.

(F) Based upon the information available at time of the emergency, the employer shall evaluate the incident and the site response capabilities and proceed with the appropriate steps to implement the site emergency response plan.

(q) *Emergency response to hazardous substance releases.* This paragraph covers employers whose employees are engaged in emergency response no matter where it occurs except that it does not cover employees engaged in operations specified in paragraphs (a)(1)(i) through (a)(1)(iv) of this section. Those emergency response organizations who have developed and implemented programs equivalent to this paragraph for handling releases of hazardous substances pursuant to section 303 of the Superfund Amendments and Reauthorization Act of 1986 (Emergency Planning and Community Right-to-Know Act of 1986, 42 U.S.C. 11003) shall be deemed to have met the requirements of this paragraph.

(1) *Emergency response plan.* An emergency response plan shall be developed and implemented to handle anticipated emergencies prior to the commencement of emergency response operations. The plan shall be in writing and available for inspection and copying by employees, their representatives and OSHA personnel. Employers who will evacuate their employees from the danger area when an emergency occurs, and who do not permit any of their employees to assist in handling the emergency, are exempt from the requirements of this paragraph if they provide an emergency action plan in accordance with § 1910.38(a) of this part.

(2) *Elements of an emergency response plan.* The employer shall develop an emergency response plan for emergencies which shall address, as a minimum, the following to the extent that they are not addressed elsewhere:

(i) Pre-emergency planning and co-ordination with outside parties.

(ii) Personnel roles, lines of authority, training, and communication.

(iii) Emergency recognition and prevention.

(iv) Safe distances and places of refuge.

(v) Site security and control.

(vi) Evacuation routes and procedures.

(vii) Decontamination.

(viii) Emergency medical treatment and first aid.

(ix) Emergency alerting and response procedures.

(x) Critique of response and follow-up.

(xi) PPE and emergency equipment.

(xii) Emergency response organizations may use the local emergency response plan or the state emergency response plan or both, as part of their emergency response plan to avoid duplication. Those items of the emergency response plan that are being properly addressed by the SARA Title III plans may be substituted into their emergency plan or otherwise kept together for the employer and employee's use.

(3) *Procedures for handling emergency response.* (i) The senior emergency response official responding to an emergency shall become the individual in charge of a site-specific Incident Command System (ICS). All emergency responders and their communications shall be coordinated and controlled through the individual in charge of the ICS assisted by the senior official present for each employer.

NOTE TO (q)(3)(i).—The "senior official" at an emergency response is the most senior official on the site who has the responsibility

§ 1910.120

for controlling the operations at the site. Initially it is the senior officer on the first-due piece of responding emergency apparatus to arrive on the incident scene. As more senior officers arrive (i.e., battalion chief, fire chief, state law enforcement official, site coordinator, etc.) the position is passed up the line of authority which has been previously established.

(ii) The individual in charge of the ICS shall identify, to the extent possible, all hazardous substances or conditions present and shall address as appropriate site analysis, use of engineering controls, maximum exposure limits, hazardous substance handling procedures, and use of any new technologies.

(iii) Based on the hazardous substances and/or conditions present, the individual in charge of the ICS shall implement appropriate emergency operations, and assure that the personal protective equipment worn is appropriate for the hazards to be encountered. However, personal protective equipment shall meet, at a minimum, the criteria contained in 29 CFR 1910.156(e) when worn while performing fire fighting operations beyond the incipient stage for any incident.

(iv) Employees engaged in emergency response and exposed to hazardous substances presenting an inhalation hazard or potential inhalation hazard shall wear positive pressure self-contained breathing apparatus while engaged in emergency response, until such time that the individual in charge of the ICS determines through the use of air monitoring that a decreased level of respiratory protection will not result in hazardous exposures to employees.

(v) The individual in charge of the ICS shall limit the number of emergency response personnel at the emergency site, in those areas of potential or actual exposure to incident or site hazards, to those who are actively performing emergency operations. However, operations in hazardous areas shall be performed using the buddy system in groups of two or more.

(vi) Back-up personnel shall stand by with equipment ready to provide assistance or rescue. Advance first aid support personnel, as a minimum, shall also stand by with medical equipment and transportation capability.

(vii) The individual in charge of the ICS shall designate a safety official, who is knowledgable in the operations being implemented at the emergency response site, with specific responsibility to identify and evaluate hazards and to provide direction with respect to the safety of operations for the emergency at hand.

(viii) When activities are judged by the safety official to be an IDLH condition and/or to involve an imminent danger condition, the safety official shall have the authority to alter, suspend, or terminate those activities. The safety official shall immediately inform the individual in charge of the ICS of any actions needed to be taken to correct these hazards at the emergency scene.

(ix) After emergency operations have terminated, the individual in charge of the ICS shall implement appropriate decontamination procedures.

(x) When deemed necessary for meeting the tasks at hand, approved self-contained compressed air breathing apparatus may be used with approved cylinders from other approved self-contained compressed air breathing apparatus provided that such cylinders are of the same capacity and pressure rating. All compressed air cylinders used with self-contained breathing apparatus shall meet U.S. Department of Transportation and National Institute for Occupational Safety and Health criteria.

(4) *Skilled support personnel.* Personnel, not necessarily an employer's own employees, who are skilled in the operation of certain equipment, such as mechanized earth moving or digging equipment or crane and hoisting equipment, and who are needed temporarily to perform immediate emergency support work that cannot reasonably be performed in a timely fashion by an employer's own employees, and who will be or may be exposed to the hazards at an emergency response scene, are not required to meet the training required in this paragraph for the employer's regular employees. However, these personnel shall be given an initial briefing at the site prior to their participation in any emergency response. The initial briefing shall include instruction in the wearing of ap-

Occupational Safety and Health Admin., Labor §1910.120

propriate personal protective equipment, what chemical hazards are involved, and what duties are to be performed. All other appropriate safety and health precautions provided to the employer's own employees shall be used to assure the safety and health of these personnel.

(5) *Specialist employees.* Employees who, in the course of their regular job duties, work with and are trained in the hazards of specific hazardous substances, and who will be called upon to provide technical advice or assistance at a hazardous substance release incident to the individual in charge, shall receive training or demonstrate competency in the area of their specialization annually.

(6) *Training.* Training shall be based on the duties and function to be performed by each responder of an emergency response organization. The skill and knowledge levels required for all new responders, those hired after the effective date of this standard, shall be conveyed to them through training before they are permitted to take part in actual emergency operations on an incident. Employees who participate, or are expected to participate, in emergency response, shall be given training in accordance with the following paragraphs:

(i) *First responder awareness level.* First responders at the awareness level are individuals who are likely to witness or discover a hazardous substance release and who have been trained to initiate an emergency response sequence by notifying the proper authorities of the release. They would take no further action beyond notifying the authorities of the release. First responders at the awareness level shall have sufficient training or have had sufficient experience to objectively demonstrate competency in the following areas:

(A) An understanding of what hazardous substances are, and the risks associated with them in an incident.

(B) An understanding of the potential outcomes associated with an emergency created when hazardous substances are present.

(C) The ability to recognize the presence of hazardous substances in an emergency.

(D) The ability to identify the hazardous substances, if possible.

(E) An understanding of the role of the first responder awareness individual in the employer's emergency response plan including site security and control and the U.S. Department of Transportation's Emergency Response Guidebook.

(F) The ability to realize the need for additional resources, and to make appropriate notifications to the communication center.

(ii) *First responder operations level.* First responders at the operations level are individuals who respond to releases or potential releases of hazardous substances as part of the initial response to the site for the purpose of protecting nearby persons, property, or the environment from the effects of the release. They are trained to respond in a defensive fashion without actually trying to stop the release. Their function is to contain the release from a safe distance, keep it from spreading, and prevent exposures. First responders at the operational level shall have received at least eight hours of training or have had sufficient experience to objectively demonstrate competency in the following areas in addition to those listed for the awareness level and the employer shall so certify:

(A) Knowledge of the basic hazard and risk assessment techniques.

(B) Know how to select and use proper personal protective equipment provided to the first responder operational level.

(C) An understanding of basic hazardous materials terms.

(D) Know how to perform basic control, containment and/or confinement operations within the capabilities of the resources and personal protective equipment available with their unit.

(E) Know how to implement basic decontamination procedures.

(F) An understanding of the relevant standard operating procedures and termination procedures.

(iii) *Hazardous materials technician.* Hazardous materials technicians are individuals who respond to releases or potential releases for the purpose of stopping the release. They assume a more aggressive role than a first responder at the operations level in that

APPENDIX 6B

§ 1910.120

they will approach the point of release in order to plug, patch or otherwise stop the release of a hazardous substance. Hazardous materials technicians shall have received at least 24 hours of training equal to the first responder operations level and in addition have competency in the following areas and the employer shall so certify:

(A) Know how to implement the employer's emergency response plan.

(B) Know the classification, identification and verification of known and unknown materials by using field survey instruments and equipment.

(C) Be able to function within an assigned role in the Incident Command System.

(D) Know how to select and use proper specialized chemical personal protective equipment provided to the hazardous materials technician.

(E) Understand hazard and risk assessment techniques.

(F) Be able to perform advance control, containment, and/or confinement operations within the capabilities of the resources and personal protective equipment available with the unit.

(G) Understand and implement decontamination procedures.

(H) Understand termination procedures.

(I) Understand basic chemical and toxicological terminology and behavior.

(iv) *Hazardous materials specialist.* Hazardous materials specialists are individuals who respond with and provide support to hazardous materials technicians. Their duties parallel those of the hazardous materials technician, however, those duties require a more directed or specific knowledge of the various substances they may be called upon to contain. The hazardous materials specialist would also act as the site liaison with Federal, state, local and other government authorities in regards to site activities. Hazardous materials specialists shall have received at least 24 hours of training equal to the technician level and in addition have competency in the following areas and the employer shall so certify:

(A) Know how to implement the local emergency response plan.

29 CFR Ch. XVII (7-1-94 Edition)

(B) Understand classification, identification and verification of known and unknown materials by using advanced survey instruments and equipment.

(C) Know of the state emergency response plan.

(D) Be able to select and use proper specialized chemical personal protective equipment provided to the hazardous materials specialist.

(E) Understand in-depth hazard and risk techniques.

(F) Be able to perform specialized control, containment, and/or confinement operations within the capabilities of the resources and personal protective equipment available.

(G) Be able to determine and implement decontamination procedures.

(H) Have the ability to develop a site safety and control plan.

(I) Understand chemical, radiological and toxicological terminology and behavior.

(v) *On scene incident commander.* Incident commanders, who will assume control of the incident scene beyond the first responder awareness level, shall receive at least 24 hours of training equal to the first responder operations level and in addition have competency in the following areas and the employer shall so certify:

(A) Know and be able to implement the employer's incident command system.

(B) Know how to implement the employer's emergency response plan.

(C) Know and understand the hazards and risks associated with employees working in chemical protective clothing.

(D) Know how to implement the local emergency response plan.

(E) Know of the state emergency response plan and of the Federal Regional Response Team.

(F) Know and understand the importance of decontamination procedures.

(7) *Trainers.* Trainers who teach any of the above training subjects shall have satisfactorily completed a training course for teaching the subjects they are expected to teach, such as the courses offered by the U.S. National Fire Academy, or they shall have the training and/or academic credentials and instructional experience necessary to demonstrate competent instruc-

398

Occupational Safety and Health Admin., Labor § 1910.120

tional skills and a good command of the subject matter of the courses they are to teach.

(8) *Refresher training.* (i) Those employees who are trained in accordance with paragraph (q)(6) of this section shall receive annual refresher training of sufficient content and duration to maintain their competencies, or shall demonstrate competency in those areas at least yearly.

(ii) A statement shall be made of the training or competency, and if a statement of competency is made, the employer shall keep a record of the methodology used to demonstrate competency.

(9) *Medical surveillance and consultation.* (i) Members of an organized and designated HAZMAT team and hazardous materials specialists shall receive a baseline physical examination and be provided with medical surveillance as required in paragraph (f) of this section.

(ii) Any emergency response employees who exhibits signs or symptoms which may have resulted from exposure to hazardous substances during the course of an emergency incident, either immediately or subsequently, shall be provided with medical consultation as required in paragraph (f)(3)(ii) of this section.

(10) *Chemical protective clothing.* Chemical protective clothing and equipment to be used by organized and designated HAZMAT team members, or to be used by hazardous materials specialists, shall meet the requirements of paragraphs (g) (3) through (5) of this section.

(11) *Post-emergency response operations.* Upon completion of the emergency response, if it is determined that it is necessary to remove hazardous substances, health hazards, and materials contaminated with them (such as contaminated soil or other elements of the natural environment) from the site of the incident, the employer conducting the clean-up shall comply with one of the following:

(i) Meet all of the requirements of paragraphs (b) through (o) of this section; or

(ii) Where the clean-up is done on plant property using plant or workplace employees, such employees shall have completed the training requirements of the following: 29 CFR 1910.38(a); 1910.134; 1910.1200, and other appropriate safety and health training made necessary by the tasks that they are expected to be performed such as personal protective equipment and decontamination procedures. All equipment to be used in the performance of the clean-up work shall be in serviceable condition and shall have been inspected prior to use.

APPENDICES TO § 1910.120—HAZARDOUS WASTE OPERATIONS AND EMERGENCY RESPONSE

NOTE: The following appendices serve as non-mandatory guidelines to assist employees and employers in complying with the appropriate requirements of this section. However paragraph 1910.120(g) makes mandatory in certain circumstances the use of Level A and Level B PPE protection.

APPENDIX A TO § 1910.120—PERSONAL PROTECTIVE EQUIPMENT TEST METHODS

This appendix sets forth the non-mandatory examples of tests which may be used to evaluate compliance with § 1910.120 (g)(4) (ii) and (iii). Other tests and other challenge agents may be used to evaluate compliance.

A. *Totally-encapsulating chemical protective suit pressure test*

1.0—Scope

1.1 This practice measures the ability of a gas tight totally-encapsulating chemical protective suit material, seams, and closures to maintain a fixed positive pressure. The results of this practice indicate the gas tight integrity of a totally-encapsulating chemical protective suit to be evaluated.

1.2 Resistance of the suit materials to permeation, penetration, and degradation by specific hazardous substances is not determined by this test method.

2.0—Definition of terms

2.1 *Totally-encapsulated chemical protective suit (TECP suit)* means a full body garment which is constructed of protective clothing materials; covers the wearer's torso, head, arms, legs and respirator; may cover the wearer's hands and feet with tightly attached gloves and boots; completely encloses the wearer and respirator by itself or in combination with the wearer's gloves and boots.

2.2 *Protective clothing material* means any material or combination of materials used in an item of clothing for the purpose of isolating parts of the body from direct contact with a potentially hazardous liquid or gaseous chemicals.

2.3 *Gas tight* means, for the purpose of this test method, the limited flow of a gas under pressure from the inside of a TECP suit to

APPENDIX 6B

§ 1910.120

29 CFR Ch. XVII (7-1-94 Edition)

atmosphere at a prescribed pressure and time interval.

3.0—Summary of test method

3.1 The TECP suit is visually inspected and modified for the test. The test apparatus is attached to the suit to permit inflation to the pre-test suit expansion pressure for removal of suit wrinkles and creases. The pressure is lowered to the test pressure and monitored for three minutes. If the pressure drop is excessive, the TECP suit fails the test and is removed from service. The test is repeated after leak location and repair.

4.0—Required Supplies

4.1 Source of compressed air.

4.2 Test apparatus for suit testing, including a pressure measurement device with a sensitivity of at least ¼ inch water gauge.

4.3 Vent valve closure plugs or sealing tape.

4.4 Soapy water solution and soft brush.

4.5 Stop watch or appropriate timing device.

5.0—Safety Precautions

5.1 Care shall be taken to provide the correct pressure safety devices required for the source of compressed air used.

6.0—Test Procedure

6.1 Prior to each test, the tester shall perform a visual inspection of the suit. Check the suit for seam integrity by visually examining the seams and gently pulling on the seams. Ensure that all air supply lines, fittings, visor, zippers, and valves are secure and show no signs of deterioration.

6.1.1 Seal off the vent valves along with any other normal inlet or exhaust points (such as umbilical air line fittings or face piece opening) with tape or other appropriate means (caps, plugs, fixture, etc.). Care should be exercised in the sealing process not to damage any of the suit components.

6.1.2 Close all closure assemblies.

6.1.3 Prepare the suit for inflation by providing an improvised connection point on the suit for connecting an airline. Attach the pressure test apparatus to the suit to permit suit inflation from a compressed air source equipped with a pressure indicating regulator. The leak tightness of the pressure test apparatus should be tested before and after each test by closing off the end of the tubing attached to the suit and assuring a pressure of three inches water gauge for three minutes can be maintained. If a component is removed for the test, that component shall be replaced and a second test conducted with another component removed to permit a complete test of the ensemble.

6.1.4 The pre-test expansion pressure (A) and the suit test pressure (B) shall be supplied by the suit manufacturer, but in no case shall they be less than: (A)=three inches water gauge; and (B)=two inches water gauge. The ending suit pressure (C) shall be no less than 80 percent of the test pressure (B); i.e., the pressure drop shall not exceed 20 percent of the test pressure (B).

6.1.5 Inflate the suit until the pressure inside is equal to pressure (A), the pre-test expansion suit pressure. Allow at least one minute to fill out the wrinkles in the suit. Release sufficient air to reduce the suit pressure to pressure (B), the suit test pressure. Begin timing. At the end of three minutes, record the suit pressure as pressure (C), the ending suit pressure. The difference between the suit test pressure and the ending suit test pressure (B–C) shall be defined as the suit pressure drop.

6.1.6 If the suit pressure drop is more than 20 percent of the suit test pressure (B) during the three-minute test period, the suit fails the test and shall be removed from service.

7.0—Retest Procedure

7.1 If the suit fails the test check for leaks by inflating the suit to pressure (A) and brushing or wiping the entire suit (including seams, closures, lens gaskets, glove-to-sleeve joints, etc.) with a mild soap and water solution. Observe the suit for the formation of soap bubbles, which is an indication of a leak. Repair all identified leaks.

7.2 Retest the TECP suit as outlined in Test procedure 6.0.

8.0—Report

8.1 Each TECP suit tested by this practice shall have the following information recorded:

8.1.1 Unique identification number, identifying brand name, date of purchase, material of construction, and unique fit features, e.g., special breathing apparatus.

8.1.2 The actual values for test pressures (A), (B), and (C) shall be recorded along with the specific observation times. If the ending pressure (C) is less than 80 percent of the test pressure (B), the suit shall be identified as failing the test. When possible, the specific leak location shall be identified in the test records. Retest pressure data shall be recorded as an additional test.

8.1.3 The source of the test apparatus used shall be identified and the sensitivity of the pressure gauge shall be recorded.

8.1.4 Records shall be kept for each pressure test even if repairs are being made at the test location.

CAUTION

Visually inspect all parts of the suit to be sure they are positioned correctly and secured tightly before putting the suit back into service. Special care should be taken to examine each exhaust valve to make sure it is not blocked.

Care should also be exercised to assure that the inside and outside of the suit is completely dry before it is put into storage.

Occupational Safety and Health Admin., Labor § 1910.120

B. Totally-encapsulating chemical protective suit qualitative leak test

1.0—Scope

1.1 This practice semi-qualitatively tests gas tight totally-encapsulating chemical protective suit integrity by detecting inward leakage of ammonia vapor. Since no modifications are made to the suit to carry out this test, the results from this practice provide a realistic test for the integrity of the entire suit.

1.2 Resistance of the suit materials to permeation, penetration, and degradation is not determined by this test method. ASTM test methods are available to test suit materials for these characteristics and the tests are usually conducted by the manufacturers of the suits.

2.0—Definition of terms

2.1 *Totally-encapsulated chemical protective suit (TECP suit)* means a full body garment which is constructed of protective clothing materials; covers the wearer's torso, head, arms, legs and respirator; may cover the wearer's hands and feet with tightly attached gloves and boots; completely encloses the wearer and respirator by itself or in combination with the wearer's gloves, and boots.

2.2 *Protective clothing material* means any material or combination of materials used in an item of clothing for the purpose of isolating parts of the body from direct contact with a potentially hazardous liquid or gaseous chemicals.

2.3 *Gas tight* means, for the purpose of this test method, the limited flow of a gas under pressure from the inside of a TECP suit to atmosphere at a prescribed pressure and time interval.

2.4 *Intrusion Coefficient* means a number expressing the level of protection provided by a gas tight totally-encapsulating chemical protective suit. The intrusion coefficient is calculated by dividing the test room challenge agent concentration by the concentration of challenge agent found inside the suit. The accuracy of the intrusion coefficient is dependent on the challenge agent monitoring methods. The larger the intrusion coefficient the greater the protection provided by the TECP suit.

3.0—Summary of recommended practice

3.1 The volume of concentrated aqueous ammonia solution (ammonia hydroxide NH_4OH) required to generate the test atmosphere is determined using the directions outlined in 6.1. The suit is donned by a person wearing the appropriate respiratory equipment (either a positive pressure self-contained breathing apparatus or a positive pressure supplied air respirator) and worn inside the enclosed test room. The concentrated aqueous ammonia solution is taken by the suited individual into the test room and poured into an open plastic pan. A two-minute evaporation period is observed before the test room concentration is measured, using a high range ammonia length of stain detector tube. When the ammonia vapor reaches a concentration of between 1000 and 1200 ppm, the suited individual starts a standardized exercise protocol to stress and flex the suit. After this protocol is completed, the test room concentration is measured again. The suited individual exits the test room and his stand-by person measures the ammonia concentration inside the suit using a low range ammonia length of stain detector tube or other more sensitive ammonia detector. A stand-by person is required to observe the test individual during the test procedure; aid the person in donning and doffing the TECP suit; and monitor the suit interior. The intrusion coefficient of the suit can be calculated by dividing the average test area concentration by the interior suit concentration. A colorimetric ammonia indicator strip of bromophenol blue or equivalent is placed on the inside of the suit face piece lens so that the suited individual is able to detect a color change and know if the suit has a significant leak. If a color change is observed the individual shall leave the test room immediately.

4.0—Required supplies

4.1 A supply of concentrated aqueous ammonium hydroxide (58% by weight).

4.2 A supply of bromophenol/blue indicating paper or equivalent, sensitive to 5–10 ppm ammonia or greater over a two-minute period of exposure. [pH 3.0 (yellow) to pH 4.6 (blue)]

4.3 A supply of high range (0.5–10 volume percent) and low range (5–700 ppm) detector tubes for ammonia and the corresponding sampling pump. More sensitive ammonia detectors can be substituted for the low range detector tubes to improve the sensitivity of this practice.

4.4 A shallow plastic pan (PVC) at least 12":14":1" and a half pint plastic container (PVC) with tightly closing lid.

4.5 A graduated cylinder or other volumetric measuring device of at least 50 milliliters in volume with an accuracy of at least ± 1 milliliters.

5.0—Safety precautions

5.1 Concentrated aqueous ammonium hydroxide, NH_4OH, is a corrosive volatile liquid requiring eye, skin, and respiratory protection. The person conducting the test shall review the MSDS for aqueous ammonia.

5.2 Since the established permissible exposure limit for ammonia is 35 ppm as a 15 minute STEL, only persons wearing a positive pressure self-contained breathing apparatus or a positive pressure supplied air respirator shall be in the chamber. Normally only the person wearing the totally-encapsulating suit will be inside the chamber. A stand-by person shall have a positive pressure self-contained breathing apparatus, or a

§ 1910.120

positive pressure supplied air respirator available to enter the test area should the suited individual need assistance.

5.3 A method to monitor the suited individual must be used during this test. Visual contact is the simplest but other methods using communication devices are acceptable.

5.4 The test room shall be large enough to allow the exercise protocol to be carried out and then to be ventilated to allow for easy exhaust of the ammonia test atmosphere after the test(s) are completed.

5.5 Individuals shall be medically screened for the use of respiratory protection and checked for allergies to ammonia before participating in this test procedure.

6.0—Test procedure

6.1.1 Measure the test area to the nearest foot and calculate its volume in cubic feet. Multiply the test area volume by 0.2 milliliters of concentrated aqueous ammonia solution per cubic foot of test area volume to determine the approximate volume of concentrated aqueous ammonia required to generate 1000 ppm in the test area.

6.1.2 Measure this volume from the supply of concentrated aqueous ammonia and place it into a closed plastic container.

6.1.3 Place the container, several high range ammonia detector tubes, and the pump in the clean test pan and locate it near the test area entry door so that the suited individual has easy access to these supplies.

6.2.1 In a non-contaminated atmosphere, open a pre-sealed ammonia indicator strip and fasten one end of the strip to the inside of the suit face shield lens where it can be seen by the wearer. Moisten the indicator strip with distilled water. Care shall be taken not to contaminate the detector part of the indicator paper by touching it. A small piece of masking tape or equivalent should be used to attach the indicator strip to the interior of the suit face shield.

6.2.2 If problems are encountered with this method of attachment, the indicator strip can be attached to the outside of the respirator face piece lens being used during the test.

6.3 Don the respiratory protective device normally used with the suit, and then don the TECP suit to be tested. Check to be sure all openings which are intended to be sealed (zippers, gloves, etc.) are completely sealed. DO NOT, however, plug off any venting valves.

6.4 Step into the enclosed test room such as a closet, bathroom, or test booth, equipped with an exhaust fan. No air should be exhausted from the chamber during the test because this will dilute the ammonia challenge concentrations.

6.5 Open the container with the pre-measured volume of concentrated aqueous ammonia within the enclosed test room, and pour the liquid into the empty plastic test pan.

Wait two minutes to allow for adequate volatilization of the concentrated aqueous ammonia. A small mixing fan can be used near the evaporation pan to increase the evaporation rate of the ammonia solution.

6.6 After two minutes a determination of the ammonia concentration within the chamber should be made using the high range colorimetric detector tube. A concentration of 1000 ppm ammonia or greater shall be generated before the exercises are started.

6.7. To test the integrity of the suit the following four minute exercise protocol should be followed:

6.7.1 Raising the arms above the head with at least 15 raising motions completed in one minute.

6.7.2 Walking in place for one minute with at least 15 raising motions of each leg in a one-minute period.

6.7.3 Touching the toes with a least 10 complete motions of the arms from above the head to touching of the toes in a one-minute period.

6.7.4 Knee bends with at least 10 complete standing and squatting motions in a one-minute period.

6.8 If at any time during the test the colorimetric indicating paper should change colors, the test should be stopped and section 6.10 and 6.12 initiated (See ¶4.2).

6.9 After completion of the test exercise, the test area concentration should be measured again using the high range colorimetric detector tube.

6.10 Exit the test area.

6.11 The opening created by the suit zipper or other appropriate suit penetration should be used to determine the ammonia concentration in the suit with the low range length of stain detector tube or other ammonia monitor. The internal TECP suit air should be sampled far enough from the enclosed test area to prevent a false ammonia reading.

6.12 After completion of the measurement of the suit interior ammonia concentration the test is concluded and the suit is doffed and the respirator removed.

6.13 The ventilating fan for the test room should be turned on and allowed to run for enough time to remove the ammonia gas. The fan shall be vented to the outside of the building.

6.14 Any detectable ammonia in the suit interior (five ppm ammonia (NH_3) or more for the length of stain detector tube) indicates that the suit has failed the test. When other ammonia detectors are used a lower level of detection is possible, and it should be specified as the pass/fail criteria.

6.15 By following this test method, an intrusion coefficient of approximately 200 or more can be measured with the suit in a completely operational condition. If the intrusion coefficient is 200 or more, then the

Occupational Safety and Health Admin., Labor § 1910.120

suit is suitable for emergency response and field use.

7.0—Retest procedures

7.1 If the suit fails this test, check for leaks by following the pressure test in test A above.

7.2 Retest the TECP suit as outlined in the test procedure 6.0.

8.0—Report

8.1 Each gas tight totally-encapsulating chemical protective suit tested by this practice shall have the following information recorded.

8.1.1 Unique identification number, identifying brand name, date of purchase, material of construction, and unique suit features; e.g., special breathing apparatus.

8.1.2 General description of test room used for test.

8.1.3 Brand name and purchase date of ammonia detector strips and color change data.

8.1.4 Brand name, sampling range, and expiration date of the length of stain ammonia detector tubes. The brand name and model of the sampling pump should also be recorded. If another type of ammonia detector is used, it should be identified along with its minimum detection limit for ammonia.

8.1.5 Actual test results shall list the two test area concentrations, their average, the interior suit concentration, and the calculated intrusion coefficient. Retest data shall be recorded as an additional test.

8.2 The evaluation of the data shall be specified as "suit passed" or "suit failed," and the date of the test. Any detectable ammonia (five ppm or greater for the length of stain detector tube) in the suit interior indicates the suit has failed this test. When other ammonia detectors are used, a lower level of detection is possible and it should be specified as the pass fail criteria.

CAUTION

Visually inspect all parts of the suit to be sure they are positioned correctly and secured tightly before putting the suit back into service. Special care should be taken to examine each exhaust valve to make sure it is not blocked.

Care should also be exercised to assure that the inside and outside of the suit is completely dry before it is put into storage.

APPENDIX B TO § 1910.120—GENERAL DESCRIPTION AND DISCUSSION OF THE LEVELS OF PROTECTION AND PROTECTIVE GEAR

This appendix sets forth information about personal protective equipment (PPE) protection levels which may be used to assist employers in complying with the PPE requirements of this section.

As required by the standard, PPE must be selected which will protect employees from the specific hazards which they are likely to encounter during their work on-site.

Selection of the appropriate PPE is a complex process which should take into consideration a variety of factors. Key factors involved in this process are identification of the hazards, or suspected hazards; their routes of potential hazard to employees (inhalation, skin absorption, ingestion, and eye or skin contact); and the performance of the PPE *materials* (and seams) in providing a barrier to these hazards. The amount of protection provided by PPE is material-hazard specific. That is, protective equipment materials will protect well against some hazardous substances and poorly, or not at all, against others. In many instances, protective equipment materials cannot be found which will provide continuous protection from the particular hazardous substance. In these cases the breakthrough time of the protective material should exceed the work durations.

Other factors in this selection process to be considered are matching the PPE to the employee's work requirements and task-specific conditions. The durability of PPE materials, such as tear strength and seam strength, should be considered in relation to the employee's tasks. The effects of PPE in relation to heat stress and task duration are a factor in selecting and using PPE. In some cases layers of PPE may be necessary to provide sufficient protection, or to protect expensive PPE inner garments, suits or equipment.

The more that is known about the hazards at the site, the easier the job of PPE selection becomes. As more information about the hazards and conditions at the site becomes available, the site supervisor can make decisions to up-grade or down-grade the level of PPE protection to match the tasks at hand.

The following are guidelines which an employer can use to begin the selection of the appropriate PPE. As noted above, the site information may suggest the use of combinations of PPE selected from the different protection levels (i.e., A, B, C, or D) as being more suitable to the hazards of the work. It should be cautioned that the listing below does not fully address the performance of the specific PPE material in relation to the specific hazards at the job site, and that PPE selection, evaluation and re-selection is an ongoing process until sufficient information about the hazards and PPE performance is obtained.

Part A. Personal protective equipment is divided into four categories based on the degree of protection afforded. (See Part B of this appendix for further explanation of Levels A, B, C, and D hazards.)

403

APPENDIX 6B

§ 1910.120

I. *Level A*—To be selected when the greatest level of skin, respiratory, and eye protection is required.

The following constitute Level A equipment; it may be used as appropriate;

1. Positive pressure, full face-piece self-contained breathing apparatus (SCBA), or positive pressure supplied air respirator with escape SCBA, approved by the National Institute for Occupational Safety and Health (NIOSH).
2. Totally-encapsulating chemical-protective suit.
3. Coveralls.[1]
4. Long underwear.[1]
5. Gloves, outer, chemical-resistant.
6. Gloves, inner, chemical-resistant.
7. Boots, chemical-resistant, steel toe and shank.
8. Hard hat (under suit).[1]
9. Disposable protective suit, gloves and boots (depending on suit construction, may be worn over totally-encapsulating suit).

II. *Level B*—The highest level of respiratory protection is necessary but a lesser level of skin protection is needed.

The following constitute Level B equipment; it may be used as appropriate.

1. Positive pressure, full-facepiece self-contained breathing apparatus (SCBA), or positive pressure supplied air respirator with escape SCBA (NIOSH approved).
2. Hooded chemical-resistant clothing (overalls and long-sleeved jacket; coveralls; one or two-piece chemical-splash suit; disposable chemical-resistant overalls).
3. Coveralls.[1]
4. Gloves, outer, chemical-resistant.
5. Gloves, inner, chemical-resistant.
6. Boots, outer, chemical-resistant steel toe and shank.
7. Boot-covers, outer, chemical-resistant (disposable).[1]
8. Hard hat.[1]
9. [Reserved]
10. Face shield.[1]

III. *Level C*—The concentration(s) and type(s) of airborne substance(s) is known and the criteria for using air purifying respirators are met.

The following constitute Level C equipment; it may be used as appropriate.

1. Full-face or half-mask, air purifying respirators (NIOSH approved).
2. Hooded chemical-resistant clothing (overalls; two-piece chemical-splash suit; disposable chemical-resistant overalls).
3. Coveralls.[1]
4. Gloves, outer, chemical-resistant.
5. Gloves, inner, chemical-resistant.
6. Boots (outer), chemical-resistant steel toe and shank.[1]
7. Boot-covers, outer, chemical-resistant (disposable)[1].

---

[1] Optional, as applicable.

29 CFR Ch. XVII (7-1-94 Edition)

8. Hard hat.[1]
9. Escape mask.[1]
10. Face shield.[1]

IV. *Level D*—A work uniform affording minimal protection, used for nuisance contamination only.

The following constitute Level D equipment; it may be used as appropriate:

1. Coveralls.
2. Gloves.[1]
3. Boots/shoes, chemical-resistant steel toe and shank.
4. Boots, outer, chemical-resistant (disposable).[1]
5. Safety glasses or chemical splash goggles*.
6. Hard hat.[1]
7. Escape mask.[1]
8. Face shield.[1]

Part B. The types of hazards for which levels A, B, C, and D protection are appropriate are described below:

I. *Level A*—Level A protection should be used when:

1. The hazardous substance has been identified and requires the highest level of protection for skin, eyes, and the respiratory system based on either the measured (or potential for) high concentration of atmospheric vapors, gases, or particulates; or the site operations and work functions involve a high potential for splash, immersion, or exposure to unexpected vapors, gases, or particulates of materials that are harmful to skin or capable of being absorbed through the skin;
2. Substances with a high degree of hazard to the skin are known or suspected to be present, and skin contact is possible; or
3. Operations are being conducted in confined, poorly ventilated areas, and the absence of conditions requiring Level A have not yet been determined.

II. *Level B*—Level B protection should be used when:

1. The type and atmospheric concentration of substances have been identified and require a high level of respiratory protection, but less skin protection;
2. The atmosphere contains less than 19.5 percent oxygen; or
3. The presence of incompletely identified vapors or gases is indicated by a direct-reading organic vapor detection instrument, but vapors and gases are not suspected of containing high levels of chemicals harmful to skin or capable of being absorbed through the skin.

NOTE: This involves atmospheres with IDLH concentrations of specific substances that present severe inhalation hazards and that do not represent a severe skin hazard; or that do not meet the criteria for use of air-purifying respirators.

III. *Level C*—Level C protection should be used when:

1. The atmospheric contaminants, liquid splashes, or other direct contact will not adversely affect or be absorbed through any exposed skin;
2. The types of air contaminants have been identified, concentrations measured, and an air-purifying respirator is available that can remove the contaminants; and
3. All criteria for the use of air-purifying respirators are met.

IV. *Level D*—Level D protection should be used when:
1. The atmosphere contains no known hazard; and
2. Work functions preclude splashes, immersion, or the potential for unexpected inhalation of or contact with hazardous levels of any chemicals.

NOTE: As stated before, combinations of personal protective equipment other than those described for Levels A, B, C, and D protection may be more appropriate and may be used to provide the proper level of protection.

As an aid in selecting suitable chemical protective clothing, it should be noted that the National Fire Protection Association is developing standards on chemical protective clothing. These standards are currently undergoing public review prior to adoption, including:

NFPA 1991—Standard on Vapor-Protective Suits for Hazardous Chemical Emergencies (EPA Level A Protective Clothing)

NFPA 1992—Standard on Liquid Splash-Protective Suits for Hazardous Chemical Emergencies (EPA Level B Protective Clothing)

NFPA 1993—Standard on Liquid Splash-Protective Suits for Non-emergency, Nonflammable Hazardous Chemical Situations (EPA Level B Protective Clothing)

These standards would apply documentation and performance requirements to the manufacture of chemical protective suits. Chemical protective suits meeting these requirements would be labelled as compliant with the appropriate standard. When these standards are adopted by the National Fire Protection Association, it is recommended that chemical protective suits which meet these standards be used.

APPENDIX C TO § 1910.120—COMPLIANCE GUIDELINES

1. *Occupational Safety and Health Program.* Each hazardous waste site clean-up effort will require an occupational safety and health program headed by the site coordinator or the employer's representative. The purpose of the program will be the protection of employees at the site and will be an extension of the employer's overall safety and health program. The program will need to be developed before work begins on the site and implemented as work proceeds as stated in paragraph (b). The program is to facilitate coordination and communication of safety and health issues among personnel responsible for the various activities which will take place at the site. It will provide the overall means for planning and implementing the needed safety and health training and job orientation of employees who will be working at the site. The program will provide the means for identifying and controlling worksite hazards and the means for monitoring program effectiveness. The program will need to cover the responsibilities and authority of the site coordinator or the employer's manager on the site for the safety and health of employees at the site, and the relationships with contractors or support services as to what each employer's safety and health responsibilities are for their employees on the site. Each contractor on the site needs to have its own safety and health program so structured that it will smoothly interface with the program of the site coordinator or principal contractor.

Also those employers involved with treating, storing or disposal of hazardous waste as covered in paragraph (p) must have implemented a safety and health program for their employees. This program is to include the hazard communication program required in paragraph (p)(1) and the training required in paragraphs (p)(7) and (p)(8) as parts of the employers comprehensive overall safety and health program. This program is to be in writing.

Each site or workplace safety and health program will need to include the following: (1) Policy statements of the line of authority and accountability for implementing the program, the objectives of the program and the role of the site safety and health supervisor or manager and staff; (2) means or methods for the development of procedures for identifying and controlling workplace hazards at the site; (3) means or methods for the development and communication to employees of the various plans, work rules, standard operating procedures and practices that pertain to individual employees and supervisors; (4) means for the training of supervisors and employees to develop the needed skills and knowledge to perform their work in a safe and healthful manner; (5) means to anticipate and prepare for emergency situations; and (6) means for obtaining information feedback to aid in evaluating the program and for improving the effectiveness of the program. The management and employees should be trying continually to improve the effectiveness of the program thereby enhancing the protection being afforded those working on the site.

Accidents on the site or workplace should be investigated to provide information on how such occurrences can be avoided in the future. When injuries or illnesses occur on

§ 1910.120

the site or workplace, they will need to be investigated to determine what needs to be done to prevent this incident from occurring again. Such information will need to be used as feedback on the effectiveness of the program and the information turned into positive steps to prevent any reoccurrence. Receipt of employee suggestions or complaints relating to safety and health issues involved with site or workplace activities is also a feedback mechanism that can be used effectively to improve the program and may serve in part as an evaluative tool(s).

For the development and implementation of the program to be the most effective, professional safety and health personnel should be used. Certified Safety Professionals, Board Certified Industrial Hygienists or Registered Professional Safety Engineers are good examples of professional stature for safety and health managers who will administer the employer's program.

2. *Training.* The training programs for employees subject to the requirements of paragraph (e) of this standard should address: the safety and health hazards employees should expect to find on hazardous waste clean-up sites; what control measures or techniques are effective for those hazards; what monitoring procedures are effective in characterizing exposure levels; what makes an effective employer's safety and health program; what a site safety and health plan should include; hands on training with personal protective equipment and clothing they may be expected to use; the contents of the OSHA standard relevant to the employee's duties and function; and, employee's responsibilities under OSHA and other regulations. Supervisors will need training in their responsibilities under the safety and health program and its subject areas such as the spill containment program, the personal protective equipment program, the medical surveillance program, the emergency response plan and other areas.

The training programs for employees subject to the requirements of paragraph (p) of this standard should address: the employers safety and health program elements impacting employees; the hazard communication program; the medical surveillance program; the hazards and the controls for such hazards that employees need to know for their job duties and functions. All require annual refresher training.

The training programs for employees covered by the requirements of paragraph (q) of this standard should address those competencies required for the various levels of response such as: the hazards associated with hazardous substances; hazard identification and awareness; notification of appropriate persons; the need for and use of personal protective equipment including respirators; the decontamination procedures to be used; preplanning activities for hazardous substance incidents including the emergency reponse plan; company standard operating procedures for hazardous substance emergency responses; the use of the incident command system and other subjects. Hands-on training should be stressed whenever possible. Critiques done after an incident which include an evaluation of what worked and what did not and how could the incident be better handled the next time may be counted as training time.

For hazardous materials specialists (usually members of hazardous materials teams), the training should address the care, use and/or testing of chemical protective clothing including totally encapsulating suits, the medical surveillance program, the standard operating procedures for the hazardous materials team including the use of plugging and patching equipment and other subject areas.

Officers and leaders who may be expected to be in charge at an incident should be fully knowledgeable of their company's incident command system. They should know where and how to obtain additional assistance and be familiar with the local district's emergency response plan and the state emergency response plan.

Specialist employees such as technical experts, medical experts or environmental experts that work with hazardous materials in their regular jobs, who may be sent to the incident scene by the shipper, manufacturer or governmental agency to advise and assist the person in charge of the incident should have training on an annual basis. Their training should include the care and use of personal protective equipment including respirators; knowledge of the incident command system and how they are to relate to it; and those areas needed to keep them current in their respective field as it relates to safety and health involving specific hazardous substances.

Those skilled support personnel, such as employees who work for public works departments or equipment operators who operate bulldozers, sand trucks, backhoes, etc., who may be called to the incident scene to provide emergency support assistance, should have at least a safety and health briefing before entering the area of potential or actual exposure. These skilled support personnel, who have not been a part of the emergency response plan and do not meet the training requirements, should be made aware of the hazards they face and should be provided all necessary protective clothing and equipment required for their tasks.

There are two National Fire Protection Association standards, NFPA 472—"Standard for Professional Competence of Responders to Hazardous Material Incidents" and NFPA 471—"Recommended Practice for Responding to Hazardous Material Incidents", which are excellent resource documents to aid fire departments and other emergency response or-

Occupational Safety and Health Admin., Labor § 1910.120

ganizations in developing their training program materials. NFPA 472 provides guidance on the skills and knowledge needed for first responder awareness level, first responder operations level, hazmat technicians, and hazmat specialist. It also offers guidance for the officer corp who will be in charge of hazardous substance incidents.

3. *Decontamination.* Decontamination procedures should be tailored to the specific hazards of the site, and may vary in complexity and number of steps, depending on the level of hazard and the employee's exposure to the hazard. Decontamination procedures and PPE decontamination methods will vary depending upon the specific substance, since one procedure or method may not work for all substances. Evaluation of decontamination methods and procedures should be performed, as necessary, to assure that employees are not exposed to hazards by re-using PPE. References in appendix D may be used for guidance in establishing an effective decontamination program. In addition, the U.S. Coast Guard's Manual, "Policy Guidance for Response to Hazardous Chemical Releases," U.S. Department of Transportation, Washington, DC (COMDTINST M16465.30) is a good reference for establishing an effective decontamination program.

4. *Emergency response plans.* States, along with designated districts within the states, will be developing or have developed local emergency response plans. These state and district plans should be utilized in the emergency response plans called for in the standard. Each employer should assure that its emergency response plan is compatible with the local plan. The major reference being used to aid in developing the state and local district plans is the *Hazardous Materials Emergency Planning Guide*, NRT-1. The current Emergency Response Guidebook from the U.S. Department of Transportation, CMA's CHEMTREC and the Fire Service Emergency Management Handbook may also be used as resources.

Employers involved with treatment, storage, and disposal facilities for hazardous waste, which have the required contingency plan called for by their permit, would not need to duplicate the same planning elements. Those items of the emergency response plan that are properly addressed in the contingency plan may be substituted into the emergency response plan required in 1910.120 or otherwise kept together for employer and employee use.

5. *Personal protective equipment programs.* The purpose of personal protective clothing and equipment (PPE) is to shield or isolate individuals from the chemical, physical, and biologic hazards that may be encountered at a hazardous substance site.

As discussed in appendix B, no single combination of protective equipment and clothing is capable of protecting against all hazards. Thus PPE should be used in conjunction with other protective methods and its effectiveness evaluated periodically.

The use of PPE can itself create significant worker hazards, such as heat stress, physical and psychological stress, and impaired vision, mobility, and communication. For any given situation, equipment and clothing should be selected that provide an adequate level of protection. However, over-protection, as well as under-protection, can be hazardous and should be avoided where possible.

Two basic objectives of any PPE program should be to protect the wearer from safety and health hazards, and to prevent injury to the wearer from incorrect use and/or malfunction of the PPE. To accomplish these goals, a comprehensive PPE program should include hazard identification, medical monitoring, environmental surveillance, selection, use, maintenance, and decontamination of PPE and its associated training.

The written PPE program should include policy statements, procedures, and guidelines. Copies should be made available to all employees, and a reference copy should be made available at the worksite. Technical data on equipment, maintenance manuals, relevant regulations, and other essential information should also be collected and maintained.

6. *Incident command system (ICS).* Paragraph 1910.120(q)(3)(ii) requires the implementation of an ICS. The ICS is an organized approach to effectively control and *manage* operations at an emergency incident. The individual in charge of the ICS is the senior official responding to the incident. The ICS is not much different than the "command post" approach used for many years by the fire service. During large complex fires involving several companies and many pieces of apparatus, a command post would be established. This enabled *one* individual to be in charge of managing the incident, rather than having several officers from different companies making separate, and sometimes conflicting, decisions. The individual in charge of the command post would delegate responsibility for performing various tasks to subordinate officers. Additionally, all communications were routed through the command post to reduce the number of radio transmissions and eliminate confusion. However, strategy, tactics, and all decisions were made by one individual.

The ICS is a very similar system, except it is implemented for emergency response to all incidents, both large and small, that involve hazardous substances.

For a small incident, the individual in charge of the ICS may perform many tasks of the ICS. There may not be any, or little, delegation of tasks to subordinates. For example, in response to a small incident, the individual in charge of the ICS, in addition to normal command activities, may become

APPENDIX 6B

§ 1910.120

the safety officer and may designate only one employee (with proper equipment) as a back-up to provide assistance if needed. OSHA does recommend, however, that at least two employees be designated as back-up personnel since the assistance needed may include rescue.

To illustrate the operation of the ICS, the following scenario might develop during a small incident, such as an overturned tank truck with a small leak of flammable liquid. The first responding senior officer would implement and take command of the ICS. That person would size-up the incident and determine if additional personnel and apparatus were necessary; would determine what actions to take to control the leak; and, determine the proper level of personal protective equipment. If additional assistance is not needed, the individual in charge of the ICS would implement actions to stop and control the leak using the fewest number of personnel that can effectively accomplish the tasks. The individual in charge of the ICS then would designate himself as the safety officer and two other employees as a back-up in case rescue may become necessary. In this scenario, decontamination procedures would not be necessary.

A large complex incident may require many employees and difficult, time-consuming efforts to control. In these situations, the individual in charge of the ICS will want to delegate different tasks to subordinates in order to maintain a span of control that will keep the number of subordinates, that are reporting, to a manageable level.

Delegation of task at large incidents may be by location, where the incident scene is divided into sectors, and subordinate officers coordinate activities within the sector that they have been assigned.

Delegation of tasks can also be by function. Some of the functions that the individual in charge of the ICS may want to delegate at a large incident are: medical services; evacuation; water supply; resources (equipment, apparatus); media relations; safety; and, site control (integrate activities with police for crowd and traffic control). Also for a large incident, the individual in charge of the ICS will designate several employees as back-up personnel; and a number of safety officers to monitor conditions and recommend safety precautions.

Therefore, no matter what size or complexity an incident may be, by implementing an ICS there will be *one individual in charge* who makes the decisions and gives directions; and, all actions, and communications are coordinated through one central point of command. Such a system should reduce confusion, improve safety, organize and coordinate actions, and should facilitate effective management of the incident.

7. *Site Safety and Control Plans.* The safety and security of response personnel and others in the area of an emergeny response incident site should be of primary concern to the incident commander. The use of a site safety and control plan could greatly assist those in charge of assuring the safety and health of employees on the site.

A comprehensive site safety and control plan should include the following: summary analysis of hazards on the site and a risk analysis of those hazards; site map or sketch; site work zones (clean zone, transition or decontamination zone, work or hot zone); use of the buddy system; site communications; command post or command center; standard operating procedures and safe work practices; medical assistance and triage area; hazard monitoring plan (air contaminate monitoring, etc.); decontamination procedures and area; and other relevant areas. This plan should be a part of the employer's emergency response plan or an extension of it to the specific site.

8. *Medical surveillance programs.* Workers handling hazardous substances may be exposed to toxic chemicals, safety hazards, biologic hazards, and radiation. Therefore, a medical surveillance program is essential to assess and monitor workers' health and fitness for employment in hazardous waste operations and during the course of work; to provide emergency and other treatment as needed; and to keep accurate records for future reference.

The *Occupational Safety and Health Guidance Manual for Hazardous Waste Site Activities* developed by the National Institute for Occupational Safety and Health (NIOSH), the Occupational Safety and Health Administration (OSHA), the U.S. Coast Guard (USCG), and the Environmental Protection Agency (EPA); October 1985 provides an excellent example of the types of medical testing that should be done as part of a medical surveillance program.

9. *New Technology and Spill Containment Programs.* Where hazardous substances may be released by spilling from a container that will expose employees to the hazards of the materials, the employer will need to implement a program to contain and control the spilled material. Diking and ditching, as well as use of absorbents like diatomaceous earth, are traditional techniques which have proven to be effective over the years. However, in recent years new products have come into the marketplace, the use of which complement and increase the effectiveness of these traditional methods. These new products also provide emergency responders and others with additional tools or agents to use to reduce the hazards of spilled materials.

These agents can be rapidly applied over a large area and can be uniformly applied or otherwise can be used to build a small dam, thus improving the workers' ability to control spilled material. These application techniques enhance the intimate contact be-

Occupational Safety and Health Admin., Labor § 1910.120

tween the agent and the spilled material allowing for the quickest effect by the agent or quickest control of the spilled material. Agents are available to solidify liquid spilled materials, to suppress vapor generation from spilled materials, and to do both. Some special agents, which when applied as recommended by the manufacturer, will react in a controlled manner with the spilled material to neutralize acids or caustics, or greatly reduce the level of hazard of the spilled material.

There are several modern methods and devices for use by emergency response personnel or others involved with spill control efforts to safely apply spill control agents to control spilled material hazards. These include portable pressurized applicators similar to hand-held portable fire extinguishing devices, and nozzle and hose systems similar to portable fire fighting foam systems which allow the operator to apply the agent without having to come into contact with the spilled material. The operator is able to apply the agent to the spilled material from a remote position.

The solidification of liquids provides for rapid containment and isolation of hazardous substance spills. By directing the agent at run-off points or at the edges of the spill, the reactant solid will automatically create a barrier to slow or stop the spread of the material. Clean-up of hazardous substances is greatly improved when solidifying agents, acid or caustic neutralizers, or activated carbon adsorbents are used. Properly applied, these agents can totally solidify liquid hazardous substances or neutralize or absorb them, which results in materials which are less hazardous and easier to handle, transport, and dispose of. The concept of spill treatment, to create less hazardous substances, will improve the safety and level of protection of employees working at spill clean-up operations or emergency response operations to spills of hazardous substances.

The use of vapor suppression agents for volatile hazardous substances, such as flammable liquids and those substances which present an inhalation hazard, is important for protecting workers. The rapid and uniform distribution of the agent over the surface of the spilled material can provide quick vapor knockdown. There are temporary and long-term foam-type agents which are effective on vapors and dusts, and activated carbon adsorption agents which are effective for vapor control and soaking-up of the liquid. The proper use of hose lines or hand-held portable pressurized applicators provides good mobility and permits the worker to deliver the agent from a safe distance without having to step into the untreated spilled material. Some of these systems can be recharged in the field to provide coverage of larger spill areas than the design limits of a single charged applicator unit. Some of the more effective agents can solidify the liquid flammable hazardous substances and at the same time elevate the flashpoint above 140 °F so the resulting substance may be handled as a nonhazardous waste material if it meets the U.S. Environmental Protection Agency's 40 CFR part 261 requirements (See particularly § 261.21).

All workers performing hazardous substance spill control work are expected to wear the proper protective clothing and equipment for the materials present and to follow the employer's established standard operating procedures for spill control. All involved workers need to be trained in the established operating procedures; in the use and care of spill control equipment; and in the associated hazards and control of such hazards of spill containment work.

These new tools and agents are the things that employers will want to evaluate as part of their new technology program. The treatment of spills of hazardous substances or wastes at an emergency incident as part of the immediate spill containment and control efforts is sometimes acceptable to EPA and a permit exception is described in 40 CFR 264.1(g)(8) and 265.1(c)(11).

APPENDIX D TO § 1910.120—REFERENCES. The following references may be consulted for further information on the subject of this standard:

1. OSHA Instruction DFO CPL 2.70—January 29, 1986, *Special Emphasis Program: Hazardous Waste Sites.*

2. OSHA Instruction DFO CPL 2–2.37A—January 29, 1986, *Technical Assistance and Guidelines for Superfund and Other Hazardous Waste Site Activities.*

3. OSHA Instruction DTS CPL 2.74—January 29, 1986, *Hazardous Waste Activity Form, OSHA 175.*

4. *Hazardous Waste Inspections Reference Manual,* U.S. Department of Labor, Occupational Safety and Health Administration, 1986.

5. Memorandum of Understanding Among the National Institute for Occupational Safety and Health, the Occupational Safety and Health Administration, the United States Coast Guard, and the United States Environmental Protection Agency, *Guidance for Worker Protection During Hazardous Waste Site Investigations and Clean-up and Hazardous Substance Emergencies.* December 18, 1980.

6. *National Priorities List,* 1st Edition, October 1984; U.S. Environmental Protection Agency, Revised periodically.

7. *The Decontamination of Response Personnel,* Field Standard Operating Procedures (F.S.O.P.) 7; U.S. Environmental Protection Agency, Office of Emergency and Remedial Response, Hazardous Response Support Division, December 1984.

§ 1910.132

8. *Preparation of a Site Safety Plan*, Field Standard Operating Procedures (F.S.O.P.) 9; U.S. Environmental Protection Agency, Office of Emergency and Remedial Response, Hazardous Response Support Division, April 1985.

9. *Standard Operating Safety Guidelines*; U.S. Environmental Protection Agency, Office of Emergency and Remedial Response, Hazardous Response Support Division, Environmental Response Team; November 1984.

10. *Occupational Safety and Health Guidance Manual for Hazardous Waste Site Activities*, National Institute for Occupational Safety and Health (NIOSH), Occupational Safety and Health Administration (OSHA), U.S. Coast Guard (USCG), and Environmental Protection Agency (EPA); October 1985.

11. *Protecting Health and Safety at Hazardous Waste Sites: An Overview*, U.S. Environmental Protection Agency, EPA/625/9-85/006; September 1985.

12. *Hazardous Waste Sites and Hazardous Substance Emergencies*, NIOSH Worker Bulletin, U.S. Department of Health and Human Services, Public Health Service, Centers for Disease Control, National Institute for Occupational Safety and Health; December 1982.

13. *Personal Protective Equipment for Hazardous Materials Incidents: A Selection Guide*; U.S. Department of Health and Human Services, Public Health Service, Centers for Disease Control, National Institute for Occupational Safety and Health; October 1984.

14. *Fire Service Emergency Management Handbook*, International Association of Fire Chiefs Foundation, 101 East Holly Avenue, Unit 10B, Sterling, VA 22170, January 1985.

15. *Emergency Response Guidebook*, U.S Department of Transportation, Washington, DC, 1987.

16. *Report to the Congress on Hazardous Materials Training, Planning and Preparedness*, Federal Emergency Management Agency, Washington, DC, July 1986.

17. *Workbook for Fire Command*, Alan V. Brunacini and J. David Beageron, National Fire Protection Association, Batterymarch Park, Quincy, MA 02269, 1985.

18. *Fire Command*, Alan V. Brunacini, National Fire Protection Association, Batterymarch Park,, Quincy, MA 02269, 1985.

19. *Incident Command System*, Fire Protection Publications, Oklahoma State University, Stillwater, OK 74078, 1983.

20. *Site Emergency Response Planning*, Chemical Manufacturers Association, Washington, DC 20037, 1986.

21. *Hazardous Materials Emergency Planning Guide*, NRT-1, Environmental Protection Agency, Washington, DC, March 1987.

22. *Community Teamwork: Working Together to Promote Hazardous Materials Transportation Safety*. U.S. Department of Transportation, Washington, DC, May 1983.

23. *Disaster Planning Guide for Business and Industry*, Federal Emergency Management Agency, Publication No. FEMA 141, August 1987.

(The Office of Management and Budget has approved the information collection requirements in this section under control number 1218–0139)

[54 FR 9317, Mar. 6, 1989, as amended at 55 FR 14073, Apr. 13, 1990; 56 FR 15832, Apr. 18, 1991]

Appendix 10A
Example: Company Inspection Procedure

APPENDIX 10A

OSHA INSPECTION POLICIES AND PROCEDURES OF

_____

POLICY

It is the policy of _____ to permit inspections by representatives of the Occupational Safety and Health Agency (OSHA). Such inspections shall be accomplished in accordance with the following procedures.

PROCEDURES

1. Upon arrival at any company workplace, the OSHA inspector shall be directed to report to [location of first contact with the designated company representative], the "key person."

Optional: All company managers should be immediately informed of the presence of the OSHA inspector.

2. The inspector is to wait for the company's key person.

3. If the key person will not be available within a reasonable period of time (for example, 30 to 60 minutes) the inspector is to be informed of that fact. The inspector should be told that the company does *not* require an inspection warrant, but that policy requires the presence of the company representative during the inspection and that the inspection may *not* proceed without this individual. It should be politely suggested that the inspection take place on another day.

Optional: If a back-up or substitute key person has been appointed and is available, that individual would assume responsibility for the inspection.

4. Before the commencement of the opening conference, if the inspector is unknown to the key person, the key person is to review the identification documents of the inspector and verify the inspector's identity with an appropriate OSHA official.

5. If the key person is available, it is likely that the inspector will immediately commence an opening conference.

6. During the opening conference, attempt to determine the reason for the inspection.

If the key person does learn of the basis for the inspection, try and limit the scope of the inspection to the subject matter which is the basis for the inspection. That is, if the inspector wants to inspect a given machine, try to limit the inspection to that machine.

Remember: An OSHA inspector does have the right to conduct an inspection of the entire company workplace.

7. During or upon completion of the opening conference, the inspector should seek consent to begin the investigation. If the company has a policy to deny the inspection without an inspection warrant, the inspector should be informed of the policy at this point in time, if not already so informed. If the company policy is to permit the inspection without an inspection warrant, the inspection will then commence.

8. The key person should accompany the inspector *throughout* the inspection.

The only exception to this requirement is when the inspector desires to talk to company employees in private. Employees are entitled to privacy when being questioned by the inspector. This right of privacy is for the protection of *the employees*. If the employees have no objection to the presence of the key person during such an interview, they have effectively waived their right to confidentiality, and the key person does have a right to be present. It may be that the employee would feel more comfortable if the key person is present during any such interview.

If the OSHA inspector objects, however, to the presence of the key person at any employee interviews, even though acceptable to the employee(s), allow the interview to proceed in private. You may always talk with the employees after the inspector has left the workplace.

9. It is not advisable to include other company representatives during any stage of the inspection procedure; rather, limit the management team to the key person;

10. Throughout the inspection, the key person should be courteous to the inspector and respond to questions *if* authorized by the company to do so. It may be that the key person will be considered to "speak for management." If so, his/her statements could be considered to be "authorized admissions" by the employer and, therefore, admissible in evidence in a later judicial proceeding.

If the key person has not been expressly authorized by the company to speak "for the company," the inspector should be informed of that fact.

11. Under no circumstances is the key person, or any other employee of the company, to guess or speculate when responding to questions of an inspector. If an answer if to be given, the key person or any employee should answer *only* what he/she *knows* to be the facts. If the key person or employee has no knowledge regarding the question, that should be the response.

12. Detailed explanations are not encouraged as they may tend to confuse or unduly prolong the scope of the investigation. Answer the question and only the question, and then only with known facts. **Do not volunteer information.**

APPENDIX 10A

13. The company representative should never admit or concede the existence of an unsafe condition. If corrective measures are taken during an inspection, the key person should either make no statement regarding the abatement action or should state that the corrective measures are to be taken *only* as a result of the inspector's demands.

14. **Never admit a violation.**

15. If the company has commenced its own investigation of an accident regarding a given operation or procedure but has not completed that investigation at the time of the OSHA inspection, answers to any questions regarding the accident, operation, or procedure should be deferred pending the completion of the company investigation.

16. An inspector is allowed to take samples, photographs and/or videotapes (except of trade secrets) during the inspection. If the inspector does perform one of these actions, the company should also consider taking such actions. See paragraph 22 below for instructions regarding the samples, photographs, etc.

17. If, during the inspection or any time thereafter, the inspector asks for copies of written documents or materials, consider *the source* of the document or material.

If the company prepared the document in question, for example, an OSHA Log (200), the inspector should be provided with a copy as soon as reasonably possible.

Remember: Some regulations require *immediate accessibility* to various written documents; for example, a copy of the company's written hazard communication program.

If the company did *not* prepare the document (for example, manufacturer's specifications of a piece of equipment) copies of the document may need to be made available, but only when accompanied by disclaimer language. (See: Attachment 1.)

If a copy of a document from a source other than your company is turned over to the inspector without disclaiming its reliability, it may subsequently be concluded that the company believed in and, therefore, adopted all of the representations included in the document.

18. The key person should keep a record of the scope of the inspection, including the identities of employees to whom the inspector spoke, items of apparent interest to the inspector (for example, a specific machine or machine operation), comments made by the inspector, and individual observations of the key person. See paragraph 22 below for instructions regarding these notes, records, etc.

19. If, at any time during the inspection, it is decided by the key person or other designated company representative that the inspection should be terminated, inform the inspector of the fact, and the inspector will immediately stop the inspection and depart the scene. Realize that such an action may force the inspector to obtain an inspection warrant.

20. Upon completion of the inspection, the inspector should hold a closing conference. If there is some question whether such a conference is to take place, the key person should request the scheduling of a closing conference. It is advisable that more than one company representative attend the closing conference to ensure that the company understands the statements of the inspector.

21. During the closing conference, the inspector should be asked if any citations are to be issued as a result of the inspection. If citations are to be issued, determine what safety orders were allegedly violated. Also attempt to determine the classification of any citations which may be forthcoming as a result of the inspection; for example, "serious," etc. The closing conference is not the time not the place to argue with the inspector. Make no concessions nor admissions during the closing conference. **Never admit a violation.**

22. Upon completion of the inspection and closing conference, the key person should prepare a report of the inspection incorporating any records, notes, samples, photographs, etc., made or taken during the inspection. This report is to be made at the request of the company's attorney and must be labeled or designated as having been so prepared. The report should be forwarded to the attorney. Copies of this report are *not* to be circulated.

[Company name]

Date: _____   by _____
                         Name:

ATTACHMENT 1

[Company] makes no representations regarding the truth or accuracy of the contents of the attached document(s). [Company] makes no representations that it or any authorized representative has knowledge of the contents of the attached document(s), that it or any authorized representative of [Company] admits to, acknowledges or adopts the contents of, or any representations contained in said document(s).

By providing a copy, or access to a review, of the attached document(s), [Company] does not and has not authorized any employee to make a statement for [Company] concerning the subject matter of the document(s) or material(s) in question.

INDEX

A

Abatement, 75, 313–314, 323–329
Access to records, 22–23, 123, 136
Accident Prevention Plan, 51–54
Accidents, 299, see also specific types
  chemical, 48
  investigation of, 314, 330–333
  prevention of, 51–54
  spill-type, 48, 299
ACGIH, see American Conference of Governmental Industrial Hygienists
Action Level for airborne contaminants, 56
Acute toxicity, 49, 301–302
Administrative agency allegations, 87–88
Administrative law judges, 87, 90, 91
Aerosols, 153
Affirmative defenses, 89–90, 91
Agriculture, 3, 38, 151
Airborne contaminants, 56
Air compressors, 38
Air contaminants limits, 221–231
Air monitoring, 38, 41, 47, 347, 352
Air quality, 38
Air sources, 38
Alarm systems, 38, 144
Alaska, 215
Alienation of inspector, 90
Alleged Imminent Danger Notice, 64–65
Allergens, 301
American Conference of Governmental Industrial Hygienists (ACGIH), 29
American National Standards Institute (ANSI), 36
American Red Cross, 27
Animal work, 302–303

Annual Survey of Occupational Injuries and Illnesses, 8, 122, 124
ANSI, see American National Standards Institute
Appeals, 71, 85–93
  costs of success of, 89–90
  likelihood of success of, 89–90
  Notice of Contest, 90, 91, 92
  of penalties, 85–93
  possible defenses in, 89–90
  procedural steps in, 90–92
  reasons for, 86–90
  timing of, 91, 92
Area Director, 19, 64, 65, 66–67, 68, 69, 71, 72, 79, 90–91, 92
Area Office location, 19
Arizona, 215
Arkansas, 215
Arsenic, 36, 42
Asbestos, 35, 36, 42, 56, 232–255
  fit testing and, 247–255
  measurement of, 246–247
  medical surveillance and, 241
  monitoring of, 234
  permissible exposure limits for, 233–234
  quality control and, 243–244, 245
  recordkeeping and, 249, 251, 252
  respiratory protection and, 236
  sampling of, 243, 244–245
  smoking cessation and, 273
Assistant Regional Director, 67
Assistant Secretary, 152
Atmospheric oxygen concentration, 184
Atmospheric testing, 194
Attorney expenses, 89
Automotive brake repair operations, 268–273
Available abatement measures, 75

385

B

Biological hazards, 152, 285, see also specific types
Biological monitoring, 134, 136
Blood, defined, 43
Bloodborne pathogens, 43–46, 55, 56, 373–374
Bodily fluids, 43
Brief Guide to Recordkeeping Requirements for Occupational Injuries and Illnesses, A, 5
Burden of proof, 70, 86, 88
Bureau of Labor Statistics, 5, 108, 124

C

California, 54, 215
  sample program from, 306–338
    accident investigation in, 314, 330–333
    communications in, 316–323
    hazard abatement in, 313–314, 323–329
    hazard evaluation in, 313–314, 323–329
    Injury and Illness Prevention Program in, 309–315
    recordkeeping in, 315
    training in, 310, 334–338
Carcinogens, 40, 49, 292, see also specific types
Case analysis, 115–120
Catastrophes, 65–66
Ceiling Limits, 41
Certification, 124
CFR, see Code of Federal Regulations
Changes in workplace, 57
Chemical accidents, 48
Chemical explosions, 48
Chemical hazards, 36, see also specific types
Chemical Hygiene Officer, 47–48, 297
Chemical Hygiene Plan, 47–48, 293, 298–300
Chemical manufacturers, 152, 155, 156
Chemical names, 152
Chemicals, see also specific types
  of acute toxicity, 49, 301–302
  air contaminant limits for, 221–231
  of chronic toxicity, 301–303
  defined, 152
  hazardous, 46–49, 153, 156, 158, 292
  laboratory use of, 46–49, 292, 297
  occupational exposure to, 46–49
  rules and procedures for working with, 300–303
  standard operating procedures for, 47, 293
  threshold limit values for, 29, 155
Chronic toxicity, 301–303
Citation and Notification of Penalty, 85
Citations, see also specific types
  appeals of, 71, 85–93
  consequences of, 87–88
  gravity of, 71
  lesser gravity, 71
  other-than-serious, 69, 70, 93
  posting of, 85–86
  for probability of deaths, 88
  proposed penalties for, 69–72
  reclassification of, 87, 88, 89, 93
  repeated, 69–71
  serious, 69–70, 88, 93
  timing of posting of, 86
  willful, 69–70, 71
Civil fines, 87
Civil litigation, 87
Clean Air Act of 1970, 2
Clean-up operations, 342
Clean Water Act of 1972, 2
Clinical laboratory, defined, 276
Closing conference, 82–83
Coal Mine Health and Safety Act of 1969, 1, 2
Coal tar pitch volatiles, 273
Code of Federal Regulations (CFR), 126
  1903.1, 63
  1903.3, 63
  1903.4(a), 79
  1903.19, 92
  1904, 5
  1904.16, 7
  1910, 29
  1910.20, 22
  1910.22, 27–28
  1910.38, 23–26
  1910.95, 39–40, 86
  1910.120, 60–62
  1910.132, 35–36
  1910.134, 36–39
  1910.146, 38–39
  1910.151, 27
  1910.176, 27–28
  1910.1000–1001, 40–42
  1910.1030, 43–46
  1910.1200, 29–33
  1910.1450, 46–49

INDEX

1926.21, 55
1926.25, 27–28
1926.50, 27
Codes of Safe Practices, 316, 317–318,
    319–320, 321
Colorado, 215
Combustible liquids, 152
Commercial accounts, 152
Communications, see also specific types
    Accident Prevention Plan and, 52
    in California sample program,
        316–323
    for emergency medical assistance, 27
    Exposure Control Plan and, 44–45
    on hazards, 29–33, 285, see also
        Hazard Communication
        Program
Community Right-to-Know, 31
Complaint inspections, 66–67
Compliance Safety and Health Officers,
    63
Comprehensive inspections, 67–68
Compressed gas, 152
Compressed Gas Association Commodity
    Specification G-7.1–1966, 38
Confidentiality, 43, 67, 82
Confined spaces, 38–39, 185, 192, 193,
    194–198, 199–200
Connecticut, 4, 215
Consent, 135
Consequences of citations, 87–88
Construction industry, 28, 38, 55, 79,
    317–318
Consultants for training, 58
Consultation Service Offices, 306
Contaminated laundry, 276
Control measures, laboratory chemicals,
    47
Cooperative program, 124
Corrective measures under Accident
    Prevention Plan, 53
Corrosive materials, 27, see also specific
    types
Cosmetics, 151
Court orders, 65
Criminal charges, 87

D

Danger, 64–65
Deaths
    citations for probability of, 88
    under General Duty Clause, 74
    on injury portion of Log, 15

investigations of, 65–66, 68
oral reporting of, 19, 66
recordkeeping for, 121
reporting of, 5, 8, 16, 19, 66, 122
Declaration of Proof of Service, 90
Decontamination, 276, 342, 355, 358, 372
Defenses, 89–90, 91
Delaware, 215
Department of Labor, 5, 63, 91, 108
Diligence, 88
Disciplinary provisions of Accident
    Prevention Plan, 52–53
Discrimination, 67
Disposables, 279
Distilled spirits, 151
Distributors, 152
Documentation, 81, see also
    Recordkeeping
Dust masks, 37
Dusts, 37, 231–232, see also
    specific types

E

Electrical hazards, 36
Embryotoxins, 301
Emergencies, 66, see also specific types
Emergency Action Plan, 23–26, 55
Emergency response, 342, 348–349, 355,
    358–359
    hazardous waste and, 364–375
Emergency Response Plan, 61, 372
Employee exposure records, 22–23, 43,
    134, 135, 136
Employee medical records, see Medical
    records
Employee representatives, 79, 82, 124,
    136–137, 152
Employees
    communications to, see Communications
    defined, 124, 134, 152–153
    hospitalization of, 8, 66, 122
    notification of, 17, 23, 47, 92
    safety checklist for, 334
    training of, see Training
Employer representatives, 79
"Employer Rights and Responsibilities
    Following an OSHA Inspection",
    82–83
Employers
    defined, 124, 153
    exempted, 3, 126
    premises of, 125–126
    small, 3, 6–7, 16, 126

Engineering controls, 37, 44, 276, 277–278, 351
Environmental monitoring, 134, 299
Environmental Pollution Control Act of 1972, 2
Environmental Protection Agency (EPA), 21, 31
EPA, See Environmental Protection Agency
Establishment, defined, 124
Evacuation, 144
Exempted employers, 3, 126
Exemptions from recordkeeping requirements, 6–8
Existing hazard, 73–74
Explosions, 48
Explosives, 153, see also specific types
Exposure, see also specific types
   air monitoring for determination of, 47
   to bloodborne pathogens, 43–46
   to chemicals, 46–49
   control of, 277
   defined, 124, 153, 276
   determination of, 47, 277, 293
   to hazardous substances, 41, 46–49
   investigations of, 331–333
   to noise, see Noise
   to pathogens, 43–46
   permissible limits of, 40–41, 47, 61, 293, 343
   published level of, 343
   short-term, 41
   to toxic substances, 41
Exposure Control Plan, 43–45, 277, 287
Exposure records, 22–23, 43, 134, 135, 136
Eye protection, 176–178, 280

F

Face protection, 176–178, 280
Facial hair, 37
Falling objects, 36
Family farms, 3
Fatalities, see Deaths
Feasible abatement measures, 75
Federal agencies, 3, see also specific types
Federal Register, 124
Field Operations Manual, 78
Fines, 69, 87
Fire extinguishing equipment, 353
Fire fighting, 66
Fire Protection Plan, 23–26, 55, 144
First aid, 12–13, 14, 15, 27–28, 43, 124
First report of injury, 124

First responder training, 61–62, 362
Fit testing, 37, 247–255
Flammable, 153
Flashpoint, 153
Florida, 215
Formaldehyde, 42
Fumes, 37

G

Gases, 153
General Duty Clause, 73–75
General Industry Standards, 21
Georgia, 215
Gloves, 279
Goals of OSHA, 2
Grade D breathing air, 38
Guam, 215

H

Handwashing facilities, 276, 278
Hawaii, 215
Hazard Communication Program, 29–33, 68, 78, 156
   changes and, 57
   implementation of, 170–174
   location of written, 33
   preparation of, 170–174
   training for, 55, 172–173
Hazard Communication Standard, 22–23, 29, 30–33, 168
Hazardous atmosphere, defined, 184
Hazardous chemicals, 46–49, 153, 156, 158, 292, see also Hazardous substances;
   Hazardous waste; specific types
Hazardous energy control, 201
Hazardous materials response team, 342–343
Hazardous materials specialists, 62, 363
Hazardous materials technicians, 62, 362–363
Hazardous substances, 29, 40–42, 150–151, 152, see also Hazardous chemicals;
   Hazardous waste; Hazards; specific types
   control of exposure to, 41
   defined, 29
   employee notification on, 42
   EPA Community Right-to-Know and, 31
   exposure to, 46–49

INDEX

inventory of, 31–32
labeling of, 30, 32
local regulatory requirements for, 31–32
mixtures as, 30
training for, 32–33
Hazardous Substances Act of 1966, 2
Hazardous waste, see also Hazardous chemicals; Hazardous substances; specific types
defined, 343–344
disposal of, 60
emergency response and, 364–375
storage of, 60
treatment of, 60
uncontrolled, 344
Hazardous Waste and Emergency Response Standard, 60–62
Hazardous Waste Operations and Emergency Response (HAZWOPER), 56, 60
Hazards, see also Hazardous substances; specific types
abatement of, 75, 313–314, 323–329
assessment of, 35–36, 313
biological, 152, 285
chemical, 36
communications on, 29–33, 285, see also Hazard Communication Program
determination of, 155, 164–165
electrical, 36
evaluation of, 313–314, 323–329
existing, 73–74
health, 154, 163–164
identification of, 346
physical, 154, 158, 292
protection from, 33
recognizable, 74
reduction of, 2
Hazard warning, 153–154
HAZWOPER, See Hazardous Waste Operations and Emergency Response
HBV, see Hepatitis B virus
Healthcare professionals, 134, 276
Health conditions, 2
Health hazard, 154, 163–164
Health inspections, 53
Health insurance claims records, 135
Health programs, see Safety and health programs
Health standards, 2, 82, 86
Health violations, 82
Hearing Conservation Program, 39–40
Hepatitis B virus (HBV), 45, 276, 283, 284, 288
High-hazard employment, 67
HIV, see Human immunodeficiency virus
Hospitalization of three or more employees, 8, 66, 122
Hot work permits, 184
Housekeeping, 27–28, 45, 280, 299
Human immunodeficiency virus (HIV), 45, 276, 283, 284, 286

I

IARC, see International Agency for Research on Cancer
Idaho, 215
Identity, 154
Illnesses, see also specific types
Annual Survey of, 8, 122, 124
defined, 15, 125
Log and Summary of Occupational, see Log and Summary of Occupational Injuries and Illnesses
overreporting of, 12
prevention of, 54, 309–315
recordkeeping for, 5–8, 13
records of, 68
reporting of, 12, 122
Supplementary Record of, 5, 17–18, 112
Immediate use, 154
Imminent danger, 64–65
Importers, 155
Incentives, 52
Incidence rate, 124
Indiana, 215
Indifference, 71–72
Infection control, universal precautions, 44
Infectious materials, 43, 45, 276, see also specific types
Informal conference, 92–93
Information for workers, 55–62, see also Communications
Information sources, 165–167
Injuries, see also specific types
Annual Survey of, 8, 122, 124
defined, 15, 125
first report of, 124
Log and Summary of Occupational, see Log and Summary of Occupational Injuries and Illnesses

overreporting of, 12
prevention of, 54, 309–315
recordkeeping for, 5–8, 13
records of, 68
reporting of, 5, 12, 19, 122, 124
serious, 19
Supplementary Record of, 5, 17–18, 112
Injury and Illness Prevention Program, 54, 309–315
Inspections, 63–68, 299, 309
  under Accident Prevention Plan, 53
  avoiding, 77–83
  closing conference, 82–83
  complaint, 66–67
  comprehensive, 67–68
  conduct of, 77–83
  in construction industry, 79
  employer and employee representatives in, 79
  health, 53
  imminent danger, 64–65
  no advance warning of, 68
  opening conference, 78–79
  partial, 67–68
  procedure recommendations, 80–81
  programmed, defined, 67
  purpose of, 78–79
  referral, 66–67
  review of documents, 78–79
  safety, 53
  scheduling of, 63–64
  scope of, 67–68, 78–79
  unprogrammed, 64
  walk-around, 78–79, 81–82
  warrants for, 79–80
Inspection warrant, 79–80, 81
Inspector
  alienation of, 90
  conduct of, 78–83, 90
  dealing with, 78–80
Intentional violations, 71
International Agency for Research on Cancer (IARC), 29, 49
Inventory of hazardous substances, 31–32
Investigations, 310, see also specific types
  accident, 314, 330–333
  catastrophe, 65–66
  of deaths, 65–66, 68
  of exposure, 331–333
Ionizing radiation, 152
Iowa, 215
Isolation, 184

K

Kansas, 215
Kentucky, 215
Key persons, 80–81
Knowing violations, 71–72
Knowledge lack, 18

L

Labeling, 150, 171, 299
  defined, 154, 156
  Hazard Communication Standard and, 30
  of hazardous substances, 30, 32
Laboratory chemicals, 46–49, 292, 297
Laboratory design, 298
Laboratory scales, 292
Laboratory Standards, 46–49, 55
Laboratory waste, 354
Laboratory work, 35
Labor Secretary, 91
Lack of knowledge, 18
Laundry, 45, 276
Lead, 36, 42
Line breaking, 185
Litigation, 18, 87
Local governments, 3, 31–32
Lockout/tagout program, 68
Log and Summary of Occupational Injuries and Illnesses, 5, 8–17, 78, 79, 112
  asterisks in, 16
  changes to previous year's, 12
  completion of, 8–17
  death and, 16
  defined, 124
  for each establishment, 9
  first aid treatment and, 15
  illness portion of, 16
  lining out entries in, 12
  location other than covered by, 9
  loss of consciousness and, 15
  lost work days and, 15, 16–17
  maintenance of, 12
  medical treatment and, 15
  modification of totals in, 12
  new recordable injury, 12
  restriction of work and, 15
  retention of, 12
  revision of, 17
  termination and, 16
  time of recording in, 9
Lost workdays, 15, 16–17, 121, 124–125

INDEX

Louisiana, 215
Low-hazard employment, 67, 125

M

Maine, 215
Maintenance, 144, 299
Maryland, 215
Massachusetts, 215
Material Safety Data Sheets, 29, 30–32, 57, 136, 158, 160, 171–172, 303
   defined, 134, 154
   destruction of, 22
   employee requests for, 30–31
   location of, 30–31
   retention of, 22
Medical consultations, 48–49, 292, 294, 350
Medical examinations, 294, 350
Medical questionaires, 256–267
Medical records, 137
   analyses using, 136
   defined, 22, 134, 135
   employee access to, 22–23
   questionaires for, 256–267
   release form for employee's use, 22
   retention of, 22
Medical services, 27
Medical surveillance, 61, 241, 348, 349, 358, 373
Medical treatment, 12–13, 14, 125
Medical wastes, 45
Metal and Nonmetallic Mine Safety Act of 1966, 1
Michigan, 215
Mineral dusts, 231–232
Mines, 3
Mine Safety and Health Administration, 38
Minnesota, 216
Mississippi, 216
Missouri, 216
Mists, 37
Mixtures, 30, 154, see also specific types
Monitoring, 293
   air, 38, 41, 47, 347, 352
   of asbestos, 234
   biological, 134, 136
   environmental, 134, 299
   of noise, 213–214
   periodic, 293
   termination of, 293
Montana, 216
MSDS, see Material Safety Data Sheet
Multi-employee hospitalization, 8, 66, 122

N

National Advisory Committee on Occupational Safety and Health, 3
National Commission on State Workers' Compensation Laws, 3
National Environmental Policy Act of 1969, 2
National Institute for Occupational Safety and Health (NIOSH), 2–3, 23, 38
National Toxicology Program (NTP), 29, 49, 155
Nebraska, 216
Nevada, 216
New Hampshire, 216
New Jersey, 216
New Mexico, 216
New York, 4, 216
NIOSH, See National Institute for Occupational Safety and Health
4-Nitrobiphenyl, 273–274
Noise, 35, 204–214, 218
   acceptable exposure to, 39
   computation of exposure to, 208–210
   employers exempt from regulations, 39
   exposure to, 39–40
   measurement of, 211, 214
   monitoring of, 213–214
   permissible, 204
   protection from, 210–211
   tolerance of, 212
Nonionizing radiation, 152
North Carolina, 216
North Dakota, 216
Notice of Alleged Imminent Danger, 64–65
Notice of Contest, 90, 91, 92
Notification of employees, 17, 23, 47, 92
Notification of Failure to Abate an Alleged Violation, 72
NTP, see National Toxicology Program
Nuisance particulates, 152

O

Occupational Safety and Health Administration (OSHA), 2, 104, 125
Occupational Safety and Health Review Commission, 3, 91
Ohio, 216
Oklahoma, 216

On-scene incident commander, training of, 62
Onsite Consultation Project, 215–217
Onsite training requirements, 56
Opening conference, 78–79
Oral reporting, 19, 66
Oregon, 216
Organic peroxide, 154, 292
OSHA, See Occupational Safety and Health Administration
OSHA-8, see Notice of Alleged Imminent Danger
OSHA-2B, see Notification of Failure to Abate an Alleged Violation
OSHA No. 101, see Supplemental Record of Occupational Injuries and Illnesses
OSHA No. 200, see Log and Summary of Occupational Injuries and Illnesses
Other-than-serious citations, 69, 70, 93
Overreporting of injuries and illnesses, 12
Overview of OSHA, 1–4
Oxidizers, 154, 292
Oxygen, 38
Oxygen concentration, 184
Oxygen deficiency, 38–39, 185, 343
Oxygen enriched atmosphere, 185

P

Partial inspections, 67–68
Pathogens, 43–46, 55, 56, 373–374, see also specific types
PELs, see Permissible Exposure Limits
Penalties
   appeal of, 85–93
   civil, 72
   mandatory, 70
   proposed, 69–72
   for recordkeeping failures, 123
   reduction of, 87
   for serious citations, 70
   for willful citations, 71
Pennsylvania, 216
Performance-oriented training requirements, 56
Periodic monitoring, 293
Periodic training, 56
Permanent transfer, 16
Permissible Exposure Limits (PELs), 40–41, 47, 61, 293, 343
   for asbestos, 233–234

Peroxide, 154, 292
Personal protective equipment, 35–36, 44–45, 279–280, 351, 364–365
Physical harm, 74, 88
Physical hazards, 154, 158, 292
Plain indifference, 71, 72
Post emergency response, 343–344
Posters, 79
Posting, 17, 86, 125
Potentially infectious materials, 43, 276
Premises, 125–126
Prescription medications, 126
Preservation of records, 135
Principal tenet of OSHA, 2
Probable cause, 80
Produce, 154
Proof, burden of, 70, 86, 88
Protection, see also specific types
   equipment for, 35–36, 44–45, 279–280, 351, 364–365
   eye, 176–178, 280
   face, 176–178, 280
   fire, 23–26, 55, 144
   from hazards, 33
   from noise, 210–211
   respiratory, 36–39, 178–182, 236
Protective laboratory practices and equipment, 292, 299
Published exposure level, 343
Puerto Rico, 216
Punch press, 35
Purchase of business, 23
Pyrophoric, 154

Q

Quality control, 243–244, 245

R

Radiation, 152
Radioactive waste, 354
Railroads, 3
RCRA, See Resource Conservation and Recovery Act
Reasonable diligence, 88
Reasonably foreseeable standard, 74
Reclassification of citations, 87, 88, 89, 93
Recognizable hazard, 74
Recordable cases, 121, 126
Recordkeeping, 5–19, 287, 350, see also Records
   for Accident Prevention Plan, 53–54
   agencies involved in, 108

asbestos and, 249, 251, 252
brief guide to, 5
in California sample program, 310, 315
for deaths, 121
defined, 126
employers subject to, 110–111
exemptions from, 6–8
forms for, 112
guide to, 5
for illnesses, 5–8, 13
for infectious materials, 43, 46
for injuries, 5–8, 13
for lost workdays, 121
penalties for failure to comply with, 123
for training, 59
Recordkeeping Guidelines for Occupational Injuries and Illnesses, 5, 15
Records, 299, see also Recordkeeping; specific types
access to, 22–23, 123, 136
confidentiality of, 43
defined, 135
establishment of, 113
exposure, 22–23, 43, 134, 135, 136
health insurance claims, 135
illness, 68
of illnesses, 68
of injuries, 68
location of, 113–114
maintenance of, 114
medical, see Medical records
preservation of, 135
retention of, 22–23, 113–114
supplementary, 5, 17–18, 112
transfer of, 23, 140
Referenced documents, 217
Referral inspections, 66–67
Refresher training, 48
Regional Director, 79
Regularly exempt employers, 126
Regulated waste, 45, 276
Release form, 23
Repeated citations, 69–71
Repeated violations, 88–89
Reporting
of accident investigations, 331–333
of deaths, 5, 8, 19, 66, 122
of exposure investigations, 331–333
forms for, 126
of hospitalization of three or more employees, 8, 66, 122
of illnesses, 122

of injuries, 5, 12, 19, 122, 124
oral, 19, 66
of permanent transfer, 16
of serious injury, 5
of termination, 16
Reproductive toxins, 49, 292
Reputation with OSHA, 78
Rescue work, 66, 185
Research laboratory, 276–277
Resource Conservation and Recovery Act (RCRA), 21, 60
Respirators, 37, 38
Respiratory protection, 36–39, 178–182, 236
Respiratory Protection Standard, 37–39
Responsible party, 154
Restraining orders, 65
Restriction of work or motion, 126
Retention
of exposure records, 22–23
of Log and Summary of Occupational Injuries and Illnesses, 12
of Material Safety Data Sheets, 22
of records, 22–23, 113–114
of Summary of Occupational Injuries and Illnesses, 17
Retrieval system, 185
Rhode Island, 216
Right-to-Know, 31

S

Safe Drinking Water Act of 1974, 2
Safety and health inspections, 53
Safety and health management program, 68
Safety and health programs, 2, 78, 316, 344–346
Safety and health supervisors, 344
Safety checklist, 334
Safety conditions, 2
Safety inspections, 53
Safety meetings, 52, 335
Safety standards, 2, 82
Safety training, 336
"Safety Training and Education," OSHA, 55
Safety violations, 82
Sale of business, 23
Sampling of asbestos, 243, 244–245
Scaffolding, 35
Secretary of Labor, 91
Self-employed persons, 3
Serious citations, 69–70, 88, 93

Serious injuries, 19
Settlement, 92
Sewer system entry, 201
Sharps, 36, 276, 278
Shipyards, 38–39
Short Term Exposure Limits (STELs), 41
SIC, see Standard Industry Classification
Single dose, 126
Small emloyers, 3, 6–7, 16, 126
Small quantity generators, 344
Source individuals, 277
South Carolina, 216
South Dakota, 216
Specific chemical identity, 135, 154, 160–161
Specific written consent, 135
Spills, 48, 299, 373–374
Standard Industry Classification (SIC), 7, 126
Standard operating procedures for laboratory chemicals, 47, 293
Standards, see also specific types
　General Industry, 21
　Hazard Communication, 22–23, 29, 30–33, 168
　Hazardous Waste and Emergency Response, 60–62
　health, 2, 82, 86
　Laboratory, 46–49, 55
State, defined, 126
State agencies, 108, 126, 127–128
State employees, 3
State governments, 3
State occupational safety and health plans, 3
Sterilization, 277
Summary of Occupational Injuries and Illnesses, 16–17
Supervisory training, 57, 60
Supplementary Record of Occupational Injuries and Illnesses, 5, 17–18, 112

T

Tagout program, 68
Temporary restraining orders, 65
Tennessee, 216
Termination, 16
Testing, 185, 194, see also specific types
　atmospheric, 194
　fit, 37, 247–255
Texas, 216

Threshold Limit Values for Chemical Substances and Physical Agents in the Work Environment, 29, 155
Timing
　of appeals, 91, 92
　of citations posting, 86
　of closing conference, 83
　of training, 45, 56, 60
Toxicity, see also Toxic substances; specific types
　acute, 49, 301–302
　chronic, 301–303
　embryo-, 301
　reproductive, 49
　unknown, 49
Toxic substances, 29, 40–42, see also Toxicity; specific types
Toxic Substances Control Act of 1976, 2, 151
Trade secrets, 135, 138, 154, 160, 167–168
Training, 2, 52, 55–62, 160–161, 299–300, 310, 314–315, 362, see also specific types
　Accident Prevention Plan, 52
　awareness level, 61–62
　on bloodborne pathogens, 55, 56
　in California sample program, 310, 334–338
　certificate for completion of, 62
　completion of, 62
　consultants for, 58
　defined, 144
　detection and observation, 33
　documentation of, 33, 36
　Emergency Action Plan, 24, 55
　Fire Protection Plan, 26, 55
　first responder, 61–62, 362
　Hazard Communication Program, 55, 172–173
　hazardous materials, 29
　of hazardous materials specialists, 62
　of hazardous materials technicians, 62
　hazardous substances, 32–33
　under Hazardous Waste Operations and Emergency Response (HAZWOPER), 60
　infectious materials, 45
　laboratory chemicals, 47, 48
　levels of, 57, 61–62
　one-time, 56
　onsite, 56
　performance-oriented, 56
　periodic, 56

INDEX

personal protective equipment, 35–36
on physical and health hazards, 33
preparation for, 57–58
presentation of topics in, 57, 58–59
on protection from hazards, 33
recordkeeping for, 59
refresher requirements for, 56–57
request for, 335
requirements for, 56–57
on respirators, 37
safety, 55, 336
supervisory, 57, 60
timing of, 45, 56, 60
Transfer of records, 23, 140

U

Uncontrolled hazardous waste, 344
Unfounded complaints, 78
Universal precautions, 44, 277
Unprogrammed inspections, 64
Unstable, 154
U.S.C.A. 660, 67
U.S.C.A. 662, 64
U.S.C.A. 658(c), 83
U.S.C.A. 666(k), 70, 88
Utah, 216

V

Vaccinations, 45, 276
Vermont, 216
Violations, 82, see also specific types
  alleged, 82
  failure to abate, 72
  health, 82
  intentional, 71–72
  knowing, 71–72
  repeated, 88–89
  of safety regulations, 87
Virginia, 217
Virgin Islands, 217
Viruses, 45, 276, 283, 284, 286, see also specific types
Volunteers, 126

W

Walk-around inspections, 78–79, 81–82
Warrants for inspections, 79–80
Washington, 217
Washington, DC, 215
Waste, see also specific types
  disposal of, 300
  hazardous, see Hazardous waste
  laboratory, 354
  medical, 45
  radioactive, 354
  regulated, 45, 276
Water-reactive, 155, 293
West Virginia, 217
Willful citations, 69–70, 71, 88
Wisconsin, 217
Work area, 155
Work environment, defined, 126
Workers' compensation, 12, 87, 126
Workplace, defined, 155
Workplace changes, 57
Work practice controls, 44, 77
Written consent, 135
Written hazard communication program, 156
Wyoming, 217

Z

Z tables, 41, 42

Materia dispuesta terminó de imprimirse en
marzo de 1997, en Litográfica Ingramex, S.A. de C.V.
Centeno 162, Col. Granjas Esmeralda, C. P. 09810,
México, D.F. Cuidado de la edición: Sandra Hussein y
Freja I. Cervantes.

toldos y braseros en las esquinas, muchos más de los necesarios; la ciudad destruida parecía un inmenso pretexto para transformarse en fonda y llenar el aire con nubes de maíz cocido.

Al ver los afanes dispersos, las manos seleccionando las ricas basuras, Mauricio sintió que todo encajaba de otro modo; lentamente, como si debiera atesorar el instante, cedió a ideas que fluían sin prisa y pensó que para su padre la Calle del Oro hubiera sido un tema de reconstrucción, un motivo ideal para subir materia. Lo vio ante el espejo, frotándose la espalda con furia, y en la profusión de las cosas sueltas, del cascajo, de lo que reposaba sin autoridad, Mauricio entendió lo que significaba el otro lado de la toalla: podía dividirlo todo a la manera de las toallas: el lado áspero para quienes construían y se adelantaban al destino; el lado suave para los testigos que recogían las porciones dispersas, rotas: una naranja un yeso una llave un botón una piedra un alfiler una obsidiana.

Durante horas, Mauricio hurgó en el polvo. Cuando ya casi no quedaban escombros, encontró un pequeño círculo de cobre, una moneda de otro tiempo, como los quintos que fueron a dar a la ventana de Verónica. Justo entonces la vio a ella; se frotaba los ojos con los puños, como si acabara de despertarse.

Amanecía en la calle, amanecían de nuevo, se acercaban al borde de las cosas, a lo que empieza a ser distinto, futuro, definitivamente real.

Cuando despertó, una luz rayada se colaba por las persianas. Sobre una mesa de marquetería, vio un vaso con café y un pan dulce.

Las paredes estaban decoradas con retratos en forma de medallón. Casi todos representaban a mujeres de pelo recogido con fuerza y labio superior ensombrecido por un bigote honesto. Parecían escogidas para representar una decencia antigua; mujeres de las que emanaba el perfume dulzón de las ropas que habían lavado.

Había quinqués en las mesas. En un rincón, la luz del sol inquietaba una vitrina. Mauricio se acercó a ver medallas, diplomas, cintas de colores, distinciones vagas. Estaba en una casa museo, no había duda. Probablemente aquellos cuartos honraban a un prócer menor, con descendientes adinerados, capaces de sacrificar una propiedad para perpetuar una gloria incierta con pergaminos, los rostros de las tías, muebles incómodos.

Escuchó el rumor de palas allá afuera; los trabajos proseguían. Verónica debía estar en la calle desde el amanecer. Bebió el café de un trago y comió el pan a dentelladas.

Buscó un baño. Orinó en la taza de porcelana, jaló la cadena y oyó la precipitación gutural de los desagües viejos. Salió a la Calle del Oro.

La zona estaba casi despejada, como si un ejército de centinelas hubiera impuesto el orden. Volvió al sitio en el que estuvo el día anterior. Buscó a Verónica con la vista, sin querer encontrarla todavía, tratando de posponer el beneficio central de esa jornada, la promesa de volver a sus manos menudas y sangradas.

Subió a un promontorio de ladrillos que en unas cuatro horas recuperaría el nivel de la calle. En Insurgentes circulaban carretillas cargadas de piedras. El aire olía a tamales, a atole, a gases raros. Había

el piso y Carlos y él en la cama diminuta. A pesar de la incomodidad, Mauricio disfrutó la reunión forzada, las respiraciones que se confundían en la oscuridad, el olor limpio y un poco agrio de las cosas de la sirvienta. Estaban asustados, incómodos, felices. Al día siguiente todos se veían cansados, salvo su madre, que ya había hecho el desayuno y tarareaba una canción sobre la primavera en el campo.

Luego Mauricio recordó un momento anterior, cuando abrió los ojos y la casa vibraba. En ese instante pensó que su padre caminaba por el pasillo y sus pasos poderosos estremecían los muros. La casa era la concha de su caminata. ¿Por qué nunca le dijo a su padre que de niño confundía los temblores con sus pasos? ¿Por qué sólo ahora eso era importante?

¿Dónde se habría metido Verónica? Abrió los ojos y no vio nada. Prefirió cerrarlos. Estaba a punto de dormirse cuando sintió los dedos rasposos que pasaban por su rostro. También ella se había despellejado.

—Desde que desperté quería hacer esto —dijo Verónica.

Seguramente se refería a esa mañana, pero él pensó que hablaba de su otro sueño, del letargo que la borró durante tanto tiempo de las calles de Terminal Progreso.

Le sorprendió la palidez lunar de Verónica. Su cuerpo delgado apenas se distinguía del de una adolescente por el vello púbico, una mata revuelta y densa.

Verónica lo desvistió sin acariciarlo. Mauricio se sintió incorporado al sillón, fue uno con los cojines mientras su sexo crecía entre los dedos de Verónica. Sintió un ardor ácido al entrar en ella y tuvo la rara impresión de presenciar la escena desde un rincón del cuarto. Vio los cuerpos unidos, como si formaran un tercer animal, una sola bestia que jadeaba apenas.

confusión, alguien ofrecía una resistencia endeble y decisiva entregando galletas a los brigadistas.

Encontró unas vendas entre las piedras del laboratorio y se cubrió las manos para seguir excavando. Movió trozos de cascajo hasta que la espalda lo hizo detenerse. Se quedó fijo, incapaz de lograr movimiento alguno, con los músculos paralizados. El dolor lo ayudó a conservar la presencia de ánimo porque en ese momento volvió a temblar. Cuatro o cinco rescatistas se arrodillaron a su lado y rezaron en voz alta, viendo el edificio de enfrente.

Un rumor de plaza recorrió la calle cuando el temblor se detuvo.

Le costó mucho trabajo ponerse en pie; la sangre parecía detenida en sus piernas. Entonces llegó Verónica:

—Por aquí —dijo, como si hubieran quedado en algo.

Caminaron al fondo de la calle. Verónica se detuvo un poco antes de la esquina, en una casa de principios de siglo. Empujó la puerta, pasaron a un vestíbulo húmedo y oscuro; él tropezó con una piedra.

—Cuidado —Verónica se movía con familiaridad en ese sitio. Lo condujo a un espacio grande; la sala, de seguro. Aun en la penumbra, Mauricio distinguió los muebles viejos, raídos. En esa habitación todo lucía tan gastado que no se extrañaba la electricidad. ¿Quiénes vivían ahí? Una pareja de ancianos, tal vez.

Mauricio se sentó en un sofá; se preguntó si ése sería el mueble que se llamaba "canapé". Los cojines parecían rellenos de aserrín.

Cerró los ojos y por un momento recuperó una escena remota de Terminal Progreso: había temblado a media noche y la familia se refugió en el cuarto de servicio, detrás del patio de lavado. Su padre decidió que era la habitación más segura. La sirvienta se había ido a su tierra y pudieron dormir ahí, sus padres en

Saltaron un Akenathón volcado como un escarabajo y empezaron a levantar piedras. Un olor químico flotaba en el aire.

—Aquí sólo ha salido un muerto —informó un hombre de chamarra verde que pertenecía a una corporación indescifrable—, de seguro era el velador de los laboratorios. Hay que sacar las sustancias.

Nadie sabía lo que eran las sustancias; el laboratorio estaba reducido a un montón de cascajo. Después de horas de escarbar entre el polvo y la argamasa, Mauricio encontró una factura, con la dirección del local; su región de piedras correspondía a un sexto piso. Entonces escuchó un ruido inverosímil: un teléfono bajo sus pies. Se arrodilló y excavó con desesperación. Cuando finalmente descolgó el aparato, con las manos despellejadas, no había nadie al otro lado.

Permaneció un rato de rodillas. Resopló, vencido por el esfuerzo, y tuvo la impresión de que le salía polvo de los pulmones.

Volvió a trabajar hasta que una mano le tocó el hombro:

—Toma, güero —un hombre le tendió un vaso de plástico con sopa de pasta, en forma de pepitas.

Comió golosamente; sólo entonces supo que tenía mucha hambre.

En la tarde se encendieron hogueras en tambos oxidados. Los depósitos de sustancias corrosivas fueron hallados al anochecer, peroles enormes con un aspecto extrañamente casero, de cocina económica.

Un poco más tarde hubo una pausa en la que se repartieron galletas. La ciudad estaba devastada, humos extraños se alzaban en derredor, se hablaba de miles de muertos, de recién nacidos atrapados en los escombros del Hospital General, de los lugares de siempre destruidos para siempre, y en medio de la

—¿Qué pasó en Terminal?

—Nada, como siempre —respondió Verónica—. Tu mamá está juntando cosas para los damnificados —Mauricio vio sus manos fuertes, mil veces lavadas, reuniendo ollas, vendas, ropas viejas, trastos que de pronto resultaban esenciales.

Verónica le dijo que los brigadistas llevaban un listón amarillo en el brazo. Subieron al departamento y Mauricio recordó la camiseta con la que dormía Lorena, recordó la última noche que pasaron juntos, recordó la maravillosa entrega que se debía a que los dos ya se sabían en otro sitio.

—Déjame ver si tengo algo amarillo —le dijo a Verónica.

Encontró una franela gruesa, para secar los trastes. La cortó en dos con unas tijeras.

Ya sabía que su nudo le iba a parecer flojo a Verónica y sonrió cuando ella insistió en que lo apretara más.

Escucharon las noticias en un radio de transistores: el presidente decía que México no necesitaba ayuda, un locutor acostumbrado a hablar con una alegría descolocada dijo que la Cruz Roja pedía voluntarios y recomendó hervir veinte minutos el agua y reportar fugas de gas. Un poco después, escucharon que los montañistas de la universidad invitaban a formar brigadas.

Subieron a una camioneta en Ciudad Universitaria y recorrieron Insurgentes en sentido contrario. La brigada se dividió en la colonia Roma. Los montañistas se armaron de sogas para escalar fachadas en la plaza Río de Janeiro y los reclutas del momento fueron llevados a la Calle del Oro, una diagonal de una cuadra, que desembocaba en la glorieta con la réplica de La Cibeles.

Insurgentes, se agitaban las banderolas colocadas para las fiestas de septiembre. Cerca de su edificio, se detuvo un Grial 600; tres hombres bajaron del auto y se arrodillaron en la acera. Entonces oyó la campana del vecino; llamaba con una insistencia inusual, tocaba sola, agitada por la tierra. Algo cayó en la cocina, un platón amortiguado por las frutas. Mauricio corrió al pasillo.

Encontró a un vecino en camiseta de basquetbolista y a una niña con clara de huevo en la cabeza. La luz se apagó en el descanso de la escalera. Alguien gritó en el piso de abajo y fue como si esa garganta los succionara a la salida. Un gato pasó entre los pies de Mauricio, los escalones se volvieron sombra y él rodó hasta el siguiente descanso. Llegó al estacionamiento golpeado, en calzones, sin aliento, vivo.

En la calle la gente miraba los edificios, tratando de detenerlos con los ojos. En el asfalto había cosas dispersas, vidrios, latas de conservas, zapatos, botellas asombrosamente enteras, naipes, un reloj de pared detenido en las 7:19, un fierro que podía ser una refacción.

Un perro enloquecido corría a lo lejos como una ráfaga negra. Sólo entonces Mauricio advirtió que había dejado de temblar.

Fue de una cabina a otra tratando de hablar con su madre y con Verónica, pero las líneas estaban muertas.

Caminó de regreso, concentrado en las grietas de la acera. Cuando alzó la vista, tardó en reconocerla. Verónica estaba de espaldas, las manos en bocina, gritando con una voz que creía capaz de llegar al cuarto piso.

Él le tocó la espalda con suavidad, para no asustarla. Los brazos le temblaban tanto que abrazarla le pareció un acto muy complejo.

reconocida. Llevaba un traje sastre negro, lentes oscuros, pañoleta en la cabeza. Una de esas figuras que no pueden faltar en los panteones o en algunos andenes de ferrocarril y llegan a despedirse para siempre.

¿Había alguna posibilidad de que fuera Rita? Mauricio no se atrevió a acercarse.

Verónica lo tomó del brazo:

—La gente que tiene tornillos en los pies camina mal en la tierra.

Llegaron a la calle y Verónica no lo soltó, como si también ahí fuera difícil caminar.

Mauricio había perfeccionado ese instante previo al despertar, la escena en que la 7 le decía "cómeme" y él devoraba el leotardo con deliciosa lentitud, mientras ella le decía cosas desagradables que lo excitaban mucho: "muerdes como Javier", "al fin me lo comen sabroso". Aunque él tuviera un mordisco superior, la frase sugería a una legión de devoradores. Justo cuando empezaba a disfrutar los humillantes elogios de la mujer, Mauricio descubría que el leotardo estaba hecho de materia orgánica: una membrana que crecía para ser comida.

Daba el último mordisco cuando sintió un empellón. El rostro se le cubrió de un polvo fino. ¿Qué extraña caricia se añadía a su duermevela? Tardó en acomodar la sensación. Una sacudida lo tiró al suelo. Abrió los ojos: el caliche caía del cielo raso y el foco desnudo se balanceaba encima de él. Estaba temblando. Se incorporó sin mucha prisa; caminó entre bostezos, rascándose el calzón, en busca de una trave resistente.

Dudó entre la cocina y la puerta de salida. Sintió una sacudida aún más fuerte y se asomó a la ventana, como si la ciudad pudiera decirle qué hacer. Vio palmeras que oscilaban; a lo lejos, en

Subieron al cuarto. Lo primero que vio fue un plato de cereal a medio comer. En el carrito de las medicinas, en lugar de la habitual profusión de frascos, había sólo dos goteros. El reloj despertador producía un ruido casi imperceptible. La frazada de cuadros había sido doblada con cuidado; las manos de Jesús Guardiola reposaban fuera de la manta. Mauricio recordó que su padre lo acostaba en esa absurda posición, con las manos fuera de la cobija. El sol daba de lleno en el rostro de su padre. La nariz se le había afilado mucho; un diente mordía el labio inferior. Mauricio pasó sus dedos por la boca y corrigió el gesto de su padre. Un olor tenue flotaba en el cuarto, el olor de las cosas usadas y fragantes, un olor a talco en cueros muy gastados.

Cristina Ferrán abrió una maleta y empezó a guardar objetos: un florero, una carpeta tejida, dos servilletas color durazno, dos juegos de cubiertos, el reloj despertador, un chal espumoso, un misal, un frasco con sal de ajo, unas pantuflas. Sólo entonces Mauricio advirtió todo lo que ella había llevado al cuarto. Tomó la mano de su padre, los dedos finos, las uñas recién arregladas.

—Mira nomás —Cristina había encontrado unos caramelos en el saco. Los vio con los ojos encendidos, con el orgullo protector de quien sorprende a un niño en una inútil travesura.

Mauricio registró mal lo que pasaba en el entierro; sin embargo, le pareció que todo era demasiado sencillo para los gustos de su padre. Un par de coronas de los colegas, dos hombres de gris en representación del deshonrado Gutiérrez Pool, el rostro sin maquillaje de Rocío, algunos amigos fieles.

Junto a la barda del cementerio, crecía una hilera de cipreses. Mauricio vio a una mujer que caminaba a la distancia, como si deseara participar sin ser

plantas. Además, el programa lo ayudó a que su vida sexual le pareciera complicada: una vez a la semana dormía con la número 4 y en ocasiones con la temperamental número 3. En sus fantasías numéricas, Mauricio codiciaba a la imposible 7. También imaginaba un momento compensatorio: acostarse simultáneamente con la 4 y la 3.

Por la hora de estudio, era obvio que el programa le importaba muy poco a los productores. A las 7:15 de la mañana, el ingeniero de audio le pasó una llamada de Verónica:

—¡Ya vi la basura que haces!

—¿Prendes la tele en las mañanas? —Mauricio desvió la vista al estudio donde las mujeres número bailaban en sus brevísimos leotardos.

—Busqué el programa por ti, idiota. Me imagino que lo único más bajo que trabajar con esas nalgonas es transmitir el Informe—. Verónica guardó silencio, como si tuviera un motivo real de celos.

Mauricio iba a responder algo, pero en eso llegó el productor, con un rostro atónito, como si los hubieran sacado del aire. Traía una tarjeta en la mano que arrugó con fuerza. Quería decir algo pero no podía. Mauricio vio el papel oprimido en el puño del productor, el mensaje arruinado, y entendió de golpe. Dejó caer el auricular. Verónica siguió hablando con la alfombra hasta que una voz anónima, cualquiera de los operadores, tomó el teléfono y explicó lo que sucedía.

Encontró a su madre en la rampa del hospital. Una camilla rodante pasó junto a ella sin alterar su postura. Sólo al ver a Mauricio torció la boca, de un modo controlado y sin embargo triste.

Él la abrazó con fuerza y respiró en su cuello un inconfundible olor a *Aqua ardens*. Supo que ella había abrazado a su padre. También supo que nunca lo iba a confesar.

les regalaba una vecina de asiento, la esposa de un acribillado. El dulce dejaba un rastro café en la lengua y la sensación de comer un caucho indebido, pero Mauricio lo aceptaba para no romper la red de gestos y pequeñas cortesías y por el gusto elemental de que una golosina fuera tan negra.

En el hospital encontró un periódico olvidado en una silla y se enteró del estreno de *Abraxas* en el Festival de Avignon. Había algunos extractos de la crítica: "la obra corrobora la convulsa capacidad de soñar de América Latina"... "no en balde Breton encontró en México el surrealismo en la vida diaria" ... "celebremos la utopía posible de la modernidad mestiza"...

Apartó la vista del periódico y vio otra imagen de la victoria. Una niña de unos diez años sostenía un trofeo, rematado por una figura tan pequeña que no se distinguía si se trataba de un ángel, un hombre con los brazos en V o un clavadista. Seguramente lo llevaba para alegrar a un familiar enfermo.

Mauricio fue al baño y se lavó la cara con agua muy fría; sentía un extraño ardor en la cara, como un efecto retardado de los baños infrarrojos. Se empapó con rabia, haciendo mucho ruido para borrar el llanto, el absurdo misterio de que una niña con un trofeo pobre volviera a ser importante.

Después de dos semanas, dejó de ir al hospital todos los días. El video del Niñopa le abrió una puerta que nada tenía que ver con los documentales; un productor de Teleprimaria lo creyó capaz de dirigir las cámaras en un programa de matemáticas donde unas bailarinas disfrazadas de números se dividían y multiplicaban en extravagantes coreografías.

La rutina era tediosa pero le dio un sueldo fijo y pudo rentar un departamento que Verónica llenó de

Al cabo de un rato se abrió la puerta. Mauricio se retiró el antifaz; la mujer de facciones orientales sostenía dos jarritos de barro:

—Contra la deshidratación.

Mauricio esperaba un líquido; le sorprendió probar una sustancia densa, muy dulce.

—¿Sabes lo único que me preocupa? Que pase algo importante mientras no estoy aquí —incluso como testigo Pancho se sentía protagonista—. Hay una conjunción rara en el cielo, nos lo dijo el astrólogo de Ferreira. Vamos a volver a la zona de los desastres plutonianos. De por sí México es muy plutoniano —hizo una pausa para beber la pócima.

Mauricio pensó que los focos habían calado demasiado hondo en Pancho.

—¿Y cómo le van a hacer en Europa para seguir morenos? —preguntó para cambiar de tema.

—Tenemos una lista mundial de baños infrarrojos. Vamos a dedicar más tiempo a broncearnos que a ensayar —luego, como si hubiera una curiosa conexión entre ambos asuntos, dijo—: ¿Supiste lo de Gutiérrez Pool, el cuate de tu padre? Le quitaron la gubernatura de Oaxaca. Estaba quemadísimo.

Unos minutos después se despidieron con un pegajoso apretón de manos. Sus sexos lacios, pendulares, oscilaban en la luz de Marte.

A las seis de la mañana, la hora en que salía a visitar sus obras, Jesús Guardiola sufrió un segundo infarto. Esta vez, Cristina Ferrán no tuvo oportunidad de llevarle guisos. El enfermo permaneció en Terapia Intensiva y ella pasó noches en vela en la sala de espera, con un rosario entre las manos: "Felipe, le debes una", murmuraba.

Mauricio la acompañó en esas jornadas sin noticias, compartió con ella el café en vasos de poliuretano, los chiclosos duros, de negro orosuz, que

opuesta: la piedra pómez, el zacate, las esponjas que despellejaban.

Pasaron por una sala de baños colectivos; había unos veinte camastros bajo los soles infrarrojos; Mauricio creyó reconocer a un actor de Ferreira.

—Aquí —la mujer llamó a una puerta de plástico.

Entraron a una cabina para dos personas. Pancho estaba tendido sobre una estera de hule; se había untado una sustancia que le inflaba ampollas harinosas. El cuarto olía a coco.

—¿Qué te echaste?

—Solución Doble Equis, para activar la melanina.

Mauricio recordó la melamina ponderosa; los muslos de su amigo eran color triplay.

—Acuéstese.

Sólo entonces advirtió que la mujer seguía con ellos.

Se tendió en la estera de hule y se puso el antifaz mientras la mujer le untaba la sustancia contrastante; tenía unas manos chicas y eficaces.

—¿Cómo sigue? —preguntó Pancho.

Mauricio se dio cuenta de que su padre se había convertido en una desgracia implícita; no hacía falta mencionar su nombre.

Sin esperar la respuesta de Mauricio, Pancho habló de la gira y de su nuevo romance, nada menos que con el empresario de la crin:

—Lo estoy ayudando a dejar la coca. Se metía kilos.

¿Era posible que Pancho, incapaz de concebir que había mentes ajenas, pudiera ayudar a alguien? Quizá suponía que su sola presencia sustituiría una adicción por otra. De algún modo, Mauricio había sido víctima de ese efecto; su amistad con Pancho ya era tan resistente como un mal hábito.

ra nada. "Lo importante es el viejo", decía en sus largas distancias. Era incapaz de vivir una historia sin percibirla como un éxito.

Cuando Mauricio lo recibió en la sala F del aeropuerto, Carlos sonreía al empujar la silla de ruedas. El rostro de su padre era de una fragilidad agónica, las manos le temblaban, sus ojos llorosos no respondían a la emoción de estar de vuelta sino a algún desarreglo interno. Mauricio sintió las uñas de Rocío encajadas en el antebrazo.

—¡Salió perfecto! —exclamó Carlos, con énfasis miserable.

Con la excusa de saber cómo seguía su padre, y la intención oculta de ponerlo al tanto de su protagonismo en la reordenación racial de *Abraxas*, Pancho le hablaba a Mauricio todos los días pero nunca tenía tiempo de verlo. Llegado el momento de la despedida, se limitó a incluirlo en su agenda: citó a Mauricio en un sitio llamado Grito Amarillo.

En la vitrina, vio la fotografía de una rubia supermorena. Abrió la puerta y respiró un aroma a plantas aromáticas. En el mostrador, una mujer de aspecto vietnamita doblaba toallas. Mauricio tuvo que repetir el nombre de su amigo (tal vez la muchacha poseía una calma excepcional o tal vez le parecía muy cortés escuchar todo dos veces).

—Está en la cabina doce —dijo con voz dulce y le tendió un antifaz, unas sandalias, una bata de toalla—. Yo lo llevo.

Caminaron sobre una rejilla de madera que impedía el contacto con el suelo húmedo. La atmósfera era dominada por un aire rojizo, que recordaba fotografías de Marte.

Los empleados eran gente pobre, naturalmente morena; sus baños debían responder a la obsesión

entre a Cardiología. ¿Cómo chingados se le ocurrió lo de Baltimore? ¡Es un pinche orate!

Mauricio admiró la capacidad de Gutiérrez Pool para apoderarse de su hermano; tal vez los abogados de Houston también tenían que ver en el asunto y le dieron información para sustituir a William Archer en el manejo de desastres. ¿Había llegado Carlos a los círculos conspiratorios que tanto anhelaba? Quizá aún no le debía favores a Gutiérrez Pool, pero quería debérselos.

Durante un par de semanas Mauricio y Carlos se dejaron de hablar, pero el pleito sirvió de muy poco. Jesús Guardiola volvió a sorprenderlos; viajó a Baltimore sin avisarle a nadie. Una doctora puertorriqueña habló a los pocos días para informar que había sido intervenido con éxito.

Con su gusto por las emergencias, Carlos logró estar en el aeropuerto media hora después de la llamada. Mauricio lo consideró un acelerado hasta que leyó los periódicos y comprobó que, al menos en parte, las aprehensiones de su hermano eran fundadas: después de citar las frases nacionalistas de Gutiérrez Pool y Guardiola, un articulista que debía llevar meses esperando la ocasión informaba que el arquitecto no había confiado en los médicos nacionales, formados con el dinero de los contribuyentes, y que el gobernador de Oaxaca, que no podía tomarse una foto sin sostener un jarrito de barro negro, era dueño de un departamento en Manhattan y un chalet para esquiar en Vail. Al día siguiente se publicaron dos desmentidos tan solemnes y tan favorables al político oaxaqueño que resultaron peores que cualquier calumnia.

Una vez desatado el vendaval que había previsto, muy en su estilo, Carlos actuó como si no pasa-

un flanco contra Gutiérrez Pool. La tiene muy difícil en Oaxaca, por cualquier mamada lo acusan de vender el estado; concesionó unas pinches grutas para un parque de diversiones gringo, con dinosaurios mecánicos, y todo el mundo defendió las cuevas como si fueran el olimpo de los zapotecas; la situación está cabrona: en Obras Públicas, donde fue ministro, hay una oficina dedicada exclusivamente a calumniarlo; lo acusan de favorecer proveedores, de aprovecharse de los terremotos para pedirle renovaciones a sus amigos, de construir más caro con el pretexto de usar materiales más auténticos, ¡hazme el chingado favor! Las cosas no son tan simples como piensas —otra estrategia de Carlos: imputarle lo que no había dicho; los nuevos políticos, los tecnócratas amaestrados en Chicago, están dispuestos a lo que sea para joder a los nacionalistas.

—¿Gutiérrez Pool es nacionalista?

—Sus edificios lo son. ¿Qué no entiendes?

Mauricio no pudo contener una carcajada. La situación era aún más grotesca que la de Ferreira y sus huestes bronceadas. ¿Era posible que sucediera precisamente eso, que forzaran a su padre a abrirse el corazón como mexicano? Carlos lo vio con desprecio y volvió a la carga con un aforismo que podía usar en cualquier circunstancia:

—Hay quienes comen mal para cagar bien —bebió un trago de whisky—. Gutiérrez Pool representará lo que se te antoje, te puede caer en la punta de los huevos, se ha enlodado hasta la coronilla, pero también ha levantado un chingamadral de arcos mayas, cimientos en equis y otras mexicanadas cortesía del arquitecto Guardiola. Piensa por un segundo en el bufet: los planos se protegen con carpetas de papel amate, las secretarias se visten de lila, ¡la camioneta está adornada con grecas!, todas esas mamadas tienen consecuencias. Hay que convencerlo de que

—A Gutiérrez le importa —Carlos disminuyó el apellido, como si esto significara que había hablado con él. Sostenía el vaso con el pulgar y el índice, un gesto que Mauricio acababa de ver en una película y que le pareció típico del estafador agradable, que bebe con sus víctimas y las divierte mucho. Carlos tenía los mismos dientes grandes, la mirada encendida, la capacidad de explotar en gritos convincentes, de insultar sin envilecerse demasiado, casi en tono fraternal; estaba hecho para joder en una forma que acababa por hacerlo popular, era la opción preferible de todo grupo ruin.

—No entiendo nada —dijo Mauricio.

—No te hagas pendejo. ¿Quieres pruebas fuertes? —Carlos chasqueó los labios, como si el whisky contuviera un éter que tenía que entrarle a las encías; habló en frases precisas, ofreció pruebas: Jesús Guardiola era un símbolo de la arquitectura mexicana, a ellos podía importarles un carajo, no habían visto gran cosa de su dinero, pero su trayectoria era seguida con atención en otros sitios.

—Ya viste lo que le pasó a Félix Barrientos —Carlos disfrutaba las alusiones para los entendidos, pero disfrutaba más tener que explicar con hartazgo que Barrientos fue secretario de Hacienda, lanzó un estricto programa de austeridad y acababa de morir en una clínica de San Francisco—: tal vez para ti ninguna de estas cosas esté conectada, pero se armó un desmadre bastante grueso. El ministro estaba desahuciado, tenía un cáncer del tamaño de una cachucha, pero insistió en ir a San Francisco; en vez de tirarse en un catre del Seguro Social como un mártir del ahorro interno, se fue a un hospital de cinco estrellas en el extranjero. Obviamente la prensa lo hizo mierda. No importa cómo vivió: murió como traidor.

—¿Y eso qué tiene que ver con nosotros?

—La operación en Estados Unidos puede abrir

Avanzó por una calle rodeada de prados que brillaban bajo la escarcha. Llegó a una puerta verde con aldaba color oro. Pulsó el previsible timbre de campanilla.

Rocío le ofreció una mejilla tibia. Mauricio olió una mezcla de alcohol y perfume dulzón. Su cuñada llevaba mallas moradas, una pequeña blusa, anudada arriba del ombligo, el pelo recogido con un moño.

La cena fue una curiosa sucesión de galletas untadas de patés. Rocío comía como si llevara semanas sin alimento y aquellas masas fueran deliciosas. Carlos apenas probó el paté. Tenía una botella de whisky en la mesa de centro y a cada rato se servía en un vaso corto, facetado, una de las pocas cosas que parecían escogidas por él en esa casa donde una fila de seis pingüinos de porcelana podía considerarse decorativa.

Después de una hora aburrida, Carlos le pidió a Rocío que los dejara solos. Mauricio vio los platones que ella había vaciado; le pareció casi perverso que una mujer delgada se alimentara con tal desmesura. Carlos lo miró a los ojos y temió otra revelación de intimidades familiares, la siniestra historia de ese apetito. Pero su hermano se sirvió otro trago y preguntó en tono rutinario:

—¿Cómo va el viejo?

Hablaron de la posible operación, los paquetes médicos de Houston y Baltimore, hasta que Carlos dijo:

—Se me hace que no va a ir ahí.

—¿Por qué?

—Hay presiones —Carlos llenó la pausa con un trago lento—; no importa mucho quién mueve estos hilos, pero si quieres un nombre piensa en Gutiérrez Pool; son socios, la mitad de sus edificios vienen de contratos que él consiguió.

—¿Y qué carajos importa que se vaya a Houston?

Club de Polo, pensó en Rita, la única mujer a la que quiso y a la que renunció por razones ya insondables.

Mauricio conocía bien al médico de su padre, un internista lóbrego, afecto a curaciones que en su misma duración parecían prometer una vida larga. "¡No tengo su tiempo!", exclamaba Guardiola a la menor provocación. Había leído lo suficiente para saber que una operación podía ayudarlo y ponerlo en riesgo. Conocía el dolor y la carnicería que significaba sacarle venas de la pierna y abrirle el corazón, pero también estaba harto de que le recomendaran ejercicios suaves, dietas, abandonarse a los dictados de su cuerpo, aguardar a que un grupo de células, alguna glándula perdida, empezara a mejorarlo.

Un día en que fue a recoger correspondencia al bufet, Mauricio escuchó que una secretaria hablaba por teléfono con una clínica extranjera. El arquitecto había optado por un atajo. ¿Había forma de contradecirlo? Nadie sabría nunca lo que significaba padecer las resequedades, los humores, los pálpitos, los vahídos, el aire en las entrañas, las pústulas, la sangre densa, las descargas interiores del cuerpo que se tenía enfrente.

Los hospitales de Estados Unidos parecían compartir la premura del paciente. Guardiola disfrutó las cartas de respuesta que se disputaban el privilegio de abrirle el pecho.

Carlos vivía en un fraccionamiento de nombre engañoso, Cipreses del Lago, una colina donde los matrimonios jóvenes y ambiciosos pasaban sus años de formación, antes de descender a los barrios que no necesitaban anunciarse como imaginarios paraísos.

En la reja de entrada, un policía que parecía no tener lengua o chupar un dulce descomunal, solicitó una identificación a Mauricio. Hacía frío: la aprobación del policía fue una sonora nube de vaho.

importa muy poco la persona, ¡sólo ven cambios químicos! —dijo esto como si la química fuera un veneno contra el carácter—; me piden que tenga paciencia, pero no están en mi piel, no saben lo que se siente. Pensé que no me afectaría, *Panza*, pero ya ves, estoy hecho un viejo jodido —volvió a sollozar, se pasó las palmas por el rostro, embarrándose las lágrimas—: ¡perdí la verga! No me mires así, eso era lo que quería decirte el otro día, pero no pude, no me atreví, me ganó el miedo, la vergüenza. Ahora ya me vale. Déjame gritarlo: ¡no tengo verga!

La enfermera entró al cuarto:

—¿Arquitecto?

—¡A la chingada! —Guardiola le dio la espalda, abrazó un cojín, lloró de un modo parejo, inconsolable.

¿Había manera de asimilar esa confesión? Mauricio no podía creer que hubieran ido al Club de Polo para hablar de eso. Algo (las pastillas, el alcohol, la comida, un recuerdo) llevó a su padre a la insensatez de Trudy y ahora quería borrarlo a toda costa, incluso al precio de humillarse. Era imposible dudar de su desarmante franqueza, pero la explicación llegaba a destiempo, como si quisiera cancelar el ridículo con un drama superior. De no haber sucedido lo del Club, ese desplante de sinceridad hubiera sido innecesario. ¿Y qué podía contestar Mauricio? Pensó que las revelaciones íntimas desnudan más a quien las oye; una vez compartidos, los secretos fisiológicos responsabilizan al testigo. ¿Fue Trudy una inspiración del momento o su padre le destinó ese apodo desde siempre? Nunca lo sabría. En segundos, Mauricio pasó de la compasión a la rabia; una vez más, su padre lo obligaba a seguir los caprichosos avatares de su sexo. "La Zona de Jesús", recordó con ironía, y le pareció un acto de justicia que la impotencia de su padre no tuviera un origen venéreo sino cardiaco. Tal vez por eso, en la insegura mesa del

Jesús Guardiola retrocedió a las rutinas de meses atrás. Tenía una enfermera de día y otra de noche y pasaba horas viendo una planta o acariciando la frazada de cuadros. Aquella prenda había sobrevivido muchas mudanzas y era una de las pocas cosas que él conservaba de Terminal Progreso. La tela tenía una textura fibrosa, una de esas cobijas que pesan demasiado y huelen rancio hasta que resulta imposible prescindir de ellas, dormir sin su olor de campamento, de caporal en el desierto, de fugitivo cuyo cobertor es ya un sudario.

Una tarde Guardiola pidió a la enfermera que lo dejara solo con Mauricio, desvió la vista a las medicinas colocadas en un plato de madera de Michoacán; al cabo de un rato dijo:

—Estoy en deuda contigo, *Panza*.

Fijó la vista, como si buscara algo entre las medicinas.

—Cuando eras chico me acompañaste mucho. Te pregunté por Rita el otro día... no sabes lo que es —su voz se quebró de repente—, de veras... no sabes... —empezó a sollozar, muy quedo, como si le faltaran fuerzas para estar a la altura de su tristeza—, perdón... —desvió la vista a la pantalla apagada del televisor—, perdón... ya no puedo...

—¿No puedes qué? —Mauricio vio las manos retorcidas en la frazada y fue como si su padre extrajera un último impulso de ese gesto tumefacto; vio a Mauricio y pronunció las sílabas con cuidado:

—No tengo verga. No se me para.

Mauricio sintió una presión en el pecho; le costó mucho trabajo preguntar:

—¿Qué dicen los doctores?

—Habladurías, como siempre, que me puedo recuperar... ¡una escuela de charlatanes! Según ellos, en algunos casos tarda más después del infarto. Les

¿Recordaría en detalle lo ocurrido en el Club de Polo? Mauricio repasó la escena en el restorán; su padre lucía bien, había asumido el holgado papel de quien representa una desaparecida "época de oro". Las conferencias en su honor fueron un éxito; por alguna razón, el público requería de una reserva de nostalgia, una prueba de que mejorar significaba retroceder; los desafíos nacionales no ameritaban inventos sino recuperaciones: el retorno de los días grandes en que los toros embestían con más fuerza, el cine ofrecía iconos que respiraban y la arquitectura era más tradicional, más típica, "¡más lo de uno!", según exclamó un conferencista. Pero justo cuando Guardiola había resuelto su retiro y avanzaba hacia una paz interesante, ocurrió lo del Club de Polo.

El cardiólogo advirtió que un segundo infarto sería letal, por el momento sólo se trataba de un susto, pero tenían que estar alertas, era necesario *arroparlo* con cariño (¿realmente usó la palabra o fue Mauricio quien incorporó esa tibia carencia?).

Mauricio soñó con ovejas. No vio la serie numerosa de los insomnes ni el apático rebaño al que su padre atribuía las desgracias del país, sino una oveja voraz, que comía carne de caballo:

—Tienes pésimo carácter por tanta carne dulce —su padre le decía en el sueño.

Mauricio descubría que en el Club de Polo había comido un caballo destazado en el hipódromo.

—Es carne inyectada para ganar la novena carrera —su padre tomaba un trozo con sus uñas esmaltadas.

Los médicos aparecían de golpe, con delantales de carniceros.

Al fondo, una oveja a la que su padre llamaba "la asesina" porque había matado un caballo, empezaba a dar leche, una leche tibia que inundaba el piso y de la que emanaba un suave vapor.

¡beeeeee, qué rico vacilón! —movió los brazos, a ritmo de mambo.

—¡¿Hay un médico?! —gritó Mauricio.

—Aquí está tu pastor, Trudy, a ver, a ver, co-
sita —masculló su padre, con espantosa ternura.

Dos hombres de pelo cano se acercaron a la
mesa.

—Es ella la que está en peligro, pero no lo
sabe —señaló a Mauricio—. Es la sublime, la estúpida... ¡Qué ojitos pela en el matadero!

Tomaron a Guardiola de las axilas y los pies y
lo cargaron a una oficina cercana. Le revisaron las
pupilas con un lápiz-linterna. El enfermo no opuso
resistencia; tenía la mirada perdida, la camisa empapada de sudor.

Uno de los médicos fue a su coche por un
"parche de pólvora".

Guardiola respiraba por la boca:

—Trudy... Trudy —acarició la mano de Mauricio.

—Aquí estoy.

—¡Tan linda!

—Ya, papá —más que a su padre, Mauricio se
dirigía a los médicos, pero ellos no tenían el menor
interés en los vericuetos íntimos del paciente; explo-
raron las bolsas del saco y dieron con las pastillas para
el corazón; le pusieron el parche en el pecho, sin
perder un segundo.

—No te preocupes, hijo —uno de ellos palmeó
la espalda de Mauricio.

Una ambulancia llevó a Jesús Guardiola al hospital.
Veintiséis horas después, bebía agua con desesperación, chorreándose el pecho.

—Perdón —fue lo primero que le dijo a Mauricio.

—Quiero que te vaya bien como taxista.

—No soy taxista, papá.

—Cada oveja con su pareja. Sí, beeeeee...

—Voy a pedir la cuenta.

Su padre lo vio con una sonrisa descolocada. Estaba borracho, tal vez cruzado con sus pastillas. De repente cerró los puños, como si sufriera un espasmo. Resopló con suficiente fuerza para sacudir la orquídea que flotaba en una cuenca de agua al centro de la mesa. Pareció reponerse de un cólico; por fin dijo, con voz articulada y mirada errante:

—Las ovejas creen que la pasividad es la perfección. ¿No es así, Trudy?

—¿Trudy?

—¡Ay, siempre tan estúpida, Trudy, tan fuera de ti, con tus rizos y tu panza pachona! Dime una sola cosa, ¿te acuerdas de mí?

Mauricio asintió con esfuerzo.

—¿Te acuerdas de mí, *entonces*?

—Sí.

—¿De veras, Trudy?

¿Con quién lo confundía? ¿Qué había detrás de esa mirada de vidrio?

—Sí, papá —contestó, pero la aclaración sirvió de poco.

—¡Mi ovejita! —su padre parecía al borde de la asfixia; tenía los carrillos enrojecidos; se aflojó el nudo de la corbata, con una rabia torpe. Luego vio a su hijo como si tratara de fijar un rostro en espiral:

—¡Siempre he odiado la pasividad de las ovejas! —golpeó la mesa; la copa de coñac se volcó.

En las mesas cercanas se hizo el silencio. Mauricio se puso de pie; desabotonó la camisa de su padre. Él sonrió, con alegría inconexa:

—¿No conoces el peligro, verdad? ¡Tan vacilona! Para ti el mundo no es sino vacilar y vacilar,

Hizo un gesto desmañado que el mesero interpretó como "coñac". Guardaron silencio durante un rato, viendo las migajas hasta que un mozo las recogió con una espátula plateada.

—¿Te acuerdas de cuando me acompañabas con Rita? —su padre tenía la lengua adormilada.

—Claro.

—¿De veras te acuerdas?

¿Se refería a algo más? ¿Advirtió que su hijo estaba en el umbral durante aquel temblor?

—Sí, me acuerdo, si no era tan chico.

—Esa época fue muy importante para mí, quiero que lo sepas. Casi tenía tu edad —sorbió el café, dejó un rastro cremoso en la servilleta, tomó la copa de coñac—: ¿me guardas rencor?

Mauricio hizo un silencio suficientemente largo para poner en duda la sinceridad de su "no".

—Hice algunas locuras, ojalá me perdones, mano, pero fue importante estar contigo; en todos estos años lo único que he aprendido es que para encontrar un camino hay que perderse; tienes que seguir tu estrella; te apartas de la ruta hasta que encuentras algo inesperado, que sin embargo buscabas en secreto; lo canijo es distinguir cuándo sigues perdido y cuándo encuentras algo. Yo busqué y encontré, busqué y encontré, busqué y encontré... —movió la cabeza como un péndulo absurdo; tomó otro trago de coñac—. Pasa lo mismo contigo; te sales del camino, te desvías y das con algo que era tu meta sin que lo supieras; de seguro lo aprendiste como taxista: tu ruta era perderte —la última frase salió en tono de reproche, pero su padre siguió hablando como si su voz careciera de una intención determinada—: no hay patrones en las calles, ibas a donde te llevaran, medio veleta, según el favor del viento... supongo que todo destino es eso, una desviación propicia. Fue bueno... todo es bueno...

—¿Pedimos la cuenta?

algo que modificar, hasta en eso se comportaba como arquitecto. Acaso pensaba en las posibilidades del video que él no utilizaba; la época no había creado un aparato más certero para cazar mujeres. ¿Le diría que perdía el tiempo con peregrinos cansados de llevar a cuestas un Niño-Padre de madera?

Jesús Guardiola pidió otro Etiqueta Negra y calma para ver el menú. Después de dos rondas de aperitivos ordenó un potaje sustancioso y un filete rojo, muy rojo.

—*Saignant*—murmuró, con repentina melancolía—. Siempre te cayó mal, ¿verdad? —la palabra francesa lo había llevado a Roberta.

Revisó la libreta forrada de un cuero que anticipaba los tonos del borgoña. Escogió un vino denso, que adormeció la lengua de Mauricio desde el primer trago. Entonces se atrevió a decirle a su padre que no podía comer ni beber de esa manera.

—¡Un día del año, *Panza*; un día del año, Panchita!

Mauricio desvió la vista: una mujer salió del restorán; su ráfaga suave combinó bien con el olor del vino.

Su padre comía a dentelladas. Mauricio recordó el consejo de su madre: 30 masticadas por bocado.

—¡Y las gaviotas no se detienen en el hielo! —dijo su padre. A saber de qué hablaba. Mauricio había perdido el hilo de la conversación.

Guardiola apuró su copa, alzó la mano, castañeteó los dedos. Quería islas flotantes, un exprés doble, el carrito de los licores.

Con el café le trajeron un chocolate de menta, envuelto en papel de estaño. Lo abrió de prisa. Aún le quedaba una cucharada de postre y la crema se mezcló con la pastilla negra. Mauricio lo vio masticar un poco más despacio, con la boca abierta. Por un momento su quijada se detuvo; le faltaba energía para seguir comiendo de ese modo.

Mauricio vio los dedos manicureados que tomaban el pan para untarle la mantequilla prohibida. Luego Guardiola alzó la mano y pidió un Etiqueta Negra.

—Es una noche especial —sonrió.

Mauricio se dispuso a escuchar una historia vinculada con Gutiérrez Pool, que acababa de asumir la gubernatura de Oaxaca, un estado con suficientes playas para la imaginación de Jesús Guardiola.

Incorporado al tibio confort del restorán, el arquitecto lucía bien, masticaba con fuerza, desviaba la vista en busca de conocidos, con clara conciencia de estar ahí, festejando su sobrevida con su hijo menor.

Las paredes cubiertas de caoba oscura mostraban cuadros con escenas hípicas, en los dinteles de las puertas había trompetas, uno de esos sitios donde la palabra "derby" alude a una opulenta solidaridad masculina. Los comensales parecían pertenecer a una clase de abogados a la que nunca llegaría Carlos; quizá él iba a ser más poderoso, pero difícilmente adquiriría el empaque de los que ultrajan sin alzar la voz. Carlos se identificaba con los momentos de Hollywood donde el héroe grita la verdad con histérica justicia; en cambio, los vecinos de mesa generaban un ambiente sosegado, de tranquila exclusión. Algunos se reconocían con un discreto alzar de cejas; sin embargo, en la contenida atención de los que escuchaban, era posible intuir las amenazas, los fraudes, los contratos vencidos que se decían tan quedo.

—Prueba el pan, lo hacen aquí —su padre señaló la cesta con el cuchillo de la mantequilla. Comía con raro apetito.

Mauricio mordió la punta de un cuerno y su padre lo vio con repentina curiosidad, como si reflexionara en la voracidad sin pasión que había llevado a su hijo a la gordura. Tal vez estaban ahí para hablar de eso, o de sus años sin estudio; su padre siempre tenía

cierto: nadie ignoraba que en la escena del desnudo colectivo Ferreira la había situado al frente para que su dorado vello púbico se viera con precisión de la fila uno a la doce.

Mauricio se concentró en la piel de su amigo, color adobe. ¿Cómo hacía para conservar el bronceado?

—Tomo baños infrarrojos —explicó Pancho—. No creas que todos aguantan: Sylvia se puso como un camarón; su alternativa era el despido o el cáncer de piel. Por si te interesa: Lorena sí resistió los focos.

Mauricio la imaginó bronceándose más de la cuenta, rociándose Coca-Cola y aceites que aceleraban la fritura. La vio negra, supertostada en las nieves de Europa, y no le importó.

De repente, se encontró rodeado de gente eufórica. Pancho le hablaba cada dos días para contarle sus preparativos de viaje, Carlos hacía progresos económicos vertiginosos que ponían en riesgo su vida planeada de antemano y Verónica se recibió con honores.

También Jesús Guardiola había adquirido un aire satisfecho y no puso el menor reparo en que le dedicaran un ciclo de conferencias; revisó la lista de invitados y tachó con entusiasmo el nombre de Felipe Jurado. En la mesa de clausura, tenía el gesto algo ausente de quien está acostumbrado al éxito. Después de la última ovación, invitó a Mauricio a cenar al Club de Polo. Rocío y Carlos regresaron a su nueva casa en una colina adinerada y los colegas se conformaron con un rápido apretón de manos.

Guardiola llegó al restorán como si pensara en otras cosas; tal vez recordaba que ahí conoció a Roberta. El capitán lo saludó como si lo reconociera, aunque el protocolo del lugar debía exigir que cada visita fuera tratada como un regreso.

opinión que la perplejidad—... pero de nada sirve darle a los europeos lo que ellos también hacen, con unos ajustes la obra puede ser perfecta."

—¿Y cuál es la solución? ¿Disfrazarse de mexicanos? —Mauricio quería ser irónico, pero no había forma de frenar el entusiasmo de Pancho. Las razones podían ser confusas y arbitrarias, pero el resultado, ¡el detalle!, era magnífico: en la nueva versión de la obra, él pasaría de las sombras que danzaban al fondo a la gloria del primer plano. Después de años de posar para Friendly Fire, Pancho parecía el más emblemático de los latinos: su rostro de guerrilla al sol resultaba imprescindible para la exportación de *Abraxas*.

—¿Y qué dijo Ferreira? —preguntó Mauricio.

Pancho describió la escena: el director había aguardado a que el empresario comunicara las noticias difíciles. Lo que él dijera a continuación sería visto como un remedio necesario. Habló del *I Ching* y recordó que el hexagrama de la Modestia tenía su mutación en la Fuerza; había que trabajar con humildad, sin atender a protagonismos ni caprichos personales. Todo mundo estuvo de acuerdo y todo mundo se preguntó si sería suficientemente latino.

Ferreira contrató a nuevos percusionistas, dos mulatos de Las Antillas que parecerían mexicanos en Europa. La coreografía recibió modificaciones sustanciales: se introdujeron números de ritmo febril en los que se alzaban plumas de colores. Al final, unos sacerdotes con máscaras aztecas pintarían de verde a una mujer; no se servirían de pinceles sino de una serpiente de plástico, remojada en una cuenca ceremonial.

Lo decisivo, sin embargo, fueron los cambios de reparto. Corría el rumor de que Charlie Xuárez pasaba los jueves con Ferreira, y tal vez recibió información confidencial porque fue el primero en teñirse el pelo de negro. Sylvia Hauser lo miró con descon-

las manos como si sus dedos fueran fascinantes. El asunto que provocaba tanto ademán era la próxima gira de *Abraxas*:

—"Sé que levantaron un buen billete en provincia —Pancho imitó la voz del promotor—; el problema es saber si podremos cumplir la siguiente meta".

Mauricio sabía que en el Círculo no había otra meta que Ferreira. Un fracaso de estruendo hubiera provocado el mismo orgullo de contribuir a sus geniales transgresiones. Pero Jimmy o Fredy era de otra opinión; habló de los meses de ensayos sin sueldo, de teatros donde se iba la luz a media función, de camerinos sin agua corriente, del sacrificio y los ejercicios dolorosos. Tenía algo del entrenador que busca un resorte mental para superar el desgaste colectivo. La palabra que podía llegarle con mayor rapidez era "equipo", pero buscó otra, y en vez de "tribu", que hubiera sonado muy bien, dijo "familia". Los cigarros apagados por disciplina volvieron a encenderse. Fredy se acarició el pelo morosamente:

—"La siguiente meta es Estados Unidos; la siguiente meta es Europa."

—¿Y eso qué? —a Mauricio el tema empezaba a aburrirle.

—"Los empresarios extranjeros están entusiasmados con las ráfagas de luz y sonido de *Abraxas*, pero hay un detalle" —Pancho hizo una pausa significativa y volvió a imitar al promotor—: "El problema... hay que decirlo... es la mera neta... el problema es que no parecen mexicanos. Sí, sí, ya lo sé: a nadie le importa que los noruegos parezcan suecos o los finlandeses húngaros, pero nosotros no podemos negar la cruz de nuestra parroquia" —Jimmy torció el argumento para que la falta de color local pareciera una traición al origen—. "Respeto sus opiniones —añadió, aunque en ese momento nadie tenía otra

Martínez?) que Lorena, recién regresada a la capital, abriera el periódico ese día.

Le molestó que le dejara tres recados en seis horas. No devolvió las llamadas. Aquel interés a destiempo le dolió, no tanto porque revelaba un perfil oportunista en Lorena, sino porque le recordó que también él había abandonado a alguien, en un lugar seguramente inencontrable, La Copa de Bronce.

Pasó horas ante su atlante de Tula, su pipa y su Artemisa sin gracia, sorprendido de la infinita tristeza que podían darle los trofeos.

Pancho llegó a visitarlo con un bronceado espectacular:

—¿Te cuento qué onda? —le preguntó, con ojos encendidos.

¿Servía de algo decir que no?

El Círculo de Ferreira había tenido una sesión plenaria. Con voz de actor, Pancho contó lo ocurrido.

Como siempre, el director llegó tarde a la reunión. Cuando sus botas martillearon las duelas, todo mundo se sacó los cigarros y los chicles de la boca. Ferreira se sentó en el estrado, con un aplomo que revelaba décadas de meditación en flor de loto. Tras él llegó un tipo difícil de describir, un hombre de porte atlético, enfundado en un traje de seda cruda, camisa sin cuello, con botones elípticos de hueso, que usaba una loción fuerte, muy fuerte. Su pelo era largo pero no tenía el desorden de los actores que aguardaban en un silencio expectante; una costosa navaja le había esculpido una crin de caballo de exhibición.

—El promotor de la gira internacional —explicó al fin Pancho.

El hombre de la crin era uno de esos Jaimes o Federicos a los que les encanta que les digan Jimmy o Fredy. Empezó a hablar sin que Ferreira lo introdujera; al hacer una pausa, se frotaba las palmas y abría

Despertó con los primeros pájaros y urgencia de grabar algo en su cámara. Desconfiaba de su habilidad para dar con un relato azaroso y pensó en una fiesta trazada de antemano, el paseo del Niñopa por las calles de Xochimilco.

Durante dos meses estudió las locaciones de la fiesta; sin embargo, en forma imprevista, al registrar la ceremonia se concentró en los detalles que más le molestaban.

Verónica fue la primera en ver el resultado. Cuando la imagen se dobló en zigzag al final del video, ella guardó un silencio pensativo. Luego habló del cultivo del durazno:

—La planta da siempre los mismos kilos de fruta, digamos que son siete. Si crece mucho, los siete kilos se reparten en muchos duraznos chicos; en cambio, si se mantiene chica, los duraznos son mayores. Los siete kilos son constantes, el problema es cómo se reparten —Verónica sonrió, disfrutando la incomprensión de Mauricio. ¿Lo invitaba a editar con furia o festejaba que su visión limitada produjera el fruto gordo?

Mauricio estaba desesperado por conocer su opinión, pero no se atrevió a hacer preguntas. Extrañó a la sietemesina Lorena, que decía las cosas antes de que fueran necesarias.

La referencia a los duraznos resultó ser un elogio. Con su habitual ignorancia de los términos medios, Verónica mandó hacer diez copias del videocasete y las envió a otros tantos festivales.

Pedro Martínez le regaló una de sus pipas cuando Mauricio obtuvo dos estatuillas por su video del Niñopa. Recibió la primera (un atlante de Tula) de manos de un licenciado; la segunda le llegó por correo (su triunfo fue internacional pero pobre).

Los premios lo llevaron por un día a las páginas culturales. Quiso la casualidad (¿el azar de

La palabra "chiripa" era el dogma de su pedagogía. Las conexiones secretas de lo real trataban de exorcizarse con los nombres de "suerte", "azar", "casualidad", "chiripa", y la misión profunda del documentalista consistía en descubrir las conectivas, los vínculos sutiles.

Una tarde en que llovía como si por los méritos de su nombre Aldea Global fuera capaz de convocar climas lejanos, Martínez dijo:

—Las cosas están ahí para probar nuestra disponibilidad. Sólo al atento le entregan su relato —dirigidas a Mauricio, aquellas palabras eran un reproche; si algo lo caracterizaba era su capacidad de observar en forma ilimitada.

Un silencio siguió a esa lección bajo la lluvia. Mauricio bajó el cubo de la escalera y entró al agua. Realmente sintió que ingresaba a otra sustancia.

Caminó a lo largo de Insurgentes, en espera de que algo le revelara su aventura escondida. ¿Era posible lograr esto en una calle mil veces vista? Le entró agua por el cuello; sus pies parecían envueltos por empanadas rechinantes, hojas negras de las que salía espuma.

Alzó la vista y vio una estatua. No leyó la inscripción; aquella figura destinada a conmemorar el coraje vencido se significaba a sí misma con excesiva dureza.

Bajó la vista y vio charcos, celofanes, papeles en fuga. La boca de la alcantarilla los tragaba en espasmos golosos. Los trozos dispares, sorpresivos, iban a dar allá.

Esa noche soñó que iba en un tren y Martínez recorría los vagones. En el pasillo soplaba un viento que le abultaba el pelo. En cada compartimiento, el profesor buscaba un sitio disponible. Al llegar a Mauricio, decía: "tu vacío ocupa mucho espacio".

sus años, lo que hiciera en el futuro sería un regalo adicional. "No esperen más: estudien mi trayectoria", eso decían sus ojos, de una tristeza altiva que sugería un pasado muy distinto al suyo.

La gira de *Abraxas* se prolongó mucho en provincia; luego vinieron presentaciones en el Festival de Cartagena y en un encuentro de teatro latino en Estados Unidos.

Mauricio había pasado de la nostalgia por Lorena y las noches en su torre a imaginar las muchas formas en que podía fracturarse en el escenario. Buscaba noticias de la obra esperando un accidente o el atentado de algún grupo de criminales moralistas.

Junto a un artículo sobre Ferreira, Mauricio encontró un anuncio donde la escuela Aldea Global se ofrecía a capacitar para un oficio que sonaba a una nueva perversión: "videoasta".

Aldea Global estaba en un edificio cubierto de hiedra. En forma extraña, la enredadera también trepaba por dentro hasta llegar al descanso en el primer piso. Las húmedas aulas sugerían una gimnasia oriental: cojines, esteras de bambú, colchonetas, lámparas con pantallas de papel y un inmenso póster donde una actriz posaba sin otra prenda que 365 agujas de acupuntura.

La clase estaba a cargo de Pedro Martínez, un sonorense obsesionado con el azar. El núcleo de su enseñanza era el documental narrativo. Martínez vivía para registrar el relato deliberado de la casualidad. No pudo lograrlo en Sonora porque tenía los ojos prejuiciados y todo le parecía común. En cambio, la ciudad de México era una oportunidad de mirada fresca, aquí podía buscar lo que el mundo deseaba decir bajo la marea de los objetos. "¡El caos es consecuente!", exclamaba entre el humo de su pipa que olía a excremento con especias.

Carlos traía noticias positivas (acuerdos sin cláusulas precisas con Archer, Roberta, Gutiérrez Pool), algunos discípulos fieles llegaban a pedir consejos que no necesitaban, las sirvientas procuraban mejorarle los guisos sin sal y Cristina le enviaba mensajes escuetos con sus hijos, frases breves y directas que hacían pensar que Terminal Progreso era un desierto donde se decían muy pocas cosas, y ninguna de ellas se olvidaba.

Poco a poco, Jesús Guardiola recuperó el gusto por afeitarse y usar costosas lociones. Una mañana tomó un taxi y gastó una fortuna "terapéutica" en ropa italiana. Aunque su casa estaba adornada con precisión casi fanática, compró tres óleos que no tenía dónde poner.

Una tarde volvió al bufet. Le sentó bien oír que estaba más delgado, con un color espléndido. Su primera actividad fue despedir a una pasante de arquitectura que trabajaba en la sala de dibujo. Tal vez era su amante en turno y no se comportó como él deseaba en la convalecencia; el caso es que le sentó bien disponer de un destino ajeno. Al salir del despacho tenía una voz firme, recompuesta.

Un nuevo corte de pelo —la mata densa y blanca echada hacia atrás— reforzó su aspecto orgulloso, como si se hubiera salvado por una tenacidad ejemplar. Las facciones acusadas, las manos quebradizas, cubiertas de una piel casi translúcida, le otorgaron un noble deterioro. El cardiólogo había dicho que los infartos llegaban por buscarlos a pulso o por temerlos en exceso: una vida de derroche o una vida sin desfogues. Jesús Guardiola pertenecía a la primera condición pero convalecía en la segunda. No inspiraba la compasión de los hombres acabados sino el respeto, incluso la envidia, de una vida lograda, virtuosa. Sus arrugas de expresión, su olor a perfumado desván, eran signos de experiencia. Se conducía como si ya no tuviera nada que demostrar: había usado bien

Carlos encontró una curiosa forma de convertir el litigio con William Archer en un remedio para su padre. La casa se llenó de asesores legales, documentos, contratistas. La estrategia para minimizar el daño fue multiplicar sus posibles soluciones. Guardiola necesitaba saberse rodeado de un equipo competente, enterarse de opciones peores que hacían que los despidos y el pago de deudas parecieran decisiones amargas pero útiles, casi buscadas.

La mayor parte del día, Guardiola dormitaba en un sillón reclinable, una frazada de cuadros en las piernas y el control remoto del televisor entre sus dedos.

Detestaba hablar de edificios; las construcciones se habían convertido para él en sitios llenos de escaleras, lugares para el agotamiento. En cambio, cuando visitaba al cardiólogo, experimentaba una extraña satisfacción en la sala de los electrocardiogramas; siempre quería permanecer más tiempo ante las pantallas donde los corazones trazaban líneas luminosas.

Una de sus pocas actividades era regar las plantas con una jarrita ligera; se detenía ante los nuevos brotes durante mucho tiempo, la mano repasaba su mejilla, produciendo un sonido rasposo en la barba de tres días. Los libros de su estudio lo aburrían y cobró interés por las novelas policiacas. Curiosamente, detestaba los momentos de sangre y era capaz de arrancar la página que incluyera una puñalada. Pedía crímenes inteligentes, misterios que se descifraran sin ruido, oprobios ingleses, como si anhelara un último contacto con Roberta.

En ocasiones, Mauricio lo encontraba con la novela cerrada entre las manos; gruesos lagrimones le recorrían el rostro. El cardiólogo había advertido que la fase postoperatoria podía traer descompensaciones emotivas. El arquitecto no podía dormir en total oscuridad y Mauricio tenía que estar atento a los focos que se gastaban con asombrosa rapidez.

lugar tranquilo, llevadero, que por primera vez Mauricio asoció con su propia colonia. La ventana llegaba como la postal de un mundo fugitivo, donde los árboles que vio de chico empezaban a valer porque eran los árboles que vio de chico; aquel sitio odiado se inscribía en una primera nostalgia.

Volvió a la sala. En una bandeja de plata encontró el correo acumulado, sobres con la estampilla de la reina. Roberta pidió el divorcio por correo, como si perteneciera al gran mundo de los que tienen demasiadas propiedades para coincidir en un sitio de disputa.

William Archer demandó al bufet por incumplimiento de contratos, pero no aplicó a fondo sus recursos: abrió un resquicio humillante, una puerta de servicio para que su yerno salvara el pellejo.

Tal vez Roberta depositó demasiadas esperanzas en el jardín; lo cierto es que parecía el último motivo para acompañar a su marido. Mauricio imaginó las presiones de Roberta, su decepción abismal, las amenazas que llevaron a su padre al infarto. Tal vez enfermó para desplazar toda la responsabilidad a la mujer que huyó de México como de la peste. Ya sólo sabía de ella por Clarita:

—Para Roberta es muy difícil entender que una piedra azteca detenga todo, después del esfuerzo que ella invirtió. Es una mujer excepcional, Mauricio, tuve que decírselo a tu padre. Estamos planeando la edición en inglés de *El jardín como metáfora*, no se lo digas a tu madre, que no tolera esas verdades.

Cristina se negaba a hablar con ella pero no se la podía sacar de encima. Al sazonar un guiso, al escoger un vestido, al decidir un asunto cualquiera, escogía la opción que menos le hubiera gustado a su antigua amiga: "¡el coraje que le daría a Clarita!", era su frase triunfal.

—¿No te parece un supercabrón? —Carlos estaba fascinado con su padre; la historia de engaños e influencias revelaba su magnífica capacidad de violar las normas.

Sin embargo, a Mauricio le costaba trabajo entender todos esos años con Roberta; las tensiones superaban en mucho a las conveniencias. Como Carlos, su padre necesitaba gente dócil al lado. Su hermano no falló con Rocío, que sólo tenía ideas firmes en materia de porcelanas o macramés.

En la mesa de junto, los chinos terminaban su helado rosa. ¿Era el mismo o habían comido bolas sucesivas sin deleite aparente?

Cuando Jesús Guardiola fue dado de alta, Cristina cerró la tapa del portaviandas y salió con una parca despedida, como si perteneciera al personal médico.

Mauricio y Carlos acompañaron a su padre a la casa. Allí estaban los óleos de siempre: la calavera, los perros aullándole a la luna, las sandías en colores terrosos; sin embargo, aquel espacio de pensada elegancia parecía en renta; faltaban huellas que lo habitaran, la agenda abierta junto al teléfono, el periódico en la mesa, el aro de café que aún no detectaba la sirvienta.

Carlos llevó a su padre a la recámara y Mauricio se entretuvo en el estudio. Se sentó al escritorio, abrió cajones: papeles en orden, con olores importados, sobres aéreos, clips recubiertos de plástico. En las repisas, los libros se alineaban por temas. Dos secciones llamaban la atención: una dedicada a los jardines, otra a los *bunkers*, las casamatas, los baluartes.

El estudio daba a una terraza, semicubierta por las frondas del jardín vecino. Enmarcada en la ventana, aquella naturaleza menor sugería otra ciudad, no las calles numerosas que rodeaban la casa, sino un

la imagen después de catástrofes como la de Union Carbide en la India, pero Archer lo logra.

Carlos siguió narrando, sin prescindir de los detalles: los ojos del abogado, de un azul sereno, no se apartaban de su colega mexicano. ¿Por qué le contaba esa historia? Hablaba como si le hiciera un favor, como si abriera un expediente en su exclusivo beneficio. Seguramente conocía la relación de su padre con Roberta; sabía bastantes cosas de Carlos, había "hecho su tarea", como él decía; dejaba caer los datos con calculado descuido: cifras, contactos, nombres de funcionarios, nóminas en el extranjero que al día siguiente relegaría a un cuidadoso olvido.

—¿Tiene algo en México? —le preguntó Carlos.

—Dime un país sin problemas, es el único donde no conocen a William Archer. Su trabajo es demostrar que nunca pasa nada.

Carlos encendió otro cigarro. Su expresión de intoxicada curiosidad contrastaba con los chinos en la mesa de junto.

—¿Entiendes el enjuague? —Carlos estaba feliz: había encontrado la razón de su padre para casarse con Roberta—. ¿Sabes cuánto le pagó Obras Públicas el año pasado? ¡Ocho melones de dólares! —Gutiérrez Pool era la pieza que cerraba el cuadro: el mismo gobierno que promovía edificios de corte nacional y comisionaba hoteles color sandía, desviaba millones al extranjero para que los desastres nacionales no cancelaran las reservaciones de los turistas. Archer pagaba reportajes en periódicos y cadenas de televisión; con precisión quirúrgica, suprimía informes nocivos. Su capacidad de cabildeo era enorme y podía exigir que la constructora de Guardiola se hiciera cargo de mejorar la fachada del país.

Tal vez por eso a Roberta le gustaba tanto inventariar calamidades; había crecido con la idea de que el trabajo estaba en los desastres.

los rostros de anuncios sanos, el ambiente que imitaba con excesiva precisión las perfumadas páginas de las revistas sobre la buena vida. A las once en punto, las mujeres se despidieron con un discreto beso en la boca de cada abogado: "gracias por la diversión", dijeron.

El abogado con el anillo de *fullback* (a esas alturas Carlos estaba al tanto de todas las yardas que devoró en favor de Notre Dame), sirvió la ronda de despedida. Sus manos tenían la autoridad, algo desprendida del cuerpo, del *croupier* o del mecánico.

Desde la *suite*, se veían los contornos de la zona hospitalaria. Carlos se concentró en los focos rojos en el lomo de un hospital, pensó en su padre y justo entonces escuchó un nombre inconexo, absurdo. Creyó haber oído mal, o tal vez se trataba de otro William Archer.

—Por cierto, su hija está en México —añadió el abogado—. Archer preside una compañía que "asegura desastres" —el abogado vio a Carlos, como para cerciorarse de que lo seguía—: Archer maneja crisis de credibilidad de empresas y gobiernos. En la Foreign Office hizo espléndidos contactos diplomáticos y su trabajo depende de una cuidadosa red de influencias; obviamente no todo es encanto personal; Archer tiene el respaldo de una enorme cartera de inversionistas: cuando le sugiere a una cadena de televisión que evite ciertas noticias, todo mundo sabe que podría retirar los anuncios de un refresco de trascendencia mundial. Si estás a punto de que te lleve el carajo, no hay mejor recurso que darle unos millones a Archer: las malas noticias regresan como palomas con nuevos contratos. Nosotros lo representamos en el caso de *La Brea Texon*, el tanquero que hizo mierda esta bahía. Dos meses después, ningún periódico hablaba del tema. Archer limpió el caso antes de que los petroleros recogieran su porquería. He visto a muy pocos profesionales como él. Cuesta un huevo recuperar

Durante un rato, Carlos guardó silencio. Nunca haría el esfuerzo de agradar, no necesitaba el elogio gratuito, el perdón anticipado, las gentilezas protectoras de los otros. Exhaló el humo de su cigarro con desdén mientras Mauricio se distraía en la mesa de al lado, donde dos chinos comían helados color de rosa; se llevaban la cucharita a la boca con disciplina, como si cumplieran una tarea algo abstracta.

Cuando el silencio empezaba a hacerse insoportable, Carlos inició la historia de su viaje. Hablaba como si la hubiera repetido varias veces en su mente. Después de firmar el acuerdo, acabó con unas *call girls* "de locura", en la *suite* de un hotel que dominaba la bahía de Galveston. Describió los cuartos rentados por su socio norteamericano, un hombre de unos cincuenta años, pelo blanco, un pesado anillo de campeón colegial en la mano derecha y aire extrañamente infantil. El abogado retó a Carlos a unas *vencidas*; con la mano libre, le tiraba caramelos y papas ranuradas a las putas (por un reflejo paranoico, Carlos le había dicho que no le gustaba pagar por el sexo y su colega lo vio con asombro: "si sólo vamos a jugar, ¿quién habla de coger?"). Y en efecto, en la *suite* se entretuvieron con un juego electrónico en el que se competía por llegar a Marte entre una lluvia de rayos láser; también había mesas con felpa verde para el *bridge*, sala de billar, tres o cuatro televisiones. El sexo sólo estuvo presente como una extensión de los juegos. Las largas piernas de las mujeres, sus pieles tostadas, los vestidos satinados que realzaban cuerpos adictos a las piscinas, los caballos, las canchas de arcilla, eran el complemento, la tensión necesaria para que la *suite* realmente fuera de cinco estrellas. Las mujeres estaban ahí como un certificado de éxito, agregaban el lujo natural de una pantera o un acuario con peces excelentes. Al cabo de un rato, Carlos lamentó no estar en un burdel reglamentario; se aburrió ante las sonrisas,

de vez en cuando, la voz del micrófono sacaba a alguna señora del tejido espumoso que progresaba en sus agujas.

Mauricio aceptó esa zona sin responsabilidades definidas, anterior y posterior a las tragedias. Mientras no lo llamaran, todo sería dichosamente transitorio.

Al volver de Estados Unidos, Carlos lo encontró en su puesto de espera y lo vio con admiración. Tal vez medía la escena con su propio temperamento; le repugnaba estar quieto y la pasividad de su hermano le asombró como un triunfo de la voluntad.

Mauricio sabía que sólo alguien que desconociera por completo su indolencia, su magnífica capacidad de contar cerillos, soplar sobre un peine o ver el techo mientras chupaba una galleta, podía pensar que su espera en esa sala requería de disciplina. Carlos lo abrazó con emoción inusitada. Aunque su respeto venía de más de veinte años de desinterés, Mauricio no vaciló en aceptarlo.

Fue una de las pocas ocasiones en que Carlos se dio el lujo de ser sorpresivo. Vivía para controlar los imprevistos, de acuerdo con un plan inquebrantable. En cuanto se recibió de abogado, obtuvo un trabajo con un penalista al que elogió como "un auténtico perro" y empezó a ahorrar con fines definidos (la casa propia, el condominio de tiempo compartido en Vallarta, la casa de campo en el valle de Morelos). Moldeaba su destino con tal autoridad que los accidentes le parecían un defecto de carácter.

Detestaba tanto el fracaso que convertía los obstáculos en "pruebas de éxito". Obviamente le fue muy bien en Houston.

—Averigüé datos duros —le comentó a Mauricio.

Pensó que se refería a los litigios del bufet, pero su hermano le pidió que bajaran a la cafetería para hablar en privado.

una casa con la luz encendida en los páramos donde no debía haber nada, por qué se arrancaban raíces y se preparaban fogones en las orillas más lejanas, por qué se encendía un cerillo lejos del mundo, una flama débil que no apagaba el viento.

Carlos se había casado con una mujer capaz de representarlo con ventaja. En cualquier situación que no fuese extrema, era preferible ver a Rocío.

El abogado Guardiola había llevado su habilidad conspiratoria al erotismo; según él, las mujeres que aparentaban más recato (Rocío hojeaba cualquier revista femenina como si se tratara de un Libro de Horas) siempre sorprendían en la cama. Las apasionadas que discutían de todo y prometían lumbres con la mirada, soltaban tanta energía en asuntos insulsos que llegaban menoscabadas a la intimidad. En cambio, las mujeres quietas, capaces de dedicarle a un anuncio la atención de un milagro y a un milagro la serenidad de un anuncio, necesitaban compensarse en plan fogoso. Carlos podía aburrirse durante meses con una mujer olla exprés con tal de llegar al precioso instante de quitarle la válvula de seguridad.

Al salir del cuarto 303, sus tacones puntiagudos se apagaban lentamente en el pasillo.

—Es un dulce —decía Jesús Guardiola, mientras Mauricio comía las galletas espolvoreadas de azúcar *glass* de Rocío.

Poco a poco, el hospital se convirtió en las llamadas corteses de Roberta (algo importante y triste y difícil de explicar la retenía en Londres), la resistencia dura de su madre, la enfermera joven e ineficiente que prefería su padre. Mauricio pasaba horas en la sala de espera, donde los familiares de los pacientes dormitaban y compartían sándwiches, barajas, diarios de la tarde;

contacto entre ellos. Quizá a su madre le bastaba con demostrar la superioridad de ese caldo, ser dueña de los recuerdos que llegaban con el sazón inconfundible de cuando fueron jóvenes. O quizá lo envenenaría lentamente, lo sometería a su sabrosa justicia, se vengaría del abandono, la disparidad de sus destinos, la casa que nunca le construyó.

—No hables, Chupito —la sopa chorreaba por la barbilla—. Así, así, —y sin el menor sentido de lo público añadía—: mi Chupis, mi Chupis pechocho.

Carlos entró al cuarto 303 como si fuera un vestidor deportivo, aplaudió con fuerza y dijo que le habían encargado un caso "gordo", "muy gordo". Su padre sonrió con melancolía, absorto ante ese derroche de vitalidad.

Carlos fue a Houston por unos días como representante legal del bufet que acababa de convertirlo en asociado. Mauricio quedó a cargo de contestar las llamadas de Roberta. Su padre prefería no hablar con ella; dormitaba muchas horas y miraba el entorno —las flores de plástico, la cortina color azafrán, el carrito con medicamentos— como si cada objeto le doliera.

Cuando Mauricio acompañaba a su madre a la cafetería del sótano, ella se refería a la inglesa con tranquila objetividad. El sitio parecía decorado en su favor: un refectorio práctico y anticuado, para reclutas en alguna película de la Segunda Guerra.

Al cabo de unos días, Mauricio se convenció de que su madre no había ido al hospital en busca de venganza, sino a demostrar lo mucho que podía contribuir a la sobrevivencia difícil. La vio acariciar el rostro enjuto de su padre, subirle la frazada, afeitarlo con esmero, quitarle los pelos de la nariz con sus pinzas para cejas, ponerle loción, cortarle las uñas de las manos y los pies, peinarlo cuatro veces al día, abotonarle la piyama con una constancia que revelaba por qué la gente no moría en los desiertos, por qué había

—Quiso verla —repitió Carlos en el tercer piso del Hospital Britania, mientras fumaban en una terraza, viendo la ciudad gris, seca, extraviada en el polvo y la luz incierta de la tarde.

—¿Y Roberta? —preguntó Mauricio.

—En Londres, ¿dónde más?

Mauricio pensó que su madre se negaría a ir al hospital; sin embargo, a las pocas horas estaba ahí, preocupada de que se le hubiera corrido el *rimmel*:

—¿No parezco mapache? —era difícil no admirar sus inseguridades, su preocupación de mujer joven que revisa una y otra vez los pliegues de su vestido.

El asistente del cardiólogo la llevó al cuarto, señalando el camino con su bitácora de triplay. Las enfermeras ignoraban la existencia de Roberta, trataron a Cristina con grave respeto y no entendieron que rechazara el sofá-cama del cuarto y prefiriera dormir en el pasillo, como una silueta extenuada en el asiento de vinilo.

Tres semanas después del infarto, Cristina abría un traste de metal ante su ex marido:

—No hables tanto, Chus.

Cristina llegaba armada de un portaviandas, como si visitara a un enfermo pobre o de otra época. Al ver la cuchara que entraba y salía de la boca exangüe, Mauricio se preguntó si volvería a haber otro

7. Las pieles infrarrojas

Carlos mantuvo los dedos tensos en su nuca, la versión rígida, destruida, de la mano que alguna vez le acarició el pelo con el orgullo del propietario que reconforta a su lebrel.

tó de buscar alguna causa para aquel confuso placer. ¿La inaudita manera de perjudicar a su padre? ¿La venganza final del testigo? No, eso era demasiado simple. Acabar con el proyecto le dolía, o más bien le dolía y lo excitaba; deseaba aniquilarse en el jardín, ser una viva escoria, el infame al que habría que expulsar de la colonia; sin embargo, esta suposición suntuosa no era auténtica: no decidió nada, fue el brazo ejecutorio, el instrumento de Verónica, el rayo de luz del tío Felipe, y esto le quitaba la posibilidad de arruinarse adrede, de elegir su ruina, una espléndida tragedia de la cual arrepentirse.

Lorena le envió una postal con las frases rápidas de quien tiene demasiadas actividades dichosas para compartirlas en detalle.

Mauricio recorrió los campos de Terminal Progreso con la postal en la mano. Parecía increíble que ese paisaje decrépito se hubiera salvado de algo.

Cuando vio la silueta a la distancia, tardó en distinguir que era Carlos. Caminaba con la boca abierta, jalando aire con desesperación.

Mauricio quiso que oscureciera de repente, deseó una ceguera bondadosa que lo librara de ver a su hermano con la camisa mal fajada, los zapatos cubiertos de tierra, la boca, sobre todo la boca que no quería cerrar, y las lágrimas que le mojaban la cara, la expresión absurda de ese rostro hecho para otras circunstancias, nunca para la tristeza, las manos temblorosas que tomaban al hermano menor de la camisa, lo abrazaban con una furia descolocada, insoportable. Mauricio quiso empujarlo, aplastar el sollozo, ese vahído torpe y desgraciado. No le importó otra cosa que silenciar a su hermano hasta que sintió los dedos en la nuca, la presión que lo incluía de otro modo en ese llanto y explicaba todo en su peor opción.

Mauricio sintió una sacudida; una mano recia lo sacó de la siesta:

—Vamos a dar gracias.

Tardó en volver a la afilada realidad de la sala comedor. Su madre se había vestido de negro.

Después de un bostezo largo, que su madre aprovechó para encender un cigarro con la colilla del anterior, Mauricio se abrochó el pantalón para ir a la iglesia.

En el trayecto, pensó que también él merecía vestirse de negro: de no ser por su video, el escalón difícilmente se habría vuelto noticia. ¿Qué lo impulsó a traicionar a su padre de ese modo? ¿Verónica? ¿Los ruegos de su madre? ¿El deseo de silenciar a Clarita? ¿La apatía de Stefan Dezman? Aunque todo se debía a la casualidad (el *zoom* sobre la zanja en el momento oportuno, el video solicitado por el escrupuloso jefe de cuadrilla, la gira que le impidió a su padre intervenir a tiempo, la disponibilidad del arqueólogo, el interés de la televisión de transmitir cinco minutos de patriotismo en horario triple A, el hecho de que el secretario de Educación viera el programa), él tuvo la oportunidad de recuperar el video en la camioneta; ése era el punto fundamental.

Su madre rezaba con solemne responsabilidad: el tío Felipe había hecho lo suyo, el obispo recamado de oro guió a Mauricio para que captara la certera anunciación.

—Te damos gracias...

Mauricio vio los músculos desgarrados del redentor, sus ojos en éxtasis, sus elaboradas heridas, y experimentó una excitación incontenible. Tenía los pulmones llenos de humo y la mirada llorosa de tanto ver las velas. Se aferró a un barandal de madera, pulido por las muchas manos que lo habían tocado. Tra-

—Un café con *piquete* para el arquitecto —dijo un hombre de camisa color caqui—, ¡mire nomás qué preciosura!

Con ojos inyectados de sangre, Guardiola vio la piedra. No pronunció palabra. Se llevó la taza de zinc a los labios y bebió el líquido que echaba humo, como si quisiera despellejarse la boca.

Un escueto boletín de Obras Públicas anunció la suspensión del parque.

—Como mexicano, me felicito por el hallazgo —dijo Gutiérrez Pool al ser abordado por la prensa afuera de sus oficinas. No había forma de que los muros de Guardiola valieran más que un escalón azteca. El parque se transformaría en zona arqueológica aunque no hubiera otro hallazgo.

—Estoy de plácemes por el resultado; nuestra intuición fue correcta: aquí se podía establecer un contacto con los ancestros. Instalaremos una comisión para transmitir los trabajos a Antropología —anunció Gutiérrez Pool.

En su refrigerador, Cristina Ferrán colgó el lema: POR SU BOCA MUERE EL PEZ. Mauricio sintió una repentina simpatía por su padre.

Fue a verlo al despacho y lo encontró abatido, junto a la maqueta del proyecto. Acariciaba un arbolito como si fuera la cola de un animal muerto.

—Hay que quemar esto —Jesús Guardiola señaló la maqueta. Se pasó la mano por la cabeza; un pelo blanco quedó entre sus dedos; lo vio con triste detenimiento.

—Roberta está hecha pedazos —añadió.

Mauricio quiso abrazarlo, alargó la mano y derribó una empalizada en miniatura, de madera de balsa. Jesús Guardiola la acomodó en su sitio, como si las cosas debieran quemarse en orden.

exigencia de su profesión. Bastaba verla para saber que su dueño había descubierto criptas decisivas y que desde ese momento la excavación era famosa.

Esa noche, el arqueólogo presentó en televisión el video de Mauricio:

—Como todos los escalones del pasado, éste lleva hacia abajo; tal vez estemos ante una ciudadela o un entierro ceremonial; la orientación de la piedra revela un cuidadoso cálculo astronómico y las hendiduras sugieren un ala de mariposa, símbolo de los guerreros —el arqueólogo hablaba con una voz certera, que no conocía las pausas ni las vacilaciones; en pleno estudio recibió una llamada del secretario de Educación y con notable presencia de ánimo criticó la errática política del ramo y exigió fondos de emergencia para "el nuevo bastión del mundo mesoamericano".

El locutor de turno se refirió a la grandeza prehispánica; habló de posibles pectorales de oro enterrados en Xochimilco y de la técnica azteca que revelaba avances desconocidos en la Europa de la época.

—A esto ya no le echan tierra —comentó el arqueólogo al despedirse de la nación.

Al día siguiente, cuando un equipo de camarógrafos profesionales recorrió el área, la zanja ya había sido acordonada. En la casamata de los constructores había gran bullicio, pero el resto del jardín estaba en paz. Los albañiles y los jardineros jugaban futbol; las porterías eran unos cipreses que no llegaron a plantar.

Jesús Guardiola estaba ausente porque había ido a inaugurar clínicas rurales en una de las "giras temáticas" de Benjamín Gutiérrez Pool. Fue localizado en una ranchería donde hacía mal tiempo. Llegó empapado, en un helicóptero del ejército.

Envuelto en una cobija, se acercó a la zona controlada por el Instituto de Antropología. La boca le temblaba y los arqueólogos lo atribuyeron a la fiebre:

de control. El silencio generaba una sensación de caos.

En la rampa de salida, una *pick-up* luchaba por salir del fango. Dos hombres empujaban en la parte trasera, los rostros bañados de lodo. El hombre que pidió el video iba al volante.

Mauricio vio la marca de la camioneta, Satori, y la leyenda en la portezuela: ENCIERRO: LUZ SAVIÑÓN 253, la dirección del bufet de su padre.

—¡Ayúdale a ésos! —el conductor le gritó a Mauricio.

Se asomó a la parte trasera y vio una mochila abierta, con un pantalón de mezclilla y el video que había grabado. Por un momento pensó en quedarse con él y dejar que la camioneta fuera en balde a la ciudad, pero luego desvió la vista y distinguió a Stefan Dezman en el camino; avanzaba con indolencia, las manos en los bolsillos y un incómodo cigarro en los labios; parecía capaz de tardar diez minutos en llegar a la camioneta. Tal vez fue la imagen de Stefan Dezman lo que le impidió tomar el video, como si liquidara sus muchas negativas con otra negativa.

Ayudó a los que empujaban, recibió el lodo en la cara, cayó de bruces y alzó la vista para ver al Satori que partía y a Stefan Dezman que no acababa de acercarse.

Horas después, una cuadrilla de Antropología limpiaba la piedra con escobetas. Clarita especuló en la posibilidad de que estuvieran sobre una gigantesca necrópolis; Stefan dijo: "muertos son vitamina de raíces". Era posible que un vasto cementerio azteca contribuyera a preservar las plantas.

Oscurecía cuando llegó un arqueólogo rubicundo, de gran barba canosa. Aquella barba no parecía responder a un gusto personal sino a una arquetípica

amigas fundaron un grupo de té, galletas y protesta: Tercer Día, para recordar la jornada en la que Dios creó las plantas. Repartían volantes escritos por Verónica en los que se enlistaban especies en peligro de extinción y se pedía la clausura del parque recreativo.

Nada de esto podía quitarle el sueño a Jesús Guardiola. La frase LA PATRIA ES PRIMERO, que había cubierto los muros de la ciudad, tenía varias formas de ser verdadera en la región: el parque aludía al esplendor interrumpido por la Conquista y ofrecía una reserva de autenticidad para los turistas; en las gruesas carpetas preparadas por Clarita, el parque servía simultáneamente para explicar el atraso (los antiguos responsables ya eran polvo en sus armaduras) y para ofrecer un "futuro viable" (los nuevos responsables rentarían coches, se hospedarían en los nuevos hoteles, comprarían artesanías, comerían el pan de pulque de la zona).

La cámara produjo un ronroneo tranquilo en el hombro de Mauricio hasta que la casualidad lo llevó a unos trabajadores que habían interrumpido su labor de zapa y miraban el suelo con extraña reverencia. Alguien se quitó el casco, tal vez en previsión de un esqueleto. Mauricio inclinó la cámara y registró lo que había al fondo: un escalón de piedra.

—Hay que dar parte a Antropología —ordenó el jefe de cuadrilla—. Préstame el video —le dijo a Mauricio.

Todo ocurrió con curioso automatismo: los tráileres dejaron de echar humo, los dibujantes, asesores e ingenieros se reunieron junto a la zanja.

Mauricio caminó hacia los terraplenes que custodiaban el jardín y encontró una flecha que no había visto: RUTA DE EVACUACIÓN. Le sorprendió que el parque tuviera señas de salida, y de algún modo, ése fue el primer indicio de que el lugar estaba fuera

escapadas, lo que era sin él, su ausencia viva, y por primera vez gritaba con la confianza abierta de no ser oída, mientras su resuello de gordo, de alcoholes, de certidumbres rotas, decía lo que no debía decir, "te quiero", "te quiero mucho", porque la piel extenuada, las uñas en la tela, los párpados ardientes, la mugre deliciosa, el pelo lleno de humo ya eran la sombra de esa fecha, el aire que fue Lorena, la partida que él recordaba desde una hora todavía futura.

—Toma, tienes que ser testigo —Verónica le tendió un aparato de video—: mi papá lo compró cuando estaba desmayada, para grabar mis primeros pasos.

Mauricio acababa de devolver las llaves del Zoas IV. Vio la cámara como un azar favorable.

Grabó los llanos sin nadie, las brigadas de excavadoras, los órganos y los pirules que llegaban en tráileres. Lo que más le gustó fue que el video pudiera borrarse; cazar imágenes significaba recoger desechos y borrar sus vínculos. Verónica mejoraba al ser filtrada por el lente. Mauricio la observó con fascinación, como si al fin se asomara a su ventana.

El arquitecto Guardiola disfrutó la cercanía de su hijo; quizá recordó los años en que fue su mejor acompañante.

Fue su madre quien le otorgó un sentido insospechado a su nueva actividad:

—Felipe está contigo —palmeó el aparato, como si el tío hubiera encontrado allí otro pequeño ataúd.

El comentario descubrió las intenciones de Verónica: le había prestado la cámara para que grabara la destrucción del campo; él podía estar cerca del arquitecto, Clarita, los asesores de Gutiérrez Pool.

Poco a poco, el clima de tensión se convirtió en otra forma de la costumbre. Cristina Ferrán y sus

Los muros de cal estaban decorados con máscaras, fotos de zapatistas, judas de cartón. Mauricio se concentró en un tigre amarillo, con espejos en los ojos y pecas rojas. Bebió sin apartar la vista de la fiera hasta que Lorena se le acercó y abrió la mano para mostrar una pastilla. Mauricio vio el círculo lila y la mano que se cerraba, creando un estuche suave.

Iba a ser su última noche juntos, la gira empezaba al día siguiente, pero no mencionaron el tema, subieron las escaleras en la torre; ella apenas podía andar y sonreía con una felicidad descolocada. Mauricio la besó y su boca le supo a algo bueno y mordido de antemano. Las manos chicas lo acariciaron con soltura, como si pasaran por una materia exigua, un paño difícil de encontrar. El pelo castaño de Lorena retenía los humos de la noche, el incienso de *Abraxas*, el tabaco, la mariguana de la fiesta. Mauricio le respiró el pelo mientras ella se desvestía. Vio con tristeza su espalda endurecida, las momentáneas huellas rojas que aparecían a la menor presión. Ella se entregó sin la prisa que lo desconcertaba tanto; abrió mucho la boca, liberando un quejido hondo, una fragancia vegetal, la mezcla que llevaba dentro; una tensión interior la arqueaba, la sumía ventajosamente en otra zona, libre ya de los roces que la hacían reír, su cuerpo se gastaba por dentro, asimilaba algo dulcemente, un misterio sofocado, o tal vez era que se iba, empezaba a estar lejos y sentía las manos que la tocaron y la tocarían en otros tiempos, un instante intermedio, sin matices ni color, o que en todo caso correspondía al verde que nunca se escoge pero está allí y gusta de un modo ambiguo, como un recuerdo superado y doloroso, o inquieta sin apremio, como una enfermedad aún lejana. Los gestos de Lorena llegaban duplicados, entregaban las huellas dormidas de otras manos, los pies ya eran los pasos que la sacarían de esa recámara; poco a poco Lorena revelaba gestos, sus manos

rias, una mujer que nunca sería Lorena, si acaso un poco más Verónica, un rostro casi muerto para exprimirse en soledad, y hundirse en la noche donde ningún peligro era suyo, para devolver el Zoas al punto de partida.

En el estreno de *Abraxas*, los actores cumplieron la dolorosa plasticidad ideada por Ferreira. En primera fila destacaba un hombre de cabeza rapada. "Lucien está aquí", había dicho Neri, "vino de París".

Alguien tan famoso no necesitaba apellido. Cuando Crystalda salió a escena, Lucien soltó la carcajada a destiempo de los que entienden "algo más".

Mauricio encendió un cerillo para leer lo que Lucien había escrito en el programa de mano: "Crystalda o la comicidad de la era plástica/un adorable monstruo escénico/un bibelot deconstruido/una oxigenada diosa africana/la definitiva negra blanca/King-Kong y la rubia en un solo cuerpo/el triunfo del sujeto sin referente."

Abraxas recibió una larga ovación, interrumpida por abucheos tan escasos que parecían contratados por Ferreira para preservar su fama de "maldito".

En el coctel, los meseros lucharon para entregarle copas a los actores que se saludaban con cuatro besos y se abrazaban durante medio minuto.

Mauricio ubicó a Lorena entre dos enormes cantantes de ópera. Sintió una repentina ternura por su esfuerzo para integrarse a ese elenco marcado por la desmesura física; la recordó haciendo ejercicios, bebiendo agua a todas horas. La abrazó, y sintió que también él era inmenso para ella.

La fiesta siguió en una mansión colonial en las barrancas del Olivar de los Padres. Desde una terraza se veían las luces de la ciudad; las zonas de oscuridad eran cementerios, colinas, parques.

Abrió la ventana.

—Ya estamos en Avenida Juárez —dijo.

Ella abrió los ojos.

—Ahí adelantito.

Mauricio vio el reloj de la Torre Latinoamericana al final de la avenida. Apagó el motor.

—¿Cuánto te debo?

—Nada.

La mujer le dirigió una mirada plana. Estaban bajo un farol y Mauricio comprobó que la línea en el cuello era una cicatriz. Luego vio un círculo de piel que asomaba por la media rota. El deseo de protegerla se mezclaba con el de causarle el siguiente daño; ése era el secreto que la muchacha guardaba bajo su suéter raído, la confusa invitación a hundirse rescatándola.

—Adiós —dijo Mauricio, y arrancó antes de que ella cerrara la puerta.

No buscó la silueta en el retrovisor; aceleró hacia los números dorados de la Torre, viendo el cielo, y se pasó el alto de San Juan de Letrán, como si pudiera permitirse un alarde, como si de veras le importara ponerse en riesgo. De cualquier forma, no sintió miedo. Atravesó la avenida, escuchó un claxon que rompía el aire, esquivó una sombra colorida, siguió de largo, y se detuvo, indiferente, triste, cada vez más triste de su indiferencia, y lloró, quizá por el simple hartazgo de recorrer la noche, de buscar cosas, distracciones, correspondencias, algo para saber que no importaba lo que había dicho Neri Castellanos, que la compañía se podía ir de gira sin que eso fuera un problema, que todo era tan normal como la aceptación de Lorena, "ya lo sabíamos, gordo", tan natural como ese recorrido en el taxi, el último de todos, porque tenía que ser el último, no podía seguir merodeando al grupo que se iba, un paseo final en busca de un cuerpo que sirviera de borrador a otras histo-

los reflejos de neón sobre su cara. Todo llegaba de otro modo a esa piel. No era necesario tocarla, ni siquiera olerla. ¿Podía haber algo más perfecto y simple que la sombra de su mano en un cuerpo desconocido? Estudió el dibujo de sus labios, los párpados vibrando apenas, los destellos suaves de la ciudad en sus mejillas, la frente rendida ante la delicada fábrica de la noche.

Tardó en distinguir la línea en el cuello, muy fina, una marca de nacimiento, tal vez, o la cicatriz de una herida, la huella de la belleza vulnerada. Entonces supo que una persona podía justificar el pasado de otra. La mujer era como Verónica pudo haber crecido.

Recordó a la puta con la que hizo el amor por primera vez, recordó su cara de alumna de preparatoria, la fresca normalidad con que tomó los billetes. En cambio, la mujer a su lado, como Verónica de niña, hacía que el solo hecho de mirarla fuera doloroso, un anticipo de las muchas cosas de las que sería inútil protegerla. Aun al sonreír, la boca parecía desviarse hacia un suave reclamo.

La mujer arrugó el rostro de pronto, como si padeciera un cólico. No abrió los ojos; se tocó el bajo vientre con los dedos, como si el dolor fuera algo de costumbre. Luego se humedeció los labios y Mauricio vio la punta blanca de la lengua. Debía estar enferma, tal vez acababa de tomar pastillas o se había drogado y subió al taxi para cumplir su sobredosis sin rumbo fijo. No, el cuerpo lacio y el dolor bajo control sugerían desarreglos de otro orden, parecía habituada a filos invisibles, desastres cotidianos, mordeduras que él no iba a conocer. Estuvo a punto de tocarla, pero eso hubiera roto el embrujo, la delgada película que los unía.

Al llegar al centro, Mauricio tenía una erección insoportable. Se acarició sobre el pantalón; eyaculó, viendo una sombra morada en el rostro de la mujer, la punta dura de su lengua sucia.

Sir William estaba ahí por motivos de trabajo; sus asistentes no dejaron de tomar notas y él hizo preguntas que suponían un detallado estudio del terreno; escuchó las respuestas como si todos los argumentos fuesen el mismo, agradable crepúsculo.

La muchacha había perdido un zapato; caminaba con dificultad, se apoyó en un poste, recargó la cabeza con alivio. Mauricio detuvo el taxi. Ella no había extendido la mano; de cualquier forma, subió a bordo. Se dejó caer en el asiento delantero. Su cabeza golpeó en el marco de la puerta, pero no se quejó, ni siquiera se llevó los dedos a la sien. Respiraba con trabajo, reponiéndose de algo que le había pasado calles atrás. Mauricio vio sus muslos fuertes; la mujer tenía un cuerpo pequeño y firme, que contrastaba con la fragilidad del rostro y la expresión algo ausente en los ojos. El pelo, muy corto y negro, estaba revuelto en la nuca, como si se hubiera rascado con fuerza.

—Voy al centro —dijo de un modo genérico.

Mauricio vio sus dedos maltratados. Lorena se mordía las uñas, pero eso sólo fue importante en el primer encuentro, cuando buscó en su oreja el punto secreto de la visión; no tenía el temperamento de las que necesitan comerse un poco para estar en paz; incluso su premura, su facilidad para atar y desatar la vida, rara vez llegaba a la desesperación. En cambio, los ojos evasivos de la pasajera, el aire difícil que le entraba a la nariz, sugerían algo quebrado, las fisuras que Lorena imitaba al ver un drama en la pantalla y que alguna vez llevaría al teatro.

A las pocas calles, la muchacha cerró los ojos; su respiración cobró un tono parejo, como si soñara o quisiera inhalar el rastro de mariguana que flotaba en el coche. Mauricio aprovechó su sueño para fingir semáforos. Se detuvo en cualquier sitio a contemplar

El trabajo de la doctora Rendón asomó en las nuevas declaraciones del arquitecto:

—Un edificio sólo se completa con el tiempo. Las construcciones deben contaminarse con la vida, entregarse al diseño final del deterioro, como la pintura que prevee la pátina —parecía convencido de que toda alteración iba a ser benéfica; la historia era una textura que matizaría sus obras.

Mauricio lo escuchó recitar esto ante la rolliza grabadora de un periodista de la radio. A pesar de sus crecientes dificultades para recorrer la construcción, estaba dispuesto a hablar durante horas. Sólo la aparición de una camioneta en el horizonte interrumpió su entrevista, la tercera de ese día.

—Acompáñame —se apoyó en Mauricio y se esforzó en caminar de prisa.

Roberta descendió del vehículo y abrió un parasol color champaña. La seguía un hombre de unos setenta años, de porte atlético.

—Sir William —dijo Roberta, enfatizando el "Sir", como si su padre perteneciera a otra familia.

Dos ejecutivos jóvenes venían detrás de William Archer. Saludaron a Mauricio y al jefe de ingenieros en un español perfecto y recorrieron las obras sin dirigirle la palabra a nadie.

Archer caminó por taludes, subió cuestas, resistió un sólido discurso de Clarita, preguntó hacia dónde quedaban los volcanes y pasó largo rato viendo la neblina café que los ocultaba. En ningún momento la sonrisa se descongeló en sus labios.

Mauricio no veía a Archer desde la boda de su padre; la edad entre ambos se había acortado. Después de dos horas, la enérgica amabilidad de Sir William agotó a su anfitrión. Jesús Guardiola se pasaba el paliacate por el cuello y la frente.

diaba la forma de infectar el jardín con plagas, parásitos, hormigas nocturnas.

Mauricio vio las heridas que aproximaban a Cristo a su hora definitiva, las tres de la tarde tan mencionadas por el maestro de Moral, la carne castigada, ya sin habla. Cualquier cosa parecía solicitable, incluso lo que dijo Cristina Ferrán:

—Felipe, intercede por nosotros.

El obispo niño, el inmutable tío en los cielos, era la última esperanza para alejar a las huestes del arquitecto Jesús Guardiola.

—"Cordero de Dios que quitas el pecado del mundo..."

A Mauricio le conmovió la fuerza con que su madre se golpeaba el pecho. Estaba acostumbrada a rezar y se sumía en larguísimas plegarias circulares. A él le empezó a sobrar el tiempo; más que de fe, carecía de la dilatada táctica para pedir, de la resistencia para un intercambio promedio con la divinidad. Vio a hombres de setenta, casi ochenta años, encender cirios y permanecer de rodillas en el piso de piedra durante un lapso extenuante. Las mujeres enfundadas en rebozos susurraban letanías con una entereza perturbadora, como si no solicitaran otra cosa que su derecho a susurrar letanías.

Él merecía estar fuera de *Abraxas*, de cualquier ceremonia que exigiese entrega física. Podía asumir supersticiones extremas, temerle al gato negro o a la sal derramada, podía admirar las salamandras de fuego de religiones desconocidas, pero no podía lograr que el cuerpo le doliera en favor de los rezos.

Cristina Ferrán le habló a Felipe, murmuró "muchas hormigas", con ojos pulidos por la indignación.

—¿No se te antoja un sándwich? —preguntó al salir.

Tanto rezo le había abierto el apetito.

Mauricio quiso felicitar a Lorena, pero ella salió sin despedirse.

Cristina Ferrán llevaba semanas pidiéndole que la acompañara a la iglesia. Desde que se inició la construcción del jardín, tenía una palidez de sábanas lloradas y cigarros angustiosos. Su mejor amiga la había traicionado con su ex marido y la afrenta transcurría "en sus narices". ¿Qué les hubiera costado conspirar en otros rumbos?

En la capilla, Mauricio volvió a ver el copete del santo en sus elevaciones simbólicas. Contempló los extremos ejemplares de Cristo: el bebé en el pesebre y el cuerpo agónico en la cruz. Un dios mudo, asfixiado por la ignorancia o el sufrimiento.

De rodillas ante el altar, su madre le pidió algo extraño:

—Ruega por Verónica.

Verónica había recogido firmas contra el jardín y aportó a las vecinas datos para exclamar "¡es un ecocidio!" en su tono de "¡se tira la leche!" Las mujeres de Terminal Progreso habían cerrado filas contra el proyecto. Más que impedir una desgracia, querían confirmar su existencia; en la colonia, una mujer que "valía lo suyo" ejercía su derecho al drama; lo más horrendo, la auténtica desgracia, hubiera sido no sufrir.

Las madres hablaban de Verónica con progresiva admiración. Era lo contrario a las mujeres que se pintaban las uñas de los pies y colocaban algodoncitos en sus entrededos, es decir, a las que vivían para irse. Verónica estaba allí, dispuesta a luchar por plantas próximas. Se vestía como un muchacho, una camiseta cubría sus senos sin relieve, sus zapatos estaban enlodados y casi siempre tenía briznas en el pelo; todo en ella apuntaba al esfuerzo, a la dedicación sin placeres evidentes. En su laboratorio de la universidad, estu-

el momento de la madurez. El día del estreno cumpliré 56.

En ese momento volvió la luz. Los actores miraron absortos al director, como si las vueltas del siete fuesen las vendas que se quitaba un herido.

Ferreira se sentó al borde del estrado y explicó que en el inmóvil Abraxas se fundían el espíritu y la materia, el bien y el mal. Una muralla de amplificadores garantizaría un sonido como el de Santana en Woodstock; el final sería una ceremonia gnóstica, una liberación del ser al fin admitido a los 365 círculos de la creación. La música en vivo estaría a cargo de un conjunto que conocía a Devadip desde sus años de Tijuana, reforzado con un saxofonista de San Francisco y un multipercusionista de Las Antillas. La escenografía iba a rendir homenaje a los elementos de la Tierra; el último, por supuesto, sería el fuego; los cuerpos progresivamente desnudos brindarían una versión encarnada de las llamas, un campo de energía capaz de liberar a Abraxas de miércoles a domingos.

A continuación, Neri Castellanos leyó el reparto de la obra. Lorena y Pancho quedaron dentro. Quienes más aplaudieron el triunfo fueron los escogidos como suplentes. Mauricio desvió la vista a los desechados; a casi todos, el pelo les había crecido en la espera, como si estar disponibles fuera una preparación para papeles de profetas. Un chileno, que solía elogiar los relatos de Neri en el tono de un dulcísimo rabí, sonreía de un modo obsecuente que en su código de expresiones equivalía a "me lo merezco".

—No canten derrota —Neri se dirigió a los eliminados—, mañana se muere uno de estos cabrones y empiezan a entrenar como suplentes.

En ese momento entraron los periodistas que habían esperado en el vestíbulo. Crystalda fue la más solicitada y se comportó con una sencillez incalculable en una giganta célebre.

Mauricio nunca tuvo una oportunidad real, lo sabía demasiado bien. Aun así, sintió tristeza cuando el director mencionó el título de la obra:

—*Abraxas*.

En ese momento se fue la luz (¿o Ferreira le pidió al iluminador que apagara las diablas?). El auditorio se unió en un siseo admirativo.

—Allá arriba están de acuerdo —la voz del director cobró un tono trascendente: "arriba" podía ser la tramoya, el techo, el cielo, el límite ulterior donde se decidía el destino—. Lo bueno es que las palabras y las ideas son luminosas en sí mismas.

En plena oscuridad, el director describió su proyecto. La obra rendiría homenaje a Carlos Santana, el prófugo de Autlán, Jalisco, que después de renovar la música de rock había accedido a una transfiguración del espíritu: las siete letras inertes de su apellido ahora formaban el nombre religioso de "Devadip":

—El siete será nuestro mantra —en la penumbra, Mauricio buscó el perfil de la sietemesina Lorena—. También "Abraxas" tiene siete letras —el director hizo una pausa y la mente de Mauricio se vio asaltada por una fuga en siete, como si algo insólito se ordenara en ese instante: el año del temblor, las siete colinas de Roma, el juego de los siete errores que nunca pudo resolver en los estacionamientos de los moteles donde aguardó a su padre, las siete puertas de Clarita, el tequila Siete Leguas del tío Roberto, la tribu de las siete cuevas que fundó la ciudad, los perros de San Andrés, su eterno promedio escolar, el insulto de siete letras que el maestro de Moral leía en las miradas de sus alumnos, el domingo en que Neri habló de los siete mares y él durmió por primera vez con Lorena.

Ferreira también estaba absorto en la numerología:

—A los 28 años —continuó—, una iluminación marcó mi vida: son las cuatro vueltas del siete,

minarían a él y que en el fondo sólo le interesaban como palabra, como acústica rareza, "diabla", una luz prohibida.

—¿Y cómo se llama la obra? —preguntó Mauricio.

—Gerónimo nos va a decir mañana.

Neri Castellanos lo recibió con sospechosa solidaridad, un abrazo fuerte que significaba exilio, las muchas Siberias que él podría recorrer en el taxi mientras los demás obedecían a Ferreira.

Pancho lucía uno de los modelos más aguerridos de Friendly Fire. Su chaleco no sólo parecía prelavado sino preincendiado. Sus brazos fuertes de tanto subir sogas contrastaban con sus ojos huidizos, como si se arrepintiera de haber llevado a su amigo a las puertas del edén, al picaporte que nunca sería suyo. O tal vez no, tal vez dudaba de su propia permanencia en el Círculo y se preparaba para la decepción superándola de antemano: su chaleco demostraba que ya tenía otro trabajo.

Los demás actores especulaban en voz baja, se tomaban de la cintura, sonreían con nerviosismo. Un ambiente de intensidad sectaria. Eran pocos pero podían ser menos. Lorena se concentraba en las agujetas de sus botas, como si pudiera desatarlas con energía mental.

Crystalda, que en los ensayos no hizo otra cosa que desvestirse para mostrar el pubis afeitado en triangulito y la piel pulida en la que aparecían extrañas manchas violáceas, era la única indiferente; mataba el tiempo tratando de que su enorme rostro entrara a un espejo circular.

Después de media hora, el lugarteniente les pidió que se ubicaran en la luneta. Jerónimo Ferreira apareció al fondo del escenario. Su cabellera rojiza parecía contener nuevos injertos.

nociste Punta del Este? Un paisito amable, el Uruguay. Menos caca, ¡oh sí!

Mauricio dejó al argentino en un hotel del centro. En el camino de regreso, sintió que el pasajero tenía razón. De golpe, el paisaje parecía una extensión que sólo se justificaba si alguien llegaba a verla de muy lejos. Gracias a los extraños, las calles saturadas de horrores podían ser típicas, representativas de algo profundo, que valía la pena por su inasible diferencia.

En un semáforo, se demoró ante una barda que terminaban de pintar unos hombres de uniforme anaranjado: LA PATRIA ES PRIMERO.

Encontró el mismo mensaje un poco más adelante, con crédito para el héroe que lo había pronunciado, Vicente Guerrero. No se decía más. Una campaña de fervor abstracto, donde se urgía a que la patria estuviera antes, sin explicar qué amenazaba su primer lugar. ¿Acaso los turistas, esos seres de países sin grandes cortesías, sin los cuales sería imposible demostrar que lo nacional era auténtico?

Lorena salía de las películas como si hubiera actuado en ellas. Después de una de esas sesiones de mímesis (con el civilizado calvario de un matrimonio sueco en el rostro), le dijo a Mauricio:

—Ferreira ya encontró su obra.

Lorena escogió bien el momento de la revelación; la película mitigaba las frases que en otra circunstancia hubieran sido deprimentes.

—En parte me da gusto —prosiguió—; hemos trabajado mucho, pero se me hace que ya no tienes ningún chance. Te voy a extrañar.

Mauricio casi había olvidado que fue al teatro en busca de un papel, y ahora Lorena tiraba de esa punta con sueca sensatez, hablaba del estreno, la gira posible, las luces ardientes, las diablas que no lo ilu-

idea era absurda. Nada se acumulaba en los taxis, las vidas en tránsito decían lo mismo que su colección de basuras, podían juntarse pero no reunirse, una cantidad sin estadística, que sólo existía desprendida del resto; imposible saber cómo eran esas gentes cuando estaban fijas. Entendió algo que le pareció absurdo no haber sabido desde el principio: las historias de Neri venían de una época en que fue taxista; se limitaba a inventar un entorno marino para las cosas que oyó al volante, por eso tenían una variedad inconcebible en una sola vida. Las costas y los huracanes le otorgaban prestigio a las anécdotas de sus pasajeros.

Repasó la biografía de Neri, donde sólo los tatuajes eran reales, hasta que oyó una voz a sus espaldas:

—Como la hiena, se ríe solo.

El pasajero era un argentino ebrio. Lo recogió en un bar y en el camino al centro criticó la comida mexicana:

—El picante nos deja sin opción.

México lo había defraudado. También el tráfico, la contaminación, la fealdad de la gente, la altura eran terribles. Luego contemporizó:

—Eso sí, ustedes son de amables. Como los uruguayos. En Buenos Aires no encuentra tanta amabilidad, pero es que ustedes dependen del turismo. *Tienen* que ser amables, como los uruguayos. ¡México es de lindo! ¡Pero el picante! ¡Las amebas! ¡Diez días con diarrea!

Mauricio recordó una idea de Stefan Dezman: los territorios sin árboles favorecen los delirios mentales ("sin espesor vegetal, el alma escapa"). Tal vez era ésta la condición espiritual de la pampa; el argentino hablaba sin dejarse perturbar por su interlocutor—. ¡Qué *iettatura* la de ustedes! ¡Una lechuguita nomás, y dale a cagar! ¡Diez días de cagada! ¡Claro que aquí todos son de amables! ¡Y bueh...! ¿Vos co-

taba cómo sería la vida de los choferes titulares. Por la identificación sobre el taxímetro, sabía que se llamaban Pedro Jiménez o José López: por las fotos, que tenían caras de gángsters coreanos.

Lo único que le disgustó de este trabajo ocasional fue que al trasladar voluntades ajenas hacía que el diagnóstico de la orientadora pareciera verdadero.

Una noche en que asaltaron a un taxista y le encajaron un desarmador en el esófago, Mauricio no tuvo más remedio que hacerse cargo de su coche. Llovía torrencialmente y él hubiera preferido seguir en el teatro, viendo el cuerpo descomunal de Crystalda, pero ya sabía que las noches de lluvia eran las mejores para el negocio y no tuvo más remedio que arrancar el Zoas para recoger pasajeros con ropas empapadas que despedían un olor agrio. Por primera vez comparó esa tarea con su colección de basuras; los tripulantes nocturnos respondían a la característica esencial del desperdicio: estaban sueltos, no alcanzaban a formar un orden, no había un dibujo que articulara sus vidas, personas arrancadas de la red, a las que nada les quedaba cerca. Aunque había frases comunes, un rencor medio, las historias de los clientes variaban mucho, comunicaban miedos y excesos que tal vez sólo se atrevían a decir en el trayecto, como anécdotas suspendidas, libres de un desenlace que forzara responsabilidades. También los silencios eran expresivos; algunos pasajeros caían en un torpor ebrio, otros miraban con ojos que se volvían hostiles con el avance del taxímetro, o callaban por mera estupidez, por falta de curiosidad, por demasiadas razones.

Ferreira usaba los corales como "sondeo de opinión"; le pedía a Neri reportes sobre las "vibraciones de la ciudad". Mauricio advirtió esa noche que la

—Claro —contestó Ferreira, incapaz de contradecirla en algo.

Neri Castellanos le entregó las llaves del coral, sin preguntarle si tenía licencia o el signo del zodiaco propicio para trasladar al hallazgo de Ferreira.

Buscó el rostro de Crystalda en el espejo retrovisor. Después de pronunciar una dirección en el Pedregal, ella se quedó dormida, con la boca muy abierta.

Mauricio se extravió en las calles llenas de curvas. Finalmente dio con una casa sobre un farallón de piedras, vigilada por un coche negro, con antena en la cajuela.

Un guardaespaldas estaba recargado en el coche; se servía de una linterna para leer un *comic*. En cuanto vio a Crystalda, silbó con fuerza para que otro guardia abriera la puerta.

—Gracias, gordito —dijo la giganta, y subió una escarpada escalera entre la lava volcánica.

Al volver al teatro, Neri Castellanos le habló con un entusiasmo lleno de anfetaminas:

—¿Viste qué chulada? Una joya del bisturí: le inventaron la nariz al estilo Nefertiti, le quitaron dos costillas para dejarle una cintura de poca madre, la nueva sonrisa le sobra un poco pero le da un encanto vulgar, de salón de belleza ranchero, ¡una naquita gigantesca!, ¿puede haber mayor delicia?, y ya verás las tetas, ¡silicón del bueno!

Los actores se despedían en ese momento. Neri llevó a Mauricio al cuarto de tramoya:

—Te he cobrado afecto, pinche gordo. Está grueso que entres a la obra, pero si quieres te aflojo uno de los corales cada que me falle un chofer. Puedes levantar un buen billete como relevista.

A partir de esa noche, cuando un taxista se enfermaba, Mauricio se hacía cargo de un Zoas IV.

Le gustó la flama en el tablero, la pelota de golf de la que emanaba un olor a vainilla. Se pregun-

La giganta se movía muy despacio, como si el suelo fuera de vidrio, pero no pudo evitar que su tacón de aguja se encajara en una alcantarilla.

—¿No es divina? —Ferreira se arrodilló a ayudarla.

—¡Tú siempre tan cochino! —exclamó ella, con voz aguda.

—Niños, les presento a Crystalda, mi nueva mejor amiga.

—¿De dónde la sacó? —Mauricio le preguntó a Neri.

—Del Teatro Iris.

Mauricio se quedó de piedra. Después de viajar por Nepal y la sierra zapoteca, de comulgar con hongos sagrados, buscar los designios ocultos del *Tarot* y el *I Ching*, sobrevivir a la heroína y los sanguíneos expolios de Venus, Ferreira descubría a una desnudista de barrio, acaso una de las que Mauricio vio con Tehui y su tío.

El director la colmó de amabilidades, la llevó al centro del escenario, le preguntó cómo se sentía en su nuevo ambiente.

Ella dijo que estaba harta de desnudarse "porque sí". Quería clase, categoría, "mucha catego".

—Aquí lo que sobra es catego —sonrió Ferreira.

—¡Te digo que eres repuerco! —Crystalda movió la cintura, con agilidad de rumba.

Ferreira le prometió un rito de paso, una segunda virginidad, un punto sin retorno que ella festejó llamándolo "cochino" por tercera vez.

La voz de Crystalda parecía capaz de pulir metales; por suerte, Ferreira no incluía parlamentos en sus puestas.

La giganta se despidió después de media hora. Todo el elenco la siguió al Uroboros.

—¿Quién me va a llevar? —preguntó ella—. ¿El gordito? —sus dedos atenazaron las mejillas de Mauricio.

Jerónimo Ferreira pasó por una fase que llamaba "plástica" y que fundamentalmente consistía en explorar el umbral de dolor de sus actores.

Lorena se fortaleció entre torceduras. Se desmañanaba para ir a correr, compró unas barras moradas para hacer pesas, su espalda se dividió en músculos que tal vez ya estaban ahí pero que adquirieron sorpresivo relieve.

En sus relatos nocturnos, Neri Castellanos solía hablar de una "flotilla de corales". Mauricio pensó que se trataba de otro de sus alardes marinos hasta que una madrugada lo ayudó a pasar la cadena en la reja del teatro y lo acompañó rumbo a la virgen de neón que presidía un sitio de taxis. Neri era dueño de cinco coches pintados en color coral que le permitían vivir con desahogo.

No se avergonzaba de su negocio porque parecía inmune a la vergüenza, pero rara vez hablaba de él. De vez en cuando, un chofer llegaba al teatro con algún problema y él despachaba el asunto sin quitarse el cigarro de los labios.

Una noche Neri le ordenó a un taxista que fuera a tal dirección, exigió máxima puntualidad y empezó a ver su reloj de buzo. Reunió a los actores y a los aspirantes y les dijo que Ferreira había encontrado a su protagonista. Resultaba curioso tener protagonista sin tener obra, pero así eran las leyes del Círculo.

—Vas a enflacar de la sorpresa —Neri le susurró a Mauricio.

El Uroboros llegó con suficiente parsimonia para que los actores reunidos en la banqueta estudiaran su serpiente cromada en el cofre.

El propio Ferreira abrió la portezuela del taxi. Del auto descendió una mujer con el pelo pintado en un rubio cremoso, aretes con flores de plástico, vestido de lentejuelas. Su boca era color cereza; su cuerpo, el más grande que Mauricio había visto.

buena o la canela; necesitaba contrastes, superar un obstáculo para llegar al insólito disfrute de los refinados; tal vez el reto mayor del olfato consistía en acceder al aire donde los aromas desagradables aportaban placer.

¿Qué recuerdos tuvo Clarita ante esa suntuosa podredumbre? ¿Regresaba a intimidades del pasado o el olor le gustaba en sí mismo, como un turbador exceso de presente?

Mauricio se preguntó si habría un aprendizaje para ese tipo de placer. La revelación de Pancho (amar es superar el asco) lo acompañaba desde la infancia; con Lorena había avanzado otro poco; no sólo podía ignorar sus secreciones sino que prefería acostarse con ella después de los ensayos, quitarle las ropas empapadas de sudor. De cualquier forma, era obvio que tenía una escala perceptiva mucho más burda que la de Clarita.

En una ocasión ella le dijo: "El truco del perfume depende de intuir a la persona que va a usarlo; no hay dos pieles iguales y los olores combinan de distinta forma; el secreto del perfumista no es la fragancia, sino la mujer añadida."

¿Llegaría él a anticipar un cuerpo por un aroma? A Clarita la planta de pétalos grasosos le traía una piel tan auténtica que no necesitaba tocarla.

Lo más cerca que él estuvo del dominio olfativo fue el descubrimiento de que algo faltaba en la sección de las *impatient*. No pudo definirlo con precisión, pero las flores casi no olían, como si el yugoslavo hubiera instalado un sistema de absorción de aire. Todo parecía demasiado pulcro. Un sitio ordenado y triste.

Stefan Dezman le dio la noticia al poco rato: Verónica había renunciado a ser su asistente.

dactaba incontables reportes sobre los beneficios del jardín. Mauricio prefería pasar las tardes escuchando a Clarita. Se despedía de ella con la sensación de que cualquier cosa que ocurriera después sería extrañamente real y racional.

El único motivo para volver a la Estación era acompañar a la doctora. Siempre dispuesta a exponer sus ideas en sitios donde la repudiaban, Clarita agobiaba al botánico con incesantes correcciones gramaticales:

—Porque usted habla español, ¿verdad? —preguntaba después de cada comentario.

Stefan sorbía su alcohol:

—Principal arma de jardines es lentitud. Al final siempre se impone lo más lento.

A Clarita le irritaba este argumento: las teorías que daban lustre al jardín no eran nada ante la pausada respiración de la Tierra. Entonces se ponía de pie y revisaba el vivero. Solía detenerse ante los cultivos de genciana, cuyo aroma debía recordarle remedios de la infancia.

Luego pasaba al invernáculo de las plantas delicadas. El techo de cristal conservaba el calor, y las mallas de tela, la humedad. En aquel microclima, Clarita hizo un hallazgo especial. Mauricio la vio alzar una maceta con una flor de pétalos brillantes y grasosos. La doctora abrió los pétalos y encajó la nariz en el corazón cárdeno y pulposo. Los pétalos mostraron un instantáneo relajamiento, como si anhelaran ser respirados.

Cuando devolvió la planta a su lugar, Clarita tenía una mirada ausente, casi al borde del desmayo.

Mauricio se agachó en dirección a la maceta y percibió una peste inclasificable. De todos los aromas posibles, Clarita elegía esa descomposición; su nariz de conocedora no podía conformarse con la hierba-

para alejarse de los problemas terrenales, ¡y allí fue donde Voltaire perdió los dientes! La paz enferma, o mejor dicho, la sensación de calma despierta otros intríngulis. Los jardines que parecen más apacibles son los que más quebrantan: recintos para el sexo, fórmulas del poder... —entonces, como si recordara que llevaba puesto el casco verde, agregaba—: es preciso trabajar con estas categorías: las calzadas de tierra deben responder a ideas claras; el solo hecho de apartar la naturaleza, de dividirla, revela fuerza. Cuando el vulgo municipal llegue con sus zapatos de plástico, debe venerar a los constructores del jardín, sentir el impacto acumulado de las tradiciones necesarias para dominar las plantas hasta el último detalle. ¡Un motor orgánico! Sí, la ciudad concluirá con un símbolo nítido del poder que la controla."

Fiel a su sentido más desarrollado, Clarita propuso un "calendario de estaciones aromáticas". En primavera, el jardín olería a jacintos, narcisos y lilas; esta etapa delicada cedería su sitio al popular verano de las rosas y los claveles; el otoño empezaría con aires un tanto exóticos, cargados de jazmines y gladiolos, para desembocar en la soberanía de los lirios; durante el invierno, todo olería a boj dulce y a laurel.

En cuanto a los colores, era decisivo que las partes externas del proyecto imitaran a la bandera: las hojas garantizarían el verde; el naranjo mexicano, que florecía en primavera y otoño, los pétalos blancos, y las peonías y las amapolas, el rojo de temporada.

Obviamente, Cristina Ferrán no podía explicarse la traición de su amiga. Al ver el interés que Mauricio tenía en ella, escribió en el refrigerador: EL VICIO HACE ESCUELA.

La Estación de Floricultura se había convertido en el sitio aburrido donde Dezman se emborrachaba y re-

oír durante horas argumentos que no compartía, pero que al cabo de muchas revisiones asimilaba como propios. Mauricio había tardado en darse cuenta de que su padre prefería servirse de ideas que en el fondo repudiaba, como si de este modo se adelantara a las críticas y privara de razones a sus enemigos. Clarita, que siempre le pareció una delirante, podía brindarle los espesores de un segundo jardín, hecho de las ideas feraces e intrincadas en las que era especialista.

En la casamata donde se revisaban los planos y se discutían los mil asuntos pendientes (representados en un pizarrón por alfileres rojos y azules que Guardiola procuraba no ver), la historiadora de las ideas fue tratada con una deferencia fundada en el absurdo. Estaba tan fuera de lugar que los demás asesores no tuvieron trabajo en imaginar las causas que la habían llevado ahí. Seguramente pertenecía a círculos de enorme influencia; su repentina inclusión en el proyecto y la agresividad con que trataba a todo mundo respondían a la más elevada condición de la política nacional: la impunidad.

Aceptada como una imposición que no requería de explicaciones, Clarita habló de Le Notre, el arquitecto de jardines de los Luises de Francia y mostró en botánica la misma actitud que en gastronomía: las plantas sólo adquirían sentido al ser pensadas, al revelar propósitos ajenos a la naturaleza.

La Estación de Floricultura le pareció una reserva bienintencionada, anterior a la lógica; el yugoslavo la mantenía en una barbarie amable, incapaz de dejar huellas. Era lo que el mundo esperaba del país: "una utopía hacia atrás, una reserva del atraso". Luego, sin reparar en el grado de atención de su interlocutor, añadía: "La primera falacia de la jardinería es que se trata de un sitio para estar en paz; en eso se equivocan Dezman y todos los ecologistas. Federico el Grande construyó el arbolado palacio de Sans-Souci

apariencia, todos estos asuntos lo llevaron a buscar un apoyo insospechado.

La historiadora de las ideas llegó a Terminal Progreso con casco verde. Mauricio llevaba años sin verla y le sorprendió la correosa estabilidad de sus facciones.

—¿Todavía me odias? —fue el sorpresivo saludo de Clarita.

—Claro que no —contestó Mauricio.

—¡Me caes bien por hipócrita!

Desde su primera visita al jardín en proceso, la doctora Rendón se dirigió a todo mundo con eficiente paranoia. Se consideraba una mujer odiada; su "conciencia lúcida" hería a la masa acrítica. Lo interesante es que esto no le parecía un obstáculo sino una razón para socializar: los demás necesitaban sus adversos saberes.

Jesús Guardiola mostraba cierta dificultad para caminar por los terraplenes y los desniveles que creaban sus obreros; usaba un retorcido bastón tlaxcalteca y, al ganar la cima de una empalizada, pasaba minutos recuperando la respiración. Su pelo abundante era completamente blanco.

Desde que lo vio frotarse con una toalla en su primera infancia, Mauricio había sido incapaz de imaginarle debilidades físicas; sin embargo, ahora su padre se veía sobrado de peso, falto de energía, incapaz de seguir no sólo las caminatas de su maestro de obras sino de concentrarse en todo lo que le decía.

Curiosamente, al debilitarse, adquirió otras cualidades; parecía un hombre reposado, que juzga con cautela, incapaz de ceder al arrebato. Su proyecto más ambicioso coincidía con un ablandamiento del carácter. Tal vez esto explicaba la idea, para muchos extravagante, de contratar a Clarita Rendón. Él podía

ciones orientales (con desarmante naturalidad, Lorena opinaba que el frijol de soya olía como el semen de Mauricio). Todo estaba más o menos bien, pero podía estar mejor. Después de años de anhelar otro sitio donde dormir, los mágicos siete números de teléfono que lo llevaran sin sobresaltos a otro sexo, Mauricio se sentía a gusto sin que eso implicara otra cosa que sentirse a gusto. ¿Era ésta la sustancia oculta de la dicha, transcurrir sin dejar huellas memorables?

Poco a poco se fue acostumbrando a ese bienestar tranquilo, a verla desayunar media toronja con la fruición de quien se lleva una mascarilla de oxígeno al rostro, a sus manías para dormirse con dos almohadas y despertar sin ellas, al té que llevaba al buró y a la mañana seguía intacto, al pulgar en la boca que ya le había desviado los incisivos, a sus pies descalzos y a los misteriosos calcetines que tenían en la mañana, a su certeza, sin pruebas ni garantías, de que su camiseta para dormir tenía que ser amarilla, porque ese color la ayudaba mucho, mucho.

Una madrugada en que Lorena describió las escenografías de Ferreira, Mauricio sospechó que él iba a la torre por una fascinación de utilero, para atrapar las claves menudas e inertes que definen una vida, el té helado en el buró, el refrigerador repleto de apios y jugos diuréticos, el juguete de peluche grasoso al cabo de los años, los trozos sueltos de una conducta, cosas que valía la pena memorizar, como si lo más valioso de ellas fuera el temor de perderlas.

Semanas después de la conferencia de prensa, los nombres herméticos de Tenayuca e Ixtlahuaca volvieron a aparecer en los periódicos en relación con el jardín de Xochimilco.

El arquitecto Guardiola hablaba mucho de control de medios, cabildeo, crisis de legitimidad. En

pareció apenas regular; también a que ella tomaba todas las iniciativas; según Lorena, esto se debía a que era sietemesina y andaba siempre anticipada. La prisa no era una urgencia, era su carácter.

La familia de Lorena vivía en Gómez Palacio y ella rentaba un departamento en un castillo medieval recién construido. Por fuera, el edificio no podía ser más absurdo; sus almenas daban a una barranca polvosa que servía como deshuesadero de automóviles; sin embargo, dentro de la torre, las habitaciones circulares suscitaban una agradable irrealidad.

La primera noche en que Mauricio se descalzó sobre los tapetes de lana cruda y los cojines hindúes, sufrió con la luz prendida. ¿Durante cuánto tiempo podría sumir la panza? Para colmo, Lorena quiso convencerlo de que no le importaba su gordura y se limitó a acariciarle el estómago.

Las siguientes noches transcurrieron con mayor fluidez. Mauricio se acostumbró a la risa de Lorena, una risa extraña, que brotaba cuando él la penetraba, como si no hubiera mayor placer que las cosquillas.

Todo era tan sencillo, tan falto de dramatismo, que Mauricio sintió que le faltaba plenitud a sus encuentros. ¿Cuál era la carencia? ¿Qué fibra oculta se resistía a ser tocada? Estropeó esas noches fáciles pensando que Lorena carecía de imaginación para los problemas o los disgustos. Desde que ella demostró su pericia ambidiestra para abrir la puerta del castillo mientras le abría la bragueta, Mauricio pensó que se necesitaban más complicaciones para que eso calificara como pasión. El viejo dogma de Pancho volvió a alcanzarlo: "lo que te gusta te da nervios". ¿Dónde estaban los pálpitos, el vacío en el estómago, el sudor absurdo, el escalofrío en el espinazo, las palabras rotas, las infinitas molestias del amor certero?

Hablaban horas del teatro, recortaban con pericia a los demás actores, comían ensaladas de aspira-

En sus relatos, los símbolos náuticos eran decisivos. Tenía los brazos tatuados y una cadena de plata con un diente de tiburón pendía de su cuello. Había trabajado en barcos camaroneros y en mercantes que hacían rutas de cabotaje; los actores lo oían como si secretamente su destino dependiera del océano. Neri poseía el carisma de los solitarios que han estado en muchos sitios. Las mujeres lo veían con ánimos de que esta vez se quedara ahí.

Mauricio se presentó como aspirante y adquirió el privilegio de ver los ensayos y oír a Neri Castellanos. Un día de tantos, con la naturalidad de quien cambia una vela en alta mar, Neri sugería a un nuevo actor. No daba explicaciones ni se rebajaba a usar términos teatrales. Ferreira le hacía caso por razones demasiado profundas para ser verbalizadas. Neri había visto suficientes islas. Eso bastaba.

El lugarteniente llevaba dos décadas al lado de Ferreira, un tiempo excesivo para haber protagonizado todas las historias que contaba; sin embargo, su rostro áspero y sus brazos tatuados lo hacían creíble, brindaban una prueba física a tanta habladuría.

Durante semanas todo ocurrió en zigzag. La mariguana olvidada en el buró llevó a Mauricio a la orientadora vocacional y luego al teatro, o por lo menos a su sombra. Pensó que allí recuperaría la amistad de Pancho, pero el Círculo le deparó otras proximidades.

Lorena lo miró de frente y dijo:

—¿Por qué no te pones un arete? Mira —le pellizcó el lóbulo de la oreja—: te fortalece la vista; la oreja es el lugar secreto de la visión.

Mauricio soportó la presión sin filo (Lorena se mordía las uñas) y por primera vez sintió que la calma superaba al nerviosismo en su trato con una mujer. En parte, esto se debía a que la belleza de la actriz le

recién descubiertas o un oficiante de sadismos prolongados. A sus cincuenta años, el rostro comunicaba una terca voluntad de ser distinto. Llevaba botas de motociclista con cadena en el empeine que redondeaban su estatura en un impresionante 1.95. Bajo el pantalón de mezclilla debía tener una concha protectora; sólo así se explicaba el promontorio que compensaba al frente sus nalgas de bailarín. Estaba en camiseta y el reflector daba a sus brazos una consistencia de cera y resaltaba su orografía de venas azules. En una silla, al borde del estrado, reposaba su chamarra de cuero.

Durante el ensayo, Ferreira hizo anotaciones en una bitácora de triplay; luego imitó a los actores, sobreactuando sus defectos. Había algo humillante en su simulación, pero todo mundo parecía convencido de que la parodia era una gran pedagogía.

Mauricio pensó que Pancho lo iba a presentar con él. Tragó saliva, previendo la frase torpe e irracional que mascullaría ante el supremo búfalo de las tablas, pero su amigo le dijo:

—Tienes que hablar con Neri. Jerónimo no se ocupa de esas cosas.

El lugarteniente de Ferreira tenía una respiración nerviosa. Había sido buzo y perdió medio pulmón en un accidente. Esa noche, al término del ensayo, rodeado de escuchas que encendían cigarros y se frotaban el cuello con toallas, comparó la inmersión profunda con un viaje en heroína:

—Hay muchos adictos al mar hondo —comentó, como si aún no saliera a la superficie.

Los actores oían a Neri hasta la madrugada. El asistente parecía conocer a cada uno en detalle; estaba al tanto de sus inciertas trayectorias, sus pequeños vicios, sus desmedidas ilusiones.

asumir riesgos enormes podía usar a los demás como un lienzo para plasmar sus adoloridos paisajes.

Mauricio aceptó, si no la genialidad de Ferreira, al menos el impacto genial que producía en su amigo.

—Hace días que no ensayamos —dijo Pancho—. Llegas en mal momento. Jerónimo se esfumó.

Ni siquiera Neri Castellanos, que llevaba veinte años de ser su asistente, sabía dónde hallarlo. Algunos decían que estaba con los monjes tibetanos; se mencionaron sobredosis, un contrato en el *off-off* Broadway, un ingreso a la Secta de los Naranjas o a la iglesia secular de los dianéticos. Tampoco faltaron las hipótesis de quienes llevaban años tratando de demeritarlo; hubo rumores de enfermedades, fraudes al fisco, problemas de narcotráfico, una oscura conexión con el gobierno.

—El karma de la notoriedad es la envidia; uno escoge a sus amigos pero no a sus enemigos —comentó Pancho, como si recitara un parlamento de Ferreira.

La reaparición del director provocó aún más historias que su partida. Había estado en el desierto, en Montreal, en Manila. Excesos de droga, dólares, marineros, extrañas ceremonias.

Después de varias tardes de café exprés dedicadas a perfeccionar el mito de Ferreira, Pancho aceptó que Mauricio entrara con él al teatro.

La primera impresión del director no pudo ser más emblemática. En el proscenio, Ferreira recibía la luz de un *seguidor*. Su aspecto era una prueba de su carácter; sólo alguien convencido de ser una Personalidad podía llevar esos injertos de pelo anaranjado. Varias cirugías menores otorgaban una contradictoria tersura a sus mejillas. Parecía un paciente de pastillas

ficó con los gordos confesionales de las telenovelas: gente que no inspira el menor deseo y sirve para que se desahoguen los protagonistas. En este papel escuchó a Pancho, que veía a Ferreira los jueves. En rigor, su amigo era el masajista de Ferreira; el genio se tendía en una mesa de mármol mientras él procedía a cumplir las más exigentes caricias. En materia de sexo, Ferreira había llegado a una perfección brahamánica: eran otros los que se movían. Pancho adoptó la posición meditativa maya para satisfacerlo y se esforzó en tocar todas las escalas del deseo ajeno.

Mauricio celebró que su amigo se subordinara por primera vez a otra persona, pero al segundo cigarro le alarmó el grado de control que ejercía Ferreira. Por culpa de uno de esos vacíos en que se extingue el cigarro y no hay algo específico que decir, se atrevió a pronunciar la palabra "manipulador" en relación con Jerónimo Ferreira. Pancho lo vio con ojos encendidos y le soltó una andanada sobre la maravillosa crueldad del espíritu: Ferreira era un ungido, conocía el sufrimiento ajeno y el propio, su pasado era una colección de heridas, los navajazos de la mucha luz. Todavía no se recuperaba de un pésimo viaje de ácido en las costas de Oaxaca; el amor de su vida murió ahogado y él pasó una semana en la cárcel de Pinotepa, sin otra actividad que leer el *I Ching*. Había ayunado con monjes en sierras inaccesibles, había meditado para salvar enfermos, había participado en ritos de sangre, había cambiado el destino de seres que parecían irredimibles, había encontrado claves en semillas, animales, sueños y tapices. Jamás se entregaría al sosiego; una cuerda, las líneas de una mano, una campana, eran signos atendibles; leía el mundo con sus ojos insomnes para otorgarle sentido; sus arrebatos no surgían de caprichos sino de su condición hipersensible; se la "había jugado" tantas veces que tenía derecho a exigir lo mejor de los otros; sólo alguien capaz de

—Sólo se vive una vez —como si la congruencia fuera una obligación de los que reencarnan.

Curiosamente, Pancho cumplió su promesa de llamarlo, pero habló como si le hubiera pedido que le recuperara un coche robado:

—No te garantizo nada. El Círculo es muy selecto.

Se encontraron en el vestíbulo del teatro. La leyenda de Jerónimo Ferreira se remontaba a los tempranos años sesenta, cuando sorprendió al Festival de Nancy con *Alicia en los fosfenos*, una producción psicodélica para quince cuerpos y tres baterías. Los privilegiados que vieron la puesta mexicana, en la pirámide de Cuicuilco, aún recordaban el final con reflectores de luz negra, los tambores redoblando al máximo, los quince cuerpos en la "posición meditativa maya" redescubierta por el director.

En sentido estricto, Ferreira no usaba actores; su teatro era un alfabeto físico; su montaje más reciente había sido *Corpori fabrica*, en honor al anatomista y dibujante Andreas Vesalius. Pancho insistió tanto en que se acostó con el director *después* del estreno de la obra, que Mauricio se convenció de lo contrario. *Corpori fabrica* tuvo la respuesta habitual para el agente provocador del teatro mexicano: los premios compitieron con el escándalo. Sin embargo, algo curioso ocurrió al final de la temporada; Ferreira no habló de otro proyecto, se negó a dar las entrevistas que tanto le gustaban (su momento cumbre: leerle el *I Ching* al entrevistador), incluso rechazó una invitación de los indios coras para pasar con ellos su Semana Santa.

Aunque se habían visto poco en los últimos tiempos, Mauricio seguía siendo el confidente erótico de Pancho. Tal vez por acercarse al teatro, se identi-

pronunció un nombre que en apariencia justificaba cualquier sacrificio: Jerónimo Ferreira.

Ferreira había revolucionado el teatro mexicano. La gente le temía, lo admiraba, lo calumniaba por pura envidia.

—¿Has conocido a un genio? —Pancho habló como si el tema fuera contagioso.

—No, pero me gustaría. La orientadora me dijo que podía ser actor. Hay muchos gordos en el cine, puedo ser un bulto adecuado, un blanco fácil para los espadachines...

—Hoy tengo sesión de fotos, mañana te hablo —dijo Pancho, como si marcar los números de Mauricio fuera algo dichosamente imposible.

Para pagar sus estudios con el renovador del arte dramático, Pancho trabajaba de modelo. Adquirió notoriedad en el Anillo Periférico por sus anuncios de un extraño paté de pescado, se había bañado con un jabón de pepino en el horario Triple A de la televisión y adornó los aparadores de la cadena norteamericana Friendly Fire, que ofrecía ropas de combatiente de trinchera, o por lo menos de corresponsal de guerra. Mauricio pensó en el fuego en cruz de San Andrés y se decepcionó al saber que el "fuego amistoso" eran las balas que un ejército recibía de sus propias tropas. La tragedia militar había saltado con fortuna a la moda; la gente parecía urgida de negar sus jornadas urbanas con chalecos llenos de bolsas para granadas, ojales para sogas y zípers donde encajar rollos de película.

Las poses que Pancho deseó para *Leandro* se cumplieron en las fotos de Friendly Fire; estaba muy bronceado; los maquillistas le untaban carbón en las mejillas y gotas de glicerina en la frente. Se veía sucio de un modo heroico.

Cuando Mauricio le recordó su antiguo afán de cambiar el mundo, él contestó:

Las artes escénicas también ofrecían algo a los ejecutores de iniciativas ajenas. La mujer no parecía muy segura al respecto; pronunció la palabra "doble", y Mauricio escuchó "actor".

En aquel consultorio de paredes color pistache vio el teatro como una oportunidad de pacificar a su padre, pero sobre todo como un pretexto para volverse a acercar a Pancho.

Después de años de militancia, Pancho experimentó algo que llamaba "el castigo de la coherencia". La misma persona que en la infancia y en la primera adolescencia vivió para lo múltiple, para suscitar deseos de amplio espectro, había tenido que someterse a mandatos cada vez más unilaterales. Su destino se disciplinó hasta que las "convicciones" se convirtieron en el nombre oculto del dogmatismo: "El castigo de la coherencia", repetía en voz baja, como un gurú que casi no respira. ¿No era una lástima que alguien con tantas posibilidades para lo difuso se limitara por culpa de sus ideales? Los grupos progresivamente chicos en los que militaba lo habían llevado a un túnel cuya única salida era la clandestinidad, el bautismo de fuego y dinamita: ser *Leandro*.

Pancho dedicó meses a imaginarse de uniforme; se vio en las portadas de los diarios que repudiarían sus atentados, pero algo lo detuvo, quizá el simple afán de supervivencia o el temor de que los otros nunca supieran que él era *Leandro*.

Al cabo de varios años de elogiar la "acción directa", descubrió las virtudes de la acción fingida y estudió teatro con una dedicación ejemplar en alguien a quien le hubiera bastado ofrecer su rostro para enriquecerse en las telenovelas.

En una ocasión en que se encontraron en la tintorería de Terminal Progreso (Mauricio iba a recoger la mantilla que adornaba el televisor de su casa y Pancho diez camisas espectaculares), el nuevo actor

—No me extraña ni tantito.

Carlos arrancó el Zohar y llevó el caso a su padre.

—No sobrerreacciones —dijo Roberta, cuando su esposo exclamó ¡*Panza*!—, de nada sirve hacer huesos del asunto, pongamos su mente en manos profesionales.

Nadie ignoraba que Mauricio llenaba su vida sin estudios ni trabajo con el humo de la mariguana, pero sólo el hallazgo de Carlos los obligó a actuar. Roberta estaba en su elemento, feliz de tratar el desastre como un asunto de familia:

—Debe ver una psicóloga, una que busque profesiones.

El arquitecto asintió, mientras revisaba el carrujo con aire de conocedor.

La mujer tenía un rostro simbiótico; se diría que los destinos que analizaba habían encontrado la manera de combinarse en su cara; sus espejuelos inseguros, su nariz diminuta, su bigote de cerdas escasas, su trompa de marmota, su frente, de una amplitud impía, hicieron que entre las profesiones del mundo, Mauricio descartara de entrada la de orientador vocacional.

Recibió una batería de preguntas y sospechó que sus hábitos tenían la parda monotonía de un animal estudiado en un documental educativo.

A la semana siguiente, supo que disponía de una personalidad reactiva, ideal para devolver las pelotas enviadas por los otros. Madera de traductor, intérprete, recepcionista, mensajero, bibliotecario o incluso médium, en caso de tener una apertura espiritual que la orientadora no podía juzgar. La invención de las pantallas había ampliado el rango de las tareas reactivas: podía trabajar ante una moviola de edición, en una sala de censura o en la torre de control de un aeropuerto.

El *pusher* llevaba portafolios de piel de cocodrilo y una camisa de satín concebida para soltar brillos tornasolados en las discotecas del momento. No vendía droga por necesidad económica sino auditiva. Con errabundo narcisismo se refirió a las granjas que su familia tenía en la Costa Chica de Guerrero y ponderó la calidad de sus cosechas:

—Es materia finísima, maestro, puro elíxir, polen de lujo... —siguió hablando, como el mensajero de un dios apícola.

Mauricio sacó unos billetes para que se callara.

Fumó en los llanos de Terminal Progreso, cerca del jardín que construía su padre, viendo las hogueras de los trabajadores, los árboles con las copas envueltas en lona, llegados de muy lejos, los agujeros fantásticos que hacían pensar en las cuevas de una tribu por venir.

Regresó a la casa al anochecer; las flores de San Andrés vibraban con un resplandor fluorescente; el aire olía a alcoholes magníficos.

Se sacó la ropa como pudo y se tendió en su cama, boca arriba. El salitre en el techo fue un espectáculo fascinante hasta que se quedó dormido. Un golpe lo sacó del milagro. En efecto: Carlos.

Mauricio tardó en enfocar lo que su hermano sostenía en la mano, a una proximidad excesiva. El cartón con mariguana. La droga lo había relajado al punto de olvidar que tenía que esconderla.

Carlos pellizcó a su hermano como un anticipo de los rigores que lo adelgazarían en la prisión y citó una ley vejatoria. Luego vino lo peor: le ofreció protección.

—Vete a la chingada —masculló Mauricio.

Al día siguiente Carlos le contó todo a su madre. Una vez más, ella demostró lo poco que importaba saber algo. Su castigo, su insalvable dolor, era la normalidad:

—Se trata de un jardín cerrado, un *hortus conclusus*.

Un periodista preguntó entonces:

—¿No están tratando de impedir la invasión de tierras? Los terrenos están subiendo de precio en la zona y hay problemas con los colonos. Ahí está lo de Tenayuca —esta última palabra cayó con especial autoridad, pero no tanta como la que vino después—. ¿Y qué me dicen de Ixtlahuaca?

Un rumor recorrió las sillas de lona: si se había localizado algo en aquellas rancherías, seguramente se trataba de cosas espantosas.

Gutiérrez Pool no perdió la compostura. Reiteró que sólo le interesaba el equilibrio entre el agua, el aire y la tierra:

—Además, la solución es muy mexicana, como lo prueba el apoyo del arquitecto Guardiola. Hace 500 años que nadie se atrevía a tocar el tema; pero no podemos escamotear el asunto de la Conquista. Hay que decirlo, a calzón quitado: el jardín siguió ahí de milagro, o mejor dicho, porque fue muy bien planeado. Es hora de que le echemos una ayudadita, ¿no creen? Tengo un reporte del Dr. Dezman, que como ustedes saben trabaja para la ONU, donde enlista los riesgos de la zona. ¡Una carpeta de 500 páginas! Una por cada año de Conquista. También las plantas son la nación que queremos.

—¿Y Tenayuca?

—No está en la agenda de hoy —Gutiérrez Pool brindó una sonrisa suave y le cedió la palabra a una reportera que lo elogió diez minutos antes de hacer una pregunta.

En sus incursiones a comprar mariguana en las "islas" de Ciudad Universitaria, Mauricio conoció a un vendedor que no paraba de hablar.

prometió "incentivos para coadyuvar" ni reiteró su "voluntad para cumplimentar acciones". Sonrió con dientes perfectos y habló del Valle de México con una mirada quieta y agradable. Se refirió a la luz del paisaje, al delgado aire de los 2 200 metros, a la cuenca lacustre entre los volcanes; poco a poco, pasó a los problemas que se cernían sobre esa orilla de la ciudad:

—El equilibrio ecológico es frágil, dramático, si me apuran un poco. No tiene caso ocultarlo, hay que decir las cosas por su nombre, ya terminó la era de la demagogia: estamos al borde del desastre; necesitamos un pulmón para combatir los vientos contaminados, pero sobre todo una zona que absorba el deshielo de los volcanes. No podemos asfaltar el valle entero sin riesgo de inundaciones —a sus sesenta años, Gutiérrez Pool había adquirido un aire chino, de aficionado a las flores y las metáforas; su rostro apenas se movió al hablar con un aplomo contemplativo de las garzas que poblarían el nuevo estanque.

Hubo aplausos al fin de su discurso y al patio llegó un olor a botanas con mole. El arquitecto tomó la palabra. Después de maratones en congresos, juntas y entrevistas, no había perdido su arrobo esencial, la actitud de descubrir las cosas al momento de decirlas. Rara vez usaba un término técnico; sus ladrillos, sus terrosos colores, dependían de otras fuerzas: la Historia, la naturaleza, el destino inescapable.

Su misión en la conferencia consistía en vincular el jardín con los aztecas. Xochimilco, abandonado durante tantos años, recibiría el apoyo que reclamaban los ancestros. Había que proteger los ahuejotes (sus manos se movieron hacia arriba, como si acariciaran un ciprés), había que garantizar que el viento, que siempre soplaba de norte a sur, no acabara con esa delicada foresta, había que construir farallones que por su textura y espesor recordarían a las pirámides.

frecuentación, el arquitecto hablaba con la estudiada naturalidad del político.

Mauricio apenas visitaba la casa de su padre. Le costaba trabajo pensar que todos esos alardes decorativos tuvieran que ver con su familia. Su madre seguía viviendo en Terminal Progreso, con una austeridad que realzaba la ostentación paterna y un sentido del sacrificio que recordaba la lejana Esparta; con enorme eficacia, había logrado que a sus hijos les pareciera no sólo aburrido sino injusto visitar a su padre.

Pero en ocasiones no podía salvarse de entrar a aquella reserva del papel amate, los juguetes de palo, las ollas de barro negro de Oaxaca. La conferencia sobre el jardín fue una de ellas.

El patio de la casa mostraba guirnaldas de papel picado para bienvenir a los periodistas. Un mesero ofrecía *margaritas*.

Carlos llegó en el Zohar que acababa de comprarse, un auto excesivo para sus ingresos como pasante de abogado. Cerró la puerta con el desdén con el que demostraba que algo era suyo. Alcanzó a Mauricio junto a una maqueta que hacía hablar mucho a Roberta. Por primera vez le interesaba un proyecto de su esposo. Entre los muchos problemas mexicanos, había detectado la incapacidad de "organizar la intemperie". Los edificios con el sello Guardiola carecían no sólo de plantas sino de ventanas para verlas, como si asomarse al exterior fuera un acto crítico.

—Pienso el mundo de esto —Roberta señaló los árboles en miniatura. Aparentemente se trataba de un elogio.

Los periodistas se sentaron en sillas de lona en el patio de la casa y recibieron servilletas moradas para limpiarse la sal de los *margaritas*.

Gutiérrez Pool fue el primero en tomar la palabra. También él había aprendido de su socio. No

—Ya estoy viejo; la rebeldía no se lleva con el colesterol.

—¡¿Eso te dijo?!

Le gustó que Verónica se enardeciera con el relato.

Estaban a la orilla del campo, no muy lejos de la zona donde se habían estacionado cuatro excavadoras.

—Van a acabar con esto —las manos de Verónica se abrieron para abarcar la extensión de arbustos y abrojos. El terreno era espantoso, pero Mauricio prefirió no opinar—. ¿Sabes los insectos y las plagas que controlan estas plantas?

La mente de Verónica se parecía a ese campo, una extensión donde las revolturas y los trozos se volvían funcionales. Su trabajo en la Estación de Floricultura no requería de gran empeño físico, pero se las arreglaba para tener los brazos vendados o rayados de merthiolate. El yugoslavo le decía "mi chamaco", y le acariciaba el pelo corto con camaradería. Le había confiado unas flores que renovaban sus pétalos varias veces al año, en muchos colores, y llevaban un nombre ideal para ella: *impatient*.

—¿Y no piensa hacer nada? —preguntó Verónica.

—Nada.

La acompañó un rato en silencio. Ella parecía pensar en cosas rápidas, intensas, alejadas de ese sitio.

—Te pido que estés conmigo, *Panza* —su padre quebró la voz para acentuar el sentimentalismo—. Benja quiere hablar en un círculo reducido, sin tapabocas; está harto de la solemnidad —después de años de

—Ya sé —contestó Dezman con hastío.

¿Dónde quedaban el interés mundial, los propósitos de la FAO, los subsidios que hacían hablar a Dezman de rábanos para el futuro y cultivos flotantes para países con poca tierra?

—¿Qué quieres que haga? Nadie deja teta gratuita.

En sus depresiones sin fondo, Stefan hablaba de México como del "país nodriza". Tenía una larga historia para justificar el conformismo. Todo empezaba del otro lado del mar: "Somos bosnios, macedonios, serbios, montenegrinos, yo soy esloveno; entre nosotros sólo hubo un yugoslavo verdadero: el mariscal Tito; él inventó un país para su rebaño." De acuerdo con Dezman, el culto a la personalidad de Tito fue posible gracias a la inmensa cantidad de huérfanos que dejó la Segunda Guerra: "era padre mítico, patriarca perfecto, en cambio mamá tenía defecto de sólo ser real". Esta explicación cautivó a Mauricio; de golpe, se sintió yugoslavo psicológico.

"En México no hay líder que sea padre sustituto", proseguía Dezman, "pero hay sistema inmutable, guardería para huérfanos obedientes: México es nodriza, teta impuesta, anónima; un día será paraíso de soviéticos con nostalgia".

—Ni modo —Stefan señaló el invernáculo al fondo, como un empresario que debe cancelar su temporada. Mauricio supo que la gente de Gutiérrez Pool había estado en el búngalo. Seguramente renovaron los subsidios de Dezman a cambio de que no se entremetiera. El 33 es el 33 —añadió; el artículo que permitía expulsar a los extranjeros indeseables le brindaba una excusa para no luchar.

—¿Y el 56? ¿Y el 68? —Mauricio mencionó las fechas que para Stefan significaban "Hungría" y "Checoslovaquia".

Era la expresión que más le gustaba de su nuevo idioma. Según él, ninguna de las lenguas de Yugoslavia disponía de una frase tan compacta para la resignación.

Sus demás aficiones mexicanas eran extrañamente yugoslavas; curaba el tequila con ciruelas de su cosecha y oía sin tregua discos de mariachis en esloveno. "Yugoslavia es segunda patria de canción ranchera", le decía a Mauricio. Lo extraño es que una vez en la cuna del mariachi, siguiera escuchando a los Cadetes de Lubliana.

Stefan estaba en México porque la ONU y la FAO tenían un interés sostenido, aunque no muy urgente, en Xochimilco. Había llegado a conocer y luchar por la preservación del jardín de los aztecas.

Mauricio pensaba que su colonia desembocaba en un campo y Stefan le reveló algo esencial: las plantas no crecían al azar; conformaban un elaboradísimo jardín, cada brote obedecía a un designio, los árboles definían el curso de los canales, las frondas arrojaban la sombra exacta para los cultivos en las chinampas flotantes. El mecanismo operaba con tal perfección que incluso había resistido a los irresponsables fraccionamientos que lo rodeaban. Estaban ante un reloj vegetal cuya principal virtud era no parecerlo. Stefan le explicó que el jardín "para ser mirado", el jardín "evidente" era una idea tardía; los aztecas no habían querido que sus huellas se notaran.

—Ni modo —repitió Stefan Dezman, acariciando el cactus de fieltro que adornaba su escritorio.

Esa mañana, el bufet del arquitecto Guardiola y el secretario de Obras Públicas, Benjamín Gutiérrez Pool, habían anunciado que recuperarían el vivero de los aztecas con un parque lleno de estatuas alusivas al esplendor histórico de la zona.

—La semana que entra empiezan las obras —insistió Mauricio.

El camino a la Estación de Floricultura era una senda polvosa la mayor parte del año; en los meses de lluvias, se cubría de flores silvestres, muy pequeñas, con pétalos en equis. "Flores de San Andrés", le había explicado el yugoslavo.

La reja estaba abierta. Mauricio se dirigió al búngalo de Stefan Dezman. Lo encontró bebiendo el primer trago del día, un "simbólico", como él lo llamaba.

—¿Viste luna llena? Plantas tienen insomnio del carajo.

El motivo real para visitar la Estación era Verónica, pero rara vez coincidían ahí. Ella estaba ocupada el día entero. En un tiempo en el que nadie sabía hacia dónde torcer su destino, Verónica descubrió una vocación precisa; estudiaba para microbióloga y en sus ratos libres trabajaba como asistente de Stefan. El yugoslavo la ayudaba a despreciar el conocimiento genérico: "Que cada quien domine su Balcán", decía con fervor por la hortaliza pequeña y detallada.

Mauricio había rebasado los veinte años sin enterarse dónde quedaba su Balcán.

—¿Ya supo lo del jardín? —le preguntó a Dezman.

El botánico resopló con un aliento que anunciaba el tercer "simbólico":

—Ni modo.

6. El jardín regulado

Mauricio le creyó. Cuando finalmente se detuvieron en una banca y escucharon una sirena distante, quiso explicar lo que había ocurrido, pero fue incapaz de pronunciar palabra. ¿Cómo contar que el camión al fin lo había encontrado? Dijera lo que dijera, su secreto saldría como una banalidad. Supo que nunca se atrevería a narrar esa historia. También supo que por eso le había ocurrido; no se la sacaría de encima, tendría que atesorarla, con una angustia incomunicable, viajaría con él, uniría otras cosas pero no revelaría su secreto.

Fue la última vez que se enfrentó al camión y que vio un Nausicaa '62.

La nube blanca, los torsos desnudos, los turbantes de tela sucia se hundieron definitivamente hacia el fondo de la noche.

seguía en la forma más precaria posible, como si el hospital necesitara un cinturón enfermo, gente dormida entre cartones, perros en busca de sobras, una larga fila en espera de una camioneta que iría muy lejos (resultaba imposible pensar que los hombres que dormían de pie, sosteniendo mochilas y herramientas, aguardaran un transporte de cercanías). Sin embargo, encima de este cuadro deplorable, flotaba un olor abundante y sabroso: el cerdo y el cilantro olían de maravilla.

Pancho condujo el Nausicaa con calma, como si fuera suyo. Respetó los semáforos, la mano derecha en el volante y la izquierda con un cigarro mentolado. Pero el motor vibraba como por arreglo propio. ¿Sería posible que ese auto fuera el fantasma del que tuvo su padre?

Se detuvieron en una tienda de abarrotes que tenía abierta una ventana en su cortina de metal. Compraron una botella de tequila y recorrieron la ciudad, tratando de olvidar al tío Roberto y, sobre todo, de esquivar una certeza: el coche los había buscado. En la última legua del tequila Mauricio supuso que aquel coche lo perseguía, pero no era una aparición tan obvia ni ruidosa como el camión materialista.

Abrió la ventanilla y tiró la botella.

—¡Serás pendejo! —le gritó Pancho—. ¿Quieres que nos detengan por pedos en un coche robado?

—No es robado —Mauricio eructó; un ardor de flama le oprimía el pecho.

Estaban con la luz en rojo, cuando el coche avanzó y se detuvo. Hubo un estruendo, giraron en círculo, dieron contra el camellón de la avenida. Un silencio denso, corrosivo, se apoderó del auto. Pancho y Mauricio se vieron después del choque, con el asombro de estar vivos.

—¡Yo no aceleré! —gritó Pancho mientras corrían para alejarse del auto.

—Te traje en el Nausicaa. ¡El coche fantasma!

Roberto lo vio como si no entendiera.

Mauricio fue al vestíbulo. Pancho lucía descompuesto de tanto ver el piso ajedrezado.

—¿Cómo está? —preguntó.

—Mejor.

Fue la última vez que pudo decir esto de su tío. Roberto salió del pabellón de urgencias y regresó a Zacatecas a las pocas semanas, sin que nadie lo obligara.

Tal vez escogió el retorno como un último castigo. Sus hijos lo internaron en una granja llamada "psiquiátrica" sólo porque tenía enfermeras. Mauricio nunca fue allí. Su padre le describió la hacienda de piedras calizas, entre un laberinto de cactus, un escondite más que un hospital.

Roberto Guardiola no intentó otra forma de suicidio; el veneno le había causado un daño secundario, una apatía de fondo que lo llevó a aceptar el encierro con resignación. Al cabo de unos meses perdió el habla. Quien llegara a la granja podía verlo sentado en el tronco de un pirul, la mirada fija en el agua de un apantle. Murió casi una década después, infinitamente gordo, muy tranquilo.

En sus últimos años tenía la costumbre de reírse a solas y trazar una A en la arena del desierto.

Aquella noche en la Cruz Verde Mauricio pensó que su tío se repondría.

—Él no es así —murmuró.

Pancho le tendió un pañuelo para que se secara las lágrimas.

Caminaron entre ambulancias desvencijadas. En las aceras había vendedores de tacos, la Cruz Verde colindaba con un mercado nocturno, donde la vida

Al abrir la puerta, Mauricio vio un rastro de azúcar en la alfombra y respiró un olor a encierro y podredumbre:

—¿Tío?

No hubo respuesta. En la mesa de la sala encontró una botella de leche, vacía. Aquel frasco salido de algún expendio pobre le pareció más preocupante que la habitual botella de whisky.

—Espérame aquí —trató de mitigar el momento dejando atrás a Pancho, como si privarlo de ver lo que estaba en la recámara fuera una forma de cancelar minucias agraviantes, como si las cucarachas desaparecieran al no tener testigos y el cuerpo en la cama recuperara su color.

Aunque sus manos estaban muy hinchadas, el rostro de Roberto se había afilado. Una barba incipiente le cubría los carrillos. En la entrepierna, tenía una mancha húmeda. Lo peor, sin embargo, estaba en sus manos. Mauricio se estremeció al ver el tamaño de las uñas. Por un momento pensó que su tío llevaba semanas muerto; apoyó la oreja en el pecho y bajo la reforzada camisa de explorador, escuchó latidos tenues, acompasados. En el buró había un polvo blanco, sobre un papel de estraza. En el piso, junto a un zapato, encontró una lata de veneno. "Para roedores", decía la etiqueta, evitando la palabra "ratas".

Mauricio sintió que nada tenía remedio y estuvo a punto de dejar a su tío en el departamento, pero Pancho ya estaba en el vértigo de la acción, lo convenció de seguir adelante y condujo con pericia suicida hasta la rampa de emergencias de la Cruz Verde.

Roberto se salvó. Le lavaron el estómago con sondas y tres horas después bromeaba sobre su torpeza para cazarse a sí mismo.

—No sabes lo difícil que es morirte —le dijo a Mauricio.

Mauricio había bebido mucho pero de golpe recuperó la lucidez. Bajó la aleta que servía para proteger del sol y vio un espejo elíptico, idéntico al del Nausicaa de su padre. Recordó a Rita corrigiéndose el maquillaje y se vio reflejado, con diez años menos. En forma sorprendente, Pancho pareció adivinar sus pensamientos; aceleró con fuerza, y como si la velocidad lo obligara a volver mentalmente atrás, le contó a Mauricio:

—¿Sabes qué? Una vez vi a tu padre en su Nausicaa en el camino de tierra que llevaba al arroyo, ¿te acuerdas? Estaba en el asiento de atrás, cogiéndose a una vendedora de flores. El cayuco estaba junto a la orilla, con ramos de azucenas. ¡Tu jefe se cogía a todo lo que se movía, dicho sea con todo respeto! Los coches y las viejas lo volvían loco. Antes de que tuviera lana, ya traía un carrazo de poca madre, como que le servía de motel rodante. Me acuerdo que lo espié hasta que la mujer salió del coche. Una chamaquita descalza, de rebozo, como de quince años. Debes tener un chingo de hermanos en los canales; tal vez ahí todos son hijos de Jesús Guardiola, tal vez también tú saliste de un coche. ¡¿Imagínate que fuera éste?! ¡A lo mejor viajamos en el carro que te trajo al mundo! ¡Es un honor estar contigo, me cae!

Pancho estaba intoxicado con el robo y las posibilidades de ser *Leandro* por una noche; aunque divagaba sin freno, Mauricio sintió que sus palabras eran verdaderas. Desvió el espejo hacia el techo y vio la cajuela de guantes. ¿Qué tal si la abría y encontraba un recuerdo lejano? La cajuela era una pequeña cripta de la que podía salir cualquier reliquia.

Sólo cuando llegaron al edificio del tío Roberto, Mauricio dejó de torturarse con la identidad del auto.

cido de las virtudes de la clandestinidad? Su nombre de barricada, su *alias* de secuestrador de aviones, sería *Leandro*. Obviamente resultaba extraño que alguien dispuesto a asumir el anonimato se encargara de esparcir su fama de terrorista célebre.

La revolución se había transformado para él en una película de gran presupuesto en la que se probaba sucesivos uniformes verdes. Era bastante difícil que Pancho llegara a ser póster sin ser mártir, pero en ese momento confundía la belleza con el carisma.

Al salir de la cantina, con el improbable *Leandro* apoyado en su hombro, Mauricio vio un coche de carrocería rosácea, llantas blancas, aletas con molduras de cromo.

—¡El Nausicaa de mi tío! —gritó Mauricio. Luego le pidió a Pancho—: tienes que robártelo.

Su amigo vio el auto y aquella elegancia pasada de moda le pareció digna de su guerrilla, o por lo menos del desfile que haría a su regreso. Se acercó al coche, con pasos vacilantes; para no caerse, apoyó las manos en el cofre. Estaba tibio.

—Deben estar cerca —se refería a los conductores del auto.

—No seas pendejo: ¡es un coche fantasma!

Pancho no lo escuchó: ya estaba en su futuro de *Leandro*, gobernado por los gestos de la acción directa. Sacó una lima y la introdujo por el costado de la ventanilla. Unos segundos bastaron para que encendiera el Nausicaa. Un bramido de grasas y aceites bien carburados.

—Vamos a enseñárselo a mi tío —dijo Mauricio.

A bordo del coche, pensó en la sucesión de autos que circulaban por una vida. Ishtar. Uroboros. Tarot. Nausicaa. ¿Era necesario que tuvieran esos nombres, que inspiraran ese oscuro respeto? Los autos comunicaban, reunían a los otros sin revelar su propio mensaje.

la vista de una mancha de humedad en el techo. Hizo una pausa al llegar al fondo color champaña, y luego descubrió los pechos, redondos, de pezones rosas, ligeramente alzados. Sonrió un poco, de lado, para sí misma. No vio a Mauricio, no necesitaba verlo.

Lo desvistió con más rapidez de la que él hubiera logrado. Le acarició el pelo con la punta de las uñas. Uñas firmes, filosas. Lo besó muy despacio, en sitios raros, la nuca, los antebrazos. Se introdujo el pene en la boca y a Mauricio le pareció increíble que el dinero de su hermano pudiera comprar a la muchacha que lo bebía deliciosamente.

—Pruébate —le dijo. Mauricio recogió en su boca un sabor acre y recordó que las putas no se dejaban besar.

Para envilecerse, para sobrellevar el embrujo arruinándolo, pensó que su hermano había negociado cada detalle, cada gesto, cada caricia de ese guión que terminó con una hermosa palma sobre su pecho y la pregunta "¿satisfecho?" en el tono neutro del comercio.

Ella se limpió con la toalla, otra vez de cara al techo, y se arregló el pelo con las manos, de un modo perfecto.

Mauricio se quedó solo junto a la cortina que le daba al cuarto un aire rojizo. Vio el vaso donde la muchacha agitó los glóbulos de azúcar y luego su propio cuerpo, blando, vencido, abrillantado en la sombra, en la parte inmunda de una maquinada maravilla.

Al día siguiente, sin permitir que Mauricio narrara su encuentro con la mujer, Pancho volvió con su nube materialista. Lo invitó a una cantina para contarle que había renunciado a la asamblea. Ahora pertenecía a un grupo de "acción directa", cuyos primeros golpes consistían en robar coches para cambiarlos por armas. ¿La desaparición de Martín Cifuentes lo había conven-

El edificio estaba en un barrio viejo sin ser antiguo, de casas descascaradas, vecindades con el patio lleno de tanques de gas, balcones con macetas atadas con cuerdas, pequeños negocios en las plantas bajas. Zapateros, sastres de zurcidos invisibles, cerrajeros. ¿Cómo sería la mujer que oficiaba en ese cuarto?

Mauricio llevaba una cajetilla de cigarros, un curioso talismán para darse ánimos. Sólo fumaba mariguana pero anhelaba el momento de encender un cigarro después del coito. No amar sino *haber amado*. El humo compartido. Pasar la prueba.

Luego pensó en dormir, deseó un sueño profundo, como los que lo asaltaban de chico.

Entonces oyó la puerta. Un nudillo débil tocaba para él, como si fuera propietario de ese cuarto. Pensó que era el viejo y le sorprendió encontrar a la muchacha en el umbral. Llevaba un traje sastre y perlas falsas. Parecía una azafata, apenas tres años mayor que él. El pelo castaño se le veía limpísimo. Supuso que se necesitaba una fortuna para contratar a una puta idéntica a las mujeres que su madre deseaba para él.

Ella lo vio con ojos inseguros, como si quisiera cerciorarse de algo y luego se arrepintiera. Fue el único signo de que estaba ahí por un convenio. Luego sacó una botellita y una cuchara de su bolso; escogió cuatro glóbulos homeopáticos; los depositó en un vaso de agua.

—No dilato nada —sonrió hacia Mauricio.

La muchacha contó un minuto en el reloj, revolvió el agua cinco veces a la derecha y luego tres veces a la izquierda. Bebió despacio pero sin despegar el vaso de los labios. Mauricio vio el líquido que le entraba al cuello, la piel blanca con una marca vinosa, como un golpe no muy fuerte.

Luego ella se desvistió; dobló sus ropas con un cuidado extremo, en forma automática, sin apartar

—Andas recaliente, ¿verdad? —su hermano puso la mano en un moretón, como para sacarle una confesión adicional, y prometió ayudarlo.

El edificio era casi tan oscuro como el de los asambleístas. Mauricio escuchó un goteo pero no pudo localizar el charco. Poco a poco se acostumbró a las sombras; distinguió una escalera con barandal de piedra. No sabía a qué clase de sitio lo enviaba su hermano; en el papel llevaba escrito, "tercer piso, puerta verde". Eran las cinco de la tarde y los niños jugaban en la calle. Hasta él llegaron gritos, el botar de una pelota.

Había algo de cromo en el pasillo del primer piso, un patín olvidado, tal vez.

Llamó a la puerta y le abrió un anciano muy bajito. El departamento tenía gruesos cortinajes y la luz encendida. El hombre lo escrutó con ojos muy pequeños.

—A las cinco, ¿verdad? —le dijo.

—Sí.

—Pásele.

Era una sala común, quizá más pobre de lo que él esperaba.

—Al fondo —el hombre señaló un pasillo.

Mauricio sintió que ser lento era ser natural; caminó muy despacio hasta la puerta del fondo, llamó una, dos veces, giró el picaporte. No había nadie. Una cama con colcha de color arenoso, un buró con dos vasos de agua, una silla con dos toallas, un aguamanil, una cortina vertical, de plástico, con un paisaje absurdo, un desierto odioso, de cielo rojo.

Se sentó en el colchón, el tambor tenía los resortes vencidos.

Carlos había preparado las cosas a su manera, sin explicaciones largas, ignorando que eran otros los protagonistas de la escena.

En el Salón de los Abanicos, Mauricio se sintió en una película con lujos de otra época. La orquesta tocaba *swing*, los *smokings* iban del negro al "azul Las Vegas", hubo vals vienés y pirámides de copas de champaña.

En la madrugada, se incorporó a un grupo que caminaba rumbo al centro. Se detuvieron en La Alameda, ante la estatua *Malgré tout*. El cuerpo desnudo que reptaba sobre el mármol, aquel esfuerzo sin futuro, la espalda blanca, dolorida, lunar, excitaron tanto a Mauricio que besó a la muchacha equivocada. María no le gustaba pero estaba junto a él, ebria, feliz de cualquier cosa.

Se sentaron en una banca de piedra que seguía agradablemente la curva de una rotonda. Mientras se besaban, Mauricio veía el reloj de la Torre Latinoamericana.

María llevaba un vestido rosa, con encajes que le abultaban el pecho. No tenía botones adelante, quizá un broche atrás, el caso es que a él le costó mucho trabajo introducir los dedos para tocar el primer seno de su vida, un globito flojo, con un pezón apenas discernible. De vez en cuando, alzaba la vista para ver la progresión de los números dorados. Tal vez María no supiera a quién besaba y tal vez lo hubiera seguido ignorando hasta entregarse en la banca de piedra, de no ser porque un bulto ensombreció sus rostros. Mauricio se apartó de María y vio a Rubén Juanes. Rubén no tenía que ver con María ni tenía por qué estar ahí, pero golpeó a Mauricio. Un gesto ocioso, como todo lo que había ocurrido esa noche.

En su primera madrugada de bachiller, Mauricio regresó a casa con un rostro que parecía maquillado para una película de mutantes. Por primera vez, Carlos lo vio con interés y lo interrogó a fondo. Mauricio recuperó la historia como pudo.

—Se lo llevaron —en boca de Verónica, las palabras tenían una extraña forma de ser verdaderas.

Lejos de ella, Mauricio pensó en otras posibilidades para la desaparición de Martín. Tal vez murió de una sobredosis y su familia quiso prevenir un escándalo, tal vez huyó al otro extremo de la ciudad y preparó las cuidadas claves que dibujarían su leyenda, tal vez había gente que se iba sólo para demostrar el peso de su ausencia. Martín nunca fue importante; nadie lo consideraba su mejor amigo, y sin embargo su sosegado segundo plano le daba espesor a la vida de Terminal Progreso; sólo su desaparición reveló su verdadera utilidad; sus destinos posibles ampliaban ese mundo reducido, lo abrían a historias múltiples; tal vez Martín maduró lo suficiente para entender que su huida sería una desgracia muy superior al beneficio de su presencia, tal vez ahora disfrutaba su venganza desde Ciudad Satélite, Matamoros, Arizona o como se llamara su fin de mundo.

Sólo en sueños, Martín era idéntico a sí mismo. Mauricio veía una silueta inmodificable que arrojaba la moneda a la ventana.

La nueva escuela admitía alumnos en cualquier periodo del año y su nombre prometía un destino sin obstáculos: Instituto Avance.

Por primera vez Mauricio tuvo condiscípulas y pasó mucho tiempo imaginando las estrategias que lo llevarían a placeres supremos e ignorados y demostrarían la cordura del mundo.

Los últimos meses de preparatoria transcurrieron a un ritmo vertiginoso, muy ayudado por la falta de exigencia de los maestros.

Quizá por ser tan ajeno a la enseñanza, el Instituto Avance celebraba una fiesta de graduación desmesurada, una ceremonia para simbolizar lo mucho que se había estudiado.

nes raros, el cuerpo intuido a partir de la ropa íntima de Rita, el escalofrío que le provocaba el recuerdo de la muchacha inyectando la naranja, tenían más relieve que sus pocos escarceos reales; por más que tratara de preservarlos, los olores y los roces se volvían progresivamente fugaces, como paisajes escapados por la ventana de un tren.

Desgraciadamente, tuvo que dejar la escuela cuando empezaba a gustarle y se quedó sin ahondar en los secretos de las esencias no vistas. Después de mucho discutir, su madre aceptó una escuela laica que por lo menos tenía techo.

La primera señal de que Martín Cifuentes se comunicaba con lo negro fueron los dientes. Sus incisivos tenían bordes oscuros; por efecto de la heroína, según Pancho.

Todo mundo conocía su cualidad de copia mitigada, de modelo alcanzable, perfecto para la medianía circundante. Ahora Martín buscaba estímulos que no pertenecían a la colonia ni a este mundo. Al término de cada viaje interior se encontraba con los hombres de negro que lo visitaban desde niño. Martín le dijo a Verónica que esta vez sí venían por él: el Anillo Periférico que se interrumpía en los campos de Terminal Progreso era una pista de aterrizaje.

¿Qué interés podían tener otras civilizaciones en Martín? ¿Les pertenecía desde siempre y lo enviaron como una copia de prueba, una materia informe, un espejo que absorbía los parecidos y regresaría a informar de los muchos humanos que pudo ser?

Mauricio encontró a Verónica en la calle un día de mucho viento. Ella trató de arreglarse el pelo que después de la rapada le crecía de un modo salvaje.

Mientras tanto, Mauricio fue a ver a su madre, que lloraba en el sofá. El vestido se le había subido y mostraba unas piernas largas, torneadas. Mauricio jamás la había visto en traje de baño, ni siquiera en un tenue camisón. Pensó en su padre, que seguramente no llegó a verla desnuda durante el noviazgo, y admiró su capacidad para intuir aquel cuerpo bajo la tela. El involuntario escote revelaba el nacimiento de unos senos firmes; el pelo desgreñado, de un negro astral, prometía una pasión impensable a otras horas. Su madre recogió las piernas y sus muslos quedaron a unos centímetros de Mauricio. Ella lo besó, varias veces, con labios mojados, trémulos. Sus manos fuertes parecían abarcar toda la espalda de Mauricio. Fue un momento de significación futura, que Mauricio iba a repasar incontables veces hasta cargarlo de sentido. Sus edades tenían la combinación perfecta para desordenar sus vidas de una vez por todas, pero en ese momento Carlos volvió a la sala, con los ojos inyectados de ira.

Un nuevo terremoto resolvió el tema de la escuela. El bastión marista sufrió graves daños y las clases tuvieron que continuar en un parque. El maestro de Moral parecía un explorador en el campamento equivocado. En esta situación les habló de San Agustín y de la materia informe, "una nada que es algo", "un ser que es un no-ser".

—Las formas de lo invisible —dijo fabulosamente.

También había materia y sustancia en lo no visto. Mauricio creyó encontrar una forma de rebatir a Pancho. Además, la materia informe también tenía una atractiva resonancia sexual; ninguna expresión mejor para los deseos donde la imaginación estaba más comprometida que la piel. El ideal masculino que ocupó sus primeras masturbaciones y sus fantasías en jardi-

La época parecía compartir la pasión de Martín por las jeringas: los deportistas mejoraban con hormonas, los árboles con injertos (la fruta del momento era la tangerina), el Ishtar paterno con un motor de inyección. Una película famosa trataba de una tripulación de humanos inyectada a un cuerpo gigantesco.

En este clima, la madre de Mauricio se tiñó el pelo de supernegro con jeringas desechables, Jesús Guardiola se inyectó un líquido de glándulas de mono que prolongaba la vida, Verónica se sometió a una terapia de electroacupuntura que la obligó a raparse y a confundir a Mauricio (de nuevo quedó absorto ante su belleza castigada), Pancho habló del erotismo de la *espada suave* y los maristas compraron una bomba novedosa para calibrar sus pedagógicos balones. Un tiempo enamorado de las soluciones a presión que Roberta aprovechó para inyectar "sentido común". A todas horas.

Entre otras cosas, no entendía que su marido enviara a sus hijos a una escuela católica. Aquello era síntoma del atraso latino.

Cuando él iniciaba una réplica, ella lo atajaba:

—Tú ni hables, *Catedral*.

Estaba descalificado por haber construido una iglesia.

Para mantener la precaria paz en la casa de las sandías y las peritas de anís, Jesús Guardiola aceptó cambiar a sus hijos de escuela. El problema era que su ex mujer había hecho del catolicismo un asunto personal; con la religión recuperó un pasado intacto, aún no perturbado por Guardiola. Sólo esto explicaba la furia con que discutieron. Cristina Ferrán no quería interrumpir la tradición de *su* familia, como si buscar un colegio laico significara un cambio genético.

Mauricio oyó los gritos desde su cuarto. Sus padres se insultaron tanto que Carlos entró a la sala, tomó al arquitecto de las solapas y lo llevó a la calle.

El problema arreció cuando la inglesa los acusó de bañarse demasiado. Soltó un discurso sobre las células muertas y las bacterias que protegen la piel. ¿Qué pecado querían lavar los mexicanos? El uso de la piedra pómez como instrumento de limpieza resultaba acusatorio: deshollarse bajo la ducha era negar la raza y el origen.

—Europa nos trajo los virus —dijo con cierta tibieza Jesús Guardiola.

Luego, para no parecer agresivo, habló con el mayor tedio posible de la infinita soledad en que vivieron los pueblos prehispánicos, ignorantes de las otras civilizaciones. La eterna cuarentena de los indios fue rota por las infecciones españolas; las bacterias, tan defendidas por Roberta, fueron el arma mortal de la conquista.

¿Si Jesús Guardiola entendía tan bien el aislamiento de los aztecas, por qué tuvo que abrirse a Roberta y sus comidas de tres tenedores?, ¿qué complejo pagaba con la inglesa que sustituyó el postre de calabaza en *tacha* por quesos de compleja ranciedumbre? El arquitecto, que no podía alzar una pared sin apelar a los colores de la patria, en las noches abrazaba un cuerpo extraño y cremoso (Roberta usaba una leche dérmica que la humectaba *sin quitarle células*).

Carlos y Mauricio debían pasar el viernes y el sábado con su padre, pero las discusiones con Roberta acerca de los ilimitados desastres nacionales generaron tal tensión que Jesús Guardiola fue el primero en sugerir, con aire de falsa camaradería, que lo visitaran "cada que les latiera".

A Mauricio nada le estimulaba los latidos mejor que la mariguana. Martín Cifuentes le habló de las propiedades superiores de la heroína, pero a él le faltó dinero y arrojo para buscar placeres intravenosos.

Antes de Pancho, habló un veterano, un hombre de cuello fuerte y pelo ensortijado, que había sobrevivido a un simulacro de fusilamiento y dos años de cárcel; inspiraba un afecto protector. En cambio, Pancho no estaba ahí porque confiaran en él; su atractivo consistía en brindar una oportunidad de futuro y horizonte, algo esencial para un grupo que todo lo planeaba hacia adelante. La asamblea no se identificaba con él, al contrario, lo contemplaba como una prueba vacía, conjetural, de que esa historia, su acordado estar juntos, iba a seguir más allá de ese mediodía.

Después de la boda, Jesús Guardiola se mudó a un barrio donde los jardineros iniciaban el día regando tres autos y construyó la única casa *mexicana* en diez cuadras a la redonda.

Mauricio estudió la decoración con odio estimulante. Los óleos de texturas terrosas representaban soles, alacranes y perros gordos; sobre los muebles de madera de ayacahuite, había juguetes populares y dulces estéticos (peritas de eucalipto en un frasco de vidrio soplado, una pirámide de merengues en un platón de Talavera).

Roberta Archer estaba fascinada por las artesanías y los guisos rociados de ajonjolí, pero detestaba otras cosas de su país de adopción. En casi todo, el pasado le parecía muy superior al presente, lo que antes fue magia se volvía miseria; las ruinas significaban esplendor y las costumbres, espanto.

Al hablar con Roberta, Mauricio se sentía oscuramente responsable de las calamidades nacionales y trataba de explicar hábitos que iban de los billetes deslizados en las manos de los policías a las voces que decían por teléfono "¿a dónde hablo?", como si marcaran los números al azar.

lían las articulaciones. La lengua se le había dormido. Vio un vaso en la mesa y bebió el agua con desesperación.

Pancho llegó con los cafés y una canasta de pan dulce.

Mauricio sintió un apetito repentino. Entre los panes, había uno color café, con forma de puerco.

"Marrano de anís." ¿En verdad le habían dicho eso? Mauricio sonrió.

—¿Ahora qué te pasa? —le dijo Pancho.

—Sabe a anís —contestó Mauricio, como si eso explicara todo.

Aunque culpó a la mariguana de su errática conducta, Pancho tardó meses en perdonarlo. Mauricio hizo méritos de militante de la materia, leyó hojas mimeografiadas donde cada letra parecía tener un fantasma cirílico y se afilió a la asamblea (recibió la credencial 1732, un número suficientemente bajo para sugerir valentía).

En su calidad de líder juvenil, Pancho aceptaba su superioridad como un dato objetivo y ejercía una suerte de desprecio solidario ("aunque podría estar lejos, *todavía* sigo con ustedes"). Lo más extraño era que los comités de base lo consideraran su representante, como si la suma de voluntades igualitarias condujera, por anulación, a una singularidad: Pancho ante la multitud.

Cuando Mauricio volvió a la asamblea, le sorprendió que su visita en lucidez se pareciera tanto a la anterior. De nuevo se ubicó en el semicírculo de planchado, pero esta vez sí escuchó a los oradores, entre ellos Pancho, que habló con voz pausada y frases cortas, como si administrara sus recursos. Tenía algo de líder televisivo, que llega de lejos y mejora en los *close-ups*.

En torno a su cuerpo se formó un charco de sudor. Un charco grande, profundo, que hizo que abrieran paraguas en el piso de abajo.

Cuando abrió los ojos, el primer detalle de la realidad le pareció una nueva alucinación: una hilera de pasteles de bodas. Mauricio preguntó:

—¿Qué onda?

—Eso digo yo —Pancho se picó el pecho, con rabioso pundonor.

¿Había ofendido sus convicciones, su liderazgo?

—Voy por un café —Pancho se dirigió a la barra.

Mauricio tenía la espalda pegada al asiento de plástico. La cabeza le dolía, las luces de neón le atravesaban los ojos.

Estaban en un café donde se vendían pasteles sobre pedido. Había uno en forma de pato, un coliseo romano, una cigüeña con un bebé de crema. Costaba trabajo creer que así fuera la vida real.

Frente a Mauricio había una puerta de cromo, con ventanas circulares, como una puerta de barco. Cuando se abrió, pudo ver a un hombre de torso desnudo, con una tela en la cabeza a modo de turbante. Desvió la vista antes de que aparecieran los otros dos.

¿Era posible que sus fantasmas fueran panaderos y harina el polvo que despedía el camión? Había algo decepcionante en eso, como si sus pesadillas fuesen incapaces de grandeza y hubiera algo superior en ser perseguido por albañiles, esclavos de las construcciones que modificaban la ciudad, enemigos de los huecos abiertos por la negligencia y los terremotos. Los hombres que hacían pan eran demasiado cotidianos.

Las sienes le latían con fuerza, el calor era tan fuerte como en el semicírculo de planchado. Le do-

¿Se refería a su gordura, realzada por el sudor, o a que la había visto?

—¿Te plancho la grasa? —mostró su palma, alarmantemente roja—. Marrano de anís, puerco de goma, cerdillo en tamaño, brasero de estaño. Puto, puto, puto.

—¡Échale, Yasmín! —gritó otra planchadora.

Mauricio no supo qué era más raro, el acoso de la gorda enrojecida, o que se llamara Yasmín. Ese nombre lleno de menta, joyas de plástico y sedas exageradas iba muy mal con la mujer que ahora llevaba sus dedos al cuello y trataba de estrangularlo:

—¡Marrano de anís!

—¡Mucho, Yasmín! —gritaron las planchadoras.

El acoso se hizo más próximo y Mauricio tuvo otra certeza: Yasmín olía a chicharrón.

¿Dónde estaba Pancho?

De pronto, la mujer abrió la boca, una bocaza ejemplar, como para simbolizar la furia en un mural, y le mordió la oreja con fuerza inusitada.

Las planchadoras rieron a carcajadas. En eso llegó Pancho:

—Ya basta.

Los separó y vio a Mauricio como si fuera el único culpable de lo ocurrido:

—Eres una bestia —lo tomó de la oreja mordida y lo sacó del cuarto. Mauricio escuchó que las planchadoras lo insultaban con alegre furia:

—¡Siete letras, siete letras!

Llegaron a un cuarto vacío. No se escuchaba el menor susurro de la asamblea vecina.

—¿Qué te pasa?

Mauricio vio que su amigo tenía cara de chino, de chino perfecto. Se rió tanto que cayó al suelo.

Al cabo de un rato, un hombre pequeño se convirtió en el centro de la asamblea.

—Un líder ferrocarrilero —explicó Pancho.

Mauricio pensó en la plancha de carbón que avanzaba a sus espaldas.

El líder habló con una voz de pato que se oyó mejor que las anteriores:

—Compañeritos... —dijo y fue arrollado por una salva de aplausos y vítores. El entusiasmo fue enorme. Los zapatos produjeron una aprobatoria estampida en el suelo de madera.

Entre tanto ruido, Mauricio tardó en escuchar el jadeo a su derecha. Cuando desvió la vista, encontró a Pancho detrás de una planchadora. Ella recargaba los brazos en el burro y sostenía la plancha hacia adelante, para no quemar la camisa de mezclilla. Pancho le había subido la falda —una falda espesa, de tela para cortina—; Mauricio pudo ver los muslos enrojecidos por el calor. La mujer le mordía un dedo a Pancho y susurraba un "aiiiiiiiiiiiii" parejo. Las demás planchadoras proseguían su trabajo, con ritmo regular: la mano derecha embestía el burro, la izquierda se quitaba el sudor de la frente. Llevaban pañoletas azules en la cabeza.

Cuando Pancho terminó con la planchadora, Mauricio volvió su atención a la asamblea. Un viejo de barbas tocaba un violín tristísimo y todos aplaudían, a contratiempo, con insólita coordinación.

—Qué bonito —se conmovió una de las mujeres.

Mauricio vio a la planchadora que había recibido a Pancho. Seguía en la misma posición, con la plancha hacia el frente, como una estatua confusa. Luego parpadeó, como si volviera repentinamente en sí, dejó la plancha en un recipiente de metal, se acercó a Mauricio, puso sus brazos en jarras y dijo:

—Marrano.

El hombre tenía la cara echada hacia atrás y una toalla en los ojos. No se la quitó cuando pasaron junto a él. Mauricio respiró el aromático aire de las plantas.

Al fondo había otra puerta. Esta vez Pancho no esperó a que le dijeran "puerta". Giró el picaporte y les llegó el ruido de una multitud. Fue una sensación curiosa, como si la puerta cerrara en forma hermética y ocultara el batir del océano.

Pasaron a un galerón inmenso, de doble altura. El público gritaba y gesticulaba. ¿Por dónde habían llegado los demás? ¿Cada quien siguió una ruta personal, tan sigilosa como la de ellos?

Al centro había un tapanco donde un hombre juntaba los dedos de la mano derecha sobre la palma de la izquierda:

—¡Moción, compañeros!

—Por aquí —dijo Pancho.

Tuvieron que empujar chamarras y sacos (todos con un periódico en la axila) para abrirse camino hasta un semicírculo, situado en un nivel superior, desde el que se podía ver la sala entera. El sitio estaba lleno de mujeres que planchaban ropa. Mauricio tardó en advertir que sólo había camisas en los burros de planchar. Todas eran de mezclilla y todas parecían del mismo tamaño, como si las mujeres se ocuparan del inmodificable vestuario de un gran líder.

Una de las planchadoras usaba un aparato de fierro, lleno de ardientes tizones, del que emanaba un humo acre.

En unos minutos, Mauricio sudaba tanto que tenía que limpiarse las cejas para que las gotas no le taparan la vista.

La multitud gritaba consignas revueltas y parecía discrepar de lo que decían los oradores. En el tapanco no había micrófono y a veces las palabras se perdían antes de llegar al semicírculo de planchado.

apática, ahora el alcohol y la mariguana atemperaban su ansiedad hasta dejarlo inmóvil frente a los sándwiches de triangulito. Los contemplaba con sonrisa beatífica, como si la aceituna rellena de pimiento morrón fuese un mandala.

Encontró a la pelirroja junto al cisne de hielo. En un español perfecto ella le dijo que no hablaba español. Se sintió tranquilo; una vez más había tratado de abordar a una mujer, hizo lo suyo aunque ya no importara, extendió la mano, un gesto vano y necesario, un último deber, como los dedos que arrojan un puño de tierra en una tumba.

Mauricio luchaba con la cruda después de la boda de su padre, cuando Pancho le habló para invitarlo a una "asamblea materialista". La cita era al mediodía. Sabía que nada podía calmarlo tanto como la mariguana. A las 11, fumó un cigarro preventivo.

A bordo del metro supo que había fumado demasiado. Una tonadilla le ocupaba la oreja izquierda, una voz rara, de enana melodiosa.

Llegaron a un edificio del centro y tuvieron que entrar de puntitas porque el suelo estaba tapizado de libros en oferta.

Tomaron una escalera en forma de hélice. El edificio era muy oscuro. En el descanso del segundo piso, Pancho llamó a una puerta. Del otro lado contestó una voz cascada:

—¡Puerta!

Se trataba de una contraseña; pasaron a un departamento tan pequeño que Mauricio recordó la casa de Regina. Las ventanas, cubiertas de periódicos, velaban la luz del mediodía. Al centro de la habitación, un hombre remojaba los pies en una bandeja de zinc. El agua soltaba un vapor espeso. Unas plantas, parecidas a algas, flotaban en torno a los gruesos tobillos.

pendiente, como si el trabajo concluido fuera una impaciencia y desearan volver a las seguridades de la fatiga, la tiranía del peso, los costales llenos. Había algo atrozmente suelto en esa imagen: el camión avanzaba como una pesadilla ligera que casi hacía preferible la boda, el viento tirando cosas ciertas.

Mauricio se volvió hacia la fiesta. Un remolino se hacía cargo de las mesas, los toldos, las inseguras faldas de las mujeres. Las hermanas de Roberta habían llegado enfundadas en telas nunca vistas, géneros vaporosos, pensados para una veranda que recibe un sol denso, junto a un río quieto. Corrieron al tendajón que hacía las veces de cocina; el viento les levantó las faldas. En el momento en que Mauricio pensaba en sus carnes de pavo, comprobó que los gustos no son cosa estable:

—Están buenérrimas —dijo su primo segundo.

En la cámara lenta proporcionada por la mariguana, Mauricio contempló las gardenias que se venían abajo y a un colibrí fijo, desconcertado por los pétalos que se desvanecían ante su pico.

La fiesta se transformó en un campo salpicado de servilletas. En medio del desastre, Mauricio buscó a una muchacha pelirroja que le había llamado la atención al inicio de la boda (mientras la juez recitaba la epístola de Melchor Ocampo: "el matrimonio es el único medio moral de fundar la familia...", ella sonreía con fascinante desprecio).

Al final de las fiestas, Mauricio solía buscar a una muchacha de belleza limitada, y se tranquilizaba al saber que vivía hasta Ciudad Satélite, sus padres eran estrictos, la esperaban en media hora, ya sólo podía bailar una pieza.

Nada en él propiciaba la sanguínea embestida, la urgencia de escupir adjetivos para llegar a un seno. Si los mejorales aceleraron el fin de una infancia

ña. Por contraste, su contenida amabilidad ante Benjamín Gutiérrez Pool tuvo un aire de servilismo.

El tío Roberto se puso un traje color marfil, que acaso compró en Nairobi. Al quinto whisky, una mancha de sudor le cubría la espalda. Su rostro encendido y sus historias de elefantes y negras servidumbres en el corazón de África dieron a la boda un toque de colonia inglesa. Roberta se fascinó con su tocayo, pero sólo por ese día.

Mauricio se ubicó junto al cisne de hielo que adornaba la mesa de las bebidas y aceptó una cuba tras otra, sin pensar que el alcohol pudiera saber a algo. Luego, un primo segundo llegó a ofrecerle mariguana. Fumaron detrás de un cactus. Con lenta precisión, Mauricio vio que su primo sacaba los cuchillos de la tierra. Al poco rato sintió un viento helado. Se acercó a la barda de piedra, que apenas le daba al pecho, y se asomó al otro lado.

El terreno quedaba en las afueras de la ciudad, junto a un arrabal de lámina y cartón. Los postes de luz estaban mal sumidos; travesaños en diagonal que sostenían una intrincada red de cables. El viento alzaba papeles pero los cables los detenían. Muy cerca del terreno, había una fila de mujeres con rostros embozados en chales; parecían esperar que la boda terminara para romper su formación y abalanzarse por las sobras.

Más allá del viento sucio y las casas náufragas, Mauricio vio un desplazamiento. La nube blanca del materialista. Los hombres de turbante parecían maniquíes, cuerpos disecados por algún castigo musulmán. La aparición duró lo suficiente para que Mauricio pensara en los peligros de mezclar la mariguana y el alcohol.

¿Por qué jamás veía el camión con carga? Los hombres ya habían hecho su trabajo, y sin embargo recorrían la ciudad de prisa, como si tuvieran algo

—¡Al carajo! —dijo Carlos junto a la fuente de piedra.

Mauricio entendió que se refería a su padre. ¿En qué agujero había caído para que la presencia de Roberta significara una ayuda?

Jesús Guardiola se abandonó a su fase *Cheri*, es decir, estuvo de acuerdo en todo con Roberta; le pareció estupendo casarse en domingo, al aire libre, y organizó un delirio de papel picado, para que el jardín pareciera Xochimilco en fiesta. Por desgracia, salvo los cactus, todas las plantas parecían rentadas.

Unos días antes de la boda hubo presagios ominosos. Carlos contrajo una salmonelosis que dio pie a que Roberta hablara de la inusual relación de los mexicanos con el agua. El lago enterrado bajo la ciudad y las nieves de los volcanes que ya no se podían ver por el esmog, habían volcado a los capitalinos a una fruición compensatoria. De ahí tanto gollete chupado con urgencia, tanta paleta helada, tanta agua fresca. El Popocatépetl y el Iztaccíhuatl eran recuperados en los pocillos de zinc en los que se servían nieves de sabores. De estas pérdidas estaba hecha la descuidada sed de Carlos.

El domingo de la boda amaneció nublado. Desde que Mauricio llegó al jardín advirtió la amenaza en el aire, un jirón polvoso entre la tierra y el cielo. Alguien sugirió enterrar cuchillos para contener la lluvia: los rosales recibieron su estocada.

Los colegas de Jesús Guardiola llegaron con gaznés y sacos de pana con coderas de gamuza; los de la escuela mexicanista, llevaban un paliacate al cuello. El anfitrión palmeaba a todo mundo en la espalda, como apoderado taurino o político en campa-

humedad que no mojaba, una actividad suave y sin objeto que contribuía a que sus ideas se dispersaran.

Carlos se frotó las sienes, como si padeciera un eczema incontenible. En la infancia, Mauricio había admirado su ignorancia del peligro, su habilidad para ser el primero en escalar una barda y entrar en la casa abandonada, para tirarse desde un trampolín suicida o abrir refrescos con los dientes. Sin embargo, en la secundaria Carlos sorprendió a todo mundo con su talento para las matemáticas: sus manos golpeadas de tanto golpear, resolvían teoremas con pulcra elegancia.

Llegó un momento en que los cuatro años que los separaban se convirtieron en un abismo, como si la cama a unos pasos fuese una isla sin correo.

Mauricio conoció algunos rasgos del carácter de Carlos sólo porque en él estaban ausentes. Al ver lo que los profesores esperaban del apellido Guardiola (ecuaciones y remates despejados con idéntica presteza), entendió las cualidades de su hermano. Aunque la gordura lo descartaba para los deportes, la huella de Carlos era tan honda que el profesor de gimnasia desperdiciaba clases enteras buscándole al menos *una* virtud: el especialista en cobrar tiros de veinte metros, el pítcher de relevo, el poste bajo la canasta.

Mauricio había visto suficientes películas de juicios para saber que en ciertos momentos críticos los abogados tenían que hablar, y le costaba trabajo imaginar a su hermano convenciendo a los doce ciudadanos de no mandar a su cliente a la silla eléctrica. Su idea de la justicia se había forjado en Hollywood, donde Carlos hubiera perdido cualquier proceso; sin embargo, estaba perfectamente equipado para abrirse camino en un sistema dominado por billetes rápidos, sordas amenazas, valores entendidos que servían para medir, no los argumentos, sino la fuerza del adversario.

Por alguna razón, a Roberta el giro le pareció fabuloso y decidió que ese hombre sería *su* materia. Una confusión del lenguaje había torcido su destino.

De golpe, Mauricio sintió algo peculiar, como si hubiera visto el mundo con ojos entrecerrados y enfocara las cosas en su exacta nitidez. En su cama de meditación, había sido un bulto en busca de sentido, y ahora la vida se ordenaba en su beneficio, todo encajaba en el equívoco de Roberta: la piel negra de Vulcano, la obsidiana como cronómetro absoluto, la salamandra latente en el ajolote, el cuerpo creciente y fijo de Verónica, la biblioteca circular de Clarita, el Bello Durmiente y la suprema melamina, las cosas que venturosamente ocurrían por ósmosis, el obispo niño, las mujeres abiertas en la pasarela del teatro, los trofeos pobres de Regina y los falsos trofeos del tío Roberto, la naranja en la que entraba la aguja, los encajes íntimos y la aun más íntima ropa "de estar" de Rita, el ser social de Pancho, su cuidada colección de basuras, todo era materia dispuesta, su vida se ordenaba con la fuerza reveladora de las confusiones.

Sin embargo, al ver el dibujo de conjunto, al saber que su destino no era producto de la casualidad sino de una ley profunda, sintió un doble fracaso: eso no le había *sucedido*, él lo había buscado, era su signo.

Roberta no pudo intuir lo que su español fracturado produjo en su futuro hijastro; lo miró con un interés mitigado por su educación y su miopía; luego consultó su reloj y abrió mucho la boca. Era tardísimo. Jesús Guardiola firmó el aire hasta que le trajeron la cuenta.

Carlos y Mauricio salieron al Bosque de Chapultepec. Era el día de lavado de las fuentes; los estanques rezumaban espuma. Mauricio sumió las manos en esa

Desde que entró a estudiar Derecho, Carlos estaba convencido de que sus interlocutores necesitaban ablandarse con alguna provocación: limpió el dedo en la servilleta, con calma, como si puliera el cañón de una pistola. No apartó los ojos de Roberta; ella le sostuvo la mirada, con frío aplomo.

Cheri sudaba, midiendo las consecuencias del encuentro. Aunque iban a una comida, Roberta dijo que había tiempo para *hors d'œuvres*. En consecuencia, Mauricio pidió un *hot-fudge*. El helado desentonó con la orden que compartían Roberta y su padre (un jamón del diablo que ella llamaba *terrine*); sin embargo, ella lo miró con simpatía. Su tendencia al silencio (por tener la boca casi siempre llena) y a darle la razón a los demás (por mera conservación de la energía), hicieron que Mauricio mereciera el comentario de *a very sweet child*.

Al terminar su plato, Roberta dijo:

—Hay que trespasar el silencio, ¡romper turrones! —golpeó el mantel con energía— ¿Les cuento el *first date* con *Cheri*? *What a chance rendezvous!*

Mauricio trató de llegar al relato que ocultaban las palabras. De algún modo entendió la anécdota que, por supuesto, trataba de malentendidos idiomáticos.

—Todo empezó en el Club de Polo. Tuvimos la conversa casual de arquitectura; me explicó todo lo de las pirámides. Estoy en el secreto —Roberta sonrió como si los uniera una profecía de Teotihuacán—; ¡fue un encuentro así de mágico! Pero esto no oírlo raro porque México es país mágico, ¡y un pelín surrealista! —agregó con acento español.

Total que el arquitecto la hizo sentir que todo era "muy Buñuel, muy Frida Kahlo, *a bit à la* torero". Luego ella habló de su temor a los asaltos y pidió ser "escoltada" al coche.

—Soy materia dispuesta —contestó Jesús Guardiola.

Al poco rato llegó una mujer de sombrero de ala ondulada. Tendió una mano flaca y dijo:

—Pardonen.

En primera instancia, Roberta Archer fue un episodio lingüístico. Aprendió español básico en Valencia, de modo que pronunciaba la *ce* y la *zeta*. A esto había que agregar sus expresiones de emergencia en inglés, los adornos en francés y las malformaciones de su cosecha.

Desde Carmello, el improbable "rey del bocado con tomate", Mauricio no había visto a nadie tan felizmente ajeno a las convenciones del habla:

—Gosto el que me da, conocerla a ti —le dijo a Mauricio y se volvió a su novio—: *What a lovely place, mon petit.*

Aunque no era particularmente fea, Mauricio pensó que sus bucles cobrizos y su nariz aguileña habrían lucido mejor en los Luises de Francia que detestaba Clarita.

Cuando el sol cambió de orientación, Roberta pidió otra mesa:

—El sol salpica pecas, *cheri* —la frase resultó extraña, no por el verbo sino porque ya tenía los brazos cubiertos de pecas.

Pero *Cheri* obedeció y fueron a la sombra.

Roberta era hija de diplomáticos, había vivido en demasiados sitios y estaba dispuesta a hacer de cada lugar una embajada; tomaba las copas con educada rigidez y sólo adoptaba posturas que le dolieran.

Jesús Guardiola, por lo común tan desatado, estaba mudo. Miraba a su novia con una extrañeza admirativa. Roberta jugaba con la cadenita de su collar; Carlos hacía movimientos equivalentes con el índice en su nariz.

—*How disgusting*, Carlis —se volvió a su novio—: *franchement. Cheri, je t'en prie*!

so automatismo y chupaba un cigarro para simbolizar un alma atribulada, Mauricio recordaba a su madre mecanógrafa.

Cristina Ferrán lograba que gestos nimios —rebanar un limón, frotar una superficie— parecieran producto de una ardua voluntad. Su condena era hacer de todo una condena. Mauricio no podía verla sin sentirse lento, inútil, incapaz de los muchos sacrificios que llevaban a la estufa limpia y la mesa puesta.

Cuando ella supo que su ex marido se iba a casar, reaccionó con una normalidad ultrajante. Mauricio esperaba el grito, los platos rotos, el dedo mordido hasta la sangre. Pero su madre fue como Verónica resucitada, un cuerpo impasible, que desplaza sus sufrimientos a la mente de los otros.

—Es inglesa —informó Jesús Guardiola, como si esto adelantara explicaciones.

Roberta Archer había ido a su patria por su *menage* y regresó a México con una notable capacidad para complicar la geografía; no encontró vuelo directo de ningún lado a ningún lado; después de varias conexiones, llegó a Los Ángeles y tomó un avión de Quantas que hacía la ruta Sidney-Los Ángeles-México y que a Mauricio le recordó los koalas de otros tiempos.

Mauricio quiso ir al aeropuerto, pero después de diecisiete años su padre había descubierto los momentos privados.

Guardiola pensó mucho en el sitio para presentar a su prometida con sus hijos. Sólo así se explicaba la elección de esa cafetería a la que nunca habían ido, al borde del Lago de Chapultepec.

A Mauricio le gustó entrar a la cafetería de manteles color durazno, ataviado con una corbata de nudo eterno.

En Quinto Sol se entonaban himnos muy agudos. Mauricio había visto cantar a grupos de bomberos y enfermeras, y sabía que todo coro institucional acepta a miembros con más convicción que oído, pero entre sus muchos caprichos, la sociedad teosófica ignoraba que había aztecas incapaces de trinar.

Con seriedad e ineficiencia, Roberto buscaba llevar al más fino éter el vocabulario nahua:

—*Pantli... ílhuitl* —en los salones emplumados de Quinto Sol aquello debía escucharse de otro modo, pero en el departamento era difícil de justificar.

El tío Roberto hacía poco más que beber, esparcir azúcar tras los muebles de la cocina, ver a las sirvientas con sus miras telescópicas y cantar con frenesí.

Tal vez fue este caos lo que precipitó a Jesús Guardiola a su segundo matrimonio. Un jueves le ofreció un cigarro cómplice a Mauricio y con su habitual sentido del rodeo dijo:

—Me voy a casar. Tengo que rehacer mi vida —añadió, como si acabara de salir de la prisión. Se pasó la mano por el pelo prematuramente blanco que le daba una dignidad molesta en ese momento.

Para Mauricio, el primer efecto de la noticia fue pensar en su madre: la vida le costaba un trabajo enorme; los continuos consejos en el refrigerador, sus esfuerzos para fumar y dejar de fumar, las cuentas que revisaba con Carlos, su arrojada forma de conducir, su catolicismo renovado y duro, las ropas que hacían pensar en lo que las mujeres discretas preferían en otro sistema solar, todo apuntaba al esfuerzo.

Había conseguido un trabajo de mecanógrafa; transcribía textos para políticos y gente rica que aún no había hecho su tesis; escribía con todos los dedos, sin ver las teclas, con un cigarro torcido en la boca. En el cine, cada vez que un "escritor" tecleaba con furio-

segura de lo que hacía: "¡Me ataron con nudo Blackwall!", exclamó, como si ése fuera un dogma del mundo práctico.

Esta vez lucía aun más sofocado. Como ya se había vuelto costumbre, fueron a una cantina donde les trajeron una botella de Siete Leguas.

—Cinco para mí, dos para ti — Roberto repartió el nombre del tequila.

Tuvo que llegar a su segunda "legua" para hablar del tema que lo alteraba:

—¡Descubrí un coche fantasma! Le vendí un Nausicaa, como el primero que tuvo tu padre, a un cliente de Matehuala. Llevaba mucho tiempo "seco", casi desde que le vendí el coche a tu madre, ¡bendita sea!, total que el cliente durmió en su hotel y al salir, ¡ni las luces del coche! Así como lo oyes. "Coche robado", pensé yo, pero lo recuperaron en Reforma, sin señas de uso. A la noche siguiente le quitó las bujías, y así y todo lo encontraron en los Indios Verdes. ¿Cómo ves que me lo trajo de regreso? Se lo aceptamos a mitad de precio. Lo sensacional es que el coche se nos volvió a ir: se largó solito, debe andar carburando por cualquier lado. ¡El fantasma se nos fue a mitad de precio!

Luego habló de buques que recorrían el Caribe con una tripulación de esqueletos y de un avión *jumbo* que perdió presión y quedó a la deriva con setecientos pasajeros asfixiados. El *jet* le recordó a un elefante:

—¿Sabías que *Jumbo* fue un elefante de pronóstico, que vivió en el zoológico de Londres? De 1865 a 1882. ¿A que no? Ya ves, sobrino, en la última legua del tequila hay que manejar muchos datos, muchos datos... *Jumbo* acabó en el circo Barnum, y ahí tienes a los elefantes que vuelan. ¡Qué fregada suerte, la de tomar un vuelo fantasma!

Siguió de tan buen ánimo que perdió la oportunidad de asociar al elefante con su fracaso en África.

la cama conveniente. Pancho mostraba un soberano
desdén por los organismos vivos a los que les cortaba
la respiración; en cambio, Mauricio conservaba un
recuerdo diluido y simple del futbolista en el bosque,
consolaba su deseo con figuras de hule espuma, vivía
entre cuerpos inciertos, imaginaba ninfas ataviadas de
tules y un rubí en el ombligo, jardines ilusorios que
podaba con obsesiva cursilería. En rigor, se oponía a
la realidad con mayor fuerza que su amigo. Pero Pancho no aceptaba réplicas; durante el rato que pasó en
la recámara, se comportó en plan grande: tenía razón
de antemano, hablaba desde sus triunfos futuros. No
mostraba el fervor del fanático sino algo más molesto,
la superioridad del que ya leyó esa escena y vio su
adaptación en película.

Se pasó la mano por el pelo y señaló el libro
que había llevado:

—Ahí te lo dejo de tarea.

Pese a todo, algo quedaba del viejo Pancho.
También en esta faceta mostraba una indudable originalidad. ¿Cómo explicar, si no, que alguien con ánimos de convencer fuera tan detestable?

Cuando abrió el *Manifiesto*, Mauricio leyó tres palabras: "Un fantasma recorre ..." No pudo seguir porque
sonó el teléfono. Era su tío Roberto:

—Te tengo una sorpresa de pronóstico. Ven a
SUPER REMATE.

La frase del *Manifiesto* resultó profética: El tío
habló de fantasmas. Mauricio no lo veía tan contento
desde la tarde en que asaltaron el lote de autos usa-
dos: "Unos tipazos, no creas que ladrones normales,
gente de traje, muy bien plantada." El atraco a mano
armada le permitió apreciar el calibre de las metralle-
tas y le brindó una versión urbana de sus cacerías; le
fascinó estar en manos de una banda profesional,

ro lo consideraba un enemigo. La sociedad Quinto
Sol era un nido de idealistas.

—Es comprensible que lo quieras, después del
"padrotismo" de tu padre.

La palabra "padrote" siempre le había sugeri-
do una expansión erótica de la paternidad; Jesús
Guardiola necesitaba un suave rebaño. ¿Cómo lo sabía Pancho? Por una fuente irrefutable: el propio Mauricio. Cada vez que Pancho le contaba sus escarceos
eróticos, a falta de experiencias propias, Mauricio
presumía los lances de su padre.

Cuando el arquitecto Guardiola empezó a favorecer las camisas negras, Pancho fue el primero en
descubrir que eso no señalaba humor de exequias ni
su incorporación a la mafia de Sinaloa, sino una nueva táctica de seducción:

—Los cuervos se visten de negro —Mauricio
se había encargado de mistificar a tal grado a su padre
que cualquier comparación con otra especie significaba una sola cosa: voracidad sexual.

Durante el discurso de la pastilla de menta,
Mauricio supo que los enemigos no tenían opiniones
sino "ideología". Además de "padrote", Jesús Guardiola
"nadaba en las aguas del cálculo egoísta": era un ex-
plotador de albañiles.

—Tienes que ser más "autocrítico" —le dijo
con la voz que antes usó para aconsejarle que aprove-
chara "sus instantes".

Mauricio se detestaba en el espejo, en el salón
de clases, en los camiones repletos donde sabía que
nadie tocaba su estómago por gusto. En este sentido,
era más autocrítico que Pancho, cuyo interés por la
materia resultaba sumamente parcial. Su biografía era
una cadena de alardes físicos: su boca recibió al magnífico Vulcano, sus manos rechazaron los senos su-
perpopulares de Eduarda, la estrella de las fotonovelas
lo embarró de lodo; hiciera lo que hiciera acabaría en

obvia que Pancho se ocupó de otros temas; durante una hora o más disertó con una pastilla de menta en la boca; la palabra "materialismo" surgió con la misma constancia con que la menta se le pegaba al paladar.

Mauricio recuperó la atención cuando su amigo habló del "modo de producción asiático". Los arrozales a medio camino entre el feudalismo y la primera industria, aquel intermedio en el programa de explotación del hombre por el hombre, se parecían asombrosamente a Terminal Progreso, la orilla asiática de la ciudad de México.

—"No es la conciencia la que determina al ser" —citó Pancho, como si las palabras le fuesen comunicadas por una imposible deidad de la materia.

Unos minutos después su discurso cobró mayor intensidad: *tenían* que defender a la Materia, como si la Conciencia fuera una niebla corrosiva que se apoderara de los pueblos.

—"El ser social determina la conciencia" —había adoptado un tono pedagógico en el que las comillas se oían con claridad.

¿Qué accidentes explicaban la lumbre en sus ojos? ¿Qué billar había desencadenado esas correspondencias? El primer impulso materialista de su amigo podía localizarse en aquel comentario sobre el deseo como superación del asco (la mierda del cuerpo amado). No era extraño que alguien con un sentido tan orgánico de los afectos dijera:

—Sólo hay "condiciones objetivas" —aplaudió para matar un mosquito. Mostró la palma con la gota de sangre, como un argumento a su favor.

Luego añadió con énfasis sobreactuado, de intrigante de telenovela:

—¿Cómo está tu tío Roberto?

Sólo entonces Mauricio entendió el sentido de la visita. Pancho quería ganarlo para su causa, no por sus virtudes radicales, sino porque de un modo oscu-

Martín Cifuentes le recomendó masturbarse con un bistec crudo, pero él no había crecido en una casa donde el refrigerador era un centro moral.

El encuentro con el futbolista se diluyó pronto. Mauricio quería tener una herida, una ostensible cicatriz, pero aquellas caricias se habían vuelto más tenues que los velos imaginados en sus tardes de hule espuma. Por más que trataba de complicar su experiencia, no podía alejarse del hecho, bastante banal, de haber frotado una piel con otra.

La noche del Teatro Iris lo perturbaba con mayor fuerza; los cuerpos circenses, los sexos extraños, su punitiva desnudez, volvían a él con insólita vivacidad, en oleadas de fascinación y vergüenza. En cuanto a la choza de Palenque, sentía la repulsión excedida de las pesadillas, una inmundicia demasiado real.

Las explicaciones a medias de Pancho "protegieron" a Mauricio de peligros políticos hasta que llegó en un plan completamente distinto; le dio un abrazo que pareció afectuoso y en realidad fue proselitista. Subieron al cuarto y Pancho le entregó un gastadísimo ejemplar del *Manifiesto comunista*. A la manera de San Andrés, venía como pescador de almas, al fin lo consideraba digno de su red.

Pancho se quitó los zapatos, se tendió en la cama de Carlos y contó que había cambiado de grupo. Ya no estaba en la "célula" a la que había que llegar salvando contraseñas en oscuros socavones, sino en una "asamblea" donde representaba nada menos que a la Juventud. Ahora su eficacia dependía del número de adeptos.

Mauricio temió que hablara de campesinos con gangrena y sirvientas torturadas en los quemadores de la estufa. Por suerte, la miseria nacional era tan

uno de ellos salió una mujer de facciones achinadas; la seguía un hombre de mirada estrábica (hizo un gran esfuerzo para fijar su ojo en los recién llegados).

—¿Una *cheva*? —les dijo una mujer gorda, de blusa morada.

Bebieron cuatro Victorias tibias.

Nadie se les acercó. Las mujeres miraban el techo, tendidas en las hamacas, en un descanso incómodo. Los que hablaron en la fogata tenían miradas huidizas.

—Vámonos —dijo el hermano.

Salieron de la barraca sin decir palabra.

No volvieron a mencionar el tema en lo que duró el campamento. ¿Cómo relacionar los protocolos de la pasión, sus fotogénicas exigencias, con ese corral inerte?

En la terminal de autobuses, un poco antes de emprender el regreso, bebieron refrescos en un tendajón y vieron la miseria a punto de desplazarse con ellos: las cajas de cartón atadas con mecates, las cobijas enrolladas, las moscas que se pegarían a sus rostros y beberían su sudor hasta el altiplano. El refresco les dejó las lenguas rojas. En la pared del establecimiento había un calendario donde se asoleaba una mujer imposible. Mauricio se preguntó cuánto dinero sería necesario para que el elemental gusto de chupar a otra persona pareciera un éxito de vida. ¿Podía ser el mundo tan distinto a sus promesas?

Al regresar a la ciudad, otra pregunta inquietó a Mauricio: ¿cómo se ayudaban los solitarios de tecnologías anteriores al hule espuma? Él recurría a los apachurrones suaves con objetos de distintos formatos, un erotismo de juguetería que regresaría años después con el olor de los preservativos.

samente extraño. Los leños crepitaron entre la lumbre, puntuando el penoso silencio que siguió a las "confesiones"; el aire tenía el hálito sucio de las historias plagiadas. Por fin alguien propuso:

—Vamos al putero. Seguro hay una "figura antropomorfa" para el gordo.

En la mañana, habían visto la misma cédula insulsa en un sinfín de piezas mayas: "figura antropomorfa".

Mauricio se volvió en derredor; las ruinas se confundían con la maleza; la luna estaba casi llena; las ramas de las ceibas se alzaban en arabescos nítidos.

Un hermano marista aceptó llevarlos en la *pick-up*. La virginidad de Mauricio le pareció un motivo extremo para ahorrarse el laberinto de los pecados y las absoluciones.

Mauricio subió atrás y en la carretera, el pelo revuelto por el viento, sintió un frío intenso. Le pareció extraño que la selva pudiera ser tan fría. Luego, cuando la camioneta se detuvo, recuperó la sensación de calor, de húmedo agobio y pantalones untados a las piernas.

Llegaron a una choza con techo de palma, junto a un arroyo que corría en forma lateral al pueblo. Un gruñido de cerdos llegaba de un corral vecino. La brisa despejaba apenas un olor estancado, a descomposiciones vegetales. De la choza salía la música de una sinfonola. Las paredes de varas dejaban pasar sombras; alguien bailaba.

Una cortina hacía las veces de puerta. El hermano la descorrió y pasaron a un local de tierra apisonada. Una guirnalda de focos desnudos recorría el techo. Un perro, vencido por un sueño de piedra, dormía junto a la rocola. Adentro hacía más calor, tal vez a causa de los focos. Había dos hamacas donde las putas se abanicaban con trozos de cartón. A la derecha, Mauricio vio los entrepaños encortinados. De

taría a la altura de los sacrificios imaginados durante
tantos años, las deliciosas torturas carnales que inspiraba el cuerpo de San Andrés. Con asombro, se concentró en la caprichosa precisión de sus reacciones:
le molestó el aliento que olía más a ceniza que a tabaco y le gustó el olor de los genitales que lamió con
delectación. Sintió menos dolor y menos placer de lo
esperado. Al cabo de un rato todo perdió interés.
Fumaron en silencio de cara a los pastizales amarillos.
El futbolista mantuvo la mano en el pene de Mauricio;
una costosa alianza le abultaba el dedo anular.

La escena perdía consistencia minuto a minuto. Resultaba difícil, casi imposible, pensar que estaba
del otro lado: sus detalladas fantasías habían encarna-
do en la borrosa realidad del sexo. Acaso lo que más
le gustó fue la forma en que el otro respetó la distancia, su capacidad de unirse sin historias.

Volvieron a la ciudad.

El Uroboros se detuvo en la esquina del principio, como si ese punto cerrara el azar.

—Nos vemos, güero —el hombre le dio una
palmada, un gesto de solidaridad en los vestidores,
antes de entrar a las regaderas.

A las pocas semanas estuvo a punto de perder su otra
virginidad. Los maristas organizaron un campamento
cerca de las ruinas de Palenque. En la noche, rodeados de la vibrátil presencia de la selva, cuatro amigos
juntaron leños y entraron en las confesiones del fuego. Mauricio dijo la verdad: no había cogido. Quizá
precipitó su franqueza para no aclarar que se lo habían cogido. Los otros tres hablaron de una gringa
extraviada en Acapulco, una precoz prima de Tijuana,
una puta que no había querido cobrar, alardes muy
poco creíbles, aunque toda historia de sexo hetero-
sexual exigiera un componente desconocido, forzo-

final de un código cuyas premisas obvias eran los chocolates, las flores, los signos del Zodiaco. Sabía que cuando sus calcetines se rindieran al fin al pie de un lecho, tendría que comportarse en forma específica. En el supermercado compró un Kama-Sutra de bolsillo para retorcerse de amor con instrucciones. Necesitaba manuales, guías, mapas sensuales. ¿Cómo acercarse a una mujer sin todas las películas que tenían inquilinato en su cabeza? Había que empezar por los dedos entrelazados, seguir por la boca, como una pintura que se ilumina por números. Amar era compararse: en cines de limitada pornografía estudió escenas donde los amantes jadeaban con amplitud de onda. ¿Qué hacer si su pareja no llegaba a esa elocuencia?

Las delicias de chupar un codo o sentir que un índice practicaba en su organismo lo que en el ensayo solitario practicó un lápiz, estaban fuera de cálculo y, sobre todo, de noción del éxito. Coger era el grito simultáneo entre las sábanas de satín; haber cogido, fumar exultantes cigarrillos.

Tal vez por ceder a un gusto que no era necesario medir con los comunicativos amantes de la pantalla, Mauricio optó por un cuerpo cuyas reacciones conocía por experiencia propia. Le asombró la tranquilidad con que subió al coche en Insurgentes. El Uroboros se había detenido junto a él, un modelo del año. El conductor era un futbolista retirado, calvo pero todavía fuerte. Sin mayor preámbulo, sugirió que fueran a "picar". Mauricio asintió, respirando el agradable olor del coche último modelo. Le divirtió destruir de una vez por todas la visión del futbol como ejercicio moral de los maristas; subieron a las faldas del Ajusco, tomaron un camino de terracería y se estacionaron en el bosque. El hombre sacó un frasco de vaselina de la cajuela de guantes y besó a Mauricio. A partir de ese momento supo que el encuentro no es-

En la preparatoria Pancho descubrió unos libros color naranja consagrados a la "economía política" y asistió a reuniones llenas de misterio que primero llamó "círculos" y luego "células". Sus anécdotas avanzaban de un modo lateral porque la vida estaba llena de soplones y teléfonos intervenidos:

—Te conviene saber poco —le decía a Mauricio. Ahora no completaba sus historias por seguridad política.

A Pancho ya sólo le interesaban las "condiciones objetivas"; los chismes, los rumores, las insinuaciones y la mala leche se habían vuelto "asuntos fenoménicos". Habría sido insoportable de no ser por su probada capacidad para contradecir sus teorías en la vida diaria (ahora llamada "praxis"). Mauricio seguía siendo su confidente erótico y sabía que sus impulsos carecían de la menor coherencia. Después de declarar que ya sólo le interesaban los hombres, Pancho se fugó con una actriz de fotonovelas, diez años mayor que él. Pasaron dos semanas en un balneario de aguas termales (dada la pobreza del entorno, esto pareció un viaje a los nocturnos delitos de Las Vegas). Probablemente Pancho recurrió a esa escapada para tranquilizar a sus padres; habló por teléfono desde una poza medicinal, cubierto de lodo y aguas sulfurosas, y le dijo a su familia que estaba con una mujer (y que ella pagaba las cuentas). Con idéntica vulgaridad, su padre le habló al de Mauricio para "festejar la noticia".

—A ver si aprendes, *Panza* —dijo el arquitecto.

La opinión pública de Terminal se revertía en forma caprichosa; Pancho dejó de ser "el del modito" y se convirtió en motivo de imitación.

Mauricio dedicaba la mejor parte de sus horas de meditación a los protocolos amorosos; trataba de precisar la escena íntima (que, según la inaccesible moda del momento, incluía cama circular), la escala

Un camión materialista avanzaba a gran velocidad; los tablones en la parte trasera despedían polvo, como si hubiesen transportado cal. Tres hombres viajaban de pie (era de madrugada pero llevaban los torsos desnudos y trapos en la cabeza a modo de turbante); la cabina de vidrios opacos impedía ver al conductor.

Mauricio quería realizar un acto imposible: cruzar la calle. Había bebido lo suficiente para que el asfalto fuera una realidad convulsa. Se volvió a la derecha y vio un perro, tendido como un dios egipcio. Las cruzas callejeras logran pelos inclasificables. Su dios testimonial era amarillo.

El perro bostezó largamente, enrollando la lengua; se estiró con la precisión de las bestias flacas y cruzó la calle. Lo hizo con tal tersura que Mauricio juzgó que su problema eran los zapatos.

Se estaba descalzando cuando vio un taxi. Subió a bordo, se tendió en un cobertor de hilachas *tutti-fruti* y murmuró "Terminal Progreso". Al cabo de un rato se incorporó. Algo vibraba junto al taxi. Un motor ronco y profundo. Otra vez los fanales turbios, los torsos desnudos, los turbantes en la nube blanca.

El materialista lo perseguía. Aunque rechazaba las invitaciones de su padre a ver obras negras, el camión lo asediaba, como una sombra enviada por el arquitecto, o por Pancho, que en un sentido muy distinto se acababa de convertir en un materialista desbocado.

5. El materialista fantasma

la sangre, sentí como si alguien me hablara hacia dentro. Luego vino un silencio ajeno, seco.

Roberto miraba como esperando un comentario, como si yo fuera capaz de humillarlo a fondo por sus cebras perdidas y los insectos que mantenía vivos, y sobre todo, como si necesitara la ofensa de un canalla para demostrar que aún podía resistir. En ese momento un insulto lo hubiera ayudado. Podía soportar a su familia con su temple de Tizoc, podía sobrellevar sus heridas invisibles como su pie de cuatro dedos. Me vio con ojos de rencilla, que invitaban a no compadecerlo, a descartarlo como el idiota conveniente que había sido para nosotros.

Cerró el puño. Un rastro de azúcar cayó de su mano y desapareció en el aire, antes de llegar al suelo.

Busqué algo que decir pero Mauricio se me calló. Me detesté en él. No teníamos voces. La vida me iba a brindar un tono en el que ya no era posible decir "más mejor" ni "demasiado bueno" pero en ese momento ni yo ni Mauricio tuvimos boca, algo se separaba y el tío me pedía, nos pedía, seguir ahí, ayudarlo, así fuera con un regaño. Sonreí canalla, como anunciando un duro escarnio; él aguardó, desafiante, pero no hubo voz. Yo quería seguir ahí, recuperarme, decir las blandas tonterías que susurraba al oído de mi madre y la hacían feliz, y luego repetiría en otros oídos como una imitación del que ya no era, como quien pide asilo en el tiempo, volver atrás, ser el que confió tanto en la hierba y miró el techo como si siempre fuera a estar ahí, regresar a esa zona rota, mejor: rompida. Mi lengua pesaba, como algo que se degolla, se forza, se torce. Un simple insulto bastara para que el tío sonriera. Quise que lo dijéramos. Algo. Lo que saldría. El tío aguardaba lo que fuera, la voz destemplada, el arranque gutural. Yo quería quedarme. Pero la garganta de Mauricio tragaba silencio, rompida. Asquerosa. Definitivamente rompida.

Tal vez para acabar de envilecerse habló con el agraviante cariño del Inspector Autoridad.

—¡Y ahora me quitaron el dinero! Te pensaba invitar con unas amigas y sólo quedó para marranilla.

Al fondo de la cantina fumaban dos mujeres gruesas, de pelo color paja. Sentí un enorme alivio de que no tuviéramos dinero, pero el hipócrita de Mauricio dijo:

—Para otra noche.

Había comido demasiado antes de salir de casa y llevaba varias rondas de alcohol. Fui al baño. Una cubeta hacía las veces de inodoro. Vomité, mientras pensaba en las mujeres descoyuntadas en el teatro.

Cuando regresé a la mesa, mi tío había dejado de llorar; parecía dormir sobre su antebrazo.

—Ni una cebra —repitió Tehui.

Hasta entonces, el pasado de Roberto había tenido un aire melancólico, una región perdida, siempre mejor que el presente. Ahora se convertía en una zona persecutoria y ruin, el momento que no dejaría de castigarlo.

Tehui tomó el mando de la expedición. Convenció al patrón de que cambiara mi llavero por otro café para el tío. El llavero era un círculo de vidrio, con un *cowboy* que alzaba un lazo, una de las pocas cosas que a Mauricio aún le gustaban de su infancia, y que terminó junto a la botella sin etiqueta de la marranilla.

Al llegar al departamento, Mauricio despertó a su tío. Con las llaves, Roberto sacó unos diez sobres de azúcar.

Al día siguiente, Mauricio y yo vimos la última escena del safari: el cazador espolvoreaba azúcar en la cocina.

Tal vez por el gas que salía de un piloto apagado, tal vez por la cruda, tal vez por un arrebato de

Desde la salida del palco Mauricio me había despreciado en silencio. Con qué odio repasó mi cuerpo tirado en el cemento, mi voz tipluda, mis gimoteos; me odiaba sin poder hacer otra cosa, con una lumbre que se alimentaba de sí misma. Cuando el tío empezó a llorar y se convirtió en el extremo vulnerable de la mesa, Mauricio volvió a su territorio, a la voz grave que no tuvo ante la autoridad.

—Estuve en África de puro farsante, de puro lengualarga...

Mauricio recordó los años preparando el safari, la expedición a la sabana de las fieras grandes.

—No maté nada. Me la pasé bien pedo. Sólo salía de la tienda para mear. ¡Me abrí, carajo, me abrí, como una mujercita!

Apoyó la cabeza en los antebrazos y lloró con un gemido insoportable. Mauricio le acarició la espalda, empapada de sudor.

—Me rajé...

La bebida, la ruptura con la familia, el envejecimiento prematuro venían de esa cobardía, ése era su secreto de África; sin embargo, Mauricio pensó que exageraba en su beneficio, que magnificaba el desastre en Kenia para protegerlo. Aun dominado por la borrachera, Roberto se sentía responsable de los "picos pardos", casi tan anunciados como la expedición a África; falló como guía y deseaba combatir la humillación de Mauricio con otra superior.

—¿Y los cuernos que trajiste? —preguntó Mauricio.

—¡Cuernos de ñandú! Eso les dije, ¿y sabes qué?, los ñandúes no tienen cuernos, ni siquiera viven en África. Compré lo que pude, un revoltijo de pieles y cuernos raros.

Roberto sonrió en forma inconexa, los ojos no tenían que ver con la boca, la frente estaba en otra cara.

—Los compré, corazón.

Dos horas más tarde, la mano del tío se aferraba a unas bolsitas de azúcar.

—¿Qué te pasa, Tizoc? —Tehui tuvo que repetir la pregunta. El tío había bebido mucho.

Los veinte pesos se nos fueron en comprar algo que Tehui definió como "pura marranilla". El reloj de mi tío sirvió para saldar las siguientes rondas.

Cuando Roberto ya estaba muy ebrio, Tehui le pidió un café, y mi tío atrapó las bolsitas de azúcar como un raro tesoro.

Mi padre había descubierto a su hermano rociando azúcar en los muebles de la cocina. Con el pésimo pulso de la borrachera, Roberto dejaba caer el alimento para insectos. "Son criaturas del Señor", explicaba, y mi padre no le preguntaba más por miedo a que el Señor fuera Mictlantecuhtli.

El departamento se había llenado de cucarachas y teníamos que ocultar el azúcar como antes ocultábamos el alcohol.

—¿Tizoc? —insistió Tehui.

—Ni una pinche cebra —contestó por fin mi tío, apretando con furia el azúcar.

—¿Otra ronda? —preguntó el cantinero.

En esa cantina yo tenía edad legal para lo que fuera. Un hombre cubierto de andrajos me pidió un cigarro y el cantinero me servía como si nada.

—¿Ya se acabó lo del reloj? —Tehui puso un cortauñas en la mesa. El cantinero lo vio con detenimiento.

—Dos rondas por la corbata —señaló el trapo que no me había servido de nada y que rendí con gusto.

—Ni una cebra de mierda —mi tío golpeó la mesa—. Nada. Me abrí. ¿No te das cuenta? —me jaló de la camisa—. ¡Me abrí!

—¿Quieres otro lleguecito?

El tío jalaba oxígeno por la boca, incapaz de responder. Tehui, por supuesto, estaba paralizado.

El Inspector se volvió hacia mí:

—¡Encuérate, hijo de tu pinche madre!

Fueron las últimas palabras que me dirigió la Ley.

Hubiera bastado que le mostrara la zona insuficiente, pero un extraño sentido del rigor me hizo desnudarme por entero.

Para subrayar la inversión de mi destino, oí el grito que salía del auditorio:

—¡Pe-los, pe-los!

El Inspector se rió tanto que creí que arrancaría el solitario pelo que despuntaba en mi pubis.

—¿Conque dieciocho? —le dijo a mi tío—. ¿Cuánto dinero traes? —añadió, como si el trámite empezara a aburrirlo.

Entonces, el tío se comportó con una entereza admirable.

—Ventajoso de mierda —pronunció despacio. La elección de la palabra "ventajoso" reveló tanta grandeza como la calma con que esperó el macanazo.

Me lancé a protegerlo, desnudo como estaba, y un golpe me alcanzó en los testículos. Me doblé en el piso de cemento y pensé intensamente en mi hermano Carlos.

Me quedé, con la boca pegada al piso arenoso hasta que el Inspector pronunció la palabra que por lo visto siempre me dirían en los momentos inapropiados:

—Vístete.

Luego tomó la cartera del tío, sacó los billetes y le devolvió dos de a diez, como si hubiera una cuota fija por no consignarlo como corruptor de menores.

La foto de un balón era pésima señal; me recordó a los inquisidores del colegio.

El hombre leyó el periódico, como si de ahí dimanara su fuerza. La lentitud era su técnica.

Finalmente nos miró con unos ojos que recordaban que nuestros antepasados salieron de una laguna.

—¿El de la corbatita? —preguntó a los policías, como si fuera necesario aclarar que yo era el sospechoso—. ¿Una identificación?

—No tengo —fingí una voz grave, Mauricio me había abandonado con una cobardía sin freno.

—Ya cumplió dieciocho, mi jefe —la voz del tío se había debilitado.

—"Dieciocho", mis huevos —el Inspector Autoridad se puso de pie. Tenía una barriga inmensa. Al decir "mis huevos" quiso tocarse en concordancia, pero sólo llegó al bajo vientre.

Luego llevó su mano a mi cara y pude oler un desodorante de lima.

—¿Qué edad tienes, mi vida? —me oprimió las mejillas como si deseara extirpar un diente.

Produje un ruido inclasificable, que ya no importaba en lo más mínimo.

—A ver gordito, demuéstrame que tienes *pelícanos.*

No me moví.

—¿Qué esperas, corazón? ¿Que te anuncien por el sonido "Pasarela monumental presenta..."?

—Hijo de la chingada —mi tío trató de zafarse y recibió dos macanazos en la cara. Entonces comprendí la falacia de las películas donde los héroes se levantan a pelear después de ser golpeados con mazos y llaves de tuercas. Aquellos golpes secos, propinados con calculada intensidad, frenaban a cualquiera. Los labios de mi tío temblaban, al borde de la convulsión.

El Inspector tomó la macana y la frotó lentamente en la sien de mi tío:

go le dio la espalda al público para exhibir el culo, se colocó el tubo del micrófono entre las nalgas y empezó a moverse con una furia descomunal.

Estuve a punto de rezar para diluir lo que miraba; la imagen de mi tío de cuatro años, muerto como un obispo de porcelana, las misteriosas novenas de mamá, la iglesia construida por mi padre, se impusieron para alejarme de esa hondonada en la que el tío capturaba presas, seguro de que la vida no era sino una ruda sucesión de cuerpos, heridas, pieles que merecían abrirse.

Mauricio buscó remedio en la cantimplora (había olvidado que su tío se la acabó al entrar); no recogió más que un aire etílico.

Tenía la cantimplora en la nariz cuando sintió una tibia caricia en la mejilla. Una linterna alumbraba el palco. Tizoc y Tehui se volvieron hacia la fuente luminosa:

—¡Fuímonos! —gritó Tehui.

Sólo al ponerse de pie, Mauricio advirtió otra complicación de la noche. A pesar del espanto, una erección le abultaba la bragueta; correr en ese estado era algo tan grotesco como las genuflexiones que la giganta producía en la pasarela.

Siguió como pudo a los hombres de Quinto Sol, y fue detenido en el pasillo.

—¡Pinche gordo caliente! —dictaminó un policía.

—¿Qué edad tiene el escuincle? —preguntó su compañero.

—Dieciocho —Roberto habló con una templanza que fue derrotada por un eructo.

—¿No le da vergüenza, venir tan pedo y con menores? Vamos con el Inspector Autoridad.

Detrás de su escritorio, un hombre estaba absorto en las páginas cafés y blancas de un periódico deportivo.

miento de sombras, un reflector seguía al cuerpo blanco y las cabezas del público oscilaban como anémonas al fondo del mar.

Las mujeres llegaban precedidas por un nombre de leyenda, bailaban sin gracia, se quitaban las breves lentejuelas y pasaban a la parte central del espectáculo, que consistía en abrirse numerosas veces, en no ser más que un sexo, un filo rojo precisado por los binoculares. Con un espanto reverencial vi esa zona cruda, mientras Tehui, con parda monotonía, repetía los sinónimos de vagina que escuché en aquella primera comunión.

Si en el guardarropa de Rita sentí la atracción de las veladuras, los cierres, los broches, los encajes que podían llevar a un cuerpo, ahí el espectáculo funcionaba por reducción; las mujeres se desvestían hasta no ser más que unos centímetros de sexo expuesto.

Una jovencita fue despedida entre silbidos.

—Le faltan chichis —explicó Tehui.

Sólo entonces, cuando la vio desaparecer de prisa hacia la cortina negra, con el bikini de lentejuelas aferrado al pecho, Mauricio supo que era el cuerpo que más le había gustado.

La mujer pequeña debía tener un efecto de contraste porque después vino una giganta a escala perfecta para un teatro de 500 butacas.

—Glenora *la Imposible* —fue la única contribución de Roberto a la discusión de los cuerpos.

La mujer tenía una flexibilidad impensable en alguien de su tamaño. Se contorsionó como si tratara de batir un récord oriental. El público se enardeció al verla pasar los pies atrás de la cabeza y caminar con las manos por la pasarela.

—¡Pe-los, pe-los! —era la básica urgencia de la multitud.

Sin cambiar de postura, la giganta se sacó el calzoncito, y avanzó como una aterradora araña. Lue-

En cuanto a la clase de Moral, el profesor estaba en desventaja. Nadie estaba dispuesto a entregarse al vicio, no se diga de aprender, sino de permitir que el maestro hablara.

Moral estaba a cargo de un marista semihistérico, que desde la primera sesión admitió su falta de control:

—¡¿Qué me ven una P en la frente?! —exclamó al ser alcanzado por una cáscara de naranja.

Todo mundo le vio la P en la frente.

Tal vez porque pensaba que el sacrificio era el nombre oculto de la moral, soportó las cerbatanas, las burlas, las risotadas, sin expulsar a nadie. Se golpeaba la frente con el puño cerrado, entre una lluvia de papeles, la mirada húmeda hacia el techo de asbesto. Quizá sentía un oscuro placer de ser humillado por cuarenta pupilos; lo cierto es que jamás logró inculcarle a Mauricio el temor de Dios que la Constitución prohibía y su madre deseaba.

Mientras tanto, por descuido, o porque ya había sido expulsado de tantas escuelas que ésa resultaba la única opción, los padres de Pancho inscribieron a su hijo en un colegio activo. Sus diferencias se agrandaron; en lo que Mauricio miraba sin ganas los balones inflados por la fe, Pancho se enteraba de métodos anticonceptivos y perfeccionaba sus tesis olfativas.

En el palco del teatro sentí un vago orgullo por la forma en que pecaba: estar ahí era salvar distancias con Pancho.

—*Pelícanos* —dijo Tehui, sin despegarse de su mira telescópica. Sólo entonces Mauricio entendió que se refería al vello púbico de las desnudistas.

La mujer se había desvestido de prisa y ahora abría las piernas. En las primeras filas había un movi-

Cuando en Terminal Progreso se corrió la voz de que Jesús Guardiola se llevó sus camisas negras a otra parte, Mauricio recurrió a una prueba técnica y patética:

—¡Pero si ahí está su cama!

Las camas gemelas seguían en el cuarto, pero eso no probaba nada. Por entonces, Mauricio vio el primer Informe de Gobierno de su vida, y entre las cuatro horas de tedio entresacó una frase que le hizo daño: México era "una isla en el mar convulso de América Latina". Pensó en la cama de su padre, que conservaba su olor de perfumado desván, una balsa en la tormenta de los otros.

De cualquier forma, nada pudo impedir que en las calles cristalizara la palabra "divorciados", el último fracaso de una familia expulsada por los terremotos. En el refrigerador, la nueva moral materna agravó las cosas; las frutas imantadas sostuvieron mensajes sobre Mundo, Demonio y Carne. Además, Cristina Ferrán cambió a sus hijos a un colegio católico. Hasta entonces Mauricio había usado el uniforme color cartón de la escuela de gobierno Héroes de la Reforma que desde su nombre celebraba a quienes se calentaron las manos en las hogueras de santos y altares.

La nueva escuela, única en su género en Terminal Progreso, no admitía mujeres e ignoraba la existencia de los Libros de Texto; allí había dos cursos cuyos rigores se confundían: Futbol y Moral. Para los hermanos maristas "formarse como hombre" implicaba saber entrar al área chica. Mauricio odiaba el deporte, era pésimo en cualquier sector de la cancha, pero el futbol resultó una disciplina insoslayable; había que correr para no imaginar largas pepas, había que cabecear para no masturbarse, había que romperse la rodilla para evitar las visitaciones de la carne suave; sus jadeos de gordo y sus caídas sobre la hierba se convirtieron en constantes de esa educación bárbara.

qué Zapata, Carranza y Obregón, si eran héroes, se persiguieron hasta el asesinato— que su familia era conservadora, es decir, que coleccionaba fotos donde los hombres miraban a la cámara con énfasis de propietarios y las mujeres se recogían el pelo con una enjundia destinada, no a despejar el rostro, sino a hacerse daño. Cuando Tranquilino, el hermano mayor de mamá, se refería al país decente en el que alguna vez íbamos a vivir, me maravillaba que en sus labios el futuro se pareciera tanto a una época sin electricidad. La decencia no admitía enchufes ni diversiones. Cuando mis parientes ahorcaran a los políticos corruptos, México sería un país honesto y lento. Poco a poco Mauricio fue entendiendo que el terror de su familia materna provenía de una doble certeza: que la Revolución mexicana fue socialista y que no había terminado.

Para Tranquilino las mujeres que se pintaban las uñas de los pies (salvo Amelia, el colorido enigma familiar) eran putas. Mamá no cayó en un fundamentalismo semejante, pero la separación la hizo buscar "lo suyo", es decir, avanzar hacia el pasado. Los meses que pasó en Culiacán, velando la agonía de su tío, le revelaron lo lejos que estaba de su esposo. Ya en México, recuperó a suficientes condiscípulas de su colegio de monjas ursulinas para fundar una rondalla. Al conocerme, las "muchachas", como las llamaba mamá, se ponían la mano en la boca (esto significaba que me parecía a mi madre); luego hablaban de mi pelo largo (esto significaba que me parecía demasiado).

A mí no me importaba hablarle a Pancho de nuestras visitas a los moteles, y me reía como un zombi feliz cuando Martín acusaba a mi padre de *caliente*. En cambio, Mauricio empezó a ponerse nervioso por cosas raras; de repente caía en una ansiedad de apariencias; su padre lo representaba, en su conducta hablaba nuestra sangre.

Un disco herido por mil agujas propagó la canción "El cubanito". Un hombre delgado en extremo, de pantalón amarillo y saco rojo, se contoneó ante el público. Ajusté mi mira de cazador y pude ver las arrugas en torno a los ojos, el pelo de un negro artificial, carbónico, la sonrisa amarillenta, la piel en la que parecía no correr la sangre. Todo se empeñaba en ser antiguo esa noche.

La tarea del bailarín consistía en enardecer al auditorio. El abucheo y la injuria eran su sueldo. Tenía una sonrisa falsa, pegada al rostro, y miraba con coquetería a las primeras filas. Algunos se ponían de pie para escupirle. Él se llevaba un dedo a la solapa en la que supuestamente había caído la saliva y lo chupaba con deleite.

El tío miraba el espectáculo con calma; en su sonrisa se dibujaba la experiencia de quien ha visto toda clase de extremos naturales; conocía las vísceras, las pieles frescas, el apareamiento de los tapires y las heces de los reptiles. Tehui conservaba el noble aplomo de las piedras. Yo tenía el estómago lleno de comida y vacío al mismo tiempo, la seña inconfundible de que cualquier cosa que pasara sería desconocida.

En el teatro recordé la vocación que el cura J creyó ver en mí y los extenuantes esfuerzos de mamá por hacernos vivir "de otro modo". Las ráfagas de los reflectores me llevaron a otros ámbitos, a escenarios que debían recordarme la existencia del pecado.

Mamá se independizó lo suficiente para ir en coche a lugares a los que podía ir a pie, pero también se afianzaron en ella creencias que de tan profundas habían pasado inadvertidas: colgó un rosario del espejo retrovisor del Lyngam Bis y encajó unas palmas secas en el marco de la puerta de su cuarto. Ya sabíamos —incluso yo, que nunca lograba entender por

tentar en foto su tersura de obispo niño. De algún modo, su quietud era la síntesis de los letargos que Mauricio empezaba a abominar: mis tardes en la cama, la obligada inmovilidad del Bello Durmiente, los años sin mundo de Verónica.

Mauricio decidió hablar con Pancho de sus nuevas aprehensiones. Su mejor amigo se limitó a decir: "Aprovecha tus instantes, sólo se vive una vez." Pancho había superado el miedo a la muerte con este lema vitalista; saltaba de un momento a otro, lo exprimía como si fuese el último. (Mauricio sospechó que le contaba sus lances con hombres y mujeres porque su gordura lo convertía en un bulto asexuado, incapaz de comprometer al deseo.)

Mauricio y yo no coincidíamos en nada. ¿Cómo encontrar "nuestros" instantes? Yo me divertía pateando un charco de agua y Mauricio siempre quería algo impreciso pero definitivamente distinto; se asustaba de lo que le gustaba y al mismo tiempo despreciaba mis ganas de extender los brazos y tronar la boca como un aeroplano. "No sé si me gusta alguien", le confesé a Pancho, con infantil brutalidad.

Él mostró que podía rivalizar con Clarita en pedagogía olfativa: "Piensa en su mierda; si caga y no te da asco, es que te gusta."

Todo esto se mezcló en el rancio aire del palco. Mauricio pensó en la muerte para que la tristeza lo calmara, pero sólo recuperó la inquietud de su vida sin instantes.

Se volvió a su derecha: Tehui asomaba medio cuerpo del palco, como una gárgola, o más precisamente, como el mascarón de alguna pirámide al dios de los pantanos.

Las luces se apagaron entre un alarido ensordecedor.

—¡Pasarela monumental presenta...! —la voz del micrófono fue cubierta por una lluvia de silbidos.

profetizada por Clarita, un terremoto superior al de su nacimiento, una magna tragedia de la especie. Lo insoportable era el mundo donde él desaparecía y los tranvías seguían corriendo, ajenos e insaciables, como los trenes de Felipe Jurado.

Supuso que su madre, tan proclive al sufrimiento, podría ayudarlo. Mauricio quiso tratar el tema con entereza, pero yo me rebelé y hablé con escabroso deleite de la muerte con gusanos.

Mamá me vio con ternura conventual:

—Todos pensamos cosas raras. Te voy a mostrar algo muy bonito.

Trajo una fotografía vieja: una familia alineada tras una mesa en la que reposaba un niño con extraña vestimenta.

—Es tu tío Gilberto. Mi hermanito. Murió a los cuatro años. Lo vistieron de obispo para la foto. ¿Verdad que parece un angelito?

Mamá tenía entonces dos años y aparecía en brazos de su abuelo, muy sonriente.

—Es de mala suerte llorar mientras toman la foto; nos vemos recontentos. Mira nomás el brocado, no creas que cualquier familia puede vestir de obispos a sus muertes niñas.

Observé con detenimiento las ropas de luto de los familiares, la mitra y el cetro en miniatura. Una sensación de sarcófago de cristal, de muerte enjoyada. Me pregunté qué hubiera sido de mí en caso de morir en el terremoto, ¿me habrían vestido de obispo? Me identifiqué a fondo con las pequeñas manos enguantadas y los anillos de pedrería hasta que descubrí, con más horror, que para mamá la muerte era un acto sin otras molestias que escoger las ropas adecuadas y decidir la categoría eclesiástica con la que el difunto viajaría a "mejor vida".

El tío Gilberto no tuvo tiempo de pecar. Como las novias del Café Shangai, estaba condenado a os-

se movieran con simiesca rapidez. En la intrincada gestualidad del graderío, predominaba el piquete a las costillas.

Mauricio sintió un latido en las sienes, activado por las pastillas y el nerviosismo. Sabía que la forma de salvarse, de salir mentalmente de allí, era asumir un temor mucho más profundo, la certeza que lo perseguía en los últimos meses: el muerto que iba a ser.

Aquel recinto era un buen testimonio de la descomposición; la tela hecha jirones en los respaldos de los asientos, el olor marino de las duelas, los focos fundidos convertían al teatro en un hueco donde las cosas tenían su término. Mientras veía el foso lleno de sogas y desperdicios, trató de sentir la lenta, inescapable caricia de la muerte.

Mauricio podía pasar horas viendo las torres de alta tensión, los esqueletos que anunciaban el inevitable fin de la ciudad. La muerte llenaba sus días; la fascinación que me despertaban las torturas se había vuelto intolerable para él; Mauricio sólo pensaba en el momento final, el eclipse de las vidas, la de la increíble Rita, la de Verónica, sin una ventana a la cual llamar, la de Martín, que se llevaría todos sus parecidos. Incluso el hermoso cuerpo de Pancho tenía, en algún sitio recóndito, la seña fatal, el destino que lo vencería.

Traté de superar esta crisis solazándome en los detalles escabrosos, buscando la intoxicante belleza del mal en el pelo y las uñas que crecían en la tumba. Algo me quedaba del gusto por las estatuas de santos con cabello auténtico porque estuve a punto de superar el nihilismo por el camino de la necrofilia. Sabía que a cualquiera le gustan sus propios pedos y ensayé una estética de la descomposición para disfrutar mi propio cadáver.

Mauricio pensaba todo el día en la muerte porque no la soportaba. Tal vez hubiera tolerado la idea de una caída de conjunto, la explosión nuclear

—¡Sus anteojos para ver *pelícanos*! —gritaba un vendedor de binoculares.

—No sabes lo que es pureza de alma —le dijo Tehui, refiriéndose, en este caso, a nuestras miras telescópicas.

Mi tío entregó los boletos y no tuve el menor problema en pasar: él se veía tan sospechoso que nadie reparó en mí; su chamarra con bolsas de campaña fue inspeccionada hasta que apareció la cantimplora de whisky.

—Está prohibido introducir bebidas. Si quiere se la guardo —ofreció el policía.

—No se preocupe, yo *me la guardo* —Roberto procedió a beber ahí mismo lo que quedaba en la cantimplora. La volteó, para demostrar que estaba vacía: una gota lenta se formó en el borde y cayó al suelo.

El policía no lo detuvo porque la gente, harta de aguardar tras la corpulenta chamarra del tío, empezó a colarse sin presentar boleto.

Mi tío llegó a donde lo esperábamos:

—Fuímonos —Tehui señaló las escaleras.

Nos ubicamos en un palco. El teatro tenía demasiados focos fundidos en los candiles. Las figuras entre mitológicas y eróticas apenas se intuían en el techo y evocaban un lujo de otros tiempos. Un espacio cubierto de terciopelos color borgoña, panas, finas telas raídas. El foso para la orquesta se había transformado en un depósito de tramoya; las sogas y los tablones se enredaban en la sombra. El ambiente tenía ese aroma que se encajona en los túneles de los estadios, una atmósfera de trabajo duro, ropas muy usadas, antojitos en los que abundaban la cebolla y el cilantro. De vez en cuando el aire era roto por una carcajada brutal o un grito abstracto, un chirrido de tucán.

Ni siquiera en los días del Bello Durmiente conocí a una multitud tan expectante. Sin embargo, la tensa espera no impedía que los brazos y las piernas

adolescentes con hilo y aguja de maguey, una versión bárbara del "elefantito". Para el tío Roberto las heridas tenían un valor moral. No era extraño que un cazador pensara que los tajos fuesen plegarias. Mauricio toleraba sus descripciones porque estaba seguro de que jamás volvería el siniestro esplendor azteca.

—Fuímonos —dijo Tehui.

—Ahorita vengo —dije.

En el baño del Café Shangai saqué dos mejorales y los tragué en seco. Tenía taquicardia y sabía que las pastillas no me ayudarían en lo más mínimo, pero necesitaba que algo me alterara. Me miré al espejo, gordo, joven hasta la náusea. Luego vi mi medalla de la Virgen. Para calmarme pensé en mi solución favorita de los quince años: la muerte. Algún día, los turgentes cuerpos que anunciaba el Teatro Iris seguirían el destino de las novias del Café Shangai. ¿Para qué preocuparse si no éramos más que el anticipo de nuestras calaveras? Esta consideración, que tantas veces me ayudó a seguir en la cama y olvidarme del examen del día siguiente, ahora sirvió para encarar al tío Roberto:

—Vamos —dijo Mauricio, y recogió una última visión de la anciana que atendía la caja.

—Toma —Roberto-Tizoc le tendió una mira telescópica, que había pertenecido a un rifle 30.06.

En tardes de ocio habían usado las miras para espiar el baño de unas sirvientas en el edificio de enfrente. Los cuerpos morenos, regordetes, ranurados por la mira, tenían algo frutal: el ojo practicaba gajos en esa desnudez de chicozapote.

—Pon cara de adulto —dijo el tío.

No se me ocurrió otra solución que ver el piso.

De nuevo encontré a la multitud masticadora de pepitas, seña inequívoca del Acontecimiento.

—Calma, Tizoc —dijo Tehui.

Había mucha gente en el estacionamiento pero aún era temprano.

—Espérenme aquí —Roberto fue a comprar las entradas. De reojo, Mauricio vio los carteles que anunciaban mujeres envueltas en plumas, con nombres de fábula: Glenora *la Imposible*, Perséfone, Rebis Star.

Mataron el tiempo en el Café Shangai. Tal vez por influencia del teatro, las paredes estaban decoradas con fotos de mujeres, casi todas tenían rasgos achinados. Las caritas polveadas miraban a la cámara con preocupación, como si temieran los efectos de su belleza.

Roberto preguntó por las "chamacas" y el dueño, un chino con peluca rojiza, habló de una agencia de novias; las fotos venían de un catálogo de propaganda.

Al tío le pareció estupendo que en su primera noche de picos pardos, Mauricio encontrara a las famosas novias de la suerte.

—¿Podemos pedir una para mi sobrino?

El dueño rió a carcajadas; movió los hombros como un muñeco descoyuntado, tosió, tuvo que tomar agua. ¡Las novias de la pared ya tenían sesenta años! Mauricio trató de asociar esas pieles tersas con la vieja que atendía la caja. Tal vez ella había salido del catálogo. También Roberto la miró largo rato y dijo:

—Las novias chinas *traían* suerte.

Para cambiar de tema sacó las piedras de jade que llevaba en los bolsillos del pantalón para conservar su "eje magnético" y habló del esplendor azteca.

Le pregunté de África, aunque sabía que era de lo único que nunca hablaba. Se hizo el desentendido y habló de un castigo (aunque en el sistema de recompensas prehispánico podía tratarse de un premio) que consistía en atar los penes de un grupo de

Bajo los banderines multicolores de super remate, el tío encontró a un cliente improbable. Lo más
interesante del coche que le compró mamá era que
no lo necesitaba.

Hay vidas tan sosegadas que la adopción de
una manía parece un cambio de carácter. Con la separación, mamá empezó a usar su apellido, insólito de
tan postergado, se dejó crecer el pelo y compró vestidos con muchos botones, de tela gruesa, que la hacían verse moderna de un modo subordinado, como
una recepcionista del futuro.

Roberto le vendió un Lyngam Bis color agua
de jamaica. Como le faltaban sitios a dónde ir, mamá
decidió enseñarle a manejar a sus amigas. Mauricio
vio con desconfianza esa escuela con malos frenos. Al
igual que su madre, las mujeres de Terminal carecían
de un destino que las obligara a llegar, no se diga
rápido, sino siquiera a tiempo. El auto fue una acade-
mia circular: aprender a conducir servía para enseñar
a conducir.

A Lupe Beltrán los nervios la hacían tartamu-
dear cada vez que tenía que decidir entre té o café.
Para tranquilizarla en su primera lección, mamá le dijo:

—Te tengo tanta confianza que traje a mi hijo.

Si durante años su padre usó a Mauricio para
que su esposa no sospechara de él, su madre lo usó
para que sus amigas no sospecharan de sí mismas.

La presencia de Mauricio le dio a Lupe y a otras
tardías conductoras suficiente presencia de ánimo para
lanzarse a las calles a producir choques menores.

El Lyngam Bis se llenó de abolladuras y fue
imposible imitar la extraña pintura color jamaica. En
unos meses quedó tan victimado como el lanchón de
Tehui, en el que Mauricio evocó las tardes de pánico
en las que él simbolizó confianza.

—"Ya vamos llegando a Pénjamo" —canturreó
Roberto.

—En *De inmenso et innumerabili*, Giordano Bruno habla de serpientes enroscadas para representar la unión del Sol y la Tierra.

¿Eran los hermanos Guardiola iguales a las serpientes? ¿Aludía a la secta de Quinto Sol y su entusiasmo por el dios reptil?

Lo cierto es que las citas y los latinajos estaban de parte de mamá. Cualquier cosa que oliera a *Aqua ardens* debía arrojarse a la basura. El mapa de París y la reproducción de Palladio acabaron en el patio trasero, junto a una acacia secada por un trueno.

Cristina Ferrán seguía viendo al tío Roberto porque tenían un enemigo y un patrocinador común. En una ocasión el cazador coincidió frente a un té de tila con Clarita. Aunque la atmósfera era perfumada, ella olió con sospecha las botas de taxidermista y volvió a la carga con Giordano Bruno.

—Con todo respeto, señora, pero las serpientes que se aparean traen buena suerte —Roberto enroscó el índice y el cordial—; se lo dice alguien que nunca tuvo la suerte de encontrarlas.

—Tal vez las serpientes animales son positivas, pero no las imaginarias —dijo la doctora.

Todo mundo se refugió en su taza y la incomprensión tuvo un olor fragante.

Roberto trabajaba en SUPER REMATE DE AUTOS. Tal vez llegó ahí atraído por el nombre cinegético o por los venados que decoraban el establecimiento. Se sentaba en una silla plegadiza y de vez en cuando se acercaba a un coche para patearle una llanta, un gesto canónico que significaba "solidez y velocidad". Trabajaba por comisión y conseguía apenas lo suficiente para pagar el whisky, las cuotas de Quinto Sol y la búsqueda de chinas de la suerte.

parte de mamá, como antes lo estuve de Rita. Por desgracia, Mauricio también envenenó esta preferencia. Con inquina, con detallada crueldad, me hizo sentir que yo cambiaba de bando en el último momento. En mi vanidad de sombra, de testigo hiperpresente, quería compartir las culpas dé mi padre, como si también yo hubiera regalado hipócritas koalas de peluche, como si hubiera arrebatado algo, los mejores años de una vida, la exigua reserva de felicidad de las mujeres que se arreglaban para nosotros con un entusiasmo sin límites. Así, en el momento final, al intuir a la mujer que fumaría a solas después de tantas mentiras y tantos discos de *twist*, me sentía en el equipo de las víctimas; entreveía con pavor el momento en que mi padre me dejara en un cuarto de alquiler, llorando sobre una colcha de peluche, mordiendo la almohada con una desesperación de fin de mundo.

Mauricio estaba de parte de mamá por razones muy distintas. Con la separación, mi padre la expondría a la posibilidad de ser penetrada por otro hombre. Mauricio era capaz de imaginar con repugnante minucia las aberraciones a las que podía llegar aquel cuerpo abandonado. A mí no me preocupaba en lo más mínimo que una mano grande y cubierta de pelos pudiera hacerse cargo de los catorce botones del camisón color tuna; al contrario, sabía que eso podía significarme regalos y la oportunidad de ver cosas raras. Pero Mauricio llegaba a mí como una peste que todo lo cuestiona. ¿Alguna vez sería capaz de abandonarse a mis deleites, de lamer sin remilgos el dulce de tamarindo que unté en las axilas de Regina?

A partir de la separación, Clarita visitó a mamá más seguido. Decía cosas terribles que no sabíamos interpretar. Por ejemplo:

Tres horas después, los mejorales habían aminorado su efecto y en el atrio no quedaba sino una sirvienta que recogía los platos sucios. Al pie de la fuente, me costó trabajo conservar la perspectiva segura de la azotea. Había recuperado mi rostro de aflicción y me trajeron un libro. Me concentré en la ilustración de un submarino apresado por un calamar gigante. Empezaba a identificarme con la asfixia de los hombres de escafandra, cuando una sombra oscureció el libro. Alcé la vista y aun a contraluz distinguí los ojos húmedos de mi padre. Me abrazó con fuerza.

Lloré tanto que le empapé la camisa y le arranqué un botón de un mordisco.

Gemí, con los labios cerrados para no escupir el botón, sintiendo la tela húmeda y fría en mi mejilla.

Cuando nos separamos, el atrio se encendía con la luz de las doce. ¡Con cuánto cuidado planeó mi padre aquella hoguera! Repasé el botón con la lengua, y decidí tragármelo.

A una semana de esta precipitada comunión, Jesús Guardiola se mudó al departamento que le había instalado a su hermano Roberto. Para Mauricio, esta convivencia fue una extravagancia mayor que abandonar a la familia. ¿Cómo era posible que alguien que apreciaba la forma en que el jugo de naranja combinaba con las servilletas de papel solferino, tolerara a un hermano que desayunaba latas de carne?

La separación de mis padres coincidía con mis propios conflictos de separación; Mauricio no se decidía a desprenderse; se limitaba a despreciar mi pericia para hurgar en la nariz y encontrar algo aún en temporadas secas.

Yo amaba a mi padre con parcialidad, pero rara vez le daba la razón en sus pleitos. Estuve de

en hablar de los "materiales nobles" como si fueran barro místico.

Uno de tantos sábados hubo un banquete en el atrio. Me divertí mucho porque un desconocido de 17 años decidió beneficiarme con un consejo: en el mundo no había nada mejor que mezclar mejorales con Coca-Cola.

La droga me ayudó a subir sin miedo, una y otra vez, los estrechos escalones que llevaban a la azotea (había que avanzar de lado, como en las pirámides mayas, para no darle la espalda al invisible dios).

En una de mis ascensiones me detuve a ver el atrio. El corazón me latía con fuerza, el sudor me chorreaba por la cara y yo bebía el refresco en tragos golosos, como si participara de la histérica vitalidad de un anuncio de televisión. Tenía los dedos llenos de tierra y los lamí con deleite.

Mauricio distinguió a sus padres allá abajo; se habían apartado del resto de los comensales y discutían con un interés que nunca les había visto. Se les acercó un párroco y el arquitecto lo empujó con fuerza.

Cristina Ferrán se cubrió la cara y abandonó el atrio. En la mesa todos dejaron de masticar; durante un segundo denso los tenedores quedaron quietos en el aire y una mosca gorda se detuvo a beber en la patilla de Mauricio. Luego volvió el murmullo distante de los cubiertos, el zumbido próximo al oído, los treinta sinónimos que el amigo de ocasión ofreció para "vagina".

Algo se fracturó en ese momento en que Mauricio estaba en lo alto, seguro, lleno de energía, viendo la separación de sus padres mientras una boca fanática pronunciaba "papaya", "chocho", "pepa"...

Jesús Guardiola se acercó al sacerdote que había empujado, hizo ademanes largos, juntó las manos en señal de súplica y se alejó de ahí, con pasos resueltos.

tón, a la vasta franja de los normales. Sin embargo, al reflejarse en Verónica, esa educación semejaba un esfuerzo tan inútil como el del maniaco de la primera fila que memorizó 54 dígitos de Pi.

—"Picos pardos" —la reiterada promesa del tío Roberto olió a whisky.

De un modo gráfico, la expresión aludía a un paisaje para cazadores; de un modo vago, a las correrías nocturnas; de un modo hermético, al sexo.

—¿Otro traguito? —preguntó Roberto.

—El tráfico está de pronóstico —dijo Tehui, para quien lo estupendo y lo pésimo eran "de pronóstico".

Roberto-Tizoc chasqueó los labios con deleite. Una tibieza alcohólica flotaba en el Kan. El tío siempre había sido un bebedor fuerte, y regresó de África con una mirada borrosa que se le fijaba al tercer whisky. Estuvo tanto tiempo allí que los trofeos que trajo parecieron pobres (una piel de cebra, los salomónicos cuernos de un ñandú, una pelambre casi abstracta). Resultaba difícil justificar sus meses de ausencia y la casa hipotecada en Zacatecas.

—¡Puro frijol negro! —dijo Tehui después de la explosión en el escape.

—Ojalá encontremos una chinita —comentó Roberto.

—A lo mejor llegamos tarde —dije.

—No te preocupes, las chinas son pacientes —sonrió mi tío.

No sé cuántas veces visité la iglesia de mi padre. Tengo la impresión de que nos invitaban a bautizos y primeras comuniones de gente que no conocíamos y donde la función del arquitecto Guardiola consistía

Verónica volvió como si nada a los fogones de Terminal Progreso, metió su cuchara en los caldos donde flotaba el cilantro y apartó los trocitos de cebolla que seguían sin gustarle.

Los años de sondas no cambiaron sus preferencias. Ni la cebolla ni Martín eran lo suyo.

Sus ojos seguían siendo tristes y les atribuí causas inciertas. Tenía que sufrir mucho, no era posible que regresara sin alaridos, sin mensajes del "otro lado", sin un extraño placer de chupar tornillos. Sin embargo, las únicas pruebas de que algo singular le había ocurrido eran que iba al hospital cada quince días y que tomaba clases especiales a todas horas.

—Está rarísima —comentó Martín a los pocos días.

Estuve de acuerdo con Martín. Lo raro era su falta de tragedia.

Yo quería una loca, una beata profética, una visionaria muy dañada, una gritona incontenible o una pálida dispuesta a nuevos sufrimientos, a soportar sin pasmo los filos, las agujas, nuestra mala sangre. Verónica estuvo "privada", como decía mamá, y en el fondo de su encierro mental debieron pasar cosas. No podía ser como los que íbamos al pan, perdíamos un *gallito* de badmington en los llanos o memorizábamos faraones de Egipto.

Lamenté que desperdiciara sus opciones de pesadilla, y Mauricio sufrió otra clase de decepción: se comparó con ella, la comparó con los demás, y apenas encontró diferencias. ¡Nada había cambiado lo suficiente para que Verónica fuera extraña! Se alejó de los estudios y la experiencia sensible sin alcanzar notoriedad negativa. Más que resucitada, parecía descendida de cualquier camión. Y esto hablaba peor de Mauricio que de ella. ¿De qué le servía haber estado despierto? En su boleta de calificaciones el número 7 se repetía como un grito de que pertenecía al mon-

Sol aprendió la leyenda de Quetzalcóatl, "la criatura dual, pareja de sí misma, la serpiente emplumada que vinculaba la tierra y el aire". Su mente de safari se entusiasmaba con los dioses animales y le otorgaba al ajolote muchas posibilidades simbólicas. Lo híbrido, lo anfibio era algo que yo debía entender por "cursar la adolescencia". Pasaba horas describiéndome los ritos de iniciación aztecas; luego me preguntaba si ya tenía novia:

—De colega a colega, te recomiendo una china. Las novias chinas traen suerte.

En Terminal Progreso no abundaban las chinas. Sin embargo, una tarde en que llovió fuerte y el sol levantaba vapor del asfalto, ocurrió una aparición que equivalía a la llegada de alguien, no del otro lado del mundo, sino de otro planeta.

Supe que era ella porque al lado estaba su padre, con el pelo pajizo de siempre, y el rostro arrugado de un modo feliz.

Sólo entonces advertí lo acostumbrado que estaba a su presencia ausente, a que creciera detrás de su ventana, inescrutable, intacta.

Nunca fui capaz de darle actualidad; la imaginaba con un rostro de ocho años y un cuerpo conservado con esfuerzo, como una momia inyectada de plásticos perfectos.

Ahí, en la calle, me pareció larga, excedida; su estatura promedio tenía una naturalidad atroz. Me hubiera impresionado menos un fenómeno, una jorobada, una enana coja, un cuerpo que justificara el encierro y la enfermedad. Alguien tan llena de años faltantes merecía verse de otro modo.

—Está de mi vuelo —sólo el comparativo Martín se midió en ella.

poniendo trampas para coyotes en San Luis Potosí o guiando a turistas norteamericanos a cazar ocelotes y tigrillos en las selvas de Nayarit. Los pocos libros que había leído trataban de África y estaban resecos de tanto llevarlos a las excursiones.

Sin embargo, una y otra vez pospuso su expedición a las sabanas de Kenia. Siempre tenía deudas o un *jeep* que reparar.

En tierras pobrísimas, donde un jabalí era una presa extraordinaria, Roberto soñaba en las mesetas donde el viento traía el olor de los antílopes, en ríos calientes donde se sumergía a esperar que los leones llegaran a beber.

Cuando finalmente fue a África, no encontró lo que esperaba, o lo encontró demasiado tarde. El caso es que regresó vencido, casi mudo, con la mente en otra parte, como si padeciera un mal cuya condena incluía olvidar su causa. No pudo recuperar su vida en Zacatecas, le habló a su hermano menor y llegó a la ciudad de México como alguien salido de otro tiempo. Había perdido la costumbre de usar "calzado civil"; llevaba botas a prueba de reptiles. Para mí, sus ropas olían perfecto, curtidas por la muerte, los soles de Sonora, la sal gruesa de los taxidermistas.

Tal vez debió escoger la compañía de Carlos (compartían la pasión por dormir sobre las piedras y encender fogatas cuando no hay cerillos y la leña está húmeda); sin embargo, para Carlos los desafíos silvestres estaban en el presente, y Roberto era puro pasado. Conmigo podía replegar las aventuras a un territorio que lentamente se enriquecía con la imaginación. Además, a las evocaciones memoriosas agregaba las ideas de su sociedad teosófica.

Roberto desconfiaba del mexicanismo de su hermano, que sólo servía para alzar la cruz de los encomenderos o imitar haciendas coloniales. Él era un purista que defendía un país arcaico. En Quinto

—¡No saben lo que es pureza de alma! —Tehui esquivó su propia embestida a un taxi.

El tío Roberto sacó la cantimplora que siempre llevaba en la chamarra. Tomó un largo trago, luego sirvió un poco en la tapa para que Mauricio bebiera; el sabor y el efecto tranquilizante empezaban a gustarle.

Las historias del tío Roberto solían incluir bebidas. En una de sus expediciones pasó días persiguiendo un borrego cimarrón, durmió en riscos y huecos de piedra hasta que finalmente logró derribar al animal. Durante tres jornadas, arrastró la presa al campamento. ¿Qué fue lo que hizo después de este lance épico? Bebió una jarra de vodka con jugo de naranja y se desmayó 36 horas. Todas sus anécdotas eran puntuadas por excesos masoquistas —alimentarse de raíces, orinar sangre después de recorrer la sierra a lomo de mula, quedarse inmóvil seis horas, descansar a la sombra de una biznaga, alejarse seis meses de su familia, volver a Zacatecas con el pie dormido por un piquete de víbora, sin saber que había un nuevo presidente—. No fue extraño que envejeciera rápido; en su género de vida calificaba como un retirado, ya no podía ir a los parajes de la caza mayor y su orgullo le impedía confinarse al rango menor de las escopetas.

Su cuerpo marcado por cicatrices se prestaba para los relatos. En Zacatecas, rodeado de sus nietos, con el infaltable paliacate para secarse el sudor, podría haber contado historias para sobrevivir con el honor de los parientes postergados, de quienes no se espera otra herencia que su condición de sombras narrativas.

Toda familia necesita sus "anécdotas locas". Roberto fue capaz de abastecer a su grey con historias excesivas hasta que un impulso, que para muchos llegó a destiempo, lo llevó a África. Sus mejores amigos habían matado elefantes mientras él se ganaba la vida

Mi única diversión en ese recinto austero fue robar hostias. Sin embargo, el sabor a engrudo contrarió a Mauricio (entre los vergonzosos agravios del mundo, había descubierto el mal aliento).

Sin embargo, los críticos de arte, del todo ajenos a mi sentido del exceso visual, festejaron la despojada elegancia de la obra. Nuestra casa se llenó de revistas costosas que hablaban de aquel "proyecto de ruptura".

El ambiente recoleto de la capilla, pensado para que los fresnos inquietaran con sus sombras el atrio blanco, para que el sol se refractara en las celosías y chorreara como una quemante sombra por la fachada naranja, participaba de las duplicidades del arquitecto Guardiola. De algún modo, la iglesia le sirvió para expiar culpas pasadas y pagar en piedra su felicidad futura.

Cristina Ferrán fumaba poco pero con extraña importancia: retenía el humo mucho tiempo y miraba a su marido como si ahumara las palabras que pensaba dirigirle. Hacía mucho que no le decía "Chus". No tenía nada qué pedirle.

Cuando él trataba de tocarla, ella retiraba la mano.

—Es mi cruz —le decía por teléfono a sus parientes—, no, no tengo cara para eso.

Sabíamos lo que iba a pasar en cuanto tuviera "cara". En la casa ya se respiraba esa enfermedad insólita en los hogares de Terminal Progreso. Me sentía culpable de que mis padres siguieran juntos (mi romance con Regina los había empujado a una lealtad suicida); en cambio, Mauricio temía que se separaran, anticipaba la vergüenza, los chismes corrosivos, el desprestigio que llegaría con la palabra "divorcio".

diendo con la contaminación, hacía que los sacerdotes hablaran mucho de santos en las nieves. San Goar Alpino era de los favoritos; lo mismo que el tocayo de nuestro patrono, San Bernardino de Aosta, cuyo hospicio en los Alpes salvó a numerosos extraviados en las tormentas. Me cautivaban los especializados heroísmos de la santidad: San Cristóbal era patrono de los navegantes, pero si uno viajaba entre la nieve, más valía encomendarse a San Bernardino (no en balde un paso de los Alpes y los perros rescatistas se llamaban como él). La prédica general podía aburrirme pero los detalles me cautivaban. Todo esto era absurdo para Mauricio, que parecía tener una atención de conjunto; las situaciones le disgustaban en bloque; si lo demás estaba mal, era incapaz de concentrarse en mirar el techo o hundir el pulgar en un frasco de miel. Tenía una inquietud fundamental, buscaba un centro que, sin saber cómo, se le había perdido. Mis sándwiches de tres mostazas, mis historias galácticas, las fantasías eróticas en las que intervenía una columna de fuego y la resistente ropa de azafata de Rita, eran intolerables para Mauricio; en su inseguro afán de perfección, en su ajuste a una realidad desconocida, temía que su camisa se manchara de sudor en las axilas (había descubierto que la gente era capaz de mirarlo con sospecha). Su voz fuerte llegaba cargada de ansias y debilidades. A veces, al despertar de madrugada, me dirigía al sofá al que antes me llevaron mis pasos de sonámbulo, y de rodillas, los codos apoyados en el cobertor de plástico, rezaba para no ser él.

La iglesia de mi padre parecía pensada para Mauricio, no para mí: se abstuvo de las truculencias, las cavidades umbrías, los adornos sin freno. Los reclinatorios seguían un diseño tan sobrio que sugerían una oficina para rezar.

un rebote histórico: gracias a la química y a los preceptos de la escuela Bauhaus haría su "contraconquista del espacio". El hecho de que las pirámides se hubieran despintado, no lo desanimaba; al contrario: la contraconquista se pintaría de *rojo resistente*, un tono azteca con técnica alemana.

En todo caso, la característica central de su arquitectura era que requería de explicación.

Del catálogo de tonos típicos, los dominicos escogieron un naranja que se llamaba "mostaza maya".

Por dentro, la nave era de una austeridad extrema, nada de altares laterales ni santos con ropajes recamados o agujeros sangrantes, nada de vitrales ni misteriosas escalinatas rumbo a la cripta de las reliquias.

Por aquellos meses, muchas de las cosas que me gustaban empezaban a ser detestadas por Mauricio. Mi fascinación por las estatuas de santos con pelo auténtico o por la ampolla de cristal, que contenía una astilla de la estaca que había logrado vulnerar el pulmón de un mártir, empezaba a darle asco. Tampoco compartía mi afición a tocar los blandos ajolotes. Mauricio era remilgoso y me sorprendía que crecer fuese adoptar sus fragilidades. Se preocupaba de sus olores y el estado de sus uñas; sentía obligaciones absurdas, por ejemplo "decir algo". Yo podía estar como una entidad de piedra, sin otra expresión que morderme la manga del suéter; pero a él le costaba sobrellevar los silencios. Tal vez su nueva voz reclamaba mayor presencia; cuando estaba acompañado y no mezclaba suficientes palabras en el aire, sentía un hondo fracaso.

Otro problema eran los intereses fáciles. Los sermones de la iglesia me aburrieron pero me distraje pensando en los distintos San Bernardos. La presencia de los volcanes, la impresionante vista que se iba per-

a los veinte años tendría ya la firmeza de un axioma; entre las muchas promesas que podía brindarle una mujer, su padre encontró en ella una primordial: salvarlo de la vida convulsa que tanto le gustaba.

Jesús Guardiola pasó del diseño de hoteles hedonistas a la iglesia donde sus escuetas ventanas lucieron más apropiadas. Los muros recibieron varias capas de pintura "mexicana". En las sobremesas, Mauricio se había familiarizado con las tesis pictóricas del arquitecto. La tríada verde-blanco-rojo se usaba para el patriotismo declarado (el uniforme de la Selección, los sobres aéreos, el escudo del Partido Oficial, el confeti del 16 de septiembre). Cuando lo auténtico servía de adorno, había que ampararse en el lila, el rojo tierra, el azul añil, el amarillo cremoso y, por supuesto, en el rosa. Cada tono tenía su historia; los frescos de Bonampak, los barrocos oros de Tepotzotlán, los neobarrocos blancos de Tonanzintla, las cajas laqueadas de Olinalá y las pinturas en amate de San Pablito brindaban un bazar retórico. Algunos colores incluso tenían el mérito de representar algo inexistente; el "rojo cochinilla", por ejemplo, trataba de emular el polvillo cárdeno, conseguido con la pulverización de gusanos de nopal, que dejó de fabricarse cuando los alemanes inventaron la anilina. La historia de Europa se apoderaba de este momento de la cátedra paterna: el rojo de la bandera de la Revolución Francesa provenía de cochinilla mexicana (sus ojos se desviaban al mapa de *París a vuelo de pájaro*, como si buscaran un sitio para un monumento al nopal de México y sus cromáticos gusanos). Pero los químicos alemanes, que jodieron el emporio henequenero de Yucatán con la invención del nylon, volvieron a joder con la anilina. México dejó de exportar colores, pero el arquitecto Jesús Guardiola preparaba

le fascinaba una puta; habló con cautivante desprecio del cuerpo enfermo que no podía dejar. Ya en la noche, con su linterna de ex Amigo del Bosque, le mostró a Mauricio su pene lastimado y el goteo que le solidificaba los calzones.

Gracias a Carlos, yo era un santo comparativo. Después del suspiro del padre J, mamá recordó que mis primos de Sinaloa eran monaguillos y empezó a llevarme a la iglesia de San Bernardino para fomentar mi vocación; nos arrodillábamos ante el retablo de Xochimilco donde el santo de Siena bendice con la mano izquierda y protege con la derecha. Lo más singular era el pelo, encrespado en tres momentos simbólicos: las tres potencias de Cristo. En los tempranos años setenta, cuando no había nada tan decisivo como el pelo, aquel copete que denotaba Sabiduría, Bondad y Misericordia tenía un valor estratégico.

Aunque el padre J aseguraba que San Bernardino fue un orador de "pico de oro", sus sucesores carecían de habilidad retórica y no fomentaban el atractivo espanto de las estampas de la papelería. Una vez más comprobé mi capacidad para los sueños rápidos: me dormí de rodillas, sentado y de pie. Mamá dejó de llevarme a la iglesia.

Más que devota, ella era beata. En caso de poder elegir, su religión favorita hubiera sido la que incluyera el manual de conducta más cargado. No se vestía de uniforme porque nadie se lo había asignado, pero actuaba como si perteneciera a una corporación llena de reglas. Quizá anticipaba un futuro ajeno a los caprichos individuales, lo cierto es que resultaba difícil entender su vida sin preferencias, manías, arrebatos, artistas de moda, antojos dulces. Mauricio se preguntaría muchas veces cómo fue que se enamoró de su padre, tal vez un oscuro sentido del deber la llevó a aceptar el cortejo. ¿Y por qué escogió él a Cristina Ferrán? Mauricio fue refinando una conjetura que

Durante el postre, el padre sólo se dirigió a mí. Mi pasión erótica me había llevado de los *comics* a buscar estampas de la hagiografía cristiana en la papelería. Mauricio tardaría años en saber que el San Andrés que más le gustó en la papelería era una desafocada reproducción de Rubens; en forma retrospectiva, iba a prestigiar su deseo, a compararse al fin con los selectos que tuvieron erecciones ante el San Sebastián de Guido Reni.

Cuando comimos con el sacerdote, yo sabía de mártires por un morbo puro y bastante cultivado; memorizaba las lanzas y los tizones que les habían hundido, los pechos y los ojos extirpados.

—¡Quedan muy pocas vocaciones! —el cura suspiró con aire melancólico.

La observación pareció apropiada, sobre todo porque también Carlos estaba en la mesa. Yo pasaba horas en la cama, y en aquella aldea donde sobraban formas nefastas de descargar las calorías, mi cuerpo postrado podía confundirse con una búsqueda religiosa. Carlos me realzaba por contraste.

En las situaciones más dispares, Mauricio iba a recordar la tarde de lluvia en que su padre reunió a los "hombres de la casa", se quitó el saco color atún, de solapa gigante, y habló del sexo con extraña naturalidad médica.

De todos modos Carlos no quería usar preservativo:

—Es como comer paleta con todo y papel —fue la primera metáfora que pronunció en años, o al menos la única que recordó Mauricio.

A diferencia de Pancho, que se hacía el interesante dejando inconclusas las historias, Carlos era incapaz, no sólo de adornar una anécdota, sino de saber que la estaba contando. En forma pedregosa dijo que

ceptos de refrigerador, mamá había escrito LOS SANTOS COMEN EN SILENCIO. El cura hacía un ruido abundoso, estupendo.

En la familia, sólo el tío Roberto comía en silencio absoluto, pero no por educación, sino para no espantar a los animales que podían acercarse al campamento.

Mamá decía que cada bocado debía masticarse treinta veces (no sé cómo llegó a esa estadística, supongo que escogió una cifra que causara la suficiente molestia para ser edificante).

El cura fue la única persona a la que vi masticar sus bocados más de treinta veces. Obviamente le pregunté acerca de mi favorito San Andrés:

—¡El magnífico Andrés! Fue el primero en unirse a Nuestro Señor. Se conocieron en la playa, entre los pescadores; las redes de Andrés atraparon muchas almas. En el *Timeo* de Platón, el demiurgo une las partes del alma del mundo con dos suturas que forman una cruz de San Andrés... —el padre se apartaba del tema; quise que volviera al aspecto técnico de la santidad de Andrés:

—¿Qué milagros hizo?

—Milagros sin número. En Niza liberó a la ciudad de siete perros que encarnaban el espíritu de Satanás; en Tesalónica salvó a un converso de una casa en llamas (sus padres lo habían dejado allí para morir). Escogió la cruz en equis para que su suplicio no rivalizara con el de Jesús. Todas las voces de "*cruz*", "*cross*", "*kreuz*", "*crux*" provienen de *ak ur os*, "luz del Gran Fuego". Andrés ardió pero no quiso que su luz opacara a la de nuestro Señor.

Me cautivaron los siete perros del diablo, el hijo lanzado a las llamas por sus padres, la voluntad de Andrés de encontrar un fuego cruzado, digno del mejor Vulcano.

Para nosotros la religión era una presencia obvia e impensada, como el ronroneo del refrigerador. En el censo, mamá nos definió como católicos, pero la auténtica fe sólo aparecía en los momentos de emergencia: mi padre se persignaba en los aviones y Carlos cuando jugaba el América.

El tío llegó a la capital en el momento en que la religión favorecía a mi padre. Los dominicos creyeron que tanta capacidad de encierro se sustentaba en la fe y le encargaron una capilla.

Jesús Guardiola pasó semanas "concibiendo" una cruz simplísima y un altar cúbico. Una tarde me dijo que la cruz era un "patíbulo", y la palabra me intrigó porque la primera expulsión de Pancho tuvo lugar cuando le encontraron unas fotos de la película *Los doce del patíbulo*; no me "completó la historia" y la mistificación se agrandó en mi mente; pensé que los doce eran "orgiastas" (esta palabra provenía de la tía Amelia; la pronunciaba con un énfasis más perturbador que su excesivo maquillaje).

La época patibularia de mi padre se extendió durante meses; no podía trazar una vertical sin añadirle un pío travesaño. Al ver sus desvelos, le hablé de la cruz de San Andrés.

—No seas raro —me dijo.

La equis se había vuelto inconveniente.

Cientos de hojas y trazos carbónicos pasaron de la casa al estudio y del estudio a la casa, como si la reiteración y los traslados convocaran al Divino.

En medio de estos trajines se hizo amigo de un sacerdote al que invitó a comer a la casa.

Mauricio recordaría siempre la calva perfecta, la piel protegida por aceites sólo asequibles en la diócesis, como si aquella pulida superficie fuese una constatación física de la fe.

El padre Jerónimo (¿o Julián?) tenía unos dientes fuertes que trituraban la comida. Entre sus pre-

años cabalgando por cuestas indómitas con mochilas y tiendas de campaña al hombro. Su piel se había secado con soles extremos y el polvo de los breñales. Su historial de heridas era largo: sordera del oído derecho por las detonaciones de alto calibre, una rodilla rota "en seis", que ahora le arruinaba los días de frío o de lluvia, una hernia inguinal, dos vértebras torcidas a causa de una caída, una cicatriz terrible en el pie derecho (se voló un dedo cuando la pistola se le disparó por accidente).

Sin embargo, lo que desesperaba a Jesús Guardiola era la crisis emocional de su hermano. Quizá pensaba que los hombres rústicos eran refractarios a los conflictos interiores; el caso es que no toleraba que alguien tan sujeto a los elementos, a buscar una cueva en la tormenta, a seguir el rastro del pavón por sus inconfundibles excrementos, a enterrarse de noche para sobrevivir al frío del alto desierto, tuviera las neurosis de la gente inmóvil.

Roberto pasó treinta y cinco años de su vida pelando liebres. Esta tarea ruda y pareja lo convirtió en alguien con pocas curiosidades y menos temas de conversación; sin embargo, no le otorgó el temple firme de quien sabe que no hay otros desafíos que pelar una liebre. A los ojos de su hermano, Roberto reunía lo peor de ambos mundos, las heridas del campo y los arrebatos emocionales de la ciudad.

Mauricio lo conoció como un hombre depresivo, que hablaba con melancolía del venado bura y miraba sus años futuros con nostalgia anticipada.

Cuando las noticias de Quinto Sol llegaron a Zacatecas, la esposa de Roberto habló por cobrar a casa de Mauricio. "Ácrata", "hereje", "apóstata", "iconoplasta" fueron algunas de las costosas palabras con que definió a su marido.

lazo en la camisa, pero Tehui opinó que era de mala suerte deshacerlo:

—El nudo es lo cerrado, el infinito, la ligadura.

Ninguna de estas tres cosas sonaban atractivas, pero tuvieron suficiente carga de solemnidad para frenar a Mauricio.

El Kan estaba mal alineado y amenazaba con invadir el carril de junto:

—¡Díscolos, no saben lo que es pureza de alma! —gritaba Tehui ante cada claxonazo.

Era incapaz de decir algo una sola vez. Quizá esto le venía de la sociedad Quinto Sol, donde él y Roberto recitaban eternas letanías en náhuatl.

El tío estaba en la ciudad porque se separó de su esposa en Zacatecas. No tenía mucho qué hacer, añoraba los parajes rurales y el pasado le parecía una región en la que aún había ciervos que cazar. Tal vez ésta fue una de las causas que lo llevó con los teósofos de Quinto Sol. La sociedad equivalía a una expedición a una zona oscura, una época que se decidía en pantanos y desiertos.

El ideario de Roberto-Tizoc incluía curas a base de magnetismo, la posibilidad de cargarse de energía viendo el cerro del Tepozteco (al que nunca iba), el retorno de los valores de Aztlán y el difusionismo sin fronteras (aseguraba que los vikingos habían estado en América, los mayas en la India, los tibetanos en Perú; su historia de las civilizaciones era un planeta de tribus sueltas).

Lo que Roberto afirmaba bajo el nombre de batalla de Tizoc servía, básicamente, para desquiciar a su hermano menor. El arquitecto Guardiola pasaba por una etapa decisiva en su trabajo, uno de esos momentos de "salto" en que nada agravia tanto como el origen.

El tío no llegaba a los cuarenta y cinco pero se veía mayor de cincuenta. Era completamente calvo y tenía una barriga injusta en alguien que pasó treinta

dos alumnas arrodilladas frente a él (las núbiles bocas se disputaban su sexo) y luego en el baño de hombres con el pene del profesor de gimnasia en su boca.

Siempre estaba presentando exámenes en la Secretaría de Educación. Las calificaciones le llegaban por correo, lo cual magnificaba aún más sus resultados: 9.5 en la época de los números, MB más tarde.

Si en mi infancia mamá no podía hablar de Pancho sin añadir "tan chulo", ahora le tenía pavor a algo que, a falta de mayor vocabulario, llamaba "su modito".

La verdad, era un modo único. Me asombraba su capacidad de hacer todo en forma imprevista. Lo desagradable eran esos vacíos: "luego te completo la historia".

En mi fiesta, me dejó con lo de las "niñas rudas" y fue a hablar con Eduarda y Martín de algo que llamaba "filosofía oriental" y en realidad era una gimnasia para sentarse con las piernas torcidas.

—Almuerza bien —me advirtió el tío Roberto, como si encabezara una excursión. Había sido cazador profesional y nada le parecía tan grave como "agarrar monte" con el estómago vacío.

El incierto Tehui tenía un Kan muy averiado, un lanchón que cada tantos minutos soltaba una flatulencia por el escape:

—¡En vez de gasolina le pongo frijoles!

Repitió lo de los frijoles hasta que tuve ganas de contribuir al ruido. Había cenado seis quesadillas sin hambre, por ciega obediencia al tío. Otro de sus consejos fue llevar corbata. Por alguna razón pensó que luciría mayor. No supe hacer el nudo; mi tío quiso ayudarme y sólo demostró que había tenido demasiadas sogas en sus manos. Quedé con un extraño

El futuro le parecía un sitio ajeno, como si ser "al fin él" fuese una suplantación, un disfraz para borrarme, para abandonar mis hormigas, mis cuadernos forrados de hule mordisqueado, mis noches de sonámbulo, mi imposibilidad de ganar la carrera o encontrar el escondite, mi temor sin freno a lo que de veras me gustaba.

Apagué las quince velas con gran revuelo de merengue, un zapato húmedo, todavía hundido en mis pasatiempos de ajolotes, y otro lustrado para elegancias que aún desconocía.

En la fiesta el tío Roberto sorbió su refresco de toronja con ruidosa ostentación, para que todo mundo advirtiera que no bebía otra cosa.

Luego me preguntó en voz baja:

—¿Todavía eres *quinto?*

Mauricio pensó en la virginidad. Yo pensé en la moneda que Martín arrojaba a la ventana de Verónica. Asentimos.

—Te voy a llevar al Iris —sonrió Roberto.

En la mente de Mauricio apareció un burdel circense, al que se entraba por un ojo gigantesco.

Esa misma tarde, Pancho ayudó a enrarecer la promesa del tío:

—Es un lugar de niñas rudas —al ver mi cara de confusión, agregó—: luego te completo la historia.

Ésta era su frase favorita. Llegaba con su camisa roja, de motas negras, y sus pantalones de mezclilla llenos de parches —un arco iris, un pez japonés, un círculo con las curvaturas del *yin-yang*— y dejaba sus historias inconclusas para subrayar que su interlocutor carecía de experiencia para "saberlo todo".

Pancho llevaba tres expulsiones escolares por su conducta de escándalo. En academias donde era delictivo llevar fotos de mujeres desnudas, se las arreglaba para compensar excesos en tercera dimensión: primero lo encontraron en el baño de mujeres con

—Nos vamos de picos pardos —repitió el tío Roberto.

No tenía coche y le había pedido a un compañero de su sociedad teosófica que nos llevara. Entre ellos estaba prohibido decir sus verdaderos nombres. Creo que el conductor se llamaba Tehui; en todo caso, Mauricio estaba seguro de que a su tío le decían Tizoc.

—Mira nomás —Roberto-Tizoc señaló los pechos minerales de la Diana Cazadora, como un anticipo de lo que íbamos a ver.

Cumplí quince años con ambivalencia; me esforzaba en ser otra persona, sabiendo que el proceso no dependía enteramente de mí. Mi voz oscilaba según las horas: en la mañana Mauricio habló en tono grave pero a las cuatro de la tarde, por teléfono, volvieron a decirme señorita.

Mauricio anhelaba la ronquera, el cambio de voz que llevó a Martín Cifuentes a parecerse a ese francés de gabardina, triste y acribillable. De cualquier forma, sentía que algo se quedaba detrás, perdido en el lejano andén de Terminal Progreso: una mano pálida, los cinco dedos que se abrían y se cerraban, la despedida favorita de los niños, el adiós que para él significaba "yo".

Durante meses, Mauricio se despidió de partes de su cuerpo que recuperaba cuando ya las creía perdidas.

4. Último safari

En su regazo, tal vez atraída por el calor del cuerpo o el diseño vegetal del vestido, reposaba una húmeda salamandra.

—Ahorita vengo —le dije a mi padre.

Corrí por calles que por primera vez me parecieron mías. Pero no calculé lo que sentiría al entrar a la tienda de trofeos. Regina sonrió con una felicidad que me hizo pedazos el estómago. No me atreví a decirle que me iba. Me dio un beso fuerte, me acarició el pelo:

—¿Qué crees?

Estaba contenta porque su hermana se había vuelto a embarazar. Aquel cuerpo extenuado era de una extraña fertilidad, como si procrear fuera su inacabable forma de consumirse.

—Tienes los ojos rojos —dijo, mientras yo pensaba en escribirle una carta.

Nunca había explicado nada por correo. Vi el sobre con ribetes tricolores, las hojas de mi cuaderno, las palabras lejanas que me iban a salvar y demostrarían que eso no era una huida.

La besé, despacio, con labios resecos.

—Luego vengo —prometí, y adentro se me rompió algo, un siseo de papel, el sobre que nunca llegaría.

Mi padre ya había encendido el motor del Kybalión. Subí sin darme cuenta de que lo hacía. Pensaba en Regina, la carta, Regina.

Fue un trayecto sin tiempo. De pronto vi la farmacia, la pecera con dulces de colores, como si despertara de un letargo.

—Te tengo una sorpresa —informó mi padre en la puerta de la casa.

Se refería a mamá. Mi tío abuelo había expirado en Culiacán y ella estaba de regreso.

Sin embargo, la auténtica sorpresa fue encontrarla desmayada en medio de la sala; respiraba con ritmo parejo, el pelo extendido en abanico, como una diva en su sobredosis.

Progreso que podían mutar con el yodo y el agua salada.

En los casi dos meses que estuve en el centro, crecí y engordé lo suficiente para que Clarita donara mis ropas a alguna Causa Justa (uno de los comités de solidaridad que le pedían firmas de apoyo a la salida de sus conferencias). Después me llevó al almacén El Tranvía. Aquel nombre anticipaba mi retorno a Terminal Progreso, y sus ropas grises, que lo haría en calidad de cobrador de boletos.

Sólo Regina fue capaz de elogiar mi descenso hacia esas prendas impersonales, severas, que tenían aire de uniforme por falta de otros atributos; el azul, el gris, el café sin variantes que suelen usar los huérfanos o los sordomudos.

Después de cambiar mi guardarropa, Clarita fue invitada a un congreso, y temí que me dejara hospedado entre sus siete puertas.

La doctora Rendón terminaba su ponencia sobre "El discurso de las flores en el siglo de las luces" cuando mi padre llegó a buscarme:

—Empaca tus cosas.

Fui a la cocina y recogí las cápsulas de hígado de bacalao que olvidé tomar desde mi llegada, metí las ropas tranviarias en la maleta, y al regresar a la sala encontré un espectáculo inusitado: Clarita lloraba, sin secarse las lágrimas, como si nunca lo hubiera hecho y desconociera la técnica de pasarse las manos por el rostro. Abracé su cuerpo de olor inconfundible.

¿Es posible entender la tristeza que suscita la pérdida de una vida odiosa? Mientras abrazaba a Clarita busqué asideros para ese tiempo cuya principal virtud era que ya había ocurrido. Sólo entonces pensé en la consecuencia más grave de mi regreso. Tenía que despedirme de Regina.

Yo sabía que mamá lloraba al otro lado de la línea. Aunque esta situación era mala, la visita de mi padre reveló que podía ser peor. La doctora y mi padre se aliaron en contra de Regina, como si también yo padeciera de servidumbre amorosa. Las llamadas a Culiacán fueron matizadas:

—Recapacita, mujer —decía Clarita, dispuesta a unir a mis padres con tal de que me llevaran con ellos a Xochimilco—. Tu hijo es más importante —la enemiga de los "instintos surgidos de la leche" recurría a cualquier bajeza con tal de privarme de lo que más me gustaba.

Empecé a aprovechar cualquier momento para besar el estómago blando y enrojecido de Regina. Ni ella ni yo alcanzamos a saber que estas acometidas se alimentaban de la fugacidad, de la amenaza, cada vez más cierta, de que nos iban a separar.

El Bello Durmiente salió de la mueblería en camilla. Quizá nunca recuperó la posición vertical; el reposo en público lo desgastó en tal forma que la residencia llena de melamina parecía un premio insignificante.

Terminado el concurso, también el hombre de los *hot-cakes* se fue con su ardiente parrilla a otros rumbos. Sus dientes triangulares, la voz hueca que me decía "princesa", las llamas que asomaban en el vientre de su carro y recordaban a la hornilla de Vulcano, me produjeron un pánico al que costaba trabajo renunciar; la tentación de ser su víctima, de arruinarme adrede, de convertir mi placidez en un drama escogido, se iba con la lengua roja y enrollada que prometía tragarme. Todo acababa en las calles del centro.

Empecé a comer pepitas en mis ratos libres (casi todos), como un adiestramiento para las sales de la madurez. Mi modelo evolutivo eran los ajolotes de Terminal

cuentas no era su tipo. Él, que pasó los mejores años de su juventud abandonando a las "existencialistas" que se atrevieran a decirle "no, chato", ahora, por necesario contraste, admiraba el rostro inteligente y aun el libro en la mano de la escritora.

—Nunca había tragado tanto —dijo Regina—. ¿Puedo pedir un postre?

—Adelante —mi padre extendió su mano de uñas manicureadas.

La curiosidad intelectual de sor Juana se concentró en nuestra mesa. ¿Qué postres escogería Regina? En la vitrina de la calle había fuentes con higos rellenos de coco, acitrones cristalizados, natillas, crujientes alegrías, pepitorias como hostias de fábula, barras de canela, blandas capirotadas. Por primera vez sentí que mi apetito por lo dulce armonizaba con la escuela a la que pertenecía mi padre. Sin embargo, él fumaba y aplastaba granos de azúcar.

Regina optó por la leche quemada y me encantó la forma en que sorbió la papilla *beige*.

Mi padre dejó la propina excesiva con la que ocultaba su disgusto en los restoranes.

A la salida tomé la mano de Regina, suave y pegajosa, como la huella que abría las puertas.

Mi padre se preocupó por mi destino pero no lo suficiente para abandonar sus obras y volver a la ciudad. ¡Tal vez si Regina hubiera comido más...!

En forma confusa yo sabía que mis padres no querían verse. Clarita era su absurda intermediaria. En las llamadas a Culiacán, enfatizaba la libertad individual y otras virtudes que aparentemente mamá no quería tener:

—Donde hay servidumbre no hay amor —fue una de las famosas frases que copié en mi cuaderno.

roce con tantos suéteres de hebras gruesas, entre las bocas trabajadas por pésimos dentistas, las manos con uñas negras que en cualquier momento pasarían del elote con crema a su cartera de becerro, las chamarras con la azulgrana escudería del Atlante, los zapatos salidos de Dios sabe qué subsuelo, las cabezas de pelos tiesos, en los que parecía sedimentarse la cal de los techos, pero por encima de todo, le repugnaba mi entusiasmo por el hombre execrado en la jaula de cristal, él, que vivía para rendirle cuentas al buen gusto, había engendrado al zombie que aplaudía las cagadas del Bello Durmiente.

La voz se estabilizó en las bocinas:

—Y ahora, el menú confeccionado por Carmello...

—Vámonos —ordenó mi padre.

Como yo quería ir al Café Superleche, fuimos al Café Tacuba.

Regina pidió tres platos fuertes y con la salsa del segundo en la boca se dirigió a mi padre:

—'tá usté reguapo —el piropo borboteó en sus labios; mi padre lo recibió como el húmedo beso de una mongólica.

Recordé la discusión de mi padre y Rita acerca de la belleza. ¿Lo que amamos es hermoso o nos parece hermoso? Regina no era ninguna de las dos cosas, no podía usar con ella el delator encubrimiento de la fealdad: "para mí es hermosa". No, para mí era fea, y me gustaba. La sabía grande, simple, enrojecida, extraordinaria.

Mi padre desvió la vista al óleo de sor Juana que decoraba la pared de enfrente y estudió a fondo los labios sensuales, el rosicler de las mejillas contrastado con el áspero hábito de la monja, la mano que sostenía la pluma con curioso equilibrio, el reloj quieto, los ojos de inteligencia sin reposo. Para desmarcarse de nosotros buscó virtudes en una mujer que a fin de

Tuvo que repetir la pregunta.

—'ien —contestó una boca sin lengua.

El locutor parecía hallarse en un trópico feliz:

—Nada más que dormir y comer. ¡La buena vida, amigos míos! ¡El *dolce far niente*, como dice nuestro querido Carmello, el rey del bocado con tomate! ¡La fiaca vegetativa, mis leales tocayos!

El locutor se llamaba Juan y se consideraba tocayo de la humanidad, al menos de la mexicana.

El Bello recibió las palabras como una llovizna. Ante su extenuante no hacer nada, pensé en los trofeos fáciles de Regina:

—¡Qué bonito! —dijo ella.

Podía referirse a cualquier cosa, a la destrucción del Bello, al saco color atún de mi padre, incluso al vendedor de los *hot-cakes* (me había descubierto y besaba el aire, ¿o se dirigía a otro y yo *quería* que la grasienta amenaza fuera para mí?).

El locutor volvió a la carga:

—¡Qué sueños fantásticos habrá tenido nuestro amigo! ¡Sueños de oro! Como que está a punto de ganar una residencia amueblada, a todo lujo, en legítimo estilo provenzal campestre, con un estudio de entrepaños empotrados... —un avión atravesó el cielo y la transmisión se enrareció—... ¡en finísima melamina, pero qué ponderosa, tocayos... el Bello gana y su sueño reparador es el México de aquí, el México que vibra y siente, el México todo del pondero sueño, el tocayo vibrador, el Bello en el México durmiente!

El inestable discurso no detuvo a un público que a la menor provocación se convertía en su propio espectáculo:

—¡Mé-xi-co, Mé-xi-co, Mé-xi-co!

Pensé que este arrebato despertaría la pasión representativa de mi padre, pero su mirada se parecía demasiado a la del Bello. Le repugnaba estar allí, en

Copa de Bronce se alarmó tanto que elogió la inteligencia, la sensatez y hasta la simpatía de Clarita.

Propuso ir al cine, seguramente para que la oscuridad borrara todo vínculo entre nosotros. Insistí en que fuéramos al teatro vivo de la mueblería.

El Bello Durmiente había bajado de peso; lamparones de salsa boloñesa le cubrían la piyama.

Muchos años después, al bajarme a deshoras en andenes y terminales de autobuses, veía a los hombres que siempre están allí, sin esperar nada ni a nadie, chupando un cigarrillo para combatir el frío, con la mirada en una lejanía sin rumbo, y en cada escala recordaría al concursante en sus días finales, su estar tendido, quieto, ajeno, sin otro propósito que enrarecer el escenario, volverlo más duro y difícil de explicar.

—¡Qué náusea! —fue lo único que dijo mi padre.

Y aún faltaba lo peor. En un rincón del escaparate había una caseta de madera, un baño ideal para la casa de Regina. El público había adquirido la costumbre de ovacionar las idas al baño del concursante; en aquel teatro lentísimo, la escapada al cubo de madera equivalía a un lance impetuoso.

—¡Be-llo... Be-llo! —coreó la gente.

Cuando regresó a la cama, el hombre vio el cristal como si no estuviéramos al otro lado. Ojos extáticos, sin párpados. Ser visto por los transeúntes y el ojo insomne de la televisión, le había vaciado la expresión. Sólo entonces entendí la severidad del concurso. El Bello se consumía, gastado por nosotros. Tal vez de haber sido el único en la calle, hubiera sentido lástima, pero ahí, en medio de tantas bocas de las que asomaban filos de oro y cáscaras de pepita, sentí el placer de ultrajarlo, de pulirlo hasta la demencia.

La voz del locutor se escuchó en las bocinas:

—¿Cómo va ese sueñito?

laureles metálicos destinados a simbolizar, por encima de todas las cosas, los escasos billetes que los habían adquirido.

Los premios baratos hicieron que Regina mirara la calle, sus afanes sin tregua, como una región de triunfos asequibles: una copa para cada mano lastimada, cada piel abierta, cada cuerpo sudoroso.

Estaba dispuesta a elogiar a Clarita sin causas definidas. En cambio, Clarita la vio como una amenaza irracional, otra prueba de mi incapacidad para aprender o escarmentar.

Mi padre, que detestaba a la mejor amiga de su esposa, se predispuso en mi favor: anticipó descalabros impulsivos, el escándalo que demostraba que yo era su hijo y sabía jugar con fuego. Tal vez recordó a su primera novia, el caso es que cuando nos encontramos me abrazó con un cariño preocupante, me plantó dos besos en la mejilla y me invitó a comer a una cafetería que daba al Zócalo.

Nos tocó la ceremonia de la bandera. Vimos a un batallón de uniformes desteñidos doblar la tela con mucho cuidado. El aire vibró con una trompeta de hojalata y una voz quebrada hizo volar a tres palomas. El acto sugería un país pequeño, recién liberado, que aún no encontraba la forma de entusiasmarse a sí mismo.

Mi padre me mostró fotos del ciclón que lo retuvo en la costa y luego pasó a lo que le interesaba, el "enredo" que lo hizo cerrar un ojo solidario:

—¡Qué calladito te lo tenías, *Panza*! ¡Vamos a pasear con ella!

Por primera vez nuestros destinos se invertían; él aceptaba acompañarme, ser mi testigo. Pero la nueva situación fue un desastre.

Hasta entonces él pensaba que Clarita era una neurótica intratable pero conveniente para mi formación. Sin embargo, al ver a Regina en la puerta de La

Como siempre, Regina desperdició la oportunidad de mentir:

—Catorce.

Clarita la miró, sonriente, como si hubiera dicho un proverbio a su favor.

Le mostré a Regina las partes visitables de la casa. Abrió la boca ante los miles de volúmenes encuadernados en piel y creyó que los cuatro ilustrados en la pared eran miembros de la familia Rendón.

En la mesa, Clarita se acercó a mi novia sin miramientos. Entre el vapor de las hojas de plátano y elote, buscó el aroma enemigo.

Regina ignoró la existencia de los cubiertos; cubrió sus dedos con una hoja de maíz y comió el tamal con saludables dentelladas. El chocolate le dejó bigotes que borró con el dorso de la mano.

Clarita la observaba en silencio. Tal vez para protegerse del olor que ya había clasificado, mordisqueó un queso azul.

Unas semanas después, mi padre hizo una breve visita a la ciudad. Tenía que rendirle cuentas a Benjamín Gutiérrez Pool y aprovechó para llamar por teléfono a Clarita Rendón.

—Ha ocurrido un asunto enojoso —dijo ella.

Curiosamente, mi "asunto enojoso" hablaba maravillas de Clarita. Le entusiasmaron sus libros, sus tamales, sus aretes (yo no advertí que los tuviera puestos), su olor a crema rosa. Quizá a todos nos está deparado un solo encuentro con la bondad irrestricta y ése fue el mío. Supongo que en su tienda Regina aprendió a desconfiar de las competencias, los honores, las metas. El mismo nombre del negocio prevenía a los clientes: La Copa de Bronce, un apropiado sitio de tercera, con entrepaños cubiertos de papel lustre, trofeos de incierto baño de oro, bases de marmolina,

nuestros suéteres de estambre y nuestros lisos rompevientos, se desplazó hacia la mueblería. Avancé, aferrado a la franela de Regina y a una espalda guinda con la P del Politécnico; atisbé muebles, variados candiles, un entresuelo con ofertas. La masa rodeó los islotes en los que se alzaban salas y recámaras, pensé que llegaríamos a la bodega, pero la corriente cambió de pronto, hubo un reflujo hacia atrás y quedé junto a un filo liso, una mesa con el esforzado brillo de un material que no quiere ser descubierto. Por vez primera estaba entre la melamina y el mundo.

El concursante se hallaba de espaldas a nosotros, encarando a quienes seguían afuera. Muy cerca de la cama, brillaba el ojo de una cámara de televisión. Dos bocinas pendían del techo.

—¿Cómo se siente? —preguntó el locutor, a control remoto.

—Rebién —contestó el Bello.

—¡Treinta días!

En el estudio de televisión había una orquesta. Las últimas palabras del locutor fueron seguidas por una marcha eufórica cuyo estribillo era, precisamente, "treinta días..."

A este ritmo salimos de la mueblería.

Llegamos a casa de Clarita Rendón tomados de la mano. Antes de entrar, Regina me pidió que le "planchara" el pelo. Respiró muy hondo, como si estuviera a punto de cargar algo importante. Ahí, en la primera puerta de Clarita, me gustó más que nunca.

Obviamente, mi celadora fue de otra opinión. No tenía prejuicios mundanos y cualquier muchacha le hubiese parecido digna de mí. Cualquiera, menos Regina.

—¿Qué edad tienes? —le preguntó al ver que me sacaba la cabeza.

Dos veces al día, el dudoso italiano prepararía pastas en el escaparate para promover su nuevo restorán en la Zona Rosa. El Bello parecía conforme con sus futuros treinta días de cama y espaguetis, pero se mordía los labios, como si la piyama le raspara.

Al terminar el programa corrí a La Copa de Bronce. Regina me esperaba, vestida con sudadera de manga larga y chaleco de franela. Parecía una extraña beisbolista.

En la esquina vimos a unos hombres que caminaban de prisa, con los dedos en pinza frente a la boca. En la mano izquierda llevaban la bolsa de pepitas de los Grandes Acontecimientos. Comían sin detenerse, escupiendo cáscaras. Los seguimos hasta Salto del Agua.

Afuera de la mueblería la multitud alzaba rehiletes, matracas, serpentinas, trompetas de cartón con hilachas tricolores de antiguos 16 de septiembre.

Cuando el carro alegórico —una fantasía de hules y poliuretanos que imitaban el merengue— despuntó junto al semáforo, tronaron vítores y aplausos.

No había otro competidor; una vez escogido, el Bello *tenía* que ganar, era nuestro seguro representante en la infalible tarea de tenderse treinta días en la cama color cielo.

—¡Se ve, se siente, el Bello está presente! —gritó un grupo, con chamarras de sindicalistas atravesadas por un rayo rojo.

El concursante entró al escaparate con mirada huidiza. La gente seguía llegando; pronto tuve un codo y el palito de un elote encajados en las costillas.

—Pinche bodoque —masculló un anciano que me llegaba al hombro.

El Bello se tendió en la cama con parsimonia. Probó el muelleo del colchón. En vano, un soporte tenso, tal vez ortopédico.

El cuerpo acostado activó a la multitud. Éramos demasiados; la trama inseparable que formaban

Wagram que solía lanzar a mi captora a los tiempos del Directorio, el Imperio y la Restauración. Pero esta vez se limitó a inclinarse y a decir en voz baja, como si se dirigiera a la cuenca de porcelana con chiles chipotles:

—¿Cómo se llama?

Pensé en el nombre de Clarita, en las tres letras, las tres puertas de clausura que la separaban de una mujer extraordinaria.

—Regina —contesté sin ganas.

Los ojos le brillaron mucho.

—Invítala a cenar —su curiosidad iba en aumento: quería olfatearla—. ¿Qué tal el miércoles?

El miércoles el Bello Durmiente sería trasladado de los estudios de televisión a la mueblería.

—¿Tamales? —su nariz se afilaba, pálida, tensa, anticipando olores deliciosamente adversos.

Estuve de acuerdo y sus labios delgados y voraces pronunciaron:

—¿De dulce?

Tuve un sueño en el que Clarita me comía. En premio, era nombrada Caballero de la Cuchara. El hombre de los *hot-cakes* observaba la escena tras su emblemático vapor; chasqueaba la lengua y decía: "pica dos veces".

El miércoles estuvo lleno de acontecimientos; el Bello Durmiente fue ungido en una ceremonia televisiva. Ganó el sorteo un hombre moreno, de mediana estatura, que lucía incómodo en la piyama.

—Tenemos una sorpresa —el locutor del programa hablaba como si las palabras le quemaran el paladar—...¡¡¡el Bello será alimentado por el sensacional Carmello!!!

Carmello era un hombre con pelo de borrego:

—¡Qué meraviglia, cari amici! ¡Mangiare tutto riquísimo!

—Te voy a comer, princesa.

Vi su lengua gorda y roja. La enrolló como un taquito para acabar de dominarme.

—¿Dónde estuviste? —me preguntó Clarita esa misma noche.

—¿Por qué?

—¿Hueles raro? ¿Con quién estuviste?

Su nariz inquisitiva me recorrió los hombros, la nuca, subió a mi coronilla. Oí la voz que salía de un estómago profundo: "prin-ce-sa", vi los dientes de caníbal que prometían tragarme. Para alejar este horror, pensé en Regina, grande, enfranelada, sudando de felicidad junto al vapor de los *hot-cakes*:

—Tengo una novia.

Regina me lamía, me dejaba tocar sus trofeos, se interesaba en el Bello Durmiente, pero nunca la vi como novia. En realidad ni siquiera la vi como mujer; costaba trabajo ubicarla entre las personas, su tibieza era buena de un modo fronterizo, que no se agotaba en sí mismo, era una mediación hacia otra cosa; sus pardas franelas tenían algo de los koalas que tanto regaló mi padre, una mascota, un juguete rumbo a la mujer.

Quizá por estar conforme con su mundo, la tienda donde los enanos y los paralíticos compraban premios baratos, Regina tenía una actitud de intercesora, actuaba con total desprendimiento, como si me entrenara para otras dichas. Yo la abrazaba con un entusiasmo que no se detenía en ella; su sonrisa, su olor a tamarindo, sus manos endurecidas en las palmas anunciaban algo todavía impreciso. Empezaba a quererla con gran confusión y en aquella cena emergió con un nombre falso y soso:

—Una novia —repitió Clarita.

Los *hot-cakes* tragados con terror me habían quitado el hambre, pero aun así comí el *omelette*

—Mi hermana —dijo Regina.

La mujer parpadeó a modo de saludo. La cabeza calva le chupaba un seno inconcebible.

Como Clarita, y acaso como las demás mujeres, Regina era fanática de lo dulce: me acompañó a la mueblería porque enfrente vendían churros con chocolate y en la esquina *hot-cakes* con cajeta.

Me detuve ante el carrito de lámina de los *hot-cakes*. El vendedor me pareció una profecía; en el futuro, si no caía la bomba, yo tendría esa inmensa obesidad. Al cabo de un rato advertí que sus facciones se afilaban al hablar; sonreía con dientes triangulares, como pulidos por una lima, y alargaba una quijada de títere dislocado. No tenía los ojos de Buda de tantos gordos sino una mirada fogosa, firme. Arrojaba la masa con fascinante precisión, el rostro abrillantado por el humo. Las cejas espesas, la nariz angulosa, la barbilla en punta, contradecían la carne oculta bajo la grasosa camiseta. Sin embargo, era la voz lo que causaba la impresión definitiva de que había otro hombre atrapado en su cuerpo. Sus gritos rompían el aire, tipludos, molestos. En cambio, cuando le pedí mi *hot-cake* me miró con sus intensas pupilas y habló con una voz que parecía venirle de otro estómago:

—¿Con azúcar, señorita?

Asentí, mientras él formaba un cono de papel y espolvoreaba azúcar. Me vio a los ojos. Abrió su boca de dientes triangulares:

—Toma, princesa.

Las manos me temblaban tanto que tiré las monedas en su comal. Él rió con una potencia que se impuso al tráfico de los camiones.

Me pregunté si habría oído bien pero al día siguiente me dijo:

más en caso de tener que avanzar con un llavero por su propia casa. En cambio, Clarita veía en las puertas un privilegio de la individualidad y ejercía su derecho de cerrojo.

Curiosamente, la arquitectura de mi padre tenía algo de la obsesión de Clarita; sus bardas y contrafuertes, sus ventanas pequeñas, protegidas por celosías de madera, eran la mezcla de tres influencias: la hacienda, el cuartel y el convento. Si esos muros inexpugnables eran "típicos", se podía inferir que los mexicanos temíamos que nos robaran algo.

Por vía negativa, en casa de Clarita estimé como nunca la televisión y entendí la delicia de abrir alcobas, de interceder entre una zona y otra; vulnerar un espacio, separarlo a discreción era el placer que no conocerían los reyes.

En La Copa de Bronce los picaportes conservaban las huellas húmedas y azucaradas de la vendedora. Una tarde Regina dejó su buñuelo junto a la caja registradora, se lamió los dedos, señaló un oscuro rincón de la trastienda y dijo:

—Vamos a la casa.

Giré el picaporte impregnado de azúcar. La perilla de metal, que debía ser dura y fría, conservaba un soplo tibio, el aliento de Regina.

Pasamos al departamento donde vivía su familia. La tienda, de por sí pequeña, era dos veces mayor que esos cubiles. La cama de Regina tocaba tres paredes, la "cocina" era un rincón donde las flores del papel tapiz se habían ahumado. Pero lo importante estaba en una silla, a la derecha. Una mujer de rostro enjuto y expresión de indecible cansancio amamantaba a un bebé. Que ese cuerpo consumido sirviera para alimentar a otro me pareció tan absurdo como que la tienda de trofeos sirviera para mantener esa pocilga.

casa) mi segunda mamá (sólo entonces le conferí esa dignidad) fue a la cocina y leyó la última leyenda en el refrigerador: SÓLO LOS REYES NO TOCAN LAS PUERTAS. Se rascó la cabeza, como el poeta en la *Anatomía de la razón*.

Mamá consideraba que la monarquía era intensamente pedagógica. LA PUNTUALIDAD ES LA CORTESÍA DEL REY invitaba a ser puntual como los reyes; en cambio, SÓLO LOS REYES NO TOCAN LAS PUERTAS revelaba que el pueblo llano tenía otras obligaciones. Mamá confiaba en la naturaleza ejemplar de la monarquía y en el sentido común del Tercer Estado para distinguir cuándo los reyes eran imitables y cuándo no.

A Clarita los reyes le gustaban muertos, reducidos a sus guisos o patrocinando jardines racionales. En cualquier otra circunstancia era regicida. Cuando le confesé mi afición a las inacabables torturas de Superman y San Andrés, me mostró espléndidos grabados de fines del XVIII donde la turbamulta sostenía cabezas en picas. Me interesaron poco los tajos rápidos, ajenos a la matizada alteración de un cuerpo.

Ante el mensaje real de mamá actuó con decisión: retiró la fruta imantada y destruyó el papel con un cuidado que no hubiera puesto para romper algo en su casa.

Por las palabras que decía Clarita y que yo copiaba en mi cuaderno, tal vez debí pensar en una oposición entre la república y la monarquía; sin embargo, en esas vacaciones donde la transmisión de valores se volvía tan ardua, pensé en la disyuntiva, más pragmática, de cerrar las puertas con o sin cerrojo.

Mamá estaba harta de que yo entrara a todas partes sin avisar (esta mala costumbre me permitió ver a mi padre y a Rita formando una carnal variante de la equis), pero no cerraba las puertas con llave. Esperaba que tocáramos y dijéramos "¿se puede?".

Las llaves yacían en desorden en un antiguo frasco de mayonesa; mamá se hubiera deprimido aún

todo, al día siguiente volví a verla. Sus ropas ardieron al embestirme.

A la tercera vez me enseñó sus tobillos, redondos, blanquísimos, llenos de piquetes de mosco.

—Tengo la sangre dulce —informó—. Vienen de muy lejos a buscarme.

Terminal Progreso era el sitio de donde venían los moscos. No se lo dije a Regina, pero conocía de sobra los jirones en torno a los canales que velaban el aire como un mosquitero.

Regresaba de besar a Regina cuando me encontré a Clarita en plena calle.

—Iba a buscarte. Habló tu mamá.

Una vez más Clarita reveló su desesperación ante la vida práctica. Como ya empezaba a ser costumbre, mamá le dijo que pasaría otras semanas en Culiacán, y Clarita consideró que yo necesitaba ropa de recambio, ese mismo día, a esa hora. El asunto, sin ser urgente, era espantosamente concreto, y ella quiso solucionarlo con la mayor rapidez.

Fuimos al lugar de los moscos. El taxi le salió carísimo y llegó de pésimo humor.

También le molestó el orden de la casa. Mamá acomodaba los frascos por estaturas y doblaba la punta del papel de baño en un triángulo, como si preparara la casa para alquilarla con todo y cepillos de dientes.

Hasta ese día pensé que las mujeres disponían de un talento innato para empacar. Mamá arreglaba las ropas con una exactitud que no podía ser adquirida, su habilidad era un don como tener ritmo o buen oído.

Clarita arrojó mi ropa a la maleta como si manipulara un cajón de verduras.

Mientras yo me entretenía con los ajolotes (vivos gracias a la sirvienta que iba cada tercer día a la

tienda, cualquiera podía obtener una copa de campeón. Sólo los vendedores me parecieron atléticos: un hombre de unos cincuenta años bien llevados, a quien incluso el pelo le crecía en forma enérgica (una cabeza de entrenador) y una muchacha de catorce años (su piel gastada y joven sugería un agotador rendimiento en pista y campo, sus manos gruesas achicaban las monedas).

A pesar de mis pocos intercambios comerciales, sabía que los vendedores de la capital sienten que los clientes son sus enemigos y que cualquier favor adicional —entregar una bolsa más grande, dejarlos hacer una llamada— equivale a una vergonzosa rendición. Ella era distinta. En mis primeras visitas revisé los trofeos con calma y me acerqué a la caja:

—¿Me cambia uno de a cinco?

—A ver si tengo.

Siempre tenía.

Se llamaba Regina y se parecía algo a las búlgaras que durante las Olimpiadas lanzaron jabalinas récord en Ciudad Universitaria. Su constitución pertenecía al modo hercúleo; al alzar un paquete apretaba los labios, su piel enrojecía, la frente era rajada en vertical, y luego sobrevenía el instante perfecto, el soplido, la burbuja suelta después de tanta contención, los labios entreabiertos.

Nueve días antes del concurso supe que su lengua era más grande que la mía. No había clientes en la tienda y me pidió que fuera atrás del mostrador. Me subió a una caja y quedé de su estatura, me rodeó con sus brazos cubiertos de franela, el corazón le latía en forma inusitada. Aunque me había entrenado besando muñecos, nada podía prepararme para la boca de Regina. La quijada se me trabó tratando de acomodar su lengua. Fue una sensación extraña, inclasificable, más cerca de una revelación técnica, la exploración fina de otras texturas, que del placer. Con

era como recibir una carta de mis padres. Desde su raciocinio, compadeció mi idolatría:

—Está bien, pero no vayas más lejos.

Así, mi hora de televisión fue seguida por las visitas a la mueblería. Me aprendí los comerciales en los que un locutor señalaba una repisa para gritar:

—¡Cien por ciento melamina ponderosa! —su boca sonreía con franqueza, como si ése fuera el nombre oculto del oro.

Cada vez que se acababan las virtudes comprensibles de un mueble, el locutor recurría a la melamina.

Faltaban catorce días para el concurso cuando tomé una nueva calle en el camino de regreso y descubrí la tienda de trofeos.

Lo primero que me sorprendió de La Copa de Bronce fue que un trofeo pudiera comprarse. Yo suponía que los trofeos se preparaban en una forma secreta, o por lo menos complicada, y eran supervisados en alguna Oficina de Triunfos.

La Copa de Bronce ofrecía premios a precios deprimentes; había uno para cada efecto, desde un tenista con raqueta al aire hasta un hombre de traje para los campeones de oratoria o los empleados del mes. Vi copas rematadas por perros, locomotoras, aviones. Si uno no quería ser tan específico, allí estaban los laureles o el dorado número uno.

La tienda me pareció una estafa tan flagrante que la visité todos los días. En una ocasión encontré a un hombre pequeño que tomé por un *jockey* (su camisa púrpura reforzaba la hipótesis) hasta que descubrí las alarmantes suelas de sus zapatos. Sin esa monstruosa ortopedia, el hombre sería un "liliputiense" (una de las muchas palabras que Clarita me inculcó después de declararme "refractario"). Sentí una decepción equivalente a la de la grácil trapecista que descendió como anciana al aserrín del circo. En esa

alegorías del amor, en la poesía china las mangas húmedas son alegorías del sufrimiento, la señal de que alguien ha llorado. ¿Has visto las batas de los chinos?

—¿Dónde queda Salto del Agua?

La doctora Rendón dio una conferencia sobre el periodo colonial y la forma en que la ciudad flotante de los aztecas se secó hasta "inventar el polvo", el horror atravesado de tolvaneras en el que ahora vivíamos.

—Veneras el agua porque la perdiste —me acusó, con mirada firme, como si me hubiera comido su postre—. Salto del Agua es lo único que queda del viejo acueducto, un monumento al lago enterrado. Tú vienes de Xochimilco.

—De Terminal Progreso.

—Es casi lo mismo; el agua está en tu imaginario.

—¿Dónde queda Salto del Agua? —insistí, después de apuntar sus palabras en mi cuaderno.

—A cinco cuadras.

La respuesta me pareció alegórica.

Clarita me llevó a ver los peces de piedra que abrían sus bocas secas en torno al escudo de la ciudad.

De reojo, miré mi auténtico objetivo, la mueblería y un anuncio gigante: FALTAN 25 DÍAS.

Lo poco que observé en el centro me pareció decrépito y abigarrado. Clarita empezaba a contagiarme su pericia olfativa: mientras ella disertaba, pensé que la ciudad azteca se pudría blandamente en el subsuelo y la ciudad española era arrasada por humos pestilentes.

De cualquier forma, me quedaron ganas de volver a la mueblería. Al día siguiente pedí permiso de ir por mi cuenta. Clarita se conmovió mucho, sin duda porque sobreinterpretó mis intenciones: yo venía de los últimos canales y ver el monumento al agua

Esperé que la cámara se acercara sin compasión a su piel porosa. Estaba harto de ella, quería que el país la contemplara horrenda y tartamuda durante la *Anatomía de la razón*. Pero su triunfo fue mayúsculo. Agredió a cada participante con una técnica distinta; el moderador no pudo arrebatarle la palabra, los sacerdotes se quedaron perplejos ante sus latinajos, el poeta fue descrito como una bestia intuitiva (exasperado, se quitó la boina para rascarse como una bestia intuitiva), la mujer de chaquira recibió un trato de infinita lástima. Al finalizar el programa incluso el pastor, de porte tan atlético, se veía descompuesto. Clarita se despidió citando a Montesquieu en un francés que nadie entendió y que seguramente bajó el *rating* de la emisora.

Quedó tan satisfecha que dejó la televisión encendida. En su mente debía proyectarse la repetición de sus grandezas. Cualquier cosa que yo viera en ese momento tendría el atractivo del hurto: las imágenes secuestradas ganaban la fuerza de anunciaciones. Sentí una suave taquicardia, disfrutando el regusto de la manzanilla en mis labios. Entonces vi el anuncio de una competencia singular: El Bello Durmiente. La televisión desafiaba al pueblo mexicano a acostarse durante un mes en el aparador de una mueblería.

Tal vez porque el sonambulismo me impidió entrar a los Amigos del Bosque, concebí el sueño inmóvil como un mérito superior. A partir de esa noche célebre, dediqué mis sesenta minutos de televisión a perseguir noticias del Bello Durmiente.

La mueblería que patrocinaba el concurso tenía su central en Salto del Agua. El ganador iría de los estudios de televisión a la tienda en un carro alegórico.

—¿Qué es alegórico? —le pregunté a Clarita.

—Cuando algo simboliza otra cosa: las calaveras de azúcar son alegorías de la muerte, las rosas son

de los presos por lo menos teníamos televisión. El aparato era tan nocivo para Clarita que acabó por resultarme indispensable. Lo guardaba bajo llave en el cajón grande de su escritorio. Se diría que, de dar rienda suelta a sus impulsos, no habría hecho otra cosa que ver la pantalla violácea.

El aparato era absurdamente pequeño y la antena de conejo tan débil que los vaqueros siempre mordían el polvo en compañía de su fantasma. Aun así, yo codiciaba los sesenta minutos en los que podía ver programas sin que se me "reblandeciera el cerebro". Clarita calculaba el tiempo con el despertador que le servía para medir cocciones de guisos y huevos duros; al escuchar la campanilla, suspendía mi "lobotomía frontal".

Ni el encierro ni la obligación de limpiar sus libros fueron tan exasperantes como el cajón de la tele que ella pateaba rítmicamente al escribir.

En ocasiones, mi celadora salía a la calle y me dejaba bajo llave. De un modo cada vez más nítido supe que no estaba de visita; era su prisionero, su insalvable enemigo.

Una noche, cuando ya había visto mi hora legal, Clarita propuso sacar la tele. Preparó sándwiches de pavo y me sirvió un dedal de manzanilla. Tanta pompa no era desinteresada: cuando la imagen dejó de vibrar en la pantalla, vi a Clarita con su fantasma. Había sido invitada al programa *Anatomías*. El panel de discusión incluía a un sacerdote de barbas de chivo, un poeta con boina y anteojos de piloto de la primera guerra, un pastor protestante que aun en blanco y negro tenía las mejillas de quien acaba de atravesar a nado el Canal de la Mancha, una mujer con collares de chaquira y pelos de tirabuzón y a Clarita, pálida, intensa.

siquiera las ideas, que valen más que los hombres: el futuro está hipotecado.

La noción de vivir en un planeta con alquiler vencido se me grabó porque compartía con Clarita la obsesión por el futuro. Mi días sólo se justificaban como algo "anterior", una sala de espera para lo que vendría después. Las visiones catastróficas de mi educadora me hicieron pasar del sonambulismo al insomnio. Encerrado entre siete puertas, escuchaba los ronquidos de la doctora como tajos que segaban el futuro.

—¡Sólo vivimos en el presente! —decía ella a cada rato, lo cual significaba que yo tenía que limpiar su biblioteca de inmediato. Una bomba podía caer del cielo, y Voltaire y los otros debían llegar limpios al fin del futuro.

Armado de un plumero esmeralda, me convertí en esclavo de los lomos forrados con piel de becerro.

—No soporto el picor del polvo; mi nariz es sensibilísima —decía Clarita—. ¿En qué letra vas?

De poco servía señalar mi ubicación en la biblioteca. Cuando terminé de frotar a Zurita y Castro, me enteré de que Aristófanes había vuelto a juntar polvo. La biblioteca era cíclica, incesante.

El segundo pasatiempo que me asignó Clarita fue llevar un diario. Me regaló un cuaderno en el que me limité a hacer dos listas: las rarezas que decía mi anfitriona y las cosas en las que soñaba Verónica.

Como el yeso firmado por la enfermera, el cuaderno sobrevivió a muchos cajones: "Agosto 20: Clarita platicó del pequeño paté de Fourier. Verónica soñó que hacía caballos de mazapán."

El 28 de agosto celebramos el cumpleaños de Goethe con un chucrut de tres pimientas. Para entonces, Terminal Progreso se había transformado en el sitio don-

aceite, aquel ruido le encendió la mirada, como si descubriese una variante perversa de la música.

Por aquellos tiempos, Clarita preparaba un libro sobre la Ilustración y las plantas: *El jardín como metáfora*. Yo venía de los alrededores de Xochimilco, un campo sin otros méritos que ofrecer flores para la ciudad y recordar los canales aztecas. A ella le interesaba poco el desorden natural; admiraba los jardines como prueba de la razón organizada. Mi mundo crudo, silvestre, la hacía musitar con cierta lástima: "cultívate". Cultivarse significaba salir del campo, transformarlo en una región portátil y ordenada, el jardín que ella y Voltaire llevaban en la mente. Las mejores plantas y los mejores hombres cedían al dominio; en el caso de la naturaleza, se trataba de un orden impuesto (alguien pensaba el jardín); en el caso del hombre, no había mejor autoridad que la de uno mismo.

Cada vez que yo chupaba un cuchillo con mayonesa o elogiaba algo como "más mejor", la profesora me decía:

—Domínate a ti mismo.

Esto me hacía pensar en mi padre; le había visto suficientes arrebatos para saber que se dominaba poco. Luego pasaba a otra preocupación: yo no tenía nada de qué dominarme.

—Ya verás en el futuro, si es que hay futuro.

Éste era otro de sus temas recurrentes. En la época en que la gente valía la pena (o sea, hasta el siglo XVIII), las ideas se comunicaban con la certeza de que llegarían a la posteridad. Los genios podían padecer exilios y mazmorras sabiendo que sus ideas rebeldes serían el sentido común del porvenir.

—Esta confianza ya no existe. Después de Hiroshima, no hay garantía de que algo sobreviva, ni

Voltaire, se dejaba afectar por esa región en la que había lavadoras automáticas y nuevos remedios infructuosos contra la gripe. Tal vez necesitaba esa cuota de cotidianidad extrema, de parco siglo xx, para volver a sus libros y a su imperturbable encierro.

La casa de la doctora estaba en el centro. La primera mañana oí las campanas de cuatro iglesias. Abrí la ventana y respiré el delicioso aire de la gasolina quemada. Escuché voces rotas, silbidos, el anhelado estruendo de la ciudad.

Por desgracia, Clarita temía, no sólo mis fugas de sonámbulo, sino que me perdiera de día. "Salir" equivalía a acompañarla, y como apenas se movía, en un principio el centro fue para mí un simple programa de efectos sonoros.

Pero también tuve problemas para abrir ventanas; los ruidos desquiciaban a Clarita. Los olores le gustaban porque podía clasificarlos, el *Atlas de los quesos* la ayudaba a trazar una cartografía de aromas, otorgaba a las fragancias una precisa superficie. En cambio, su sentido del oído era casi inexistente; para ella, "escuchar" equivalía a padecer un desarreglo atmosférico; ni siquiera la música le revelaba un orden. Tal vez por vanidad intelectual descartaba los estímulos que sólo comprendía a medias. Ante un ruido repentino, su lengua roja asomaba de la boca, como si quisiera probar el éter. Luego venía una sucesión de portazos rumbo a la cocina. En sus momentos de mayor desesperación se encajaba tapones de nadador en los oídos y ponía a hervir agua; el ruido parejo le servía de filtro.

Sólo en una ocasión me pareció que disfrutaba un sonido. Había puesto a freír especias y escuchaba el chisporroteo como una abstracción fascinante. Tal vez por conocer los aromas que se desprendían del intelecto, y acaso por llevar una dieta diferente a la de Rousseau se desesperaba pronto:

—¡Ni aprendes ni escarmientas! —gritaba cuando no comprendía sus errabundos discursos (muchas veces por quedarme dormido).

Mi incapacidad educativa la hizo cuestionar el ideario de Juan Jacobo:

—¡Qué podía saber ese antropófago! —se refería a un pasaje de las *Confesiones* donde "el loco de la leche" mostraba su interés en los Caballeros de la Cuchara, los hidalgos de Saboya dispuestos a "comerse" a sus adversarios.

Seguramente también le molestaba que Rousseau elogiara los instintos que sólo despiertan con la maternidad.

Después de varios fracasos intelectuales, mi educadora me llevó ante el retrato del "supremo Voltaire":

—La tesis del buen salvaje le pareció tan "convincente" que la leyó en cuatro patas. Por cierto, ¿qué estará haciendo Carlos, nuestro salvaje de cabecera? —mi anfitriona rió con la pregunta, asombrada de que yo no la siguiera—: ¡Eres refractario! "Cultiva tu jardín", Mauricio, son palabras de Voltaire, ¿o tienes el coco lleno de arena?

Lo dicho, las vacaciones eran un largo desierto, al menos en mi mente.

Para mamá, Clarita representaba una inversión femenina, la enemiga de las amigas de mi padre. Resultaba más difícil saber lo que la historiadora de las ideas encontraba en su amiga de Culiacán. Quizá para Clarita las tardes de té eran una curiosa expedición a la vida diaria. Mamá podía hablar con eficiencia de telas convenientes, aparatos domésticos, pechugas de pollo que huelen y pechugas que no huelen, era el supermercado de lo real donde Clarita se abastecía. Durante dos horas, la mujer que aún no se recuperaba del exilio de

comida y sus olores el principio y el fin de la sensualidad. Con frecuencia hablaba de la "comida de tesis" y la "gastrosofía". Curiosamente, en la comida se oponía a sus autores favoritos. Hasta yo, que apenas lograba seguir sus desvaríos, entendí la disparidad entre su mente y su apetito. Los ingredientes finos, la pimienta verde, el eneldo y el orégano, eran su forma de vengarse de los intelectos que tanto admiraba. Hablaba pestes de las "habas republicanas", la "democrática papa", las "empanadas del vulgo municipal y espeso". En la cocina repudiaba lo igualitario, el "arroz rascuache", y exaltaba las "divinas mayonesas" de los Luises de Francia y la dieta impar de Moctezuma, que jamás probó un platillo por segunda vez.

Los espíritus racionales rara vez entendían los méritos del ajo, las pizcas de tomillo, el vaporoso batido de las claras de huevo. Su condena sumaria a las mesas de los ilustrados era:

—¡La leche de Rousseau!

Una noche, después de comparar a Carlos con el buen salvaje, Clarita me dijo que según Rousseau la leche, aunque se producía en la vaca, pertenecía al reino vegetal. Abrió su ejemplar de *Emilio* para citar: "Las mujeres comen pan, legumbres y lacticinios; las perras y las gatas comen lo mismo, y hasta las lobas cuando pastan. Buscan jugos vegetales para su leche".

Cuando habló de la residencia de lo vegetal en la carne, pensé en su cuerpo donde lo salado se alimentaba de lo dulce, y en mi deseo incumplido de sustituir lo dulce por lo salado para mejorar mi carácter.

Clarita admiraba a Rousseau por muchas razones. Una de las pocas que recuerdo es su disposición a educar al huérfano Emilio. Quizá sólo me recibió en su casa para poner a prueba los recursos de la educación. Pero enfrentarse a un ser menor significaba un esfuerzo supremo, una especie de maratón del

rojos sino que "enrojecen de rabia en el sartén". Aquellos intercambios en las insoladas tardes del norte se habían ennoblecido en la cabeza de Clarita. Ella, que creía que la humanidad fue algo que existió del Renacimiento a la Ilustración, atesoraba los consejos básicos que le dio una niña de rodillas peladas.

Más extraño aún era que se siguieran frecuentando; cada dos o tres meses se reunían a tomar té helado. ¿Qué podían decirse? Tal vez mamá disfrutaba la cercanía de la doctora porque encarnaba el reverso del ideal femenino de mi padre. Dura y erudita, la Rendón era una suerte de contramujer, el negativo de las muchachas con las que íbamos a los moteles. Sus ojos ponían en duda lo que miraban. En cambio, salvo Rita Terreros, que siempre lo excedió, las amigas de mi padre confiaban tanto en la armonía del mundo que creían que las ropas fosforescentes las hacían verse, no se diga bien, sino normales.

Si Clarita disfrutaba lo dulce y las salsas complicadas, mi padre era un pionero de las granolas y los jugos de betabel. Entonces nada de eso se consideraba especialmente sano, pero él necesitaba renunciar a algo en el desayuno para ganar su relajamiento a otras horas. Ni siquiera sus tendencias nacionalistas lo llevaron a revalorar los chiles:

—No me gusta la comida que quema dos veces —le decía a mamá, que ahogaba sus huevos en salsa de chile pasilla.

Ella lo miraba con ojos pulidos por el picante y la humillación de no poder contestarle; en ese pleito los nombres exactos estaban prohibidos y le resultaba imposible defenderse de la indirecta acusación de que el segundo fuego no sólo existía sino que le gustaba.

A diferencia de mi padre, que vivía para los placeres externos, la solitaria Clarita encontraba en la

eran inmensos, de modo que mandó hacer un atril de madera que se colocaba a horcajadas en el vientre. Sus pies descalzos reposaban en almohadones de seda; sus dedos gordos eran escuálidos, de una piel muy suave, como si nunca caminara o sólo lo hiciera en pantuflas supercómodas; en el baño tenía piedritas de varios grosores para lavarse los "entrededos".

Una tarde en que ella repasaba la *Crítica del juicio* vi sus pies limpísimos y no resistí la tentación de chuparlos. Era aun más salada que su aroma. Ignoro si para ella el contacto tuvo un toque sensual, para mí fue una degustación que me dio mucha sed y hubiera repetido de buena gana. Pero al día siguiente ella decidió leer a puerta cerrada.

Ésta no fue la única barrera entre nosotros. Clarita consideraba que las puertas existen porque se cierran. Le avisaron de mi sonambulismo y esto le dio pretexto para "protegerme".

La casa carecía de pasillos y seguía un plano telescópico; la entrada era la parte más ancha y la cocina el punto final, la mirilla para poner el ojo. De la calle a la cocina había siete puertas, y mi anfitriona se deleitaba pasando pestillos. Para salir de ahí en las noches, además de sonámbulo, hubiera tenido que ser el Conde de Montecristo.

Lo extraño es que el sonambulismo cesó en cuanto puse un pie en la casa. Estar lejos de mamá bastó para mantenerme en la cama y reveló mi condición de sonámbulo satélite, cuyo único interés era llorar rumbo al camisón color tuna.

¿Qué tenía que ver Clarita con mamá? Casi nada. Se conocieron en la lejana Culiacán, donde Clarita pasó cinco "veranos imposibles". A los diez años mamá le habló de temas prácticos que hasta la fecha recordaba; por ejemplo, que la flor de calabaza no es una planta aparte sino que crece "como un copete en la calabacita", o que los camarones no son

Sus extremos favoritos eran los quesos putre-factos y los perfumes; le gustaba revisar un tomo gor-do que llevaba el título de *Atlas de los quesos de Francia* y usaba un desodorante cuyo nombre no he olvidado: *Canela Vetiver*.

Pero lo más singular en ese museo de los olo-res era el propio cuerpo de Clarita. Me bañaba des-pués que ella y en el aire vaporoso reconstruía la figura de mi anfitriona. Tal vez alguien tan sensible a los aromas merecía oler menos; no había suficiente *Ca-nela Vetiver* para mitigarla. De modo fragmentario, nunca en su fresca plenitud, he recuperado su olor en ciertas cajas de madera que despiden un aroma entre salino y vegetal.

Su cuerpo flaco tenía un apetito ilimitado por los dulces pero exudaba una fragancia alcalina. La frase de Feuerbach en la "portada del refri", como ella de-cía, cobraba un acento irónico. ¿Si el hombre es lo que come, por qué una dieta tan rica en mermeladas producía ese humor de sales?

Tal vez se trataba de un desarreglo de la edad. Mamá solía decirme: "pronto te va a gustar lo salado". Crecer era abandonar los dulces que me engordaban. Incluso los ajolotes apoyaban su teoría: al remojarlos en agua salada tenían más posibilidades de mutar en salamandras. Secretamente yo también esperaba la mañana en que unas galletas duras me interesaran más que la mermelada.

Tres veces al día observaba la masticación fir-me de Clarita; hasta los chocolates con *nougat* pro-vocaban el batir de sus quijadas. Tensas. Implacables.

Comer era un proceso enérgico; en cambio, su trabajo me parecía una forma de la desocupación; pasa-ba el día entero en casa, hojeando libros. Yo no era muy activo pero me atribuía la intensidad del pez piloto.

Clarita leía en todos los lugares de la casa pero de preferencia en la cama. La mayoría de sus libros

En su cuerpo nada destacaba tanto como la nariz. Aguda más que larga. Porosa. Aletas de piel fina. Rojiza en el nacimiento, blancuzca, casi translúcida en la punta.

Desde entonces, cada vez que encuentro una nariz que palidece hacia abajo, sé que estoy ante un olfato de cacería.

—Sudas agrio —me dijo en la primera tarde, y pasó sus dedos por mi pelo, sin el menor asco.

Aunque olfateaba en exceso, ningún aroma la molestaba. Sus libros despedían un aire rancio y las cortinas apestaban a humedad; no había un cojín de felpa que no oliera a cosa usada y vagamente femenina (siempre un dejo de perfume en la tela raída).

Después de la primera cena se sintió obligada a contarme un cuento para niños. Repasó su memoria y consideró que lo más aproximado era la estatua de Condillac. Se ató un pañuelo en los ojos y anunció:

—Soy la estatua, entiendo el mundo por los olores.

Me pidió que le pusiera cosas ante su ávida nariz.

Fui al refrigerador y casi me desmayé al ver la leyenda en la puerta. ¡Ahí estaba la fuente intelectual de la pedagogía materna! Sin embargo, en las semanas por venir me enteraría de que, en el caso de Clarita, se trataba de una cita inmutable: DER MENSCH IST WAS ER ISST. Sin que yo lo ameritara, la doctora me diría que Ludwig Feuerbach era un mediocre que por accidente, llevado por un juego de palabras, dio con el mejor lema para las despensas: "el hombre es lo que come".

Abrí el refrigerador y encontré complicadas jaleas. Yo provenía, no sólo de las orillas de la ciudad, sino de una cultura constante donde la mermelada siempre era de fresa. Tomé dos tarros. Para mi asombro, Clarita olió la diferencia entre la grosella y la frambuesa.

Carlos se sintió aliviado de que me rechazaran como Amigo del Bosque; hubiera sido un lastre para él, un bulto que sacar de zanjas y avisperos.

Las oficinas de los Amigos eran unos tétricos cuartos en el centro: un mapa amarillento y arrugado en la pared, luz mortecina, repisas con frascos llenos de reptiles. La asociación ofrecía una bronca respuesta a los Boy Scouts y su disciplina de kermés; los Amigos luchaban cuerpo a cuerpo con la naturaleza, encarnaban un código viril donde el músculo adquiría rango ético: podían ser vencidos pero no derrotados. Carlos es de quienes se engrandecen cuando sobran insectos y falta comida, de modo que se convirtió en Amigo básico, pasó de una excursión a otra, nadó en pozas de lodo, durmió con la cabeza en una piedra, se volvió inmume a los mosquitos y alérgico a las abejas, una garrapata le pasó una enfermedad y se curó con un tratamiento de estiércol que parecía otra enfermedad.

Comparados con los Amigos del Bosque, los miembros del Lienzo del Charro eran de una rebuscada coquetería agraria. El agua fría y las telas ásperas que tanto promovió mi padre al fin eran la cotidianidad de su hijo mayor.

Mientras tanto, yo enfrenté el mundo lento de Clarita Rendón. Supongo que me dejaron con ella porque vivía sola; para mamá, la soledad nunca es una condición buscada; Clarita sufría su aislamiento y yo iba a aliviarla. La verdad es que mi anfitriona estaba hecha para vivir sin otra compañía que sus cinco mil libros. La doctora Rendón enseñaba Historia de las ideas y en su única pared sin libreros había colgado una ilustrada galería. Voltaire, Campanella, Kant y Condorcet supervisaban su escritorio. Ella era suficientemente fea para parecerse a los cuatro. Lo peculiar es que los genios no se parecían entre sí, Clarita era la combinatoria que los unía; como Martín Cifuentes, tenía la cualidad de atraer dispares semejanzas.

Por primera vez la ausencia de mamá me pareció más grave. Su tío fue aplastado por una prensa en Culiacán (estaba inmóvil, atrozmente enyesado, pero en su boca asomaba un termómetro que marcaba un febricular 37). Mamá tenía que aguardar a que esa última señal de vida se extinguiera; compró más ropas negras y habló a casa de Clarita para decir cómo debía portarme:

—Estáte sosiego.

El sosiego era la forma heroica de la calma. Aunque me atraía más la postura de Rita, a quien las turbulencias le sugerían otro martini, me resultaba fácil cumplir el mandato de mamá. Ser educado era moverse poco, asemejarse al pariente herido, cuya sola actividad parecía ser la de fumar vidrio.

Mi quietismo venía de una inclinación natural pero también de un rechazo. No pude entrar a los Amigos del Bosque porque mamá no desperdició la oportunidad de contar que era sonámbulo. El Amigo de turno consideró imprudente tenerme en su tienda de campaña; cualquier noche de ésas podía salir roncando y sumirme en las lagunas de Zempoala.

Lo cierto es que *apenas* fui sonámbulo. Cuando mi padre dejó de ver a Rita, tuve sueños en los que la mataba o la salvaba y empecé a caminar dormido. Despertaba llorando, frente a la recámara de mis padres. El asunto duró un par de meses, sin otras consecuencias que esta discusión:

—Déjalo entrar, Chus —pedía mamá (en su código personal aquella abreviatura sólo tenía una función: implorar).

—¡Que se curta! —respondía mi padre, como si hablara de un salami.

No me abrieron y me curtí en la puerta, lo cual quiere decir que los perjudicados fueron ellos. Mamá, que carecía de cultura cinematográfica, empezó a soñar con *El peñón de las ánimas*.

Las vacaciones eran un largo desierto. El primer día de libertad despertaba cargado de energía, a las seis de la mañana palpaba la nueva atmósfera, alerta, seguro de que algo me iba a sacudir. Un gallo de latón en espera del viento y sus rumbos. Dos horas después ya conocía la sustancia de las vacaciones. Arena, infinita arena.

Mis vacaciones más inolvidables coincidieron con el alejamiento de mis padres; mamá tuvo que ir a su tierra a velar la agonía de un tío abuelo y mi padre interrumpió la construcción de su hospital para remodelar un hotel en la costa, propiedad de Benjamín Gutiérrez Pool (un ciclón anegó los sótanos de planchado y avanzó hasta la suite presidencial; aunque resultaba improbable que un dignatario se hospedara en ese hotel de cuatro estrellas, un espacio cívico sin una cama para el presidente se hubiera visto como una plaza de toros sin un altar para los matadores; el nicho tenía que estar ahí, como un símbolo tranquilizador, y mi padre debía repararlo).

Carlos se fue de campamento con los Amigos del Bosque y yo acabé en casa de Clarita Rendón, una amiga de mamá.

En sus llamadas de larga distancia, mi padre decía con énfasis de canción ranchera: "no tengo para cuándo volver".

3. El Bello Durmiente

—¿Qué llevas? —preguntó.

Iba a acercarle la bolsa para que le diera asco pero en ese momento la sangre le escurrió de la nariz. Una gota cayó sobre mi zapato.

—Perdón —Eduarda me pidió que abriera la bolsa, ahuecó la mano y me mojó el empeine hasta dejarlo hecho un desastre.

Regresé a la casa, con el molesto rechinido de mis pasos nones. Al secar mi zapato, el olor a toalla húmeda me trajo una época que ya no existía y también, de un modo incalificable, la promesa de una piel futura. Pensé en Eduarda sangrada, en Verónica dormida, en la desconocida de la jeringa.

Cuando me secaba (durante más tiempo del que tardaba en bañarme) buscaba entre el vapor un rastro de *Aqua ardens*. De lejos me llegaba el estruendo del tocadiscos de Carlos, un aparato inestable, del tamaño de un portafolios. Me froté, con innecesaria lentitud, pensando en la niña que inyectaba naranjas, hasta que algo se trabó en el aire. Las toallas eran como los discos de 45 revoluciones que compraba Carlos. La parte de mi padre me hacía pensar en la canción de éxito, saturada de raspaduras.

Al reverso, el lado B, negro, intacto, aguardaba las agujas que lo llenarían de tiempo.

ba gabardina negra, un hombre honesto y descontento, al que siempre mataban por la espalda.

La voz de Pancho y la melancólica semejanza de Martín iban bien con mi estado de ánimo.

Nada me interesó hasta que fui al consultorio donde me quitaron el yeso. Ahí conocí a la hija de una enfermera; quería ser doctora y entrenaba el pulso inyectando una naranja. No he olvidado los lunares en el cuello, los dientes separados, la mano torturando la fruta. Un nudo extraño se trabó en mí; sentí electricidad en las plantas de los pies, un hueco en mi estómago de gordo. Murmuré unas palabras rotas para que me firmara el yeso. Tomó un plumón y trazó letras seguras e incomprensibles.

Durante años conservé en mi caja plateada su caligrafía de doctora, su rápido nombre con vocales en equis.

Las vacaciones se aproximaban, mi padre seguía en Reynosa y mamá hablaba cada vez más seguido con los parientes de Sinaloa que parecían darle consejos drásticos. "No es el momento", contestaba ella, "el gordo no ha terminado los exámenes". De un modo vago, supe que algo importante sucedería cuando acabara de memorizar la ruta de Hidalgo y la sucesión de emperadores aztecas. Las vacaciones iban a dividir nuestra vida. La tía Amelia me dijo que "pediría por mí" en el verano, como si el descanso fuese una tragedia.

En lo que llegaba el fin de cursos, sumía los dedos en la pecera, rozaba los cuerpos fríos que flotaban sin gracia, prehistóricos, inalterables, estudiaba sus ojos cristalinos, sus manos torpes, la aleta superior que medía diez, doce centímetros.

Una tarde saqué a pasear un ajolote en una bolsa de hule llena de agua. Encontré a Eduarda Ramos Nielsen recargada contra una barda.

Pero no lo hizo. Al contrario, sintió que beneficiarse era una forma de congruencia, de darle sentido a sus arrebatos: alejarse de Rita sería aún más provechoso que haberla conocido.

Nos avisó que se iba a Reynosa, a levantar un "nosocomio" donde el auditorio imitaría la pirámide del caracol de Uxmal.

Esa misma noche bajé a la sala y le pedí a mamá que soltara su libro (leía tomos inmensos, que acaso fueran un solo libro inagotable cuyo nombre nunca supe). La vi a los ojos y le hablé de Rita, del Lienzo del Charro, de los martes y los jueves, de los koalas de tres tamaños, de la mariguana y del incienso en el pequeño Buda.

Esperaba que me odiara, o mejor dicho, que se odiara en mí, pero ocurrió algo mucho peor. Encendió un Raleigh y dijo con total compostura:

—Ya lo sabía.

Su existencia era menos desabrida y más atroz de lo que yo suponía. Ni siquiera le molestó mi actitud de intrigante; su perdón inmenso, su bondadosa asfixia, me privaba de cualquier maldad.

Pero algo gané en ese intercambio. Si mamá toleraba a Rita, ¿por qué no iba a aceptar una pecera con ajolotes?

El día de su partida, mi padre dio consejos que no quise oír: los ajolotes podían mutar, no todos, sino los escogidos. Yo tenía que vigilarlos, cuidar la temperatura del agua, revisar que siguieran siendo tres.

Aunque salía poco de casa supe que Eduarda Ramos Nielsen se enamoró de Pancho y que él la rechazó con su nueva voz, una voz grave, de locutor que transmite para las "almas perdidas en la noche". Esto me lo dijo Martín, que seguía obsesionado con los extraterrestres y ahora se parecía a un actor francés que usa-

En el camino de regreso, al cabo de media hora, masculló:

—Tengo que cambiar. No soy así.

Lo dijo con total extrañamiento. ¿Cómo se comportaría cuando al fin fuera él?

Mi padre quería averiguarse, descubrirse. Yo no quería nada especial, pero desde la despedida en el aeropuerto pensaba en cambiar las rutas de los otros, en decir cosas que en forma indirecta me afectaran. Le conté de la visita a Ciudad Satélite. No sé por qué le di el argumento que le faltaba para terminar con Rita. Describí la droga, la cara del hombre moreno. Mi padre estacionó el coche junto a un terreno con pastos amarillos. ¿Por qué siempre había un hueco como paisaje de los momentos duros?

Habló de ella en forma extraña, llena de insinuaciones, de molestias imprecisas. Quería ser sincero pero temía maleducarme; un último resabio pedagógico lo llevó a explicar la "clase de persona que era Rita" con una confusión que pretendía preservar mi inocencia, pero donde las atrocidades se insinuaban con eficacia; entreví manos que la tomaban del pelo y la ataban dolorosamente, entreví abusos, un puñal que abría su espalda. Entonces le pedí que siguiera con ella:

—Por favorcito...—mi súplica fue tan auténtica que lo asustó y sólo contribuyó a reforzar su decisión de abandonarla.

Mi padre liquidó su traje de charro en un bazar y Benjamín Gutiérrez Pool, feliz de tenerlo en una segura periferia y sin la intermediación de Rita, le ofreció construir un hospital lleno de grecas y alardes prehispánicos. Era un momento ideal para la dignidad herida y el dramatismo que siempre le gustó a mi padre; podía mandar a Benja a las oficinas del carajo.

siasmaban a mamá? Martín comía tantos pellejos de Resistol que pensé que sus visiones se alimentaban del color opuesto; eran las pesadillas del blanco.

—Ella sí entiende —me dijo, y sus ojos se ensombrecieron.

Ella, por supuesto, era Verónica.

No tenía la menor intención de volver a la casa de mosaicos árabes, pero mi padre me obligó a ser testigo de sus muchos pleitos con Rita. Invariablemente me puse de parte de ella.

Una tarde, al regresar de una fiesta en el Lienzo donde el subsecretario lo presentó con unos amigos de la clase política "¡como si fuera una res de su establo!", mi padre azotó la puerta, impidió que Rita se acercara a la licorera, la tomó del antebrazo, la insultó, le imputó amantes y drogas que no podía probar.

—Me haces daño —dijo Rita y esto le dio ideas a mi padre.

Le lanzó un golpe que ella esquivó tirándose al sofá, la acorraló y trató de sofocarla con un cojín. Las piernas largas de Rita se movieron mucho, lanzando sus zapatos al techo. Yo grité, como para pulverizar las copas de cristal cortado. Mi padre aflojó su intento de asesinato, ella consiguió zafarse y corrió a su recámara.

Salí al jardín, donde estaba el columpio innecesario. Me entretuve pisoteando hormigas; al cabo de un rato alcé la vista y vi que el columpio se movía. Me volví hacia la casa; las paredes y las ventanas se estremecían por el temblor. Sólo pensé en salvar a Rita.

Subí las escaleras, abrí la puerta y fue entonces que presencié la cruda reconciliación de los amantes. Mi padre, semivestido de charro, se hundía en la adorable Rita.

con su regreso que con su partida. Cuando finalmente lo recibimos en la Sala B del aeropuerto, vimos a un hombre rejuvenecido, bronceado por los soles de Colima, que exudaba un entusiasmo incompatible. Me felicitó por mi fractura, como si hubiera caído en la batalla de Puebla, y le guiñó un ojo a Carlos por su herida de amor.

Venía eufórico y no perdió tiempo en incluirme en sus alarmantes iniciativas. En algún cabaret se había vuelto amigo íntimo de un ejecutivo de PEMEX; el monopolio petrolero usaba a un charro de mascota y mi padre se enteró de que habría una campaña publicitaria con un niño charro. A pesar de mi brazo enyesado me consideró aspirante ("¡si sólo se va a ver la cara con sombrero!"). Así, el lunes de San Juan fuimos a un estudio fotográfico donde encontramos suficientes niños charros para garantizar un futuro de fanatismo nacionalista. No me escogieron por gordo.

Una nueva leyenda apareció en el refrigerador: EL HOMBRE CONSTA DE ALMA, CUERPO Y ROPAS, lo cual significaba que el tercer elemento era el importante. Mamá estaba harta de recibir calcetines terrosos:

—Aprendan de Martín, tan bien plantado.

Martín Cifuentes se vestía con esmero por los extraterrestres. Había sido abordado por tres hombres vestidos de negro, con trajes de oficinistas:

—Tenían ojos con luz, dijeron que volverían por mí. Desde entonces no duermo. Tampoco me canso.

Su mirada estaba fija, lo cual no resultaba tan extraño, si se pensaba en su afición a comer pegamento.

Nadie tomó en serio aquella expedición sin ovnis ni rayos láser, pero él siguió vestido de negro.

¿Era posible que una tecnología superior llegara con esas ropas de funcionarios que sólo entu-

pero me sabía incapaz de un remedio drástico. Desde el clóset, mi traje de charro anunciaba una violencia inútil: ningún caballo recibiría mi aguijón en sus ijares. Las telenovelas repetían, insaciables, una frase que obligaba a disculpar cualquier atrocidad hecha en familia: "pero si es tu padre..." Cada vez que la oía aumentaba mi sed de venganza; la rabia me limaba, ácida, voraz, pero mi única salida fue renunciar a lo que más me gustaba.

Un jueves, cuando regresaba de un paseo entre ajolotes, la señora que iba a planchar me dijo:

—Le habló una Rita, joven Mauricio —(mamá insitía en el trato de "joven Mauricio" para darle a la casa un aire de grandeza esclavista; sin embargo, ella respondía el teléfono como una empleada: "casa del arquitecto Guardiola...").

No quise devolver la llamada de Rita; me asumí como un mártir intenso, abierto en canal por una obsidiana.

Fui a la papelería y descubrí una imagen ideal para el momento: una estampa de San Andrés, crucificado en equis. Compensé la realidad con sufrimientos imaginarios aun peores. Como si intuyera mis dilemas, mamá escribió en el refrigerador: LA DESGRACIA NUNCA VIAJA SOLA. Allí estaba el anuncio de los meses de borrasca en los que todo iría mal: los desastres conocidos perdurarían —Verónica sin abrir los ojos, Pancho indiferente, Rita lejana— y cualquier novedad sería nefasta.

Para colmo, Carlos y yo tuvimos padecimientos que en cierta forma podían considerarse voluntarios. Él contrajo su primera gonorrea y yo me rompí el brazo. Por gordo, me escogieron de "base" para la *pirámide humana* del 5 de mayo. Aunque estaba muy cerca del suelo, me las arreglé para fracturarme ante la Sociedad de Padres de Familia.

La ausencia de mi padre duró lo suficiente para que yo perfeccionara mi rencor y sufriera más

"¿Quién es?" "¿Qué le pasó?", me preguntaban. ¿Podía explicar que estaba disfrazado para que mamá no supiera que visitaba a la idolatrada amante de mi padre? Un hombre me preguntó dónde vivía; logré mencionar mi barrio y todos me miraron con asquerosa naturalidad, como si venir de esa orilla justificara mi atuendo rural y mi desesperación de fin de mundo. Nadie se ofreció a llevarme.

Un pequeño cortejo me acompañó al tranvía. Me regalaron una pastilla que se me fue intacta al esófago y un anciano cortés extendió su bastón, como si fuese menester señalar la parada.

Subí al vagón amarillo. Al frente, un rótulo anunciaba una remota dirección azteca.

Al martes siguiente aproveché que Rita habló durante media hora por teléfono para explorar sus cajones. Buscaba bolsas y frascos de droga, pero encontré algo inesperado: una obsidiana. La sostuve como un raro cristal, tratando de alterarla, de convencerme de que no se trataba de la flecha que le di a mi padre. Sin embargo, ahí estaba la rajada, nítida, acusatoria. Aunque ya no era idéntica, era la misma: él había mandado pulir las aristas para darle forma de corazón. Con su gusto por las suplantaciones, transformó el arma en el órgano que debía extirpar. Pero entonces sólo me importó que regalara mi regalo. Salí de la casa antes de que Rita colgara y no volví a visitarla.

Le dije a mamá que mis clases en el Lienzo se habían suspendido por temporada de lluvias. En Terminal Progreso el cielo estaba despejado, pero me creyó porque para ella la ciudad era una abstracción extensa que podía incluir todos los climas.

Alejarme de Rita fue una solución estúpida; ella no sufría mi ausencia y yo la extrañaba. Además, el culpable de todo era mi padre; no podía perdonarlo

Arrancó el coche y me recosté en sus muslos calientes. Tardamos mucho en volver a casa. Ella iba despacio, sin quejarse del tráfico; sus lágrimas me caían en la nuca.

De vez en cuando yo levantaba la vista y miraba un trozo de cielo por el parabrisas. Tenía ganas de llorar. Para no hacerlo, pensé que el cielo estaba en otra parte. Entonces "otra parte" siempre era Acapulco. Nunca había ido ahí, pero la televisión promovía sin tregua las playas y los acantilados frente al Pacífico. Imaginé que avanzábamos entre palmeras y el ruido de los motores se convirtió en un oleaje.

Fue un momento extrañamente triste y feliz. Al llegar a la casa, Rita me dijo "vístete", como si la escena estuviera en otra vida. Tal vez por sentir una cercanía adulta le pregunté quién era el hombre de Ciudad Satélite.

—Equis... —respondió para restarle importancia, pero la letra que mandó a mi padre a Colima se me grabó como una afrenta.

Me puse el traje de charro mientras ella se bañaba.

Algo se rompió entonces. No me despedí. Caminé como un autómata a la parada del tranvía, con la mente en el frasco de droga, la mano que dominaba el cuerpo de Rita, los ojos vencidos, aquel insulto babeante, monocorde.

Un poco antes de llegar a la parada encontré un poste de madera. Por alguna razón me pareció mejor que los de cemento. Lo abracé y lloré como un perro. La expresión es idiota pero así lloré, como una bestia sumisa, alimentada de tortillas secas. La brea del poste se me untó a la cara, una señora se acercó, dijo "niño", preguntó qué me pasaba.

Al cabo de un rato había cinco curiosos tratando de descifrar mis balbuceos. Una palabra profunda me salía del estómago en dos golpes: "Ri-ta, Ri-ta."

mi casa podía estar horas sin otra diversión que ver el techo y rara vez caía dormido; sin embargo, la tensión de espiar a mi padre o a Rita, de buscar un sentido en sus escenas lentas, solía sumirme en un sueño profundo y mínimo. Cuando abrí los ojos, ella salía de la casa, con pasos inseguros, como si tuviera una piedra en el zapato. Abrió la puerta del coche y se desplomó en el asiento.

Yo no pensaba decir nada pero ella abrió la mano frente a mi rostro, un gesto de "ni preguntes".

Pensé que saldríamos de allí a toda prisa, pero ella vio la calle durante tanto tiempo que me entretuve contando las cagadas en el solar de junto.

Esa tarde excepcional y horrenda conocí el cuerpo de Rita y descubrí otro tipo de deseo. También entreví a una mujer humillada, frágil, insoportable; Rita miró la calle como si la calle no fuera nada y al cabo de un rato las lágrimas le bajaron por las mejillas con un rastro negro. Poco a poco una palabra se formó en su boca, un insulto preciso que repitió en silencio, los labios unidos por un hilillo de saliva. Sus manos se aferraban al volante como para librarse de un mareo. Luego pareció recordar que estaba allí, en su coche oloroso a alfombras y hules nuevos. Se limpió los ojos de un modo absurdo, con el dorso de las manos, y quedó como los koalas de tres tamaños que le había dado mi padre.

Abrió su bolso, sacó las llaves del coche y un frasco con un polvo blanco. Hundió la llave en el frasco y se la llevó a la nariz. Aspiró con fuerza, dos o tres veces.

—No has visto nada —me dijo, justo cuando empezaba a preguntarme por qué me dejaba ver todo.

Se chupó un dedo, lo sumió en el frasco y se lo frotó en las encías. Entonces me miró como si redescubriera mi presencia, me acarició el pelo y me estrechó contra ella. Me cautivó su olor sucio.

Me preparé para los asombros de Ciudad Satélite, pero después de tomar un trébol de autopistas, entramos a una colonia idéntica a la mía.

Rita condujo por calles que revelaban improvisación: lotes baldíos, construcciones a medias, un taller mecánico con un coche cubierto de óxido y un perro flaco encadenado, casitas donde una reja dorada, una pequeña fuente de piedra o un David de porcelana luchaban por lograr un toque de señorío.

Nos detuvimos junto a un coche negro, de vidrios oscuros.

—Espérame aquí.

Pulsó el timbre de una casa de ventanas con vidrios polarizados y marcos de aluminio. Abrió la puerta un hombre de unos cuarenta años; su camisa arremangada dejaba ver unos brazos gruesos, muy morenos; en la muñeca le brillaba un reloj costoso. Tenía un bigote espeso, el pelo húmedo, una toalla floja en el cuello. Yo no perdía detalle, y Rita lo sabía; desvió la mirada hacia el coche y puso las palmas en el pecho del hombre para posponer el abrazo, pero él la estrechó con fuerza. Se besaron de un modo goloso, abriendo las bocas y moviendo mucho las lenguas. Nunca había visto que mi padre la besara de ese modo. Ella alzó un zapato cereza, como hacían las mujeres en el cine.

La mano grande de aquel hombre recorrió la espalda de Rita, le acarició las nalgas, muy despacio, y le hundió el índice en la raya. Sólo al ver las nalgas controladas por esa mano impositiva tuve ganas de hacer lo mismo. En el coche de Rita experimenté la primera erección no provocada por un *comic* ni por los sueños donde el vulcanizador me lamía con su lengua de fuego.

Rita estuvo bastante rato dentro de la casa. Ignoro si pueda llamarse "narcolepsia" a mi capacidad para dormirme en las escenas de los adultos. En

imposible valorar una emoción inédita: no supe lo que sentí. Estaba alterado, nervioso, trataba de pensar lo que veía, de entender ese raro portento. Aunque hubiera preferido menos vellos en el pubis, la misma mente que tasó la objetiva belleza de Eduarda tenía que reconocer la supremacía de Rita.

Ella actuó con fascinante desesperación, pasó un rato revolviendo cajones e insultando a la lavandera, finalmente encontró unos zapatos color cereza y un vestido de estambre que se puso por arriba, como una camiseta. Le quedó muy ceñido. Luego se recogió el pelo con una pinza, dejando mechones sueltos en la frente y las orejas, se colgó un collar dorado, unos aretes grandes.

—¿Cómo me veo?

Desde mi perspectiva en el piso pude contemplar un brote de vello púbico.

—¿No te vas a poner calzones?

—Se me marcan —sonrió de un modo avasallante, pero sólo por un segundo.

Escogió cinco o seis pulseras y me jaló hacia la puerta.

Manejó de pésimo humor, mentándole la madre a los coches que embestía. Íbamos hacia el norte, de modo que la ciudad empeoraba con su carácter.

Después de casi una hora avizoramos las torres de Ciudad Satélite. Su diseño era futurista —flotaban en el aire, como hechas de papel— y sus colores, una declaración de que el porvenir sería mexicano o no sería.

Para la escuela nacionalista a la que pertenecía mi padre, aquellas torres eran un adoratorio; el hecho de que sirvieran de depósitos de agua reforzaba su condición trascendente (en la segunda prédica del Lienzo del Charro, el arquitecto Guardiola dijo: "tenemos nostalgia de los canales, del lago que enterramos en la ciudad").

bajaba la falda para no mostrar demasiado los muslos. No me interesaba su cuerpo pero me halagaba que ella pensara lo contrario. Las mujeres suaves seguían lejos de mi interés, por lo demás en Terminal Progreso las niñas no salían de sus casas y las únicas piernas que se acercaban a las mías eran las de los amigos, llenas de costras y manchas de merthiolate. Exhaustos, sudorosos después de correr sin ningún propósito, escogíamos un claro entre los árboles y nos acariciábamos con dedos terrosos y uñas mordidas. En las tardes de lluvia nos desnudábamos para jugar al "elefantito". Desfilábamos en círculo, tomados de nuestras trompas. Estas rondas, de una irrecuperable tristeza zoológica, terminaban con masturbaciones en algún arroyo; las gotas de semen se hundían como crías albinas de los ajolotes.

En aquel grupo Pancho sobresalía en tal forma que me sorprendía su renuencia a usar su poder. Yo me hubiera aprovechado en forma cruenta. Él se limitaba a tenderse en el pasto, boca abajo; sus nalgas recibían la lluvia, sus ojos permanecían cerrados. Un dios imbécil, ajeno a la adoración.

Un jueves toqué el timbre de Rita (uno de esos timbres "femeninos", de doble campanilla) y abrió con una expresión que jamás le había visto:

—Tienes que acompañarme —el comentario fue absurdo; ya sabíamos que mi llegada en traje de charro significaba que estaría varias horas a su disposición.

Me llevó al vestidor en el piso de arriba y me desnudó de prisa, casi con furia. Me senté en el piso, para amarrarme los zapatos. Entonces ocurrió algo insólito: Rita se desvistió frente a mí. Supongo que ante el primer cuerpo desnudo de otro sexo y otra edad, el asombro siempre antecede al deseo. Resulta

pelería me causaron mayor efecto, tal vez por ser portátiles, o porque me recordaban la narrativa en cuadros de las historietas. Buscaba en ellas una figura intermedia, apta para recibir un sadismo de *comic* —el vejatorio rayo láser—, los clavos abandonados en los campos de la colonia y los tizones del vulcanizador.

La expulsión de Vulcano, su ultraje final, completó su figura de leyenda. Me detuve ante su local como si mirara un secreto incendiado. El repudio que inspiraba en los demás le otorgó un curioso espesor. Se hablaba de él con un odio rutinario. Lo amé, no como se ama al débil, sino al que sabe soportar las heridas que merece. Su fuerza se alimentaba del desprecio que sobrellevaba como un segundo hollín.

El cierre de la vulcanizadora me hizo buscar a Pancho. Me olvidé de un rencor que de cualquier forma él nunca advirtió.

Apenas había reparado en el asunto; la suerte del ídolo le importaba poco.

—¿Te gusta lo que no conoces? —me interrogó con insidia.

Pancho había crecido en los meses en que dejamos de vernos. Que expresara algo en forma de pregunta ya era una excentricidad adulta. Además, la frase me caló hondo. A Pancho le interesaba una idea si con ella podía romper al menos un florero; estaba hecho para repercutir, para lograr algo tangible; en cambio, yo sólo parecía capaz de disfrutar las cosas en su ausencia. Estuve tan lejos del vulcanizador que su partida significó un acercamiento. Pensé en él a todas horas. La puerta condenada ofrecía un segundo acceso, una eficaz manera de sufrir los anhelos incumplidos.

El coche de Rita era muy grande, un Tarot de asiento corrido. Me sentaba muy cerca de ella y la ayudaba a cambiar las velocidades. De cuando en cuando se

hasta tocarse la nuca y bebió el líquido de un tirón. Desde antes de este capricho su trapecio nos mantuvo absortos y aterrados; un silencio espléndido llenaba la carpa, la multitud torcía el cuello para verla, en un pacto de inmovilidad, y sin embargo, como si eso fuera poco, decidió beber el refresco sin perder el equilibro.

Siempre asocié ese rasgo adicional con Rita. Vivía, no sólo para encontrar las llaves y los boletos en el último momento, sino para disfrutar el vértigo, para beber algo dulce al filo del vacío.

Pero la trapecista también me deparó una decepción. En lo alto de la carpa parecía una grácil adolescente. Cuando descendió de cabeza, atada a una cuerda, vi su rostro lleno de arrugas. La elástica mujer tenía dentro una anciana. Como la asociaba con Rita, este nuevo prodigio me hizo esperar algo terrible. ¿Había otra mujer adentro de ella? Soñé que me llevaba a otra fiesta del Niño Peregrino y secuestraba al muñeco para sentarlo en un columpio de su casa:

—Mécelo —me pedía.

Yo me convertía en esclavo del dios de un año.

Un lunes la cortina de Vulcano permaneció cerrada. El miércoles escuché los rumores: lo habían expulsado, nadie decía cómo ni por qué, pero las miradas me recordaron el desprecio con que el padre de Pancho habló de la Zona de Jesús. Alguien, poderoso y lejano, dio la orden. Los fierros fueron sacados de noche, tal vez para evitar la defensa de sus idólatras. El vulcanizador se convirtió al fin en un héroe castigado, en un mártir semejante a los que acababa de descubrir en la papelería.

Aunque la iglesia de San Bernardino ofrecía su ración de sangre —estatuas abiertas con eficacia por los encarnadores virreinales—, las estampas de la pa-

Ignoraba el poder que me confería. Yo era su hijo consentido, tenía el rostro de la mujer que una vez quiso y me llevaba bien con la mujer que ahora idolatraba; lo que él no sabía era que en esos urinarios donde se eliminaban líquidos bebidos en tres continentes, estaba ante otra persona. Es absurdo hablar de un instante de elección, pero si hubo uno en mi infancia fue ése; durante años mi padre me tuvo cerca, en una proximidad que empezaba a ser excesiva; al irse, confiaba en alguien que ya no existía.

En la escuela, un maestro tuvo el tino de hablar del pez piloto. De inmediato me identifiqué con él; mi padre y Carlos disponían de una fuerza incompatible, pero yo podía torcer sus destinos, conducirlos, comer sus desperdicios. En el momento menos pensado, bajo el blanco vientre y la dentada hendidura, sería el dueño de la ruta.

Martes y jueves me puse el traje café con leche. Supongo que mi padre deseaba que mi presencia tuviera un efecto inhibitorio y que cualquier desliz saliera a relucir en la conducta de Rita (ya anticipaba las preguntas que me haría sobre regalos, llamadas telefónicas, un viaje inesperado, nombres dichos sin querer).

No sé qué misterio de la bondad hizo que ella aceptara mi compañía. Al llegar a su casa me quitaba el traje absurdo, me ponía una camiseta y me llevaba a todas partes en calidad de "sobrino".

Su horario estaba lleno de citas y compras de emergencia, como si nada pudiera anticiparse. En una ocasión le pareció que el circo era una actividad urgente y fuimos a un lote baldío en las afueras donde una carpa se alzaba entre jaulas viejas. Recuerdo con exactitud a una trapecista. Lo que más me impresionó fue un gesto gratuito: una vez en las alturas, recibió una soga con un refresco color naranja, alzó un pie

Para efectos del discurso, convenía que la pasión fuera mucho más definida que los argumentos. Cada quien entendió lo que quiso. Sólo el aplauso fue unánime.

Por desgracia, al día siguiente supe que mi padre estaba lejos de alcanzar en su vida las alianzas que celebraba en la ortografía nacional. El campeón unitario estaba escindido:

—No soy así.

Me pregunté si no era "él" en casa de Rita o en Terminal Progreso, y fue como si escuchara mis pensamientos porque se rascó la cabeza con tal fuerza que unos cabellos blancos se le enredaron en los dedos.

—Tengo que irme —agregó, como si su identidad esperara a su cuerpo en otro sitio.

Decidió salir a Colima al día siguiente de su cumpleaños. Mi padre se veía cada vez peor y se me ocurrió darle un regalo. Nunca antes había querido compensar su vida con un objeto; escogí mi mejor flecha de obsidiana, una pieza grande, aplanada con cuidado por un azteca. Él le dio tanta importancia que la guardó en su saco, en la bolsa del pañuelo, donde nunca guardaba nada.

Fuimos a despedirlo al aeropuerto y mamá me puso corbata, como si se tratara de una ceremonia. Mi hermano no perdió la oportunidad de conquistar nuevos territorios y le picó el culo a una azafata sueca. Mientras mamá pedía disculpas en un inglés deplorable, mi padre me llevó al baño "a hablar de hombre a hombre". Entre el olor a orines y alcanfor me pidió que vigilara a Rita:

—Ya hablé con ella, te espera los martes y los jueves. Tienes que ir de charro: le dije a tu mamá que ibas a tomar clases en el Lienzo.

estaba lejos y se replegaría aún más si tratábamos de alcanzarlo. Pero mi padre opinaba distinto y ante cada nombre mencionado por ella descubría la opción que más lo humillaba.

—¡Pero si tú eres casado, Chuy! —esta sentencia irrefutable hizo que mi padre me mandara a comprarle unos chicles. Me tardé unos veinte minutos para que explicara cómo pensaba divorciarse.

Creo que jamás calculó lo mucho que llegaría a amar a Rita. En un principio, cuando alababa las licoreras y los espadines de Toledo de la planta baja, parecía aceptar, e incluso celebrar, que ella recibiera dinero de otros hombres, pero con el tiempo odió esa relación que funcionaba tan bien bajo el cinismo y tan mal bajo la pasión.

La segunda conferencia en el Lienzo del Charro fue un acto trascendente. Tal vez el apoyo de Benjamín Gutiérrez Pool animó a mi padre a decir cosas que ignoraba; habló como si todo se le ocurriera en ese instante. Un reflector alumbró su pelo de charro recién desmontado, y durante dos horas fue un impecable gurú de lo "nuestro". Dijo que los materiales nobles eran la mezcla de lo masculino y lo femenino: la tierra y el agua madres embestidas por el azadón. Describió al horno de los ladrillos como "matriz" y al cemento como "maridaje". No fue muy claro, pero la gente deseaba oscuridades en esa segunda sesión. Las rugosas uniones aludían a un ideal aún desconocido. La equis, símbolo de la dualidad, unía dos pueblos, dos razas, dos géneros. "Letra criolla", pronunció mi padre, y yo pensé en otras mezclas raras, el Hombre Perfecto descrito como "dama" por la tía Amelia, el Niñopa que ejercía su paternidad de un año, el Valiente que acuchillaba, Martín, idéntico a tantos modelos distintos.

En el camino de regreso discutieron mucho a causa de la blusa:

—Pareces turista —dijo mi padre, y su crítica me dejó perplejo.

No volví a ver aquella blusa típica que misteriosamente convirtió a Rita en extranjera. Yo dominaba cada rincón de su vestidor y me concentraba en la sección de lencería. Tal vez Rita sabía que revisaba sus calzones, pues me costaba trabajo dejarlos en el mismo orden que mamá pedía para sus alacenas; en todo caso, ése no era el mejor sitio para guardar aquella bolsa de celofán con un polvo blanco, brillante, muy fino. Antes de entrar en otra boca, mi lengua entró en una bolsa de cocaína.

La taquicardia me hizo salir al jardín y acostarme en el pasto con energía. La expresión es contradictoria pero real: tenderme era algo más intenso y vibrante que activar los columpios; yací con fuerza, alerta, aliado de las mil hormigas.

Un suave olor a podredumbre me recordó la colección de objetos que solía colocar en mi cama, como si tratara de formar un dibujo que me explicara.

En vísperas de su viaje a Colima, mi padre acosó a Rita con reproches; el temor a dejarla sola lo volvió imaginativo en exceso; sospechaba de todos y de todo, la involucraba en situaciones precisas, siempre imaginarias. En una ocasión, harta de sus plurales desvaríos, ella le respondió con una frase inolvidable:

—Si eres el preferido, ¿para qué quieres ser el único?

Los destinos de Rita, sus escenografías impares, tenían que ver con varios hombres. A mí me pareció perfecto que ella tuviese alternativas; su horizonte

Peregrino, o Niño Padre, o Niño Dios custodiado por una familia que lo sacaba a pasear el 2 de febrero.

No había el menor riesgo de que nos vieran con Rita porque los habitantes de Terminal Progreso nunca iban a las fiestas de Xochimilco.

Al único que vimos de lejos fue al padre de Verónica, con una expresión tensa, como si un perro callejero hurgara entre sus piernas.

Tal vez pensaba en su hija desmayada. La gira del Niño Dios, y la algarabía de palmas y confeti, eran el triunfo de un pequeño tirano inerte. El padre de Verónica miraba la escena con fanático descontento, como si ese veneno pudiera ayudarlo a comprender su situación, como si deseara aceptar la idolatría de un bulto joven, convencerse de que el sufrimiento es algo parejo, inescapable, que alcanza a cualquiera y sólo sorprende en sus detalles.

Ante el padre de Verónica, pensé que la "tradición" —palabra favorita de mi padre— consistía en escoger por capricho lo que para otros era una fatalidad.

La muchedumbre llevó en hombros al Niñopa, un muñeco arropado con terciopelos; los fieles se empujaban para recibir el peso del niño fundador, el patriarca de un año, el Dios sin idioma, que mi padre miraba como una aparición.

Desde entonces, al escuchar las distantes trompetas de Xochimilco, imaginaba al Niño Peregrino y su rebaño de adultos, las manos arrugadas, llenas de pecas, que le ofrecían juguetes.

Rita se divirtió con el Niño Padre como si estuviera en un buen hipódromo. Para ella, lo importante era la alegría manifiesta, la exacta combinación de ruido y movimiento.

Antes de llegar al Kybalión, se detuvo en un puesto callejero a comprar una blusa con un bordado que parecía un muestrario de los colores que mi padre propuso para su edificio en equis.

autobuses que llevaban el pensado nombre de *refu-
giatones*. Aunque el edificio se levantaría en Colima,
el país entero debía saber lo que el gobierno hacía
para combinar los valores nacionales con los ladrillos.
La letra equis, que nos distinguía de los pueblos par-
cos que sólo usaban la jota, era la nueva inicial de
Jesús Guardiola.

Rita asumió el proyecto como un logro personal y dio un desayuno donde dos meseros sirvieron
chocolate en jarras de plata y donde resultó obvio que
ese éxito le quedaba chico. Ella merecía las esbeltas palmeras de Beverly Hills, los jardines con antorchas de
Tailandia, un yate en altamar, algo más que los hombres
que ocupaban las cabeceras de la mesa como los respec-
tivos dueños de la planta baja y la planta alta.

En un momento en que mi padre se apartó de
la mesa, el licenciado Gutiérrez Pool dijo algo que me
dejó frío:

—Es una dama —el elogio de la tía Amelia cayó
como una daga.

Mi padre estuvo muy tenso en el desayuno. Le
molestaba la mantequilla en forma de caracol, el vestido de Rita, el amplio escote, la acidez del jugo de
naranja, lo que fuera, literalmente lo que fuera. Quería a Rita, como nunca quiso a nadie, y se dejaba afectar por nimiedades que no hubiera advertido en otras
mujeres; ella le importaba lo suficiente para que las
minucias fueran irritantes, y para soportarlas.

Rita tenía tal pasión por las fiestas populares que iba
a todas, sin reparar en las tradiciones que las susten-
taban. Un 2 de febrero decidió celebrar la Candelaria
cerca de nuestra colonia:

—Vamos a ver al Niño Peregrino.

Mi padre sabía algo del asunto y me explicó
que en Xochimilco se veneraba al Niñopa, o Niño

rápido como sus palabras. Seguramente le preocupaba que Rita desconfiara de su talento; la letanía "no son enchiladas" empezó a trabajar en su contra. Nos convenció de que el asunto era muy complejo, y de que no estaba a su alcance.

Una madrugada en que tenía un sueño tranquilo a pesar de su contenido (una oveja negra a punto de ser degollada), mi padre me despertó para que bajara a ver algo que, a esa hora incierta, se reveló como una gigantesca equis. Su edificio, visto desde arriba.

—Miren la entrada —mostró un triángulo incómodo—: ¡el arco maya!

Según supimos en el anticipado desayuno, aquella unidad habitacional lograba el mejor aprovechamiento del espacio para celebrar la equis. Sólo entendimos el valor trascendental de esa letra cuando gritó:

—¡México se escribe con equis!

Curiosamente, este detalle de patriótica ortografía hizo que le soltaran millones. El licenciado Gutiérrez Pool volvió a ser Benja, organizó un concurso en el que primero exigió que el bufet presentara el proyecto de Jesús Guardiola y luego eliminó a los contrincantes. El Ishtar se desbieló de tanto ir de Terminal Progreso a San Ángel, y mi padre lo sustituyó por un Kybalión con carburador de dos gargantas. Hubo que discutir mucho hasta que un agremiado al Lienzo del Charro ofreció sus terrenos y otro importó de Estados Unidos máquinas para hacer adobes ("por el factor velocidad", explicó mi padre, con énfasis científico, para no discutir por qué lo auténtico venía de lejos).

Como se necesitaba visión aérea para distinguir la equis, Gutiérrez Pool mandó tomar fotos en helicóptero y el proyecto se promovió en carteles en el Anillo Periférico y en los techos de las paradas de

virtudes a su nuevo aspecto. Además, desde la visita al subsecretario dormía poco, pasaba horas extra en el despacho o en la mesa del comedor y le gritaba a Rita con cariñosa desesperación:

—¡Si no son enchiladas, mi vida!

Benjamín Gutiérrez Pool le había dado una oportunidad que parecía una condena. Las enchiladas se cocinaban por gusto y en dos minutos. Aquello era algo gordo, muy gordo.

Seguramente lo que le interesó a Gutiérrez Pool no fue tanto el discurso de mi padre como su impacto en el público: trescientos inversionistas en traje de charro aplaudieron con furor, y él calculó lo que podía sacarles. Tal vez también deseaba favorecer a Rita en una forma que refrendara su dominio, recordarle quién mandó hacer sus retratos. En todo caso, su buena voluntad sirvió para que mi padre y Rita se trataran con una tensión desconocida.

Casi extrañé los días en que el arquitecto Guardiola no tenía otra ambición constructiva que transformar un desván en un medio baño. Mamá, en cambio, le preparaba termos con café, le dejaba guisos en el horno por si la desvelada le abría el apetito, bajaba a verlo envuelta en una burda frazada de cuadros que hacía pensar que dormía en el suelo.

Los meses en los que la cabeza de mi padre se llenó de canas fueron los más felices de mamá. El terapeuta la dio de alta y fuimos a celebrar a una cafetería donde pidió un *banana split*, un postre que no le gustaba mucho pero que era la representación más gráfica de su entusiasmo. Luego fue al salón de belleza, donde le pintaron las uñas de los pies, y se compró un vestido hasta los tobillos, de tela sintética, con un enorme zíper al frente. Se necesitaba estar muy contenta para usarlo.

Mi padre llevaba proyectos del bufet a la oficina de San Ángel, pero sus diseños no convencían tan

Mi nombre selló las paces y le dio a sus propósitos un tono de valores profundos, de herencia irrenunciable.

Tal vez por eso a los pocos días me pidieron que los acompañara a la oficina privada del subsecretario de Obras Públicas.

Benjamín Gutiérrez Pool recibía en una casa de San Ángel, circundada de un enorme jardín. Hicimos antesala en sillones de cuero guinda y un mozo de librea nos ofreció "un whisquicito" extraño a las once de la mañana. En la mesa de centro había un caballo de plata y en las paredes serigrafías que mi padre contempló con aprobación (un coyote aullándole a la luna, una reunión de sandías). Los gustos públicos de Gutiérrez Pool diferían mucho de los retratos que encargaba para sus amigas.

Aunque debíamos sentirnos honrados de estar en el sitio donde el subsecretario despachaba los asuntos "fuertes", que se resolvían "en corto", las dos horas de espera demostraron que podíamos ser afines pero no urgentes. Me torcí el cuello ensayando posturas para dormir en los sillones. Cuando abrí los ojos supe que me había perdido la entrevista: mi padre y Rita salían de la junta. Me concentré en los zapatos del licenciado, tan brillantes que sospeché que mi padre había entrado a darle lustre.

Fue en ese tiempo que dejé de usar goma para el pelo y tuve caspa por primera vez. Curiosamente, los copos blancos me hicieron sentir orgulloso, como si revelaran una moral de la edad; la caspa era un predicamento adulto, y nada me parecía mejor que crecer, aunque fuera para contagiarme.

Usaba el peine de mi padre y entre los dientes de plástico encontraba pelos que pasaban del rubio al cenizo. Aunque un charro canoso es mucho más convincente que uno rubio, él no le encontraba

Las palabras "cuates" y "changarro" salieron de aquella boca como regalos carísimos.

Benja se dirigió al fondo de la sala. Aun después de que salió, varios charros siguieron viendo la puerta. En aquel ambiente de amistades impulsivas, resultaba extraña la admiración que rodeaba al calvo.

Me sorprendió que sólo fuera subsecretario de Obras Públicas.

—¿No ves que maneja un presupuesto mayor que el de Costa Rica? —explicó mi padre en el camino de regreso, con una enjundia que casi nos estrelló contra un trolebús.

En casa de Rita me mandaron al piso de arriba. Bajé a gatas, oculto por el borde de la escalera. A esa hora, el vitral era un filtro violáceo. No encendieron la luz.

Mi padre le preguntó por Benjamín Gutiérrez Pool.

—Lo conocí en Nogales, cuando era muy chamaca.

Benja y Rita eran paisanos. Él siempre la había apoyado; la apadrinó para que participara en un concurso de belleza, le consiguió un puesto en el ballet folklórico del estado, la conectó con la gente de Aeroméxico.

—Los retratos, ¿los mandó hacer él?

—Eso fue hace siglos...

No vi lo que hizo mi padre pero ella gritó "Jesús" en un tono totalmente profano.

Luego escuché el tintineo de las licoreras. Bebieron en silencio; imaginé a mi padre rascarse el pelo y a Rita en su ballet, meciéndose como una lánguida tehuana.

Quizá me dormí un rato, el caso es que, de un modo inconexo, escuché que ella decía "por nosotros" y mi padre, sin ceder del todo, contestaba "por Mauricio".

elocuencia seducía por el ritmo y por sus ojos, que confiaban mucho en la distancia, el horizonte donde se edificarían sus anhelos. Era tan articulado que parecía hablar de otra cosa, de algo tan cercano que no hacía falta mencionar; su voz sobrecogía como una tristeza buena e indefinible, un rumor nuestro, un silbido que se pierde en el altiplano, entre la tierra llovida. Así recupero esas palabras evanescentes, mi padre nos hizo sentir muy solos, emocionados de tocar el polvo con las manos, recoger piedras, levantar la casa. El auditorio lo escuchó como si fuera un gurú del espacio mexicano; al final de su discurso, "adobe" quería decir "patria" y "azul añil", "nosotros".

Hubo una ovación que compartí con total oportunismo. Mi padre me subió al estrado y alcé una mano para demostrar que nuestro éxito era rutina, pero produje un nervioso movimiento de mecanógrafo. Desde ahí vi a un colega de mi padre, el arquitecto que lo llevó al bufet, compartiendo las felicitaciones en la puerta de salida.

Sólo entendí el alcance de esta prédica cuando el hombre que llevaba el calendario azteca en el índice saludó con aspavientos a un calvo de corbatín color perla que apenas le dirigió un parpadeo.

El calvo miraba como si los demás fueran paisaje. Sólo fijó la vista en mi padre:

—Tenemos que amarrar una cita —le dijo. Su boca dibujó una sonrisa de triunfo, como si mi padre esperara la cita desde su nacimiento.

—Hombre, licenciado... —mi padre trató de aplacarse el pelo.

—Benjamín, para los cuates —el calvo detuvo la mano en el hombro de mi padre, con afectuosa cautela. Vi sus uñas manicureadas.

—Benja es divino —comentó Rita.

—Te espero por mi changarro.

En la tarde se sirvió un bufet tumultuoso en el que se necesitaba media hora para llegar del mole a las tortillas.

Me llevé mi plato al estacionamiento. Aunque estábamos en plena ciudad, los charros favorecían camionetas de volteo, con llantas que hacían pensar en ríos crecidos y reses enlodadas. De lejos, llegaba el fragor de las trompetas y los alaridos del cuarto tequila. Oriné entre unos magueyes enormes, que me cubrían por completo; uno había floreado: vi el mástil amarillento.

Regresé despacio a la construcción donde los mariachis se escuchaban con repentina nitidez, como si cantaran en un ruedo desierto. Subí los escalones de baldosas coloradas y encontré un tablero con letras de plástico: EL ESPÍRITU MEXICANO, CONFERENCIA DEL ARQUITECTO JESÚS GUARDIOLA, SALÓN TAPATÍO.

La sala tenía aspecto de centro de convenciones; alfombra de yute y sillería con respaldos de plástico. Los charros y las chinas poblanas se abanicaban con papeles morados que, según me enteré después, informaban el cambio de domicilio del bufet donde trabajaba mi padre.

Me senté en el piso, en primera fila, entre las botas olorosas a vaca de un magnate (decidí sus ingresos al ver su anillo de oro con el calendario azteca). Mi padre subió a la tarima; llevaba el pelo en desorden por los ajetreos del día y esto le daba un aspecto atribulado, a la manera de un virtuoso del violín. Habló de pie, sosteniendo el micrófono en la mano derecha, con apostura escénica. Sus ademanes dependían de la mano izquierda: cortaba el aire como un anticipo de los ladrillos de adobe que prometía su boca.

No recuerdo las palabras pero sí la corriente de energía que circulaba entre él y el auditorio; su

se ofrecían una ayuda que ninguno de ellos parecía necesitar. En el pórtico —un arco rematado con tejas donde "Lienzo del Charro" estaba escrito en una caligrafía en forma de soga— los miembros se saludaban con solidaridad de ejecutivos; resultaba difícil saber quiénes eran amigos de mucho tiempo y quiénes se encontraban por primera vez; luego se sentaban en equipales de cuero, pedían una botana y hablaban de sus ropas con una coquetería sin freno —comparaban cinturones piteados, corbatines de seda, botones de hueso—. Supongo que ésa era su forma de refrendar valores entendidos; opinaban lo mismo sobre la familia, la religión y el Estado, y sólo disentían sobre la etiqueta charra o el efecto que las dos variantes fundamentales del tequila, la reposada y la blanca, tenían en la naturaleza humana.

Los coches en el estacionamiento y los choferes vestidos de funcionarios revelaban que los agremiados pertenecían a una clase muy superior a la nuestra; sin embargo, a mi padre le decían "Chuy" y "con todo respeto" le describían a Rita como si fuera una belleza que él desconocía. Fue ahí donde ella le presentó a uno de los arquitectos del bufet donde ahora trabajaba.

De mi primera visita recuerdo el pantalón que me apretaba, el olor a cuero en los cuartos y a humedad y estiércol en los patios, los platones de barro pletóricos de dulces mexicanos, la capilla donde los charros comulgaban (llegamos muy temprano y sin embargo la misa ya acababa). Luego fuimos al cortijo donde las mujeres desfilaron en trajes de chinas poblanas. Rita llevó una prenda tan estelar que parecía escapada de un mural de Diego Rivera.

Hubo lances con sogas y un charro de brazos alarmantes infundió una tristeza general al someter a un novillo con brutalidad de levantador de pesas.

Rita enloquecía con los caballos; los jueves y los sábados apostaba en el hipódromo, su mascada favorita tenía fuetes en miniatura, y en años no muy lejanos había participado en competencias de saltos. Además, frecuentaba el Lienzo del Charro. La asociación sólo admitía mujeres en celebraciones especiales, y Rita aguardaba esos días de equitación y folklor con el entusiasmo unificador que dedicaba a tantas cosas disímbolas.

Fue ella quien convenció a mi padre de que se inscribiera al Lienzo, y no sé si calculó las consecuencias. Pese a su continua mención de los Altos de Jalisco, él no había mostrado una tendencia natural hacia las tradiciones ni los deportes rurales. Aceptó la idea de pertenecer al Lienzo porque Rita le consiguió cartas de recomendación firmadas por gente de "alto calibre" que no se podían tirar al basurero: ese apoyo se agradecía como una orden.

Aprendió algunas suertes básicas y luego se limitó a ir a las fiestas. Aunque esporádicas, aquellas visitas al cortijo lo relacionaron con personajes extrañamente ávidos de influir en su vida. Desde la primera vez que fui con ellos, enfundado en un traje color café con leche, percibí el aire de cofradía. En la hacienda de muros encalados y baños con mosaicos de Talavera, donde las llaves de agua eran elegantes chorizos de porcelana, los charros se trataban de tú y

2. Historia de la equis

hubiera pintado un retratista de plaza. Pero el consenso local la convirtió en el dogma de la belleza. Carlos el Elocuente habló de tetas grandes, pero también esto era falso; acabó gustando porque todo mundo estaba harto de los mismos juegos, de ver la tarde como un desfile inacabable, de escuchar las voces de siempre que llamaban a cenar arroz con huevo.

Estudié a Eduarda con calma, y aunque lo que más me gustó fue la sangre que repentinamente le salía de la nariz, pude describir su cintura estrecha y sus labios carnosos, le encontré virtudes que en nada comprometían al deseo, historié su cuerpo como si explicara el funcionamiento de un sistema.

Una vez mi padre le dijo a Rita que el Partenón estaba hecho de acuerdo con las proporciones pitagóricas.

(Lo mismo podría decir de Eduarda.)

—Pero la belleza está en la mirada, no en los objetos —contradijo Rita, con una sonrisa que no admitía respuesta—: yo te veo hermoso y a lo mejor eres horrendo.

(Lo mismo podría decir de Vulcano.)

Eduarda venía de los fríos de Toluca; su nombre de pila, que rozaba la virilidad, prometía una belleza o un adefesio; de los dos extremos, nuestra colonia escogió el primero. Sabíamos muy pocas cosas; teníamos las uñas negras, las orejas tapadas de cerilla, la cabeza llena de ideas tentativas; abríamos el vientre de los gatos con vidrios sólo para entender nuestro propio horror; Eduarda gustó como si eso nos ayudara a explicarnos; la discutimos como se discute una estampa; acepté que estaba bien, estuve de acuerdo; Eduarda era algo que nos juntaba, que nos hacía ser seis o siete, a las cinco de la tarde.

Para mí, el jardín era un lugar para tenderme a oler la hierba y ver aviones en el cielo. No sabía a ciencia cierta si las cosquillas venían de las hormigas pero me gustaba estar ahí, recorrido por los insectos que me separaban del sueño. Bajo el sol denso, caía en un estado intermedio, en el que a veces levitaba y a veces oía los ruidos de los coches; la línea punteada de las hormigas separaba ambas realidades. Entonces imaginaba la laxitud de Verónica, los ojos abiertos que miraban hacia dentro. ¿Se acordaría de nosotros? ¿Sabría aún que le pagué para acariciar su tornillo en el pie? ¿Recordaría las calles, el barrio que crecía como ella en el sueño?

Carlos alardeaba de su fuerza y a mí me excitaba la fuerza ajena: me masturbé por primera vez viendo el turgente cuerpo de Superman. Más que la potencia, me atraía la potencia castigada. Un héroe victimado a fondo me provocaba una erección. Quisiera prestigiar mis tendencias pero no hubo para mí un San Sebastián de Guido Reni. Vivíamos en una franja donde los iconos no habían acabado de fijarse y tuve que conformarme con imágenes fuera de registro y orbitadas de onomatopeyas. Carlos se masturbaba con las mujeres que un periódico publicaba en azul y blanco.

La tristeza de Verónica y el locuaz dramatismo de Rita me gustaban sin excitación física. Mis primeras opiniones heterosexuales fueron forzadas por un plebiscito. De repente el mundo conocido enloqueció con Eduarda Ramos Nielsen. Este nombre impetuoso sugiere a una suerte de Regenta, una mujer con voz gruesa, cigarrillo oscuro y cejas altivas. Cuesta trabajo extraer a una niña de ese bloque nominativo. Eduarda no tenía ningún chiste, al menos para mí. Sus ojos castaños se abrían más que los de otras niñas y su nariz poseía una gracia algo forzada, como si la

mitía abrir alacenas sin ser sorprendido por el rostro solemne, mineral, de condena atávica, que solían tener las cocineras.

Me gustaba el caos de los alimentos, del todo distinto a las repisas de mi casa. En el refrigerador, mamá había puesto la leyenda DESORDENAR LA CASA ES DESTRUIR LA VIDA. ¿Realmente creía que desacomodar la salsa Búfalo era arruinar nuestro futuro? Quizá sus frascos parejos conformaban una especie de cábala que no se podía alterar sin pérdida; lo cierto es que la cocina, pintada de amarillo-naranja-amarillo, le producía un cansancio cósmico.

Semanas antes, mamá había escrito EL QUE COME Y CANTA LOCO SE LEVANTA. La frase resultaba inútil porque nadie cantaba entre nosotros, ni siquiera la pasión charra de mi padre nos llevó a entonar rancheras en colectiva tercera voz. Carlos es un épico intenso (la música es el himno que cantará cuando le den una medalla), mi padre no quería revelar el repertorio de boleros románticos y baladas de rock aprendido lejos de Xochimilco, y yo tenía una voz frágil, indigna de mi gordura. Contra la evidencia, mamá recomendaba silencio. Quizá quería educarnos para situaciones futuras, para límites desconocidos, el ebrio arrebato en que recibiríamos una sopa ajena entonando "Voz de la guitarra mía..." Sus mensajes inculcaban méritos raros, semejantes a la lotería donde el Valiente asesinaba.

Si el tabaquismo de mamá, y la consecuente ceniza sobre sus guisos, me cerraron el apetito, la casa de Rita me compensó hasta el exceso. Abría latas de mangos y comía con las manos. Mientras ellos se entretenían arriba, salía al jardín trasero y disfrutaba la luz de la tarde que combinaba bien con el almíbar. El jardín tenía columpios, algo raro en una casa sin hijos. "Mécete", me pedía Rita, como si deseara darle sentido a ese juego.

hechos con estambres estridentes, carteles op que contemplé casi hasta el estrabismo, un equipo de sonido en el que palpitaban luces rojas y verdes, un árbol de Metepec que crecía en arabescos de barro multicolor, semejando parras y frutos imposibles.

Mi sitio favorito era el vestidor; podía pasar horas viendo uniformes y acariciando calzones. Rita tenía una extensa colección de lencería y toda clase de payasitos semitransparentes. Aunque el cuerpo carbónico del vulcanizador me perturbaba de un modo más eficaz, ante los delicados broches y botones no tardé en advertir la superioridad textil de desvestir a las mujeres.

En el vestidor había una sección que Rita describió de modo sugerente:

—Es ropa de estar.

Me gustó que hubiera prendas para envolver a una persona sin más propósito que estar allí. En rigor, esas ropas eran más íntimas que las lencerías, calculadas para la mirada ajena. Los auténticos secretos de Rita estaban en las batas y camisolas de mujer cansada, algo aburrida, que se cubre con un abandono infantil.

Rita vivía como dos personas en su casa: un lujo subordinado abajo y una región de caprichos en la parte alta. Cuando colocaba una varita de incienso de frambuesa en su Buda de cobre yo sabía que al poco rato un olor acre y quemante saldría de la recámara. Unas horas después ella me miraba con ojos aborregados y sonrisa inconexa.

En las tardes de mariguana, mi padre se mojaba la cabeza con agua fría antes de salir a la calle. Vivíamos tan lejos que el pelo se le secaba en el camino.

En la cocina de Rita yo movía frascos en busca de dulces importados. No tenía sirvienta de planta ("me choca que un bulto pase por la casa") y esto me per-

ciones ganaderas, lugares para improvisar un picnic. Se entretenía sin remordimientos ni saciedad.

Nunca cuestioné las duplicidades de mi padre, en gran parte porque mi propia vida hubiera sido siniestra sin ellas, y cuando tuve edad para establecer las primeras diferencias, Rita le dio lógica, coherencia retrospectiva, a las muchachas que sirvieron de borrador para llegar a la versión definitiva. Las tardes en moteles y cafés de enamorados habían sido un camino de perfección rumbo a Rita Terreros. Ella encarnaba los ideales cinematográficos de mi padre, sus excesos de escenografía (ninguna otra mujer se hubiera visto mejor en casa de Felipe Jurado).

La casa de Rita era contradictoria. La parte de abajo seguía la moda de principios de siglo que incluía salones "arábigos"; los azulejos subían a una cúpula de yeso decorada con escritura sufi y las rejas de las ventanas imitaban celosías. En el cubo de la escalera, un vitral de vidrios verdes y púrpuras enrarecía la atmósfera. En la sala había un carrito con copas y licoreras de cristal cortado, ceniceros de oro, una cimitarra, un abanico de plumas de pavo real, el busto de un furibundo Beethoven y una mantilla en el respaldo del sofá. En los muros, tres óleos le atribuían fantasiosas encarnaciones: "Rita en los alegres veinte", "Rita en el esplendor helénico", "Rita, reina de Java."

Mi padre, de sobra está decirlo, se había aficionado a la pintura mexicana, cuyas figuras axiales son la sandía y la calavera. En una ocasión le preguntó a Rita si sus retratos tenían "una historia".

—¿No te gustan? Los mandó hacer un amigo. Él mismo los colgó. Me dijo que esos hoyos siempre serían suyos —y sonrió en una forma que trastornó a mi padre (se rasguñó la palma de la mano como cuando hablaba del borreguismo).

El segundo piso sugería a una persona enteramente distinta. Había mandalas, cuadros huicholes

Durante casi dos años Rita iba a llenar nuestras cabezas de planes imposibles. A su lado, mi padre estaba de un humor estupendo. Al enfilar hacia nuestra colonia, mostraba un rictus terrible, como si fuéramos deportados.

Rita había sido aeromoza, conocía parajes de locura, había visto toda clase de espectáculos y deportes que no me interesaban pero que en sus labios adquirían otro valor. En ella la vida era una posibilidad amplísima, una rara opción de que lo recóndito (nosotros) se situara al centro.

Tenía fotos en toda clase de sitios; mi memoria selecciona escenas que convocan un lujo de cinco estrellas: clubes hípicos, estaciones de esquí, una playa en la que señalaba un pez vela colgado de una horquilla, calandrias tropicales, carritos de golf, restoranes con cascadas. A mí me atraían poco esos lugares (salvo el restorán con cascada) en los que Rita se divertía hasta fracturarse, encajarse una cuña de madera, abrirse las manos con el hilo de nylon. Le gustaba mucho hablar de sus heridas; en su caso, el dolor era un riesgo deportivo.

Las mujeres no me atraían de un modo físico pero al entrar al vestidor de Rita admiré sus uniformes de aeromoza, hechos con telas antinflamables. Mi padre me había puesto al tanto de que el espíritu, si era *nuestro*, se vestía de colores chillones. Rita había volado para una aerolínea nacional y sus trajes eran maravillosamente anaranjados. Vivía para infundir serenidad en las turbulencias que ella misma creaba; sus jornadas de horarios cruzados y su energía para el enredo eran compensadas por su pulso firme para preparar cocteles en las bolsas de aire. Perdía las llaves y los boletos para el cine y los recuperaba un segundo antes del desastre. Sería absurdo hablar de sus aficiones porque en realidad todo le gustaba, el mundo era una infinita cartelera con óperas, exposi-

desmañanarse para hablar con maestros de obras, le pedían que bardeara un terreno o diseñara una escalera, pero no aceptaban sus casas mexicanas.

La constructora estaba en manos de una célebre mancuerna de arquitectos; por desgracia, entre ellos y los dibujantes había una red de hombres timoratos:

—¡Pinche país de borregos! —se quejaba mi padre—. Lo nuevo les aterra.

Era difícil entender que quisiera ser "típico" y al mismo tiempo "novedoso". ¿Cómo podía esperar que su originalidad fuera representativa? En un momento de vejación heroica se definió como Oveja Negra. El pueblo paciente, que avanzaba con mansedumbre al matadero, necesitaba de caudillos. Algún día el rebaño seguiría a la Oveja Negra.

Una de las pocas cosas que aprendí en esa etapa en que él buscaba dejar el restirador de dibujante para encargarse de un proyecto, fue que el Valiente y la Oveja eran formas básicas de lo mexicano. En las barajas y los tableros de la lotería, el Valiente sostenía un cuchillo ensangrentado: el valor exigía matar de cerca. Cuando una feria llegó a Terminal Progreso, mi padre nos llevó a jugar lotería; en la casilla del Valiente, tapé el cuchillo con mi frijol, la sangre que seguramente venía de alguna oveja.

Mi padre sustituyó el Nausicaa por un Ishtar de asientos reclinables. Cuando subí al coche y me dijo "Mauricio" supe que me presentaría a otra mujer. Llevaba meses sin acompañarlo, y no sé por qué pospuso tanto ese encuentro; tal vez se sentía a prueba, nervioso, sorprendido de las ricas alternativas que le exigía su emoción. El caso es que el nuevo trabajo y las curiosas aficiones que trataba de comunicarnos tenían que ver con Rita Terreros.

zo. Cuando finalmente corrimos la cortina de plástico vimos algo insólito. En la atmósfera insegura, cargada de sombras y vapor, emergió una figura imposible.

Era un charro negro, y olía a *Aqua ardens*.

Con la misma infatuación con que detenía el coche frente al mural del Teatro Insurgentes para explicarnos la historia de México, mi padre aseguró que llevaba la charrería en las venas; su familia materna provenía de los Altos de Jalisco. Esto le daba cierta prosapia a su nueva afición pero también revelaba un impedimento: en los Altos hay sangre francesa y él era demasiado rubio para convencer como charro.

Cuando mi padre empezaba con sus peroratas de gurú nacionalista, yo corría a refugiarme en mi colección de basuras. En ocasiones me seguía por el pasillo, me tomaba de la oreja que lamentablemente no perdí con el granizo y me obligaba a regresar a la mesa donde se discutía la traición de los tlaxcaltecas.

Fueron tantas las pruebas de incomprensión que dimos Carlos y yo que empezó a decirnos "Masiosares". Los lunes en la mañana, al jurar bandera y cantar el himno en el patio de la escuela, el desajuste familiar llegaba en la estrofa "Mas si osare un extraño enemigo".

Al margen de nuestro desconcierto, él tomó muy en serio su faceta charra. Se inscribió a un lienzo en el que aprendió a hacer lazos que reprodujo con gracia en la mesa y compró trajes progresivamente lujosos, destinados a realzar sus nalgas perfectas.

En cuanto al trabajo, mostraba un raro fervor; consultaba libros sobre casas de adobe, asistió a un seminario en Antropología para que sus planos "salieran de la Historia", amanecía en el comedor ante sus hojas borroneadas. Sin embargo, sus "proyectos gordos" eran rechazados en el bufet. Lo obligaban a

chas de aceite, yo rezaba para que la moneda al fin rompiera el vidrio.

Luego vinieron las lluvias y yo pasé las tardes con la cara untada a mi propia ventana. Caían tormentas de dos o tres horas y los relámpagos hacían que las torres de alta tensión parecieran esqueletos del futuro. Una de esas tardes en que me pegaba al cristal con un abandono de sonámbulo, sentí la mano de Carlos en el hombro.

Era incapaz de tocar a otro hombre sin estrujarlo (el roce sin daño pertenecía al mundo puto):

—Arriba está la acción.

Subí a la azotea con sus dedos encajados en la espalda.

Salimos al descubierto. Granizaba con furia y nos expusimos a la metralla. Carlos empezó a gritar: "¡que se caiga... que se caiga!" No supe si se refería a una torre de electricidad, a la casa o al fraccionamiento entero, pero grité con él como un fanático del hielo.

El granizo nos golpeaba como una tortura deliciosa, nuestros zapatos aplastaban hielo, todo se abandonaba a una suntuosa destrucción.

Un rayo verde partió el cielo. No me hubiera sorprendido que los montes letrados se desgajaran.

—¡Aaaaaaaaaaaaaaaaaaa... ! —Carlos estaba en su elemento, ofrecía el pecho desnudo a la lluvia y se golpeaba, como si la granizada no fuera suficiente.

Sentí que un perdigón me tiraba la oreja pero resistí hasta el final.

Bajamos exhaustos. Se había ido la luz y mamá sostenía una vela. Su rostro, orlado de sombras, lucía cadavérico; su índice blanquísimo señaló la puerta del baño. La obedecimos sin decir palabra.

Colocó la vela en una botella de refresco y durante un buen rato nos frotamos las huellas del grani-

La cara seca y triste del padre de Verónica revelaba que todo seguía igual. En el espacio exterior y en las profundidades marinas pasaban cosas repentinas; sin embargo, entre nosotros sólo los ajolotes parecían dignos de ósmosis.

Martín Cifuentes fue el único que buscó un remedio directo, una campanilla para la oreja de Verónica.

Martín era el perfecto Segundo Lugar. Nadie como él para el triunfo matizado; en cualquier categoría sería sublíder, empezando por su aspecto físico y su extraña capacidad de parecerse a alguien. En un par de años, Martín se asemejó al portero del Guadalajara, a un baladista romántico y al asesino múltiple que sedujo a sus víctimas a sólo unas calles de distancia. El hecho de que los tres modelos apenas se parecieran entre sí era otro de los enigmas de la copia. Curiosamente, el primero en detectar los parecidos era Pancho. Acaso para realzar su incomparable singularidad, le gustaba que hubiera imitadores, sombras sin cuerpo verdadero. A su manera, Martín aprovecharía las comparaciones; años después iba a conquistar mujeres enseñando fotografías ajenas, adoptando cortes de pelo y tics que lo transformaban en la opción local de una fama distante.

Durante muchas tardes no tuve otra diversión que seguir a Martín a casa de Verónica, como una copia de la copia. Cuando creía que nadie lo miraba, Martín arrojaba una moneda a la ventana; siempre usaba la misma, un quinto que producía un ruido suave en el cristal. Verónica debía estar sola en su alcoba porque nadie se asomaba.

Oculto tras la defensa cromada de un coche, veía el metal tocando la ventana, una y otra vez, como si su valor se acumulara. ¿Oía algo ella? ¿Sentía el reloj de los que estábamos afuera, el tiempo que se iba? Martín tiraba, con obstinada puntería; junto a las man-

puestos con toldos blancos que rodeaban los canales de Xochimilco, prefiguraba cambios que aún no podíamos advertir.

Dejó pasar semanas, tal vez meses, sin invitarme al "cine". Trabajaba con súbito denuedo, volvía a la casa de madrugada, diseñaba patios decorados con ánforas inmensas, ideales para que en ellas durmieran aborígenes de Australia, dormitorios sin ventanas (o con ventanucos que sugerían una ardua penitencia), discutía sus proyectos con curioso énfasis, como si nosotros pudiéramos frenarlo o, más bien, como si ahí estuvieran otras personas.

Yo seguía molesto con Pancho, y lo peor del caso es que él no lo había notado. Mi tiempo avanzaba como en un cronómetro de obsidiana. Me dedicaba a vagar por los canales, hundía las manos en el agua turbia, esperando el contacto frío y blando de un ajolote.

Al regresar a la colonia, me dirigía a casa de Verónica y aguardaba a que su padre saliera. Buscaba en su rostro alguna noticia de su hija, pero sus facciones parecían cortadas por algo frío. Todo en él apuntaba a un resignado fracaso; su coche era un Eureka del 56 y su casa tenía aspecto de ruina recién comprada. Nunca habíamos visto que un rubio se arruinara y la relativa pobreza de aquel hombre adquiría un aire de tragedia buscada.

Durante un tiempo pensé que un sacrificio de mi parte ayudaría a Verónica. Abandonar algo que me gustara era una forma de sufrir por ella, de repartir el dolor hasta que Dios se apiadara de nosotros. Hice una lista de los alimentos cuya ausencia me perjudicaría pero no prescindí de ninguno.

La palabra del momento era "ósmosis". Lo que pasaba de golpe, sin esfuerzo alguno, recibía ese nombre que armonizaba con los ovnis. Confié en que un acceso de ósmosis me llevara al sacrificio o despertara a Verónica.

eran legítimas si servían para liquidar extranjeros como el enigmático Masiosare del himno nacional.

En las cátedras de sobremesa supimos que el ajolote *Siredon tigrina* había escogido nuestra colonia para salir al mundo. Mi padre nos mostró un par de láminas del "célebre paisajista" José María Velasco que ilustraban la metamorfosis del ajolote en salamandra. Ante los platos con migajas, luchaba por "subirnos de nivel". Mi colección de obsidianas recibió el nombre de "Lapidario" y tuve que oír que en el libro 36 de su *Historia natural* Plinio el Viejo informaba que el cristal negro debía su nombre a su similitud con una piedra descubierta por Obsidio en Etiopía. Ningún otro mineral tenía una edad tan fácil de calcular: la obsidiana era un *cronómetro absoluto*, su "línea de humedad" permitía leer el tiempo. Yo no quería saber tanto, pero mi padre continuaba con que Plinio murió ahogado por las cenizas del Vesubio, mamá desviaba la vista ante la mención de un volcán y yo pensaba en la lanza al rojo vivo del vulcanizador. "Las piedras son el mayor exponente de la locura humana", citaba mi padre, en el momento en que estábamos a punto de reivindicar mis obsidianas como flechas.

En las tardes lentas en que mi padre buscaba lo "nuestro" en su *Diccionario enciclopédico* aprendí el significado de aprender: mitigar asombros, fingir que se está de acuerdo, acercarse a quienes, desde mucho tiempo atrás, aceptan lo improbable.

El arquitecto mexicanista soltaba datos que nos rebasaban; en rigor, no se dirigía a sus tres parientes más cercanos sino a sí mismo; buscaba, en forma casi desesperada, convencerse de algo que apenas conocía. Esta fase, que llegó con floreros de vidrio soplado, elogios a la plata de Taxco y expediciones a comprar pan de pulque y gorditas de hormiga en los

co fanatismo, como si hubiese creído en un sistema del mundo y descubriera otro superior.

—¡Mira nomás! —señaló un muro de adobe, con ventanas diminutas.

Pensé que si existiera Esparta, así serían sus cárceles.

Cuando habló de trojes y otros depósitos de granos, pensamos que era su nueva idea de la sala comedor.

A mamá no le importó tanta tontería con tal de que él trabajara sin tregua; admiraba el trabajo duro y sentía que todo estaba bien cuando la noche encontraba a la familia exhausta. Mi padre se quedaba dormido sobre sus planos en papel albanene y ella sonreía como no lo había hecho en mucho tiempo, convencida de que la virtud cansa.

En cosa de semanas, mi padre se volvió experto en pueblos de artesanos y compró unos platos de barro crudo que soltaban tierra. En las enfrijoladas de esa noche conocimos el sabor del patriotismo.

Hasta entonces ningún miembro de la casa había sentido una obligación especial con el país; si acaso, el entorno nos inspiraba repugnancia. Tener éxito significaba largarse. Carlos y yo sabíamos que el mundo se dividía en mexicanos y turistas, pero jamás cruzó por nuestras mentes que tuviéramos que demostrar de qué lado estábamos. Sin embargo, desde que entró al bufet, mi padre pasó horas tratando de despertar en nosotros algo que sólo puedo llamar "pasión representativa". No bastaba con haber nacido en la república de las serpientes y las aguas frescas, teníamos que parecernos a nosotros mismos, y celebrarlo a voz en cuello. La noche del 15 de septiembre nos llevó al Zócalo y bajo una lluvia de confeti tricolor gritamos: "¡Viva México, hijos de la chingada!" Las groserías

en rebanadas de pay; cada una correspondía a un grupo alimenticio. En el próximo número se hablaría de la vejiga. Mi silueta de conjunto se parecía mucho a la vejiga de Juan.

Me pusieron a dieta de legumbres y pollos hervidos, pero las amantes de mi padre se encargaron de que las mieles y las mayonesas siguieran llegando a mi organismo.

Jesús Guardiola parecía no tener otra ambición arquitectónica que ampliar cocheras y ganar lo suficiente para complicarse la vida. Ninguno de nosotros sospechó los cambios que se gestaban en su interior. Un día llegó fuera de sí, con una felicidad inédita: le había pasado algo bueno que no tenía que ver con su cuerpo.

Golpeó la mesa de formica con las palmas y dijo que se había pasado a la escuela mexicana de arquitectura. La noticia nos sorprendió porque ignorábamos que estuviese en otra escuela. Con un fervor que superó el de sus noticias de Esparta, describió los estilos arquitectónicos en pugna: la modernidad sin rostro definido (representada por destructores como Felipe Jurado) y el rescate de los valores nacionales (representado por el bufet que le acababa de dar trabajo).

Llevaba una carpeta con fotografías de casas mexicanas. Yo jamás había visto esas paredes de cal rugosa, pintadas en azul celeste y rosa pálido, con estanques de agua cristalina y mesas adornadas con sandías, pero según el arquitecto Guardiola eso no sólo era más hermoso sino que era "nuestro".

Mi padre no dejaba de confundirnos; había puesto una reproducción de Palladio en la sala, admiraba el mapa cartesiano de París, y ahora se refería a las casas con aspecto de hacienda en un tono de fran-

gasto adicional en una expiación para proseguir su ronda de engaños.

El primer resultado ostensible del tratamiento fue que un sábado mamá se dirigió a la cocina, regresó con un cenicero y encendió un Raleigh sin filtro.

—¡Pero chaparra! —protestó mi padre.

—Cada quien sus vicios —pensé que se refería a las muchachas que me acariciaban la coronilla con sus veloces uñas—... a ti te gusta el vino —añadió mamá, que le decía "vino" a cualquier bebida alcohólica, como si viniera de un sitio mucho más apartado que su ciudad natal. Cada vez que la he visto rechazar una cerveza diciendo que no bebe "vino" he sentido por ella una emoción intensa e inconfesable que sólo puedo llamar "piedad agraria". La expresión es ridícula pero real. Mamá fracasaba como se fracasa en un llano.

De haber tenido afición al cine, le hubiera sacado buen provecho a su papel de esposa sufrida, pero sólo se le ocurrió fumar y tomar el tranvía dos veces a la semana para deprimirse en la terapia.

En sus diálogos con el psicólogo se activó un resorte relacionado con mi apetito. Hasta entonces, sus consejos en el refrigerador estaban de parte de la comida. Cuando Carlos tuvo hepatitis escribió: ENFERMO QUE COME NO MUERE. ¿Qué dijo de mí en la terapia? Supongo que algo relacionado con la desidia, la molicie, la apatía vegetativa. Mi escenografía básica incluía la cama de meditación, un tubo de galletas Marías y dos litros de leche. Seguramente el terapeuta advirtió que mis meriendas, sólo interrumpidas para cenar, eran una forma de la inutilidad; el caso es que mamá entró al cuarto armada de un ejemplar de *Selecciones* y lo abrió en un artículo estratégico: "El estómago de Juan."

Juan era un personaje al que el cuerpo le funcionaba de maravilla. Una gráfica dividía su estómago

idolatraban por ser un pésimo estudiante y sobrellevar su libreta salpicada de notas rojas como las cicatrices de un combatiente. En una ocasión le oí decir "ese putito se saca puro 10"; el estudio pertenecía al mundo puto. El complemento de su vacío mental era, por supuesto, su habilidad para patear balones o condiscípulos. En una ocasión sus botas con punteras metálicas fracturaron el peroné de un compañero y mi padre tuvo que pedir disculpas y pagar el yeso.

A los ojos de Carlos, yo pertenecía a medias al mundo puto (mis malas calificaciones me daban cierta dignidad viril). En términos generales me consideraba un desperdicio, lo cual no estaba muy lejos de la opinión que yo tenía de mí mismo. Cuando el Nausicaa siempre sobrecalentado vibraba rumbo a la ciudad, yo sabía que los desechos iban de regreso.

De haber conocido mi pasión por el vulcanizador, Carlos me habría corregido a puntapiés. Sin embargo, al ahorrarme esta tortura me sumió en otra forma de la desgracia: yo me sentía merecedor de una golpiza, y tal vez conservaba mi secreto, no para ponerme a salvo, sino para herirme al prescindir de la violencia que tanto ameritaba.

No es de sorprender que mamá encontrara pocas satisfacciones en nosotros. Una tarde, después de preguntar si alguien quería más guisado, informó que estaba en terapia, una noticia que ese día, y sobre todo en ese lugar, sonó como el anuncio de que se iba a Australia o la confesión de que bebía a solas.

Mi padre guardó silencio y vio el chile en su plato como si estuviera relleno de culpas:

—¿Cuánto cuesta?

A partir de entonces, trabajó horas extra para pagar el psicólogo y, muy a su manera, transformó el

cáscaras de mango; los trozos sólo contaban su historia de conjunto si seguían siendo trozos; por eso detestaba la inútil grandeza del estadio como basurero y procuraba que mi colección de restos fuera pequeña. En la caja plateada guardaba algunas obsidianas, cerillos, un botón de cobre, otro azul ultramarino, un silbato, lo suficiente para suponer una conexión entre ellos, y para que esa conexión no fuera lógica.

De modo inmejorable, mamá hablaba de mi "colección de basuras".

Dejé de ver a Pancho y, con ello, de jugar a la colonia como isla en riesgo, habitada por accidente (ya no mandaba mensajes en globos, con un mapa de la región y una improbable recompensa). Por unos días traté de acercarme a las aficiones de Carlos. Desgraciadamente mi hermano sospechaba de cualquier juego que tuviera una parte imaginaria y no desembocara en un marcador. Vivía para sudar con reglas y vitorear a sus equipos favoritos. Para colmo, me llevaba cuatro años excesivos; llegué a su vida como una criatura ilógica que se arrastraba por el tapete, y años después de la primera infancia me miraba con la misma extrañeza: yo odiaba los deportes, no quería atrapar víboras de agua, pasaba horas en la cama, con los pies apoyados en la pared, viendo el techo como una función impresionante.

En nuestra evolución hubo algo que nos separó al modo de las toallas. Cuando nací, Carlos volvió a pedir el pecho de mamá. Ella accedió y así nos diferenció para siempre: Carlos ya tenía dientes y conciencia para recordar la succión. A mí me faltó un hermano menor para imponer mi edad y regresar al pezón con la capacidad de morderlo y memorizarlo.

Durante años asocié su fuerza con los dientes, los filos, las rugosidades. Sus compañeros de clase lo

estar junto a ese nombre que mamá no podía pronunciar sin añadir "tan chulo" en dos golpes asmáticos, se transformó en un odio parejo, que se alimentaba de sí mismo.

Esta etapa de celos y despecho significó, entre otras cosas, abandonar nuestras fantasías de náufragos. Veíamos un programa de televisión sobre un grupo de sobrevivientes en una isla desierta; los aparatos rescatados del naufragio eran comparables a la incipiente tecnología de Terminal Progreso, pero sobre todo nos identificábamos por estar a la orilla, en espera del rescate. Para los náufragos la vida se hallaba lejos, en las voces crujientes que a veces llegaban al radio de onda corta; para nosotros, en los resplandores mercuriales que avistábamos desde la azotea, aferrados a las jaulas para colgar la ropa.

Al apartarme de Pancho dejé de confundir las antenas distantes con los mástiles de los barcos que venían a salvarnos. La ciudad que durante los últimos meses había adquirido una condición marina, empezó a volverse subterránea. Cuando mi padre y yo íbamos en el Nausicaa, los túneles, las bardas, los edificios en incesante construcción, nos envolvían, nos tragaban. Estos desplazamientos me descubrieron la capacidad de entraña de la ciudad, su resistencia estomacal; estábamos en la zona de los residuos finales y el camino de regreso implicaba el paso por los grises intestinos en busca de la boca donde todo se decidía, el Zócalo, la plaza bajo el sol.

Una publicidad insistía en que la ciudad generaba suficiente basura para llenar el Estadio Azteca todos los días. En el camino de regreso imaginaba el estadio convertido en un bote de deyecciones, pero el amontonamiento me dejaba del todo insatisfecho; la riqueza de la basura está en su dispersión: el relato de los desechos debía estar suelto; avanzaba en los celofanes atropellados en el asfalto, en la botella que agregaba un brillo repentino a los canales, en el olor de las

Pancho y yo solíamos jugar con felicidad mongólica. Una tarde su padre atajó nuestras correrías y nos llevó a la sala de su casa.

—¿Saben lo que dijo Jesús? —preguntó.

Jesús había dicho suficientes cosas para llenar las iglesias de imágenes alusivas, pero no para extraer una respuesta de nuestras bocas tibias.

—Que de aquí para abajo no se toca —colocó su mano en la cintura.

Pancho y yo nos habíamos picado el sexo y el culo como todos los días sin saber que registrábamos la Zona de Jesús.

En las construcciones los albañiles jugaban del mismo modo sin que nadie llegara a evangelizarlos; sin embargo, en aquella sala que hospedaba a unos payasos gemelos de porcelana, el padre de Pancho se sintió obligado a decir:

—Tu familia es decente, Mauricio.

Lo mejor de mi vida familiar eran las cocheras de los moteles, el suave susurro de la manta que caía tras el auto y la oscuridad en la que yo aguardaba sin aburrirme. Ése era mi secreto, el edén oloroso a carburantes en el que de vez en cuando atrapaba un quejido.

Pancho miró a su padre con descarada osadía, como si estuviera ante un demente de registro limitado. Más que el regaño fue esta superioridad lo que me impidió volver a frecuentar su Zona de Jesús. Pancho se sabía por encima de nosotros, lo que yo hacía por distracción, por reflejo maquinal, para él era algo calculado; más que el roce de los cuerpos parecía disfrutar del efecto que causaba en los demás, empezando por su padre. Entendí que la suya era una región superior, destinada a despertar famas y rumores, y que mis manos le habían rendido vasallaje.

Recordé su éxito con Vulcano y dejé de verlo por un tiempo. La envidia que normalmente me daba

ña, hacía frío y me imaginaba en otro país; además, allí vendían las tortas de chorizo verde de Toluca que primero me dieron náuseas y a las que me aficioné tanto que le di náuseas a mi padre.

La más "existencialista" de sus amigas fue una flaca que se cortaba el pelo en forma de nuez, fumaba cigarros sin filtro, desviaba la vista cuando yo comía y tenía voz de hombre. Por suerte fue sustituida por una entusiasta con un suéter de angora idéntico a un algodón de azúcar.

Como es de suponerse, en la casa todo iba mal. Mi padre contraía deudas, trabajaba poco, gastaba mucho en gasolina, cafeterías, moteles, los increíbles koalas de peluche que regalaba a sus amantes y una loción de rara etiqueta: *Aqua ardens, essentia exaltada*.

En ocasiones, al entrar a la cocina, sorprendía a mamá llorando. Por las aletas de cristal translúcido, encargadas de ventilar los guisos, ella miraba un trozo de Terminal Progreso. Sin embargo, no era ése el motivo de sus lágrimas, o sólo lo era en parte. Me conmovía verla en su camisón color tuna, con encajes en los hombros y botones gruesos al frente, una prenda para que una mujer muy ingenua se sintiera "reina de la noche". Sus labios, tan parecidos a los míos, vibraban como aquejados por la fiebre, por uno de los virus que había en su tierra y que en dos días aniquilaba al ganado. Lloraba sin saber que la miraban; sufría, y yo tenía parte de la culpa.

En esos momentos pensaba en la manera de delatar a mi padre; luego veía el cuchillo con el que ella subdividía las zanahorias y el silencio me parecía un motivo de supervivencia. Engañarla era amargo, pero al menos posponía la tragedia y me daba oportunidad de salir a la ciudad.

sino que fuese el último en disfrutarla; pasaba la mayor parte del tiempo en su despacho y muchas veces dormía allí; casi le suplicaba a sus amigos que usaran su casa; en la entrada había un clóset con "blancos" para los visitantes, y en la lavandería un cesto para las toallas y las sábanas usadas; su verdadera excitación provenía de ser el locatario del placer ajeno.

Aunque ésta es una especulación tardía, algo me hizo pensar desde entonces en los extraños pliegues de Jurado; tenía un cuarto consagrado a sus trenes eléctricos. Una mesa de cuatro por cuatro soportaba a una nación en miniatura; los árboles, los vigías con sus linternas, los puentes levadizos, el molino de agua, la cabaña del guardabosques, el castillo en la colina, las puntuales locomotoras eran de una perfección que invitaba a ser destruida.

Por desgracia, el hijo de otro padre infiel tuvo la misma idea: un vagón comedor recibió un delicioso martillazo y Jurado dejó de renovarle las sábanas a amantes con hijos.

La casa, que conocí en sus excesivos detalles (el restirador con 11 lápices afilados como un perverso equipo, la larga foto de generación donde mi padre era el único entre 75 que podía ser reconocido como "el de las patillas") me hizo odiar para siempre la arquitectura cúbica.

La ciudad ha sido aniquilada por los idólatras del rectángulo y en cada edificio que se alza para agraviar a la casa de junto veo a Felipe el Desmedido, lo imagino con sus trenes de juguetería, comiendo pan con una jalea inclasificable, oliendo las sábanas de sus amigos.

Sin el apoyo de Jurado, mi padre volvió a llevar a sus amigas a los moteles. Los que más me gustaban eran los de la carretera a Toluca; estaban casi en la monta-

padre sobre las pirámides hundidas en el subsuelo. Xochimilco era otra prueba del fracaso; en unos años sólo quedaría un ojo de agua que adoraríamos como un altar.

Dos veces por semana mi padre y yo subíamos al Nausicaa —techo verde clorofila, cuerpo blanco— para enfilar a los variables rumbos de su pasión. De los sitios que conocí ninguno igualó a la casa del arquitecto Felipe Jurado.

Jurado estudió con mi padre pero él sí construía. Su especialidad eran los edificios cúbicos que contrastaban con el perfil urbano. En México no había límites de altura, y él lo sabía.

—Fíjate bien —mi padre señalaba un nuevo rascacielos en Insurgentes, junto a una cafetería, La Vaca Negra, que en su nombre bucólico y en su pequeñez anunciaba que sería arrasada por las hordas de Jurado.

Mi padre no admiraba las construcciones sino el éxito de su condiscípulo. Como el monumento a la Revolución, las inmensidades de Jurado eran derrotas estéticas que triunfaban de otro modo.

Jurado era soltero y se había construido una mansión en el Pedregal, con un jardín interior de roca volcánica, alberca techada y una sala para fiestas épicas (que en los momentos apacibles albergaba tres juegos de sofás). La decoración respondía a los imperativos del "hombre de mundo", un modelo de conducta que en aquella época incluía la coctelera para martinis, camas circulares y teléfono blanco. Todo en la casa había sido calculado para que el dueño se viera natural con gazné y bata china.

De niño me impresionaron los lujos decorativos y pasé por alto la psicología del dueño. Sin embargo, lo peculiar de Jurado no era la escenografía

Para desviar la atención, mi padre colgó en la sala un mapa de *París a vuelo de pájaro*. Así, la Ciudad Ideal se confundió en mi mente: el Coliseo emergía entre los recios bulevares del barón Haussmann y los canales navegables del esplendor azteca. Lo único cierto es que estábamos lejos, muy lejos de las ciudades verdaderas.

A mi padre le gustaba repetir que al terminar el siglo México sería "la urbe más grande del mundo". Esto reforzaba nuestro malestar. Si la capital era tan vasta, ¿por qué teníamos que ser los últimos? Las casas numeradas a partir de Correo Mayor hacían cola para llegar al centro; lo extraño, lo humillante, era que nadie se formara detrás de nosotros.

En la colonia incluso los brotes de modernidad adquirían un aspecto agrario. A doscientos metros de nuestra casa se iniciaba una hilera de torres de alta tensión. Cada torre estaba rodeada por una reja con letreros que no habíamos leído (bastaba ver la calavera con los huesos). Instalaciones hechas para los desiertos, las cañadas, los paisajes rápidos que pasan junto al tren. Las armazones sugerían en forma temible que las calles no iban a avanzar hasta ahí; resultaba improbable que la vida se ordenara entre las torres de metal que soltaban gruesas chispas azules.

Si las torres de alta tensión eran nuestro signo moderno, el contacto con el pasado era Xochimilco. De vez en cuando pedaleábamos hacia un canal donde un lanchero insistía en cambiarnos su cayuco por una bicicleta. Los domingos las trajineras se llenaban de mariachis y gringos insolados. Ocultos tras un pirul aguardábamos el momento de lanzarles una lluvia de piedras.

Las desgracias de México tenían que ver con la muerte del agua; lo sabíamos por los maestros que comparaban a Tenochtitlan con Venecia (otra confusión en la Ciudad Ideal) y por las anécdotas de mi

mis trapos cagados hervían en peroles medievales; mamá tomaba tranquilizantes para mitigar el mal olor de mi llegada y hablaba horas con sus familiares de Sinaloa. Mi padre, con su insólita energía para referirse a lo que nunca va a ocurrir, prometía una terraza para asolearse, una alberca en forma de riñón, un *garage* doble.

No me culparon en forma directa pero cada vez que apagaba las velas en mi pastel, alguien recordaba el 57, las grietas en el suelo, el miedo, la expulsión al arrabal que mi padre llamaba "campestre" y donde juraba haber visto un águila.

Al llegar a la casa junto al campo mamá se convirtió en la mujer desesperada y sin chiste que conocí. Tal vez desde antes tenía la habilidad de odiar la vida sin que eso fuera interesante, pero en todo caso necesitaba precisar su caída y aludía al "Ángel del 57" como al momento en que su gráfica personal se vino abajo.

Tal vez por un afán compensatorio, o por sentir una secreta complicidad con las placas subterráneas, disfruté cada temblor que sacudió la casa de Terminal Progreso. Mamá se colocaba en el quicio de una puerta, con un rostro de martirio que no aceptaba mejorías.

En las comidas edificantes, mi padre evitaba hablar de Roma para impedir que la antigua colonia volviera a nosotros como un edén abandonado. En cambio, mamá recitaba las cuatro letras al derecho y al revés, con sostenida pasión. Su tristeza, su futuro roto, otorgó a aquel barrio una condición de dorada antigüedad. Se diría que en otro tiempo vivimos junto a la columna de Trajano, a orillas del Tíber, rodeados de las siete colinas de fábula. "Roma" era el nombre, eterno y convulso, del sitio que perdimos. Las depresiones de mamá lograron que una zona que en el mejor de los casos aspiraba a ciertos triunfos *art nouveau*, se transformara en tierra clásica.

nadie pedía la sal porque sabíamos que lo desabrido era positivo.

Cuando llevé la primera obsidiana al comedor, mi padre abrió su libro color vino y habló de los cristales que se forman en las zonas volcánicas. Mamá nos vio como si la piedra se transformara en un blando ajolote. Su mente siguió una cadena más o menos de este estilo:

1.- La ciudad de México se fundó en una cuenca volcánica.

2.- En las regiones rodeadas de volcanes hay terremotos.

3.- El temblor de 1957 era la causa de nuestra desgracia.

Esta secuencia significaba que el auténtico aguafiestas de la familia era yo; nací el año en que las placas telúricas se desplazaron unos centímetros y el corazón de la ciudad padeció un cataclismo que, aunque no fue fatal, tuvo su carga simbólica; en Paseo de la Reforma el Ángel de la Independencia perdió la orientación y voló en picada, como un anticipo de la inversión celeste que ocurriría en los próximos años (en las noches de esmog, el Ángel entendería que las estrellas estaban abajo).

Vivíamos en la colonia Roma y durante el sismo un edificio se recargó en nuestra casa. Mamá, que por mi culpa padecía de depresión *postpartum*, cayó en un delirio de fin de mundo.

Obviamente no recuerdo los días en que mis padres buscaban alternativas para esa casa semidestruida. Según me enteré por reproches posteriores, ella quería mudarse a toda costa y él insistía en reforzar la casa. Prevaleció la tenacidad materna y la capacidad de engaño paterna: nos fuimos, pero no a la zona residencial que ella quería, sino a Terminal Progreso, la orilla de la nada. Puedo imaginar las semanas que siguieron al terremoto. No había pañales desechables y

—¡Basura buena! —protestaba ante el ordenado tambo que le tendía mamá.

Ella gozaba el momento de salir con la basura; escuchaba la campana del camión como una iglesia en movimiento. Tenía una fijación tan fuerte por limpiar la casa que seguramente tiraba de más, como el cocinero que no resiste la pizca adicional.

El camión olía a putrefacción pobre; éramos pocos y nuestras cosas demasiado recientes para lograr un deterioro de interés.

Aunque mi padre hablaba sin parar de casas y edificios, yo intuía que la fuerza de una ciudad se calculaba de otro modo: por lo que podía tirar, por su desfogue, su capacidad de soltar lastre, el resto espumoso de lo que ocurre con intensidad.

Recogía los botones, los peines, los cerillos que perdía mi padre, y no los devolvía; los atesoraba en una caja plateada que había contenido galletas. Lo curioso es que él no se ocupaba de sus pérdidas. Nunca lo vi extrañar un objeto; se diría que perder algo era una prueba del impulso que lo guiaba; desprenderse del paraguas plegadizo o la tapa de una pluma era el resultado, el resto necesario, de su fricción con el ambiente.

Los consejos de mamá aspiraban al sentido común, a la conciencia compartida; los descubrimientos, el avance de lo nuevo, eran propiedad paterna. Él tenía un *Diccionario enciclopédico*, color vino, del que sacaba bastante información. En las comidas solía hablar de icebergs, jeroglíficos, las siete maravillas del mundo. Exponía con sencillez los argumentos y los encaramaba en orden; sus ideas se articulaban en forma espaciosa: "ésta es la recámara, por aquí se sube a la azotea". Hablaba de Esparta como quien se mueve en una casa. Luego venían las albóndigas y el silencio en el que

Vivir en las afueras equivalía a crecer contra la naturaleza; anhelaba el día en que las milpas donde verdeaba el maíz fueran sustituidas por cines y centros comerciales. Estábamos en la incierta frontera de las familias recién perjudicadas o que mejoraron apenas lo suficiente para salir de una decrépita vecindad en el centro. Terminal Progreso era una sucesión de casas hechas en serie, con paredes de tabla-roca y candiles dorados en las puertas que sólo servían para enfatizar que no eran mansiones.

Las diversiones locales consistían en desenterrar flechas de obsidiana en los lotes baldíos o pescar ajolotes en los arroyos y meandros cercanos a Xochimilco. Larvarios, fríos, gelatinosos, los ajolotes recordaban una era de volcanes activos y saurios fabulosos; por desgracia, su hábitat se reducía al agua castigada de Xochimilco, lo único que quedaba del lago de los aztecas. Aquel paraje era un híbrido sin gloria; la ciudad sitiaba al campo sin derrotarlo y llegaba a nosotros en forma precaria: en los riachuelos, los celofanes de golosinas devoradas desde hacía varios meses, flotaban junto a los lirios.

Soñábamos con el bosque de neón que cancelaría los pastos pero no podíamos celebrar las escasas señales urbanas. ¿De qué servía encontrar clavos y tornillos en los sembradíos? Hubiera sido mejor un campo intacto, la roca, la víbora y el fresco ajolote. Estábamos de parte de la urbe pero sufríamos su lentitud; éramos el borde nunca rebasado, el lote sin nadie donde las tuzas construían sus túneles nocturnos.

El hombre de la basura contrastaba con la negra limpieza de Vulcano. Lo que en mi héroe era disfraz, en él parecía un agravio. Llegaba como si hubiera hecho su camino por las alcantarillas y se quejaba de que Terminal Progreso sólo brindara desechos orgánicos; él quería cristales, varillas, aceros inoxidables:

las nalgas de sus amigos, secretamente me resignaba a que la revelación no tuviera que ver conmigo.

Un viernes en la tarde Pancho me acompañó a reparar la bicicleta. El vulcanizador se lavaba las manos con cuidado, en una lata grande que había contenido leche en polvo. Se volvió hacia nosotros y nos pidió que bajáramos la cortina de metal. En vez de encender el foco desnudo que pendía del techo, prendió la hornilla que le servía para cauterizar hules. El cuarto era muy pequeño pero las sombras se alzaron como en una gruta infinita. En nuestras narices infantiles, afectas a los héroes entallados, el aire olió a carbones magníficos, a la oscura sustancia de los gigantes. Un calor saturado de fierros y acideces. Sin decir palabra, el vulcanizador se bajó el pantalón. Nos mostró el sexo, un sexo enorme y enrojecido de tanto acercarse a los fuegos. Pancho y yo nunca habíamos visto nada más hermoso. Aquella verga nos tenía hipnotizados. Sentí un vacío en el estómago, los labios me temblaban de pánico y fascinación, pero de nada sirvió tanto nerviosismo. Las manos gruesas acariciaron el pelo de Pancho y fue mi amigo quien posó sus labios impecables en el pene y lo chupó despacio, como si fuera un experto en la tarea. Se interrumpió un momento antes de que Vulcano eyaculara y el semen salió disparado a la pared, al auto deportivo que soportaba a dos rubias desnudas. Aquel tiro de guerra nos fascinó pero Pancho no quiso regresar allí, o al menos no regresó en mi compañía.

La colonia se llamaba como la última parada del tranvía: Terminal Progreso. Los canales de Xochimilco quedaban cerca pero la zona carecía de encanto rural. Un planeta abandonado a la suerte de cápsulas inferiores.

De frente teníamos el campo y los cerros con las iniciales del dignatario; a nuestras espaldas vibraba, eléctrica, la ciudad.

Un acontecimiento central de mi infancia fue crecer junto a un amigo que vivía para excitar al prójimo. No he conocido a nadie que ejerza una atracción tan unánime. A nuestro Vulcano le gustaban las mujeres expansivas que al entrar a un almacén escogían los vestidos con más flores (los sábados en la noche regresaba del brazo de una morena de vestido color piña, con hojas estampadas en las nalgas y los pechos). Pero también le gustaba Pancho.

Mi amigo no decía gran cosa al respecto. Idolatraba al vulcanizador por su recubrimiento de carbón, su aspecto fabuloso, escapado de un *comic*, de los planetas donde los guerreros usaban mallas.

Vivíamos en las afueras de la ciudad, donde el Anillo Periférico traicionaba su nombre y moría en un campo de pastos amarillos. Al fondo, los cerros mostraban enormes letras de cal, las iniciales que un presidente mandó rubricar durante su campaña.

Nada resultaba tan fácil como ponchar las llantas en los campos que rodeaban la colonia (uno de los muchos misterios en la ronda de las civilizaciones eran aquellos pastizales llenos de clavos, como si nuestro fraccionamiento sucediera a una tribu de carpinteros nómadas). En las ruedas de mi bicicleta giraban cámaras llenas de parches rosas y azules. Vulcano se burlaba de mi torpeza y me pasaba su extraordinaria mano por la nuca (¡si hubiera sabido con qué astucia robaba el dinero para pagar sus preciadas y demasiado rápidas reparaciones!).

Ciertos lugares prometen cambios, sitios cargados de misteriosa inminencia; de un modo confuso, sabía que en la vulcanizadora iba a ocurrir algo que no tendría que ver con las llantas ni la lanza de hierro que desprendía los rines. Aunque anhelaba la camaradería con que el hombre de carbón jugaba con

Verónica me gustaba como tragedia. Ella afianzó mi aprecio por la belleza desmejorada. En los comerciales de remedios contra la gripe disfrutaba la parte negativa, cuando las modelos estornudaban con ojos hinchados, labios resecos, narices afligidas, voces rotas, infinitamente superiores a la banal alegría con que se aliviaban.

Amaba a Verónica como se ama un estilo, una abstracción dolorosa que se extendía en la cama. En esa época sólo me gustaba el cuerpo de los hombres.

Sería un facilismo psicológico atribuir esta tendencia al lado suave de la toalla; ningún cambio en mi formación hubiera impedido que me enamorara del dueño de la vulcanizadora, un hombre musculoso, con el cuerpo cubierto de hulla. Usaba pantalón corto en un lugar donde nadie usaba pantalón corto. En las paredes renegridas de su local había un centenar de mujeres desnudas, de pechos rosados y nalgas enormes, muy distintas a las flaquitas que le gustaban a mi padre.

Podía pasar horas viéndolo martillear el aro donde colocaba los neumáticos, hundir cámaras de hule en cubetas de agua para probar si echaban burbujas, lamer con su lengua roja los sitios donde luego ponía un cemento espeso y brillante que parecía una condensación de su saliva. Sudaba mucho pero su piel seguía cubierta de tizne; el carbón se filtraba en su cuerpo como un tatuaje definitivo. De vez en cuando lo visitaban amigos y ejercía con ellos una camaradería perturbadora; les pasaba las manos por la cintura, les picaba el fundillo, les apretaba el pene. Ellos se reían mucho.

Una vez a la semana ponchaba adrede las llantas de mi bicicleta y entraba en ese cuarto que olía a sudor, a trabajo duro.

Por desgracia, la fascinación era relevada por el momento en que me preguntaba por "Francisco". Todos le decíamos Pancho pero él le decía Francisco.

brarse de la maldita inocencia que dejó en nuestra colonia.

El padre de Verónica era un hombre de pelo pajizo y piel reseca, con un eterno traje café, de vendedor fracasado. Tenía la expresión fija de alguien hecho para trabajos fuertes y tragedias largas. Levantó a Verónica en vilo, sin derramar lágrimas ni preguntar por el dueño del balón. Se la llevó, como si cumpliera una condena premeditada. Minutos más tarde oímos un alarido de mujer en su casa y platos que se rompían en el piso.

Unas semanas después me atreví a acercarme al coche de su padre, un modesto Eureka. Le pregunté por su hija. Me vio de un modo extraño, como si la culpa hablara por mi boca. Tal vez me vio igual que siempre pero sus pestañas amarillas me desconcertaron.

—Respira, pero no despierta —dijo.

No supe qué decir. Hubo una pausa lenta, llena de ruidos de moscas. Luego agregó:

—Sigue creciendo. Ayer la medí. Medio centímetro más. Estoy seguro.

Tal vez hubiera preferido que al perder el conocimiento, su hija dejara de crecer. Los dedos cada vez más largos, los zapatos que ya no le quedaban medían la vida que se iba.

Pasé horas imaginando sus cosas, sus muebles, sus ropas desmayadas; con indecible torpeza, pues conocía mal sus pertenencias y apenas captaba las variaciones entre una decoración y otra. En mi mente su cuarto se llenaba de triques con los que pretendía darle relieve; sillas y juguetes imperfectos que aguardaban el momento de volver a lastimarla.

Me sentaba en la banqueta frente a su casa, chupando un caramelo con curiosa intensidad, como si chupar me apartara del delirio.

y se desvió violentamente hacia la izquierda. Vi la escena con la lentitud de las crueldades imborrables. El faro izquierdo del Lyngam, rematado por una fina aleta de metal, se acercó a Verónica. Un segundo después escuchamos otro golpe, muy suave.

A pesar de la lentitud con que el accidente se produjo ante mis ojos, tardé en armar la triangulación: para salvarse de un balonazo en esa calle sin autos el Lyngam golpeó apenas a Verónica (un milagro que la aleta de cromo no le entrara al rostro). Veo los detalles en su precisa confusión: la pelota que rueda y se moja en el charco dejado por el vendedor de jícamas y Verónica tendida en el asfalto. No gritó. Se quedó ahí, con los ojos cerrados.

Lo que siguió después fue como la vuelta a una película sonora (sólo entonces advertí que el pánico no tiene ruido): el aire atravesado por pasos, llantos, la petición de una ambulancia.

El hombre que la atropelló tenía un rostro destruido; con gesto automático se llevó la mano al bolsillo y sacó una cartera con documentos y billetes, en un gesto de rendición que nadie atendió.

Luego apoyó la cabeza sobre el techo color betabel y masculló: "hijo de puta". Sabíamos que si de repartir culpas se trataba, el que pateó el balón saldría peor parado que el conductor, pero el hombre asumió con firmeza su conducta degradada, como si desde un principio supiera que entraba a esa calle a torcer su vida. La amenaza de un linchamiento lo hubiera aliviado más que la ignorancia que lo rodeó.

Al cabo de unas horas tuvieron que convencerlo de que se fuera. Dejó unos billetes en una mano equivocada y arrancó el Lyngam con pulso torpe. Lo vimos doblar en una curva donde crecía el maíz, a punto de embestir un caballo que pastaba hierbas largas. Necesitaba una desgracia mayor, algún desastre que lo hiciera detenerse y merecer su castigo, li-

Amelia fumaba sin tregua y sus colillas ribeteadas de carmín me daban asco. Al oír sus tacones de aguja en el vestíbulo huía a otros sitio, de preferencia con mi padre.

Me divertían las alternancias que complicaban mi vida sin mayor esfuerzo. Comparaba con cuidado a las amantes de mi padre pero no sentía atracción por ellas. Mi idea de la belleza femenina tenía que ver con el sufrimiento. Los ojos de Verónica eran maravillosamente tristes, como si estuviera presa ante un espectáculo que no deseaba atestiguar. Vivía a dos calles de mi casa y en un lapso breve —tres años a lo sumo— se fracturó dos veces la misma pierna y cayó de boca en el asfalto; el filo de la banqueta le limó los incisivos en un arco extraordinario que se acostumbró a acariciar con la lengua. Por ella supe que pocas cosas superan al defecto dental de una mujer hermosa. Verónica respondía a la incontrovertible verdad de ponerme nervioso. Estaba hecha para relumbrar entre filos y amenazas. Nunca supe dónde le cortaban el pelo; un tajo cruel, humillante, un casquete en desorden, como si estuviera loca. Con la segunda fractura le pusieron un tornillo en el pie y por cinco centavos nos dejaba acariciarlo. Bastaba ver su rostro pálido, sus ojos negros, su vestido azul marino, de tela barata y gruesa, para saber que la iban a operar, que se rompería otro hueso, que perdería sangre, que amarla sería sufrir mucho.

Una tarde en que ella miraba la calle como si fuera lo más gris y húmedo del mundo, un pie anónimo pateó un balón con inclemencia. La pelota fue a dar al parabrisas de un coche que avanzaba sin prisa —lo recuerdo perfectamente, un Lyngam color betabel, con defensa cromada—; el conductor no supo lo que se le venía encima, trató de esquivar aquella sombra

Mi padre tuvo a su primer hijo a los 20, cuando estudiaba arquitectura y servía de contable en un almacén. Cuatro años después, fui concebido en una recámara llena de reglas T, planos de papel albanene y bolsas rosas con electrodomésticos a mitad de precio. En su ratos libres, Jesús Guardiola revendía las licuadoras que le fiaban en el almacén. También le pedía prestado a personas que le siguieron cobrando cuando yo ya tenía uso de razón. Después de recibirse entró a un bufet en el que le confiaron remodelaciones de poca monta: cocheras para casas anteriores a la expansión automotriz. Me alimentó gracias a sus sueldos de contable, la reventa no siempre legal de aparatos y los préstamos que lo desprestigiaron durante una generación. Pero todo este esfuerzo servía de poco; en primer lugar porque el dinero llegaba a la casa menguado por los gastos de su vida paralela y en segundo porque mientras no edificara al menos una casa nada tendría sentido. Mamá estaba a su lado en espera de los muros que la protegieran y en cierto sentido la ubicaran en la vida; lo demás tenía un valor secundario. Hay que decir que su insistencia en la casa propia carecía de veleidades escenográficas, su mente era ajena a los lujos, el cultivado confort de las revistas de diseño, los colores del papel tapiz; amaba a su marido con una confianza de pionera: él alzaría la trave, haría la chimenea, la puerta para salir al mundo.

Sin embargo, el arquitecto Jesús Guardiola tenía otros ideales; se irritaba con la toalla en las mañanas para buscar mujeres en la tarde. Todo en él tendía a la fricción. Jamás mereció el extraño elogio que la tía Amelia brindaba a los hombres: "es una dama". Nunca entendí por qué nuestra pariente de párpados morados otorgaba género femenino a la caballerosidad extrema; lo cierto es que mi padre, más perfumado que mamá, no alcanzó aquella urbanidad de dama que la tía buscaba en sus favoritos.

En todo caso, la película me reveló el horror de que las mujeres siguieran existiendo más allá de cierto punto: extensas, húmedas, meritorias de la pintura de oro.

Nunca conocí la técnica con que mi padre rompía en forma definitiva con las mujeres. No vi llantos ni espasmos. Todas lucían contentas hasta el final y llegué a pensar, con helada objetividad, que las cortaba en el más literal de los sentidos. La imagen de mi padre como decapitador múltiple no me estorbaba gran cosa; correspondía a su hercúleo poderío, al círculo de fuerza que sería bueno mientras yo estuviese dentro.

Era yo quien extrañaba las uñas rosas de Katia o los perfumados sándwiches de Lorena.

Mi padre se recibió de arquitecto en 1957, el año de mi nacimiento. Entró a la década de los sesenta sin construir una sola casa; pasaba horas consiguiendo amigas en cafés que llamaba "existencialistas", y usaba un suéter de cuello de tortuga negro que le daba el atractivo aire de un cura recién decepcionado.

Decir que sus amigas se vestían en forma "vistosa" es decir muy poco. Tal vez algunas de las muchachas que me acariciaban el pelo fueran putas; en todo caso, la moda obligaba a mostrar los muslos y el maquillaje admitía anémonas en los párpados (por lo demás, al menos en mi familia, el maquillaje excesivo nunca estuvo reñido con la virtud: la beata tía Amelia se pintaba como para salir en un mural de Orozco). Las mujeres "existencialistas" fumaban mucho, decían "pendejo", no para insultar, sino para darle ritmo a la conversación, y repetían obsesivamente la palabra "neurosis". Eran de una edad movediza entre los 22 y los 35, aunque ninguna se veía mayor que mamá (sus 28 años parecían responder a otro reloj).

Ante Verónica carecía de palabras. Sus tobillos flacos y sus calcetines vencidos me llenaban de apuros. Yo era una planicie. Una hoja en blanco. Una boca perdida. El que comía hule y estaba lleno de hormigas. En cambio, las pasiones paternas avanzaban con una intensidad sin sobresaltos, y esto me hacía quererlo más. Era firme, no le llegaban traidoras lágrimas a los ojos; estaba tan cerca de él que su egoísmo me parecía una forma de la protección. Cuando pronunciaba mi nombre al salir de casa sabía que cambiaríamos de mujer. "Mauricio" era el protocolo de una conquista. En las primeras citas repetía mucho el apodo que me puso en la cuna y que resultó una profecía: *Panza*. Lo decía como para que me acostumbrara a estar ahí, con la nueva pelirroja; luego me convertía en un testigo algo anónimo y llegaba el momento en que ellos eran tan naturales como si yo no existiera.

Apenas abandonaba a una mujer (nunca me constó que ocurriera lo contrario), mi padre podía olvidar su nombre (en cambio, yo llevaba un inventario en el que ya figuraban tres Susanas).

En una de las raras ocasiones en que sí fuimos al cine descubrí una de las fuentes de su conducta. Le dio cinco pesos al encargado de romper los boletos y pude ver una escena magnífica en la que una mujer desnuda muere por asfixia dérmica, el cuerpo cubierto de pintura dorada.

También recuerdo la función del teléfono para el héroe de la película. Después de resolver un caso de espionaje dormía con una mujer, pero lo decisivo era que una llamada de Londres lo sacaba de la cama: su Majestad estaba en peligro y él tenía un motivo histórico para dejar a la rubia que empezaba a fastidiarlo. Tal vez yo cumplía un papel similar para mi padre. Era su llamada de Londres; el niño en la sala o en el estacionamiento servía como boleto de salida.

Yo inventaba una historia y ella picaba cebolla al primer muerto. Mi padre me acariciaba la nuca, en un gesto adicional de complicidad.

Pocas cosas se comparaban a la recompensa de sus dedos fuertes en mi pelo engomado. Con los años empecé a asociar el gesto con el del cazador que reconforta a su lebrel. De cualquier forma, mentir en forma convincente aún me trae esa delicia elemental, los dedos de mi padre, la confirmación de que somos aliados.

Nunca llevó a mi hermano Carlos en sus correrías porque temía que lo delatara. Carlos tiene un carácter impositivo, muy parecido al de mi padre; hasta la fecha, cree que se debilita al cumplir una voluntad ajena.

Aunque Rita fue la mejor, todas las amantes de mi padre hicieron conmigo su mejor esfuerzo. A saber qué extraña y convincente historia contaba él para incluirme en la relación. Yo era su pretexto para salir de casa pero ellas me besaban como si supieran algo más. Si íbamos a sus casas me preparaban sándwiches extradulces y si íbamos a un motel me dejaban en el coche con una batería de juegos de mesa.

En esos años estaban de moda las pelucas: mi padre tuvo una larga sucesión de rubias y pelirrojas que pudieron ser una misma castaña. Antes de Rita no amó a ninguna, o se amó de un modo parejo en todas ellas.

Mi amigo Pancho, con el que solía compartir muchas horas de suave olor a podredumbre en los lotes baldíos de la colonia, me dijo un aforismo improbable para sus siete u ocho años: "lo que te gusta te da nervios". Lo escuché con la aguda y agria sensación de entender un misterio.

Mi padre tocaba sin nerviosismo a sus mujeres; en cambio, yo veía con pánico a Verónica; en la clasificación de Pancho, yo estaba más cerca de los agravios del amor.

los pies, los dedos torcidos en la almohada, una flor de papel lila en el buró, los aditamentos de la mala hora. Eran pocos pero todos sobraban.

Hasta ese día nada me parecía mejor que acompañar a mi padre. Dos veces por semana íbamos al "cine". Mamá detestaba las películas; le tenían sin cuidado los naufragios y los tigres de Bengala que los productores pudieran llevar a la pantalla, se desprendió de la pasión de la época como de un desierto incultivable. Por entonces Estados Unidos acababa de devolvernos un pedazo de país: El Chamizal, una franja seca, que a pesar de los discursos no valía gran cosa. Mamá nos legaba algo semejante, con el fastidio de quien concede poco: la vida exterior que llamábamos "cine".

Su reino tiránico era la cocina y el refrigerador su Tabla de la Ley. La puerta blanca siempre tenía algún mandamiento bajo una fruta imantada. Por ejemplo: LA PUNTUALIDAD ES LA CORTESÍA DEL REY.

Aunque mamá quería educarnos con sus mensajes, la verdadera pedagogía estaba dentro del refrigerador: recipientes envueltos en celofanes, papeles encerados, aluminios de diversos grosores. Alzar una tapa equivalía a profanar su disciplinado edén.

Me asombra que en ese clima yo comiera tantas grasas. Guardo una borrosa memoria de las mantequillas y los licuados, pero siempre estuve gordo, siempre fui el último en las carreras y el más visible en los escondites.

Como toda cabeza de seis años la mía era demasiado grande para el cuerpo. Pero además tenía una costra de goma. Bajo aquella coraza que en verano atraía a las abejas, supuestamente había un cerebro lleno de episodios cinematográficos. Sin embargo mi mente estaba en blanco. Jamás íbamos al cine.

—¿Cómo estuvo la película? —preguntaba mamá, por decir algo.

Estoy en el jardín de una casa ajena. Soy un bulto que "juega" a ver hormigas. De pronto algo blando se desgaja en el pasto, un desmembramiento, un hormigueo de tierra. Alzo la vista y los columpios se mecen solos. Me vuelvo hacia la casa y sé que va a venirse abajo. Lo único que me importa es morir adentro.

Subo las escaleras, abro una puerta de golpe y lo que veo coincide penosamente con algo que ya sospechaba y en esencia quería comprobar. Es difícil acomodar el exceso visual de la escena. Hay un traje de charro en una silla, un corbatín tricolor se extiende sobre un tapete de peluche, junto a unas sandalias *cherokees*; el aire huele a cuero crudo, a vagas monturas. Las nalgas de mi padre son perfectas, redondas, rojizas. Con furia, con minuciosa exactitud, se hunde en la adorable Rita, a 6.3 en la escala de Mercalli. Sus ojos tienen un brillo acerado, ciego.

No advirtieron mi presencia, ni se enteraron del temblor. Cerré la puerta con cuidado. En el barandal de las escaleras descubrí el rastro de pulpa de tamarindo que dejé al subir.

La escena se me impone al barajar los años como la dura impronta de la que todo deriva. Sin embargo, fueron necesarias muchas cosas para llegar allí. Un enredo de suplantaciones, silencios, valores entendidos, me llevó a contemplar la intimidad ajena (la mayor cercanía no fue visual; más que los cuerpos, me asombraron sus impensables ruidos). En ese umbral, sin saber por qué, me sentí en total desventaja: gordo, sucio, incapaz de dejar de comer el hule con que forraba mis cuadernos, carne para las hormigas.

Pero tampoco quiero exagerar la fuerza del momento; aquella imagen no daba para un trauma profundo. ¿Entonces por qué me sentí tan mal? En principio porque el hombre que jadeaba era mi padre, pero más seguramente porque ciertas combinaciones exceden la mirada. Vi las plantas callosas de

de las telas familiares significaba dejarse llevar por la vida fácil, ceder a las presiones y a los gustos plácidos. Mucha miel de abeja, mucha televisión, muchos cojines en el sofá.

Ante el espejo, mi padre se adoraba con una pasión casi mística. Me cuesta trabajo encontrarle esa mirada en otras circunstancias; persigo el recuerdo de sus ojos en éxtasis y sé que corro el riesgo de inventarlo. Las formas de la memoria me recuerdan, de manera inevitable, a una esfera de dulces en la farmacia cercana a la casa. El aparato contenía caramelos redondos, de distintos colores. Con una moneda de veinte centavos se podían obtener tres o cuatro. Me gustaba localizar una bola roja en la pecera de cristal y verla descender rumbo a la boca del aparato, oprimida por las demás. En ocasiones, el dulce avistado llegaba a la cuenca de mi mano; sin embargo, ¿podía estar seguro de que se trataba del mismo que había escogido antes? Lo único cierto es que para obtener un dulce había que sacar otros. Algo semejante sucede con los instantes perdidos; a veces no llega el momento solicitado, o llega en compañía de otros; regresa en densidad, y al final resulta imposible saber si se trata del recuerdo auténtico o de su copia, trabajada por las manías del tiempo, las presiones de los demás instantes que pugnan por salir.

Como es de suponerse, mientras engordaba con los dulces de la farmacia no sabía que mi memoria se adiestraba en sus imposibilidades, en la azarosa contigüidad de los recuerdos.

Escojo la mirada de mi padre ante el espejo, y al girar la manivela, con los dedos pegajosos de otra hora, recibo algo que no solicité y sin embargo forma parte de ese orden.

Digo "toalla" y recupero los ojos encendidos de mi padre, pero en el lugar equivocado. El barroco desorden de ese instante no puede ser pospuesto.

Mi padre siempre usó el lado rasposo de la toalla. Si algo definía su carácter era la furia para frotar y admirar su carne enrojecida; el vapor se disolvía en el espejo, mostrando a un hombre joven (en mi primer recuerdo debe haber tenido 28 años), con la toalla firmemente atada a la cintura, satisfecho de los músculos que en su particular código de valores significaban "estar vivo". Había que mantener el cuerpo en guardia, rascarse las sienes, darse un golpe estratégico en el pecho, usar agua fría.

En la casa las toallas se planchaban hasta lograr un efecto de prensado. Al desdoblarse hacían ruido, y con ese rumor empezó mi historia general del mundo. Ignoraba casi todo, pero no que hubo una civilización con las manías paternas: Esparta.

A los seis años recibí un inútil globo terráqueo y mi índice asalchichado trató de posarse en Esparta. En vano. La nación de las molestias edificantes, donde las manzanas se comían verdes, fue derrotada por tribus confortables.

—¿Y eso qué? —preguntó mi padre.

No me atreví a responder "eso demuestra que se equivocaron". Para él los rigores eran un fin en sí mismos.

Supongo que me seguí bañando porque mamá suavizaba toallas secretas para ella y para mí. Crecí del lado opuesto, algo que en la esotérica valoración

1. Toallas ejemplares

El juego de los siete errores lo reservaba para más tarde, en la casa; lo sacaba con Franco sentado en las rodillas, mostrándole cada error; el niño se entusiasmaba, pero no había encontrado por sí mismo un solo error. Debía de haber una ceguera propia de ese juego, que se curaba con la edad. Martín no estaba seguro de haberse curado de verdad. Le daba la impresión de que lo resolvía haciendo trampas.

CÉSAR AIRA

A Pablo Friedmann
A la memoria de Xavier Cara

PQ
7298
I55
M38
1997

Índice

1. Toallas ejemplares	13
2. Historia de la equis	57
3. El Bello Durmiente	89
4. Último safari	127
5. El materialista fantasma	171
6. El jardín regulado	215
7. Las pieles infrarrojas	265

MATERIA DISPUESTA
© 1996, Juan Villoro

De esta edición:
© 1996, Aguilar, Altea, Taurus, Alfaguara, S.A. de C.V.
Av. Universidad 767, Col. del Valle
México, 03100, D.F. Teléfono 688 8966

- Ediciones Santillana S.A.
  Carrera 13 N° 63-39, Piso 12. Bogotá.
- Santillana S.A.
  Juan Bravo 38. 28006, Madrid.
- Santillana S.A., Avda San Felipe 731. Lima.
- Editorial Santillana S.A.
  4ᵗᵃ, entre 5ᵗᵃ y 6ᵗᵃ, transversal. Caracas 106. Caracas.
- Editorial Santillana Inc.
  P.O. Box 5462 Hato Rey, Puerto Rico, 00919.
- Santillana Publishing Company Inc.
  901 W. Walnut St., Compton, Ca. 90220-5109. USA.
- Ediciones Santillana S.A.(ROU)
  Boulevar España 2418, Bajo. Montevideo.
- Aguilar, Altea, Taurus, Alfaguara, S.A.
  Beazley 3860, 1437. Buenos Aires.
- Aguilar Chilena de Ediciones Ltda.
  Pedro de Valdivia 942. Santiago.
- Santillana de Costa Rica, S.A.
  Av. 10 (entre calles 35 y 37)
  Los Yoses, San José, C.R.

Primera edición en Alfaguara: enero de 1997
Primera reimpresión: febrero de 1997

ISBN: 968-19-0305-6

Diseño:
Proyecto de Enric Satué
© Foto cubierta: J. Pablo de Aguinaco
Impreso en México

Este libro fue escrito, en gran parte, gracias al apoyo del Sistema
Nacional de Creadores.

Todos los derechos reservados. Esta publicación no puede ser reproducida, ni en
todo ni en parte, ni registrada en o transmitida por un sistema de recuperación de
información, en ninguna forma ni por ningún medio, sea mecánico, fotoquímico,
electrónico, magnético, electroóptico, por fotocopia o cualquier otro, sin el
permiso previo, por escrito, de la editorial.

Juan Villoro

Materia dispuesta

Materia dispuesta

ARCADIA UNIVERSITY LIBRARY
GLENSIDE, PA 19038